NORTHANGER ABBEY, PERSUASION, EMMA

JANE AUSTEN

1775 - 1817

JANE AUSTEN

NORTHANGER ABBEY

PERSUASION

EMMA

BLITZ EDITIONS

© This edition Blitz Editions 1993

Published in this edition by Blitz Editions, an imprint of
Bookmart Ltd, Registered No. 2372865 England
Trading as Bookmart Ltd, Desford Road,
Enderby, Leicester LE9 5AD

ISBN 1 85605 184 6

Cover illustrations:
Main picture – *Mansion on a hill overlooking a village*, English
School. Reproduced by permission of Maidstone Museum and
Art Gallery, Kent/Bridgeman Art Library, London.
Inset – *Hat shop*. Reproduced by permission of Mary Evans
Picture Library, London.

Production services by
Book Production Consultants PLC, Cambridge

Printed and bound in Finland by WSOY

NORTHANGER ABBEY

NORTHANGER ABBEY

CHAPTER I

No one who had ever seen Catherine Morland in her infancy would have supposed her born to be an heroine. Her situation in life, the character of her father and mother, her own person and disposition, were all equally against her. Her father was a clergyman, without being neglected or poor, and a very respectable man, though his name was Richard, and he had never been handsome. He had a considerable independence, besides two good livings, and he was not in the least addicted to locking up his daughters. Her mother was a woman of useful plain sense, with a good temper, and, what is more remarkable, with a good constitution. She had three sons before Catherine was born and, instead of dying in bringing the latter into the world, as any body might expect, she still lived on—lived to have six children more—to see them growing up around her, and to enjoy excellent health herself. A family of ten children will be always called a fine family, where there are heads, and arms, and legs enough for the number ; but the Morlands had little other right to the word, for they were in general very plain, and Catherine, for many years of her life, as plain as any. She had a thin awkward figure, a sallow skin without colour, dark lank hair, and strong features ; so much for her person, and not less unpropitious for heroism seemed her mind. She was fond of all boys' plays, and greatly preferred cricket, not merely to dolls, but to the more heroic enjoyments of infancy, nursing a dormouse, feeding a canary-bird, or watering a rose-bush. Indeed she had no taste for a garden, and if she gathered flowers at all, it was chiefly for the pleasure of mischief, at least so it was conjectured from her always preferring those which she was forbidden to take. Such were her propensities ; her abilities were quite as extraordinary. She never could learn or understand anything before she was taught, and sometimes not even then, for she was often inattentive, and occasionally stupid. Her mother was three months in teaching her only to repeat the "Beggar's Petition," and, after all, her next sister Sally could say it better than she did. Not that Catherine was always stupid ; by no means ; she learnt the fable of " The Hare and many Friends," as quickly as any girl in England. Her mother wished her to learn music ; and Catherine was sure she should like it, for she was very fond of tinkling the keys of the old forlorn spinnet, so at eight years old she began. She learnt a year and could not bear it ; and Mrs Morland, who did not insist on her daughters being accomplished in spite of incapacity or distaste, allowed her to leave off. The day which dismissed the music-master was one of the happiest of Catherine's life. Her taste for drawing was not superior ; though whenever she could obtain the outside of a letter from her mother, or seize upon any other odd piece of paper, she did what she could in that way by drawing houses and trees, hens and chickens, all very much like one another. Writing and accounts she was taught by her father ; French by her mother. Her proficiency in either was not remarkable, and she shirked her lessons in both whenever she could. What a strange unaccountable character ! for with all these symptoms of profligacy at ten years old, she had neither a bad heart nor a bad temper, was seldom stubborn, scarcely ever quarrelsome, and very kind to the little ones, with few interruptions of tyranny. She was, moreover, noisy and wild, hated confinement and cleanliness, and loved nothing so well in the world as rolling down the green slope at the back of the house.

Such was Catherine Morland at ten. At fifteen appearances were mending ; she began to curl her hair and long for balls, her complexion improved, her features were softened by plumpness and colour, her eyes gained more animation, and her figure more consequence. Her love of dirt gave way to an inclination for finery, and she grew clean as she grew smart; she had now the pleasure of sometimes hearing her father and mother remark on her personal improvement. "Catherine grows quite a good-looking girl; she is almost pretty to-day," were words which caught her ears now and then; and how welcome were the sounds! To look *almost* pretty is an acquisition of higher delight to a girl who has been looking plain the first fifteen years of her life than a beauty from her cradle can ever receive.

Mrs Morland was a very good woman, and wished to see her children everything they ought to be: but her time was so much occupied in lying-in and teaching the little ones, that her elder daughters were inevitably left to shift for themselves; and it was not very wonderful that Catherine, who had by nature nothing heroic about her, should prefer cricket, base ball, riding on horseback, and running about the country, at the age of fourteen, to books, or at least books of information, for, provided that nothing like useful knowledge could be gained from them, provided they were all story and no reflection, she had never any objection to books at all. But from fifteen to seventeen she was in training for a heroine; she read all such works as heroines must read to supply their memories with those quotations which are so serviceable and so soothing in the vicissitudes of their eventful lives.

From Pope, she learnt to censure those who

> " bear about the mockery of woe."

From Gray, that

> " Many a flower is born to blush unseen,
> And waste its fragrance on the desert air

From Thomson, that

> ——" It is a delightful task
> To teach the young idea how to shoot."

And from Shakspeare she gained a great store of information: amongst the rest, that

> ——"Trifles light as air,
> Are, to the jealous, confirmation strong,
> As proofs of Holy Writ."

That

> " The poor beetle, which we tread upon,
>   In corporal sufferance feels a pang as great
>   As when a giant dies."

And that a young woman in love always looks

> ——" like Patience on a monument
> Smiling at Grief."

So far her improvement was sufficient, and in many other points she came on exceedingly well ; for though she could not write sonnets, she brought herself to read them ; and though there seemed no chance of her throwing a whole party into raptures by a prelude on the piano-forte of her own composition, she could listen to other people's performance with very little fatigue. Her greatest deficiency was in the pencil—she had no notion of drawing—not enough even to attempt a sketch of her lover's profile, that she might be detected in the design. There she fell miserably short of the true heroic height. At present she did not know her own poverty, for she had no lover to pourtray. She had reached the age of seventeen, without having seen one amiable youth who could call forth her sensibility : without having inspired one real passion, and without having excited even any admiration but what was very moderate and very transient. This was strange indeed ! But strange things may be generally accounted for if their cause be fairly searched out. There was not one lord in the neighbourhood ; no, not even a baronet. There was not one family among their acquaintance who had reared and supported a boy accidentally found at their door ; not one young man whose origin was unknown. Her father had no ward, and the squire of the parish no children.

But when a young lady is to be a heroine, the perverseness of forty surrounding families cannot prevent her. Something must and will happen to throw a hero in her way.

Mr Allen, who owned the chief of the property about Fullerton, the village in Wiltshire where the Morlands lived, was ordered to Bath for the benefit of a gouty constitution ; and his lady, a good-humoured woman, fond of Miss Morland, and probably aware that, if adventures will not befall a young lady in her own village, she must seek them abroad, invited her to go with them. Mr and Mrs Morland were all compliance, and Catherine all happiness.

CHAPTER II

IN addition to what has been already said of Catherine Morland's personal and mental endowments, when about to be launched into all the difficulties and dangers of a six weeks' residence in Bath, it may be stated, for the reader's more certain information, lest the following pages should otherwise fail of giving any idea of what her character is meant to be, that her heart was affectionate, her disposition cheerful and open, without conceit or affectation of any kind ; her manners just removed from the awkwardness and shyness of a girl ; her person pleasing, and, when in good looks, pretty ; and her mind about as ignorant and uninformed as the female mind at seventeen usually is.

When the hour of departure drew near, the maternal anxiety of Mrs Morland will be naturally supposed to be most severe. A thousand alarming presentiments of evil to her beloved Catherine from this terrific separation must oppress her heart with sadness, and drown her in tears for the last day or two of their being together ; and advice of the most important and applicable nature must of course flow from her wise lips in their parting conference in her closet. Cautions against the violence of such noblemen and baronets as delight in forcing young ladies away to some remote farm-house, must, at such a moment, relieve the fulness of her heart. Who would not think so ? But Mrs Morland knew so little of lords and baronets, that she entertained no notion of their general mischievousness, and was wholly unsuspicious of danger to her daughter from their machinations. Her cautions were confined to the following points : " I beg, Catherine, you will always wrap yourself up very warm about the throat when you come from the Rooms at night ; and I wish you would try to keep some account of the money you spend ; I will give you this little book on purpose."

Sally, or rather Sarah (for what young lady of common

gentility will reach the age of sixteen without altering her name as far as she can ?), must from situation be at this time the intimate friend and confidante of her sister. It is remarkable, however, that she neither insisted on Catherine's writing by every post, nor exacted her promise of transmitting the character of every new acquaintance, nor a detail of every interesting conversation that Bath might produce. Everything, indeed, relative to this important journey was done on the part of the Morlands with a degree of moderation and composure, which seemed rather consistent with the common feelings of common life, than with the refined susceptibilities—the tender emotions which the first separation of a heroine from her family ought always to excite. Her father, instead of giving her an unlimited order on his banker, or even putting an hundred pounds bank-bill into her hands, gave her only ten guineas, and promised her more when she wanted it.

Under these unpromising auspices, the parting took place and the journey began. It was performed with suitable quietness and uneventful safety. Neither robbers nor tempests befriended them, nor one lucky overturn to introduce them to the hero. Nothing more alarming occurred than a fear, on Mrs Allen's side, of having once left her clogs behind her at an inn, and that fortunately proved to be groundless.

They arrived at Bath. Catherine was all eager delight ; her eyes were here, there, everywhere, as they approached its fine and striking environs, and afterwards drove through those streets which conducted them to the hotel. She was come to be happy, and she felt happy already.

They were soon settled in comfortable lodgings in Pulteney Street.

It is now expedient to give some description of Mrs Allen, that the reader may be able to judge, in what manner her actions will hereafter tend to promote the general distress of the work, and how she will probably contribute to reduce poor Catherine to all the desperate wretchedness of which a last volume is capable—whether by her imprudence, vulgarity, or jealousy—whether by intercepting her letters, ruining her character, or turning her out of doors.

Mrs Allen was one of that numerous class of females,

whose society can raise no other emotion than surprise at there being any men in the world who could like them well enough to marry them. She had neither beauty, genius, accomplishment, nor manner. The air of a gentlewoman, a great deal of quiet, inactive good temper, and a trifling turn of mind, were all that could account for her being the choice of a sensible, intelligent man, like Mr Allen. In one respect she was admirably fitted to introduce a young lady into public, being as fond of going everywhere and seeing everything herself, as any young lady could be. Dress was her passion. She had a most harmless delight in being fine ; and our heroine's entrée into life could not take place till after three or four days had been spent in learning what was mostly worn, and her chaperon was provided with a dress of the newest fashion. Catherine, too, made some purchases herself, and when all these matters were arranged, the important evening came which was to usher her into the Upper Rooms. Her hair was cut and dressed by the best hand, her clothes put on with care, and both Mrs Allen and her maid declared she looked quite as she should do. With such encouragement, Catherine hoped at least to pass uncensured through the crowd ; as for admiration, it was always very welcome when it came, but she did not depend on it.

Mrs Allen was so long in dressing that they did not enter the ball-room till late. The season was full, the room crowded, and the two ladies squeezed in as well as they could. As for Mr Allen, he repaired directly to the card-room, and left them to enjoy a mob by themselves. With more care for the safety of her new gown than for the comfort of her protegée, Mrs Allen made her way through the throng of men by the door, as swiftly as the necessary caution would allow ; Catherine, however, kept close at her side, and linked her arm too firmly within her friend's to be torn asunder by any common effort of a struggling assembly. But, to her utter amazement, she found that to proceed along the room was by no means the way to disengage themselves from the crowd ; it seemed rather to increase as they went on ; whereas she had imagined that, when once fairly within the door, they should easily find seats, and be able to watch the dances with perfect convenience.

But this was far from being the case; and though by un-wearied diligence they gained even the top of the room, their situation was just the same: they saw nothing of the dancers, but the high feathers of some of the ladies.   Still they moved on: something better was yet in view; and by a continued exertion of strength and ingenuity, they found themselves at last in the passage behind the highest bench. Here there was something less of crowd than below; and hence Miss Morland had a comprehensive view of all the com-pany beneath her, and of all the dangers of her late passage through them.   It was a splendid sight; and she began, for the first time that evening, to feel herself at a ball: she longed to dance, but she had not an acquaintance in the room.   Mrs Allen did all that she could do in such a case, by saying very placidly, every now and then, "I wish you could dance, my dear; I wish you could get a partner." For some time her young friend felt obliged to her for these wishes, but they were repeated so often, and proved so totally ineffectual, that Catherine grew tired at last, and would thank her no more.

They were not long able, however, to enjoy the repose of the eminence they had so laboriously gained.   Every-body was shortly in motion for tea, and they must squeeze out like the rest.   Catherine began to feel something of disappointment: she was tired of being continually pressed against by people, the generality of whose faces possessed nothing to interest, and with all of whom she was so wholly unacquainted that she could not relieve the irksomeness of imprisonment by the exchange of a syllable with any of her fellow-captives; and when at last arrived in the tea-room, she felt yet more the awkwardness of having no party to join, no acquaintance to claim, no gentleman to assist them.   They saw nothing of Mr Allen; and after looking about them in vain for a more eligible situation, were obliged to sit down at the end of a table, at which a large party were already placed, without having anything to do there, or anybody to speak to, except each other.

Mrs Allen congratulated herself, as soon as they were seated, on having preserved her gown from injury.   "It would have been very shocking to have it torn," said she, "would not it ? It is such a delicate muslin. For my part, I have not seen anything I like so well in the whole room, I assure you."

"How uncomfortable it is," whispered Catherine, "not to have a single acquaintance here ! "

"Yes, my dear," replied Mrs Allen, with perfect serenity, "it is very uncomfortable, indeed."

"What shall we do ? The gentlemen and ladies at this table look as if they wondered why we came here ; we seem forcing ourselves into their party."

"Aye, so we do. That is very disagreeable. I wish we had a large acquaintance here."

"I wish we had *any* ; it would be somebody to go to."

"Very true, my dear ; and if we knew anybody, we would join them directly. The Skinners were here last year ; I wish they were here now."

"Had not we better go away as it is ? Here are no tea-things for us, you see."

"No more there are, indeed. How very provoking ! But I think we had better sit still, for one gets so tumbled in such a crowd. How is my head, my dear ? Somebody gave me a push that has hurt it I am afraid."

"No, indeed, it looks very nice. But, dear Mrs Allen, are you sure there is nobody you know in all this multitude of people ? I think you *must* know somebody."

"I don't, upon my word ; I wish I did. I wish I had a large acquaintance here with all my heart, and then I should get you a partner. I should be so glad to have you dance. There goes a strange-looking woman ! What an odd gown she has got on ! How old-fashioned it is ! Look at the back."

After some time they received an offer of tea from one of their neighbours ; it was thankfully accepted, and this introduced a light conversation with the gentleman who offered it, which was the only time that anybody spoke to them during the evening, till they were discovered and joined by Mr Allen when the dance was over.

"Well, Miss Morland," said he, directly, "I hope you have had an agreeable ball."

"Very agreeable, indeed," she replied, vainly endeavouring to hide a great yawn.

" I wish she had been able to dance," said his wife ; " I wish we could have got a partner for her. I have been saying how glad I should be if the Skinners were here this winter instead of last ; or if the Parrys had come, as they talked of once, she might have danced with George Parry. I am so sorry she has not had a partner."

" We shall do better another evening, I hope," was Mr Allen's consolation.

The company began to disperse when the dancing was over : enough to leave space for the remainder to walk about in some comfort ; and now was the time for a heroine, who had not yet played a very distinguished part in the events of the evening, to be noticed and admired. Every five minutes, by removing some of the crowd, gave greater openings for her charms. She was now seen by many young men who had not been near her before. Not one, however, started with rapturous wonder on beholding her, no whisper of eager inquiry ran round the room, nor was she once called a divinity by anybody. Yet Catherine was in very good looks, and, had the company only seen her three years before, they would *now* have thought her exceedingly handsome.

She *was* looked at, however, and with some admiration ; for, in her own hearing, two gentlemen pronounced her to be a pretty girl. Such words had their due effect : she immediately thought the evening pleasanter than she had found it before, her humble vanity was contented ; she felt more obliged to the two young men for this simple praise, than a true quality heroine would have been for fifteen sonnets in celebration of her charms, and went to her chair in good humour with everybody, and perfectly satisfied with her share of public attention.

CHAPTER III

EVERY morning now brought its regular duties ; shops were to be visited, some new part of the town to be looked at, and the Pump-room to be attended, where they paraded up and down for an hour, looking at everybody and speaking to no one. The wish of a numerous acquaintance in Bath was still uppermost with Mrs Allen, and she repeated it after every fresh proof, which every morning brought, of her knowing nobody at all.

They made their appearance in the Lower Rooms; and here fortune was more favourable to our heroine. The master of the ceremonies introduced to her a very gentleman-like young man as a partner; his name was Tilney. He seemed to be about four or five and twenty, was rather tall, had a pleasing countenance, a very intelligent and lively eye, and, if not quite handsome, was very near it. His address was good, and Catherine felt herself in high luck. There was little leisure for speaking while they danced; but when they were seated at tea she found him as agreeable as she had already given him credit for being. He talked with fluency and spirit, and there was an archness and pleasantry in his manner which interested, though it was hardly understood by her. After chatting some time on such matters as naturally arose from the objects around them, he suddenly addressed her with—" I have hitherto been very remiss, madam, in the proper attentions of a partner here; I have not yet asked you how long you have been in Bath, whether you were ever here before, whether you have been at the Upper Rooms, the theatre, and the concert, and how you like the place altogether. I have been very negligent; but are you now at leisure to satisfy me in these particulars? If you are, I will begin directly."

" You need not give yourself that trouble, sir."

" No trouble, I assure you, madam." Then forming his features into a set smile, and affectedly softening his voice, he added, with a simpering air, " Have you been long in Bath, madam ? "

" About a week, sir," replied Catherine, trying not to laugh.

" Really ! " with affected astonishment.

" Why should you be surprised, sir ? "

" Why, indeed ? " said he, in his natural tone; " but some emotion must appear to be raised by your reply, and surprise is more easily assumed, and not less reasonable, than any other. Now let us go on. Were you never here before, madam ? "

" Never, sir."

" Indeed ! Have you yet honoured the Upper Rooms ? "

" Yes, sir ; I was there last Monday."

" Have you been to the theatre ? "

" Yes, sir ; I was at the play on Tuesday."

" To the concert ? "

" Yes, sir ; on Wednesday."

" And are you altogether pleased with Bath ? "

" Yes ; I like it very well."

" Now I must give one smirk, and then we may be rational again."

Catherine turned away her head, not knowing whether she might venture to laugh.

" I see what you think of me," said he, gravely ; " I shall make but a poor figure in your journal to-morrow."

" My journal ! "

" Yes ; I know exactly what you will say. Friday, went to the Lower Rooms ; wore my sprigged muslin robe with blue trimmings, plain black shoes ; appeared to much advantage, but was strangely harassed by a queer half-witted man, who would make me dance with him, and distressed me by his nonsense."

" Indeed I shall say no such thing."

" Shall I tell you what you ought to say ? "

" If you please."

" I danced with a very agreeable young man, introduced by Mr King ; had a great deal of conversation with him ; seems a most extraordinary genius ; hope I may know more of him. *That*, madam, is what I *wish* you to say."

" But perhaps I keep no journal."

" Perhaps you are not sitting in this room, and I am not sitting by you. These are points in which a doubt is equally possible. Not keep a journal ! How are your absent cousins to understand the tenour of your life in Bath without one ? How are the civilities and compliments of every day to be related as they ought to be unless noted down every evening in a journal ! How are your various dresses to be remembered, and the particular state of your complexion, and curl of your hair to be described, in all their diversities, without having constant recourse to a journal ? My dear madam, I am not so ignorant of young ladies' ways as you wish to believe me. It is this delightful habit of journalizing which largely contributes to form the easy style of writing for which ladies are so generally celebrated. Everybody allows that the talent of writing agreeable letters is peculiarly female. Nature may have done something, but I am sure it must be essentially assisted by the practice of keeping a journal."

" I have sometimes thought," said Catherine, doubtingly, " whether ladies *do* write so much better letters than gentlemen. That is, I should not think the superiority was always on our side."

" As far as I have had opportunity of judging, it appears to me that the usual style of letter-writing among women is faultless, except in three particulars."

" And what are they ? "

" A general deficiency of subject, a total inattention to stops, and a very frequent ignorance of grammer."

" Upon my word, I need not have been afraid of disclaiming the compliment ! You do not think too highly of us in that way."

" I should no more lay it down as a general rule that women write better letters than men, than that they sing better duets, or draw better landscapes. In every power of which taste is the foundation, excellence is pretty fairly divided between the sexes."

They were interrupted by Mrs Allen. " My dear Catherine," said she, " do take this pin out of my sleeve. I am afraid it has torn a hole already. I shall be quite sorry if it has, for this is a favourite gown, though it cost but nine shillings a yard."

" That is exactly what I should have guessed it, madam," said Mr Tilney, looking at the muslin.

" Do you understand muslins, sir ? "

" Particularly well ; I always buy my own cravats, and am allowed to be an excellent judge ; and my sister has often trusted me in the choice of a gown. I bought one for her the other day, and it was pronounced to be a prodigious bargain by every lady who saw it. I gave but five shillings a yard for it, and a true Indian muslin."

Mrs Allen was quite struck by his genius. "Men commonly take so little notice of those things," said she. "I can never get Mr Allen to know one of my gowns from another. You must be a great comfort to your sister, sir."

"I hope I am, madam."

"And pray, sir, what do [you] think of Miss Morland's gown?"

"It is very pretty, madam," said he, gravely examining it; "but I do not think it will wash well. I am afraid it will fray."

"How can you," said Catherine, laughing, "be so——?" she had almost said "strange."

"I am quite of your opinion, sir," replied Mrs Allen; "and so I told Miss Morland when she bought it."

"But then you know, madam, muslin always turns to some account or other; Miss Morland will get enough out of it for a handkerchief, or a cap, or a cloak. Muslin can never be said to be wasted. I have heard my sister say so forty times, when she has been extravagant in buying more than she wanted, or careless in cutting it to pieces."

"Bath is a charming place, sir; there are so many good shops here. We are sadly off in the country: not but what we have very good shops in Salisbury, but it is so far to go; eight miles is a long way. Mr Allen says it is nine, measured nine; but I am sure it cannot be more than eight; and it is such a fag; I come back tired to death. Now, here one can step out of doors, and get a thing in five minutes."

Mr Tilney was polite enough to seem interested in what she said; and she kept him on the subject of muslins till the dancing recommenced. Catherine feared as she listened to their discourse, that he indulged himself a little too much with the foibles of others. "What are you thinking of so earnestly?" said he, as they walked back to the ball-room; "not of your partner, I hope, for by that shake of the head, your meditations are not satisfactory."

Catherine coloured, and said, "I was not thinking of anything."

" That is artful and deep, to be sure ; but I had rather be told at once that you will not tell me."

" Well, then, I will not."

" Thank you ; for now we shall soon be acquainted, as I am authorized to tease you on this subject whenever we meet, and nothing in the world advances intimacy so much."

They danced again ; and when the assembly closed, parted, on the lady's side at least, with a strong inclination for continuing the acquaintance. Whether she thought of him so much, while she drank her warm wine and water, and prepared herself for bed, as to dream of him when there, cannot be ascertained, but I hope it was no more than in a slight slumber, or a morning doze at most ; for if it be true, as a celebrated writer has maintained, that no young lady can be justified in falling in love before the gentleman's love is declared,* it must be very improper that a young lady should dream of a gentleman before the gentleman is first known to have dreamt of her. How proper Mr Tilney might be as a dreamer or a lover, had not yet, perhaps, entered Mr Allen's head, but that he was not objectionable as a common acquaintance for his young charge, he was on inquiry satisfied ; for he had early in the evening taken pains to know who her partner was, and had been assured of Mr Tilney's being a clergyman, and of a very respectable family in Gloucestershire.

CHAPER IV

WITH more than usual eagerness did Catherine hasten to the Pump-room the next day, secure within herself of seeing Mr Tilney there before the morning were over, and ready to meet him with a smile : but no smile was demanded—Mr Tilney did not appear. Every creature in Bath, except himself, was to be seen in the room at different periods of the fashionable hours ; crowds of people were every moment passing in and out, up the steps and down ; people whom nobody cared about, and nobody wanted to see ; and he only was absent. " What a delightful place Bath is," said

* *Vide* a letter from Mr Richardson, No. 97, vol. ii. Rambler.

Mrs Allen, as they sat down near the great clock, after parading the room till they were tired ; " and how pleasant it would be if we had any acquaintance here."

This sentiment had been uttered so often in vain, that Mrs Allen had no particular reason to hope it would be followed with more advantage now ; but we are told to " Despair of nothing we would attain," as " Unwearied diligence our point would gain," and the unwearied diligence with which she had every day wished for the same thing was at length to have its just reward ; for hardly had she been seated ten minutes, before a lady of about her own age, who was sitting by her, and had been looking at her attentively for several minutes, addressed her with great complaisance in these words :—" I think, madam, I cannot be mistaken ; it is a long time since I had the pleasure of seeing you, but is not your name Allen ? " This question answered, as it readily was, the stranger pronounced her's to be Thorpe ; and Mrs Allen immediately recognized the features of a former schoolfellow and intimate, whom she had seen only once since their respective marriages, and that many years ago. Their joy on this meeting was very great, as well it might, since they had been contented to know nothing of each other for the last fifteen years. Compliments on good looks now passed ; and, after observing how time had slipped away since they were last together, how little they had thought of meeting in Bath, and what a pleasure it was to see an old friend, they proceeded to make enquiries and give intelligence as to their families, sisters, and cousins, talking both together, far more ready to give than to receive information, and each hearing very little what the other said. Mrs Thorpe, however, had one great advantage as a talker, over Mrs Allen, in a family of children ; and when she expatiated on the talents of her sons, and the beauty of her daughters, when she related their different situations and views, that John was at Oxford, Edward at Merchant Taylors', and William at sea, and all of them more beloved and respected in their different [stations] than any other three beings ever were, Mrs Allen had no similar information to give, no similar triumphs to press on the unwilling and unbelieving ear of her friend ; and was forced to sit and appear to listen to all these maternal effusions, consoling herself, however, with the discovery, which her keen eyes soon made, that the lace on Mrs Thorpe's pelisse was not half so handsome as that on her own.

" Here come my dear girls," cried Mrs Thorpe, pointing at three smart looking females, who, arm in arm, were then moving towards her. " My dear Mrs Allen, I long to introduce them ; they will be so delighted to see you : the tallest is Isabella, my eldest ; is not she a fine young woman ? The others are very much admired too, but I believe Isabella is the handsomest."

The Miss Thorpes were introduced ; and Miss Morland, who had been for a short time forgotten, was introduced likewise. The name seemed to strike them all ; and, after speaking to her with great civility, the eldest young lady observed aloud to the rest, " How excessively like her brother Miss Morland is ! "

" The very picture of him, indeed ! " cried the mother ; and " I should have known her any where for his sister ! " was repeated by them all, two or three times over. For a moment Catherine was surprized ; but Mrs Thorpe and her daughters had scarcely begun the history of their acquaintance with Mr James Morland, before she remembered that her eldest brother had lately formed an intimacy with a young man of his own college, of the name of Thorpe, and that he had spent the last week of the Christmas vacation with his family, near London.

The whole being explained, many obliging things were said by the Miss Thorpes of their wish of being better acquainted with her ; of being considered as already friends, through the friendship of their brothers, etc., which Catherine heard with pleasure, and answered with all the pretty expressions she could command ; and, as the first proof of amity, she was soon invited to accept an arm of the eldest Miss Thorpe, and take a turn with her about the room. Catherine was delighted with this extension of her Bath acquaintance, and almost forgot Mr Tilney while she talked to Miss Thorpe. Friendship is certainly the finest balm for the pangs of disappointed love.

Their conversation turned upon those subjects of which

the free discussion has generally much to do in perfecting
a sudden intimacy between two young ladies ; such as
dress, balls, flirtations, and quizzes. Miss Thorpe, however, being four years older than Miss Morland, and at
least four years better informed, had a very decided advantage in discussing such points. She could compare
the balls of Bath with those of Tunbridge ; its fashions
with the fashions of London ; could rectify the opinions
of her new friend in many articles of tasteful attire ; could
discover a flirtation between any gentleman and lady who
only smiled on each other ; and point out a quiz through
the thickness of a crowd. These powers received due
admiration from Catherine, to whom they were entirely
new ; and the respect which they naturally inspired might
have been too great for familiarity, had not the easy gaiety
of Miss Thorpe's manners, and her frequent expressions
of delight on this acquaintance with her, softened down
every feeling of awe, and left nothing but tender affection.
Their increasing attachment was not to be satisfied with
half a dozen turns in the Pump-room, but required, when
they all quitted it together, that Miss Thorpe should accompany Miss Morland to the very door of Mr Allen's
house ; and that they should there part with a most affectionate and lengthened shake of hands, after learning,
to their mutual relief, that they should see each other
across the theatre at night, and say their prayers in the
same chapel the next morning. Catherine then ran directly
up stairs, and watched Miss Thorpe's progress down the
street from the drawing-room window ; admired the graceful spirit of her walk, the fashionable air of her figure and
dress, and felt grateful, as well she might, for the chance
which had procured her such a friend.

Mrs Thorpe was a widow, and not a very rich one ; she
was a good-humoured, well-meaning woman, and a very
indulgent mother. Her eldest daughter had great personal
beauty, and the younger ones, by pretending to be as
handsome as their sister, imitating her air, and dressing
in the same style, did very well.

This brief account of the family is intended to super-
sede the necessity of a long and minute detail from Mrs

Thorpe herself, of her past adventures and sufferings, which might otherwise be expected to occupy the three or four following chapters, in which the worthlessness of lords and attornies might be set forth ; and conversations which had passed twenty years before be minutely repeated.

CHAPTER V

CATHERINE was not so much engaged at the theatre, that evening, in returning the nods and smiles of Miss Thorpe, though they certainly claimed much of her leisure, as to forget to look with an inquiring eye for Mr Tilney in every box which her eye could reach ; but she looked in vain. Mr Tilney was no fonder of the play than the Pump-room. She hoped to be more fortunate the next day ; and when her wishes for fine weather were answered by seeing a beautiful morning, she hardly felt a doubt of it ; for a fine Sunday in Bath empties every house of its inhabitants, and all the world appears on such an occasion, to walk about, and tell their acquaintance what a charming day it is.

As soon as divine service was over, the Thorpes and Allens eagerly joined each other ; and, after staying long enough in the Pump-room to discover that the crowd was insupportable, and that there was not a genteel face to be seen, which everybody discovers every Sunday throughout the season, they hastened away to the Crescent, to breathe the fresh air of better company. Here Catherine and Isabella, arm in arm, again tasted the sweets of friendship in an unreserved conversation. They talked much, and with much enjoyment ; but again was Catherine disappointed in her hope of re-seeing her partner. He was no where to be met with ; every search for him was equally unsuccessful, in morning lounges or evening assemblies, neither at the upper nor lower rooms, at dressed or undressed balls was he perceivable ; nor among the walkers, the horsemen, or the curricle-drivers of the morning. His name was not in the Pump-room book, and curiosity could do no more.   He must be gone from Bath; yet he had not mentioned that his stay would be so short.   This sort of mysteriousness, which is always so becoming in a hero, threw a fresh grace, in Catherine's imagination, around his person and manners, and increased her anxiety to know more of him.   From the Thorpes she could learn nothing, for they had been only two days in Bath before they met with Mrs Allen.   It was a subject, however, in which she often indulged with her fair friend, from whom she received every possible encouragement to continue to think of him; and his impression on her fancy was not suffered therefore to weaken.   Isabella was very sure that he must be a charming young man; and was equally sure that he must have been delighted with her dear Catherine, and would therefore shortly return.   She liked him the better for being a clergyman, " for she must confess herself very partial to the profession;" and something like a sigh escaped her as she said it.   Perhaps Catherine was wrong in not demanding the cause of that gentle emotion, but she was not experienced enough in the finesse of love, or the duties of friendship, to know when delicate raillery was properly called for, or when a confidence should be forced.

Mrs Allen was now quite happy, quite satisfied with Bath.   She had found some acquaintance; had been so lucky, too, as to find in them the family of a most worthy old friend; and, as the completion of good fortune, had found these friends by no means so expensively dressed as herself.   Her daily expressions were no longer, " I wish we had some acquaintance in Bath!"   They were changed into, "How glad I am we have met with Mrs Thorpe!" and she was as eager in promoting the intercourse of the two families as her young charge and Isabella themselves could be; never satisfied with the day unless she spent the chief of it by the side of Mrs Thorpe, in what they called conversation; but in which there was scarcely ever any exchange of opinion, and not often any resemblance of subject, for Mrs Thorpe talked chiefly of her children, and Mrs Allen of her gowns.

The progress of the friendship between Catherine and

Isabella was quick as its beginning had been warm ; and
they passed so rapidly through every gradation of increasing tenderness, that there was shortly no fresh proof of
it to be given to their friends or themselves. They called
each other by their Christian name, were always arm-in-
arm when they walked, pinned up each other's train for
the dance, and were not to be divided in the set ; and, if
a rainy morning deprived them of other enjoyments, they
were still resolute in meeting in defiance of wet and dirt,
and shut themselves up to read novels together. Yes,
novels ; for I will not adopt that ungenerous and impolitic
custom, so common with novel writers, of degrading, by
their contemptuous censure, the very performances to the
number of which they are themselves adding : joining
with their greatest enemies in bestowing the harshest
epithets on such works, and scarcely ever permitting them
to be read by their own heroine, who, if she accidentally
take up a novel, is sure to turn over its insipid pages with
disgust. Alas ! if the heroine of one novel be not patronized
by the heroine of another, from whom can she expect protection and regard ? I cannot approve of it. Let us leave
it to the Reviewers to abuse such effusions of fancy at
their leisure, and over every new novel to talk in threadbare strains of the trash with which the press now groans.
Let us not desert one another ; we are an injured body.
Although our productions have afforded more extensive
and unaffected pleasure than those of any other literary
corporation in the world, no species of composition has been
so much decried. From pride, ignorance, or fashion,
our foes are almost as many as our readers ; and while
the abilities of the nine-hundredth abridger of the History
of England, or of the man who collects and publishes in
a volume some dozen lines of Milton, Pope, and Prior,
with a paper from the Spectator, and a chapter from Sterne,
are eulogized by a thousand pens, there seems almost a
general wish of decrying the capacity and undervaluing
the labour of the novelist, and of slighting the performances which have only genius, wit, and taste to recommend them. " I am no novel reader ; I seldom look into
novels ; do not imagine that *I* often read novels ; it is

really very well for a novel." Such is the common cant.
" And what are you reading, Miss —— ? " " Oh ! it is
only a novel ! " replies the young lady ; while she lays
down her book with affected indifference, or momentary
shame. " It is only Cecilia, or Camilla, or Belinda ; "
or, in short, only some work in which the greatest powers
of the mind are displayed, in which the most thorough knowledge of human nature, the happiest delineation of its
varieties, the liveliest effusions of wit and humour, are
conveyed to the world in the best chosen language. Now,
had the same young lady been engaged with a volume
of the Spectator, instead of such a work, how proudly would
she have produced the book, and told its name ! though
the chances must be against her being occupied by any
part of that voluminous publication, of which either the
matter or manner would not disgust a young person of
taste ; the substance of its papers so often consisting in
the statement of improbable circumstances, unnatural
characters, and topics of conversation, which no longer
concern any one living ; and their language, too, frequently
so coarse as to give no very favourable idea of the age
that could endure it.

CHAPTER VI

THE following conversation, which took place between
the two friends in the Pump-room one morning, after an
acquaintance of eight or nine days, is given as a specimen
of their very warm attachment, and of the delicacy, discretion, originality of thought, and literary taste which
marked the reasonableness of that attachment.

They met by appointment ; and as Isabella had arrived
nearly five minutes before her friend, her first address
naturally was : " My dearest creature, what can have made
you so late ? I have been waiting for you at least this
age ! "

" Have you, indeed ? I am very sorry for it, but really
I thought I was in very good time. It is but just one.
I hope you have not been here long ? "

"Oh! these ten ages at least. I am sure I have been here this half hour. But now, let us go and sit down at the other end of the room and enjoy ourselves. I have an hundred things to say to you. In the first place, I was so afraid it would rain this morning just as I wanted to set off; it looked very showery, and that would have thrown me into agonies! Do you know I saw the prettiest hat you can imagine in a shop window in Milsom Street just now; very like yours, only with coquelicot ribbons instead of green; I quite longed for it. But, my dearest Catherine, what have you been doing with yourself all this morning? Have you gone on with Udolpho?"

"Yes, I have been reading it ever since I woke; and I am got to the black veil."

"Are you, indeed? How delightful! Oh! I would not tell you what is behind the black veil for the world! Are not you wild to know?"

"Oh! yes, quite; what can it be? But do not tell me: I would not be told upon any account. I know it must be a skeleton; I am sure it is Laurentina's skeleton. Oh! I am delighted with the book! I should like to spend my whole life in reading it, I assure you; if it had not been to meet you, I would not have come away from it for all the world."

"Dear creature, how much I am obliged to you; and when you have finished Udolpho, we will read the Italian together; and I have made out a list of ten or twelve more of the same kind for you."

"Have you, indeed! How glad I am! What are they all?"

"I will read you their names directly; here they are in my pocket-book. Castle of Wolfenbach, Clermont, Mysterious Warnings, Necromancer of the Black Forest, Midnight Bell, Orphan of the Rhine, and Horrid Mysteries. Those will last us some time."

"Yes; pretty well; but are they all horrid? Are you sure they are all horrid?"

"Yes, quite sure; for a particular friend of mine, a Miss Andrews, a sweet girl, one of the sweetest creatures in the world, has read every one of them. I wish you knew

Miss Andrews, you would be delighted with her. She is netting herself the sweetest cloak you can conceive. I think her as beautiful as an angel, and I am so vexed with the men for not admiring her! I scold them all amazingly about it."

"Scold them! Do you scold them for not admiring her?"

"Yes, that I do. There is nothing I would not do for those who are really my friends. I have no notion of loving people by halves; it is not my nature. My attachments are always excessively strong. I told Capt. Hunt, at one of our assemblies this winter, that if he was to tease me all night, I would not dance with him, unless he would allow Miss Andrews to be as beautiful as an angel. The men think us incapable of real friendship, you know, and I am determined to show them the difference. Now, if I were to hear anybody speak slightingly of you, I should fire up in a moment: but that is not at all likely, for *you* are just the kind of girl to be a great favourite with the men."

"Oh, dear!" cried Catherine, colouring, "how can you say so?"

"I know you very well; you have so much animation, which is exactly what Miss Andrews wants; for I must confess there is something amazingly insipid about her. Oh! I must tell you, that, just after we parted yesterday, I saw a young man looking at you so earnestly; I am sure he is in love with you." Catherine coloured, and disclaimed again. Isabella laughed. "It is very true, upon my honour; but I see how it is: you are indifferent to everybody's admiration, except that of one gentleman, who shall be nameless. Nay, I cannot blame you" (speaking more seriously)—"your feelings are easily understood. Where the heart is really attached, I know very well how little one can be pleased with the attention of anybody else. Everything is so insipid, so uninteresting, that does not relate to the beloved object! I can perfectly comprehend your feelings."

"But you should not persuade me that I think so very much about Mr Tilney, for perhaps I may never see him again."

" Not see him again ! My dearest creature, do not talk of it. I am sure you would be miserable if you thought so."

" No, indeed ; I should not. I do not pretend to say that I was not very much pleased with him ; but while I have Udolpho to read, I feel as if nobody could make me miserable. Oh ! the dreadful black veil ! My dear Isabella, I am sure there must be Laurentina's skeleton behind it."

" It is so odd to me, that you should never have read Udolpho before ; but I suppose Mrs Morland objects to novels."

" No, she does not. She very often reads Sir Charles Grandison herself ; but new books do not fall in our way."

" Sir Charles Grandison ! That is an amazing horrid book, is it not ? I remember Miss Andrews could not get through the first volume."

" It is not like Udolpho at all ; but yet I think it is very entertaining."

" Do you indeed ? you surprize me ; I thought it had not been readable. But, my dearest Catherine, have you settled what to wear on your head to-night ? I am determined, at all events, to be dressed exactly like you. The men take notice of *that* sometimes, you know."

" But it does not signify, if they do," said Catherine, very innocently,

" Signify ! oh heavens ! I make it a rule never to mind what they say. They are very often amazingly impertinent, if you do not treat them with spirit, and make them keep their distance."

" Are they ? Well, I never observed *that*. They always behave very well to me."

" Oh ! they give themselves such airs. They are the most conceited creatures in the world, and think themselves of so much importance ! By-the-bye, though I have thought of it a hundred times, I have always forgot to ask you what is your favourite complexion in a man. Do you like them best dark or fair ? "

" I hardly know. I never much thought about it. Something between both, I think ; brown : not fair, and not very dark."

"Very well, Catherine. That is exactly he. I have not forgot your description of Mr Tilney : 'a brown skin, with dark eyes, and rather dark hair.' Well, my taste is different. I prefer light eyes ; and as to complexion, do you know, I like a sallow better than any other. You must not betray me, if you should ever meet with one of your acquaintance answering that description."

"Betray you ! What do you mean ? "

"Nay, do not distress me. I believe I have said too much. Let us drop the subject."

Catherine, in some amazement, complied ; and, after remaining a few moments silent, was on the point of reverting to what interested her at that time rather more than anything else in the world, Laurentina's skeleton ; when her friend prevented her, by saying : " For Heaven's sake ! let us move away from this end of the room. Do you know, there are two odious young men who have been staring at me this half hour. They really put me quite out of countenance. Let us go and look at the arrivals. They will hardly follow us there."

Away they walked to the book ; and while Isabella examined the names, it was Catherine's employment to watch the proceedings of these alarming young men.

"They are not coming this way, are they ? I hope they are not so impertinent as to follow us. Pray let me know if they are coming. I am determined I will not look up."

In a few moments Catherine, with unaffected pleasure, assured her that she need not be longer uneasy, as the gentlemen had just left the Pump-room.

" And which way are they gone ? " said Isabella, turning hastily round. "One was a very good-looking young man."

" They went towards the churchyard."

"Well, I am amazingly glad I have got rid of them. And now, what say you to going to Edgar's Buildings with me, and looking at my new hat ? You said you should like to see it.'

Catherine readily agreed. " Only," she added, " perhaps we may overtake the two young men."

" Oh ! never mind that. If we make haste, we shall pass by them presently, and I am dying to show you my hat."

" But if we only wait a few minutes, there will be no danger of our seeing them at all."

" I shall not pay them any such compliment, I assure you. I have no notion of treating men with such respect. *That* is the way to spoil them."

Catherine had nothing to oppose against such reasoning ; and therefore, to show the independence of Miss Thorpe, and her resolution of humbling the sex, they set off immediately, as fast as they could walk, in pursuit of the two young men.

CHAPTER VII

HALF a minute conducted them through the Pump-yard to the archway, opposite Union Passage ; but here they were stopped. Everybody acquainted with Bath may remember the difficulties of crossing Cheap Street at this point; it is indeed a street of so impertinent a nature, so unfortunately connected with the great London and Oxford roads, and the principal inn of the city, that a day never passes in which parties of ladies, however important their business, whether in quest of pastry, millinery, or even (as in the present case) of young men, are not detained on one side or other by carriages, horsemen, or carts. This evil had been felt and lamented, at least three times a day, by Isabella since her residence in Bath ; and she was now fated to feel and lament it once more ; for at the very moment of coming opposite to Union Passage, and within view of the two gentlemen who were proceeding through the crowds, and threading the gutters of that interesting alley, they were prevented crossing by the approach of a gig, driven along on bad pavement by a most knowing-looking coachman, with all the vehemence that could most fitly endanger the lives of himself, his companion, and his horse.

" Oh, these odious gigs ! " said Isabella, looking up

" how I detest them ! " But this detestation, though so just, was of short duration, for she looked again, and exclaimed, " Delightful ! Mr Morland and my brother ! "

" Good heaven ! 'tis James ! " was uttered at the same moment by Catherine ; and, on catching the young men's eyes, the horse was immediately checked with a violence which almost threw him on his haunches, and the servant having now scampered up, the gentlemen jumped out, and the equipage was delivered to his care.

Catherine, by whom this meeting was wholly unexpected, received her brother with the liveliest pleasure ; and he, being of a very amiable disposition, and sincerely attached to her, gave every proof on his side of equal satisfaction, which he could have leisure to do, while the bright eyes of Miss Thorpe were incessantly challenging his notice ; and to her his devoirs were speedily paid, with a mixture of joy and embarrassment which might have informed Catherine, had she been more expert in the development of other people's feelings, and less simply engrossed by her own, that her brother thought her friend quite as pretty as she could do herself.

John Thorpe, who in the meantime, had been giving orders about the horses, soon joined them, and from him she directly received the amends which were her due ; for while he slightly and carelessly touched the hand of Isabella, on her he bestowed a whole scrape and half a short bow. He was a stout young man, of middling height, who, with a plain face and ungraceful form, seemed fearful of being too handsome, unless he wore the dress of a groom, and too much like a gentleman unless he were easy where he ought to be civil, and impudent where he might be allowed to be easy. He took out his watch : " How long do you think we have been running it from Tetbury, Miss Morland ? "

" I do not know the distance." Her brother told her that it was twenty-three miles.

" *Three* and twenty ! " cried Thorpe ; " five and twenty if it is an inch." Morland remonstrated, pleaded the authority of road-books, innkeepers, and milestones ; but his friend disregarded them all ; he had a surer test of distance. " I know it must be five and twenty," said he,

" by the time we have been doing it. It is now half after one ; we drove out of the inn-yard at Tetbury as the town-clock struck eleven ; and I defy any man in England to make my horse go less than ten miles in harness ; that makes it exactly twenty-five."

" You have lost an hour," said Morland ; " it was only ten o'clock when we came from Tetbury."

" Ten o'clock ! it was eleven, upon my soul ! I counted every stroke. This brother of yours would persuade me out of my senses, Miss Morland ; do but look at my horse ; did you ever see an animal so made for speed in your life ? " (The servant had just mounted the carriage and was driving off.) " Such true blood ! Three hours and a half, indeed, coming only three and twenty miles ! Look at that creature, and suppose it possible if you can."

" He *does* look very hot to be sure ! "

" Hot ! he had not turned a hair till we came to Walcot church : but look at his forehead ; look at his loins ; only see how he moves ; that horse *cannot* go less than ten miles an hour : tie his legs, and he will get on. What do you think of my gig, Miss Morland ? A neat one, is it not ? Well hung ; town built : I have not had it a month. It was built for a Christ-church man, a friend of mine, a very good sort of fellow ; he ran it a few weeks, till I believe, it was convenient to have done with it. I happened just then to be looking out for some light thing of the kind, though I had pretty well determined on a curricle too ; but I chanced to meet him on Magdalen Bridge, as he was driving into Oxford, last term : ' Ah ! Thorpe,' said he, ' do you happen to want such a little thing as this ? It is a capital one of the kind, but I am cursed tired of it.' ' Oh ! d——,' said I, ' I am your man ; what do you ask ? ' And how much do you think he did, Miss Morland ? "

" I am sure I cannot guess at all."

" Curricle-hung, you see ; seat, trunk, sword-case, splashing-board, lamps, silver moulding, all, you see, com-plete ; the iron-work as good as new, or better. He asked fifty guineas : I closed with him directly, threw down the money, and the carriage was mine."

" And I am sure," said Catherine, " I know so little

of such things, that I cannot judge whether it was cheap or dear."

" Neither one nor t'other ; I might have got it for less, I dare say ; but I hate haggling, and poor Freeman wanted cash."

" That was very good-natured of you," said Catherine, quite pleased.

" Oh ! d—— it, when one has the means of doing a kind thing by a friend, I hate to be pitiful."

An inquiry now took place into the intended movements of the young ladies ; and, on finding whither they were going, it was decided that the gentlemen should accompany them to Edgar's Buildings, and pay their respects to Mrs Thorpe. James and Isabella led the way ; and so well satisfied was the latter with her lot, so contentedly was she endeavouring to ensure a pleasant walk to him who brought the double recommendation of being her brother's friend and her friend's brother, so pure and uncoquettish were her feelings, that, though they overtook and passed the two offending young men in Milsom Street, she was so far from seeking to attract their notice, that she looked back at them only three times.

John Thorpe kept of course with Catherine, and, after a few minutes' silence, renewed the conversation about his gig : " You will find, however, Miss Morland, it would be reckoned a cheap thing by some people, for I might have sold it for ten guineas more the next day ; Jackson, of Oriel, bid me sixty at once ; Morland was with me at the time."

" Yes," said Morland, who overheard this ; " but you forget that your horse was included."

" My horse ! oh, d—— it ! I would not sell my horse for a hundred. Are you fond of an open carriage, Miss Morland ? "

" Yes, very ; I have hardly ever an opportunity of being in one ; but I am particularly fond of it."

" I am glad of it ; I will drive you out in mine every day."

" Thank you," said Catherine, in some distress, from a doubt of the propriety of accepting such an offer.

' I will drive you up Lansdown Hill to-morrow."

" Thank you ; but will not your horse want rest ? "

" Rest ! he has only come three and twenty miles to-day ; all nonsense ; nothing ruins horses so much as rest ; nothing knocks them up so soon. No, no ; I shall exercise mine at the average of four hours every day while I am here."

" Shall you, indeed ? " said Catherine, very seriously, " that will be forty miles a day."

" Forty ! aye, fifty for what I care. Well, I will drive you up Lansdown to-morrow ; mind, I am engaged."

" How delightful that will be ! " cried Isabella, turning round ; " my dearest Catherine, I quite envy you ; but I am afraid, brother, you will not have room for a third."

" A third, indeed ! no, no ; I did not come to Bath to drive my sisters about ; that would be a good joke, faith ! Morland must take care of you."

This brought on a dialogue of civilities between the other two ; but Catherine heard neither the particulars nor the result. Her companion's discourse now sunk from its hitherto animated pitch, to nothing more than a short, decisive sentence of praise or condemnation on the face of every woman they met ; and Catherine, after listening and agreeing as long as she could, with all the civility and deference of the youthful female mind, fearful of hazarding an opinion of its own in opposition to that of a self-assured man, especially where the beauty of her own sex is concerned, ventured at length to vary the subject by a question which had been long uppermost in her thoughts : it was, " Have you ever read ' Udolpho,' Mr Thorpe ? "

" ' Udolpho ! ' oh, Lord ! not I ; I never read novels ; I have something else to do."

Catherine, humbled and ashamed, was going to apologize for her question ; but he prevented her by saying, " Novels are all so full of nonsense and stuff ! there has not been a tolerably decent one come out since ' Tom Jones,' except the ' Monk ; ' I read that t'other day ; but as for all the others, they are the stupidest things in creation.

" I think you must like ' Udolpho,' if you were to read it ; it is so very interesting."

"Not I, faith! No, if I read any, it shall be Mrs Radcliffe's; her novels are amusing enough; they are worth reading; some fun and nature in *them*."

"Udolpho was written by Mrs Radcliffe," said Catherine, with some hesitation, from the fear of mortifying him.

"No, sure; was it? Aye, I remember, so it was; I was thinking of that other stupid book, written by that woman they make such a fuss about; she who married the French emigrant."

"I suppose you mean Camilla!"

"Yes, that's the book; such unnatural stuff! An old man playing at see-saw; I took up the first volume once, and looked it over, but I soon found it would not do; indeed, I guessed what sort of stuff it must be before I saw it: as soon as I heard she had married an emigrant, I was sure I should never be able to get through it."

"I have never read it."

"You had no loss, I assure you; it is the horridest nonsense you can imagine; there is nothing in the world in it but an old man's playing at see-saw and learning Latin; upon my soul, there is not."

This critique, the justness of which was unfortunately lost on poor Catherine, brought them to the door of Mrs Thorpe's lodgings, and the feelings of the discerning and unprejudiced reader of Camilla gave way to the feelings of the dutiful and affectionate son, as they met Mrs Thorpe, who had descried them from above, in the passage. "Ah, mother, how do you do?" said he, giving her a hearty shake of the hand: "where did you get that quiz of a hat, it makes you look like an old witch? Here is Morland and I come to stay a few days with you; so you must look out for a couple of good beds some where near." And this address seemed to satisfy all the fondest wishes of the mother's heart, for she received him with the most delighted and exulting affection. On his two younger sisters he then bestowed an equal portion of his fraternal tenderness, for he asked each of them how they did, and observed that they both looked very ugly.

These manners did not please Catherine; but he was James's friend and Isabella's brother; and her judg-

ment was further bought off by Isabella's assuring her,
when they withdrew to see the new hat, that John thought
her the most charming girl in the world, and by John's
engaging her before they parted to dance with him that
evening. Had she been older or vainer, such attacks
might have done little ; but where youth and diffidence
are united, it requires uncommon steadiness of reason
to resist the attraction of being called the most charming
girl in the world, and being so very early engaged as a
partner ; and the consequence was, that when the two
Morlands, after sitting an hour with the Thorpes, set off
to walk together to Mr Allen's, and James, as the door
was closed on them, said, " Well, Catherine, how do you
like my friend Thorpe ?·" instead of answering, as she
probably would have done, had there been no friendship
and no flattery in the case, " I do not like him at all ; "
she directly replied, " I like him very much ; he seems
very agreeable."

" He is as good-natured a fellow as ever lived ; a little
of a rattle ; but that will recommend him to your sex,
I believe : and how do you like the rest of the family ? "

" Very, very much indeed : Isabella particularly."

" I am very glad to hear you say so : she is just the kind
of young woman I could wish to see you attached to ;
she has so much good sense, and is so thoroughly unaffected
and amiable ; I always wanted you to know her ; and she
seems very fond of you. She said the highest things in
your praise that could possibly be ; and the praise of such
a girl as Miss Thorpe, even you, Catherine," taking her
hand with affection, " may be proud of."

" Indeed I am," she replied ; " I love her exceedingly,
and am delighted to find that you like her too. You hardly
mentioned anything of her when you wrote to me after
your visit there."

" Because I thought I should soon see you myself. I
hope you will be a great deal together while you are in
Bath. She is a most amiable girl ; such a superior understanding ! How fond all the family are of her ; she is
evidently the general favourite ; and how much she must
be admired in such a place as this. Is not she ? "

"Yes, very much, indeed, I fancy ; Mr Allen thinks her the prettest girl in Bath."

"I dare say he does ; and I do not know any man who is a better judge of beauty than Mr Allen. I need not ask you whether you are happy here, my dear Catherine ; with such a companion and friend as Isabella Thorpe, it would be impossible for you to be otherwise ; and the Allens, I am sure, are very kind to you."

"Yes, very kind ; I never was so happy before ; and now you are come it will be more delightful than ever. How good it is of you to come so far on purpose to see *me*."

James accepted this tribute of gratitude, and qualified his conscience for accepting it too, by saying with perfect sincerity, " Indeed, Catherine, I love you dearly."

Inquiries and communications concerning brothers and sisters, the situation of some, the growth of the rest, and other family matters, now passed between them, and continued, with only one small digression on James's part, in praise of Miss Thorpe, till they reached Pulteney Street, where he was welcomed with great kindness by Mr and Mrs Allen, invited by the former to dine with them, and summoned by the latter to guess the price and weigh the merits of a new muff and tippet. A pre-engagement in Edgar's Buildings prevented his accepting the invitation of one friend, and obliged him to hurry away as soon as he had satisfied the demands of the other. The time of the two parties' uniting in the Octagon Room being correctly adjusted, Catherine was then left to the luxury of a raised, restless, and frightened imagination over the pages of Udolpho, lost from all worldly concerns of dressing and dinner, incapable of soothing Mrs Allen's fears on the delay of an expected dressmaker, and having only one minute in sixty to bestow even on the reflection of her own felicity, in being already engaged for the evening.

CHAPTER VIII

In spite of Udolpho and the dressmaker, however, the party from Pulteney Street reached the Upper-Rooms in very good time. The Thorpes and James Morland were there only two minutes before them ; and Isabella having gone through the usual ceremonial of meeting her friend with the most smiling and affectionate haste, of admiring the set of her gown, and envying the curl of her hair, they followed their chaperons, arm-in-arm, into the ball-room, whispering to each other whenever a thought occurred, and supplying the place of many ideas by a squeeze of the hand or a smile of affection.

The dancing began within a few minutes after they were seated ; and James, who had been engaged quite as long as his sister, was very importunate with Isabella to stand up ; but John was gone into the card-room to speak to a friend, and nothing, she declared, should induce her to join the set before her dear Catherine could join it too. " I assure you," said she, " I would not stand up without your dear sister, for all the world ; for if I did, we should certainly be separated the whole evening." Catherine accepted this kindness with gratitude, and they continued as they were for three minutes longer, when Isabella, who had been talking to James on the other side of her, turned again to his sister and whispered, " My dear creature, I am afraid I must leave you, your brother is so amazingly impatient to begin ; I know you will not mind my going away, and I dare say John will be back in a moment, and then you may easily find me out." Catherine, though a little disappointed, had too much good nature to make any opposition, and the others rising up, Isabella had only time to press her friend's hand and say, " Good-bye, my dear love," before they hurried off. The younger Miss Thorpes being also dancing, Catherine was left to the mercy of Mrs Thorpe and Mrs Allen, between whom she now remained. She could not help being vexed at the non-appearance of Mr Thorpe : for she not only longed to be dancing, but was likewise aware that, as the real dignity of her

situation could not be known, she was sharing with the
scores of other young ladies still sitting down all the discredit of wanting a partner. To be disgraced in the eye
of the world, to wear the appearance of infamy while her
heart is all purity, her actions all innocence, and the misconduct of another the true source of her debasement,
is one of those circumstances which peculiarly belong to
the heroine's life, and her fortitude under it what particularly
dignifies her character. Catherine had fortitude too ;
she suffered, but no murmur passed her lips.

From this state of humiliation she was roused, at the
end of ten minutes, to a pleasanter feeling, by seeing, not
Mr Thorpe, but Mr Tilney, within three yards of the place
where they sat : he seemed to be moving that way, but he
did not see her, and, therefore, the smile and the blush,
which his sudden re-appearance raised in Catherine, passed
away without sullying her heroic importance. He looked
as handsome and as lively as ever, and was talking with
interest to a fashionable and pleasing-looking young woman,
who leant on his arm, and whom Catherine immediately
guessed to be his sister ; thus unthinkingly throwing away
a fair opportunity of considering him lost to her for ever,
by being married already. But, guided only by what
was simple and probable, it had never entered her head
that Mr Tilney could be married ; he had not behaved,
he had not talked, like the married men to whom she had
been used ; he had never mentioned a wife, and he had
acknowledged a sister. From these circumstances sprang
the instant conclusion of his sister's now being by his side ;
and, therefore, instead of turning of a deathlike paleness,
and falling in a fit on Mrs Allen's bosom, Catherine sat erect,
in the perfect use of her senses, and with cheeks only a
little redder than usual.

Mr Tilney and his companion, who continued, though
slowly, to approach, were immediately preceded by a lady,
an acquaintance of Mrs Thorpe ; and this lady stopping
to speak to her, they, as belonging to her, stopped likewise,
and Catherine, catching Mr Tilney's eye, instantly received
from him the smiling tribute of recognition. She returned
it with pleasure, and then advancing still nearer, he spoke

both to her and Mrs Allen, by whom he was very civilly acknowledged. " I am very happy to see you again, sir, indeed ; I was afraid you had left Bath." He thanked her for her fears, and said that he had quitted it for a week on the very morning after his having had the pleasure of seeing her.

" Well, sir, and I dare say you are not sorry to be back again, for it is just the place for young people ; and, indeed, for everybody else too. I tell Mr Allen, when he talks of being sick of it, that I am sure he should not complain, for it is so very agreeable a place, that it is much better to be here than at home at this dull time of year. I tell him he is quite in luck to be sent here for his health."

" And I hope, madam, that Mr Allen will be obliged to like the place, from finding it of service to him."

" Thank you, sir. I have no doubt that he will. A neighbour of ours, Dr Skinner, was here for his health last winter, and came away quite stout."

" That circumstance must give great encouragement."

" Yes, sir ; and Dr Skinner and his family were here three months ; so I tell Mr Allen he must not be in a hurry to get away."

Here they were interrupted by a request from Mrs Thorpe to Mrs Allen, that she would move a little to accommodate Mrs Hughes and Miss Tilney with seats, as they had agreed to join their party. This was accordingly done, Mr Tilney still continuing standing before them ; and, after a few minutes' consideration, he asked Catherine to dance with him. This compliment, delightful as it was, produced severe mortification to the lady ; and, in giving her denial, she expressed her sorrow on the occasion so very much as if she really felt it, that had Thorpe, who joined her just afterwards, been half a minute earlier, he might have thought her sufferings rather too acute. The very easy manner in which he then told her that he had kept her waiting, did not by any means reconcile her more to her lot ; nor did the particulars which he entered into while they were standing up, of the horses and dogs of the friend whom he had just left, and of a proposed exchange of terriers between them, interest her so much as to prevent her looking very often

towards that part of the room where she had left Mr Tilney.
Of her dear Isabella, to whom she particularly longed to
point out that gentleman, she could see nothing. They
were in different sets. She was separated from all her
party, and away from all her acquaintance ; one mortification succeeded another, and from the whole she deduced
this useful lesson, that to go previously engaged to a ball
does not necessarily increase either the dignity or enjoyment
of a young lady. From such a moralizing strain as this
she was suddenly roused by a touch on the shoulder ; and
turning round, perceived Mrs Hughes directly behind her,
attended by Miss Tilney and a gentleman. " I beg your
pardon, Miss Morland," said she, " for this liberty, but I
cannot anyhow get to Miss Thorpe ; and Mrs Thorpe said
she was sure you would not have the least objection to
letting in this young lady by you." Mrs Hughes could
not have applied to any creature in the room more happy
to oblige her than Catherine. The young ladies were introduced to each other, Miss Tilney expressing a proper sense
of such goodness ; Miss Morland, with the real delicacy
of a generous mind, making light of the obligation ; and
Mrs Hughes, satisfied with having so respectably settled
her young charge, returned to her party.

Miss Tilney had a good figure, a pretty face, and a very
agreeable countenance ; and her air, though it had not
all the decided pretension, the resolute stilishness, of Miss
Thorpe's, had more real elegance. Her manners shewed
good sense and good breeding ; they were neither shy,
nor affectedly open ; and she seemed capable of being
young, attractive, and at a ball, without wanting to fix
the attention of every man near her, and without exaggerated
feelings of extatic delight or inconceivable vexation on every
little trifling occurrence. Catherine, interested at once
by her appearance and her relationship to Mr Tilney, was
desirous of being acquainted with her, and readily talked,
therefore, whenever she could think of anything to say,
and had courage and leisure for saying it. But the hindrance thrown in the way of a very speedy intimacy, by the
frequent want of one or more of these requisites, prevented
their doing more than going through the first rudiments

of an acquaintance, by informing themselves how well the other liked Bath, how much she admired its buildings and surrounding country ; whether she drew, or played, or sang, and whether she was fond of riding on horseback.

The two dances were scarcely concluded, before Catherine found her arm gently seized by her faithful Isabella, who in great spirits exclaimed, " At last I have got you. My dearest creature, I have been looking for you this hour. What could induce you to come into this set, when you knew I was in the other ? I have been quite wretched without you."

" My dear Isabella, how was it possible for me to get at you ? I could not even see where you were."

" So I told your brother all the time, but he would not believe me. Do go and see for her, Mr Morland, said I ; but all in vain, he would not stir an inch. Was not it so, Mr Morland ? But you men are all so immoderately lazy ! I have been scolding him to such a degree, my dear Catherine, you would be quite amazed. You know I never stand upon ceremony with such people."

" Look at that young lady with the white beads round her head," whispered Catherine, detaching her friend from James : " it is Mr Tilney's sister."

" Oh heavens ! you don't say so ! Let me look at her this moment. What a delightful girl ! I never saw anything half so beautiful ! But where is her all-conquering brother ? Is he in the room ! Point him out to me this instant, if he is ; I die to see him. Mr Morland, you are not to listen ; we are not talking about you."

"But what is all this whispering about? What is going on?"

" There now, I knew how it would be ! You men have such restless curiosity ! Talk of the curiosity of women, indeed ! 'tis nothing. But be satisfied ; for you are not to know anything at all of the matter."

" And is that likely to satisfy me, do you think ? "

" Well, I declare, I never knew anything like you. What can it signify to you, what we are talking of ? Perhaps we are talking about you ; therefore I would advise you not to listen, or you may happen to hear something not very agreeable."

In this common-place chatter, which lasted some time, the original subject seemed entirely forgotten ; and though Catherine was very well pleased to have it dropped for a while, she could not avoid a little suspicion at the total suspension of all Isabella's impatient desire to see Mr Tilney. When the orchestra struck up a fresh dance, James would have led his fair partner away, but she resisted. " I tell you, Mr Morland," she cried, " I would not do such a thing for all the world. How can you be so teasing ! Only conceive, my dear Catherine, what your brother wants me to do ? He wants me to dance with him again, though I tell him that it is a most improper thing, and entirely against the rules. It would make us the talk of the place, if we were not to change partners."

" Upon my honour," said James, " in these public assemblies it is as often done as not."

" Nonsense, how can you say so ? But when you men have a point to carry, you never stick at anything. My sweet Catherine, do support me ; persuade your brother how impossible it is. Tell him, that it would quite shock you to see me do such a thing ; now would not it ? "

" No, not at all ; but if you think it wrong, you had much better thange."

" There," cried Isabella, " you hear what your sister says, and yet you will not mind her. Well, remember that it is not my fault, if we set all the old ladies in Bath in a bustle. Come along, my dearest Catherine, for heaven's sake, and stand by me." And off they went to regain their former place. John Thorpe, in the meanwhile, had walked away ; and Catherine, ever willing to give Mr Tilney an opportunity of repeating the agreeable request which had already flattered her once, made her way to Mrs Allen and Mrs Thorpe as fast as she could, in the hope of finding him still with them, a hope which, when it proved to be fruitless, she felt to have been highly unreasonable. " Well, my dear," said Mrs Thorpe, impatient for praise of her son, " I hope you have had an agreeable partner."

" Very agreeable, madam."

" I am glad of it. John has charming spirits, has not he?"

" Did you meet Mr Tilney, my dear ? " said Mrs Allen.

" No : where is he ? "

" He was with us just now, and said he was so tired of lounging about, that he was resolved to go and dance ; so I thought perhaps he would ask you, if he met with you."

" Where can he be ? " said Catherine, looking round ; but she had not looked round long, before she saw him leading a young lady to the dance.

" Ah ! he has got a partner ; I wish he had asked *you*," said Mrs Allen ; and after a short silence, she added, " he is a very agreeable young man."

" Indeed he is, Mrs Allen," said Mrs Thorpe, smiling complacently ; " I must say it, though I *am* his mother, that there is not a more agreeable young man in the world."

This inapplicable answer might have been too much for the comprehension of many ; but it did not puzzle Mrs Allen ; for, after only a moment's consideration, she said, in a whisper, to Catherine, " I dare say she thought I was speaking of her son."

Catherine was disappointed and vexed. She seemed to have missed, by so little, the very object she had had in view ; and this persuasion did not incline her to a very gracious reply, when John Thorpe came up to her soon afterwards, and said, " Well, Miss Morland, I suppose you and I are to stand up and jig it together again ? "

" Oh, no ! I am much obliged to you, our two dances are over ; and, besides, I am tired, and do not mean to dance any more."

" Do not you ? then let us walk about and quiz people. Come along with me, and I will show you the four greatest quizzers in the room ; my two younger sisters and their partners. I have been laughing at them this half hour."

Again Catherine excused herself ; and at last he walked off to quiz his sisters by himself. The rest of the evening she found very dull ; Mr Tilney was drawn away from their party at tea to attend that of his partner ; Miss Tilney, though belonging to it, did not sit near her ; and James and Isabella were so much engaged in conversing together, that the latter had no leisure to bestow more on her friend than one smile, one squeeze, and one " dearest Catherine."

CHAPTER IX

THE progress of Catherine's unhappiness from the events of the evening was as follows. It appeared first in a general dissatisfaction with everybody about her, while she remained in the rooms, which speedily brought on considerable weariness and a violent desire to go home. This, on arriving in Pulteney Street, took the direction of extraordinary hunger, and when that was appeased, changed into an earnest longing to be in bed. Such was the extreme point of her distress ; for when there she immediately fell into a sound sleep, which lasted nine hours, and from which she awoke perfectly revived, in excellent spirits, with fresh hopes and fresh schemes. The first wish of her heart was to improve her acquaintance with Miss Tilney, and almost her first resolution to seek her for that purpose in the Pump-room at noon. In the Pump-room one so newly arrived in Bath must be met with ; and that building she had already found so favourable for the discovery of female excellence, and the completion of female intimacy, so admirably adapted for secret discourses and unlimited confidence, that she was most reasonably encouraged to expect another friend from within its walls. Her plan for the morning thus settled, she sat quietly down to her book after breakfast, resolving to remain in the same place and the same employment till the clock struck one ; and from habitude very little incommoded by the remarks and ejaculations of Mrs Allen, whose vacancy of mind, and incapacity for thinking, were such, that, as she never talked a great deal, so she could never be entirely silent ; and, therefore, while she sat at her work, if she lost her needle, or broke her thread, if she heard a carriage in the street, or saw a speck upon her gown, she must observe it aloud, whether there were any one at leisure to answer her or not. At about half-past twelve a remarkably loud rap drew her in haste to the window, and scarcely had she time to inform Catherine of there being two open carriages at the door, in the first only a servant, her brother driving Miss Thorpe in the second, before John Thorpe came running up stairs, calling out, " Well, Miss Morland, here I am. Have you been waiting long ? We could not come before, the old devil of a coachmaker was such an eternity finding out a thing fit to be got into, and now it is ten thousand to one but they break down before we are out of the street. How do you do, Mrs Allen ? A famous ball last night, was not it ? Come, Miss Morland, be quick, for the others are in a confounded hurry to be off. They want to get their tumble over."

" What do you mean ? " said Catherine ; " where are you all going to ? "

" Going to ! Why, you have not forgot our engagement ? Did not we agree together to take a drive this morning ? What a head you have ? We are going up Claverton Down."

" Something was said about it, I remember," said Catherine, looking at Mrs Allen for her opinion ; " but really, I did not expect you."

" Not expect me ! That's a good one ! And what a dust you would have made, if I had not come ! "

Catherine's silent appeal to her friend, meanwhile, was entirely thrown away ; for Mrs Allen, not being at all in the habit of conveying any expression herself by a look, was not aware of its being ever intended by any body else ; and Catherine, whose desire of seeing Miss Tilney again, could at that moment bear a short delay in favour of a drive, and who thought there could be no impropriety in her going with Mr Thorpe, as Isabella was going at the same time with James, was therefore obliged to speak plainer. " Well ma'am, what do you say to it ? Can you spare me for an hour or two ? Shall I go ? "

" Do just as you please, my dear," replied Mrs Allen, with the most placid indifference. Catherine took the advice, and ran off to get ready. In a very few minutes, she re-appeared, having scarcely allowed the two others time enough to get through a few short sentences in her praise, after Thorpe had procured Mrs Allen's admiration of his gig, and then, receiving her friend's parting good wishes, they both hurried down stairs. " My dearest creature," cried Isabella, to whom the duty of friendship immediately called her before she could get into the carriage, "you have been at least three hours getting ready: I was afraid you were ill. What a delightful ball we had last night! I have a thousand things to say to you; but make haste and get in, for I long to be off."

Catherine followed her orders and turned away, but not too soon to hear her friend exclaim aloud to James, "What a sweet girl she is! I quite doat on her."

"You will not be frightened, Miss Morland," said Thorpe, as he handed her in, "if my horse should dance about a little at first setting off. He will most likely give a plunge or two, and perhaps take the rest for a minute; but he will soon know his master. He is full of spirits, playful as can be, but there is no vice in him."

Catherine did not think the portrait a very inviting one, but it was too late to retreat, and she was too young to own herself frightened; so, resigning herself to her fate, and trusting to the animal's boasted knowledge of its owner, she sat peaceably down, and saw Thorpe sit down by her. Everything being then arranged, the servant who stood at the horse's head was bid in an important voice "to let him go," and off they went in the quietest manner imaginable, without a plunge or a caper, or anything like one. Catherine, delighted at so happy an escape, spoke her pleasure aloud with grateful surprize; and her companion immediately made the matter perfectly simple by assuring her that it was entirely owing to the peculiarly judicious manner in which he had then held the reins, and the singular discernment and dexterity with which he had directed his whip. Catherine, though she could not help wondering that, with such perfect command of his horse, he should think it necessary to alarm her with a relation of its tricks, congratulated herself sincerely on being under the care of so excellent a coachman; and perceiving that the animal continued to go on in the same quiet manner, without showing the smallest propensity towards any unpleasant vivacity, and (considering its inevitable pace was ten miles an hour) by no means alarmingly fast, gave herself up to all the enjoyment of air and exercise of the most invigorating kind in a fine mild day of February, with the consciousness of safety. A silence of several minutes

succeeded their first short dialogue. It was broken by
Thorpe's saying very abruptly, " Old Allen is as rich as a
Jew, is not he ? " Catherine did not understand him, and
he repeated his question, adding in explanation, " Old
Allen, the man you are with."

" Oh ! Mr Allen you mean. Yes, I believe he is very
rich."

" And no children at all ? "

" No, not any."

" A famous thing for his next heirs. He is *your* godfather, is not he ? "

" My godfather ! No."

" But you are always very much with them ? "

" Yes, very much."

" Aye, that is what I meant. He seems a good kind
of old fellow enough, and has lived very well in his time,
I dare say ; he is not gouty for nothing. Does he drink
his bottle a day now ? "

" His bottle a-day ! No. Why should you think of
such a thing ? He is a very temperate man, and you could
not fancy him in liquor last night ? "

" Lord help me ! You women are always thinking
of men's being in liquor. Why, you do not suppose a
man is overset by a bottle ? I am sure of *this*, that if everybody was to drink their bottle a-day, there would not be
half the disorders in the world there are now. It would
be a famous good thing for us all."

" I cannot believe it."

" Oh ! lord, it would be the saving of thousands. There
is not the hundredth part of the wine consumed in this
kingdom that there ought to be. Our foggy climate wants
help."

" And yet I have heard that there is a great deal of wine
drank in Oxford."

" Oxford ! There is no drinking at Oxford now, I assure
you. Nobody drinks there. You would hardly meet
with a man who goes beyond his four pints at the utmost.
Now, for instance, it was reckoned a remarkable thing at
the last party in my rooms, that upon an average we cleared
about five pints a head. It was looked upon as something

out of the common way. *Mine* is famous good stuff, to be sure. You would not often meet with anything like it in Oxford, and that may account for it. But this will just give you a notion of the general rate of drinking there."

"Yes, it does give a notion," said Catherine, warmly, "and that is, that you all drink a great deal more wine than I thought you did. However, I am sure James does not drink so much."

This declaration brought on a loud and overpowering reply, of which no part was very distinct, except the frequent exclamations, amounting almost to oaths, which adorned it, and Catherine was left, when it ended, with rather a strengthened belief of there being a great deal of wine drank in Oxford, and the same happy conviction of her brother's comparative sobriety.

Thorpe's ideas then all reverted to the merits of his own equipage, and she was called on to admire the spirit and freedom with which his horse moved along, and the ease which his paces, as well as the excellence of the springs, gave the motion of the carriage. She followed him in all his admiration as well as she could. To go before, or beyond him, was impossible. His knowledge and her ignorance of the subject, his rapidity of expression and her diffidence of herself, put that out of her power; she could strike out nothing new in commendation, but she readily echoed whatever he chose to assert, and it was finally settled between them, without any difficulty, that his equipage was altogether the most complete of its kind in England, his carriage the neatest, his horse the best goer, and himself the best coachman. "You do not really think, Mr Thorpe," said Catherine, venturing after some time to consider the matter as entirely decided, and to offer some little variation on the subject, "that James's gig will break down?"

"Break down! Oh, lord! Did you ever see such a little tittuppy thing in your life? There is not a sound piece of iron about it. The wheels have been fairly worn out these ten years at least; and as for the body, upon my soul, you might shake it to pieces yourself with a touch. It is the most devilish little ricketty business I ever beheld!

Thank God ! we have got a better. I would not be bound to go two miles in it for fifty thousand pounds."

" Good heavens ! " cried Catherine, quite frightened, " then pray let us turn back ; they will certainly meet with an accident if we go on. Do let us turn back, Mr Thorpe ; stop and speak to my brother, and tell him how very unsafe it is."

" Unsafe ! Oh, lord ! what is there in that ? They will only get a roll if it does break down ; and there is plenty of dirt, it will be excellent falling. Oh, curse it ! the carriage is safe enough if a man knows how to drive it ; a thing of that sort in good hands will last above twenty years after it is fairly worn out. Lord bless you ! I would undertake for five pounds to drive it to York and back again without losing a nail."

Catherine listened with astonishment. She knew not how to reconcile two such very different accounts of the same thing ; for she had not been brought up to under-stand the propensities of a rattle, nor to know to how many idle assertions and impudent falsehoods the excess of vanity will lead. Her own family were plain matter-of-fact people, who seldom aimed at wit of any kind ; her father at the utmost being contented with a pun, and her mother with a proverb ; they were not in the habit, there-fore, of telling lies to increase their importance, or of assert-ing at one moment what they would contradict the next. She reflected on the affair for some time in much perplexity, and was more than once on the point of requesting from Mr Thorpe a clearer insight into his real opinion on the subject ; but she checked herself, because it appeared to her that he did not excel in giving those clearer insights, in making those things plain which he had before made ambiguous, and, joining to this the consideration that he would not really suffer his sister and his friend to be exposed to a danger from which he might easily preserve them, she concluded at last that he must know the carriage to be in fact perfectly safe, and therefore would alarm herself no longer. By him the whole matter seemed entirely forgotten ; and all the rest of his conversation, or rather talk, began and ended with himself and his own concerns.

He told her of horses which he had bought for a trifle and sold for incredible sums ; of racing matches, in which his judgment had infallibly foretold the winner ; of shooting parties, in which he had killed more birds (though without having one good shot) than all his companions together ; and described to her some famous day's sport with the fox-hounds, in which his foresight and skill in directing the dogs had repaired the mistakes of the most experienced huntsman, and in which the boldness of his riding, though it had never endangered his own life for a moment, had been constantly leading others into difficulties, which, he calmly concluded, had broken the necks of many.

Little as Catherine was in the habit of judging for herself, and unfixed as were her general notions of what men ought to be, she could not entirely repress a doubt, while she bore with the effusions of his endless conceit, of his being altogether completely agreeable. It was a bold surmise, for he was Isabella's brother, and she had been assured by James that his manners would recommend him to all her sex ; but in spite of this, the extreme weariness of his company which crept over her before they had been out an hour, and which continued unceasingly to increase till they stopped in Pulteney Street again, induced her in some small degree to resist such high authority, and to distrust his powers of giving universal pleasure.

When they arrived at Mrs Allen's door, the astonishment of Isabella was hardly to be expressed on finding that it was too late in the day for them to attend her friend into the house :—" Past three o'clock ! " it was inconceivable, incredible, impossible, and she would neither believe her own watch, nor her brother's, nor the servants, she would believe no assurance of it founded on reason or reality, till Morland produced his watch and ascertained the fact : to have doubted a moment longer *then*, would have been equally inconceivable, incredible, and impossible, and she could only protest over and over again, that no two hours and a half had ever gone off so swiftly before, as Catherine was called on to confirm ; Catherine could not tell a false-hood even to please Isabella ; but the latter was spared the misery of her friend's dissenting voice by not waiting for her answer. Her own feelings entirely engrossed her; her wretchedness was most acute on finding herself obliged to go directly home. It was ages since she had had a moment's conversation with her dearest Catherine, and though she had such thousands of things to say to her, it appeared as if they were never to be together again; so with smiles of most exquisite misery, and the laughing eye of utter despondency, she bade her friend adieu, and went on.

Catherine found Mrs Allen just returned from all the busy idleness of the morning, and was immediately greeted with, " Well, my dear, here you are !" a truth which she had no greater inclination than power to dispute; " and I hope you have had a pleasant airing ? "

" Yes, ma'am, I thank you; we could not have had a nicer day."

" So Mrs Thorpe said. She was vastly pleased at your all going."

" You have seen Mrs Thorpe, then ? "

" Yes ; I went to the Pump-room as soon as you were gone, and there I met her, and we had a great deal of talk together. She says there was hardly any veal to be got at market this morning, it is so uncommonly scarce."

" Did you see any body else of our acquaintance ? "

" Yes ; we agreed to take a turn in the Crescent, and there we met Mrs Hughes, and Mr and Miss Tilney walking with her."

" Did you, indeed ? and did they speak to you ? "

" Yes ; we walked along the Crescent together for half an hour. They seem very agreeable people. Miss Tilney was in a very pretty spotted muslin, and I fancy, by what I can learn, that she always dresses very handsomely. Mrs Hughes talked to me a great deal about the family."

" And what did she tell you of them ? "

" Oh ! a vast deal, indeed ; she hardly talked of anything else."

" Did she tell you what part of Gloucestershire they come from ? "

" Yes, she did, but I cannot recollect now. But they are very good kind of people, and very rich. Mrs Tilney was a Miss Drummond, and she and Mrs Hughes were school-fellows ; and Miss Drummond had a very large fortune, and, when she married, her father gave her twenty thousand pounds, and five hundred to buy wedding clothes. Mrs Hughes saw all the clothes after they came from the warehouse."

" And are Mr and Mrs Tilney in Bath ? "

" Yes, I fancy they are, but I am not quite certain. Upon recollection, however, I have a notion they are both dead ; at least the mother is ; yes, I am sure Mrs Tilney is dead, because Mrs Hughes told me there was a very beautiful set of pearls that Mr Drummond gave his daughter on her wedding-day, and that Miss Tilney has got now, for they were put by for her when her mother died."

" And is Mr Tilney, my partner, the only son ? "

" I cannot be quite positive about that, my dear ; I have some idea he is ; but, however, he is a very fine young man, Mrs Hughes says, and likely to do very well."

Catherine inquired no further ; she had heard enough to feel that Mrs Allen had no real intelligence to give, and that she was most particularly unfortunate herself in having missed such a meeting with both brother and sister. Could she have forseen such a circumstance, nothing should have persuaded her to go out with the others ; and, as it was, she could only lament her ill-luck, and think over what she had lost, till it was clear to her that the drive had by no means been very pleasant, and that John Thorpe hmiself was quite disagreeable.

CHAPTER X

THE Allens, Thorpes, and Morlands, all met in the evening at the theatre ; and, as Catherine and Isabella sat together, there was then an opportunity for the latter to utter some few of the many thousand things which had been collecting within her for communication in the immeasurable length of time which had divided them. " Oh, heavens ! my beloved Catherine, have I got you at last ? " was her address on Catherine's entering the box and sitting by her. " Now,

Mr Morland," for he was close to her on the other side, " I shall not speak another word to you all the rest of the evening ; so I charge you not to expect it. My sweetest Catherine, how have you been this long age ? but I need not ask you, for you look delightfully. You really have done your hair in a more heavenly style than ever ; you mischievous creature, do you want to attract everybody ? I assure you, my brother is quite in love with you already ; and as for Mr Tilney—but *that* is a settled thing—even *your* modesty cannot doubt his attachment now ; his coming back to Bath makes it too plain. Oh ! what would not I give to see him ! I really am quite wild with impatience. My mother says he is the most delightful young man in the world ; she saw him this morning, you know. You must introduce him to me. Is he in the house now ? Look about, for heaven's sake ! I assure you I can hardly exist till I see him."

" No," said Catherine, " he is not here. I cannot see him any where."

" Oh, horrid ! am I never to be acquainted with him ? How do you like my gown ? I think it does not look amiss ; the sleeves were entirely my own thought. Do you know, I get so immoderately sick of Bath ! Your brother and I were agreeing this morning, that, though it is vastly well to be here for a few weeks, we would not live here for millions. We soon found out that our tastes were exactly alike in preferring the country to every other place ; really our opinions were so exactly the same, it was quite ridiculous ! There was not a single point in which we differed. I would not have had you by for the world ; you are such a sly thing, I am sure you would have made some droll remark or other about it."

" No, indeed, I should not."

" Oh, yes ! you would, indeed. I know you better than you know yourself. You would have told us that we seemed born for each other, or some nonsense of that kind, which would have distressed me beyond conception ; my cheeks would have been as red as your roses ; I would not have had you by for the world."

" Indeed, you do me injustice ; I would not have

made so improper a remark upon any account; and besides, I am sure it would never have entered my head."

Isabella smiled incredulously, and talked the rest of the evening to James.

Catherine's resolution of endeavouring to meet Miss Tilney again continued in full force the next morning; and till the usual moment of going to the Pump-room, she felt some alarm from the dread of a second prevention. But nothing of that kind occurred, no visitors appeared to delay them, and they all three set off in good time for the Pump-room, where the ordinary course of events and conversation took place. Mr Allen, after drinking his glass of water, joined some gentlemen to talk over the politics of the day, and compare the accounts of their newspapers; and the ladies walked about together, noticing every new face, and almost every new bonnet in the room. The female part of the Thorpe family, attended by James Morland, appeared among the crowd in less than a quarter of an hour, and Catherine immediately took her usual place by the side of her friend. James, who was now in constant attendance, maintained a similar position, and separating themselves from the rest of their party, they walked in that manner for some time, till Catherine began to doubt the happiness of a situation which, confining her entirely to her friend and brother, gave her very little share in the notice of either. They were always engaged in some sentimental discussion or lively dispute, but their sentiment was conveyed in such whispering voices, and their vivacity attended with so much laughter, that though Catherine's supporting opinion was not unfrequently called for by one or the other, she was never able to give any, from not having heard a word of the subject. At length, however, she was empowered to disengage herself from her friend, by the avowed necessity of speaking to Miss Tilney, whom she most joyfully saw just entering the room with Mrs Hughes, and whom she instantly joined, with a firmer determination to be acquainted, than she might have had courage to command, had she not been urged by the disappointment of the day before. Miss

Tilney met her with great civility, returned her advances with equal good will, and they continued talking together as long as both parties remained in the room ; and though in all probability not an observation was made, nor an expression used by either which had not been made and used some thousands of times before, under that roof, in every Bath season, yet the merit of their being spoken with simplicity and truth, and without personal conceit, might be something uncommon.

" How well your brother dances ! " was an artless exclamation of Catherine's towards the close of their conversation, which at once surprized and amused her companion.

" Henry ! " she replied with a smile. " Yes, he does dance very well."

" He must have thought it very odd to hear me say I was engaged the other evening, when he saw me sitting down. But I really had been engaged the whole day to Mr Thorpe." Miss Tilney could only bow. " You cannot think," added Catherine, after a moment's silence, " how surprized I was to see him again. I felt so sure of his being quite gone away."

" When Henry had the pleasure of seeing you before, he was in Bath but for a couple of days. He came only to engage lodgings for us."

" *That* never occurred to me ; and of course, not seeing him anywhere, I thought he must be gone. Was not the young lady he danced with on Monday a Miss Smith ? "

" Yes ; an acquaintance of Mrs Hughes."

" I dare say she was very glad to dance. Do you think her pretty ? "

" Not very."

" He never comes to the Pump-room, I suppose ? "

" Yes ; sometimes ; but he has rid out this morning with my father."

Mrs Hughes now joined them, and asked Miss Tilney if she was ready to go. " I hope I shall have the pleasure of seeing you again soon," said Catherine. " Shall you be at the cotillion ball to-morrow ? "

" Perhaps we—yes, I think we certainly shall."

"I am glad of it, for we shall all be there." This civility was duly returned, and they parted: on Miss Tilney's side with some knowledge of her new acquaintance's feelings, and on Catherine's without the smallest consciousness of having explained them.

She went home very happy. The morning had answered all her hopes, and the evening of the following day was now the object of expectation—the future good. What gown and what head-dress she should wear on the occasion became her chief concern. She cannot be justified in it. Dress is at all times a frivolous distinction, and excessive solicitude about it often destroys its own aim. Catherine knew all this very well; her great aunt had read her a lecture on the subject only the Christmas before; and yet she lay awake ten minutes on Wednesday night debating between her spotted and her tamboured muslin; and nothing but the shortness of the time prevented her buying a new one for the evening. This would have been an error in judgment, great though not uncommon, from which one of the other sex rather than her own, a brother rather than a great aunt, might have warned her; for man only can be aware of the insensibility of man towards a new gown. It would be mortifying to the feelings of many ladies could they be made to understand how little the heart of man is affected by what is costly or new in their attire; how little it is biassed by the texture of their muslin, and how unsusceptible of peculiar tenderness towards the spotted, the sprigged, the mull, or the jackonet. Woman is fine for her own satisfaction alone. No man will admire her the more, no woman will like her the better for it. Neatness and fashion are enough for the former, and a something of shabbiness or impropriety will be most endearing to the latter. But not one of these grave reflections troubled the tranquillity of Catherine.

She entered the rooms on Thursday evening with feelings very different from what had attended her thither the Monday before. She had then been exulting in her engagement to Thorpe, and was now chiefly anxious to avoid his sight, lest he should engage her again; for though she could not, dared not expect that Mr Tilney should ask her a third time to dance, her wishes, hopes, and plans, all centered in nothing less. Every young lady may feel for my heroine in this critical moment, for every young lady has at some time or other known the same agitation. All have been, or at least all have believed themselves to be, in danger from the pursuit of some one whom they wished to avoid ; and all have been anxious for the attentions of some one whom they wished to please. As soon as they were joined by the Thorpes, Catherine's agony began ; she fidgetted about if John Thorpe came towards her, hid herself as much a possible from his view, and when he spoke to her pretended not to hear him. The cotillions were over, the country-dancing beginning, and she saw nothing of the Tilneys. " Do not be frightened, my dear Catherine," whispered Isabella, " but I am really going to dance with your brother again. I declare positively it is quite shocking. I tell him he ought to be ashamed of himself, but you and John must keep us in countenance. Make haste, my dear creature, and come to us. John is just walked off, but he will be back in a moment."

Catherine had neither time nor inclination to answer. The others walked away. John Thorpe was still in view, and she gave herself up for lost. That she might not appear, however, to observe or expect him, she kept her eyes intently fixed on her fan ; and a self-condemnation for her folly, in supposing that among such a crowd they should even meet with the Tilneys in any reasonable time, had just passed through her mind, when she suddenly found herself addressed and again solicited to dance, by Mr Tilney himself. With what sparkling eyes and ready motion she granted his request, and with how pleasing a flutter of heart she went with him to the set may be easily imagined ! To escape, and as she believed, so narrowly escape John Thorpe, and to be asked, so immediately on his joining her, asked by Mr Tilney, as if he had sought her on purpose ! —it did not appear to her that life could supply any greater felicity.

Scarcely had they worked themselves into the quiet possession of a place, however, when her attention was claimed by John Thorpe, who stood behind her. " Hey-

day, Miss Morland!" said he, "what is the meaning of
this? I thought you and I were to dance together."

"I wonder you should think so, for you never asked
me."

"That is a good one, by Jove! I asked you as soon
as I came into the room, and I was just going to ask you
again, but when I turned round, you were gone! This
is a cursed shabby trick! I only came for the sake of
dancing with *you*, and I firmly believe you were engaged
to me ever since Monday. Yes; I remember, I asked
you while you were waiting in the lobby for your cloak;
and here have I been telling all my acquaintance that I
was going to dance with the prettiest girl in the room;
and when they see you standing up with somebody else,
they will quiz me famously."

"Oh! no; they will never think of *me*, after such a
description as that."

"By heavens! if they do not, I will kick them out of
the room for blockheads. What chap have you there?"
Catherine satisfied his curiosity. "Tilney," he repeated;
"hum; I do not know him. A good figure of a man;
well put together. Does he want a horse? Here is a
friend of mine, Sam Fletcher, has got one to sell that would
suit anybody. A famous clever animal for the road;
only forty guineas. I had fifty minds to buy it myself,
for it is one of my maxims always to buy a good horse
when I meet with one; but it would not answer my purpose,
it would not do for the field. I would give any money for
a real good hunter. I have three now, the best that ever
were backed. I would not take eight hundred guineas
for them. Fletcher and I mean to get a house in Leicester-
shire against the next season. It is so d—— uncomfortable
living at an inn."

This was the last sentence by which he could weary
Catherine's attention, for he was just then born off by the
resistless pressure of a long string of passing ladies. Her
partner now drew near, and said, "That gentleman would
have put me out of patience, had he staid with you half a
minute longer. He has no business to withdraw the attention of my partner from me. We have entered into a

contract of mutual agreeableness for the space of an evening, and all our agreeableness belongs solely to each other for that time. Nobody can fasten themselves on the notice of one, without injuring the rights of the other. I consider a country-dance as an emblem of marriage. Fidelity and complaisance are the principal duties of both ; and those men who do not chuse to dance or marry themselves, have no business with the partners or wives of their neighbours."

" But they are such very different things ! "

" That you think they cannot be compared together ? "

" To be sure not. People that marry can never part, but must go and keep house together. People that dance, only stand opposite to each other in a long room for half an hour."

" And such is your definition of matrimony and dancing. Taken in that light certainly, their resemblance is not striking ; but I think I could place them in such a view. You will allow that in both man has the advantage of choice, woman only the power of refusal ; that in both it is an engagement between man and woman, formed for the advantage of each ; and that when once entered into, they belong exclusively to each other till the moment of its dissolution ; that it is their duty each to endeavour to give no cause for wishing that he or she had bestowed themselves elsewhere, and their best interest to keep their own imaginations from wandering towards the perfections of their neighbours, or fancying that they should have been better off with any one else. You will allow all this ? "

" Yes, to be sure, as you state it, all this sounds very well ; but still they are so very different. I cannot look upon them at all in the same light, nor think the same duties belong to them."

" In one respect, there certainly is a difference. In marriage, the man is supposed to provide for the support of the woman ; the woman to make the home agreeable to the man ; he is to purvey, and she is to smile. But in dancing, their duties are exactly changed ; the agreeableness, the compliance are expected from him, while she furnishes the fan and the lavender water. *That*, I suppose, was the difference of duties which struck you, as rendering the conditions incapable of comparison."

" No, indeed, I never thought of that."

" Then I am quite at a loss. One thing, however, I must observe. This disposition on your side is rather alarming. You totally disallow any similarity in the obligations ; and may I not thence infer, that your notions of the duties of the dancing state are not so strict as your partner might wish ? Have I not reason to fear, that if the gentleman who spoke to you just now were to return, or if any gentleman were to address you, there would be nothing to restrain you from conversing with him as long as you chose ? "

" Mr Thorpe is such a very particular friend of my brother's, that if he talks to me, I must talk to him again ; but there are hardly three young men in the room besides him that I have any acquaintance with."

" And is that to be my only security ? alas ! alas ! "

" Nay, I am sure that you cannot have a better ; for if I do not know anybody, it is impossible for me to talk to them ; and, besides, I do not *want* to talk to anybody."

" Now you have given me a security worth having ; and I shall proceed with courage. Do you find Bath as agreeable as when I had the honour of making the inquiry before ? "

" Yes, quite ; more so, indeed."

" More so ! Take care, or you will forget to be tired of it at the proper time. You ought to be tired at the end of six weeks."

" I do not think I should be tired, if I were to stay here six months."

" Bath, compared with London, has little variety, and so everybody finds out every year. ' For six weeks, I allow Bath is pleasant enough ; but beyond *that*, it is the most tiresome place in the world.' You would be told so by people of all descriptions, who come regularly every winter, lenghten their six weeks into ten or twelve, and go away at last because they can afford to stay no longer."

" Well, other people must judge for themselves, and those who go to London may think nothing of Bath. But

I, who live in a small retired village in the country, can never find greater sameness in such a place as this than in my own home ; for here are a variety of amusements, a variety of things to be seen and done all day long, which I can know nothing of there."

" You are not fond of the country."

" Yes, I am. I have always lived there, and always been very happy. But certainly there is much more sameness in a country life than in a Bath life. One day in the country is exactly like another."

" But then you spend your time so much more rationally in the country."

" Do I ? "

" Do you not ? "

" I do not believe there is much difference."

" Here you are in pursuit only of amusement all day long."

" And so I am at home : only I do not find so much of it. I walk about here, and so I do there ; but here I see a variety of people in every street, and there I can only go and call on Mrs Allen."

Mr Tilney was very much amused. " Only go and call on Mrs Allen ! " he repeated. " What a picture of intellectual poverty ! However, when you sink into this abyss again, you will have more to say. You will be able to talk of Bath, and of all that you did here."

" Oh ! yes ; I shall never be in want of something to talk of again to Mrs Allen, or anybody else. I really believe I shall always be talking of Bath, when I am at home again ; I *do* like it so very much. If I could have but papa and mamma, and the rest of them here, I suppose I should be too happy ! James's coming (my eldest brother) is quite delightful ; and especially as it turns out, that the very family we are just got so intimate with are his intimate friends already. Oh ! who can ever be tired of Bath ? "

" Not those who bring such fresh feelings of every sort to it as you do. But papas and mammas, and brothers and intimate friends, are a good deal gone by, to most of the frequenters of Bath ; and the honest relish of balls and plays, and every-day sights, is past with them."

Here their conversation closed ; the demands of the

dance becoming now too importunate for a divided attention.

Soon after their reaching the bottom of the set, Catherine perceived herself to be earnestly regarded by a gentleman who stood among the lookers-on, immediately behind her partner. He was a very handsome man, of a commanding aspect, past the bloom, but not past the vigour of life ; and with his eye still directed towards her, she saw him presently address Mr Tilney in a familiar whisper. Confused by his notice, and blushing from the fear of its being excited by something wrong in her appearance, she turned away her head. But while she did so, the gentleman retreated, and her partner coming nearer, said, " I see that you guess what I have just been asked. That gentleman knows your name, and you have a right to know his. It is General Tilney, my father."

Catherine's answer was only " Oh ! " but it was an " Oh ! " expressing everything needful ; attention to his words, and perfect reliance on their truth. With real interest and strong admiration did her eye now follow the General, as he moved through the crowd, and " How handsome a family they are ! " was her secret remark.

In chatting with Miss Tilney before the evening concluded, a new source of felicity arose to her. She had never taken a country walk since her arrival in Bath. Miss Tilney, to whom all the commonly frequented environs were familiar, spoke of them in terms which made her all eagerness to know them too ; and on her openly fearing that she might find nobody to go with her, it was proposed by the brother and sister that they should join in a walk, some morning or other. " I shall like it," she cried, " beyond anything in the world ; and do not let us put it off : let us go to-morrow," This was readily agreed to, with only a proviso of Miss Tilney's, that it did not rain, which Catherine was sure it would not. At twelve o'clock, they were to call for her in Pulteney Street, and " remember, twelve o'clock," was her parting speech to her new friend. Of her other, her older, her more established friend, Isabella, of whose fidelity and worth she had enjoyed a fortnight's experience, she scarcely saw anything during the evening.

Yet, though longing to make her acquainted with her happiness, she cheerfully submitted to the wish of Mr Allen, which took them rather early away, and her spirits danced within her, as she danced in her chair all the way home.

CHAPTER XI

THE morrow brought a very sober-looking morning; the sun making only a few efforts to appear; and Catherine augured from it everything most favourable to her wishes. A bright morning so early in the year, she allowed, would generally turn to rain; but a cloudy one foretold improvement as the day advanced. She applied to Mr Allen for confirmation of her hopes, but Mr Allen not having his own skies and barometer about him, declined giving any absolute promise of sunshine. She applied to Mrs Allen, and Mrs Allen's opinion was more positive. " She had no doubt in the world of its being a very fine day, if the clouds would only go off, and the sun keep out."

At about eleven o'clock, however, a few specks of small rain upon the windows caught Catherine's watchful eye, and " Oh dear! I do believe it will be wet," broke from her in a most desponding tone.

" I thought how it would be," said Mrs Allen.

" No walk for me to-day," sighed Catherine; " but perhaps it may come to nothing, or it may hold up before twelve."

" Perhaps it may; but then, my dear, it will be so dirty."

" Oh! that will not signify; I never mind dirt."

" No," replied her friend very placidly, " I know you never mind dirt."

After a short pause, " It comes on faster and faster!" said Catherine, as she stood watching at a window.

" So it does, indeed. If it keeps raining, the streets will be very wet."

" There are four umbrellas up already. How I hate the sight of an umbrella!"

" They are disagreeable things to carry. I would much rather take a chair at any time."

" It was such a nice looking morning ! I felt so convinced it would be dry ! "

" Any body would have thought so, indeed. There will be very few people in the Pump-room, if it rains all the morning. I hope Mr Allen will put on his great coat when he goes, but I dare say he will not, for he had rather do anything in the world than walk out in a great coat ; I wonder he should dislike it, it must be so comfortable."

The rain continued, fast though not heavy. Catherine went every five minutes to the clock, threatening, on each return, that, if it still kept on raining another five minutes, she would give up the matter as hopeless. The clock struck twelve, and it still rained. " You will not be able to go, my dear."

" I do not quite despair yet. I shall not give it up till a quarter after twelve. This is just the time of day for it to clear up, and I do think it looks a little lighter. There, it is twenty minutes after twelve, and now I *shall* give it up entirely. Oh ! that we had such weather here as they had at Udolpho, or at least in Tuscany and the south of France !—the night that poor St Aubin died !—such beautiful weather ! "

At half past twelve, when Catherine's anxious attention to the weather was over, and she could no longer claim any merit from its amendment, the sky began voluntarily to clear. A gleam of sunshine took her quite by surprize ; she looked round, the clouds were parting, and she instantly returned to the window to watch over and encourage the happy appearance. Ten minutes more made it certain that a bright afternoon would succeed, and justified the opinion of Mrs Allen, who had " always thought it would clear up." But whether Catherine might still expect her friends, whether there had not been too much rain for Miss Tilney to venture, must yet be a question.

It was too dirty for Mrs Allen to accompany her husband to the Pump-room : he accordingly set off by himself, and Catherine had barely watched him down the street, when her notice was claimed by the approach of the same two open carriages, containing the same three people that had surprized her so much a few mornings back.

"Isabella, my brother, and Mr Thorpe, I declare! They are coming for me, perhaps; but I shall not go; I cannot go, indeed; for, you know, Miss Tilney may still call." Mrs Allen agreed to it. John Thorpe was soon with them, and his voice was with them yet sooner, for on the stairs he was calling out to Miss Morland to be quick. "Make haste! make haste!" as he threw open the door, "put on your hat this moment; there is no time to be lost; we are going to Bristol. How d'ye do, Mrs Allen?"

"To Bristol! Is not that a great way off? But, however, I cannot go with you to-day, because I am engaged; I expect some friends every moment." This was of course vehemently talked down as no reason at all, Mrs Allen was called on to second him, and the two others walked in, to give their assistance. "My sweetest Catherine is not this delightful? We shall have a most heavenly drive. You are to thank your brother and me for the scheme: it darted into our heads at breakfast time, I verily believe at the same instant; and we should have been off two hours ago, if it had not been for this detestable rain. But it does not signify, the nights are moonlight, and we shall do delightfully. Oh! I am in such extasies at the thoughts of a little country air and quiet! so much better than going to the Lower Rooms. We shall drive directly to Clifton and dine there; and as soon as dinner is over, if there is time for it, go on to Kingsweston."

"I doubt our being able to do so much," said Morland.

"You croaking fellow!" cried Thorpe, "we shall be able to do ten times more. Kingsweston! aye, and Blaize Castle too, and anything else we can hear of; but here is your sister says she will not go."

"Blaize Castle!" cried Catherine; "what is that?"

"The finest place in England; worth going fifty miles at any time to see."

"What, is it really a castle, an old castle?"

"The oldest in the kingdom."

"But is it like what one reads of?"

"Exactly: the very same."

" But now, really, are there towers and long galleries ? "

" By dozens."

" Then I should like to see it ; but I cannot, I cannot go."

" Not go ! my beloved creature, what do you mean ? "

" I cannot go, because " (looking down as she spoke, fearful of Isabella's smile) " I expect Miss Tilney and her brother to call on me to take a country walk. They promised to come at twelve, only it rained ; but now, as it is so fine, I dare say they will be here soon."

" Not they, indeed," cried Thorpe ; " for, as we turned into Broad Street, I saw them. Does he not drive a phæton with bright chestnuts ? "

" I do not know, indeed."

" Yes, I know he does ; I saw him. You are talking of the man you danced with last night, are not you ? "

" Yes."

" Well, I saw him at that moment turn up Lansdown Road, driving a smart-looking girl."

" Did you, indeed ? "

" Did, upon my soul ; knew him again directly ; and he seemed to have got some very pretty cattle too."

" It is very odd ! But I suppose they thought it would be too dirty for a walk."

" And well they might, for I never saw so much dirt in my life. Walk ! you could no more walk than you could fly ! It has not been so dirty the whole winter ; it is ancle deep everywhere."

Isabella corroborated it :—" My dearest Catherine, you cannot form an idea of the dirt ; come, you must go ; you cannot refuse going now."

" I should like to see the castle ; but may we go all over it ? May we go up every staircase, and into every suite of rooms ? "

" Yes, yes ; every hole and corner."

" But then, if they should only be gone out for an hour till it is drier, and call by and by ? "

" Make yourself easy, there is no danger of that ; for I heard Tilney hallooing to a man who was just passing by on horseback, that they were going as far as Wick Rocks."

" Then I will. Shall I go, Mrs Allen ? "

" Just as you please, my dear."

" Mrs Allen, you must persuade her to go," was the general cry. Mrs Allen was not inattentive to it. " Well, my dear," said she, " suppose you go." And in two minutes they were off.

Catherine's feelings, as she got into the carriage, were in a very unsettled state : divided between regret for the loss of one great pleasure, and the hope of soon enjoying another, almost its equal in degree, however unlike in kind. She could not think the Tilneys had acted quite well by her, in so readily giving up their engagement, without sending her any message of excuse. It was now but an hour later than the time fixed on for the beginning of their walk ; and, in spite of what she had heard of the pro- digious accumulation of dirt in the course of that hour, she could not from her own observation help thinking that they might have gone with very little inconvenience. To feel herself slighted by them was very painful. On the other hand, the delight of exploring an edifice like Udolpho, as her fancy represented Blaize Castle to be, was such a counterpoise of good, as might console her for almost any thing.

They passed briskly down Pulteney Street, and through Laura Place, without the exchange of many words. Thorpe talked to his horse, and she meditated by turns on broken promises and broken arches, phætons and false hangings, Tilneys and trap-doors. As they entered Argyle Buildings, however, she was roused by this address from her com- panion, " Who is that girl who looked at you so hard as she went by ? "

" Who ? where ? "

" On the right-hand pavement : she must be almost out of sight now." Catherine looked round, and saw Miss Tilney leaning on her brother's arm, walking slowly down the street. She saw them both looking back at her. " Stop, stop, Mr Thorpe," she impatiently cried, " it is Miss Tilney ; it is indeed. How could you tell me they were gone ? Stop, stop, I will get out this moment and go to them." But to what purpose did she speak ? Thorpe only lashed his horse into a brisker trot ; the Tilneys, who had soon ceased to look after her, were in a moment out of sight round the corner of Laura Place, and in another moment, she was herself whisked into the Market Place. Still, however, and during the length of another street, she entreated him to stop. " Pray, pray stop, Mr Thorpe. I cannot go on, I will not go on ; I must go back to Miss Tilney." But Mr Thorpe only laughed, smacked his whip, encouraged his horse, made odd noises, and drove on ; and Catherine, angry and vexed as she was, having no power of getting away, was obliged to give up the point and submit. Her reproaches, however, were not spared. " How could you deceive me so, Mr Thorpe ? How could you say that you saw them driving up the Lansdown Road ? I would not have had it happen so for the world. They must think it so strange, so rude of me, to go by them, too, without saying a word ! You do not know how vexed I am. I shall have no pleasure at Clifton, nor in anything else. I had rather, ten thousand times rather, get out now, and walk back to them. How could you say, you saw them driving out in a phæton ? " Thorpe defended himself very stoutly, declared he had never seen two men so much alike in his life, and would hardly give up the point of its having been Tilney himself.

Their drive, even when this subject was over, was not likely to be very agreeable. Catherine's complaisance was no longer what it had been in their former airing. She listened reluctantly, and her replies were short. Blaize Castle remained her only comfort ; towards *that,* she still looked at intervals with pleasure ; though rather than be disappointed of the promised walk, and especially rather than be thought ill of by the Tilneys, she would willingly have given up all the happiness which its walls could supply : the happiness of a progress through a long suite of lofty rooms, exhibiting the remains of magnificent furniture, though now for many years deserted : the happiness of being stopped in their way along narrow, winding vaults, by a low, grated door ; or even of having their lamp, their only lamp, extinguished by a sudden gust of wind, and of being left in total darkness. In the meanwhile, they proceeded on their journey without any mischance : and were

within view of the town of Keynsham, when a halloo from
Morland, who was behind them, made his friend pull up,
to know what was the matter. The others then came
close enough for conversation ; and Morland said, " We
had better go back, Thorpe ; it is too late to go on to-day ;
your sister thinks so as well as I. We have been exactly
an hour coming from Pulteney Street, very little more than
seven miles ; and, I suppose, we have at least eight more
to go. It will never do. We set out a great deal too late.
We had much better put it off till another day, and turn
round."

" It is all one to me," replied Thorpe, rather angrily ;
and instantly turning his horse, they were on their way
back to Bath.

" If your brother had not got such a d—— beast to
drive," said he soon afterwards, " we might have done
it very well. My horse would have trotted to Clifton
within the hour, if left to himself, and I have almost broke
my arm pulling him in to that cursed broken-winded jade's
pace. Morland is a fool for not keeping a horse and gig
of his own."

" No, he is not," said Catherine, warmly ; " for I am
sure he could not afford it."

" And why cannot he afford it ? "

" Because he has not money enough."

" And whose fault is that ? "

" Nobody's that I know of." Thorpe then said something in the loud, incoherent way to which he had often
recourse, about its being a d—— thing to be miserly ;
and that if people who rolled in money could not afford
things, he did not know who could, which Catherine did
not even endeavour to understand. Disappointed of what
was to have been the consolation for her first disappointment, she was less and less disposed either to be agreeable
herself, or to find her companion so ; and they returned
to Pulteney Street without her speaking twenty words.

As she entered the house, the footman told her, that
a gentleman and lady had called and inquired for her a
few minutes after her setting off ; that, when he told them
she was gone out with Mr Thorpe, the lady had asked

whether any message had been left for her, and on his saying
no, had felt for a card, but said she had none about her,
and went away. Pondering over these heart-rending
tidings, Catherine walked slowly upstairs. At the head
of them she was met by Mr Allen, who, on hearing the
reason of their speedy return, said, " I am glad your brother
had so much sense ; I am glad you are come back. It was
a strange, wild scheme."

They all spent the evening together at Thorpe's.
Catherine was disturbed and out of spirits ; but Isabella
seemed to find a pool of commerce, in the fate of which
she shared, by private partnership, with Morland, a very
good equivalent for the quiet and country air of an inn
at Clifton. Her satisfaction, too, in not being at the Lower
Rooms was spoken more than once. " How I pity the
poor creatures that are going there ! How glad I am that
I am not amongst them ! I wonder whether it will be a
full ball or not ! They have not begun dancing yet. I
would not be there for all the world. It is so delightful
to have an evening now and then to one's self. I dare say
it will not be a very good ball. I know the Mitchells
will not be there. I am sure I pity everybody that is.
But I dare say, Mr Morland, you long to be at it, do not you ?
I am sure you do. Well, pray do not let anybody here be
a restraint on you. I dare say we could do very well without you, but you men think yourselves of such consequence."

Catherine could almost have accused Isabella of being
wanting in tenderness towards herself and her sorrows,
so very little did they appear to dwell on her mind, and
so very inadequate was the comfort she offered. " Do
not be so dull, my dearest creature," she whispered. " You
will quite break my heart. It was amazingly shocking,
to be sure, but the Tilneys were entirely to blame. Why
were they not more punctual ? It was dirty, indeed,
but what did that signify ? I am sure John and I should
have not minded it. I never mind going through anything
where a friend is concerned ; that is my disposition, and
John is just the same ; he has amazing strong feelings.
Good heavens ! what a delightful hand you have got !
Kings, I vow ! I never was so happy in my life ! I

would fifty times rather you should have them than myself."

And now I may dismiss my heroine to the sleepless couch which is the true heroine's portion ; to a pillow strewed with thorns and wet with tears. And lucky may she think herself, if she get another good night's rest in the course of the next three months.

CHAPTER XII

"MRS ALLEN," said Catherine, the next morning, "will there be any harm in my calling on Miss Tilney to-day ? I shall not be easy till I have explained everything."

" Go by all means, my dear ; only put on a white gown. Miss Tilney always wears white."

Catherine cheerfully complied ; and, being properly equipped, was more impatient than ever to be at the Pump-room, that she might inform herself of General Tilney's lodgings ; for though she believed they were in Milsom Street, she was not certain of the house, and Mrs Allen's wavering convictions only made it more doubtful. To Milsom Street she was directed ; and having made herself perfect in the number, hastened away with eager steps and a beating heart to pay her visit, explain her conduct, and be forgiven : tripping lightly through the churchyard, and resolutely turning away her eyes, that she might not be obliged to see her beloved Isabella, and her dear family, who, she had reason to believe were in a shop hard by. She reached the house without any impediment, looked at the number, knocked at the door, and inquired for Miss Tilney. The man believed Miss Tilney to be at home, but was not quite certain. Would she be pleased to send up her name ? She gave her card. In a few minutes the servant returned, and with a look which did not quite confirm his words, said he had been mistaken, for that Miss Tilney had walked out. Catherine, with a blush of morti-fication, left the house. She left almost persuaded that Miss Tilney *was* at home, and too much offended to admit her ; and as she retired down the street, could not withhold

one glance at the drawing-room windows, in expectation
of seeing her there, but no one appeared at them. At the
bottom of the street, however, she looked back again,
and then, not at a window, but issuing from the door, she
saw Miss Tilney herself. She was followed by a gentleman
whom Catherine believed to be her father, and they turned
up towards Edgar's Buildings. Catherine, in deep mortification, proceeded on her way. She could almost be angry
herself at such angry incivility ; but she checked the resentful sensation, she remembered her own ignorance. She
knew not how such an offence as hers might be classed
by the laws of worldly politeness, to what a degree of un-
forgiveness it might with propriety lead, nor to what rigours
of rudeness in return it might justly make her amenable.
Dejected and humbled, she had even some thoughts of not
going with the others to the theatre that night ; but, it
must be confessed that they were not of long continuance ;
for she soon recollected, in the first place, that she was
without any excuse for staying at home ; and, in the second,
that it was a play she wanted very much to see. To the
theatre accordingly they all went ; no Tilneys appeared
to plague or please her ; she feared that amongst the many
perfections of the family a fondness for plays was not to
be ranked, but perhaps it was because they were habituated
to the finer performances of the London stage, which she
knew, on Isabella's authority, rendered everything else
of the kind " quite horrid." She was not deceived in her
own expectation of pleasure : the comedy so well suspended
her care, that no one observing her during the first four
acts would have supposed she had any wretchedness about
her. On the beginning of the fifth, however, the sudden
view of Mr Henry Tilney and his father joining a party
in the opposite box recalled her to anxiety and distress.
The stage could no longer excite genuine merriment, no
longer keep her whole attention. Every other look upon
an average was directed towards the opposite box ; and
for the space of two entire scenes did she thus watch Henry
Tilney, without being once able to catch his eye. No
longer could he be suspected of indifference for a play ;
his notice was never withdrawn from the stage during

two whole scenes. At length, however, he did look towards her, and he bowed, but such a bow ! no smile, no continued observance attended it : his eyes were immediately returned to their former direction. Catherine was restlessly miserable; she could almost have run round to the box in which he sat, and forced him to hear her explanation. Feelings rather natural than heroic possessed her. Instead of considering her own dignity injured by this ready condemnation ; instead of proudly resolving, in conscious innocence, to show her resentment towards him who could harbour a doubt of it, to leave to him all the trouble of seeking an explanation, and to enlighten him on the past only by avoiding his sight, or flirting with somebody else, she took to herself all the shame of misconduct, or, at least, of its appearance, and was only eager for an opportunity of explaining its cause.

The play concluded, the curtain fell ; Henry Tilney was no longer to be seen where he had hitherto sat, but his father remained, and perhaps he might be now coming round to their box. She was right : in a few minutes he appeared, and making his way through the then thinning rows, spoke with like calm politeness to Mrs Allen and her friend. Not with such calmness was he answered by the latter. "Oh, Mr Tilney, I have been quite wild to speak to you, and make my apologies. You must have thought me so rude ; but indeed it was not my own fault. Was it, Mrs Allen ? Did not they tell me that Mr Tilney and his sister were gone out in a phæton together ? and then what could I do ? But I had ten thousand times rather have been with you. Now, had not I, Mrs Allen ? "

" My dear, you tumble my gown," was Mrs Allen's reply.

Her assurance, however, standing sole as it did, was not thrown away ; it brought a more cordial, more natural smile into his countenance, and he replied in a tone which retained only a little affected reserve, " We were much obliged to you, at any rate, for wishing us a pleasant walk after our passing you in Argyle Street. You were so kind as to look back on purpose."

" But indeed, I did not wish you a pleasant walk, I never thought of such a thing ; but I begged Mr Thorpe so earnestly to stop ; I called out to him as soon as ever I saw you. Now, Mrs Allen, did not —— Oh ! you were not there. But, indeed, I did ; and, if Mr Thorpe would only have stopped, I would have jumped out and run after you."

Is there a Henry in the world who could be insensible to such a declaration ? Henry Tilney, at least, was not. With a yet sweeter smile, he said everything that need be said of his sister's concern, regret, and dependence on Catherine's honour. " Oh, do not say Miss Tilney was not angry," cried Catherine, " because I know she was ; for she would not see me this morning when I called. I saw her walk out of the house the next minute after my leaving it. I was hurt, but I was not affronted. Perhaps you did not know I had been there."

" I was not within at the time ; but I heard of it from Eleanor, and she has been wishing ever since to see you, to explain the reason of such incivility ; but, perhaps, I can do it as well. It was nothing more than that my father —— they were just preparing to walk out, and he being hurried for time, and not caring to have it put off, made a point of her being denied. That was all, I do assure you. She was very much vexed, and meant to make her apology as soon as possible."

Catherine's mind was greatly eased by this information, yet a something of solicitude remained, from which sprang the following question, thoroughly artless in itself, though rather distressing to the gentleman : " But, Mr Tilney, why were *you* less generous than your sister ? If she felt such confidence in my good intentions, and could suppose it to be only a mistake, why should *you* be so ready to take offence ? "

" Me ! I take offence ! "

" Nay, I am sure by your look, when you came into the box, you were angry."

" I angry ! I could have no right ! "

" Well, nobody would have thought you had no right who saw your face."

He replied by asking her to make room for him and talking of the play. He remained with them some time, and was only to agreeable for Catherine to be contented when he went away. Before they parted, however, it was agreed that the projected walk should be taken as soon as possible ; and, setting aside the misery of his quitting their box, she was, upon the whole, left one of the happiest creatures in the world.

While talking to each other, she had observed with some surprize, that John Thorpe, who was never in the same part of the house for ten minutes together, was engaged in conversation with General Tilney ; and she felt something more than surprize, when she thought she could perceive herself the object of their attention and discourse. What could they have to say of her ? She feared General Tilney did not like her appearance. She found it was implied in his preventing her admittance to his daughter, rather than postpone his own walk a few minutes. " How came Mr Thorpe to know your father ? " was her anxious inquiry, as she pointed them out to her companion. He knew nothing about it : but his father, like every military man, had a very large acquaintance.

When the entertainment was over, Thorpe came to assist them in getting out. Catherine was the immediate object of his gallantry ; and, while they waited in the lobby for a chair, he prevented the inquiry which had travelled from her heart almost to the tip of her tongue, by asking in a consequential manner, whether she had seen him talking with General Tilney. " He is a fine old fellow, upon my soul ! stout, active ; looks as young as his son. I have a great regard for him, I assure you. A gentleman-like, good sort of fellow as ever lived."

" But how came you to know him ? "

" Know him ! There are few people much about town that I do not know. I have met him for ever at the Bedford ; and I knew his face again to-day the moment he came into the billiard-room. One of the best players we have, by-the-bye ; and we had a little touch together, though I was almost afraid of him at first. The odds were five to four against me ; and, if I had not made one of the cleanest strokes that perhaps ever was made in this world— I took his ball exactly—but I could not make you understand it without a table : however, I *did* beat him. A very fine fellow ; as rich as a Jew. I should like to dine with him. I daresay he gives famous dinners. But what do you think we have been talking of ? You. Yes, by heavens and the General thinks you the finest girl in Bath."

" Oh, nonsense ! how can you say so ? "

" And what do you think I said ? " (lowering his voice). " Well done, General," said I, " I am quite of your mind."

Here Catherine, who was much less gratified by his admiration than by General Tilney's, was not sorry to be called away by Mr Allen. Thorpe, however would see her to her chair, and, till she entered it, continued the same kind of delicate flattery, in spite of her entreating him to have done.

That general Tilney, instead of disliking, should admire her, was very delightful ; and she joyfully thought that there was not one of the family whom she need now fear to meet. The evening had done more, much more for her than could have been expected.

CHAPTER XIII

MONDAY, Tuesday, Wednesday, Thursday, Friday, and Saturday, have now passed in review before the reader ; the events of each day, its hopes and fears, mortifications and pleasures, have been separately stated, and the pangs of Sunday only now remain to be described, and close the week. The Clifton scheme had been deferred, not relinquished ; and on the afternoon's Crescent of this day it was brought forward again. In a private consultation between Isabella and James, the former of whom had particularly set her heart upon going, and the latter no less anxiously placed his upon pleasing her, it was agreed that, provided the weather were fair, the party should take place on the following morning ; and they were to set off very early, in order to be at home in good time. The affair thus determined, and Thorpe's approbation secured, Catherine, only remained to be apprized of it. She had left them for a few minutes to speak to Miss Tilney. In that interval the plan was completed, and as soon as she came again, her agreement was demanded; but instead of the gay acquiescence expected by Isabella, Catherine looked grave, was very sorry, but could not go. The engagement which ought to have kept her from joining in the former attempt would make it impossible for her to accompany them now. She had that moment settled with Miss Tilney to take their promised walk to-morrow; it was quite determined, and she would not, upon any account, retract. But that she *must* and *should* retract was instantly the eager cry of both the Thorpes; they must go to Clifton to-morrow, they would not go without her, it would be nothing to put off a mere walk for one day longer, and they would not hear of a refusal. Catherine was distressed, but not subdued. "Do not urge me, Isabella. I am engaged to Miss Tilney. I cannot go." This availed nothing. The same arguments assailed her again; she must go, she should go, and they would not hear of a refusal. "It would be so easy to tell Miss Tilney that you had just been reminded of a prior engagement, and must only beg to put off the walk till Tuesday."

"No, it would not be easy. I could not do it. There has been no prior engagement." But Isabella became only more and more urgent; calling on her in the most affectionate manner; addressing her by the most endearing names. She was sure her dearest, sweetest Catherine would not seriously refuse such a trifling request to a friend who loved her so dearly. She knew her beloved Catherine to have so feeling a heart, so sweet a temper, to be so easily persuaded by those she loved. But all in vain; Catherine felt herself to be in the right, and though pained by such tender, such flattering supplication, could not allow it to influence her. Isabella then tried another method. She reproached her with having more affection for Miss Tilney, though she had known her so little a while, than for her best and oldest friends; with being grown cold and indifferent, in short, towards herself. "I cannot help being jealous, Catherine, when I see myself slighted for strangers; I, who love you so excessively! When once my affections are placed, it is not in the power of anything to change them. But I believe my feelings are stronger than any body's; I am sure they are too strong for my own peace ; and to see myself supplanted in your friendship by strangers does cut me to the quick, I own.   These Tilneys seem to swallow up everything else."

Catherine thought this reproach equally strange and unkind.   Was it the part of a friend thus to expose her feelings to the notice of others ?   Isabella appeared to her ungenerous and selfish, regardless of everything but her own gratification.   These painful ideas crossed her mind, though she said nothing.   Isabella, in the meanwhile, had applied her handkerchief to her eyes ; and Morland, miserable at such a sight, could not help saying, " Nay, Catherine, I think you cannot stand out any longer now.   The sacrifice is not much ; and to oblige such a friend, I shall think you quite unkind, if you still refuse."

This was the first time of her brother's openly siding against her ; and anxious to avoid his displeasure, she proposed a compromise.   If they would only put off their scheme till Tuesday, which they might easily do, as it depended only on themselves, she could go with them, and everybody might then be satisfied.   But " No, no, no ! " was the immediate answer ; " that could not be, for Thorpe did not know that he might not go to town on Tuesday." Catherine was sorry, but could do no more ; and a short silence ensued, which was broken by Isabella, who, in a voice of cold resentment, said, " Very well, then there is an end of the party.   If Catherine does not go, I cannot. I cannot be the only woman.   I would not upon any account in the world, do so improper a thing."

" Catherine, you must go," said James.

" But why cannot Mr Thorpe drive one of his other sisters ?   I dare say either of them would like to go."

" Thank ye," cried Thorpe ; " but I did not come to Bath to drive my sisters about and look like a fool.   No, if you do not go, d— me if I do.   I only go for the sake of driving you."

" That is a compliment which gives me no pleasure." But her words were lost on Thorpe, who had turned abruptly away.

The three others still continued together, talking in a

most uncomfortable manner to poor Catherine; sometimes not a word was said, sometimes she was again attacked
with supplications or reproaches, and her arm was still
linked within Isabella's, though their hearts were at war.
At one moment she was softened, at another irritated;
always distressed, but always steady.

" I did not think you had been so obstinate, Catherine,"
said James; " you were not used to be so hard to persuade;
you once were the kindest, best-tempered of my sisters."

" I hope I am not less so now," she replied, very feelingly;
" but indeed I cannot go. If I am wrong, I am doing
what I believe to be right."

" I suspect," said Isabella, in a low voice, " there is no
great struggle."

Catherine's heart swelled; she drew away her arm,
and Isabella made no opposition. Thus passed a long
ten minutes, till they were again joined by Thorpe, who,
coming to them with a gayer look, said, " Well, I have
settled the matter, and now we may all go to-morrow with
a safe conscience. I have been to Miss Tilney, and made
your excuses."

" You have not!" cried Catherine.

" I have upon my soul. Left her this moment. Told
her you had sent me to say, that having just recollected
a prior engagement of going to Clifton with us to-morrow,
you could not have the pleasure of walking with her till
Tuesday. She said very well, Tuesday was just as convenient to her; so there is an end of all our difficulties.
A pretty good thought of mine, hey?"

Isabella's countenance was once more all smiles and
good-humour, and James too looked happy again.

" A most heavenly thought, indeed! Now, my sweet
Catherine, all our distresses are over; you are honourably
acquitted, and we shall have a most delightful party."

" This will not do," said Catherine; " I cannot submit
to this. I must run after Miss Tilney directly and set her
right."

Isabella, however, caught hold of one hand, Thorpe
of the other; and remonstrances poured in from all three.
Even James was quite angry. When everything was

settled, when Miss Tilney herself said that Tuesday would suit her as well, it was quite ridiculous, quite absurd, to make any further objection.

" I do not care. Mr Thorpe had no business to invent any such message. If I had thought it right to put it off, I could have spoken to Miss Tilney myself. This is only doing it in a ruder way ; and how do I know that Mr Thorpe has — ; he may be mistaken again, perhaps. He led me into one act of rudeness by his mistake on Friday. Let me go, Mr Thorpe ; Isabella, do not hold me."

Thorpe told her it would be in vain to go after the Tilneys ; they were turning the corner into Brook Street, when he had overtaken them, and were at home by this time.

" Then I will go after them," said Catherine ; " wherever they are, I will go after them. It does not signify talking. If I could not be persuaded into doing what I thought wrong, I never will be tricked into it." And with these words she broke away and hurried off. Thorpe would have darted after her, but Morland withheld him. " Let her go, let her go, if she will go. She is as obstinate as —— "

Thorpe [?] never finished the simile, for it could hardly have been a proper one.

Away walked Catherine in great agitation, as fast as the crowd would permit her, fearful of being pursued, yet determined to persevere. As she walked, she reflected on what had passed. It was painful to her to disappoint and displease them, particularly to displease her brother ; but she could not repent her resistance. Setting her own inclination apart, to have failed a second time in her engagement to Miss Tilney, to have retracted a promise voluntarily made only five minutes before, and on a false pretence too, must have been wrong. She had not been withstanding them on selfish principles alone, she had not consulted merely her own gratification ; *that* might have been ensured in some degree by the excursion itself, by seeing Blaize Castle; no, she had attended to what was due to others, and to her own character in their opinion. Her conviction of being right, however, was not enough to restore her composure : till she had spoken to Miss Tilney, she could not be at ease ; and quickening her pace when she got clear of the Crescent, she almost ran over the remaining ground till she ganied the top of Milsom Street. So rapid had been her movements, that, in spite of the Tilney's advantage in the outset, they were but just turning into their lodgings as she came within view of them ; and the servant still remaining at the open door, she used only the ceremony of saying that she must speak with Miss Tilney that moment, and hurrying by him proceeded up stairs. Then, opening the first door before her, which happened to be the right, she immediately found herself in the drawing-room with General Tilney, his son and daughter. Her explanation, defective only in being—from her irritation of nerves and shortness of breath—no explanation at all, was instantly given. " I am come in a great hurry,—it was all a mistake ; I never promised to go ; I told them from the first I could not go ; I ran away in a great hurry to explain it ; I did not care what you thought of me ; I would not stay for the servant."

The business, however, though not perfectly elucidated by this speech, soon ceased to be a puzzle. Catherine found that John Thorpe *had* given the message ; and Miss Tilney had no scruples in owning herself greatly surprized by it. But whether her brother had still exceeded her in resentment, Catherine, though she instinctively addressed herself as much to one as to the other in her vindication, had no means of knowing. Whatever might have been felt before her arrival, her eager declarations immediately made every look and sentence as friendly as she could desire.

The affair thus happily settled, she was introduced by Miss Tilney to her father, and received by him with such ready, such solicitous politeness, as recalled Thorpe's information to her mind, and made her think with pleasure that he might be sometimes depended on. To such anxious attention was the General's civility carried, that, not aware of her extraordinary swiftness in entering the house, he was quite angry with the servant whose neglect had reduced her to open the door of the apartment herself. " What did William mean by it ? He should make a point of inquiring into the matter." And if Catherine had not most

warmly asserted his innocence, it seemed likely that William
would lose the favour of his master for ever, if not his place,
by her rapidity.

After sitting with them a quarter of an hour, she rose
to take leave, and was then most agreeably surprized by
General Tilney's asking her if she would do his daughter
the honour of dining and spending the rest of the day with
her. Miss Tilney added her own wishes. Catherine was
greatly obliged ; but it was quite out of her power, Mr and
Mrs Allen would expect her back every moment. The
General declared he could say no more ; the claims of Mr
and Mrs Allen were not to be superseded ; but on some
other day, he trusted, when longer notice could be given,
they would not refuse to spare her to her friend. " Oh,
no ; Catherine was sure they would not have the least
objection, and she should have great pleasure in coming."
The General attended her himself to the street door, saying
everything gallant as they went down stairs, admiring
the elasticity of her walk, which corresponded exactly
with the spirit of her dancing, and making her one of the
most graceful bows she had ever beheld when they parted.

Catherine delighted by all that had passed, proceeded
gaily to Pulteney Street, walking, as she concluded, with
great elasticity, though she had never thought of it before.
She reached home without seeing anything more of the
offended party ; and now that she had been triumphant
throughout, had carried her point, and was secure of her
walk, she began (as the flutter of her spirits subsided)
to doubt whether she had been perfectly right. A sacrifice
was always noble ; and if she had given way to their entreaties, she should have been spared the distressing idea
of a friend displeased, a brother angry, and a scheme of
great happiness to both destroyed, perhaps through her
means. To ease her mind, and ascertain by the opinion
of an unprejudiced person what her own conduct had really
been, she took occasion to mention before Mr Allen the
half-settled scheme of her brother and the Thorpes for the
following day. Mr Allen caught at it directly, " Well,"
said he, " and do you think of going too ? "

" No ; I had just engaged myself to walk with Miss

Tilney before they told me of it ; and therefore, you know, I could not go with them, could I ? "

" No, certainly not ; and I am glad you do not think of it. These schemes are not at all the thing. Young men and women driving about the country in open carriages ! Now and then it is very well ; but going to inns and public places together ! It is not right ; and I wonder Mrs Thorpe should allow it. I am glad you do not think of going ; I am sure Mrs Morland would not be pleased. Mrs Allen, are not you of my way of thinking ? Do not you think these kind of projects objectionable ? "

" Yes, very much so, indeed. Open carriages are nasty things. A clean gown is not five minutes' wear in them. You are splashed getting in and getting out ; and the wind takes your hair and your bonnet in every direction. I hate an open carriage myself."

" I know you do ; but that is not the question. Do not you think it has an odd appearance, if young ladies are frequently driven about in them by young men, to whom they are not even related ? "

" Yes, my dear, a very odd appearance indeed. I cannot bear to see it."

" Dear madam," cried Catherine, " then why did not you tell me so before ? I am sure if I had known it to be improper I would not have gone with Mr Thorpe at all ; but I always hoped you would tell me, if you thought I was doing wrong."

" And so I should, my dear, you may depend on it ; for, as I told Mrs Morland at parting, I would always do the best for you in my power. But one must not be over particular. Young people *will* be young people, as your good mother says herself. You know I wanted you, when we first came, not to buy that sprigged muslin, but you would. Young people do not like to be always thwarted."

" But this was something of real consequence ; and I do not think you would have found me hard to persuade."

" As far as it has gone hitherto, there is no harm done," said Mr Allen ; " and I would only advise you, my dear, not to go out with Mr Thorpe any more."

" That is just what I was going to say," added his wife.

Catherine, relieved for herself, felt uneasy for Isabella ; and after a moment's thought, asked Mr Allen whether it would not be both proper and kind in her to write to Miss Thorpe, and explain the indecorum of which she must be as insensible as herself ; for she considered that Isabella might otherwise perhaps be going to Clifton the next day, in spite of what had passed. Mr Allen, however, discouraged her from doing any such thing, " You had better leave her alone, my dear, she is old enough to know what she is about : and if not, has a mother to advise her. Mrs Thorpe is too indulgent beyond a doubt ; but, however, you had better not interfere. She and your brother chuse to go, and you will be only getting ill-will."

Catherine submitted ; and though sorry to think that Isabella should be doing wrong, felt greatly relieved by Mr Allen's approbation of her own conduct, and truly rejoiced to be preserved by his advice from the danger of falling into such an error herself. Her escape from being one of the party to Clifton was now an escape indeed ; for what would the Tilneys have thought of her, if she had broken her promise to them in order to do what was wrong in itself, if she had been guilty of one breach of propriety only to enable her to be guilty of another ?

CHAPTER XIV

THE next morning was fair, and Catherine almost expected another attack from the assembled party. With Mr Allen to support her, she felt no dread of the event ; but she would gladly be spared a contest where victory itself was painful, and was heartily rejoiced, therefore, at neither seeing nor hearing anything of them. The Tilneys called for her at the appointed time, and no new difficulty arising, no sudden recollection, no unexpected summons, no impertinent intrusion to disconcert their measures, my heroine was most unnaturally able to fulfil her engagement, though it was made with the hero himself. They determined on walking round Beechen Cliff, that noble hill, whose beautiful verdure and hanging coppice render it so striking an object from almost every opening in Bath.

"I never look at it," said Catherine, as they walked along the side of the river, "without thinking of the south of France."

"You have been abroad, then?" said Henry, a little surprized.

"Oh! no, I only mean what I have read about. It always put me in mind of the country that Emily and her father travelled through in the 'Mysteries of Udolpho.' But you never read novels, I dare say?"

"Why not?"

"Because they are not clever enough for you; gentlemen read better books."

"The person, be it gentleman or lady, who has not pleasure in a good novel, must be intolerably stupid. I have read all Mrs Radcliffe's works, and most of them with great pleasure. 'The Mysteries of Udolpho,' when I had once begun it, I could not lay down again; I remember finishing it in two days, my hair standing on end the whole time."

"Yes," added Miss Tilney; "and I remember that you undertook to read it aloud to me; and that when I was called away for only five minutes to answer a note, instead of waiting for me, you took the volume into the Hermitage Walk, and I was obliged to stay till you had finished it."

"Thank you, Eleanor; a most honourable testimony. You see, Miss Morland, the injustice of your suspicions. Here was I, in my eagerness to get on, refusing to wait only five minutes for my sister; breaking the promise I had made of reading it aloud, and keeping her in suspense at a most interesting part, by running away with the volume, which, you are to observe, was her own, particularly her own. I am proud when I reflect on it, and I think it must establish me in your good opinion."

"I am very glad to hear it, indeed; and now I shall never be ashamed of liking Udolpho myself. But I really thought before, young men despised novels amazingly."

"It is *amazingly*; it may well suggest *amazement* if they do, for they read nearly as many as women. I, myself, have read hundreds and hundreds. Do not imagine that you can cope with me in a knowledge of Julias and Louisas. If we proceed to particulars, and engage in the never-ceasing inquiry of ' Have you read this ? ' and ' Have you read that ? ' I shall soon leave you as far behind me as—what shall I say ? I want an appropriate simile ; as far as your friend Emily herself left poor Valancourt when she went with her aunt into Italy. Consider how many years I have had the start of you. I had entered on my studies at Oxford, while you were a good little girl working your sampler at home ! "

" Not very good, I am afraid. But now, really, do not you think Udolpho the nicest book in the world ? "

" The nicest ; by which I suppose you mean the neatest. That must depend upon the binding."

" Henry," said Miss Tilney, " you are very impertinent. Miss Morland, he is treating you exactly as he does his sister. He is for ever finding fault with me for some incorrectness of language, and now he is taking the same liberty with you. The word ' nicest,' as you used it, did not suit him ; and you had better change it as soon as you can, or we shall be overpowered with Johnson and Blair all the rest of the way."

" I am sure," cried Catherine, " I did not mean to say anything wrong ; but it *is* a nice book, and why should not I call it so ? "

" Very true," said Henry, " and this is a very nice day ; and we are taking a very nice walk ; and you are two very nice young ladies. Oh ! it is a very nice word, indeed ! it does for everything. Originally, perhaps, it was applied only to express neatness, propriety, delicacy, or refinement ; people were nice in their dress, in their sentiments, or their choice. But now every commendation no every subject is comprised in that one word."

" While, in fact," cried his sister, " it ought only to be applied to you, without any commendation at all. You are more nice than wise. Come, Miss Morland, let us leave him to meditate over our faults in the utmost propriety of diction, while we praise Udolpho in whatever terms we like best. It is a most interesting work. You are fond of that kind of reading ? "

" To say the truth, I do not much like any other."

" Indeed ! "

" That is, I can read poetry and plays, and things of that sort, and do not dislike travels. But history, real solemn history, I cannot be interested in. Can you ? "

" Yes, I am fond of history."

" I wish I were too. I read it a little as a duty ; but it tells me nothing that does not either vex or weary me. The quarrels of popes and kings, with wars or pestilences in every page ; the men all so good for nothing, and hardly any women at all, it is very tiresome ; and yet I often think it odd that it should be so dull, for a great deal of it must be invention. The speeches that are put into the heroes' mouths, their thoughts and designs : the chief of all this must be invention, and invention is what delights me in other books."

" Historians, you think," said Miss Tilney, " are not happy in their flights of fancy. They display imagination without raising interest. I am fond of history, and am very well contented to take the false with the true. In the principal facts they have sources of intelligence in former histories and records, which may be as much depended on I conclude as anything that does not actually pass under one's own observation ; and as for the little embellishments you speak of, they are embellishments, and I like them as such. If a speech be well drawn up, I read it with pleasure, by whomsoever it may be made : and probably with much greater, if the production of Mr Hume or Mr Robertson, than if the genuine words of Caractacus, Agricola, or Alfred the Great."

" You are fond of history ! and so are Mr Allen and my father ; and I have two brothers who do not dislike it. So many instances within my small circle of friends is remarkable ! At this rate, I shall not pity the writers of history any longer. If people like to read their books, it is all very well ; but to be at so much trouble in filling great volumes, which, as I used to think, nobody would willingly ever look into, to be labouring only for the torment of little boys and girls, always struck me as a hard fate ; and though I know it is all very right and necessary, I have often wondered at the person's courage that could sit down on purpose to do it."

"That little boys and girls should be tormented," said Henry, "is what no one at all acquainted with human nature in a civilised state can deny ; but in behalf of our most distinguished historians, I must observe, that they might well be offended at being supposed to have no higher aim ; and that by their method and style they are perfectly well qualified to torment readers of the most advanced reason and mature time of life. I use the verb ' to torment,' as I observed to be your own method, instead of ' to instruct,' supposing them to be now admitted as synonimous."

"You think me foolish to call instruction a torment ; but if you had been as much used as myself to hear poor little children first learning their letters, and then learning to spell, if you had ever seen how stupid they can be for a whole morning together, and how tired my poor mother is at the end of it, as I am in the habit of seeing almost every day of my life at home, you would allow, that to *torment* and to *instruct* might sometimes be used as synonimous words."

"Very probably. But historians are not accountable for the difficulty of learning to read ; and even you yourself, who do not altogether seem particularly friendly to very severe, very intense application, may perhaps be brought to acknowledge that it is very well worth while to be tormented for two or three years of one's life, for the sake of being able to read all the rest of it. Consider, if reading had not been taught, Mrs Radcliffe would have written in vain, or, perhaps, might not have written at all."

Catherine assented ; and a very warm panegyric from her on that lady's merits closed the subject. The Tilneys were soon engaged in another, on which she had nothing to say. They were viewing the country with the . eyes of persons accustomed to drawing ; and decided on its capability of being formed into pictures, with all the eagerness or real taste. Here Catherine was quite lost. She knew nothing of drawing—nothing of taste ; and she listened to them with an attention which brought her little profit, for they talked in phrases which conveyed scarcely any

idea to her. The little which she could understand, however, appeared to contradict the very few notions she had
entertained on the matter before. It seemed as if a good
view were no longer to be taken from the top of an high
hill, and that a clear blue sky was no longer a proof of a
fine day. She was heartily ashamed of her ignorance—
a misplaced shame. Where people wish to attach, they
should always be ignorant. To come with a well-informed
mind, is to come with an inability of administering to the
vanity of others, which a sensible person would always
wish to avoid. A woman, especially, if she have the misfortune of knowing any thing, should conceal it as well
as she can.

The advantages of natural folly in a beautiful girl have
been already set forth by the capital pen of a sister author ;
and to her treatment of the subject I will only add, in justice
to men, that though, to the larger and more trifling part
of the sex, imbecility in females is a great enhancement
of their personal charms, there is a portion of them too
reasonable, and too well-informed themselves, to desire
anything more in woman than ignorance. But Catherine
did not know her own advantages ; did not know that a
good-looking girl with an affectionate heart, and a very
ignorant mind, cannot fail of attracting a clever young
man, unless circumstances are particularly untoward. In
the present instance, she confessed and lamented her want
of knowledge ; declared that she would give anything in the
world to be able to draw ; and a lecture on the picturesque
immediately followed, in which his instructions were so clear
that she soon began to see beauty in everything admired by
him ; and her attention was so earnest, that he became
perfectly satisfied of her having a great deal of natural taste.
He talked of fore-grounds, distances, and second distances ;
side-screens, and perspectives ; lights and shades ; and
Catherine was so hopeful a scholar, that when they gained
the top of Beechen Cliff, she voluntarily rejected the whole
city of Bath, as unworthy to make part of a landscape.
Delighted with her progress, and fearful of wearying her
with too much wisdom at once, Henry suffered the subject
to decline, and, by an easy transition from a piece of rocky

fragment, and the withered oak which he had placed near its summit, to oaks in general—to forests, the enclosure of them, waste lands, crown lands and government—he shortly found himself arrived at politics ; and from politics it was an easy step to silence. The general pause which succeeded his short disquisition on the state of the nation was put an end to by Catherine, who, in rather a solemn tone of voice, uttered these words, " I have heard that something very shocking indeed will soon come out in London."

Miss Tilney, to whom this was chiefly addressed, was startled, and hastily replied, " Indeed! and of what nature?"

" That I do not know, nor who is the author. I have only heard that it is to be more horrible than anything we have met with yet."

" Good heaven ! Where could you hear of such a thing ? "

" A particular friend of mine had an account of it in a letter from London yesterday. It is to be uncommonly dreadful. I shall expect murder and everything of the kind."

" You speak with astonishing composure. But I hope your friend's accounts have been exaggerated ; and if such a design is known beforehand, proper measures will undoubtedly be taken by government to prevent its coming to effect."

" Government," said Henry, endeavouring not to smile, " neither desires nor dares to interfere in such matters. There must be murder, and government cares not how much."

The ladies stared. He laughed, and added, " Come, shall I make you understand each other, or leave you to puzzle out an explanation as you can ? No, I will be noble. I will prove myself a man no less by the generosity of my soul, than the clearness of my head. I have no patience with such of my sex as disdain to let themselves sometimes down to the comprehension of yours. Perhaps the abilities of women are neither sound nor acute, neither vigorous nor keen. Perhaps they may want observation, discernment, judgment, fire, genius, and wit."

"Miss Morland, do not mind what he says; but have the goodness to satisfy me as to this dreadful riot."

"Riot!—what riot?"

"My dear Eleanor, the riot is only in your own brain. The confusion there is scandalous. Miss Morland has been talking of nothing more dreadful than a new publication which is shortly to come out, in three duodecimo volumes, two hundred and seventy-six pages in each, with a frontispiece to the first, of two tombstones and a lantern—do you understand? And you, Miss Morland—my stupid sister has mistaken all your clearest expressions. You talked of expected horrors in London; and instead of instantly conceiving, as any rational creature would have done, that such words could relate only to a circulating library, she immediately pictured to herself a mob of three thousand men assembling in St George's Fields; the Bank attacked, the Tower threatened, the streets of London flowing with blood, a detachment of the 12th Light Dragoons (the hopes of the nation) called up from Northampton to quell the insurgents, and the gallant Captain Frederick Tilney, in the moment of charging at the head of his troop, knocked off his horse by a brick-bat from an upper window. Forgive her stupidity. The fears of the sister have added to the weakness of the woman, but she is by no means a simpleton in general."

Catherine looked grave. "And now, Henry," said Miss Tilney, "that you have made us understand each other, you may as well make Miss Morland understand yourself, unless you mean to have her think you intolerably rude to your sister, and a great brute in your opinion of women in general. Miss Morland is not used to your odd ways."

"I shall be most happy to make her better acquainted with them."

"No doubt; but that is no explanation of the present."

"What am I to do?"

"You know what you ought to do." Clear your character handsomely before her. Tell her that you think very highly of the understanding of women."

"Miss Morland, I think very highly of the understanding of all the women in the world, especially of those, who-ever they may be, with whom I happen to be in company."

" That is not enough.   Be more serious."

" Miss Morland, no one can think more highly of the understanding of women than I do.   In my opinion, nature has given them so much that they never find it necessary to use more than half."

" We shall get nothing more serious from him now, Miss Morland.   He is not in a sober mood.   But I assure you that he must be entirely misunderstood, if he can ever appear to say an unjust thing of any woman at all, or an unkind one of me."

It was no effort to Catherine to believe that Henry Tilney could never be wrong.   His manner might sometimes surprize, but his meaning must always be just ; and what she did not understand, she was almost as ready to admire, as what she did.   The whole walk was delightful, and though it ended too soon, its conclusion was delightful too.   Her friends attended her into the house, and Miss Tilney, before they parted, addressing herself with respect-ful form, as much to Mrs Allen as to Catherine, petitioned for the pleasure of her company to dinner on the day after the next.   No difficulty was made on Mrs Allen's side, and the only difficulty on Catherine's was in concealing the excess of her pleasure.

The morning had passed away so charmingly as to banish all her friendship and natural affection ; for no thought of Isabella or James crossed her mind during their walk. When the Tilneys were gone, she became amiable again, but she was amiable for some time to little effect ; Mrs Allen had no intelligence to give that could relieve her anxiety ; she had heard nothing of any of them.   Towards the end of the morning, however, Catherine having occasion for some indispensable yard of ribbon, which must be bought without a moment's delay, walked out into the town, and in Bond Street overtook the second Miss Thorpe, as she was loitering towards Edgar's Buildings between two of the sweetest girls in the world, who had been her dear friends all the morning.   From her, she soon learned that the party to Clifton had taken place.   " They set off at eight this morning," said Miss Anne, "and I am sure I do not envy them their drive. I think you and I are very well off to be out of the scrape. It must be the dullest thing in the world, for there is not a soul at Clifton at this time of the year. Belle went with your brother, and John drove Maria."

Catherine spoke the pleasure she really felt on hearing this part of the arrangement.

"Oh! yes," rejoined the other, "Maria is gone. She was quite wild to go. She thought it would be something very fine. I cannot say I admire her taste; and, for my part, I was determined from the first not to go, if they pressed me ever so much."

Catherine, a little doubtful of this, could not help answering, "I wish you could have gone too. It is a pity you could not all go."

"Thank you: but it is quite a matter of indifference to me. Indeed, I would not have gone on any account. I was saying so to Emily and Sophia when you overtook us."

Catherine was still unconvinced; but glad that Anne should have the friendship of an Emily and a Sophia to console her, she bade her adieu without much uneasiness, and returned home, pleased that the party had not been prevented by her refusing to join it, and very heartily wishing that it might be too pleasant to allow either James or Isabella to resent her resistance any longer.

CHAPTER XV

EARLY the next day, a note from Isabella, speaking peace and tenderness in every line, and entreating the immediate presence of her friend on a matter of the utmost importance, hastened Catherine, in the happiest state of confidence and curiosity, to Edgar's Buildings. The two youngest Miss Thorpes were by themselves in the parlour, and on Anne's quitting it to call her sister, Catherine took the opportunity of asking the other for some particulars of their yesterday's party.

Maria desired no greater pleasure than to speak of it ; and Catherine immediately learned that it had been altogether the most delightful scheme in the world, that nobody could imagine how charming it had been, and that it had been more delightful than anybody could conceive. Such was the information of the first five minutes ; the second unfolded thus much in detail, that they had driven directly to the York Hotel, ate some soup, and bespoke an early dinner, walked down to the Pump-room, tasted the water, and laid out some shillings in purses and spars ; thence adjourned to eat ice at a pastry-cook's, and hurrying back to the hotel, swallowed their dinner in haste, to prevent being in the dark, and then had a delightful drive back, only the moon was not up, and it rained a little, and Mr Morland's horse was so tired he could hardly get it along.

Catherine listened with heartfelt satisfaction. It appeared that Blaize Castle had never been thought of, and as for all the rest, there was nothing to regret for half an instant. Maria's intelligence concluded with a tender effusion of pity for her sister Anne, whom she represented as insupportably cross from being excluded the party.

" She will never forgive me, I am sure ; but, you know, how could I help it ? John would have me go, for he vowed he would not drive her because she had such thick ancles. I dare say she will not be in good humour again this month ; but I am determined I will not be cross ; it is not a little matter that puts me out of temper."

Isabella now entered the room with so eager a step, and a look of such happy importance, as engaged all her friend's notice. Maria was without ceremony sent away, and Isabella, embracing Catherine, thus began :—" Yes, my dear Catherine, it is so, indeed ; your penetration has not deceived you. Oh, that arch eye of yours ! it sees through everything."

Catherine replied only by a look of wondering ignorance.

" Nay, my beloved, sweetest friend," continued the other, " compose yourself. I am amazingly agitated, as you perceive. Let us sit down and talk in comfort. Well, and so you guessed it the moment you had my note ? Sly creature ! Oh ! my dear Catherine, you alone who know

my heart can judge of my present happiness. Your brother
is the most charming of men. I only wish I were more
worthy of him. But what will your excellent father and
mother say ? Oh, heavens ! when I think of them, I am
so agitated ! "

Catherine's understanding began to awake ; an idea
of the truth suddenly darted into her mind ; and, with
the natural blush of so new an emotion, she cried out,
" Good heaven ! my dear Isabella, what do you mean ?
Can you—can you really be in love with James ? "

This bold surmise, however, she soon learnt comprehended but half the fact. The anxious affection which
she was accused of having continually watched in Isabella's
every look and action, had, in the course of their yesterday's
party, received the delightful confession of an equal love.
Her heart and faith were alike engaged to James. Never
had Catherine listened to anything so full of interest, wonder,
and joy. Her brother and her friend engaged ! New to
such circumstances, the importance of it appeared un-
speakably great, and she contemplated it as one of those
grand events of which the ordinary course of life can hardly
afford a return. The strength of her feelings she could
not express ; the nature of them, however, contented
her friend. The happiness of having such a sister was
their first effusion, and the fair ladies mingled in embraces
and tears of joy.

Delighting, however, as Catherine sincerely did, in the
prospect of the connexion, it must be acknowledged that
Isabella far surpassed her in tender anticipations. " You
will be so infinitely dearer to me, my Catherine, than either
Anne or Maria. I feel that I shall be so much more attached
to my dear Morland's family than to my own."

This was a pitch of friendship beyond Catherine.

" You are so like your dear brother," continued Isabella,
" that I quite doated on you the first moment I saw you.
But so it always is with me : the first moment settles everything. The very first day that Morland came to us last
Christmas, the very first moment I beheld him, my heart
was irrevocably gone. I remember I wore my yellow gown,
with my hair done up in braids ; and when I came into the

drawing-room, and John introduced him, I thought I never saw anybody so handsome before."

Here Catherine secretly acknowledged the power of love; for, though exceedingly fond of her brother, and partial to all his endowments, she had never in her life thought him handsome.

"I remember, too, Miss Andrews drank tea with us that evening, and wore her puce-coloured sarsenet; and she looked so heavenly, that I thought your brother must certainly fall in love with her; I could not sleep a wink all night for thinking of it. Oh! Catherine, the many sleepless nights I have had on your brother's account! I would not have you suffer half what I have done! I am grown wretchedly thin, I know; but I will not pain you by describing my anxiety; you have seen enough of it. I feel that I have betrayed myself perpetually; so unguarded in speaking of my partiality for the church! But my secret I was always sure would be safe with *you*."

Catherine felt that nothing could have been safer; but ashamed of an ignorance little expected, she dared no longer contest the point, nor refuse to have been as full of arch penetration and affectionate sympathy as Isabella chose to consider her. Her brother, she found, was preparing to set off with all speed to Fullerton, to make known his situation and ask consent; and here was a source of some real agitation to the mind of Isabella. Catherine endeavoured to persuade her, as she was herself persuaded, that her father and mother would never oppose their son's wishes. "It is impossible," said she, "for parents to be more kind, or more desirous of their children's happiness; I have no doubt of their consenting immediately."

"Morland says exactly the same," replied Isabella; "and yet I dare not expect it; my fortune will be so small; they never can consent to it. Your brother, who might marry anybody!"

Here Catherine again discerned the force of love.

"Indeed, Isabella, you are too humble. The difference of fortune can be nothing to signify."

"Oh! my sweet Catherine, in *your* generous heart I know it would signify nothing, but we must not expect such disinterestedness in many. As for myself, I am sure I only wish our situations were reversed. Had I the command of millions, were I mistress of the whole world, your brother would be my only choice."

This charming sentiment, recommended as much by sense as novelty, gave Catherine a most pleasing remembrance of all the heroines of her acquaintance; and she thought her friend never looked more lovely than in uttering the grand idea. "I am sure they will consent," was her frequent declaration : "I am sure they will be delighted with you."

"For my own part," said Isabella, "my wishes are so moderate, that the smallest income in nature would be enough for me. Where people are really attached, poverty itself is wealth: grandeur I detest: I would not settle in London for the universe. A cottage in some retired village would be extasy. There are some charming little villas about Richmond."

"Richmond!" cried Catherine. "You must settle near Fullerton. You must be near us."

"I am sure I shall be miserable if we do not. If I can but be near *you*, I shall be satisfied. But this is idle talking! I will not allow myself to think of such things till we have your father's answer. Morland says that by sending it to-night to Salisbury, we may have it to-morrow. To-morrow! I know I shall never have courage to open the letter. I know it will be the death of me."

A reverie succeeded this conviction, and when Isabella spoke again, it was to resolve on the quality of her wedding-gown.

Their conference was put an end to by the anxious young lover himself, who came to breathe his parting sigh before he set off for Wiltshire. Catherine wished to congratulate him, but knew not what to say, and her eloquence was only in her eyes. From them, however, the eight parts of speech shone out most expressively, and James could combine them with ease. Impatient for the realization of all that he hoped at home, his adieus were not long, and they would have been yet shorter had he not been frequently detained by the urgent entreaties of his fair one that he would go. Twice was he called almost from the door by her eagerness to have him gone. " Indeed, Morland, I must drive you away. Consider how far you have to ride. I cannot bear to see you linger so. For Heaven's sake, waste no more time. There, go, go—I insist on it."

The two friends, with hearts now more united than ever, were inseparable for the day ; and in schemes of sisterly happiness the hours flew along. Mrs Thorpe and her son, who were acquainted with everything, and who seemed only to want Mr Morland's consent to consider Isabella's engagement as the most fortunate circumstance imaginable for their family, were allowed to join their counsels, and add their quota of significant looks and mysterious expressions, to fill up the measure of curiosity to be raised in the un-privileged younger sisters. To Catherine's simple feelings, this odd sort of reserve seemed neither kindly meant, nor consistently supported ; and its unkindness she would hardly have forborn pointing out, had its inconsistency been less their friend ; but Anne and Maria soon set her heart at ease by the sagacity of their " I know what ; " and the evening was spent in a sort of war of wit, a display of family ingenuity ; on one side in the mystery of an affected secret, on the other of undefined discovery, all equally acute."

Catherine was with her friend again the next day, en-deavouring to support her spirits, and while away the many tedious hours before the delivery of the letters : a needful exertion ; for as the time of reasonable expectation drew near, Isabella became more and more desponding, and before the letter arrived, had worked herself into a state of real distress. But when it did come, where could distress be found ? " I have had no difficulty in gaining the con-sent of my kind parents, and am promised that everything in their power shall be done to forward my happiness," were the first three lines, and in one moment all was joyful security. The brightest glow was instantly spread over Isabella's features—all care and anxiety seemed removed, her spirits became almost too high for controul, and she called herself without scruple the happiest of mortals.

Mrs Thorpe, with tears of joy, embraced her daughter,

her son, her visitor, and could have embraced half the inhabitants of Bath with satisfaction. Her heart was overflowing with tenderness. It was "dear John," and "dear Catherine," at every word; "dear Anne and dear Maria" must immediately be made sharers in their felicity; and two "dears" at once before the name of Isabella were not more than that beloved child had now well earned. John himself was no skulker in joy. He not only bestowed on Mr Morland the high commendation of being one of the finest fellows in the world, but swore off many sentences in his praise.

The letter whence sprang all this felicity was short, containing little more than this assurance of success; and every particular was deferred till James could write again. But for particulars Isabella could well afford to wait. The needful was comprised in Mr Morland's promise: his honour was pledged to make everything easy; and by what means their income was to be formed, whether landed property were to be resigned, or funded money made over, was a matter in which her disinterested spirit took no concern. She knew enough to feel secure of an honourable and speedy establishment, and her imagination took a rapid flight over its intended felicities. She saw herself, at the end of a few weeks, the gaze and admiration of every new acquaintance at Fullerton, the envy of every valued old friend in Putney, with a carriage at her command, a new name on her tickets, and a brilliant exhibition of hoop rings on her finger.

When the contents of the letter were ascertained, John Thorpe, who had only waited its arrival to begin his journey to London, prepared to set off. "Well, Miss Morland," said he, on finding her alone in the parlour, "I am come to bid you good-bye." Catherine wished him a good journey. Without appearing to hear her, he walked to the window, fidgetted about, hummed a tune, and seemed wholly self-occupied.

"Shall not you be late at Devizes?" said Catherine. He made no answer; but after a minute's silence burst out with, "A famous good thing this marrying scheme, upon my soul! A clever fancy of Morland's and Belle's.

What do you think of it, Miss Morland? *I* say it is no bad notion."

" I am sure I think it a very good one."

" Do you?—that's honest, by heavens! I am glad you are no enemy to matrimony, however. Did you ever hear the old song, ' Going to one wedding brings on another ' ? I say, you will come to Belle's wedding, I hope."

" Yes ; I have promised your sister to be with her, if possible."

" And then you know "—twisting himself about, and forcing a foolish laugh—" I say, then you know, we may try the truth of this same old song."

" May we ? but I never sing. Well, I wish you a good journey. I dine with Miss Tilney to-day, and must now be going home."

" Nay, but there is no such confounded hurry. Who knows when we may be together again ? Not but that I shall be down again by the end of a fortnight, and a devilish long fortnight it will appear to me."

" Then why do you stay away so long ? " replied Catherine, finding that he waited for an answer.

" That is kind of you, however ; kind and good-natured. I shall not forget it in a hurry. But you have more good-nature, and all that, than anybody living, I believe. A monstrous deal of good-nature, and it is not only good-nature, but you have so much—so much of everything ; and then you have such—upon my soul, I do not know any body like you."

" Oh dear ! there are a great many people like me, I dare say, only a great deal better. Good morning to you."

" But I say, Miss Morland, I shall come and pay my respects at Fullerton before it is long, if not disagreeable."

" Pray do ; my father and mother will be very glad to see you."

" And I hope—I hope, Miss Morland, *you* will not be sorry to see me."

" Oh dear ! not at all. There are very few people I am sorry to see. Company is always cheerful."

" That is just my way of thinking. Give me but a little cheerful company, let me only have the company of the people I love, let me only be where I like and with whom I like, and the devil take the rest, say I ; and I am heartily glad to hear you say the same. But I have a notion, Miss Morland, you and I think pretty much alike upon most matters."

" Perhaps we may ; but it is more than I ever thought of. And as to *most matters*, to say the truth, there are not many that I know my own mind about."

" By Jove, no more do I ! It is not my way to bother my brains with what does not concern me. My notion of things is simple enough. Let me only have the girl I like, say I, with a comfortable house over my head, and what care I for all the rest ? Fortune is nothing. I am sure of a good income of my own ; and if she had not a penny, why so much the better."

" Very true. I think like you there. If there is a good fortune on one side, there can be no occasion for any on the other. No matter which has it, so that there is enough. I hate the idea of one great fortune looking out for another ; and to marry for money, I think the wickedest thing in existence. Good day. We shall be very glad to see you at Fullerton, whenever it is convenient." And away she went. It was not in the power of all his gallantry to detain her longer. With such news to communicate, and such a visit to prepare for, her departure was not to be delayed by anything in his nature to urge ; and she hurried away, leaving him to the undivided consciousness of his own happy address and her explicit encouragement.

The agitation which she had herself experienced on first learning her brother's engagement made her expect to raise no inconsiderable emotion in Mr and Mrs Allen, by the communication of the wonderful event. How great was her disappointment ! The important affair, which many words of preparation ushered in, had been foreseen by them both ever since her brother's arrival ; and all that they felt on the occasion was comprehended in a wish for the young people's happiness, with a remark, on the gentleman's side, in favour of Isabella's beauty, and on the lady's, of her great good luck. It was to Catherine the most surprizing insensibility. The disclosure, however, of the great secret of James's going to Fullerton the day before did raise some emotion in Mrs Allen. She could not listen to that with perfect calmness, but repeatedly regretted the necessity of its concealment, wished she could have known his intention, wished she could have seen him before he went, as she should certainly have troubled him with her best regards to his father and mother, and her kind compliments to all the Skinners.

CHAPTER XVI

CATHERINE'S expectations of pleasure from her visit in Milsom Street were so very high, that disappointment was inevitable; and, accordingly, though she was most politely received by General Tilney, and kindly welcomed by his daughter; though Henry was at home, and no one else of the party, she found on her return, without spending many hours in the examination of her feelings, that she had gone to her appointment preparing for happiness which it had not afforded. Instead of finding herself improved in acquaintance with Miss Tilney, from the intercourse of the day, she seemed hardly so intimate with her as before. Instead of seeing Henry Tilney to greater advantage than ever, in the ease of a family party; he had never said so little nor been so little agreeable; and, in spite of their father's great civilities to her, in spite of his thanks, invitations, and compliments, it had been a release to get away from him. It puzzled her to account for all this. It could not be General Tilney's fault. That he was perfectly agreeable and good-natured, and altogether a very charming man, did not admit of a doubt, for he was tall and handsome, and Henry's father. *He* could not be accountable for his children's want of spirits, or for her want of enjoyment in his company. The former she hoped at last might have been accidental, and the latter she could only attribute to her own stupidity. Isabella, on hearing the particulars of the visit, gave a different explanation. "It was all pride, pride; insufferable haughtiness and pride! She had long suspected the family to be very high, and this made it certain. Such insolence of behaviour as Miss Tilney's she had never heard of in her life! Not to do the honours of her house with common good breeding! To behave to her guest with such superciliousness! Hardly even to speak to her!"

"But it was not so bad as that, Isabella; there was no superciliousness; she was very civil."

"Oh, don't defend her! And then the brother, he, who had appeared so attached to you! Good heavens! well, some people's feelings are incomprehensible. And so he hardly looked once at you the whole day?"

"I do not say so; but he did not seem in good spirits."

"How contemptible! Of all things in the world inconstancy is my aversion. Let me entreat you never to think of him again, my dear Catherine; indeed he is unworthy of you."

"Unworthy! I do not suppose he ever thinks of me."

"That is exactly what I say; he never thinks of you. Such fickleness! Oh, how different to your brother and to mine! I really believe John has the most constant heart."

"But as for General Tilney, I assure you it would be impossible for any body to behave to me with greater civility and attention; it seemed to be his only care to entertain and make me happy."

"Oh! I know no harm of him; I no not suspect him of pride. I believe he is a very gentleman-like man. John thinks very well of him, and John's judgment—"

"Well, I shall see how they behave to me this evening; we shall meet them at the rooms."

"And must I go?"

"Do not you intend it? I thought it was all settled."

"Nay, since you make such a point of it, I can refuse you nothing. But do not insist upon my being very agreeable, for my heart, you know, will be some forty miles off; and as for dancing, do not mention it, I beg; *that* is quite out of the question. Charles Hodges will plague me to death, I dare say; but I shall cut him very short. Ten to one but he guesses the reason, and that is exactly what

I want to avoid ; so I shall insist on his keeping his conjecture to himself."

Isabella's opinion of the Tilneys did not influence her friend ; she was sure there had been no insolence in the manners either of brother or sister ; and she did not credit there being any pride in their hearts. The evening rewarded her confidence ; she was met by one with the same kindness, and by the other with the same attention as heretofore. Miss Tilney took pains to be near her, and Henry asked her to dance.

Having heard the day before in Milsom Street that their elder brother, Captain Tilney, was expected almost every hour, she was at no loss for the name of a very fashionable-looking, handsome young man, whom she had never seen before, and who now evidently belonged to their party. She looked at him with great admiration ; and even supposed it possible, that some people might think him handsomer than his brother, though, in her eyes, his air was more assuming, and his countenance less prepossessing. His taste and manners were, beyond a doubt, decidedly inferior ; for, within her hearing, he not only protested against every thought of dancing himself, but even laughed openly at Henry for finding it possible. From the latter circumstance it may be presumed, that, whatever might be our heroine's opinion of him, his admiration of her was not of a very dangerous kind ; not likely to produce animosities between the brothers, nor persecutions to the lady. *He* cannot be the instigator of the three villains in horsemen's great coats, by whom she will hereafter be forced into a travelling chaise and four, which will drive off with incredible speed. Catherine, meanwhile, undisturbed by presentiments of such an evil, or of any evil at all, except that of having but a short set to dance down, enjoyed her usual happiness with Henry Tilney, listening with sparkling eyes to everything he said ; and, in finding him irresistible, becoming so herself.

At the end of the first dance, Captain Tilney come towards them again, and, much to Catherine's dissatisfaction, pulled his brother away. They retired whispering together ; and, though her delicate sensibility did not take immediate alarm, and lay it down as fact, that Captain Tilney must have heard some malevolent misrepresentation of her, which he now hastened to communicate to his brother, in the hope of separating them for ever, she could not have her partner conveyed from her sight without very uneasy sensations. Her suspense was of full five minutes' duration ; and she was beginning to think it a very long quarter of an hour, when they both returned ; and an explanation was given, by Henry's requesting to know, if she thought her friend Miss Thorpe would have any objection to dancing, as his brother would be most happy to be introduced to her. Catherine, without hesitation, replied, that she was very sure Miss Thorpe did not mean to dance at all. The cruel reply was passed on to the other, and he immediately walked away.

" Your brother will not mind it, I know," said she, " because I heard him say before that he hated dancing ; but it was very good-natured in him to think of it. I suppose he saw Isabella sitting down, and fancied she might wish for a partner ; but he is quite mistaken, for she would not dance upon any account in the world."

Henry smiled, and said, " How very little trouble it can give you to understand the motive of other people's actions."

" Why ? What do you mean ? "

" With you it is not, how is such a one likely to be influenced ? What is the inducement most likely to act upon such a person's feelings, age, situation, and probable habits of life considered ? But, how should *I* be influenced ; what would *my* inducement in acting so and so ? "

" I do not understand you."

" Then we are on very unequal terms, for I understand you perfectly well."

" Me ? yes ; I cannot speak well enough to be unintelligible."

" Bravo ! an excellent satire on modern language."

" But pray tell me what you mean."

" Shall I, indeed ? Do you really desire it ? But you are not aware of the consequences ; it will involve you in a very cruel embarrassment, and certainly bring on a disagreement between us."

"No, no; it shall not do either; I am not afraid."

"Well, then, I only meant that your attributing my brother's wish of dancing with Miss Thorpe to good-nature alone, convinced me of your being superior in good-nature yourself to all the rest of the world."

Catherine blushed and disclaimed, and the gentleman's predictions were verified. There was a something, however, in his words which repaid her for the pain of confusion; and that something occupied her mind so much, that she drew back for some time, forgetting to speak or to listen, and almost forgetting where she was; till, roused by the voice of Isabella, she looked up and saw her with Captain Tilney preparing to give them hands across.

Isabella shrugged her shoulders and smiled, the only explanation of this extraordinary change which could at that time be given; but as it was not quite enough for Catherine's comprehension, she spoke her astonishment in very plain terms to her partner.

"I cannot think how it could happen! Isabella was so determined not to dance."

"And did Isabella never change her mind before?"

"Oh! but, because —— and your brother! After what you told him from me, how could he think of going to ask her?"

"I cannot take surprize to myself on that head. You bid me be surprized on your friend's account, and, therefore, I am; but as for my brother, his conduct in the business, I must own, has been no more than I believed him perfectly equal to. The fairness of your friend was an open attraction; her firmness, you know, could only be understood by yourself."

"You are laughing; but, I assure you, Isabella is very firm in general."

"It is as much as should be said of any one. To be always firm must be to be often obstinate. When properly to relax is the trial of judgment; and, without reference to my brother, I really think Miss Thorpe has by no means chosen ill in fixing on the present hour."

The friends were not able to get together for any confidential discourse till all the dancing was over; but

then, as they walked about the room arm in arm, Isabella
thus explained herself : " I do not wonder at your surprize ;
and I am really fatigued to death. He is such a rattle !
Amusing enough, if my mind had been disengaged ; but
I would have given the world to sit still."

" Then why did not you ? "

" Oh ! my dear, it would have looked so particular ;
and you know how I abhor doing that. I refused him
as long as I possibly could, but he would take no denial.
You have no idea how he pressed me. I begged him to
excuse me, and get some other partner ; but no, not he ;
after aspiring to my hand, there was nobody else in the
room he could bear to think of ; and it was not that he
wanted merely to dance, he wanted to be with *me*. Oh,
such nonsense ! I told him he had taken a very unlikely
way to prevail upon me ; for, of all things in the world,
I hated fine speeches and compliments ;—and so—and so
then I found there would be no peace if I did not stand up.
Besides, I thought Mrs Hughes, who introduced him,
might take it ill if I did not ; and your dear brother, I am
sure he would have been miserable if I had sat down the
whole evening. I am so glad it is over ! My spirits are
quite jaded with listening to his nonsense ; and then, being
such a smart young fellow. I saw every eye was upon
us."

" He is very handsome, indeed."

" Handsome ! Yes, I suppose he may. I dare say
people would admire him in general ; but he is not at all
in my style of beauty. I hate a florid complexion and dark
eyes in a man. However, he is very well. Amazingly
conceited, I am sure. I took him down several times, you
know, in my way."

When the young ladies next met, they had a far more
interesting subject to discuss. James Morland's second
letter was then received, and the kind intentions of his
father fully explained. A living, of which Mr Morland
was himself parton and incumbent, of about four hundred
pounds yearly value, was to be resigned to his son as soon
as he should be old enough to take it ; no trifling deduction
from the family income, no niggardly assignment to one

of ten children. An estate of at least equal value, more-over, was assured as his future inheritance.

James expressed himself on the occasion with becoming gratitude ; and the necessity of waiting between two and three years before they could marry being, however un-welcome, no more than he had expected, was borne by him without discontent. Catherine, whose expectations had been as unfixed as her ideas of her father's income, and whose judgment was now entirely led by her brother, felt equally well satisfied, and heartily congratulated Isabella on having everything so pleasantly settled.

" It is very charming, indeed," said Isabella, with a grave face.

" Mr Morland has behaved vastly handsome, indeed," said the gentle Mrs Thorpe, looking anxiously at her daughter. " I only wish I could do as much. One could not expect more from him, you know. If he finds he *can* do more, by-and-bye, I dare say he will ; for I am sure he must be an excellent, good-hearted man. Four hundred is but a small income to begin on, indeed ; but your wishes, my dear Isabella, are so moderate, you do not consider how little you ever want, my dear."

" It is not on my own account I wish for more ; but I cannot bear to be the means of injuring my dear Morland, making him sit down upon an income hardly enough to find one in the common necessaries of life. For myself, it is nothing ; I never think of myself."

" I know you never do, my dear ; and you will always find your reward in the affection it makes everybody feel for you. There never was a young woman so beloved as you are by everybody that knows you ; and I dare say when Mr Morland sees you, my dear child—but do not let us distress our dear Catherine by talking of such things. Mr Morland has behaved so very handsome, you know. I always heard he was a most excellent man ; and you know, my dear, we are not to suppose but what, if you had had a suitable fortune, he would have come down with something more ; for I am sure he must be a most liberal-minded man."

" Nobody can think better of Mr Morland than I do,

I am sure. But everybody has their failing, you know; and everybody has a right to do what they like with their own money."

Catherine was hurt by these insinuations. " I am very sure," said she, " that my father has promised to do as much as he can afford."

Isabella recollected herself. " As to that, my sweet Catherine, there cannot be a doubt, and you know me well enough to be sure that a much smaller income would satisfy me. It is not the want of more money that makes me just at present a little out of spirits. I hate money; and if our union could take place now upon only fifty pounds a year, I should not have a wish unsatisfied. Ah ! my Catherine, you have found me out. There's the sting. The long, long, endless two years and a half that are to pass before your brother can hold the living."

" Yes, yes, my darling Isabella," said Mrs Thorpe, " we perfectly see into your heart. You have no disguise. We perfectly understand the present vexation ; and everybody must love you the better for such a noble, honest affection."

Catherine's uncomfortable feelings began to lessen. She endeavoured to believe that the delay of the marriage was the only source of Isabella's regret ; and when she saw her at their next interview as cheerful and amiable as ever, endeavoured to forget that she had for a minute thought otherwise. James soon followed his letter, and was received with the most gratifying kindness.

CHAPTER XVII

THE Allens had now entered on the sixth week of their stay in Bath ; and whether it should be the last, was for some time a question, to which Catherine listened with a beating heart. To have her acquaintance with the Tilneys end so soon, was an evil which nothing could counterbalance. Her whole happiness seemed at stake, while the affair was in suspense, and everything secured when it was determined that the lodgings should be taken for another fortnight. What this additional fortnight was to produce to her beyond the pleasure of sometimes seeing Henry Tilney, made but a small part of Catherine's speculation. Once or twice, indeed, since James's engagement had taught her what *could* be done, she had got so far as to indulge in a secret "perhaps," but in general the felicity of being with him for the present bounded her views : the present was now comprised in another three weeks, and her happiness being certain for that period, the rest of her life was at such a distance as to excite but little interest. In the course of the morning which saw this business arranged, she visited Miss Tilney, and poured forth her joyful feelings. It was doomed to be a day of trial. No sooner had she expressed her delight in Mr Allen's lengthened stay, than Miss Tilney told her of her father's having just determined upon quitting Bath by the end of another week. Here was a blow ! The past suspense of the morning had been ease and quiet to the present disappointment. Catherine's countenance fell ; and in a voice of most sincere concern she echoed Miss Tilney's concluding words, " By the end of another week ! "

" Yes ; my father can seldom be prevailed on to give the waters what I think a fair trial. He has been disappointed of some friends' arrival whom he expected to meet here, and as he is now pretty well, is in a hurry to get home."

" I am very sorry for it," said Catherine, dejectedly ; " if I had known this before——"

" Perhaps," said Miss Tilney in an embarrassed manner, " you would be so good—it would make me very happy if——"

The entrance of her father put a stop to the civility which Catherine was beginning to hope might introduce a desire of their corresponding. After addressing her with his usual politeness, he turned to his daughter, and said, " Well, Eleanor, may I congratulate you on being successful in your application to your fair friend ? "

" I was just beginning to make the request, sir, as you came in."

" Well, proceed by all means. I know how much your heart is in it. My daughter, Miss Morland," he continued

without leaving his daughter time to speak, " has been
forming a very bold wish. We leave Bath, as she has
perhaps told you, on Saturday se'nnight. A letter from
my steward tells me that my presence is wanted at home ;
and being disappointed in my hope of seeing the Marquis
of Longtown and General Courteney here, some of my
very old friends, there is nothing to detain me longer in
Bath. And could we carry our selfish point with you,
we should leave it without a single regret. Can you, in
short, be prevailed on to quit this scene of public triumph,
and oblige your friend Eleanor with your company in
Gloucestershire ? I am almost ashamed to make the request, though its presumption would certainly appear
greater to every creature in Bath than yourself. Modesty
such as your's—but not for the world would I pain it by
open praise. If you can be induced to honour us with a
visit, you will make us happy beyond expression. 'Tis
true, we can offer you nothing like the gaieties of this
lively place ; we can tempt you neither by amusement
nor splendour, for our mode of living, as you see, is
plain and unpretending, yet no endeavours shall be
wanting on our side to make Northanger Abbey not wholly
disagreeable."

Northanger Abbey ! These were thrilling words, and
wound up Catherine's feelings to the highest points of
extasy. Her grateful and gratified heart could hardly
restrain its expressions within the language of tolerable
calmness. To receive so flattering an invitation ! To
have her company so warmly solicited ! Everything
honourable and soothing, every present enjoyment and
every future hope was contained in it, and her acceptance,
with only the saving clause of papa and mamma's approbation, was eagerly given. " I will write home directly,"
said she, " and if they do not object, as I dare say they will
not—— "

General Tilney was not less sanguine, having already
waited on her excellent friends in Pulteney Street, and
obtained their sanction of his wishes. " Since they can
consent to part with you," said he, " we may expect philo-
sophy from all the world."

Miss Tilney was earnest, though gentle, in her secondary civilities, and the affair became in a few minutes as nearly settled as this necessary reference to Fullerton would allow.

The circumstances of the morning had led Catherine's feelings through the varieties of suspense, security, and disappointment: but they were now safely lodged in perfect bliss; and with spirits elated to rapture, with Henry at her heart, and Northanger Abbey on her lips, she hurried home to write her letter. Mr and Mrs Morland, relying on the discretion of the friends to whom they had already entrusted their daughter, felt no doubt of the propriety of an acquaintance which had been formed under their eye, and sent, therefore, by return of post, their ready consent to her visit in Gloucestershire. This indulgence, though not more than Catherine had hoped for, completed her conviction of being favoured beyond every other human creature, in friends and fortune, circumstance and chance. Everything seemed to co-operate for her advantage. By the kindness of her first friends, the Allens, she had been introduced into scenes where pleasures of every kind had met her. Her feelings, her preferences had each known the happiness of a return. Wherever she felt attachment, she had been able to create it. The affection of Isabella was to be secured to her in a sister. The Tilneys, they by whom above all she desired to be favourably thought of, outstripped even her wishes in the flattering measures by which their intimacy was to be continued. She was to be their chosen visitor, she was to be for weeks under the same roof with the person whose society she mostly prized; and, in addition to all the rest, this roof was to be the roof of an abbey! Her passion for ancient edifices was next in degree to her passion for Henry Tilney, and castles and abbies made usually the charm of those reveries which his image did not fill. To see and explore either the ramparts and keep of the one, or the cloisters of the other, had been for many weeks a darling wish, though to be more than the visitor of an hour had seemed too nearly impossible for desire; and yet this was to happen. With all the chances against her of house, hall, place, park, court, and cottage, Northanger turned up an abbey, and she was to be its inhabitant. Its long, damp passages, its narrow cells and ruined chapel, were to be within her daily reach, and she could not entirely subdue the hope of some traditional legends, some awful memorials of an injured and ill-fated nun.

It was wonderful that her friends should seem so little elated by the possession of such a home ; that the consciousness of it should be so meekly born. The power of early habit only could account for it. A distinction to which they had been born gave no pride. Their superiority of abode was no more to them than their superiority of person.

Many were the inquiries she was eager to make of Miss Tilney ; but so active were her thoughts, that when these inquiries were answered, she was hardly more assured than before of Northanger Abbey having been a richly endowed convent at the time of the Reformation, of its having fallen into the hands of an ancestor of the Tilneys on its dissolution, of a large portion of the ancient building still making a part of the present dwelling although the rest was decayed, or of its standing low in a valley, sheltered from the north and east by rising woods of oak.

CHAPTER XVIII

WITH a mind thus full of happiness, Catherine was hardly aware that two or three days had passed away, without her seeing Isabella for more than a few minutes together. She began first to be sensible of this, and to sigh for her conversation, as she walked along the Pump-room one morning, by Mrs Allen's side, without anything to say or to hear ; and scarcely had she felt a five minutes' longing of friendship, before the object of it appeared, and inviting her to a secret conference, led the way to a seat. " This is my favourite place," said she, [as] they sat down on a bench between the doors, which commanded a tolerable view of everybody entering at either, " it is so out of the way."

Catherine, observing that Isabella's eyes were continually bent towards one door or the other, as in eager expectation, and remembering how often she had been falsely accused of being arch, thought the present a fine opportunity for being really so, and therefore gaily said, " Do not be uneasy, Isabella.   James will soon be here."

" Psha ! my dear creature," she replied, " do not think me such a simpleton as to be always wanting to confine him to my elbow.   It would be hideous to be always together ; we should be the jest of the place.   And so you are going to Northanger !   I am amazingly glad of it.   It is one of the finest old places in England, I understand. I shall depend upon a most particular description of it."

" You shall certainly have the best in my power to give.   But who are you looking for ?   Are your sisters coming ? "

" I am not looking for anybody.   One's eyes must be somewhere, and you know what a foolish trick I have of fixing mine, when my thoughts are an hundred miles off.   I am amazingly absent ; I believe I am the most absent creature in the world.   Tilney says it is always the case with minds of a certain stamp."

" But I thought, Isabella, you had something in particular to tell me ? "

" Oh, yes ! and so I have.   But here is a proof of what I was saying.   My poor head !   I had quite forgot it. Well, the thing is this : I have just had a letter from John. You can guess the contents."

" No, indeed, I cannot."

" My sweet love, do not be so abominably affected. What can he write about but yourself ?   You know he is over head and ears in love with you."

" With *me*, dear Isabella ? "

" Nay, my sweetest Catherine, this is being quite absurd. Modesty, and all that, is very well in its way, but really a little common honesty is sometimes quite as becoming. I have no idea of being so overstrained.   It is fishing for compliments.   His attentions were such as a child must have noticed, and it was but half an hour before he left Bath that you gave him the most positive encouragement. He says so in this letter ; says that he as good as made you an offer, and that you received his advances in the kindest way, and now he wants me to urge his suit, and say all manner of pretty things to you. So it is in vain to affect ignorance."

Catherine, with all the earnestness of truth, expressed her astonishment at such a charge, protesting her innocence of every thought of Mr Thorpe's being in love with her, and the consequent impossibility of her having ever intended to encourage him. "As to any attentions on his side, I do declare, upon my honour, I never was sensible of them for a moment, except just his asking me to dance the first day of his coming ; and as to making me an offer, or anything like it, there must be some unaccountable mistake. I could not have misunderstood a thing of that kind, you know ; and, as I ever wish to be believed, I solemnly protest that no syllable of such a nature ever passed between us. The last half hour before he went away ! It must be all and completely a mistake, for I did not see him once that whole morning."

"But *that* you certainly did, for you spent the whole morning in Edgar's Buildings. It was the day your father's consent came, and I am pretty sure that you and John were alone in the parlour some time before you left the house."

"Are you ? Well, if you say it, it was so, I dare say ; but for the life of me, I cannot recollect it. I *do* remember now being with you, and seeing him as well as the rest ; but that we were alone for five minutes—. However, it is not worth arguing about, for whatever might pass on his side, you must be convinced, by my having no recollection of it, that I never thought, nor expected, nor wished for anything of the kind from him. I am excessively concerned that he should have any regard for me, but indeed it has been quite unintentional on my side ; I never had the smallest idea of it. Pray undeceive him as soon as you can, and tell him I beg his pardon ; that is—I do not know what I ought to say—but make him understand what I mean in the properest way. I would not speak disrespectfully of a brother of yours, Isabella, I am sure, but you know very well that if I could think of one man more than another, *he* is not the person." Isabella was silent. "My dear friend, you must not be angry with me. I cannot suppose your brother cares so very much about me ; and, you know, we shall still be sisters."

" Yes, yes " (with a blush), " there are more ways than one of our being sisters. But where am I wandering to ? Well, my dear Catherine, the case seems to be, that you are determined against poor John, is not it so ? "

" I certainly cannot return his affection, and as certainly never meant to encourage it."

" Since that is the case, I am sure I shall not tease you any further. John desired me to speak to you on the subject, and therefore I have. But I confess, as soon as I read this letter, I thought it a very foolish, imprudent business, and not likely to promote the good of either ; for what were you to live upon, supposing you came together? You have both of you something, to be sure, but it is not a trifle that will support a family now-a-days ; and after all that romancers may say, there is no doing without money. I only wonder John could think of it ; he could not have received my last."

" You *do* acquit me then of anything wrong ? You are convinced that I never meant to deceive your brother, never suspected him of liking me till this moment ? "

" Oh ! as to that," answered Isabella, laughingly, " I do not pretend to determine what your thoughts and designs in time past may have been. All that is best known to yourself. A little harmless flirtation or so will occur, and one is often drawn on to give more encouragement than one wishes to stand by. But you may be assured that I am the last person in the world to judge you severely. All those things should be allowed for in youth and high spirits. What one means one day, you know, one may not mean the next. Circumstances change, opinions alter."

" But my opinion of your brother never did alter ; it was always the same. You are describing what never happened."

" My dearest Catherine," continued the other without at all listening to her, " I would not for all the world be the means of hurrying you into an engagement before you knew what you were about. I do not think anything would justify me in wishing you to sacrifice all your happiness merely to oblige my brother, because he is my brother, and who, perhaps, after all, you know, might be just as happy without you ; for people seldom know what they would be at, young men especially, they are so amazingly changeable and inconstant. What I say is, why should a brother's happiness be dearer to me than a friend's ? You know I carry my notions of friendship pretty high. But, above all things, my dear Catherine, do not be in a hurry. Take my word for if, that it you are in too great a hurry, you will certainly live to repent it. Tilney says, there is nothing people are so often deceived in as the state of their own affections ; and I believe he is very right. Ah ! here he comes ; never mind, he will not see us, I am sure."

Catherine, looking up, perceived Captain Tilney ; and Isabella, earnestly fixing her eye on him as she spoke, soon caught his notice. He approached immediately, and took the seat to which her movements invited him. His first address made Catherine start. Though spoken low, she could distinguish, " What ! always to be watched, in person or by proxy ! "

" Psha, nonsense ! " was Isabella's answer, in the same half whisper. " Why do you put such things into my head ? If I could believe it !—my spirit you know, is pretty independent."

" I wish your heart were independent. That would be enough for me."

" My heart, indeed ! What can you have to do with hearts ? You men have none of you any hearts."

" If we have not hearts, we have eyes ; and they give us torment enough."

" Do they ? I am sorry for it ; I am sorry they find anything so disagreeable in me. I will look another way. I hope this pleases you " (turning her back on him) ; " I hope your eyes are not tormented now."

" Never more so : for the edge of a blooming cheek is still in view—at once too much and too little."

Catherine heard all this, and, quite out of countenance, could listen no longer. Amazed that Isabella could endure it, and jealous for her brother, she rose up, and saying she should join Mrs Allen, proposed their walking. But

for this Isabella, showed no inclination She was so amazingly
tired, and it was so odious to parade about the Pump-room ;
and if she moved from her seat, she should miss her sisters ;
she was expecting her sisters every moment, so that her
dearest Catherine must excuse her, and must sit quietly
down again.   But Catherine could be stubborn too ; and
Mrs Allen just then coming up to propose their returning
home, she joined her and walked out of the Pump-room,
leaving Isabella still sitting with Captain Tilney. With
much uneasiness did she thus leave them.   It seemed to
her that Captain Tilney was falling in love with Isabella,
and Isabella unconsciously encouraging him ; unconsciously
it must be, for Isabella's attachment to James was as certain
and well acknowledged as her engagement.   To doubt her
truth or good intentions was impossible ; and yet, during
the whole of their conversation, her manner had been odd.
She wished Isabella had talked more like her usual self,
and not so much about money ; and had not looked so
well pleased at the sight of Captain Tilney.   How strange
that she should not perceive his admiration ! Catherine
longed to give her a hint of it, to put her on her guard, and
prevent all the pain which her too lively behaviour might
otherwise create both for him and her brother.

The compliment of John Thorpe's affection did not
make amends for this thoughtlessness in his sister. She
was almost as far from believing as from wishing it to be
sincere ; for she had not forgotten that he could mistake ;
and his assertion of the offer, and of her encouragement,
convinced her that his mistakes could sometimes be very
egregious.   In vanity, therefore, she gained but little :
her chief profit was in wonder. That he should think it
worth his while to fancy himself in love with her was a
matter of lively astonishment.   Isabella talked of his attentions ; *she* had never been sensible of any ; but Isabella
had said many things which she hoped had been spoken in
haste, and would never be said again ; and upon this she
was glad to rest altogether for present ease and comfort.

CHAPTER XIX

A few days passed away, and Catherine, though not allowing herself to suspect her friend, could not help watching her closely. The result of her observations was not agreeable. Isabella seemed an altered creature. When she saw her indeed surrounded only by their immediate friends in Edgar's Buildings or Pulteney Street, her change of manners was so trifling that, had it gone no farther, it might have passed unnoticed. A something of languid indifference, or of that boasted absence of mind which Catherine had never heard of before, would occasionally come across her; but had nothing worse appeared, *that* might only have spread a new grace and inspired a warmer interest. But when Catherine saw her in public, admitting Captain Tilney's attentions as readily as they were offered, and allowing him almost an equal share with James in her notice and smiles, the alteration became too positive to be past over. What could be meant by such unsteady conduct, what her friend could be at, was beyond her comprehension. Isabella could not be aware of the pain she was inflicting; but it was a degree of wilful thoughtlessness which Catherine could not but resent. James was the sufferer. She saw him grave and uneasy; and however careless of his present comfort the woman might be who had given him her heart, to *her* it was always an object. For poor Captain Tilney too she was greatly concerned. Though his looks did not please her, his name was a passport to her goodwill, and she thought with sincere compassion of his approaching disappointment; for, in spite of what she had believed herself to overhear in the Pump-room, his behaviour was so incompatible with a knowledge of Isabella's engagement, that she could not, upon reflection, imagine him aware of it. He might be jealous of her brother as a rival, but if more had seemed implied, the fault must have been in her misapprehension. She wished, by a gentle remonstrance, to remind Isabella of her situation, and make her aware of this double unkindness; but for remonstrance, either

opportunity or comprehension was always against her.
If able to suggest a hint, Isabella could never understand
it. In this distress, the intended departure of the Tilney
family became her chief consolation ; their journey into
Gloucestershire was to take place within a few days, and
Captain Tilney's removal would at least restore peace to
every heart but his own. But Captain Tilney had at
present no intention of removing ; he was not to be of the
party to Northanger, he was to continue at Bath. When
Catherine knew this, her resolution was directly made.
She spoke to Henry Tilney on the subject, regretting his
brother's evident partiality for Miss Thorpe, and entreating
him to make known her prior engagement.

"My brother does know it," was Henry's answer.

"Does he ? then why does he stay here ? "

He made no reply, and was beginning to talk of something else ; but she eagerly continued, "Why do not you
persuade him to go away ? The longer he stays, the worse
it will be for him at last. Pray advise him for his own
sake, and for everybody's sake, to leave Bath directly.
Absence will in time make him comfortable again ; but he
can have no hope here, and it is only staying to be miserable."
Henry smiled, and said, "I am sure my brother would not
wish to do that."

"Then you will persuade him to go away."

"Persuasion is not at command ; but pardon me, if I
cannot even endeavour to persuade him. I have myself
told him that Miss Thorpe is engaged. He knows what he
is about, and must be his own master."

"No, he does not know what he is about," cried
Catherine ; "he does not know the pain he is giving my
brother. Not that James has ever told me so, but I am
sure he is very uncomfortable."

"And are you sure it is my brother's doing."

"Yes, very sure."

"Is it my brother's attentions to Miss Thorpe, or Miss
Thorpe's admission of them, that gives the pain ? "

"Is not it the same thing ? "

"I think Mr Morland would acknowledge a difference.
No man is offended by another's man admiration of the

woman he loves ; it is the woman only who can make it a torment."

Catherine blushed for her friend, and said, " Isabella is wrong. But I am sure she cannot mean to torment, for she is very much attached to my brother. She has been in love with him ever since they first met, and while my father's consent was uncertain, she fretted hersef almost into a fever. You know she must be attached to him."

" I understand ; she is in love with James, and flirts with Frederick."

" Oh no, not flirts ! A woman in love with one man cannot flirt with another."

" It is probable that she will neither love so well, nor flirt so well, as she might do either singly. The gentlemen must each give up a little."

After a short pause, Catherine resumed with—" Then you do not believe Isabella so very much attached to my brother."

" I can have no opinion on that subject."

" But what can your brother mean ? If he knows her engagement, what can he mean by his behaviour ? "

" You are a very close questioner."

" Am I ? I only ask what I want to be told."

" But do you only ask what I can be expected to tell ? "

" Yes, I think so ; for you must know your brother's heart."

" My brother's heart, as you term it on the present occasion, I assure you I can only guess at."

" Well ? "

" Well ! Nay, if it is to be guess-work, let us all guess for ourselves. To be guided by second-hand conjecture is pitiful. The premises are before you. My brother is a lively, and perhaps sometimes a thoughtless young man ; he has had about a week's acquaintance with your friend, and he has known her engagement almost as long as he has known her."

" Well," said Catherine, after some moments' considera-tion, " *you* may be able to guess at your brother's inten-tions from all this ; but I am sure I cannot. But is not your father uncomfortable about it ? Does not he want

Captain Tilney to go away ?   Sure, if your father were to speak to him he would go."

"My dear Miss Morland," said Henry, "in this amiable solicitude for your brother's comfort, may you not be a little mistaken ? Are you not carried a little too far ? Would he thank you, either on his own account or Miss Thorpe's for supposing that her affection, or at least her good behaviour, is only to be secured by her seeing nothing of Captain Tilney ? Is he safe only in solitude ? or, is her heart constant to him only when unsolicited by any one else ! He cannot think this, and you may be sure that he would not have you think it. I will not say, ' Do not be uneasy,' because I know that you are so, at this moment ; but be as little uneasy as you can. You have no doubt of the mutual attachment of your brother and your friend ; depend upon it, therefore, that real jealousy never can exist between them ; depend upon it that no disagreement between them can be of any duration. Their hearts are open to each other, as neither heart can be to you : they know exactly what is required and what can be borne ; and you may be certain, that one will never tease the other beyond what is known to be pleasant."

Perceiving her still to look doubtful and grave, he added, "Though Frederick does not leave Bath with us he will probably remain but a very short time, perhaps only a few days behind us. His leave of absence will soon expire, and he must return to his regiment. And what will then be their acquaintance ? The mess-room will drink Isabella for a fortnight, and she will laugh with your brother over poor Tilney's passion for a month."

Catherine would contend no longer against comfort. She had resisted its approaches during the whole length of a speech, but it now carried her captive. Henry Tilney must know best. She blamed herself for the extent of her fears, and resolved never to think so seriously on the subject again.

Her resolution was supported by Isabella's behaviour in their parting interview. The Thorpes spent the last evening of Catherine's stay in Pulteney Street, and nothing passed between the lovers to excite her uneasiness, or make her quit them in apprehension. James was in excellent spirits, and Isabella most engagingly placid. Her tenderness for her friend seemed rather the first feeling of her heart, but that at such a moment was allowable ; and once she gave her lover a flat contradiction, and once she drew back her hand, but Catherine remembered Henry's instructions, and placed it all to judicious affection. The embraces, tears, and promises of the parting fair ones may be fancied.

CHAPTER XX

MR and Mrs Allen were sorry to lose their young friend, whose good humour and cheerfulness had made her a valuable companion, and in the promotion of whose enjoyment their own had been greatly increased. Her happiness in going with Miss Tilney, however, prevented their wishing it otherwise ; and, as they were to remain only one more week in Bath themselves, her quitting them now would not long be felt. Mr Allen attended her to Milsom Street, where she was to breakfast, and saw her seated with the kindest welcome among her new friends ; but so great was her agitation in finding herself as one of the family, and so fearful was she of not doing exactly what was right, and of not being able to preserve their good opinion, that, in the embarrassment of the first five minutes, she could almost have wished to return with him to Pulteney Street.

Miss Tilney's manners, and Henry's smile, soon did away some of her unpleasant feelings : but still she was far from being at ease ; nor could the incessant attentions of the General himself entirely re-assure her. Nay, perverse as it seemed, she doubted whether she might not have felt less, had she been less attended to. His anxiety for her comfort, his continual solicitations that she would eat, and his often-expressed fears of her seeing nothing to her taste, though never in her life before had she beheld half such variety on a breakfast-table, made it impossible for her to forget for a moment that she was a visitor. She felt utterly unworthy of such respect, and knew not how

to reply to it. Her tranquillity was not improved by the
General's impatience for the appearance of his eldest son,
nor by the displeasure he expressed at his laziness when
Captain Tilney at last came down. She was quite pained
by the severity of his father's reproof, which seemed dis-
proportionate to the offence ; and much was her concern
increased, when she found herself the principal cause of
the lecture ; and that his tardiness was chiefly resented
from being disrespectful to her. This was placing her in
a very uncomfortable situation, and she felt great compassion for Captain Tilney, without being able to hope
for his good will.

He listened to his father in silence, and attempted not
any defence, which confirmed her in fearing that the inquietude of his mind, on Isabella's account, might, by
keeping him long sleepless, have been the real cause of his
rising late. It was the first time of her being decidely
in his company, and she had hoped to be now able to form
her opinion of him : but she scarcely heard his voice while
his father remained in the room ; and even afterwards,
so much were his spirits affected, she could distinguish
nothing but these words, in a whisper to Eleanor, " How
glad I shall be when you are all off ! "

The bustle of going was not pleasant. The clock struck
ten while the trunks were carrying down, and the General
had fixed to be out of Milsom Street by that hour. His
great coat, instead of being brought for him to put on
directly, was spread out in the curricle in which he was
to accompany his son. The middle seat of the chaise
was not drawn out, though there were three people to go
in it, and his daughter's maid had so crowded it with parcels
that Miss Morland would not have room to sit ; and so
much was he influenced by this apprehension when he
handed her in, that she had some difficulty in saving her
own new writing-desk from being thrown out into the street.
At last, however, the door was closed upon the three females,
and they set off at the sober pace in which the handsome,
highly-fed four horses of a gentleman usually perform a journey
of thirty miles : such was the distance of Northanger from
Bath, to be now divided into two equal stages. Catherine's

spirits revived as they drove from the door ; for with Miss
Tilney she felt no restraint ; and with the interest of a
road entirely new to her, of an abbey before, and a curricle
behind, she caught the last view of Bath without any regret,
and met with every milestone before she expected it. The
tediousness of a two hours' wait at Petty France, in
which there was nothing to be done but to eat without
being hungry, and loiter about without anything to see,
next followed ; and her admiration of the style in which
they travelled, of the fashionable chaise and four, postillions
handsomely liveried, rising so regularly in their stirrups,
and numerous outriders, properly mounted, sunk a little
under this consequent inconvenience. Had their party
been perfectly agreeable, the delay would have been nothing ;
but General Tilney, though so charming a man, seemed
always a check upon his children's spirits, and scarcely
anything was said but by himself ; the observation of which,
with his discontent at whatever the inn afforded, and his
angry impatience at the waiters, made Catherine grow
every moment more in awe of him, and appeared to lengthen
the two hours into four. At last, however, the order of
release was given ; and much was Catherine then surprized
by the General's proposal of her taking his place in his
son's curricle for the rest of the journey : " The day was
fine, and he was anxious for her seeing as much of the
country as possible."

The remembrance of Mr Allen's opinion respecting,
young men's open carriages, made her blush at the mention
of such a plan, and her first thought was to decline it ;
but her second was of greater deference for General Tilney's
judgment : he could not propose anything improper for her ;
and, in the course of a few minutes, she found herself with
Henry in the curricle, as happy a being as ever existed.
A very short trial convinced her that a curricle was the
prettiest equipage in the world ; the chaise and four
wheeled off with some grandeur, to be sure, but it was
a heavy and troublesome business, and she could not easily
forget its having stopped two hours at Petty France. Half
the time would have been enough for the curricle ; and so
nimbly were the light horses disposed to move, that, had

not the General chosen to have his own carriage lead the way, they could have passed it with ease in half a minute. But the merit of the curricle did not all belong to the horses : Henry drove so well, so quietly, without making any disturbance, without parading to her, or swearing at them ; so different from the only gentleman-coachman whom it was in her power to compare him with ! And then his hat sat so well, and the innumerable capes of his great coat looked so becomingly important ! To be driven bv him, next to being dancing with him, was certainly the greatest happiness in the world. In addition to every other delight, she had now that of listening to her own praise ; of being thanked at least, on his sister's account, for her kindness in thus becoming her visitor ; of hearing it ranked as real friendship, and described as creating real gratitude. His sister, he said, was uncomfortably circumstanced ; she had no female companion, and in the frequent absence of her father, was sometimes without any companion at all.

"But how can that be ? " said Catherine ; "are not you with her ? "

"Northanger is not more than half my home ; I have an establishment at my own house in Woodston, which is nearly twenty miles from my father's, and some of my time is necessarily spent there."

"How sorry you must be for that ! "

"I am always sorry to leave Eleanor."

"Yes ; but besides your affection for her, you must be so fond of the abbey ! After being used to such a home as the abbey, an ordinary parsonage-house must be very disagreeable."

He smiled and said, "You have formed a very favourable idea of the abbey."

"To be sure I have. Is not it a fine old place, just like what one reads about ? "

"And are you prepared to encounter all the horrors that a building such as ' what one reads about ' may produce ? Have you a stout heart ? Nerves fit for sliding panels and tapestry ? "

"Oh ! yes, I do not think I should be easily frightened,

because there would be so many people in the house;
and besides, it has never been uninhabited and left deserted
for years, and then the family come back, to it unawares
without giving any notice, as generally happens."

" No, certainly. We shall not have to explore our way
into a hall dimly lighted by the expiring embers of a wood
fire, nor be obliged to spread our beds on the floor of a
room without windows, doors or furniture, But you must
be aware that when a young lady is (by whatever means)
introduced into a dwelling of this kind, she is always lodged
apart from the rest of the family. While tney snugly
repair to their own end of the house, she is formally conducted by Dorothy, the ancient housekeeper, up a different
staircase, and along many gloomy passages, into an apartment never used since some cousin of kin died in it about
twenty years before. Can you stand such a ceremony
as this ! Will not your mind misgive you, when you find
yourself in this gloomy chamber, too lofty and extensive
for you, with only the feeble rays of a single lamp to take
in its size, its walls hung with tapestry exhibiting figures
as large as life, and the bed of dark green stuff or purple
velvet, presenting even a funereal appearance. Will not
your heart sink within you ? "

" Oh ! but this will not happen to me I am sure."

" How fearfully will you examine the furniture of your
apartment ? And what will you discern ? Not tables,
toilettes, wardrobes, or drawers, but on one side perhaps
the remains of a broken lute, on the other a ponderous
chest which no efforts can open, and over the fire-place the
portrait of some handsome warrior, whose features will
so incomprehensively strike you, that you will not be able
to withdraw your eyes from it. Dorothy, meanwhile,
no less struck by your appearance, gazes on you in great
agitation, and drops a few unintelligible hints. To raise
your spirits, moreover, she gives you reason to suppose
that the part of the abbey you inhabit is undoubtedly
haunted, and informs you that you will not have a single
domestic within call. With this parting cordial, she curtseys
off : you listen to the sound of her receding footsteps as
long as the last echo can reach you : and when, with faint-

ing spirits, you attempt to fasten your door, you discover, with increased alarm, that it has no lock."

" Oh ! Mr Tilney, how frightful.   This is just like a book ! But it cannot really happen to me.   I am sure your house-keeper is not really Dorothy.   Well, what then ? "

" Nothing further to alarm, perhaps, may occur the first night.   After surmounting your *unconquerable* horror of the bed, you will retire to rest, and get a few hours' unquiet slumber.   But on the second, or at farthest the *third* night after your arrival, you will probably have a violent storm.   Peals of thunder so loud as to seem to shake the edifice of its foundation will roll round the neigh-bouring mountains ; and during the frightful gusts of wind which accompany it, you will probably think you discern (for your lamp is not extinguished) one part of the hanging more violently agitated than the rest.   Unable of course to repress your curiosity in so favourable a moment for indulging it, you will instantly arise, and, throwing your dressing-gown around you, proceed to examine this mystery. After a very short search, you will discover a division in the tapestry so artfully constructed as to defy the minutest inspection, and on opening it, a door will immediately appear, which door being only secured by massy bars and a padlock, you will, after a few efforts, succeed in opening and, with your lamp in your hand, will pass through it into a small vaulted room."

" No, indeed ; I should be too much frightened to do any such thing."

" What ! not when Dorothy has given you to under-stand that there is a secret subterraneous communication between your apartment and the chapel of St Anthony, scarcely two miles off.   Could you shrink from so simple an adventure ?   No, no ; you will preceed into this small vaulted room, and through this into several others, with-out perceiving anything very remarkable in either.   In one, perhaps, there may be a dagger, in another, a few drops of blood, and in a third the remains of same instrument of torture ; but there being nothing in all this out of the common way, and your lamp being nearly exhausted, you will return towards your own apartment.   In repassing through the small vaulted room, however, your eyes will be attracted towards a large, old-fashioned cabinet of ebony and gold, which, though narrowly examining the furniture before, you had passed unnoticed. Impelled by an irresistible presentiment, you will eagerly advance to it, unlock its folding doors, and search into every drawer; but for sometime without discovering anything of importance; perhaps nothing but a considerable hoard of diamonds. At last, however, by touching a secret spring, an inner compartment will open, a roll of paper appears, you seize it—it contains many sheets of manuscript; you hasten with the precious treasure into your own chamber, but scarcely have you been able to decipher, ' Oh thou, whomsoever thou mayst be, into whose hands these memoirs of the wretched Matilda may fall,' when your lamp suddenly expires in the socket, and leaves you in total darkness."

"Oh no, no! do not say so. Well, go on."

But Henry was too much amused by the interest he had raised to be able to carry it farther; he could no longer command solemnity either of subject or voice, and was obliged to entreat her to use her own fancy in the perusal of Matilda's woes. Catherine, recollecting herself, grew ashamed of her eagerness, and began earnestly to assure him that her attention had been fixed without the smallest apprehension of really meeting with what he related. " Miss Tilney, she was sure, would never put her into such a chamber as he had described. She was not at all afraid."

As they drew near the end of their journey, her impatience for a sight of the abbey, for some time suspended by his conversation on subjects very different, returned in full force, and every bend in the road was expected, with solemn awe, to afford a glimpse of its massy walls of grey stone, rising amidst a grove of ancient oaks, with the last beams of the sun playing in beautiful splendour on its high Gothic windows. But so low did the building stand, that she found herself passing through the great gates of the lodge, into the very grounds of Northanger, without having discerned even an antique chimney.

She knew not that she had any right to be surprized, but there was something in this mode of approach which she certainly had not expected. To pass between lodges of a modern appearance, to find herself with such ease in the very precincts of the abbey, and driven so rapidly along a smooth, level road of fine gravel, without obstacle, alarm, or solemnity of any kind, struck her as odd and inconsistent. She was not long at leisure, however, for such considerations. A sudden scud of rain driving full in her face, made it impossible for her to observe anything further, and fixed all her thoughts on the welfare of her new straw bonnet : and she was actually under the abbey walls, was springing, with Henry's assistance, from the carriage, was beneath the shelter of the old porch, and had even passed on to the hall, where her friend and the General were waiting to welcome her, without feeling one aweful foreboding of future misery to herself, or one moment's suspicion of any past scenes of horror being acted within the solemn edifice. The breeze had not seemed to waft the sighs of the murderer to her ; it had wafted nothing worse than a thick mizzling rain, and having given a good shake to her habit, she was ready to be shown into the common drawing-room, and capable of considering where she was.

An abbey ! Yes, it was delightful to be really in an abbey ! But she doubted, as she looked round the room, whether anything within her observation would have given her the consciousness. The furniture was in all the profusion and elegance of modern taste. The fire-place, where she had expected the ample width and ponderous carving of former times, was contracted to a Rumford, with slabs of plain, though handsome, marble, and [ornaments] over it of the prettiest English china. The windows, to which she looked with peculiar dependence, from having heard the General talk of his preserving them in their Gothic form with reverential care, were yet less what her fancy had portrayed. To be sure the pointed arch was preserved, the form of them was Gothic they might be even casements, but every pane was so large, so clear, so light ! To an imagination which had hoped for the smallest divisions and the heaviest stone work, for painted glass, dirt, and cobwebs, the difference was very distressing.

The General, perceiving how her eye was employed, began to talk of the smallness of the room and simplicity of the furniture, where everything being for daily use, pretended only to comfort, &c., flattering himself, however, that there [were] some apartments in the abbey not unworthy her notice, and was proceeding to mention the costly gilding of one in particular, when, taking out his watch, he stopped short, to pronounce it, with surprize, within twenty minutes of five ! This seemed the word of separation, and Catherine found herself hurried away by Miss Tilney, in such a manner as convinced her that the strictest punctuality to the family hours would be expected at Northanger.

Returning through the large and lofty hall, they ascended a broad staircase of shining oak, which, after many flights and many landing-places, brought them upon a long wide gallery. On one side it had a range of doors, and it was lighted on the other by windows, which Catherine had only time to discover looked into a quadrangle, before Miss Tilney led the way into a chamber, and, scarcely staying to hope she would find it comfortable, left her with an anxious entreaty that she would make as little alteration as possible in her dress.

CHAPTER XXI

A MOMENT's glance was enough to satisfy Catherine that her apartment was very unlike the one which Henry had endeavoured to alarm her by the description of. It was by no means unreasonably large, and contained neither tapestry nor velvet. The walls were papered, the floor was carpeted, the windows were neither less perfect nor more dim than those of the drawing-room below ; the furniture, though not of the latest fashion, was handsome and comfortable, and the air of the room altogether far from uncheerful. Her heart instantaneously at ease on this point, she resolved to lose no time in particular examination of anything, as she greatly dreaded disobliging the General by any delay. Her habit therefore was thrown off with all possible haste, and she was preparing to unpin the linen package, which the chaise-seat had conveyed for her immediate accommodation, when her eye suddenly fell on a large high chest, standing back in a deep recess on one side of the fire-place. The sight of it made her start ; and, forgetting everything else, she stood gazing on it in motionless wonder, while these thoughts crossed her :—

"This is strange, indeed ! I did not expect such a sight as this ! An immense heavy chest ! What can it hold ? Why should it be placed here ? Pushed back, too, as if meant to be out of sight ! I will look into it ; cost me what it may, I will look into it, and directly too—by daylight. If I stay till evening my candle may go out." She advanced and examined it closely ; it was of cedar, curiously inlaid with some darker wood, and raised about a foot from the ground on a carved stand of the same. The lock was silver, though tarnished from age ; at each end were the imperfect remains of handles also of silver, broken perhaps prematurely by some strange violence ; and on the centre of the lid, was a mysterious cipher in the same metal. Catherine bent over it intently, but without being able to distinguish anything with certainty. She could not, in whatever direction she took it, believe the last letter to be a *T ;* and yet that it should be anything else in that house was a circumstance to raise no common degree of astonishment. If not originally theirs, by what strange events could it have fallen into the Tilney family ?

Her fearful curiosity was every moment growing greater; and seizing with trembling hands, the hasp of the lock, she resolved, at all hazards, to satisfy herself at least as to its contents. With difficulty, for something seemed to resist her efforts, she raised the lid a few inches ; but at that moment a sudden knocking at the door of the room made her, starting, quit her hold, and the lid closed with alarming violence. This ill-timed intruder was Miss Tilney's maid, sent by her mistress to be of use to Miss Morland ; and though Catherine immediately dismissed her, it recalled her to the sense of what she ought to be doing, and forced her, in spite of her anxious desire to penetrate this mystery, to proceed in her dressing without further delay. Her

progress was not quick, for her thoughts and her eyes
were still bent on the object so well calculated to interest
and alarm ; and though she dared not waste a moment
upon a second attempt, she could not remain many paces
from the chest. At length, however, having slipped one
arm into her gown, her toilet seemed so nearly finished,
that the impatience of her curiosity might safely be indulged.
One moment surely might be spared ; and so desperate
should be the exertion of her strength, that unless secured
by supernatural means, the lid in one moment should be
thrown back. With this spirit she sprang forward, and her
confidence did not deceive her. Her resolute effort threw
back the lid, and gave to her astonished eyes the view of
a white cotton counterpane, properly folded, reposing at
one end of the chest in undisputed possession !

She was gazing on it with the first blush of surprize,
when Miss Tilney, anxious for her friend's being ready,
entered the room, and to the rising shame of having harboured for some minutes an absurd expectation, was then
added the shame of being caught in so idle a search. " That
is a curious old chest, is not it ? " said Miss Tilney, as Catherine hastily closed it and turned away to the glass. " It
is impossible to say how many generations it has been here.
How it came to be first put in this room I know not, but I
have not had it moved, because I though it might sometimes
be of use in holding hats and bonnets. The worst of it is,
that its weight makes it difficult to open. In that corner,
however, it is at least out of the way."

Catherine had no leisure for speech, being at once blushing, tying her gown, and forming wise resolutions with
the most violent dispatch. Miss Tilney gently hinted her
fear of being late ; and in half a minute they ran down
stairs together, in an alarm not wholly unfounded, for General
Tilney was pacing the drawing-room, his watch in his hand,
and having, on the very instant of their entering, pulled
the bell with violence, ordered, " Dinner to be on table
directly ! "

Catherine trembled at the emphasis with which he spoke,
and sat pale and breathless, in a most humble mood, concerned for his children, and detesting old chests ; and the

General recovering his politeness as he looked at her, spent
the rest of his time in scolding his daughter, for so foolishly
hurrying her fair friend, who was absolutely out of breath
from haste, when there was not the least occasion for hurry
in the world ; but Catherine could not at all get over the
double distress of having involved her friend in a lecture
and been a great simpleton herself, till they were happily
seated at the dinner-table, when the General's complacent
smiles, and a good appetite of her own, restored her to
peace. The dining-parlour was a noble room, suitable in
its dimensions to a much larger drawing-room than the
one in common use, and fitted up in a style of luxury and
expense which was almost lost on the unpractised eye of
Catherine, who saw little more than its spaciousness and
the number of their attendants. Of the former, she spoke
aloud her admiration ; and the General, with a very
gracious countenance, acknowledged that it was by no
means an ill-sized room ; and further confessed, that,
though as careless on such subjects as most people, he did
look upon a tolerably large eating-room as one of the necessaries of life ; he supposed, however, " that she must have
been used to much better sized apartments at Mr Allen's ? "

" No, indeed," was Catherine's honest assurance ; " Mr
Allen's dining-parlour was not more than half as large ; "
and she had never seen so large a room as this in her life.
The General's good-humour increased. Why, as he had
such rooms, he thought it would be simple not to make use
of them ; but, upon his honour, he believed there might be
more comfort in rooms of only half their size. Mr Allen's
house, he was sure, must be exactly of the true size for
rational happiness.

The evening passed without any further disturbance, and,
in the occasional absence of General Tilney, with much
positive cheerfulness. It was only in his presence that
Catherine felt the smallest fatigue from her journey ; and
even then, even in moments of langour, or restraint, a sense
of general happiness preponderated, and she could think of
her friends in Bath without one wish of being with them.

The night was stormy ; the wind had been rising at intervals the whole afternoon ; and by the time the party

broke up, it blew and rained violently. Catherine, as she crossed the hall, listened to the tempest with sensations of awe; and when she heard it rage round a corner of the ancient building, and close with sudden fury a distant door, felt for the first time that she was really in an abbey. Yes, these were characteristic sounds: they brought to her recollection a countless variety of dreadful situations and horrid scenes, which such buildings had witnessed, and such storms ushered in; and most heartily did she rejoice in the happier circnmstances attending her entrance within walls so solemn! *She* had nothing to dread from midnight assassins or drunken gallants. Henry had certainly been only in jest in what he had told her that morning. In a house so furnished, and so guarded, she could have nothing to explore or to suffer, and might go to her bedroom as securely as if it had been her own chamber at Fullerton. Thus wisely fortifying her mind, as she proceeded upstairs, she was enabled, especially on perceiving that Miss Tilney slept only two doors from her, to enter her room with a tolerably stout heart; and her spirits were immediately assisted by the cheerful blaze of a wood fire. "How much better is this," said she, as she walked to the fender; "how much better to find a fire ready lit, than to have to wait shivering in the cold, till all the family are in bed, as so many poor girls have been obliged to do, and then to have a faithful old servant frightening one by coming in with a faggot! How glad I am that Northanger is what it is! If it had been like some other places, I do not know that, in such a night as this, I could have answered for my courage; but now, to be sure, there is nothing to alarm one."

She looked round the room. The window curtains seemed in motion. It could be nothing but the violence of the wind penetrating through the divisions of the shutters; and she stept boldly forward, carelessly humming a tune, to assure herself of its being so, peeped courageously behind each curtain, saw nothing on either low window-seat to scare her, and on placing a hand against the shutter, felt the strongest conviction of the wind's force. A glance at the old chest, as she turned away from this examination, was not without its use; she scorned the causeless fears of an idle fancy, and began with a most happy indifference to prepare herself for bed. " She should take her time ; she should not hurry herself ; she did not care if she were the last person up in the house. But she would not make up her fire : *that* would seem cowardly, as if she wished for the protection of light after she were in bed." The fire, therefore, died away ; and Catherine, having spent the best part of an hour in her arrangements, was beginning to think of stepping into bed, when, on giving a parting glance round the room, she was struck by the appearance of a high old-fashioned black cabinet, which, though in a situation conspicuous enough, had never caught her notice before. Henry's words, the description of the ebony cabinet which was to escape her observation at first, immediately rushed across her ; and though there could be nothing really in it, there was something whimsical, it was certainly a very remarkable coincidence ! She took her candle and looked closely at the cabinet. It was not absolutely ebony and gold ; but it was Japan, black and yellow Japan of the handsomest kind ; and as she held her candle, the yellow had very much the effect of gold.

The key was in the door, and she had a strange fancy to look into it ; not, however, with the smallest expectation of finding anything, but it was so very odd, after what Henry had said. In short, she could not sleep till she had examined it. So, placing the candle with great caution on a chair, she seized the key with a very tremulous hand, and tried to turn it ; but it resisted her utmost strength. Alarmed, but not discouraged, she tried it another way ; a bolt flew, and she believed herself successful ; but how strangely mysterious ! the door was still immoveable. She paused a moment in breathless wonder. The wind roared down the chimney, the rain beat in torrents against the windows, and everything seemed to speak the awfulness of her situation. To retire to bed, however, unsatisfied on such a point, would be vain, since sleep must be impossible with the consciousness of a cabinet so mysteriously closed in her immediate vicinity. Again, therefore, she applied herself to the key, and after moving it in every possible way, for some instants, with the determined celerity of hope's last effort, the door suddenly yielded to her hand : her heart leaped with ex-ultation at such a victory, and having thrown open each folding door, the second being secured only by bolts of less wonderful construction than the lock, though in that her eye could not discern anything unusual, a double range of small drawers appeared in view, with some larger drawers above and below them, and in the centre, a small door, closed also with lock and key, secured in all probability a cavity of importance.

Catherine's heart beat quick, but her courage did not fail her. With a cheek flushed by hope, and an eye strain-ing with curiosity, her fingers grasped the handle of a drawer and drew it forth. It was entirely empty. With less alarm and greater eagerness she seized a second, a third, a fourth—each was equally empty. Not one was left unsearched, and in not one was anything found. Well read in the art of concealing a treasure, the possibility of false linings to the drawers did not escape her, and she felt round each with anxious acuteness in vain. The place in the middle alone remained now unexplored ; and though she had " never from the first had the smallest idea of finding anything in any part of the cabinet, and was not in the least disappointed at her ill success thus far, it would be foolish not to examine it thoroughly while she was about it." It was some time, however, before she could unfasten the door, the same difficulty occuring in the management of this inner lock as of the outer ; but at length it did open ; and not vain, as hitherto, was her search ; her quick eyes directly fell on a roll of paper pushed back into the further part of the cavity, apparently for concealment, and her feelings at that moment were indescribable. Her heart fluttered, her knees trembled, and her cheeks grew pale. She seized, with an unsteady hand, the precious manu-script, for half a glance sufficed to ascertain written char-acters ; and while she acknowledged with awful sensations this striking exemplification of what Henry had foretold, resolved instantly to peruse every line before she attempted to rest.

The dimness of the light her candle emitted made her turn to it with alarm ; but there was no danger of its sudden extinction, it had yet some hours to burn ; and that she might not have any greater difficulty in distinguishing the writing than what its ancient date might occasion, she hastily snuffed it.   Alas ! it was snuffed and extinguished in one.   A lamp could not have expired with more awful effect.   Catherine, for a few moments, was motionless with horror.   It was done complétely ; not a remnant of light in the wick could give hope to the rekindling breath.   Darkness impenetrable and immoveable filled the room.   A violent gust of wind, rising with sudden fury, added fresh horror to the moment.   Catherine trembled from head to foot.   In the pause which succeeded, a sound like receding footsteps and the closing of a distant door struck on her affrighted ear.   Human nature could support no more.   A cold sweat stood on her forehead, the manuscript fell from her hand, and groping her way to the bed, she jumped hastily in, and sought some suspension of agony by creeping far underneath the clothes.   To close her eyes in sleep that night she felt must be entirely out of the question.   With a curiosity so justly awakened, and feelings in every way so agitated, repose must be absolutely impossible.   The storm, too, abroad so dreadful !   She had not been used to feel alarm from wind, but now every blast seemed fraught with awful intelligence.   The manuscript so wonderfully found, so wonderfully accomplishing the morning's prediction, how was it to be accounted for ?   What could it contain ?   to whom could it relate ?   by what means could it have been so long concealed ?   and how singularly strange that it should fall to her lot to discover it !   Till she had made herself mistress of its contents, however, she could have neither repose nor comfort ;   and with the sun's first rays she was determined to peruse it.   But many were the tedious hours which must yet intervene.   She shuddered, tossed about in her bed, and envied every quiet sleeper.   The storm still raged, and various were the noises, more terrific even than the wind, which struck at intervals on her startled ear.   The very curtains of her bed seemed at one moment in motion, and at another the lock of her door was agitated, as if by the attempt of somebody to enter.   Hollow murmurs seemed to creep along the gallery, and more than once her blood was chilled by the sound of distant moans. Hour after hour passed away, and the wearied Catherine had heard three proclaimed by all the clocks in the house, before the tempest subsided, or she unknowingly fell fast asleep.

CHAPTER XXII

THE housemaid's folding back her window-shutters at eight o'clock the next day was the sound which first roused Catherine; and she opened her eyes, wondering that they could ever have been closed, on objects of cheerfulness; her fire was already burning, and a bright morning had succeeded the tempest of the night. Instantaneously with the consciousness of existence, returned her recollection of the manuscript; and springing from the bed in the very moment of the maid's going away, she eagerly collected every scattered sheet which had burst from the roll on its falling to the ground, and flew back to enjoy the luxury of their perusal on her pillow. She now plainly saw that she must not expect a manuscript of equal length with the generality of what she had shuddered over in books; for the roll, seeming to consist entirely of small disjointed sheets, was altogether but of trifling size, and much less than she had supposed it to be at first.

Her greedy eye glanced rapidly over a page. She started at its import. Could it be possible, or did not her senses play her false? An inventory of linen, in coarse and modern characters, seemed all that was before her! If the evidence of sight might be trusted, she held a washing-bill in her hand. She seized another sheet, and saw the same articles with little variation; a third, a fourth, and a fifth, presented nothing new. Shirts, stockings, cravats, and waistcoats, faced her in each. Two others, penned by the same hand, marked an expenditure scarcely more interesting, in letters, hair-powders, shoe-string, and breeches-ball; and the larger sheet, which had enclosed the rest, seemed by its first cramp line, " To poultice chestnut mare," a farrier's bill! Such was the collection of papers (left, perhaps, as she could then suppose, by the negligence of a servant, in the place whence she had taken them) which had filled her with expectation and alarm, and robbed her of half her night's rest ! She felt humbled to the dust. Could not the adventure of the chest have taught her wisdom ? A corner of it catching her eye as she lay, seemed to rise up in judgment against her. Nothing could now be clearer than the absurdity of her recent fancies. To suppose that a manuscript of many generations back could have remained undiscovered in a room such as that, so modern, so habitable ! or that she should be the first to possess the skill of unlocking a cabinet, the key of which was open to all.

How could she have so imposed on herself ? Heaven forbid that Henry Tilney should ever know her folly ! And it was in a great measure his own doing, for had not the cabinet appeared so exactly to agree with his description of her adventures, she should never have felt the smallest curiosity about it. This was the only comfort that occurred. Impatient to get rid of those hateful evidences of her folly, those detestable papers then scattered over the bed, she rose directly ; and folding them up as nearly as possible in the same shape as before, returned them to the same spot within the cabinet, with a very hearty wish that no untoward accident might ever bring them forward again, to disgrace her even with herself.

Why the locks should have been so difficult to open, however, was still something remarkable, for she could now manage them with perfect ease. In this there was surely something mysterious, and she indulged in the flattering suggestion for half a minute, till the possibility of the door's having been at first unlocked, and of being herself its fastener, darted into her head and cost her another blush.

She got away soon as as she could from a room in which her conduct produced such unpleasant reflections, and found her way with all speed to the breakfast-parlour, as it had been pointed out to her by Miss Tilney the evening before. Henry was alone in it ; and his immediate hope of her having been undisturbed by the tempest, with an arch reference to the character of the building they inhabited, was rather distressing. For the world would she not have her weakness suspected ; and yet, unequal to an absolute falsehood, was constrained to acknowledge that the wind had kept her awake a little. " But we have a charming morning after it," she added, desiring to get rid of the subject ; " and storms and sleeplessness are nothing when they are over. What beautiful hyacinths ! I have just learnt to love a hyacinth."

" And how might you learn ? By accident or argument ? "

" Your sister taught me : I cannot tell how. Mrs Allan used to take pains, year after year, to make me like them ; but I never could, till I saw them the other day in Milsom Srteet ; I am naturally indifferent about flowers."

" But now you love a hyacinth. So much the better. You have gained a new source of enjoyment, and it is well to have as many holds upon happiness as possible. Besides, a taste for flowers is always desirable in your sex, as a means of getting you out of doors, and tempting you to more frequent exercise than you would otherwise take : and though the love of a hyacinth may be rather domestic, who can tell, the sentiment once raised, but you may in time come to love a rose ? "

" But I do not want any such pursuit to get me out of doors. The pleasure of walking and breathing fresh air is enough for me, and in fine weather I am out more than half my time. Mamma says I am never within."

" At any rate, however, I am pleased that you have learnt to love a hyacinth. The mere habit of learning to love is the thing ; and a teachableness of disposition in a young lady is a great blessing. Has my sister a pleasant mode of instruction ? "

Catherine was saved the embarrassment of attempting an answer by the entrance of the General, whose smiling compliments announced a happy state of mind, but whose gentle hint of sympathetic early rising did not advance her composure.

The elegance of the breakfast-set forced itself on Catherine's notice when they were seated at table ; and, luckily, it had been the General's choice. " He was enchanted by her approbation of his taste, confessed it to be neat and simple, thought it right to encourage the manufacture of his country ; and for his part, to his uncritical palate, the tea was as well flavoured from the clay of Staffordshire as from that of Dresden or Séve. But this was quite an old set, purchased two years ago. The manufacture was much improved since that time : he had seen some beautiful specimens when last in town, and had he not been perfectly without vanity of that kind, might have been tempted to order a new set. He trusted, however, that an opportunity might ere long occur of selecting one, though not for himself." Catherine was probably the only one of the party who did not understand him.

Shortly after breakfast Henry left them for Woodston, where business required and would keep him two or three days. They all attended in the hall to see him mount his horse, and immediately on re-entering the breakfast-room, Catherine walked to a window in the hope of catching another glimpse of his figure. " This is a somewhat heavy call upon your brother's fortitude," observed the General to Eleanor. " Woodston will make but a sombre appearance to-day."

" Is it a pretty place ? " asked Catherine.

"What say you, Eleanor ? Speak your opinion ; for ladies can best tell the taste of ladies in regard to places as well as men. I think it would be acknowledged by the most impartial eye to have many recommendations. The house stands among fine meadows facing the south-east, with an excellent kitchen-garden in the same aspect ; the walls surrounding which I built and stocked myself about ten years age, for the benefit of my son. It is a family living, Miss Morland ; and, the property in the place being chiefly my own, you may believe I take care that it shall not be a bad one. Did Henry's income depend solely on this living, he would not be ill provided for. Perhaps it may seem odd, that with only two younger children, I should think any profession necessary for him ; and certainly there are moments when we could all wish him disengaged from every tie of business. But though I may not exactly make converts of you young ladies, I am sure your father,

Miss Morland, would agree with me in thinking it expedient to give every young man some employment. The money is nothing, it is not an object ; but employment is the thing. Even Frederick, my eldest son, you see, who will perhaps inherit as considerable a landed property as any private man in the county, has his profession."

The imposing effect of this last argument was equal to his wishes. The silence of the lady proved it to be unanswerable.

Something had been said the evening before of her being shewn over the house, and he now offered himself as her conductor ; and though Catherine had hoped to explore it accompanied only by his daughter, it was a proposal of too much happiness in itself, under any circumstances, not to be gladly accepted ; for she had been already eighteen hours in the abbey, and had seen only a few of its rooms. The netting-box just leisurely drawn forth, was closed with joyful haste, and she was ready to attend him in a moment. "And when they had gone over the house, he promised himself, moreover, the pleasure of accompanying her into the shrubberies and garden." She curtsied her acquiescence. "But perhaps it might be more agreeable to her to make those her first object. The weather was at present favourable, and at this time of year the uncertainty was very great of its continuing so. Which would she prefer ? He was equally at her service. Which did his daughter think would most accord with her fair friend's wishes ? But he thought he could discern. Yes, he certainly read in Miss Morland's eyes, a judicious desire of making use of the present smiling weather. But when did she judge amiss ? The abbey would be always safe and dry. He yielded implicitly, and would fetch his hat and attend them in a moment." He left the room, and Catherine, with a disappointed anxious face, began to speak of her unwillingness that he should be taking them out of doors against his own inclination, under a mistaken idea of pleasing her ; but she was stopt by Miss Tilney's saying, with a little confusion, "I believe it will be wisest to take the morning while it is so fine ; and do not be uneasy on my father's account : he always walks out at this time of day."

Catherine did not exactly know how this was to be understood. Why was Miss Tilney embarrassed ? Could there be any unwillingness on the General's side to show her over the abbey ? The proposal was his own. And was it not odd that he should *always* take his walk so early ? Neither her father nor Mr Allen did so. It was certainly very provoking. She was all impatience to see the house, and had scarcely any curiosity about the grounds. If Henry had been with them, indeed ! but now she should not know what was picturesque when she saw it. Such were her thoughts ; but she kept them to herself, and put on her bonnet in patient discontent.

She was struck, however, beyond her expectation, by the grandeur of the abbey, as she saw it for the first time from the lawn. The whole building enclosed a large court ; and two sides of the quadrangle, rich in Gothic ornaments, stood forward for admiration. The remainder was shut off by knolls of old trees, or luxuriant plantations, and the steep woody hills rising behind to give it shelter were beautiful even in the leafless month of March. Catherine had seen nothing to compare with it ; and her feelings of delight were so strong, that without waiting for any better authority, she boldly burst forth in wonder and praise. The General listened with assenting gratitude, and it seemed as if his own estimation of Northanger had waited unfixed till that hour.

The kitchen-garden was to be next admired, and he led the way to it across a small portion of the park.

The number of acres contained in this garden was such as Catherine could not listen to without dismay, being more than double the extent of all Mr Allen's, as well [as] her father's, including churchyard and orchard. The walls seemed countless in number, endless in length ; a village of hot-houses seemed to arise among them, and a whole parish to be at work within the enclosure. The General was flattered by her looks of surprize, which told him almost as plainly, as he soon forced her to tell him in words, that she had never seen any gardens at all equal to them before ; and he then modestly owned that, " without any ambition of that sort himself, without any solicitude about it, he did believe them to be unrivalled in the kingdom. If he had a hobby-horse, it was *that*. He loved a garden. Though careless enough in most matters of eating, he loved good fruit ; or if he did not, his friends and children did. There were great vexations, however, attending such a garden as his. The utmost care could not always secure the most valuable fruits. The pinery had yielded only one hundred in the last year. Mr Allen, he supposed, must feel these inconveniences as well as himself."

" No, not at all. Mr Allen did not care about the garden, and never went into it."

With a triumphant smile of self-satisfaction, the General wished he could do the same, for he never entered his without being vexed in one way or other, by its falling short of his plan.

" How were Mr Allen's succession-houses worked ? " describing the nature of his own as they entered them.

" Mr Allen had only one small hot-house, which Mrs Allen had the use of for her plants in winter, and there was a fire in it now and then."

" He is a happy man ! " said the General, with a look of very happy contempt.

Having taken her into every division, and led her under every wall, till she was heartily weary of seeing and wondering, he suffered the girls at last to seize the advantage of an outer door, and then expressing his wish to examine the effect of some recent alterations about the tea-house, proposed it as no unpleasant extension of their walk, if Miss Morland were not tired. " But where are you going, Eleanor ? Why do you chuse that cold, damp path to it ? Miss Morland will get wet. Our best way is across the park."

" This is so favourite a walk of mine," said Miss Tilney, " that I always think it the best and nearest way. But perhaps it may be damp."

It was a narrow winding path through a thick grove of old Scotch firs ; and Catherine, struck by its gloomy aspect, and eager to enter it, could not, even by the General's disapprobation, be kept from stepping forward. He perceived her inclination, and having again urged the plea of health in vain, was too polite to make further opposition. He excused himself, however, from attending them : " The rays of the sun were not too cheerful for him, and he would meet them by another course." He turned away ; and Catherine was shocked to find how much her spirits were relieved by the separation. The shock, however, being less real than the relief, offered it no injury ; and she began to talk with easy gaiety of the delightful melancholy which such a grove inspired.

" I am particularly fond of this spot," said her companion, with a sigh. " It was my mother's favourite walk."

Catherine had never heard Mrs Tilney mentioned in the family before ; and the interest excited by this tender remembrance shewed itself directly in her altered countenance, and in the attentive pause with which she waited for something more.

" I used to walk here so often with her," added Eleanor ; " though I never loved it then as I have loved it since. At that time, indeed, I used to wonder at her choice. But her memory endears it now."

" And ought it not," reflected Catherine, " to endear it to her husband ? Yet the General would not enter it." Miss Tilney continuing silent, she ventured to say, " Her death must have been a great affliction."

" A great and increasing one," replied the other, in a low voice. " I was only thirteen when it happened ; and, though I felt my loss perhaps as strongly as one so young could feel it, I did not, I could not then know what a loss it was." She stopped for a moment, and then added with great firmness : " I have no sister, you know ; and though Henry—though my brothers are very affectionate, and Henry is a great deal here, which I am most thankful for, it is impossible for me not to be often solitary."

" To be sure, you must miss him very much."

" A mother would have been always present ; a mother would have been a constant friend ; her influence would have been beyond all other."

" Was she a very charming woman ? Was she handsome ? Was there any picture of her in the abbey ? And why had she been so partial to that grove ? Was it from

dejection of spirits ? " were questions now eagerly poured
forth. The first three received a ready affirmative, the
two others were passed by ; and Catherine's interest in
the deceased Mrs Tilney augmented with every question,
whether answered or not. Of her unhappiness in marriage
she felt persuaded. The General certainly had been an
unkind husband. He did not love her walk ; could he,
therefore, have loved her ? And besides, handsome as he
was, there was a something in the turn of his features
which spoke his not having behaved well to her.

" Her picture, I suppose," blushing at the consummate
art of her own question, " hangs in your father's room ? "

" No ; it was intended for the drawing-room ; but my
father was dissatisfied with the painting, and for some time
it had no place. Soon after her death I obtained it for my
own, and hung it in my bedchamber, where I shall be happy
to shew it you : it is very like." Here was another proof.
A portrait, very like, of a departed wife, not valued by her
husband. He must have been dreadfully cruel to her.

Catherine attempted no longer to hide from herself the
nature of the feelings which, in spite of all his attentions,
he had previously excited ; and what had been terror and
dislike before, was now absolute aversion. Yes, aversion !
His cruelty to such a charming woman made him odious to
her. She had often read of such characters ; characters,
which Mr Allen had been used to call unnatural and over-
drawn ; but here was proof positive to the contrary.

She had just settled this point, when the end of the path
brought them directly upon the General ; and in spite of
all her virtuous indignation, she found herself again obliged
to walk with him, listen to him, and even to smile when he
smiled. Being no longer able, however, to receive pleasure
from the surrounding objects, she soon began to walk with
lassitude : the General perceived it, and with a concern for
her health, which seemed to reproach her for her opinion of
him, was most urgent for returning with his daughter to
the house. He would follow them in a quarter of an hour.
Again they parted ; but Eleanor was called back in half a
minute to receive a strict charge against taking her friend
round the Abbey till his return. This second instance of

his anxiety to delay what she so much wished for, struck
Catherine as very remarkable.

CHAPTER XXIII

AN hour passed away before the General came in, spent,
on the part of his young guest, in no very favourable consideration of his character. " This lengthened absence,
these solitary rambles, did not speak a mind at ease, or a
conscience void of reproach." At length he appeared ;
and whatever might have been the gloom of his meditations,
he could still smile with *them*. Miss Tilney, understanding,
in part, her friend's curiosity to see the house, soon revived
the subject ; and her father being, contrary to Catherine's
expectations, unprovided with any pretence for further
delay, beyond that of stopping five minutes to order refreshments to be in the room by their return, was at last
ready to escort them.

They set forward ; and, with a grandeur of air, a dignified
step, which caught the eye, but could not shake the doubts
of the well-read Catherine, he led the way across the hall,
through the common drawing-room and one useless ante-
chamber, into a room magnificent both in size and furniture,
the real drawing-room, used only with company of consequence. It was very noble, very grand, very charming, was
all that Catherine had to say, for her indiscriminating eye
scarcely discerned the colour of the satin ; and all minuteness of praise, all praise that had such meaning, was
supplied by the General : the costliness or elegance of any
room's fitting up could be nothing to her ; she cared for
no furniture of a more modern date than the fifteenth
century. When the General had satisfied his own curiosity,
in a close examination of every well-known ornament, they
proceeded to the library, an apartment, in its way, of equal
magnificence, exhibiting a collection of books, on which
an humble man might have looked with pride. Catherine
heard, admired, and wondered with more genuine feeling
than before, gathered all that she could from this storehouse
of knowledge, by running over the titles of half a shelf, and

was ready to proceed. But suites of apartments did not spring up with her wishes. Large as was the building, she had already visited the greatest part ; though, on being told that, with the addition of the kitchen, the six or seven rooms she had now seen surrounded three sides of the court, she could scarcely believe it, or overcome the suspicion of there being many chambers secreted. It was some relief, however, that they were to return to the rooms in common use, by passing through a few of less importance, looking into the court, which, with occasional passages, not wholly unintricate, connected the different sides ; and she was further soothed in her progress by being told that she was treading what had once been a cloister, having traces of cells pointed out, and observing several doors that were neither opened nor explained to her ; by finding herself successively in a billiard-room and in the General's private apartment, without comprehending their connection, or being able to turn aright when she left them ; and lastly by passing through a dark little room, owning Henry's authority, and strewed with his litter of books, guns, and great-coats.

From the dining-room, of which, though already seen, and always to be seen at five o'clock, the General could not forego the pleasure of pacing out the length, for the more certain information of Miss Morland, as to what she neither doubted nor cared for, they proceeded by quick communication to the kitchen—the ancient kitchen of the convent, rich in the massy walls and smoke of former days, and in the stoves and hot closets of the present. The General's improving hand had not loitered here : every modern invention to facilitate the labour of the cooks had been adopted within this their spacious theatre ; and, when the genius of others had failed, his own had often produced the perfection wanted. His endowments of this spot alone might at any time have placed him high among the benefactors of the convent.

With the walls of the kitchen ended all the antiquity of the Abbey ; the fourth side of the quadrangle having, on account of its decaying state, been removed by the General's father, and the present erected in its place. All that was venerable ceased here. The new building was

not only new, but declared itself to be so ; intended only
for offices, and enclosed behind by stable-yards, no uniformity
of architecture had been thought necessary. Catherine
could have raved at the hand which had swept away what
must have been beyond the value of all the rest, for the
purposes of mere domestic economy ; and would willingly
have been spared the mortification of a walk through scenes
so fallen, had the General allowed it : but if he had a vanity,
it was in the arrangement of his offices ; and as he was
convinced, that, to a mind like Miss Morland's, a view of
the accommodations and comforts by which the labours
of her inferiors were softened, must always be gratifying,
he should make no apology for leading her on. They took
a slight survey of all ; and Catherine was impressed, beyond
her expectation, by their multiplicity and their convenience.
The purposes for which a few shapeless pantries, and a
comfortless scullery, were deemed sufficient at Fullerton,
were here carried on in appropriate divisions, commodious
and roomy. The number of servants continually appearing,
did not strike her less than the number of their offices.
Wherever they went, some pattened girl stopped to curtsey,
or some footman in dishabille sneaked off. Yet this was
an Abbey ! How inexpressibly different in these domestic
arrangements from such as she had read about : from abbeys
and castles, in which, though certainly larger than Northanger, all the dirty work of the house was to done by two
pair of female hands at the utmost. How they could get
through it all, had often amazed Mrs Allen ; and, when
Catherine saw what was necessary here, she began to be
amazed herself.

They returned to the hall, that the chief staircase might
be ascended, and the beauty of its wood and ornaments
of rich carving might be pointed out : having gained the
top, they turned in an opposite direction from the gallery
in which her room lay, and shortly entered one on the same
plan, but superior in length and breadth. She was here
shown successively into three large bed-chambers, with
their dressing-rooms, most completely and handsomely
fitted up : everything that money and taste could do, to
give comfort and elegance to apartments, had been bestowed

on these ; and, being furnished within the last five years, they were perfect in all that would be generally pleasing, and wanting in all that could give pleasure to Catherine. As they were surveying the last, the General, after slightly naming a few of the distinguished characters by whom they had at times been honoured, turned with a smiling countenance to Catherine, and ventured to hope that henceforward some of the earliest tenants might be " our friends from Fullerton." She felt the unexpected compliment, and deeply regretted the impossibility of thinking well of a man so kindly disposed towards herself, and so full of civility to all her family.

The gallery was terminated by folding doors, which Miss Tilney, advancing, had thrown open, and passed through, and seemed on the point of doing the same by the first door to the left, in another long reach of gallery, when the General, coming forwards, called her hastily, and, as Catherine thought, rather angrily back, demanding whither she were going ? And what was there more to be seen ? Had not Miss Morland already seen all that could be worth her notice ? And did she not suppose her friend might be glad of some refreshment after so much exercise ? Miss Tilney drew back directly, and the heavy doors were closed upon the mortified Catherine, who, having seen, in a momentary glance beyond them, a narrower passage, more numerous openings, and symptoms of a winding staircase, believed herself at last within the reach of something worth her notice ; and felt, as she unwillingly paced back the gallery, that she would rather be allowed to examine that end of the house than see all the finery of all the rest. The General's evident desire of preventing such an examination was an additional stimulant. Something was certainly to be concealed : her fancy, though it had trespassed lately once or twice, could not mislead her here ; and what that something was, a short sentence of Miss Tilney's as they followed the General at some distance downstairs, seemed to point out :—" I was going to take you into what was my mother's room, the room in which she died——" were all her words ; but few as they were, they conveyed pages of intelligence to Catherine.

It was no wonder that the General should skrink from the sight of such objects as that room must contain—a room, in all probability, never entered by him since the dreadful scene had passed which released his suffering wife, and left him to the stings of conscience.

She ventured, when next alone with Eleanor, to express her wish of being permitted to see it, as well as all the rest of that side of the house ; and Eleanor promised to attend her there, whenever they should have a convenient hour. Catherine understood her : the General must be watched from home, before that room could be entered. " It remains as it was, I suppose ? " said she, in a tone of feeling.

" Yes, entirely."

" And how long ago may it be that your mother died ? "

" She has been dead these nine years." And nine years, Catherine knew, was a trifle of time, compared with what generally elapsed after the death of an injured wife, before her room was put to rights.

" You were with her, I suppose, to the last ? "

" No," said Miss Tilney, sighing ; " I was unfortunately from home. Her illness was sudden and short ; and before I arrived, it was all over."

Cathcrine's blood ran cold with the horrid suggestions which naturally sprang from these words. Could it be possible ? Could Henry's father—? And yet how many were the examples to justify even the blackest suspicions ! And when she saw him in the evening, while she worked with her friend, slowly pacing the drawing-room for an hour together in silent thoughtfulness, with downcast eyes and contracted brow, she felt secure from all possibility of wronging him. It was the air and attitude of a Montoni ! What could more plainly speak the gloomy workings of a mind not wholly dead to every sense of humanity, in its fearful review of past scenes of guilt ? Unhappy man ! And the anxiousness of her spirits directed her eyes towards his figure so repeatedly, as to catch Miss Tilney's notice. " My father," she whispered, " often walks about the room in this way ; it is nothing unusual."

" So much the worse ! " thought Catherine : such ill-

timed exercise was of a piece with the strange unseasonableness of his morning walks, and boded nothing good.

After an evening, the little variety and seeming length
of which made her peculiarly sensible of Henry's importance
among them, she was heartily glad to be dismissed ; though
it was a look from the General not designed for her observation which sent his daughter to the bell. When the butler
would have lit his master's candle, however, he was forbidden. The latter was not going to retire. " I have
many pamphlets to finish," said he to Catherine, " before
I can close my eyes ; and perhaps may be poring over the
affairs of the nation for hours after you are asleep. Can
either of us be more meetly employed ? *My* eyes will be
blinding for the good of others ; and *yours* preparing by rest
for future mischief."

But neither the business alleged, nor the magnificent
compliment, could win Catherine from thinking that some
very different object must occasion so serious a delay of
proper repose. To be kept up for hours, after the family
were in bed, by stupid pamphlets, was not very likely.
There must be some deeper cause : something was to be
done which could be done only while the household slept ;
and the probability that Mrs Tilney yet lived, shut up for
causes unknown, and receiving from the pitiless hands of
her husband a nightly supply of coarse food, was the conclusion which necessarily followed. Shocking as was the
idea, it was at least better than a death unfairly hastened,
as in the natural course of things, she must ere long be
released. The suddenness of her reputed illness, the absence
of her daughter, and probably of her other children, at the
time, all favoured the supposition of her imprisonment.
Its origin—jealousy, perhaps, or wanton cruelty—was yet
to be unravelled.

In revolving these matters while she undressed, it suddenly
struck her as not unlikely, that she might that morning
have passed near the very spot of this unfortunate woman's
confinement ; might have been within a few paces of the
cell in which she languished out her days ; for what part
of the Abbey could be more fitted for the purpose than that
which yet bore the traces of monastic division ? In the

high-arched passage, paved with stone, which already she
had trodden with peculiar awe, she well remembered the
doors of which the General had given no account.   To what
might not these doors lead ?   In support of the plausibility
of this conjecture, it further occurred to her, that the forbidden gallery, in which lay the apartments of the unfortunate Mrs Tilney, must be, as certainly as her memory could
guide her, exactly over this suspected range of cells ; and
the staircase by the side of those apartments of which
she had caught a transient glimpse, communicating by some
secret means with those cells, might well have favoured
the barbarous proceedings of her husband.   Down that
staircase she had perhaps been conveyed in a state of well-
prepared insensibility.

Catherine sometimes started at the boldness of her own
surmises, and sometimes hoped or feared that she had gone
too far ; but they were supported by such appearances as
made their dismissal impossible.

The side of the quadrangle, in which she supposed the
guilty scene to be acting, being, according, to her belief
just opposite her own, it struck her that, if judiciously
watched, some rays of light from the General's lamp might
glimmer through the lower windows, as he passed to the
prison of his wife ; and, twice before she stepped into bed,
she stole gently from her room to the corresponding window
in the gallery, to see if it appeared, but all abroad was dark,
and it must yet be too early.   The various ascending noises
convinced her that the servants must still be up.   Till
midnight, she supposed it would be in vain to watch ; but
then, when the clock had struck twelve, and all was quiet,
she would, if not appalled by darkness, steal out and look
once more.   The clock struck twelve, and Catherine had
been half an hour asleep.

CHAPTER XXIV

THE next day afforded no opportunity for the proposed
examination of the mysterious apartments.   It was Sunday,
and the whole time between morning and afternoon service

was required by the General in exercise abroad or eating cold meat at home ; and great as was Catherine's curiosity, her courage was not equal to a wish of exploring them after dinner, either by the fading light of the sky between six and seven o'clock, or by the yet more partial though stronger illumination of a treacherous lamp. The day was unmarked, therefore, by anything to interest her imagination beyond the sight of a very elegant monument to the memory of Mrs Tilney, which immediately fronted the family pew. By that her eye was instantly caught and long retained ; and the perusal of the highly-strained epitaph, in which every virtue was ascribed to her by the inconsolable husband, who must have been in some way or other her destroyer, affected her even to tears.

That the General, having erected such a monument, should be able to face it, was not perhaps very strange, and yet that he could sit so boldly collected within its view, maintain so elevated an air, look so fearlessly around, nay, that he should even enter the church, seemed wonderful to Catherine. Not however, that many instances of being equally hardened in guilt might not be produced. She could remember dozens who had persevered in every possible vice, going on from crime to crime, murdering whomsoever they chose, without feeling of humanity or remorse, till a violent death or a religious retirement closed their black career. The erection of the monument itself could not in the smallest degree affect her doubts of Mrs Tilney's actual decease. Were she even to descend into the family vault where her ashes were supposed to slumber, were she to behold the coffin in which they were said to be enclosed, what could it avail in such a case ? Catherine had read too much not to be perfectly aware of the ease with which a waxen figure might be introduced, and a supposititious funeral carried on.

The succeeding morning promised something better. The General's early walk, ill-timed as it was in every other view, was favourable here ; and when she knew him to be out of the house, she directly proposed to Miss Tilney the accomplishment of her promise. Eleanor was ready to oblige her ; and Catherine reminding her as they went

of another promise, their first visit in consequence was
to the portrait in her bed-chamber. It represented a
very lovely woman, with a mild and pensive countenance,
justifying so far, the expectations of its new observer ;
but they were not in every respect answered, for Catherine
had depended upon meeting with features, air, complexion,
that should be the very counterpart, the very image, if
not of Henry's, of Eleanor's ; the only portraits of which
she had been in the habit of thinking, bearing always an
equal resemblance of mother and child. A face once taken
was taken for generations. But here she was obliged
to look, and consider, and study for a likeness. She contemplated it, however, in spite of this drawback, with much
emotion ; and, but for a yet stronger interest, would have
left it unwillingly.

Her agitation, as they entered the great gallery, was
too great for any endeavour at discourse ; she could only
look at her companion. Eleanor's countenance was dejected, yet sedate ; and its composure spoke her enured
to all the gloomy objects to which they were advancing.
Again she passed through the folding-doors, again her hand
was upon the important lock, and Catherine, hardly able to
breathe, was turning to close the former with fearful caution,
when the figure, the dreaded figure of the General himself
at the further end, of the gallery stood before her ! The
name of " Eleanor " at the same moment, in his loudest
tone, resounded through the building, giving to his daughter
the first intimation of his presence, and to Catherine terror
upon terror. An attempt at concealment had been her
first instinctive movement on perceiving him, yet she
could scarcely hope to have escaped his eye ; and when
her friend, who with an apologizing look darted hastily
by her, had joined and disappeared with him, she ran for
safety to her own room, and, locking herself in, believed
that she should never have courage to go down again. She
remained there at least an hour, in the greatest agitation,
deeply commiserating the state of her poor friend, and
expecting a summons herself from the angry General,
to attend him in his own apartment. No summons, however, arrived ; and at last, on seeing a carriage drive up

to the Abbey, she was emboldened to descend and meet him under the protection of visitors. The breakfast-room was gay with company ; and she was named to them by the General as the friend of his daughter, in a complimentary style, which so well concealed his resentful ire, as to make her feel secure at least of life for the present. And Eleanor, with a command of countenance which did honour to her concern for his character, taking an early occasion of saying to her, " My father only wanted me to answer a note," she began to hope that she had either been unseen by the General, or that from some consideration of policy she should be allowed to suppose herself so. Upon this trust she dared still to remain in his presence after the company left them, and nothing occurred to disturb it.

In the course of this morning's reflections, she came to a resolution of making her next attempt on the forebidden door alone. It would be much better in every respect that Eleanor should know nothing of the matter. To involve her in the danger of a second detection, to court her into an apartment which must wring her heart, could not be the office of a friend. The General's utmost anger could not be to herself what it might be to a daughter, and besides, she thought the examination itself would be more satisfactory if made without any companion. It would be impossible to explain to Eleanor the suspicions, from which the other had, in all likelihood, been hitherto happily exempt ; nor could she therefore, in *her* presence, search for those proofs of the General's cruelty, which, however they might yet have escaped discovery, she felt confident of somewhere drawing forth, in the shape of some fragmented journal, continued to the last gasp. Of the way to the apartment she was now perfectly mistress, and as she wished, to get it over before Henry's return, who was expected on the morrow, there was no time to be lost. The day was bright, her courage high ; at four o'clock the sun was now two hours above the horizon, and it would be only her retiring to dress half an hour earlier than usual.

It was done ; and Catherine found herself alone in the gallery before the clocks had ceased to strike. It was no time for thought : she hurried on, slipped with the least

possible noise through the folding doors, and without
stopping to look or breathe, rushed forward to the one
in question. The lock yielded to her hand, and luckily
with no sullen sound that could alarm a human being.
On tiptoe she entered : the room was before her : but it
was some minutes before she could advance another step.
She beheld what fixed her to the spot, and agitated every
feature. She saw a large, well-proportioned apartment,
an handsome dimity bed, arranged as unoccupied, with
an housemaid's care, a bright Bath stove, mahogany wardrobes and neatly-painted chairs, on which the warm beams
of a western sun gaily poured through two sash windows.
Catherine had expected to have her feelings worked, and
worked they were. Astonishment and doubt first seized
them, and a shortly succeeding ray of common sense added
some bitter emotions of shame. She could not be mistaken as to the room ; but how grossly mistaken in everything else, in Miss Tilney's meaning, in her own calculation !
This apartment, to which she had given a date so ancient, a
position so awful, proved to be one end of what the General's
father had built. There were two other doors in the
chamber, leading probably into dressing-closets, but she
had no inclination to open either. Would the veil in which
Mrs Tilney had last walked, or the volume in which she
had last read, remain to tell what nothing else was allowed
to whisper ? No ; whatever might have been the General's
crimes, he had certainly too much wit to let them sue for
detection. She was sick of exploring, and desired but to
be safe in her own room, with her own heart only privy
to its folly, and she was on the point of retreating as softly
as she had entered, when the sound of footsteps, she could
hardly tell where, made her pause and tremble. To be
found there, even by a servant, would be unpleasant, but
by the General (and he seemed always at hand when least
wanted) much worse. She listened, the sound had ceased,
and resolving not to lose a moment she passed through
and closed the door. At that instant a door underneath
was hastily opened, some one seemed with swift steps to
ascend the stairs, by the head of which she had yet to pass
before she could gain the gallery. She had no power to

move. With a feeling of terror not very definable, she fixed her eyes on the staircase, and in a few moments it gave Henry to her view. " Mr Tilney ? " she exclaimed, in a voice of more than common astonishment. He looked astonished too. " Good God ! " she continued, not attending to his address, " how came you here ? How came you up that staircase ? "

" How came I up that staircase ? " he replied, greatly surprized. " Because it is my nearest way from the stable-yard to my own chamber ; and why should I not come up it ? "

Catherine recollected herself, blushed deeply, and could say no more. He seemed to be looking in her countenance for that explanation which her lips did not afford. She moved on towards the gallery. " And may I not, in my turn," said he, as he pushed back the folding doors, " ask how *you* came here ? This passage is at least as extraordinary a road from the breakfast-parlour to your apartment, as that staircase can be from the stables to mine."

" I have been," said Catherine, looking down, " to see your mother's room."

" My mother's room ! Is there anything extraordinary to be seen there ? "

" No, nothing at all. I thought you did not mean to come back till to-morrow."

" I did not expect to be able to return sooner, when I went away ; but three hours ago I had the pleasure of finding nothing to detain me. You look pale. I am afraid I alarmed you by running so fast up those stairs. Perhaps you did not know—you were not aware of their leading from the offices in common use ? "

" No, I was not. You have had a very fine day for your ride ? "

" Very ; and does Eleanor leave you to find your way into all the rooms in the house by yourself ? "

" Oh, no ! she shewed me over the greatest part on Saturday, and we were coming here to these rooms, but only " (dropping her voice), " your father was with us."

" And that prevented you," said Henry, earnestly regarding her. " Have you looked into all the rooms in that passage ? "

" No ; I only wanted to see— Is not it very late ? I must go and dress."

" It is only a quarter past four " (shewing his watch) ; " and you are not now in Bath. No theatre, no rooms to prepare for. Half an hour at Northanger must be enough."

She could not contradict it, and therefore suffered herself to be detained, though her dread of further questions made her, for the first time in their acquaintance, wish to leave him. They walked slowly up the gallery. " Have you had any letter from Bath since I saw you ? "

" No, and I am very much surprized. Isabella promised so faithfully to write directly."

" Promised so faithfully ! A faithful promise ! That puzzles me. I have heard of a faithful performance ; but a faithful promise—the fidelity of promising ! It is a power little knowing worth, however, since it can deceive and pain you. My mother's room is very commodious, is it not ? Large and cheerful looking, and the dressing-closets so well disposed. It always strikes me as the most comfortable apartment in the house ; and I rather wonder that Eleanor should not take it for her own. She sent you to look at it, I suppose ? "

" No."

" It has been your own doing entirely ? " Catherine said nothing. After a short silence, during which he had closely observed her, he added : " As there is nothing in the room in itself to raise curiosity, this must have proceeded from a sentiment of respect for my mother's character, as described by Eleanor, which does honour to her memory. The world, I believe, never saw a better woman. But it is not often that virtue can boast an interest such as this. This domestic, unpretending merits of a person never known, do not often create that kind of fervent, venerating tenderness which would prompt a visit like yours. Eleanor, I suppose, has talked of her a great deal ? "

" Yes, a great deal. That is—no, not much, but what she did say, was very interesting. Her dying so suddenly "

(slowly, and with hesitation it was spoken), "and you—
none of you being at home ; and your father, I thought,
perhaps, had not been very fond of her."

"And from these circumstances," he replied (his quick
eye fixed on hers), "you infer, perhaps, the probability
of some negligence—some—" (involuntarily she shook her
head), "or it may be, of something still less pardonable."
She raised her eyes towards him more fully than she had
ever done before. "My mother's illness," he continued,
"the seizure which ended in her death, *was* sudden. The
malady itself one from which she had often suffered : a
bilious fever : its cause therefore constitutional. On the
third day, in short, as soon as she could be prevailed on, a
physician attended her ; a very respectable man, and one
in whom she had always placed great confidence. Upon
his opinion of her danger, two others were called in the next
day, and remained in almost constant attendance for four-
and-twenty hours. On the fifth day she died. During
the progress of her disorder, Frederick and I (*we* were both
at home) saw her repeatedly ; and from our own observation
can bear witness to her having received every possible
attention which could spring from the affection of those
about her, or which her situation in life could command.
Poor Eleanor *was* absent, and at such a distance as to return only to see her mother in her coffin."

"But your father," said Catherine "was *he* afflicted ? "

"For a time, greatly so. You have erred in supposing
him not attached to her. He loved her, I am persuaded,
as well as it was possible for him to—— We have not all,
you know, the same tenderness of disposition ; and I will
not pretend to say that while she lived, she might not often
have had much to bear ; but though his temper injured her,
his judgment never did. His value of her was sincere ;
and, if not permanently, he was truly afflicted by her
death."

"I am very glad of it," said Catherine ; "it would have
been very shocking—"

"If I understand you rightly, you had formed a surmise
of such horror as I have hardly words to—— Dear Miss Morland, consider the dreadful nature of the suspicions you have

entertained. What have you been judging from ? Remember the country and the age in which we live. Remember that we are English : that we are Christians. Consult your own understanding, your own sense of the probable, your own observation of what is passing around you. Does our education prepare us for such atrocities ? Do our laws connive at them ? Could they be perpetrated without being known in a country like this, where social and literary intercourse is on such a footing ; where every man is surrounded by a neighbourhood of voluntary spies ; and where roads and newspapers lay everything open ? Dearest Miss Morland, what ideas have you been admitting ? ''

They had reached the end of the gallery ; and with tears of shame she ran off to her own room.

CHAPTER XXV

THE visions of romance were over. Catherine was completely awakened. Henry's address, short as it had been, had more thoroughly opened her eyes to the extravagance of her late fancies than all their several disappointments had done. Most grievously was she humbled. Most bitterly did she cry. It was not only with herself that she was sunk, but with Henry. Her folly, which now seemed even criminal, was all exposed to him, and he must despise her for ever. The liberty which her imagination had dared to take with the character of his father, could he ever forgive it ? The absurdity of her curiosity and her fears, could they ever be forgotten ? She hated herself more than she could express. He had, she thought he had, once or twice before this fatal morning, shewn something like affection for her. But now—in short, she made herself as miserable as possible for about half an hour, went down, when the clock struck five, with a broken heart, and could scarcely give an intelligible answer to Eleanor's inquiry if she was well. The formidable Henry soon followed her into the room, and the only difference in his behaviour to her was, that he paid her rather more attention than usual. Cath-

erine had never wanted comfort more, and he looked as
if he was aware of it.

The evening wore away with no abatement of this soothing
politeness ; and her spirits were gradually raised to a modest
tranquillity. She did not learn either to forget or defend
the past ; but she learned to hope that it would never
transpire farther, and that it might not cost her Henry's
entire regard. Her thoughts being still chiefly fixed on
what she had with such causeless terror felt and done, nothing
could shortly be clearer, than that it had been all a voluntary,
self-created delusion, each trifling circumstance receiving
importance from an imagination resolved on alarm, and
everything forced to bend to one purpose by a mind which,
before she entered the abbey, had been craving to be frightened. She remembered with what feelings she had prepared for a knowledge of Northanger. She saw that the
infatuation had been created, the mischief settled, long
before her quitting Bath, and it seemed as if the whole
might be traced to the influence of that sort of reading
which she had there indulged.

Charming as were all Mrs Radcliffe's works, and charming even as were the works of all her imitators, it was not
in them perhaps that human nature, at least in the midland
counties of England, was to be looked for. Of the Alps
and Pyrenees, with their pine forests and their vices, they
might give a faithful delineation ; and Italy, Switzerland,
and the South of France, might be as fruitful in horrors
as they were there represented. Catherine dared not doubt
beyond her own country, and even of that, if hard pressed,
vould have yielded the northern and western extremities.
But in the central part of England there was surely some
security for the existence even of a wife not beloved, in
the laws of the land, and the manners of the age. Murder
vas not tolerated, servants were not slaves, and neither
poison nor sleeping potions to be procured, like rhubarb,
from every druggist. Among the Alps and Pyrenees,
perhaps, there were no mixed characters. There, such
as were not as spotless as an angel, might have the dispositions of a fiend. But in England it was not so ; among
the English, she believed, in their hearts and habits, there

was a general though unequal mixture of good and bad. Upon this conviction, she would not be surprized if even in Henry and Eleanor Tilney some slight imperfection might hereafter appear ; and upon this conviction she need not fear to acknowledge some actual specks in the character of their father, who, though cleared from the grossly injurious suspicions which she, must ever blush to have entertained, she did believe, upon serious consideration, to be not perfectly amiable.

Her mind made up on these several points, and her resolution formed, of always judging and acting in future with the greatest good sense, she had nothing to do but tò forgive herself and be happier than ever ; and the lenient hand of time did much for her by insensible gradations in the course of another day. Henry's astonishing generosity and nobleness of conduct, in never alluding in the slightest way to what had passed, was of the greatest assistance to her ; and sooner than she could have supposed it possible, in the beginning of her distress, her spirits became absolutely comfortable, and capable, as heretofore, of continual improvement by anything he said. There were still some subjects, indeed, under which she believed they must always tremble ; the mention of a chest or a cabinet, for instance, and she did not love the sight of japan in any shape : but even *she* could allow that an occasional memento of past folly, however painful, might not be without use.

The anxieties of common life began soon to succeed to the alarms of romance. Her desire of hearing from Isabella grew every day greater. She was quite impatient to know how the Bath world went on, and how the Rooms were attended ; and especially was she anxious to be assured of Isabella's having matched some fine netting cotton, on which she had left her intent ; and of her continuing on the best terms with James. Her only dependence for information of any kind was on Isabella. James had protested against writing to her till his return to Oxford ; and Mrs Allen had given her no hopes of a letter till she had got back to Fullerton. But Isabella had promised and promised again ; and when she promised a thing she was so scrupulous in performing it; this made it so particularly strange!

For nine successive mornings Catherine wondered over the repetition of a disappointment which each morning became more severe; but on the tenth, when she entered the breakfast-room, her first object was a letter, held out by Henry's willing hand. She thanked him as heartily as if he had written it himself. "'Tis only from James, however," as she looked at the direction. She opened it: it was from Oxford; and to this purpose:—

"DEAR CATHERINE—Though, God knows, with little inclination for writing, I think it my duty to tell you, that everything is at an end between Miss Thorpe and me. I left her and Bath yesterday, never to see either again. I shall not enter into particulars, they would only pain you more. You will soon hear enough from another quarter to know where lies the blame; and I hope will acquit your brother everything but the folly of too easily thinking his affection returned. Thank God! I am undeceived in time! But it is a heavy blow! After my father's consent had been so kindly given—but no more of this. She has made me miserable for ever! Let me soon hear from you, dear Catherine; you are my only friend; *your* love I do build upon. I wish your visit at Northanger may be over before Captain Tilney makes his engagement known, or you will be uncomfortably circumstanced. Poor Thorpe is in town: I dread the sight of him; his honest heart would feel so much. I have written to him and my father. Her duplicity hurts me more than all; till the very last, if I reasoned with her, she declared herself as much attached to me as ever, and laughed at my fears. I am ashamed to think how long I bore with it; but if ever man had reason to believe himself loved, I was that man. I cannot understand, even now, what she would be at, for there could be no need of my being played off to make her secure of Tilney. We parted at last by mutual consent. Happy for me had we never met! I can never expect to know such another woman! Dearest Catherine, beware how you give your heart.—Believe me, &c."

Catherine had not read three lines before her sudden change of countenance, and short exclamations of sorrowing wonder, declared her to be receiving unpleasant news ; and Henry, earnestly watching her through the whole letter, saw plainly that it ended no better than it began. He was prevented, however, from even looking his surprize, by his father's entrance. They went to breakfast directly ; but Catherine could hardly eat anything. Tears filled her eyes, and even ran down her cheeks as she sat. The letter was one moment in her hand, then in her lap, and then in her pocket ; and she looked as if she knew not what she did. The General, between his cocoa and his newspaper, had luckily no leisure for noticing her ; but to the other two her distress was equally visible. As soon as she dared leave the table, she hurried away to her own room ; but the housemaids were busy in it, and she was obliged to come down again. She turned into the drawing-room for privacy, but Henry and Eleanor had likewise retreated thither, and were at that moment deep in consultation about her. She drew back, trying to beg their pardon, but was, with gentle violence, forced to return ; and the others withdrew, after Eleanor had affectionately expressed a wish of being of use or comfort to her.

After half an hour's free indulgence of grief and reflection, Catherine felt equal to encountering her friends ; but whether she should make her distress known to them was another consideration. Perhaps, if particularly questioned, she might just give an idea—just distantly hint at it— but not more. To expose a friend, such a friend as Isabella had been to her ; and then their own brother so closely concerned in it ! She believed she must wave the subject altogether. Henry and Eleanor were by themselves in the breakfast-room ; and each, as she entered it, looked at her anxiously. Catherine took her place at the table, and, after a short silence, Eleanor said, " No bad news from Fullerton, I hope ? Mr and Mrs Morland, your brothers and sisters, I hope they are none of them ill ? "

" No, I thank you," (sighing as she spoke ;) " they are all very well. My letter was from my brother at Oxford."

Nothing further was said for a few minutes ; and then,

speaking through her tears, she added, " I do not think I shall ever wish for a letter again ! "

" I am sorry," said Henry, closing the book he had just opened ; " if I had suspected the letter of containing anything unwelcome, I should have given it with very different feelings."

" It contained something worse than anybody could suppose ! Poor James is so unhappy ! You will soon know why."

" To have so kind-hearted, so affectionate a sister," replied Henry, warmly, " must be a comfort to him under any distress."

" I have one favour to beg," said Catherine, shortly afterwards, in an agitated manner, " that, if your brother should be coming here, you will give me notice of it, that I may go away."

" Our brother ! Frederick ! "

" Yes ; I am sure I should be very sorry to leave you so soon, but something has happened that would make it very dreadful for me to be in the same house with Captain Tilney."

Eleanor's work was suspended while she gazed with increasing astonishment ; but Henry began to suspect the truth, and something in which Miss Thorpe's name was included, passed his lips.

" How quick you are ! " cried Catherine ; " you have guessed it, I declare ! And yet, when we talked about it in Bath, you little thought of its ending so. Isabella— no wonder *now* I have not heard from her—Isabella has deserted my brother, and is to marry yours ! Could you have believed there had been such inconstancy, and fickleness, and everything that is bad in the world ? "

" I hope, so far as concerns my brother, you are misinformed. I hope he has not had any material share in bringing on Mr Morland's disappointment. His marrying Miss Thorpe is not probable. I think you must be deceived so far. I am very sorry for Mr Morland : sorry that any one you love should be unhappy ; but my surprize would be greater at Frederick's marrying her, than at any other part of the story."

" It is very true, however ; you shall read James's letter yourself. Stay, there is one part—" recollecting, with a blush, the last line.

" Will you take the trouble of reading to us the passages which concern my brother ? "

" No, read it yourself," cried Catherine, whose second thoughts were clearer. " I do not know what I was thinking of," (blushing again that she had blushed before). " James only means to give me good advice."

He gladly received the letter ; and, having read it through with close attention, returned it, saying, " Well, if it is to be so, I can only say that I am sorry for it. Frederick will not be the first man who has chosen a wife with less sense than his family expected. I do not envy his situation, either as a lover or a son."

Miss Tilney, at Catherine's invitation, now read the letter likewise ; and, having expressed also her concern and surprize, began to inquire into Miss Thorpe's connexions and fortune.

" Her mother is a very good sort of woman," was Catherine's answer.

" What was her father ? "

" A lawyer, I believe. They live at Putney."

" Are they a wealthy family ? "

" No, not very. I do not believe Isabella has any fortune at all ; but that will not signify in your family. Your father is so very liberal ! He told me the other day, that he only valued money as it allowed him to promote the happiness of his children." The brother and sister looked at each other. " But," said Eleanor, after a short pause, " would it be to promote his happiness to enable him to marry such a girl ? She must be an unprincipled one, or she could not have used your brother so. And how strange an infatuation on Frederick's side ! A girl, who, before his eyes, is violating an engagement voluntarily entered into with another man ! Is not it inconceivable, Henry ? Frederick, too, who always wore his heart so proudly ! who found no woman good enough to be loved."

" That is the most unpromising circumstance, the strongest presumption against him. When I think of his past de-

clarations, I give him up. Moreover, I have too good an
opinion of Miss Thorpe's prudence, to suppose that she
would part with one gentleman before the other was secured.
It is all over with Frederick, indeed ! He is a deceased man ;
defunct in understanding. Prepare for your sister-in-law,
Eleanor ; and such a sister-in-law as you must delight in.
Open, candid, artless, guileless, with affections strong, but
simple, forming no pretensions, and knowing no disguise."

"Such a sister-in-law, Henry, I should delight in,"
said Eleanor, with a smile.

" But, perhaps," observed Catherine, " though she has
behaved so ill by our family, she may behave better by
yours. Now she has really got the man she likes, she may
be constant."

" Indeed, I am afraid she will," replied Henry ; " I am
afraid she will be very constant, unless a baronet should
come in her way ; that is Frederick's only chance. I will
get the Bath paper, and look over the arrivals."

" You think it is all for ambition, then ? And upon
my word, there are some things that seem very like it.
I cannot forget that, when she first knew what my father
would do for them, she seemed quite disappointed that it
was not more. I never was so deceived in any one's
character in my life before."

" Among all the great variety that you have known
and studied."

" My own disappointment and loss in her is very great ;
but, as for poor James, I suppose he will hardly ever recover
it."

" Your brother is certainly very much to be pitied at
present ; but we must not, in our concern for his sufferings, undervalue yours. You feel, I suppose, that, in
losing Isabella, you lose half yourself : you feel a void
in your heart which nothing else can occupy. Society is
becoming irksome ; and as for the amusements in which
you were wont to share at Bath, the very idea of them
without her is abhorrent. You would not, for instance,
now go to a ball for the world. You feel that you have no
longer any friend to whom you can speak with unreserve ;
on whose regard you can place dependence ; or whose

counsel, in any difficulty, you could rely on. You feel all this ? "

"No," said Catherine, after a few moments' reflection, "I do not! ought I? To say the truth, though I am hurt and grieved that I cannot still love her, that I am never to hear from her, perhaps never to see her again, I do not feel so very, very much afflicted as one would have thought."

"You feel, as you always do, what is most to the credit of human nature. Such feelings ought to be investigated, that they may know themselves."

Catherine, by some chance or other, found her spirits so very much relieved by this conversation, that she could not regret her being led on, though so unaccountably, to mention the circumstance which had produced it.

CHAPTER XXVI

FROM this time the subject was frequently canvassed by the three young people ; and Catherine found, with some surprize, that her two young friends were perfectly agreed in considering Isabella's want of consequence and fortune as likely to throw great difficulties in the way of her marrying their brother. Their persuasion that the General would, upon this ground alone, independent of the objection that might be raised against her character, oppose the connexion, turned her feelings moreover with some alarm towards herself. She was as insignificant, and perhaps as portionless as Isabella ; and if the heir of the Tilney property had not grandeur and wealth enough in himself, at what point of interest wer the demands of his younger brother to rest? The very painful reflections to which this thought led, could only be dispersed by a dependence on the effect of that particular partiality, which, as she was given to understand by his words as well as his actions, she had from the first been so fortunate as to excite in the General ; and by a recollection of some most generous and disinterested sentiments on the subject of money, which she had more than once heard him utter, and which tempted her to think his disposition in such matters misunderstood by his children.

They were so fully convinced, however, that their brother would not have the courage to apply in person for his father's consent, and so repeatedly assured her that he had never in his life been less likely to come to Northanger than at the present time, that she suffered her mind to be at ease as to the necessity of any sudden removal of her own. But as it was not to be supposed that Captain Tilney, whenever he made his application, would give his father any just idea of Isabella's conduct, it occurred to her as highly expedient that Henry should lay the whole business before him as it really was, enabling the General by that means to form a cool and impartial opinion, and prepare his objections on a fairer ground than inequality of situations. She proposed it to him accordingly ; but he did not catch at the measure so eagerly as she had expected. "No," said he ; "my father's hands need not be strengthened, and Frederick's confession of folly need not be forestalled. He must tell his own story."

"But he will only tell half of it."

"A quarter would be enough."

A day or two passed away and brought no tidings of Captain Tilney. His brother and sister knew not what to think. Sometimes it appeared to them as if his silence would be the natural result of the suspected engagement, and at others that it was wholly incompatible with it. The General, mean while, though offended every morning by Frederick's remissness in writing, was free from any real anxiety about him ; and had no more pressing solicitude than that of making Miss Morland's time as Northanger pass pleasantly. He often expressed his uneasiness on this head, "feared the sameness of every day's society and employments would disgust her with the place, wished the Lady Frasers had been in the country, talked every now and then of having a large party to dinner, and once or twice began even to calculate the number of young dancing people in the neighbourhood. But then it was such a dead time of year, no wild-fowl, no game, and the Lady Frasers were not in the country." And it all ended, at last, in his telling Henry, one morning, that when he next went to Woodston, they would take him by surprize there some day or other, and eat their mutton with him. Henry was greatly honoured and very happy, and Catherine was quite delighted with the scheme. "And when do you think, sir, I may look forward to this pleasure? I must be at Woodston on Monday to attend the parish meeting, and shall probably be obliged to stay two or three days."

"Well, well, we will take our chance some one of those days. There is no need to fix. You are not to put yourself at all out of your way. Whatever you may happen to have in the house will be enough. I think I can answer for the young ladies making allowance for a bachelor's table. Let me see; Monday will be a busy day with you; we will not come on Monday; and Tuesday will be a busy one with me. I expect my surveyor from Brockham with his report in the morning; and afterwards I cannot, in decency, fail attending the club. I really could not face my acquaintance if I staid away now; for, as I am known to be in the country, it would be taken exceedingly amiss; and it is a rule with me, Miss Morland, never to give offence to any of my neighbours if a small sacrifice of time and attention can prevent it. They are a set of very worthy men. They have half a buck from Northanger twice a year; and I dine with them whenever I can. Tuesday, therefore, we may say, is out of the question. But on Wednesday, I think, Henry, you may expect us; and we shall be with you early, that we may have time to look about us. Two hours and three-quarters will carry us to Woodston, I suppose; we shall be in the carriage by ten; so, about a quarter before one on Wednesday, you may look for us."

A ball itself could not have been more welcome to Catherine than this little excursion, so strong was her desire to be acquainted with Woodston; and her heart was still bounding with joy, when Henry, about an hour afterwards, came booted and great-coated into the room where she and Eleanor were sitting, and said, "I am come, young ladies, in a very moralizing strain, to observe that our pleasures in this world are always to be paid for, and that we often purchase them at a great disadvantage, giving ready-monied, actual happiness for a draft on the future that may not be honoured. Witness myself at this present hour. Because I am to hope for the satisfaction of seeing you at Woodston on Wednesday, which bad weather, or twenty other causes may prevent, I must go away directly, two days before I intended it."

" Go away," said Catherine, with a very long face, " and why ? "

" Why ! How can you ask the question ? Because no time is to be lost in frightening my old housekeeper out of her wits : because I must go and prepare a dinner for you, to be sure."

" Oh ! not seriously ! "

" Ay, and sadly too ; for I had much rather stay."

" But how can you think of such a thing after what the General said ? When he so particularly desired you not to give yourself any trouble, because *anything* would do."

Henry only smiled. " I am sure it is quite unnecessary upon your sister's account, and mine. You must know it to be so ; and the General made such a point of your providing nothing extraordinary ; besides, if he had not said half so much as he did, he has always such an excellent dinner at home, that sitting down to a middling one for one day could not signify."

" I wish I could reason like you, for his sake and my own. Good-bye. As to-morrow is Sunday, Eleanor, I shall not return."

He went ; and, it being at any time a much simpler operation to Catherine to doubt her own judgment than Henry's, she was very soon obliged to give him credit for being right, however disagreeable to her his going. But the inexplicability of the General's conduct dwelt much on her thoughts. That he was very particular in his eating, she had, by her own unassisted observation, already discovered ; but why he should say one thing so positively, and mean another all the while, was most unaccountable ! How were people, at that rate, to be understood ? Who but Henry could have been aware of what his father was at ?

From Saturday to Wednesday, however, they were
now to be without Henry. This was the sad finale of every
reflection; and Captain Tilney's letter would certainly
come in his absence, and Wednesday, she was very sure,
would be wet. The past, present, and future, were all
equally in gloom. Her brother so unhappy, and her loss
in Isabella so great; and Eleanor's spirits always affected
by Henry's absence! What was there to interest or amuse
her? She was tired of the woods and the shrubberies,
always so smooth and so dry; and the abbey in itself was
no more to her now than any other house. The painful
remembrance of the folly it had helped to nourish and
perfect was the only emotion which could spring from a
consideration of the building. What a revolution in her
ideas! She, who had so longed to be in an abbey. Now,
there was nothing so charming to her imagination as the
unpretending comfort of a well-connected parsonage,
something like Fullerton, but better. Fullerton had its
faults, but Woodston probably had none. If Wednesday
should ever come!

It did come, and exactly when it might be reasonably
looked for. It came; it was fine, and Catherine trod on
air. By ten o'clock the chaise-and-four conveyed the two
from the abbey, and, after an agreeable drive of almost
twenty miles, they entered Woodston, a large and populous
village, in a situation not unpleasant. Catherine was
ashamed to say how pretty she thought it, as the General
seemed to think an apology necessary for the flatness of
the country, and the size of the village; but in her heart
she preferred it to any place she had ever been at, and
looked with great admiration at every neat house above
the rank of a cottage, and at all the little chandler's shops
which they passed. At the further end of the village,
and tolerably disengaged from the rest of it, stood the parsonage, a new-built substantial stone house, with its semi-
circular sweep and green gates; and, as they drove up to
the door, Henry, with the friends of his solitude, a large
Newfoundland puppy and two or three terriers, was ready
to receive and make much of them.

Catherine's mind was too full, as she entered the house, for her either to observe or to say a great deal ; and, till called on by the General for her opinion of it, she had very little idea of the room in which she was sitting. Upon looking round it then, she perceived in a moment that it was the most comfortable room in the world; but she was too guarded to say so, and the coldness of her praise disappointed him.

"We are not calling it a good house," said he, "We are not comparing it with Fullerton and Northanger. We are considering it as a mere parsonage, small and confined we allow, but decent perhaps and habitable ; and altogether not inferior to the generality ; or, in other words, I believe there are few country parsonages in England half so good. It may admit of improvement, however. Far be it from me to say otherwise; and anything in reason—a bow thrown out, perhaps ; though, between ourselves, if there is one thing more than another my aversion, it is a patched-on bow."

Catherine did not hear enough of this speech to understand or be pained by it ; and other subjects being studiously brought forward and supported by Henry, at the same time that a tray full of refreshments was introduced by his servant, the General was shortly restored to his complacency, and Catherine to all her usual ease of spirits.

The room in question was of a commodious, well-proportioned size, and handsomely fitted up as a dining parlour ; and on their quitting it to walk round the grounds, she was shewn, first into a smaller apartment belonging peculiarly to the master of the house, and made unusually tidy on the occasion ; and afterwards into what was to be the drawing-room, with the appearance of which, though unfurnished, Catherine was delighted enough even to satisfy the General. It was a prettily-shaped room, the windows reaching to the ground, and the view from them pleasant, though only over green meadows ; and she expressed her admiration at the moment with all the honest simplicity with which she felt it. "Oh ! why do not you fit up this room, Mr Tilney ? What a pity not to have it fitted up ! It is the prettiest room I ever saw; it is the prettiest room in the world ! "

"I trust," said the General, with a most satisfied smile,

" that it will very speedily be furnished : it waits only for a lady's taste."

" Well, if it was my house, I should never sit anywhere else. Oh what a sweet little cottage there is among the trees ; apple trees too ! It is the prettiest cottage—"

" You like it : you approve it as an object ; it is enough. Henry, remember that Robinson is spoken to about it. The cottage remains."

Such a compliment recalled all Catherine's consciousness, and silenced her directly ; and, though pointedly applied to by the General for her choice of the prevailing colour of the paper and hangings, nothing like an opinion on the subject could be drawn from her. The influence of fresh objects and fresh air, however, was of great use in dissipating these embarrassing associations ; and, having reached the ornamental part of the premises, consisting of a walk round two sides of a meadow, on which Henry's genius had begun to act about half a year ago, she was sufficiently recovered to think it prettier than any pleasure-ground she had ever been in before, though there was not a shrub in it higher than the green bench in the corner.

A saunter into other meadows, and through part of the village, with a visit to the stables to examine some improvements, and a charming game of play with a litter of puppies just able to roll about, brought them to four o'clock, when Catherine scarcely thought it would be three. At four they were to dine, and at six to set off on their return. Never had any day passed so quickly !

She could not but observe that the abundance of the dinner did not seem to create the smallest astonishment in the General ; nay, that he was even looking at the side-table for cold meat which was not there. His son and daughter's observations were of a different kind. They had seldom seen him eat so heartily at any table but his own ; and never before known him so little disconcerted by the melted butter's being oiled.

At six o'clock, the General having taken his coffee, the carriage again received them ; and so gratifying had been the tenor of his conduct throughout the whole visit, so well assured was her mind on the subject of his expectations, that, could she have felt equally confident of the wishes of his son, Catherine would have quitted Woodston with little anxiety as to the How or the When she might return to it.

CHAPTER XXVII

THE next morning brought the following very unexpected letter from Isabella :—

"Bath, April ——

"MY DEAREST CATHERINE—I received your two kind letters with the greatest delight, and have a thousand apologies to make for not answering them sooner. I really am quite ashamed of my idleness ; but in this horrid place one can find time for nothing. I have had my pen in my hand to begin a letter to you almost every day since you left Bath, but have always been prevented by some silly trifle or other. Pray write to me soon, and direct to my own home. Thank God ! we leave this vile place to-morrow. Since you went away I have had no pleasure in it ; the dust is beyond anything ; and everybody one cares for is gone. I believe if I could see you I should not mind the rest, for you are dearer to me than anybody can conceive. I am quite uneasy about your dear brother, not having heard from him since he went to Oxford ; and am fearful of some misunderstanding. Your kind offices will set all right : he is the only man I ever did or could love, and I trust you will convince him of it. The spring fashions are partly down, and the hats the most frightful you can imagine. I hope you spend your time pleasantly, but am afraid you never think of me. I will not say all that I could of the family you are with, because I would not be ungenerous, or set you against those you esteem ; but it is very difficult to know whom to trust, and young men never know their minds two days together. I rejoice to say, that the young man, whom of all others, I particularly abhor, has left Bath. You will know, from this description, I must mean Captain Tilney, who, as you may remember, was amazingly disposed to follow and tease me, before you went away. Afterwards he got worse, and became quite my shadow. Many

girls might have been taken in, for never were such attentions ; but I knew the fickle sex too well. He went away
to his regiment two days ago, and I trust I shall never be
plagued with him again. He is the greatest coxcomb I
ever saw, and amazingly disagreeable. The last two days
he was always by the side of Charlotte Davis : I pitied his
taste, but took no notice of him. The last time we met
was in Bath Street, and I turned directly into a shop that
he might not speak to me : I would not even look at him.
He went into the Pump-room afterwards, but I would not
have followed him for all the world. Such a contrast between him and your brother ! Pray send me some news of
the latter ; I am quite unhappy about him ; he seemed so
uncomfortable when he went away, with a cold, or something that affected his spirits. I would write to him myself,
but have mislaid his direction ; and, as I hinted above, am
afraid he took something in my conduct amiss. Pray
explain everything to his satisfaction ; or, if he still harbours
any doubt, a line from himself to me, or a call at Putney
when next in town, might set all to rights. I have not
been to the Rooms this age, nor to the Play, except going
in last night with the Hodges's, for a frolic, at half-price :
they teased me into it ; and I was determined they should
not say I shut myself up because Tilney was gone. We
happened to sit by the Mitchells, and the pretended to be
quite surprized to see me out. I knew their spite : at one
time they could not be civil to me, but now they are all
friendship ; but I am not such a fool to be taken in by them.
You know I have a pretty good spirit of my own. Anne
Mitchell had tried to put on a turban like mine, as I wore
it the week before at the Concert, but made wretched work
of it. It happened to become my odd face, I believe, at
least Tilney told me so at the time, and said every eye was
upon me ; but he is the last man whose word I would take.
I wear nothing but purple now : I know I look hideous
in it, but no matter ; it is your dear brother's favourite
colour. Lose no time, my dearest, sweetest Catherine,
in writing to him and to me.—Who ever am, &c."

Such a strain of shallow artifice could not impose even

upon Catherine. Its inconsistencies, contradictions, and falsehood, struck her from the very first. She was ashamed of Isabella, and ashamed of having ever loved her. Her professions of attachment were now as disgusting as her excuses were empty, and her demands impudent. " Write to James on her behalf ! No ! James should never hear Isabella's name mentioned by her again."

On Henry's arrival from Woodston she made known to him and Eleanor their brother's safety, congratulating them with sincerity on it, and reading aloud the most material passages of her letter with strong indignation. When she had finished it :—" So much for Isabella," she cried, " and for all our intimacy ! She must think me an idiot, or she could not have written so ; but perhaps this has served to make her character better known to me than mine is to her. I see what she has been about. She is a vain coquette, and her tricks have not answered. I do not believe she had ever any regard either for James or for me, and I wish I had never known her."

" It will soon be as if you never had," said Henry.

" There is but one thing that I cannot understand. I see that she has had designs on Captain Tilney which have not succeeded ; but I do not understand what Captain Tilney has been about all this time. Why should he pay her such attentions as to make her quarrel with my brother, and then fly off himself ? "

" I have very little to say for Frederick's motives, such as I believe them to have been. He has his vanities as well as Miss Thorpe, and the chief difference is, that having a stronger head they have not yet injured himself. If the *effect* of his behaviour does not justify him with you, we had better not seek after the cause."

" Then you do not suppose he ever really cared about her ? "

" I am persuaded that he never did."

" And only made believe to do so for mischief's sake ? "

Henry bowed his assent.

" Well, then, I must say that I do not like him at all. Though it has turned out so well for us, I do not like him at all. As it happens, there is no great harm done, because

I do not think Isabella has any heart to lose. But suppose he had made her very much in love with him ? "

" But we must first suppose Isabella to have had a heart to lose, consequently to have been a very different creature ; and, in that case, she would have met with very different treatment."

" It is very right that you should stand by your brother."

" And if you would stand by *your's*, you would not be much distressed by the disappointment of Miss Thorpe. But your mind is warped by an innate principle of general integrity, and, therefore, not accessible to the cool reasonings of family partiality, or a desire of revenge."

Catherine was complimented out of further bitterness. Frederick could not be unpardonably guilty while Henry made himself so agreeable. She resolved on not answering Isabella's letter, and tried to think no more of it.

CHAPTER XXVIII

Soon after this, the General found himself obliged to go to London for a week ; and he left Northanger, earnestly regretting that any necessity should rob him, even for an hour, of Miss Morland's company, and anxiously recommending the study of her comfort and amusement to his children, as their chief object in his absence. His departure gave Catherine the first experimental conviction that a loss may be sometimes a gain. The happiness with which their time now passed, every employment voluntary, every laugh indulged, every meal a scene of ease and good-humour, walking where they liked and when they liked, their hours, pleasures, and fatigues at their own command, made her thoroughly sensible of the restraint which the General's presence had imposed, and most thankfully feel their present release from it. Such ease and such delights made her love the place and the people more and more every day ; and had it not been for a dread of its soon becoming expedient to leave the one, and an apprehension of not being equally beloved by the other, she would at each moment of each day have been perfectly happy ; but

she was now in the fourth week of her visit; before the
General came home, the fourth week would be turned,
and perhaps it might seem an intrusion if she staid much
longer. This was a painful consideration whenever it
occurred; and eager to get rid of such a weight on her mind,
she very soon resolved to speak to Eleanor about it at once,
propose going away, and be guided in her conduct by the
manner in which her proposal might be taken.

Aware that if she gave herself much time, she might
feel it difficult to bring forward so unpleasant a subject,
she took the first opportunity of being suddenly alone
with Eleanor, and of Eleanor's being in the middle of
a speech about something very different, to start forth
her obligation of going away very soon. Eleanor looked
and declared herself much concerned. She had " hoped
for the pleasure of her company for a much longer time—
had been misled (perhaps by her wishes) to suppose that
a much longer visit had been promised, and could not but
think that if Mr and Mrs Morland were aware of the pleasure
it was to have her there, they would be too generous to
hasten her return." Catherine explained. " Oh! as to
that, papa and mamma were in no hurry at all. As long
as she was happy, they would always be satisfied."

" Then why, might she ask, in such a hurry herself
to leave them? "

" Oh! because she had been there so long."

" Nay, if you can use such a word, I can urge you no
farther. If you think it long—"

" Oh no! I do not, indeed. For my own pleasure,
I could stay with you as long again." And it was directly
settled that, till she had, her leaving them was not even
to be thought of. In having this cause of uneasiness so
pleasantly removed, the force of the other was likewise
weakened. The kindness, the earnestness of Eleanor's
manner in pressing her to stay, and Henry's gratified look
on being told that her stay was determined, were such
sweet proofs of her importance with them, as left her only
just so much solicitude as the human mind can never do
comfortably without. She did, almost always, believe that
Henry loved her, and quite always that his father and sister

loved and even wished her to belong to them ; and believing so far, her doubts and anxieties were merely sportive irritations.

Henry was not able to obey his father's injunction of remaining wholly at Northanger, in attendance on the ladies, during his absence in London ; the engagements of his curate at Woodston obliging him to leave them on Saturday for a couple of nights. His loss was not now what it had been while the General was at home ; it lessened their gaiety, but did not ruin their comfort ; and the two girls, agreeing in occupation, and improving in intimacy, found themselves so well-sufficient for the time to themselves, that it was eleven o'clock, rather a late hour at the abbey, before they quitted the supper-room on the day of Henry's departure. They had just reached the head of the stairs, when it seemed, as far as the thickness of the walls would allow them to judge, that a carriage was driving up to the door, and the next moment confirmed the idea by the loud noise of the house-bell. After the first perturbation of surprize had passed away, in a " Good Heaven ! what can be the matter ? " it was quickly decided by Eleanor to be her eldest brother, whose arrival was often as sudden, if not quite so unseasonable and accordingly she hurried down to welcome him.

Catherine walked on to her chamber, making up her mind, as well as she could, to a further acquaintance with Captain Tilney, and comforting herself under the unpleasant impression his conduct had given her, and the persuasion of his being by far too fine a gentleman to approve of her, that at least they should not meet under such circumstances as would make their meeting materially painful. She trusted he would never speak of Miss Thorpe, and, indeed, as he must by this time be ashamed of the part he had acted, there could be no danger of it ; and as long as all mention of Bath scenes were avoided, she thought she could behave to him very civilly. In such considerations time passed away, and it was certainly in his favour that Eleanor should be so glad to see him, and have so much to say, for half an hour was almost gone since his arrival, and Eleanor did not come up.

At that moment Catherine thought she heard her step in the gallery, and listened for its continuance, but all was silent. Scarcely, however, had she convicted her fancy of error, when the noise of something moving close to her door made her start; it seemed as if some one was touching the very doorway, and in another moment a slight motion of the lock proved that some hand must be on it. She trembled a little at the idea of anyone's approaching so cautiously, but resolving not to be again overcome by trivial appearances of alarm, or misled by a raised imagination, she stepped quietly forward, and opened the door. Eleanor, and only Eleanor, stood there. Catherine's spirits, however, were tranquillized but for an instant, for Eleanor's cheeks were pale, and her manner greatly agitated. Though evidently intending to come in, it seemed an effort to enter the room, and a still greater to speak when there. Catherine, supposing some uneasiness on Captain Tilney's account, could only express her concern by silent attention, obliged her to be seated, rubbed her temples with lavender water, and hung over her with affectionate solicitude. "My dear Catherine, you must not, you must not, indeed——" were Eleanor's first connected words. "I am quite well. This kindness distracts me. I cannot bear it. I come to you on such an errand:"

"Errand! to me!"

"How shall I tell you? Oh! how shall I tell you?"

A new idea now darted into Catherine's mind, and turning as pale as her friend, she exclaimed, "'Tis a messenger from Woodston!"

"You are mistaken, indeed," returned Eleanor, looking at her most compassionately, "it is no one from Woodston. It is my father himself." Her voice faltered, and her eyes were turned to the ground as she mentioned his name. His unlooked-for return was enough in itself to make Catherine's heart sink, and for a few moments she hardly supposed there were anything worse to be told.

She said nothing; and Eleanor, endeavouring to collect herself and speak with firmness, but with eyes still cast down, soon went on. "You are too good, I am sure, to think the worst of me for the part I am obliged to perform.

I am, indeed, a most unwilling messenger. After what has so lately passed, so lately been settled between us, how joyfully, how thankfully, on my side! as to your continuing here, as I hoped, for many, many weeks longer, how can I tell you that your kindness is not to be accepted, and that the happiness your company has hitherto given us is to be repaid by——but I must not trust myself with words. My dear Catherine, we are to part. My father has recollected an engagement that takes our whole family away on Monday; we are going to Lord Longtown's, near Hereford, for a fortnight. Explanation and apology are equally impossible. I cannot attempt either."

"My dear Eleanor," cried Catherine, suppressing her feelings as well as she could, " do not be so distressed. A second engagement must give way to a first. I am very, very sorry we are to part so soon, and so suddenly too, but I am not offended, indeed I am not. I can finish my visit here, you know, at any time; or I hope you will come to me. Can you, when you return from this lord's, come to Fullerton? "

" It will not be in my power, Catherine."

" Come when you can, then."

Eleanor made no answer; and Catherine's thoughts recurring to something more directly interesting, she added, thinking aloud, " Monday; so soon as Monday; and you *all* go! Well, I am certain of——I shall be able to take leave, however. I need not go till just before you do, you know. Do not be distressed, Eleanor; I can go on Monday very well. My father and mother's having no notice of it is of very little consequence. The General will send a servant with me, I dare say, half the way; and then I shall soon be at Salisbury, and then I am only nine miles from home."

" Ah, Catherine! were it settled so, it would be somewhat less intolerable; though in such common attentions, you would have received but half what you ought. But, how can I tell you? To-morrow morning is fixed for your leaving us, and not even the hour is left to your choice; the very carriage is ordered, and will be here at seven o'clock, and no servant will be offered you."

Catherine sat down breathless and speechless. " I could hardly believe my senses when I heard it ; and no displeasure, no resentment that you can feel at this moment, however justly great, can be more than I myself—but I must not talk of what I felt. Oh, that I could suggest anything in extenuation ! Good God ! what will your father and mother say ? After courting you from the protection of real friends to this, almost double distance from your home, to have you driven out of the house, without the considerations even of decent civility ! Dear, dear Catherine, in being the bearer of such a message, I seem guilty myself of all its insult ; yet I trust you will acquit me, for you must have been long enough in this house to see that I am but a nominal mistress of it, that my real power is nothing."

" Have I offended the General ? " said Catherine, in a faltering voice.

" Alas ! for my feelings as a daughter, all that I know, all that I answer for is, that you can have given him no just cause of offence. He certainly is greatly, very greatly discomposed ; I have seldom seen him more so. His temper is not happy, and something has now occurred to ruffle it in an uncommon degree ; some disappointment, some vexation, which just at this moment seems important ; but which I can hardly suppose you to have any concern in ; for how is it possible ? "

It was with pain that Catherine could speak at all ; and it was only for Eleanor's sake that she attempted it. " I am sure," said she, " I am very sorry if I have offended him. It was the last thing I would willingly have done. But do not be unhappy, Eleanor. An engagement, you know, must be kept. I am only sorry it was not recollected sooner, that I might have written home. But it is of very little consequence."

" I hope, I earnestly hope that to your real safety it will be of none ; but to everything else it is of the greatest conse-quence ; to comfort, appearance, propriety, to your family, to the world. Were your friends, the Allens, still in Bath, you might go to them with comparative ease ; a few hours would take you there ; but a journey of seventy miles, to be taken post by you, at your age, alone, unattended ! "

"Oh! the journey is nothing. Do not think about that. And if we are to part, a few hours sooner or later, you know, makes no difference. I can be ready by seven. Let me be called in time." Eleanor saw that she wished to be alone; and believing it better for each that they should avoid any further conversation, now left her with, " I shall see you in the morning."

Catherine's swelling heart needed relief. In Eleanor's presence friendship and pride had equally restrained her tears, but no sooner was she gone than they burst forth in torrents. Turned from the house, and in such a way ! Without any reason that could justify, any apology that could atone for the abruptness, the rudeness, nay, the insolence of it. Henry at a distance; not able even to bid him farewell. Every hope, every expectation from him suspended, at least, and who could say how long ? Who could say when they might meet again ? And all this by such a man as General Tilney : so polite, so well-bred, and heretofore so particularly fond of her ! It was as incomprehensible as it was mortifying and grievous. From what it could arise, and where it would end, were considerations of equal perplexity and alarm. The manner in which it was done so grossly uncivil : hurrying her away without any reference to her own convenience, or allowing her even the appearance of choice as to the time or mode of her travelling ; of two days, the earliest fixed on, and of that almost the earliest hour, as if resolved to have her gone before he was stirring in the morning, that he might not be obliged even to see her. What could all this mean but an intentional affront ? By some means or other she must have had the misfortune to offend him. Eleanor had wished to spare her from so painful a notion, but Catherine could not believe it possible that any injury or any misfortune could provoke such ill-will against a person not connected, or, at least, not supposed to be connected with it.

Heavily passed the night. Sleep, or repose that deserved the name of sleep, was out of the question. That room, in which her disturbed imagination had tormented her on her first arrival, was again the scene of agitated spirits and unquiet slumbers. Yet how different now the source of her inquietude from what it had been then , how mournfully superior in reality and substance ! Her anxiety had foundation in fact, her fears in probability ; and with a mind so occupied in the contemplation of actual and natural evil, the solitude of her situation, the darkness of her chamber, the antiquity of the building, were felt and considered without the smallest emotion ; and though the wind was high, and often produced strange and sudden noises throughout the house, she heard it all as she lay awake, hour after hour, without curiosity or terror.

Soon after six Eleanor entered her room, eager to show attention, or give assistance where it was possible ; but very little remained to be done. Catherine had not loitered ; she was almost dressed, and her packing almost finished. The possibility of some conciliatory message from the General occurred to her as his daughter appeared. What so natural, as that anger should pass away and repentance succeed it ? and she only wanted to know how far, after what had passed, an apology might properly be received by her. But the knowledge would have been useless here, it was not called for ; neither clemency nor dignity was put to the trial ; Eleanor brought no message. Very little passed between them on meeting : each found her greatest safety in silence ; and few and trivial were the sentences exchanged while they remained upstairs ; Catherine in busy agitation completing her dress, and Eleanor, with more good-will than experience, intent upon filling the trunk. When everything was done, they left the room, Catherine lingering only half a minute behind her friend to throw a parting glance on every well-known cherished object, and went down to the breakfast-parlour, where breakfast was prepared. She tried to eat, as well to save herself from the pain of being urged, as to make her friend comfortable ; but she had no appetite, and could not swallow many mouthfuls. The contrast between this and her last breakfast in that room gave her fresh misery, and strengthened her distaste for everything before her. It was not four-and-twenty hours ago since they had met there to the same repast, but in circumstances how different ! With what cheerful ease, what happy, though false security, had she then looked around her, enjoying everything present, and fearing little in future, beyond Henry's going to Woodston for a day ! Happy, happy breakfast ! for Henry had been there ; Henry had sat by her and helped her. These reflections were long indulged undisturbed by any address from her companion, who sat as deep in thought as herself ; and the appearance of the carriage was the first thing to startle and recall them to the present moment. Catherine's colour rose at the sight of it ; and the indignity with which she was treated striking, at that instant, on her mind with peculiar force, made her for a short time sensible only of resentment. Eleanor seemed now impelled into resolution and speech.

"You *must* write to me, Catherine," she cried ; "you *must* let me hear from you as soon as possible. Till I know you to be safe at home, I shall not have an hour's comfort. For *one* letter at all risks, all hazards, I must entreat. Let me have the satisfaction of knowing that you are safe at Fullerton, and have found your family well ; and then, till I can ask for your correspondence as I ought to do, I will not expect more. Direct to me at Lord Longtown's, and, I must ask it, under cover to Alice."

"No, Eleanor, if you are not allowed to receive a letter from me, I am sure I had better not write. There can be no doubt of my getting home safe."

Eleanor only replied, "I cannot wonder at your feelings. I will not importune you. I will trust to your own kindness of heart when I am at a distance from you." But this, with the look of sorrow accompanying it, was enough to melt Catherine's pride in a moment, and she instantly said, "Oh ! Eleanor, I *will* write to you, indeed ! "

There was yet another point which Miss Tilney was anxious to settle, though somewhat embarrassed in speaking of. It had occurred to her, that after so long an absence from home, Catherine might not be provided with money enough for the expenses of her journey, and, upon suggesting it to her with most affectionate offers of accommodation, it proved to be exactly the case. Catherine had never thought on the subject till that moment ; but, upon examining her purse, was convinced that but for this kindness of her friend, she might have been turned from

the house without even the means of getting home ; and
the distress in which she must have been thereby involved
filling the minds of both, scarcely another word was said
by either during the time of their remaining together.
Short, however, was that time. The carriage was soon
announced to be ready ; and Catherine instantly rising,
a long and affectionate embrace supplied the place of language
in bidding each other adieu ; and, as they entered the hall,
unable to leave the house without some mention of one whose
name had not yet been spoken by either, she paused a
moment, and with quivering lips just made it intelligible
that she left " her kind remembrance for her absent friend."
But with this approach to his name ended all possibility
of restraining her feelings ; and, hiding her face as well
as she could with her handkerchief, she darted across the
hall, jumped into the chaise, and in a moment was driven
from the door.

CHAPTER XXIX

CATHERINE was too wretched to be fearful. The journey
in itself had no terrors for her ; and she began it without
either dreading its length, or feeling its solitariness. Leaning back in one corner of the carriage, in a violent burst
of tears, she was conveyed some miles beyond the walls
of the abbey before she raised her head ; and the highest
point of ground within the park was almost closed from
her view before she was capable of turning her eyes towards
it. Unfortunately, the road she now travelled was the same
which only ten days ago she had so happily passed along in
going to and from Woodston ; and, for fourteen miles,
every bitter feeling was rendered more severe by the review of objects on which she had first looked under impressions so different. Every mile, as it brought her nearer
Woodston, added to her sufferings ; and when within the
distance of five, she passed the turning which led to it,
and thought of Henry, so near, yet so unconscious, her grief
and agitation were excessive.

The day which she had spent at that place had been one

of the happiest of her life.   It was there, it was on that day
that the General had made use of such expressions with
regard to Henry and herself, had so spoken and so looked
as to give her the most positive conviction of his actually
wishing their marriage.   Yes, only ten days ago had he
elated her by his pointed regard—had he even confused
her by his too significant reference !   And now, what had
she done, or what had she omitted to do, to merit such a
change ?

The only offence against him, of which she could accuse
herself, had been such as was scarcely possible to reach
his knowledge.   Henry and her own heart only were privy
to the shocking suspicions which she had so idly entertained ;
and equally safe did she believe her secret with each.   Designedly, at least, Henry could not have betrayed her.
If, indeed, by any strange mischance his father should have
gained intelligence of what she had dared to think and
look for, of her causeless fancies and injurious examinations,
she could not wonder at any degree of his indignation.   If
aware of her having viewed him as a murderer, she could
not wonder as his even turning her from his house.   But
a justification so full of torture to herself she trusted would
not be in his power.

Anxious as were all her conjectures on this point, it was
not, however, the one on which she dwelt most.   There
was a thought yet nearer ; a more prevailing, more im-
petuous concern ; how Henry would think, and feel, and
look, when he returned on the morrow to Northanger,
and heard of her being gone, was a question of force and
interest to rise over every other, to be never-ceasing, alter-
nately irritating and soothing : it sometimes suggested
the dread of his calm acquiescence, and at others was
answered by the sweetest confidence in his regret and
resentment.   To the General, of course, he would not
dare to speak ; but to Eleanor, what might he not say to
Eleanor about her ?

In this unceasing recurrence of doubts and inquiries,
on any one article of which her mind was incapable of
more than momentary repose, the hours passed away, and
her journey advanced much faster than she looked for.

The pressing anxieties of thought which prevented her from noticing anything before her, when once beyond the neighbourhood of Woodston, saved her at the same time from watching her progress ; and though no object on the road could engage a moment's attention, she found no stage of it tedious. From this she was preserved, too, by another cause ; by feeling no eagerness for her journey's conclusion ; for to return in such a manner to Fullerton was almost to destroy the pleasure of a meeting with those she loved best, even after an absence such as hers : an eleven weeks' absence. What had she to say that would not humble herself and pain her family ; that would not increase her own grief by the confession of it ; extend an useless resentment, and perhaps involve the innocent with the guilty in undistinguishing ill-will ? She could never do justice to Henry and Eleanor's merit : she felt it too strongly for expression, and should a dislike be taken against them, should they be thought of unfavourably on their father's account, it would cut her to the heart.

With these feelings, she rather dreaded than sought for the first view of that well-known spire which would announce her within twenty miles of home. Salisbury she had known to be her point on leaving Northanger, but after the first stage, she had been indebted to the post-masters for the names of the places which were then to conduct her it to ; so great had been her ignorance of her route. She met with nothing, however, to distress or frighten her. Her youth, civil manners, and liberal pay, procured her all the attention that a traveller like herself could require ; and stopping only to change horses, she travelled on for about eleven hours without accident or alarm, and between six and seven o'clock in the evening found herself entering Fullerton.

A heroine returning at the close of her career, to her native village, in all the triumph of recovered reputution, and all the dignity of a countess, with a long train of noble relations in their several phaetons, and three waiting-maids in a travelling chaise-and-four behind her, is an event on which the pen of the contriver may well delight to dwell ; it gives credit to every conclusion, and the author must share in the glory she so liberally bestows. But my affair is widely different; I bring back my heroine to her home in solitude and disgrace, and no sweet elation of spirits can lead me into minuteness. A heroine in a hack post-chaise is such a blow upon sentiment as no attempt at grandeur or pathos can withstand. Swiftly, therefore, shall her post-boy drive through the village, amid the gaze of Sunday groups, and speedy shall be her descent from it.

But whatever might be the distress of Catherine's mind as she thus advanced towards the parsonage, and whatever the humiliation of her biographer in relating it, she was preparing enjoyment of no every-day nature for those to whom she went; first, in the appearance of her carriage, and secondly, in herself. The chaise of a traveller being a rare sight in Fullerton, the whole family were immediately at the window; and to have it stop at the sweep-gate was a pleasure to brighten every eye, and occupy every fancy; a pleasure quite unlooked for by all but the two youngest children, a boy and girl of six and four years old, who expected a brother or sister in every carriage. Happy the glance that first distinguished Catherine ! Happy the voice that proclaimed the discovery ! But whether such happiness were the lawful property of George or Harriet, could never be exactly understood.

Her father, mother, Sarah, George, and Harriet, all assembled at the door, to welcome her with affectionate eagerness, was a sight to awaken the best feelings of Catherine's heart; and in the embrace of each, as she stepped from the carriage, she found herself soothed beyond anything. that she had believed possible. So surrounded, so caressed, she was even happy ! In the joyfulness of family love, everything, for a short time, was subdued; and the pleasure of seeing her, leaving them at first little leisure for calm curiosity, they were all seated round the tea-table, which Mrs Morland had hurried for the comfort of the poor traveller, whose pale and jaded looks soon caught her notice, before any inquiry so direct as to demand a positive answer was addressed to her.

Reluctantly, and with much hesitation, did she then begin what might, perhaps, at the end of half an hour, be termed by the courtesy of her hearers an explanation ; but scarcely, within that time, could they at all discover the cause, or collect the particulars of her sudden return. They were far from being an irritable race ; far from any quickness in catching, or bitterness in resenting affronts ; but here, when the whole was unfolded, was an insult not to be overlooked, nor, for the first half hour, to be easily pardoned. Without suffering any romantic alarm in the consideration of their daughter's long and lonely journey, Mr and Mrs Morland could not but feel that it might have been productive of much unpleasantness to her ; that it was what they could never have voluntarily suffered ; and that, in forcing her on such a measure, General Tilney had acted neither honourably nor feelingly, neither as a gentleman nor as a parent. Why he had done it, what could have provoked him to such a breach of hospitality, and so suddenly turned all his partial regard for their daughter into actual ill-will, was a matter which they were at least as far from divining as Catherine herself : but it did not oppress them by any means so long ; and, after a due course of useless conjecture, that "it was a strange business, and that he must be a very strange man," grew enough for all their indignation and wonder ; though Sarah, indeed, still indulged in the sweets of incomprehensibility, exclaiming and conjecturing with youthful ardour—"My dear, you give yourself a great deal of needless trouble," said her mother at last ; "depend upon it, it is something not at all worth understanding."

"I can allow for his wishing Catherine away when he recollected this engagement," said Sarah ; "but why not do it civilly ?"

"I am sorry for the young people," returned Mrs Morland ; "they must have a sad time of it ; but as far anything else, it is no matter now : Catherine is safe at home, and our comfort does not depend upon General Tilney." Catherine sighed. "Well," continued her philosophic mother, "I am glad I did not know of your journey at the time ; but now it is all over, perhaps there is no great harm done. It is always good for young people to be put upon exerting themselves ; and you know, my dear Catherine, you always were a sad little shatter-brained creature : but now you must have been forced to have your wits about you, with so much changing of chaises and so forth ; and I hope it will appear that you have not left anything behind you in any of the pockets."

Catherine hoped so too, and tried to feel an interest in her own amendment, but her spirits were quite worn down ; and to be silent and alone becoming soon her only wish ; she readily agreed to her mother's next counsel of going early to bed. Her parents seeing nothing in her ill-looks and agitation but the natural consequence of morti-fied feelings, and of the unusual exertion and fatigue of such a journey, parted from her without any doubt of their being soon slept away ; and though, when they all met the next morning, her recovery was not equal to their hopes, they were still perfectly unsuspicious of there being any deeper evil. They never once thought of her heart, which, for the parents of a young lady of seventeen, just returned from her first excursion from home, was odd enough !

As soon as breakfast was over, she sat down to fulfil her promise to Miss Tilney, whose trust in the effect of time and distance on her friend's disposition was already justified, for already did Catherine reproach herself with having parted from Eleanor coldly ; with having never enough valued her merits or kindness ; and never enough commiserated her for what she had been yesterday left to endure. The strength of these feelings, however, was far from assisting her pen ; and never had it been harder for her to write than in addressing Eleanor Tilney. To compose a letter which might at once do justice to her sentiments and her situation, convey gratitude without servile regret, be guarded without coldness, and honest without resentment ; a letter which Eleanor might not be pained by the perusal of ; and, above all, which she might not blush herself, if Henry should chance to see, was an undertaking to frighten away all her powers of performance ; and, after long thought and much perplexity, to be very brief was all that she could determine on which any con-fidence of safety. The money, therefore, which Eleanor had advanced, was enclosed with little more than grateful thanks, and the thousand good wishes of a most affectionate heart.

"This has been a strange acquaintance," observed Mrs Morland, as the letter was finished; "soon made and soon ended. I am sorry it happens so, for Mrs Allen thought them very pretty kind of young people; and you were sadly out of luck too, in your Isabella. Ah, poor James! Well, we must live and learn; and the next new friends you make I hope will be better worth keeping."

Catherine coloured as she warmly answered, "No friend can be better worth keeping than Eleanor."

"If so, my dear, I dare say you will meet again some time or other; do not be uneasy. It is ten to one but you are thrown together again in the course of a few years; and then, what a pleasure it will be!"

Mrs Morland was not happy in her attempt at consolation. The hope of meeting again in the course of a few years could only put into Catherine's head what might happen within that time to make a meeting dreadful to her. She could never forget Henry Tilney, or think of him with less tenderness than she did at that moment, but he might forget her, and in that case to meet—! Her eyes filled with tears as she pictured her acquaintance so renewed; and her mother perceiving her comfortable suggestions to have had no good effects, proposed, as another expedient for restoring her spirits, that they should call on Mrs Allen.

The two houses were only a quarter of a mile apart; and, as they walked, Mrs Morland quickly despatched all that she felt on the score of James's disappointment. "We are sorry for him," said she; "but otherwise there is no harm done in the match going off; for it could not be a desirable thing to have him engaged to a girl whom we had not the smallest acquaintance with, and who was so entirely without fortune; and now after such behaviour, we cannot think at all well of her. Just at present it comes hard to poor James, but that will not last for ever; and I dare say he will be a discreeter man all his life, for the foolishness of his first choice."

This was just such a summary view of the affair as Cath-

erine could listen to : another sentence might have endangered her complaisance, and made her reply less rational ;
for soon were all her thinking powers swallowed up in the
reflection of her own change of feelings and spirits since
last she had trodden that well-known road. It was not
three months ago since, wild with joyful expectation, she
had there run backwards and forwards some ten times
a-day, with an heart light, gay, and independent ; looking
forward to pleasures untasted and unalloyed, and as free
from the apprehension of evil as from the knowledge of
it. Three months ago had seen her all this, and now, how
altered a being did she return !

She was received by the Allens with all the kindness
which her unlooked-for appearance, acting on a steady
affection, would naturally call forth ; and great was their
surprize, and warm their displeasure, on hearing how she
had been treated, though Mrs Morland's account of it
was no inflated representation, no studied appeal to their
passions. " Catherine took us quite by surprize yesterday
evening," said she. " She travelled all the way post by
herself, and knew nothing of coming till Saturday night ;
for General Tilney, from some odd fancy or other, all of a
sudden grew tired of having her there, and almost turned
her out of the house. Very unfriendly, certainly ; and he
must be a very odd man ; but we are so glad to have her
amongst us again ! And it is a great comfort to find that
she is not a poor helpless creature, but can shift very well
for herself."

Mr Allen expressed himself on the occasion with the
reasonable resentment of a sensible friend ; and Mrs Allen
thought his expressions quite good enough to be immediately
made use of again by herself. His wonder, his conjectures,
and his explanations, became in succession hers, with the
addition of this single remark : " I really have not patience
with the General," to fill up every accidental pause ; and
" I really have not patience with the General," was uttered
twice after Mr Allen left the room, without any relaxation
of anger, or any material digression of thought. A more
considerable degree of wandering attended the third repetition ; and, after completing the fourth, she immediately

added, " Only think, my dear, of my having got that frightful
great rent in my best Mechlin. so charmingly mended,
before I left Bath, that one can hardly see where it was.
I must shew it you some day or other.   Bath is a nice place,
Catherine, after all.   I assure you I did not above half
like coming away.   Mrs Thorpe's being there was such a
comfort to us, was not it ?   You know, you and I were
quite forlorn at first."

" Yes, but *that* did not last long," said Catherine, her
eyes brightening at the recollection of what had first given
spirit to her existence.

" Very true :   we soon meet with Mrs Thorpe, and then
we wanted for nothing.   My dear, do not you think these
silk gloves wear very well ?   I put them on new the first
time of our going to the Lower Rooms, you know, and I
have worn them a great deal since.   Do you remember
that evening ? "

" Do I !   Oh !   perfectly."

" It was very agreeable, was not it ?   Mr Tilney drank
tea with us, and I always thought him a great addition ;
he is so very agreeable.   I have a notion you danced
with him, but am not quite sure.   I remember I had my
favourite gown on."

Catherine could not answer ;   and, after a short trial
of other subjects, Mrs Allen again returned to—" I really
have not patience with the General !   Such an agreeable
worthy man as he seemed to be !   I do not suppose, Mrs
Morland, you ever saw a better-bred man in your life.
His lodgings were taken the very day after he left them,
Catherine.   But no wonder ;   Milsom Street, you know."

As they walked home again, Mrs Morland endeavoured
to impress on her daughter's mind the happiness of having
such steady well-wishers as Mr and Mrs Allen, and the
very little consideration which the neglect or unkindness
of slight acquaintance like the Tilneys ought to have with
her, while she could preserve the good opinion and affection
of her earliest friends.   There was a great deal of good
sense in all this ; but there are some situations of the human
mind in which good sense has very little power ;   and
Catherine's feelings contradicted almost every position

her mother advanced. It was upon the behaviour of these very slight acquaintance that all her present happiness depended ; and while Mrs Morland was successfully confirming her own opinions by the justness of her own representations, Catherine was silently reflecting that *now* Henry must have arrived at Northanger ; *now* he must have heard of her departure ; and *now*, perhaps, they were all setting off for Hereford.

CHAPTER XXX

CATHERINE'S disposition was not naturally sedentary, nor had her habits been ever very industrious ; but, whatever might hitherto have been her defects of that sort, her mother could not but perceive them now to be greatly increased. She could neither sit still nor employ herself for ten minutes together ; walking round the garden and orchard again and again, as if nothing but motion was voluntary ; and it seemed as if she could even walk about the house rather than remain fixed for any time in the parlour. Her loss of spirits was a yet greater alteration. In her rambling and her idleness, she might only be a caricature of herself ; but in her silence and sadness, she was the very reverse of all that she had been before.

For two days Mrs Morland allowed it to pass even without a hint ; but when a third night's rest had neither restored her cheerfulness, improved her in useful activity, nor given her a greater inclination for needlework, she could no longer refrain from the gentle reproof of, " My dear Catherine, I am afraid you are growing quite a fine lady. I do not know when poor Richard's cravats would be done, if he had no friend but you. Your head runs too much upon Bath ; but there is a time for everything—a time for balls and plays, and a time for work. You have had a long run of amusement, and now you must try to be useful."

Catherine took up her work directly, saying, in a dejected voice, that " her head did not run upon Bath—much."

" Then you are fretting about General Tilney, and that is very simple of you ; for ten to one whether you ever see

him again. You should never fret about trifles." After
a short silence : " I hope, my Catherine, you are not getting
out of humour with home, because it is not so grand as
Northanger. That would be turning your visit into an
evil, indeed. Wherever you are, you should always be
contented, but especially at home, because there you must
spend the most of your time. I did not quite like, at breakfast, to hear you talk so much about the French bread at
Northanger."

" I am sure I do not care about the bread. It is all the
same to me what I eat."

" There is a very clever essay in one of the books upstairs upon much such a subject, about young girls who
have been spoilt for home by great acquaintance : ' The
Mirror,' I think. I will look it out for you some day or
other, because I am sure it will do you good."

Catherine said no more ; and, with an endeavour to
do right, applied to her work ; but, after a few minutes,
sunk again, without knowing it herself, into languor and
listlessness ; moving herself in her chair, from the irritation
of weariness, much oftener than she moved her needle.
Mrs Morland watched the progress of this relapse ; and
seeing, in her daughter's absent and dissatisfied look,
the full proof of that repining spirit to which she had now
begun to attribute her want of cheerfulness, hastily left
the room to fetch the book in question, anxious to lose
no time in attacking so dreadful a malady. It was some
time before she could find what she looked for ; and other
family matters occurring to detain her, a quarter of an hour
had elapsed ere she returned down stairs with the volume
from which so much was hoped. Her avocations above
having shut out all noise but what she created herself,
she knew not that a visitor had arrived within the last
few minutes, till, on entering the room, the first object she
beheld was a young man whom she had never seen before.
With a look of much respect, he immediately rose, and being
introduced to her by her conscious daughter as " Mr Henry
Tilney," with the embarrassment of real sensibility, began
to apologise for his appearance there, acknowledging that
after what had passed he had little right to expect a welcome

at Fullerton, and stating his impatience to be assured of Miss Morland's having reached her home in safety, as the cause of his intrusion. He did not address himself to an uncandid judge or a resentful heart. Far from comprehending him or his sister in their father's misconduct, Mrs Morland had been always kindly disposed towards each ; and instantly, pleased by his appearance, received him with the simple professions of unaffected benevolence ; thanking him for such an attention to her daughter ; assuring him that the friends of her children were always welcome there, and intreating him to say not another word of the past.

He was not ill inclined to obey this request ; for though his heart was greatly relieved by such unlooked-for mildness, it was not, just at that moment, in his power to say anything to the purpose. Returning in silence to his seat, therefore, he remained for some minutes most civilly answering all Mrs Morland's common remarks about the weather and roads. Catherine, meanwhile, the anxious, agitated, happy, feverish Catherine, said not a word : but her glowing cheek and brightened eye made her mother trust that this good-natured visit would, at least, set her heart at ease for a time ; and gladly, therefore, did she lay aside the first volume of " The Mirror " for a future hour.

Desirous of Mr Morland's assistance, as well in giving encouragement as in finding conversation for her guest, whose embarrassment on his father's account she earnestly pitied, Mrs Morland had very early despatched one of the children to summon him ; but Mr Morland was from home, and being thus without any support, at the end of a quarter of an hour she had nothing to say. After a couple of minutes' unbroken silence, Henry, turning to Catherine for the first time since her mother's entrance, asked her, with sudden alacrity, if Mr and Mrs Allen were now at Fullerton ? and on developing, from amidst all her perplexity of words in reply, the meaning, which one short syllable would have given, immediately expressed his intention of paying his respects to them, and with a rising colour, asked her if she would have the goodness to shew him the way. " You may see the house from this window, sir," was information,

on Sarah's side, which produced only a bow of acknowledgment from the gentleman, and a silencing nod from
her mother; for Mrs Morland, thinking it probable, as
a secondary consideration in his wish of waiting on their
worthy neighbours, that he might have some explanation
to give of his father's behaviour, which it must be more
pleasant for him to communicate only to Catherine, would
not, on any account, prevent her accompanying him.
They began their walk, and Mrs Morland was not entirely
mistaken in his object in wishing it. Some explanation
on his father's account he had to give; but his first purpose
was to explain himself; and before they reached Mr Allen's
grounds he had done it so well that Catherine did not
think it could ever be repeated too often. She was assured
of his affection; and that heart in return was solicited,
which, perhaps, they pretty equally knew was already
entirely his own; for, though Henry was now sincerely
attached to her—though he felt and delighted in all the
excellencies of her character, and truly loved her society—
I must confess that his affection originated in nothing
better than gratitude; or, in other words, that a persuasion
of her partiality for him had been the only cause of giving
her a serious thought. It is a new circumstance in romance,
I acknowledge, and dreadfully derogatory of an heroine's
dignity; but if it be as new in common life, the credit of
a wild imagination will at least be all my own.

A very short visit to Mrs Allen, in which Henry talked
at random, without sense or connection, and Catherine,
wrapt in the contemplation of her own unutterable happiness,
scarcely opened her lips, dismissed them to the extasies
of another tête-à-tête; and before it was suffered to close,
she was enabled to judge how far he was sanctioned by
parental authority in his present application. On his
return from Woodston, two days before, he had been met
near the abbey by his impatient father, hastily informed
in angry terms of Miss Morland's departure, and ordered
to think of her no more.

Such was the permission upon which he had now offered
her his hand. The affrighted Catherine, amidst all the
terrors of expectation, as she listened to this account,

could not but rejoice in the kind caution with which Henry had saved her from the necessity of a conscientious rejection, by engaging her faith before he mentioned the subject ; and as he proceeded to give the particulars, and explain the motives of his father's conduct, her feelings soon hardened into even a triumphant delight. The General had had nothing to accuse her of, nothing to lay to her charge, but her being the involuntary, unconscious object, of a deception which his pride could not pardon, and which a better pride would have been ashamed to own. She was guilty only of being less rich than he had supposed her to be. Under a mistaken persuasion of her possessions and claims, he had courted her acquaintance in Bath, solicited her company at Northanger, and designed her for his daughter-in-law. On discovering his error, to turn her from the house seemed the best, though to his feelings an inadequate proof, of his resentment towards herself, and his contempt of her family.

John [Thorpe] had first misled him. The General perceiving his son one night at the theatre, to be paying considerable attention to Miss Morland, had accidentally inquired of Thorpe if he knew more of her than her name. Thorpe, most happy to be on speaking terms with a man of General Tilney's importance, had been joyfully and proudly communicative ; and being at that time not only in daily expectation of Morland's engaging Isabella, but likewise pretty well resolved upon marrying Catherine himself, his vanity induced him to represent the family as yet more wealthy than his vanity and avarice had made him believe them. With whomsoever he was, or was likely to be connected, his own consequence always required that theirs should be great ; and as his intimacy with any acquaintance grew, so regularly grew their fortune. The expectations of his friend Morland, therefore, from the first over-rated, had, ever since his introduction to Isabella, been gradually increasing ; and by merely adding twice as much for the grandeur of the moment, by doubling what he chose to think the amount of Mr Morland's preferment, trebling his private fortune, bestowing a rich aunt, and sinking half the children, he was able to represent the

whole family to the General in a most respectable light.
For Catherine, however, the peculiar object of the General's
curiosity and his own speculations, he had yet something more in reserve; and the ten or fifteen thousand
pounds which her father could give her, would be a pretty
addition to Mr Allen's estate. Her intimacy there had
made him seriously determined on her being handsomely
legacied hereafter; and to speak of her, therefore, as the
most acknowledged future heiress of Fullerton, naturally followed. Upon such intelligence the General had proceeded,
for never had it occurred to him to doubt its authority.
Thorpe's interest in the family, by his sister's approaching
connection with one of its members, and his own views
on another (circumstances of which he boasted with almost
equal openness), seemed sufficient vouchers for his truth;
and to these were added, the absolute facts of the Allens
being wealthy and childless, of Miss Morland's being under
their care, and, as soon as his acquaintance allowed him
to judge, of their treating her with parental kindness.
His resolution was soon formed. Already had he discerned a liking towards Miss Morland in the countenance
of his son; and, thankful for Mr Thorpe's communication,
he almost instantly determined to spare no pains in weakening his boasted interest, and ruining his dearest hopes.
Catherine herself could not be more ignorant at the time
of all this than his own children. Henry and Eleanor,
perceiving nothing in her situation likely to engage their
father's particular respect, had seen with astonishment
the suddenness, continuance, and extent of his attention;
and though latterly, from some hints which had accompanied an almost positive command to his son, of doing
everything in his power to attach her, Henry was convinced of his father's believing it to be an advantageous
connection, it was not till the late explanation at Northanger
that they had the smallest idea of the false calculations
which had hurried him on. That they were false, the General
had learned from the very person who had suggested them,
from Thorpe himself, whom he had chanced to meet again
in town; and who, under the influence of exactly opposite
feelings, irritated by Catherine's refusal, and yet more by

the failure of a very recent endeavour to accomplish a reconciliation between Morland and Isabella, convinced that they were separated for ever, and spurning a friendship which could be no longer serviceable, hastened to contradict all that he had said before to the advantage of the Morlands : confessed himself to have been totally mistaken in his opinion of their circumstances and character, misled by the rhodo-montade of his friend to believe his father a man of sub-stance and credit, whereas the transactions of the two or three last weeks proved him to be neither ; for, after coming eagerly forward on the first overture of a marriage between the families, with the most liberal proposals, he had, on being brought to the point, by the shrewdness of the relator, been constrained to acknowledge himself incapable of giving the young people even a decent support. They were, in fact, a necessitous family ; numerous too, almost beyond example ; by no means respected in their own neighbourhood, as he had lately had particular oppor-tunities of discovering ; aiming at a style of life which their fortune could not warrant ; seeking to better themselves by wealthy connexions ; a forward, bragging, scheming race.

The terrified General pronounced the name of Allen with an inquiring look ; and here, too, Thorpe had learnt his error. The Allens, he believed, had lived near them too long, and he knew the young man on whom the Fullerton estate must devolve. The General needed no more. En-raged with almost everybody in the world but himself, he set out the day next for the abbey, where his performances have been seen.

I leave it to my reader's sagacity to determine how much of all this it was possible for Henry to communicate at this time to Catherine ; how much of it he could have learnt from his father, in what point his own conjectures might assist him, and what portion must yet remain to be told in a letter from James. I have united for their ease what they must divide for mine. Catherine, at any rate, heard enough to feel, that, in suspecting General Tilney of either murdering or shutting up his wife, she had scarcely sinned against his character or magnified his cruelty.

Henry, in having such things to relate of his father,

was almost as pitiable as in their first avowal to himself. He blushed for the narrow-minded counsel which he was obliged to expose. The conversation between them at Northanger had been of the most unfriendly kind. Henry's indignation on hearing how Catherine had been treated, on comprehending his father's views, and being ordered to acquiesce in them, had been open and bold. The General accustomed on every ordinary occasion to give the law in his family, prepared for no reluctance but of feeling, no opposing desire that should dare to clothe itself in words, could ill brook the opposition of his son, steady as the sanction of reason and the dictate of conscience could make it. But, in such a cause, his anger, though it must shock, could not intimidate Henry, who was sustained in his purpose by a conviction of its justice. He felt himself bound as much in honour as in affection to Miss Morland, and believing that heart to be his own which he had been directed to gain, no unworthy retraction of a tacit consent, no reversing decree of unjustifiable anger, could shake his fidelity, or influence the resolutions it prompted.

He steadily refused to accompany his father into Herefordshire, an engagement formed almost at the moment, to promote the dismissal of Catherine, and as steadily declared his intention of offering her his hand. The General was furious in his anger, and they parted in dreadful disagreement. Henry, in an agitation of mind which many solitary hours were required to compose, had returned almost instantly to Woodston; and on the afternoon of the following day had begun his journey to Fullerton.

CHAPTER XXXI

Mr and Mrs Morland's surprize on being applied to by Mr Tilney for their consent to his marrying their daughter, was, for a few minutes, considerable; it having never entered their heads to suspect an attachment on either side; but as nothing, after all, could be more natural than Catherine's being beloved, they soon learnt to consider it with only the happy agitation of gratified pride; and, as far as they alone were concerned, had not a single objection to start. His pleasing manners and good sense were self-evident recommendations ; and having never heard evil of him, it was not their way to suppose any evil could be told. Good-will supplying the place of experience, his character needed no attestation. " Catherine would made a sad, heedless young housekeeper, to be sure," was her mother's foreboding remark ; but quick was the consolation of there being nothing like practice.

There was but one obstacle, in short, to be mentioned : but till that one was removed, it must be impossible for them to sanction the engagement. Their tempers were mild, but their principles were steady ; and while his parent so expressly forbad the connexion, they could not allow themselves to encourage it. That the General should come forward to solicit the alliance, or that he should even very heartily approve it, they were not refined enough to make any parading stipulation, but the decent appearance of consent must be yielded, and that once obtained, and their own hearts made them trust that it could not be very long denied, their willing approbation was instantly to follow. His *consent* was all that they wished for. They were no more inclined than entitled to demand his *money*. Of a very considerable fortune, his son was, by marriage settlements, eventually secure ; his present income was an income of independence and comfort, and under every pecuniary view it was a match beyond the claims of their daughter.

The young people could not be surprized at a decision like this. They felt and they deplored, but they could not resent it ; and they parted, endeavouring to hope that such a change in the General, as each believed almost impossible, might speedily take place, to unite them again in the fullness of privileged affection. Henry returned to what was now his only home, to watch over his young plantations, and extend his improvements for her sake, to whose share in them he looked anxiously forward ; and Catherine remained at Fullerton to cry. Whether the torments of absence were softened by a clandestine correspondence, let us not inquire. Mr and Mrs Morland never did ; they had been too kind to exact any promise, and whenever Catherine received a letter, as at that time happened pretty often, they always looked another way.

The anxiety which in this state of their attachment must be the portion of Henry and Catherine, and of all who loved either, as to its final event, can hardly extend, I fear, to the bosom of my readers, who will see in the tell-tale compression of the pages before them, that we are all hastening together to perfect felicity. The means by which their early marriage was effected can be the only doubt : what probable circumstance could work upon a temper like the General's ? The circumstance which chiefly availed was the marriage of his daughter with a man of fortune and consequence, which took place in the course of the summer : an accession of dignity that threw him into a fit of good humour, from which he did not recover till after Eleanor had obtained his forgiveness of Henry, and his permission for him " to be a fool if he liked it."

The marriage of Eleanor Tilney, her removal from all the evils of such a home as Northanger had been made by Henry's banishment, to the home of her choice and the man of her choice, is an event which I expect to give general satisfaction among all her acquaintance. My own joy on the occasion is very sincere. I know no one more entitled by unpretending merit, or better prepared by habitual suffering, to receive and enjoy felicity. Her partiality for this gentleman was not of recent origin, and he had been long withheld only by inferiority of situation from addressing her. His unexpected accession to title and fortune had removed all his difficulties ; and never had the General loved his daughter so well in all her hours of companionship, utility, and patient endurance, as when he first hailed her, " Your Ladyship ! " Her husband was really deserving of her, independent of his peerage, his wealth, and his attachment, being to a precision the most charming young man in the world. Any further definition of his merits must be unnecessary : the most charming young man in the world is instantly before the imagination of us all. Concerning the one in question, therefore, I have only to add (aware that the rules of composition forbid the introduction of a character not connected with my fable) that this was the very gentleman whose negligent servant left behind him that collection of washing-bills, resulting from a long visit at Northanger, by which my heroine was involved in one of her most alarming adventures.

The influence of the Viscount and Viscountess in their brother's behalf was assisted by that right understanding of Mr Morland's circumstances, which, as soon as the General would allow himself to be informed, they were qualified to give. It taught him that he had been scarcely more misled by Thorpe's first boast of the family wealth than by his subsequent malicious overthrow of it ; that in no sense of the word were they necessitous or poor, and that Catherine would have three thousand pounds. This was so material an amendment of his late expectations, that it greatly contributed to smooth the descent of his pride ; and by no means without its effect was the private intelligence which he was at some pains to procure, that the Fullerton estate, being entirely at the disposal of its present proprietor, was consequently open to every greedy speculation.

On the strength of this the General, soon after Eleanor's marriage, permitted his son to return to Northanger, and thence made him the bearer of his consent, very courteously worded in a page full of empty professions, to Mr Morland. The event which it authorized soon followed : Henry and Catherine were married, the bells rang and everybody smiled ; and, as this took place within a twelvemonth from the first day of their meeting, it will not appear, after all the dreadful delays occasioned by the General's cruelty, that they were essentially hurt by it. To begin perfect happiness at the respective ages of twenty-six and eighteen is to do pretty well ; and professing myself, moreover, convinced that the General's unjust interference, so far from being really injurious to their felicity, was perhaps rather conducive to it, by improving their knowledge of each other, and adding strength to their attachment, I leave it to be settled by whomsoever it may concern, whether the tendency of this work be altogether to recommend parental tyranny or reward filial disobedience.

PERSUASION

PERSUASION

CHAPTER I

SIR WALTER ELLIOT, of Kellynch Hall, in Somersetshire, was a man who, for his own amusement, never took up any book but the Baronetage; there he found occupation for an idle hour, and consolation in a distressed one; there his faculties were roused into admiration and respect by contemplating the limited remnant of the earliest patents; there any unwelcome sensations arising from domestic affairs changed naturally into pity and contempt as he turned over the almost endless creations of the last century; and there, if every other leaf were powerless, he could read his own history with an interest which never failed. This was the page at which the favourite volume always opened:—

" ELLIOT OF KELLYNCH HALL

" Walter Elliot, born March 1, 1760, married July 15, 1784, Elizabeth, daughter of James Stevenson, Esq. of South Park, in the county of Gloucester; by which lady (who died 1800) he has issue, Elizabeth, born June 1, 1785; Anne, born August 9, 1787; a still-born son, November 5, 1789; Mary, born November 20, 1791."

Precisely such had the paragraph originally stood from the printer's hands; but Sir Walter had improved it by adding, for the information of himself and his family, these words, after the date of Mary's birth:—" Married, December 16, 1810, Charles, son and heir of Charles Musgrove, Esq. of Uppercross, in the county of Somerset," and by inserting most accurately the day of the month on which he had lost his wife.

Then followed the history and rise of the ancient and respectable family in the usual terms; how it had been first settled in Cheshire, how mentioned in Dugdale, serving the office of high sheriff, representing a borough in three successive parliaments, exertions of loyalty, and dignity of baronet, in the first year of Charles II. with all the Marys and Elizabeths they had married; forming altogether two handsome duodecimo pages, and concluding with the arms and motto:—" Principal seat, Kellynch Hall, in the county of Somerset," and Sir Walter's handwriting again in this finale:—

" Heir presumptive, William Walter Elliot, Esq., great grandson of the second Sir Walter."

Vanity was the beginning and end of Sir Walter Elliot's character: vanity of person and of situation. He had been remarkably handsome in his youth, and at fifty-four was still a very fine man. Few women could think more of their personal appearance than he did, nor could the valet of any new made lord be more delighted with the place he held in society. He considered the blessing of beauty as inferior only to the blessing of a baronetcy; and the Sir Walter Elliot, who united these gifts, was the constant object of his warmest respect and devotion.

His good looks and his rank had one fair claim on his attachment, since to them he must have owed a wife of very superior character to anything deserved by his own. Lady Elliot had been an excellent woman, sensible and amiable, whose judgment and conduct, if they might be pardoned the youthful infatuation which made her Lady Elliot, had never required indulgence afterwards. She had humoured, or softened, or concealed his failings, and promoted his real respectability for seventeen years; and though not the very happiest being in the world herself, had found enough in her duties, her friends, and her children, to attach her to life, and make it no matter of indifference to her when she was called on to quit them. Three girls, the two eldest sixteen and fourteen, was an awful legacy for a mother to bequeath, an awful charge rather, to confide to the authority and guidance of a conceited, silly father. She had, however, one very intimate friend, a sensible, deserving woman, who had been brought, by strong attachment to herself, to settle close by her, in the village of Kellynch; and on her kindness and advice Lady Elliot mainly relied for the best help and maintainance of the good principles and instruction which she had been anxiously giving her daughters.

This friend and Sir Walter did *not* marry, whatever might have been anticipated on that head by their acquaintance. Thirteen years had passed away since Lady Elliot's death, and they were still near neighbours and intimate friends, and one remained a widower, the other a widow.

That Lady Russell, of steady age and character, and extremely well provided for, should have no thought of a second marriage, needs no apology to the public, which is rather apt to be unreasonably discontented when a woman *does* marry again, than when she does *not ;* but Sir Walter's continuing in singleness requires explanation. Be it known, then, that Sir Walter, like a good father (having met with one or two private disappointments in very unreasonable applications), prided himself on remaining single for his dear daughter's sake. For one daughter, his eldest, he would really have given up anything, which he had not been very much tempted to do. Elizabeth had succeeded at sixteen to all that was possible of her mother's rights and conse- quence; and being very handsome, and very like himself, her influence had always been great, and they had gone on together most happily. His two other children were of very inferior value. Mary had acquired a little artificial import- ance by becoming Mrs. Charles Musgrove; but Anne, with an elegance of mind and sweetness of character, which must have placed her high with any people of real understanding, was nobody with either father or sister; her word had no weight, her convenience was always to give way—she was only Anne.

To Lady Russell, indeed, she was a most dear and highly valued god-daughter, favourite, and friend. Lady Russell loved them all, but it was only in Anne that she could fancy the mother to revive again.

A few years before Anne Elliot had been a very pretty

girl, but her bloom had vanished early; and as, even in its height, her father had found little to admire in her (so totally different were her delicate features and mild dark eyes from his own), there could be nothing in them, now that she was faded and thin, to excite his esteem. He had never indulged much hope, he had now none, of ever reading her name in any other page of his favourite work. All equality of alliance must rest with Elizabeth, for Mary had merely connected herself with an old country family of respectability and large fortune, and had, therefore, *given* all the honour and received none: Elizabeth would, one day or other, marry suitably.

It sometimes happens that a woman is handsomer at twenty-nine than she was ten years before; and, generally speaking, if there has been neither ill health nor anxiety, it is a time of life at which scarcely any charm is lost. It was so with Elizabeth, still the same handsome Miss Elliot that she had begun to be thirteen years ago, and Sir Walter might be excused, therefore, in forgetting her age, or, at least, be deemed only half a fool, for thinking himself and Elizabeth as blooming as ever, amidst the wreck of the good looks of everybody else; for he could plainly see how old all the rest of his family and acquaintance were growing. Anne haggard, Mary coarse, every face in the neighbourhood worsting, and the rapid increase of the crow's foot about Lady Russell's temples had long been a distress to him.

Elizabeth did not quite equal her father in personal contentment. Thirteen years had seen her mistress of Kellynch Hall, presiding and directing with a self-possession and decision which could never have given the idea of her being younger than she was. For thirteen years had she been doing the honours, and laying down the domestic law at home, and leading the way to the chaise and four, and walking immediately after Lady Russell out of all the drawing-rooms and dining-rooms in the country. Thirteen winters' revolving frosts had seen her opening every ball of credit which a scanty neighbourhood afforded, and thirteen springs shewn their blossoms, as she travelled up to London with her father, for a few weeks' annual enjoyment of the great world. She had the remembrance of all this, she had the consciousness of being nine-and-twenty to give her some regrets and some apprehensions; she was fully satisfied of being still quite as handsome as ever, but she felt her approach to the years of danger, and would have rejoiced to be certain of being properly solicited by baronet-blood within the next twelvemonth or two. Then might she again take up the book of books with as much enjoyment as in her early youth, but now she liked it not. Always to be presented with the date of her own birth and see no marriage follow but that of a youngest sister, made the book an evil; and more than once, when her father had left it open on the table near her, had she closed it, with averted eyes, and pushed it away.

She had had a disappointment, moreover, which that book, and especially the history of her own family, must ever present the remembrance of. The heir presumptive, the very William Walter Elliot, Esq., whose rights had been so generously supported by her father, had disappointed her.

She had, while a very young girl, as soon as she had known him to be, in the event of her having no brother, the future baronet, meant to marry him, and her father had always meant that she should. He had not been known to them as a boy; but soon after Lady Elliot's death, Sir Walter had sought the acquaintance, and though his overtures had not been met with any warmth, he had persevered in seeking it, making allowance for the modest drawing-back of youth; and, in one of their spring excursions to London, when Elizabeth was in her first bloom, Mr. Elliot had been forced into the introduction.

He was at that time a very young man, just engaged in the study of the law; and Elizabeth found him extremely agreeable, and every plan in his favour was confirmed. He was invited to Kellynch Hall; he was talked of and expected all the rest of the year; but he never came. The following spring he was seen again in town, found equally agreeable, again encouraged, invited, and expected, and again he did not come; and the next tidings were that he was married. Instead of pushing his fortune in the line marked out for the heir of the house of Elliot, he had purchased independence by uniting himself to a rich woman of inferior birth.

Sir Walter had resented it. As the head of the house,

he felt that he ought to have been consulted, especially after taking the young man so publicly by the hand; "For they must have been seen together," he observed, "once at Tattersal's, and twice in the lobby of the House of Commons." His disapprobation was expressed, but apparently very little regarded. Mr. Elliot had attempted no apology, and shewn himself as unsolicitous of being longer noticed by the family, as Sir Walter considered him unworthy of it: all acquaintance between them had ceased.

This very awkward history of Mr. Elliot was still, after an interval of several years, felt with anger by Elizabeth, who had liked the man for himself, and still more for being her father's heir, and whose strong family pride could see only in *him* a proper match for Sir Walter Elliot's eldest daughter. There was not a baronet from A to Z whom her feelings could have so willingly acknowledged as an equal. Yet so miserably had he conducted himself, that though she was at this present time (the summer of 1814) wearing black ribbons for his wife, she could not admit him to be worth thinking of again. The disgrace of his first marriage might, perhaps, as there was no reason to suppose it perpetuated by offspring, have been got over, had he not done worse; but he had, as by the accustomary intervention of kind friends, they had been informed, spoken most disrespectfully of them all, most slightingly and contemptuously of the very blood he belonged to, and the honours which were hereafter to be his own. This could not be pardoned.

Such were Elizabeth Elliot's sentiments and sensations; such the cares to alloy, the agitations to vary, the sameness and the elegance, the prosperity and the nothingness of her scene of life; such the feelings to give interest to a long, uneventful residence in one country circle, to fill the vacancies which there were no habits of utility abroad, no talents or accomplishments for home, to occupy.

But now, another occupation and solicitude of mind was beginning to be added to these. Her father was growing distressed for money. She knew, that when he now took up the Baronetage, it was to drive the heavy bills of his tradespeople, and the unwelcome hints of Mr. Shepherd, his agent, from his thoughts. The Kellynch property was good, but

not equal to Sir Walter's apprehension of the state required
in its possessor. While Lady Elliot lived, there had been
method, moderation, and economy, which had just kept him
within his income; but with her had died all such right-
mindedness, and from that period he had been constantly
exceeding it. It had not been possible for him to spend
less: he had done nothing but what Sir Walter Elliot was
imperiously called on to do; but blameless as he was, he
was not only growing dreadfully in debt, but was hearing
of it so often, that it became vain to attempt concealing it
longer, even partially, from his daughter. He had given her
some hints of it the last spring in town; he had gone so far
even as to say, " Can we retrench? Does it occur to you that
there is any one article in which we can retrench? " and
Elizabeth, to do her justice, had, in the first ardour of female
alarm, set seriously to think what could be done, and had
finally proposed these two branches of economy, to cut off
some unnecessary charities, and to refrain from new furnishing
the drawing-room; to which expedients she afterwards added
the happy thought of their taking no present down to Anne,
as had been the usual yearly custom. But these measures,
however good in themselves, were insufficient for the real
extent of the evil, the whole of which Sir Walter found himself
obliged to confess to her soon afterwards. Elizabeth had
nothing to propose of deeper efficacy. She felt herself ill-
used and unfortunate, as did her father; and they were
neither of them able to devise any means of lessening their
expenses without compromising their dignity, or relinquishing their comforts in a way not to be borne.

There was only a small part of his estate that Sir Walter
could dispose of; but had every acre been alienable, it would
have made no difference. He had condescended to mortgage
as far as he had the power, but he would never condescend
to sell. No; he would never disgrace his name so far. The
Kellynch estate should be transmitted whole and entire, as
he had received it.

Their two confidential friends, Mr. Shepherd, who lived
in the neighbouring market town, and Lady Russell, were
called on to advise them; and both father and daughter
seemed to expect that something should be struck out by one

or the other to remove their embarrassments and reduce their expenditure, without involving the loss of any indulgence of taste or pride.

CHAPTER II

MR. SHEPHERD, a civil, cautious lawyer, who, whatever might be his hold or his views on Sir Walter, would rather have the *disagreeable* prompted by anybody else, excused himself from offering the slightest hint, and only begged leave to recommend an implicit reference to the excellent judgment of Lady Russell, from whose known good sense he fully expected to have just such resolute measures advised as he meant to see finally adopted.

Lady Russell was most anxiously zealous on the subject, and gave it much serious consideration. She was a woman rather of sound than of quick abilities, whose difficulties in coming to any decision in this instance were great, from the opposition of two leading principles. She was of strict integrity herself, with a delicate sense of honour; but she was as desirous of saving Sir Walter's feelings, as solicitous for the credit of the family, as aristocratic in her ideas of what was due to them, as anybody of sense and honesty could well be. She was a benevolent, charitable, good woman, and capable of strong attachments, most correct in her conduct, strict in her notions of decorum, and with manners that were held a standard of good-breeding. She had a cultivated mind, and was, generally speaking, rational and consistent; but she had prejudices on the side of ancestry; she had a value for rank and consequence, which blinded her a little to the faults of those who possessed them. Herself the widow of only a knight, she gave the dignity of a baronet all its due; and Sir Walter, independent of his claims as an old acquaintance, an attentive neighbour, an obliging landlord, the husband of her very dear friend, the father of Anne and her sisters, was, as being Sir Walter, in her apprehension, entitled to a great deal of compassion and consideration under his present difficulties.

They must retrench; that did not admit of a doubt. But she was very anxious to have it done with the least possible pain to him and Elizabeth. She drew up plans of economy, she made exact calculations, and she did what nobody else thought of doing: she consulted Anne, who never seemed considered by the others as having any interest in the question. She consulted, and in a degree was influenced by her in marking out the scheme of retrenchment which was at last submitted to Sir Walter. Every emendation of Anne's had been on the side of honesty against importance. She wanted more vigorous measures, a more complete reformation, a quicker release from debt, a much higher tone of indifference for everything but justice and equity.

"If we can persuade your father to all this," said Lady Russell, looking over her paper, "much may be done. If he will adopt these regulations, in seven years he will be clear; and I hope we may be able to convince him and Elizabeth that Kellynch Hall has a respectability in itself which cannot be affected by these reductions; and that the true dignity of Sir Walter Elliot will be very far from lessened in the eyes of sensible people, by his acting like a man of principle. What will he be doing, in fact, but what very many of our first families have done, or ought to do? There will be nothing singular in his case; and it is singularity which often makes the worst part of our suffering, as it always does of our conduct. I have great hope of our prevailing. We must be serious and decided; for after all, the person who has contracted debts must pay them; and though a great deal is due to the feelings of the gentleman, and the head of a house, like your father, there is still more due to the character of an honest man."

This was the principle on which Anne wanted her father to be proceeding, his friends to be urging him. She considered it as an act of indispensable duty to clear away the claims of creditors with all the expedition which the most comprehensive retrenchments could secure, and saw no dignity in anything short of it. She wanted it to be prescribed, and felt as a duty. She rated Lady Russell's influence highly; and as to the severe degree of self-denial which her own conscience prompted, she believed there might be little more difficulty in persuading them to a complete, than to half a reformation. Her knowledge of her father and Elizabeth inclined her to think that the sacrifice of one pair of horses would be hardly less painful than of both, and so on, through the whole list of Lady Russell's too gentle reductions.

How Anne's more rigid requisitions might have been taken is of little consequence. Lady Russell's had no success at all: could not be put up with, were not to be borne. "What! every comfort of life knocked off! Journeys, London, servants, horses, table—contractions and restrictions everywhere! To live no longer with the decencies even of a private gentleman! No, he would sooner quit Kellynch Hall at once, than remain in it on such disgraceful terms."

"Quit Kellynch Hall!" The hint was immediately taken up by Mr. Shepherd, whose interest was involved in the reality of Sir Walter's retrenching, and who was perfectly persuaded that nothing would be done without a change of abode. "Since the idea had been started in the very quarter which ought to dictate, he had no scruple," he said, "in confessing his judgment to be entirely on that side. It did not appear to him that Sir Walter could materially alter his style of living in a house which had such a character of hospitality and ancient dignity to support. In any other place Sir Walter might judge for himself; and would be looked up to, as regulating the modes of life in whatever way he might choose to model his household."

Sir Walter would quit Kellynch Hall; and after a very few days more of doubt and indecision, the great question of whither he should go was settled, and the first outline of this important change made out.

There had been three alternatives, London, Bath, or another house in the country. All Anne's wishes had been for the latter. A small house in their own neighbourhood, where they might still have Lady Russell's society, still be near Mary, and still have the pleasure of sometimes seeing the lawns and groves of Kellynch, was the object of her ambition. But the usual fate of Anne attended her, in having something very opposite from her inclination fixed on. She disliked Bath, and did not think it agreed with her; and Bath was to be her home.

Sir Walter had at first thought more of London; but Mr. Shepherd felt that he could not be trusted in London, and had been skilful enough to dissuade him from it, and make Bath preferred. It was a much safer place for a gentleman in his predicament: he might there be important at comparatively little expense. Two material advantages of Bath over London had of course been given all their weight: its more convenient distance from Kellynch, only fifty miles, and Lady Russell's spending some part of every winter there; and to the very great satisfaction of Lady Russell, whose first views on the projected change had been for Bath, Sir Walter and Elizabeth were induced to believe that they should lose neither consequence nor enjoyment by settling there.

Lady Russell felt obliged to oppose her dear Anne's known wishes. It would be too much to expect Sir Walter to descend into a small house in his own neighbourhood. Anne herself would have found the mortifications of it more than she foresaw, and to Sir Walter's feelings they must have been dreadful. And with regard to Anne's dislike of Bath, she considered it as a prejudice and mistake arising, first, from the circumstance of her having been three years at school there, after her mother's death; and secondly, from her happening to be not in perfectly good spirits the only winter which she had afterwards spent there with herself.

Lady Russell was fond of Bath, in short, and disposed to think it must suit them all; and as to her young friend's health, by passing all the warm months with her at Kellynch Lodge, every danger would be avoided; and it was in fact, a change which must do both health and spirits good. Anne had been too little from home, too little seen. Her spirits were not high. A larger society would improve them. She wanted her to be more known.

The undesirableness of any other house in the same neighbourhood for Sir Walter was certainly much strengthened by one part, and a very material part of the scheme, which had been happily engrafted on the beginning. He was not only to quit his home, but to see it in the hands of others: a trial of fortitude which stronger heads than Sir Walter's have found too much. Kellynch Hall was to be let. This, however, was a profound secret, not to be breathed beyond their own circle.

Sir Walter could not have borne the degradation of being known to design letting his house. Mr. Shepherd had once mentioned the word " advertise," but never dared approach it again. Sir Walter spurned the idea of its being offered in any manner; forbad the slightest hint being dropped of his having such an intention; and it was only on the supposition of his being spontaneously solicited by some most unexceptionable applicant, on his own terms, and as a great favour, that he would let it at all.

How quick come the reasons for approving what we like! Lady Russell had another excellent one at hand, for being extremely glad that Sir Walter and his family were to remove from the country. Elizabeth had been lately forming an intimacy, which she wished to see interrupted. It was with a daughter of Mr. Shepherd, who had returned, after an unprosperous marriage, to her father's house, with the additional burden of two children. She was a clever young woman, who understood the art of pleasing—the art of pleasing, at least, at Kellynch Hall; and who had made herself so acceptable to Miss Elliot, as to have been already staying there more than once, in spite of all that Lady Russell, who thought it a friendship quite out of place, could hint of caution and reserve.

Lady Russell, indeed, had scarcely any influence with Elizabeth, and seemed to love her, rather because she would love her, than because Elizabeth deserved it. She had never received from her more than outward attention, nothing beyond the observances of complaisance; had never succeeded in any point which she wanted to carry, against previous inclination. She had been repeatedly very earnest in trying to get Anne included in the visit to London, sensibly open to all the injustice and all the discredit of the selfish arrangements which shut her out, and on many lesser occasions had endeavoured to give Elizabeth the advantage of her own better judgment and experience; but always in vain: Elizabeth would go her own way; and never had she pursued it in more decided opposition to Lady Russell than in this selection of Mrs. Clay; turning from the society of so deserving a sister, to bestow her affection and confidence on one who ought to have been nothing to her but the object of distant civility.

From situation, Mrs. Clay was, in Lady Russell's estimate, a very unequal, and in her character, she believed, a very dangerous companion; and a removal that would leave Mrs. Clay behind, and bring a choice of more suitable intimates within Miss Elliot's reach, was therefore an object of first-rate importance.

CHAPTER III

" I MUST take leave to observe, Sir Walter," said Mr. Shepherd one morning at Kellynch Hall, as he laid down the newspaper, " that the present juncture is much in our favour. This peace will be turning all our rich naval officers ashore. They will be all wanting a home. Could not be a better time, Sir Walter, for having a choice of tenants, very responsible tenants. Many a noble fortune has been made during the war. If a rich admiral were to come in our way, Sir Walter——"

" He would be a very lucky man, Shepherd," replied Sir Walter; " that's all I have to remark. A prize, indeed, would Kellynch Hall be to him; rather the greatest prize of all, let him have taken ever so many before; hey, Shepherd? "

Mr. Shepherd laughed, as he knew he must, at this wit, and then added—

" I presume to observe, Sir Walter, that, in the way of business, gentlemen of the navy are well to deal with. I have had a little knowledge of their methods of doing business; and I am free to confess that they have very liberal notions, and are as likely to make desirable tenants as any set of people one should meet with. Therefore, Sir Walter, what I would take leave to suggest is, that if in consequence of any rumours getting abroad of your intention; which must be contemplated as a possible thing, because we know how difficult it is to keep the actions and designs of one part of the world from the notice and curiosity of the other; consequence has its tax; I, John Shepherd, might conceal any family-matters that I chose, for nobody would think it worth their while to observe me; but Sir Walter Elliot has eyes upon him which it may be very difficult to elude; and, therefore, thus much I venture upon, that it will not greatly surprise me if, with all our caution, some rumour of the truth should get abroad; in the supposition of which, as I was going to observe, since applications will unquestionably follow, I should think any from our wealthy naval commanders particularly worth attending to; and beg leave to add, that two hours will bring me over at any time, to save you the trouble of replying."

Sir Walter only nodded. But soon afterwards, rising and pacing the room, he observed sarcastically—

"There are few among the gentlemen of the navy, I imagine, who would not be surprised to find themselves in a house of this description."

"They would look around them, no doubt, and bless their good fortune," said Mrs. Clay, for Mrs. Clay was present: her father had driven her over, nothing being of so much use to Mrs. Clay's health as a drive to Kellynch: "but I quite agree with my father in thinking a sailor might be a very desirable tenant. I have known a good deal of the profession; and besides their liberality, they are so neat and careful in all their ways! These valuable pictures of yours, Sir Walter, if you chose to leave them, would be perfectly safe. Everything in and about the house would be taken such excellent care of! The gardens and shrubberies would be kept in almost as high order as they are now. You need not be afraid, Miss Elliot, of your own sweet flower gardens being neglected."

"As to all that," rejoined Sir Walter coolly, "supposing I were induced to let my house, I have by no means made up my mind as to the privileges to be annexed to it. I am not particularly disposed to favour a tenant. The park would be open to him of course, and few navy officers, or men of any other description, can have had such a range; but what restrictions I might impose on the use of the pleasure-grounds is another thing. I am not fond of the idea of my shrubberies being always approachable; and I should recommend Miss Elliot to be on her guard with respect to her flower garden. I am very little disposed to grant a tenant of Kellynch Hall any extraordinary favour, I assure you, be he sailor or soldier."

After a short pause, Mr. Shepherd presumed to say—

" In all these cases there are established usages which make everything plain and easy between landlord and tenant. Your interest, Sir Walter, is in pretty safe hands. Depend upon me for taking care that no tenant has more than his just rights. I venture to hint, that Sir Walter Elliot cannot be half so jealous for his own, as John Shepherd will be for him."

Here Anne spoke—

" The navy, I think, who have done so much for us, have at least an equal claim with any other set of men, for all the comforts and all the privileges which any home can give. Sailors work hard enough for their comforts, we must all allow."

" Very true, very true. What Miss Anne says is very true," was Mr. Shepherd's rejoinder, and " Oh! certainly," was his daughter's; but Sir Walter's remark was, soon afterwards—

" The profession has its utility, but I should be sorry to see any friend of mine belonging to it."

" Indeed! " was the reply, and with a look of surprise.

" Yes; it is in two points offensive to me; I have two strong grounds of objection to it. First, as being the means of bringing persons of obscure birth into undue distinction, and raising men to honours which their fathers and grand-fathers never dreamt of; and, secondly, as it cuts up a man's youth and vigour most horribly; a sailor grows old sooner than any other man. I have observed it all my life. A man is in greater danger in the navy of being insulted by the rise of one whose father his father might have disdained to speak to, and of becoming prematurely an object of disgust himself, than in any other line. One day last spring, in town, I was

in company with two men, striking instances of what I am
talking of: Lord St. Ives, whose father we all know to have
been a country curate, without bread to eat: I was to give
place to Lord St. Ives, and a certain Admiral Baldwin, the
most deplorable-looking personage you can imagine; his face
the colour of mahogany, rough and rugged to the last degree;
all lines and wrinkles, nine grey hairs of a side, and nothing
but a dab of powder at top. ' In the name of heaven, who
is that old fellow?' said I to a friend of mine who was standing near (Sir Basil Morley). ' Old fellow!' cried Sir Basil,
' it is Admiral Baldwin. What do you take his age to be?'
' Sixty,' said I, ' or perhaps sixty-two.' ' Forty,' replied Sir
Basil, ' forty, and no more.' Picture to yourselves my amazement: I shall not easily forget Admiral Baldwin. I never
saw quite so wretched an example of what a sea-faring life
can do; but to a degree, I know it is the same with them all:
they are all knocked about, and exposed to every climate,
and every weather, till they are not fit to be seen. It is a
pity they are not knocked on the head at once, before they
reach Admiral Baldwin's age."

" Nay, Sir Walter," cried Mrs. Clay, " this is being severe
indeed. Have a little mercy on the poor men. We are not
all born to be handsome. The sea is no beautifier, certainly;
sailors do grow old betimes; I have often observed it; they
soon lose the look of youth. But then, is not it the same with
many other professions, perhaps most other? Soldiers, in
active service, are not at all better off; and even in the quieter
professions, there is a toil and a labour of the mind, if not of
the body, which seldom leaves a man's looks to the natural
effect of time. The lawyer plods, quite care-worn: the
physician is up at all hours, and travelling in all weather;
and even the clergyman—" she stopt a moment to consider
what might do for the clergyman—" and even the clergyman, you know, is obliged to go into infected rooms, and
expose his health and looks to all the injury of a poisonous
atmosphere. In fact, as I have long been convinced, though
every profession is necessary and honourable in its turn, it is
only the lot of those who are not obliged to follow any, who
can live in a regular way, in the country, choosing their own
hours, following their own pursuits, and living on their own

property, without the torment of trying for more; it is only *their* lot, I say, to hold the blessings of health and a good appearance to the utmost: I know no other set of men but what lose something of their personableness when they cease to be quite young."

It seemed as if Mr. Shepherd, in this anxiety to bespeak Sir Walter's good will towards a naval officer as tenant, had been gifted with foresight; for the very first application for the house was from an Admiral Croft, with whom he shortly afterwards fell into company in attending the quarter sessions at Taunton; and, indeed, he had received a hint of the Admiral from a London correspondent. By the report which he hastened over to Kellynch to make, Admiral Croft was a native of Somersetshire, who having acquired a very handsome fortune, was wishing to settle in his own country, and had come down to Taunton in order to look at some advertised places in that immediate neighbourhood, which, however, had not suited him; that accidentally hearing—(it was just as he had foretold, Mr. Shepherd observed, Sir Walter's concerns could not be kept a secret)—accidentally hearing of the possibility of Kellynch Hall being to let, and understanding his (Mr. Shepherd's) connection with the owner, he had introduced himself to him in order to make particular inquiries, and had, in the course of a pretty long conference, expressed as strong an inclination for the place as a man who knew it only by description could feel; and given Mr. Shepherd, in his explicit account of himself, every proof of his being a most responsible, eligible tenant.

"And who is Admiral Croft?" was Sir Walter's cold, suspicious inquiry.

Mr. Shepherd answered for his being of a gentleman's family, and mentioned a place; and Anne, after the little pause which followed, added—

"He is rear-admiral of the white. He was in the Trafalgar action, and has been in the East Indies since; he has been stationed there, I believe, several years."

"Then I take it for granted," observed Sir Walter, "that his face is about as orange as the cuffs and capes of my livery."

Mr. Shepherd hastened to assure him, that Admiral Croft

was a very hale, hearty, well-looking man, a little weather-
beaten, to be sure, but not much, and quite the gentleman
in all his notions and behaviour; not likely to make the
smallest difficulty about terms, only wanted a comfortable
home, and to get into it as soon as possible; knew he must
pay for his convenience; knew what rent a ready-furnished
house of that consequence might fetch; should not have been
surprised if Sir Walter had asked more; had inquired about
the manor; would be glad of the deputation, certainly, but
made no great point of it; said he sometimes took out a gun,
but never killed; quite the gentleman.

Mr. Shepherd was eloquent on the subject, pointing out
all the circumstances of the Admiral's family, which made
him peculiarly desirable as a tenant. He was a married man,
and without children; the very state to be wished for. A
house was never taken good care of, Mr. Shepherd observed,
without a lady: he did not know whether furniture might
not be in danger of suffering as much where there was no
lady, as where there were many children. A lady without
a family was the very best preserver of furniture in the world.
He had seen Mrs. Croft too; she was at Taunton with the
Admiral, and had been present almost all the time they were
talking the matter over.

"And a very well-spoken, genteel, shrewd lady, she
seemed to be," continued he; "asked more questions about
the house, and terms, and taxes, than the Admiral himself,
and seemed more conversant with business; and, moreover,
Sir Walter, I found she was not quite unconnected in this
country, any more than her husband; that is to say, she is
sister to a gentleman who did live amongst us once; she told
me so herself; sister to the gentleman who lived a few years
back at Monkford. Bless me! what was his name? At
this moment I cannot recollect his name, though I have heard
it so lately. Penelope, my dear, can you help me to the
name of the gentleman who lived at Monkford: Mrs. Croft's
brother?"

But Mrs. Clay was talking so eagerly with Miss Elliot that
she did not hear the appeal.

"I have no conception whom you can mean, Shepherd;
I remember no gentleman resident at Monkford since the
time of old Governor Trent."

"Bless me! how very odd! I shall forget my own name soon, I suppose. A name that I am so very well acquainted with; knew the gentleman so well by sight; seen him a hundred times; came to consult me once, I remember, about a trespass of one of his neighbours; farmer's man breaking into his orchard; wall torn down; apples stolen; caught in the fact; and afterwards, contrary to my judgment, submitted to an amicable compromise. Very odd, indeed!"

After waiting another moment—

"You mean Mr. Wentworth, I suppose?" said Anne.

Mr. Shepherd was all gratitude.

"Wentworth was the very name! Mr. Wentworth was the very man. He had the curacy of Monkford, you know, Sir Walter, some time back, for two or three years. Came there about the year—5, I take it. You remember him, I am sure."

"Wentworth? Oh ay! Mr. Wentworth, the curate of Monkford. You misled me by the term *gentleman*. I thought you were speaking of some man of property: Mr. Wentworth was nobody, I remember; quite unconnected; nothing to do with the Strafford family. One wonders how the names of many of our nobility become so common."

As Mr. Shepherd perceived that this connexion of the Crofts did them no service with Sir Walter, he mentioned it no more; returning, with all his zeal, to dwell on the circumstances more indisputably in their favour; their age, and number, and fortune; the high idea they had formed of Kellynch Hall, and extreme solicitude for the advantage of renting it; making it appear as if they ranked nothing beyond the happiness of being the tenants of Sir Walter Elliot: an extraordinary taste, certainly, could they have been supposed in the secret of Sir Walter's estimate of the dues of a tenant.

It succeeded, however; and though Sir Walter must ever look with an evil eye on any one intending to inhabit that house, and think them infinitely too well off in being permitted to rent it on the highest terms, he was talked into allowing Mr. Shepherd to proceed in the treaty, and authorising him to wait on Admiral Croft, who still remained at Taunton, and fix a day for the house being seen.

Sir Walter was not very wise; but still he had experience enough of the world to feel, that a more unobjectionable tenant, in all essentials, than Admiral Croft bid fair to be, could hardly offer. So far went his understanding; and his vanity supplied a little additional soothing, in the Admiral's situation in life, which was just high enough, and not too high. "I have let my house to Admiral Croft," would sound extremely well; very much better than to any mere *Mr.*——; a *Mr.* (save, perhaps, some half dozen in the nation) always needs a note of explanation. An admiral speaks his own consequence, and, at the same time, can never make a baronet look small. In all their dealings and intercourse, Sir Walter Elliot must ever have the precedence.

Nothing could be done without a reference to Elizabeth: but her inclination was growing so strong for a removal, that she was happy to have it fixed and expedited by a tenant at hand; and not a word to suspend decision was uttered by her.

Mr. Shepherd was completely empowered to act; and no sooner had such an end been reached, than Anne, who had been a most attentive listener to the whole, left the room, to seek the comfort of cool air for her flushed cheeks; and as she walked along a favourite grove, said, with a gentle sigh, "A few months more, and *he*, perhaps, may be walking here."

CHAPTER IV

He was not Mr. Wentworth, the former curate of Monkford, however suspicious appearances may be, but a Captain Frederick Wentworth, his brother, who being made commander in consequence of the action off St. Domingo, and not immediately employed, had come into Somersetshire, in the summer of 1806; and having no parent living, found a home for half a year at Monkford. He was, at that time, a remarkably fine young man, with a great deal of intelligence, spirit, and brilliancy; and Anne an extremely pretty girl, with gentleness, modesty, taste, and feeling. Half the sum

of attraction, on either side, might have been enough, for
he had nothing to do, and she had hardly anybody to love;
but the encounter of such lavish recommendations could not
fail. They were gradually acquainted, and when acquainted,
rapidly and deeply in love. It would be difficult to say which
had seen highest perfection in the other, or which had been
the happiest: she, in receiving his declarations and proposals,
or he in having them accepted.

A short period of exquisite felicity followed, and but a
short one. Troubles soon arose. Sir Walter, on being
applied to, without actually withholding his consent, or
saying it should never be, gave it all the negative of great
astonishment, great coldness, great silence, and a professed
resolution of doing nothing for his daughter. He thought
it a very degrading alliance; and Lady Russell, though with
more tempered and pardonable pride, received it as a most
unfortunate one.

Anne Elliot, with all her claims of birth, beauty, and
mind, to throw herself away at nineteen; involve herself
at nineteen in an engagement with a young man, who had
nothing but himself to recommend him, and no hopes of
attaining affluence, but in the chances of a most uncertain
profession, and no connexions to secure even his farther
rise in that profession, would be, indeed, a throwing away,
which she grieved to think of! Anne Elliot, so young;
known to so few, to be snatched off by a stranger without
alliance or fortune; or rather sunk by him into a state of
most wearing, anxious, youth-killing dependence! It must
not be, if by any fair interference of friendship, any representations from one who had almost a mother's love and
mother's rights, it would be prevented.

Captain Wentworth had no fortune. He had been lucky
in his profession; but spending freely what had come
freely, had realised nothing. But he was confident that he
should soon be rich: full of life and ardour, he knew that he
should soon have a ship, and soon be on a station that would
lead to everything he wanted. He had always been lucky;
he knew he should be so still. Such confidence, powerful in
its own warmth, and bewitching in the wit which often
expressed it, must have been enough for Anne; but Lady

Russell saw it very differently. His sanguine temper, and fearlessness of mind, operated very differently on her. She saw in it but an aggravation of the evil. It only added a dangerous character to himself. He was brilliant, he was headstrong. Lady Russell had little taste for wit, and of anything approaching to imprudence a horror. She deprecated the connexion in every light.

Such opposition, as these feelings produced, was more than Anne could combat. Young and gentle as she was, it might yet have been possible to withstand her father's ill-will, though unsoftened by one kind word or look on the part of her sister; but Lady Russell, whom she had always loved and relied on, could not, with such steadiness of opinion, and such tenderness of manner, be continually advising her in vain. She was persuaded to believe the engagement a wrong thing: indiscreet, improper, hardly capable of success, and not deserving it. But it was not a merely selfish caution, under which she acted, in putting an end to it. Had she not imagined herself consulting his good, even more than her own, she could hardly have given him up. The belief of being prudent and self-denying, principally for *his* advantage, was her chief consolation under the misery of a parting, a final parting; and every consolation was required, for she had to encounter all the additional pain of opinions, on his side, totally unconvinced and unbending, and of his feeling himself ill-used by so forced a relinquishment. He had left the country in consequence.

A few months had seen the beginning and the end of their acquaintance; but not with a few months ended Anne's share of suffering from it. Her attachment and regrets had, for a long time, clouded every enjoyment of youth, and an early loss of bloom and spirits had been their lasting effect.

More than seven years were gone since this little history of sorrowful interest had reached its close; and time had softened down much, perhaps nearly all of peculiar attachment to him, but she had been too dependant on time alone; no aid had been given in change of place (except in one visit to Bath soon after the rupture), or in any novelty or enlargement of society. No one had ever come within the Kellynch circle, who could bear a comparison with Frederick Wentworth, as he stood in her memory. No second attachment, the only thoroughly natural, happy, and sufficient cure, at her time of life, had been possible to the nice tone of her mind, the fastidiousness of her taste, in the small limits of the society around them. She had been solicited, when about two-and-twenty, to change her name by the young man who not long afterwards found a more willing mind in her younger sister: and Lady Russell had lamented her refusal: for Charles Musgrave was the eldest son of a man, whose landed property and general importance were second in that country only to Sir Walter's, and of good character and appearance; and however Lady Russell might have asked yet for something more while Anne was nineteen, she would have rejoiced to see her at twenty-two so respectably removed from the partialities and injustice of her father's house, and settled so permanently near herself. But in this case Anne had left nothing for advice to do; and though Lady Russell, as satisfied as ever with her own discretion, never wished the past undone, she began now to have the anxiety which borders on hopelessness for Anne's being tempted, by some man of talents and independence, to enter a state for which she held her to be peculiarly fitted by her warm affections and domestic habits.

They knew not each other's opinion, either its constancy or its change, on the one leading point of Anne's conduct, for the subject was never alluded to; but Anne, at seven-and-twenty, thought very differently from what she had been made to think at nineteen. She did not blame Lady Russell, she did not blame herself for having been guided by her; but she felt that were any young person in similar circumstances to apply to her for counsel, they would never receive any of such certain immediate wretchedness, such uncertain future good. She was persuaded, that under every disadvantage of disapprobation at home, and every anxiety attending his profession, all their probable fears, delays, and disappointments, she should yet have been a happier woman in maintaining the engagement, than she had been in the sacrifice of it; and this, she fully believed, had the usual share, had even more than a usual share of all such solicitudes and suspense been theirs, without reference to the actual results of their case, which, as it happened, would have bestowed earlier prosperity than could be reasonably calculated on. All his sanguine expectations, all his confidence, had been justified. His genius and ardour had seemed to foresee and to command his prosperous path. He had, very soon after their engagement ceased, got employ: and all that he had told her would follow had taken place. He had distinguished himself, and early gained the other step in rank, and must now, by successive captures, have made a handsome fortune. She had only navy lists and newspapers for her authority, but she could not doubt his being rich; and, in favour of his constancy, she had no reason to believe him married.

How eloquent could Anne Elliot have been! how eloquent, at least, were her wishes on the side of early warm attachment, and a cheerful confidence in futurity, against that over-anxious caution which seems to insult exertion and distrust Providence! She had been forced into prudence in her youth, she learned romance as she grew older: the natural sequel of an unnatural beginning.

With all these circumstances, recollections, and feelings, she could not hear that Captain Wentworth's sister was likely to live at Kellynch without a revival of former pain; and many a stroll, and many a sigh, were necessary to dispel the agitation of the idea. She often told herself it was folly, before she could harden her nerves sufficiently to feel the continual discussion of the Crofts and their business no evil. She was assisted, however, by that perfect indifference and apparent unconsciousness, among the only three of her own friends in the secret of the past, which seemed almost to deny any recollection of it. She could do justice to the superiority of Lady Russell's motives in this, over those of her father and Elizabeth; she could honour all the better feelings of her calmness; but the general air of oblivion among them was highly important from whatever it sprung; and in the event of Admiral Croft's really taking Kellynch Hall, she rejoiced anew over the conviction which had always been most grateful to her, of the past being known to those three only among her connexions, by whom no syllable, she believed, would ever be whispered, and in the trust that among his, the brother only with whom he had been residing had received any information of their short-lived engagement. That brother had been long removed from the country, and being a sensible man, and, moreover, a single man at the time, she had a fond dependance on no human creature's having heard of it from him.

The sister, Mrs. Croft, had then been out of England, accompanying her husband on a foreign station, and her own sister, Mary, had been at school while it all occurred; and never admitted by the pride of some, and the delicacy of others, to the smallest knowledge of it afterwards.

With these supports, she hoped that the acquaintance between herself and the Crofts, which, with Lady Russell still resident in Kellynch, and Mary fixed only three miles off, must be anticipated, need not involve any particular awkwardness.

CHAPTER V

On the morning appointed for Admiral and Mrs. Croft's seeing Kellynch Hall, Anne found it most natural to take her almost daily walk to Lady Russell's, and keep out of the way till all was over; when she found it most natural to be sorry that she had missed the opportunity of seeing them.

This meeting of the two parties proved highly satisfactory, and decided the whole business at once. Each lady was previously well disposed for an agreement, and saw nothing, therefore, but good manners in the other; and with regard to the gentlemen, there was such an hearty good humour, such an open, trusting liberality on the Admiral's side, as could not but influence Sir Walter, who had besides been flattered into his very best and most polished behaviour by Mr. Shepherd's assurances of his being known, by report, to the Admiral, as a model of good breeding.

The house, and grounds, and furniture, were approved, the Crofts were approved, terms, time, every thing, and every body, was right; and Mr. Shepherd's clerks were set to work, without there having been a single preliminary difference to modify of all that " This indenture showeth."

Sir Walter, without hesitation, declared the Admiral to be the best-looking sailor he had ever met with, and went so far as to say, that if his own man might have had the arranging of his hair, he should not be ashamed of being seen with him any where; and the Admiral, with sympathetic cordiality, observed to his wife as they drove back through the park, " I thought we should soon come to a deal, my dear, in spite of what they told us at Taunton. The Baronet will never set the Thames on fire, but there seems no harm in him: " reciprocal compliments which would have been esteemed about equal.

The Crofts were to have possession at Michaelmas; and as Sir Walter proposed removing to Bath in the course of the preceding month, there was no time to be lost in making every dependant arrangement.

Lady Russell, convinced that Anne would not be allowed to be of any use, or any importance, in the choice of the house which they were going to secure, was very unwilling to have her hurried away so soon, and wanted to make it possible for her to stay behind till she might convey her to Bath herself after Christmas; but having engagements of her own which must take her from Kellynch for several weeks, she was unable to give the full invitation she wished, and Anne, though dreading the possible heats of September in all the white glare of Bath, and grieving to forego all the influence so sweet and so sad of the autumnal months in the country, did not think that, everything considered, she wished to remain. It would be most right, and most wise, and therefore must involve least suffering to go with the others.

Something occurred, however, to give her a different duty. Mary, often a little unwell, and always thinking a great deal of her own complaints, and always in the habit of claiming Anne when anything was the matter, was indisposed; and foreseeing that she should not have a day's health all the autumn, entreated, or rather required her, for it was hardly entreaty, to come to Uppercross Cottage, and bear her company as long as she could want her, instead of going to Bath.

" I cannot possibly do without Anne," was Mary's reasoning; and Elizabeth's reply was, " Then I am sure Anne had better stay, for nobody will want her in Bath."

To be claimed as a good, though in an improper style, is at least better than being rejected as no good at all; and Anne, glad to be thought of some use, glad to have anything marked out as a duty, and certainly not sorry to have the scene of it in the country, and her own dear country, readily agreed to stay.

This invitation of Mary's removed all Lady Russell's difficulties, and it was consequently soon settled that Anne should not go to Bath till Lady Russell took her, and that all the intervening time should be divided between Uppercross Cottage and Kellynch Lodge.

So far all was perfectly right; but Lady Russell was almost startled by the wrong of one part of the Kellynch Hall plan, when it burst on her, which was, Mrs. Clay's being engaged to go to Bath with Sir Walter and Elizabeth, as a most important and valuable assistant to the latter in all the business before her. Lady Russell was extremely sorry that such a measure should have been resorted to at all, wondered, grieved, and feared; and the affront it contained to Anne, in Mrs. Clay's being of so much use, while Anne could be of none, was a very sore aggravation.

Anne herself was become hardened to such affronts, but she felt the imprudence of the arrangement quite as keenly as Lady Russell. With a great deal of quiet observation, and a knowledge, which she often wished less, of her father's character, she was sensible that results the most serious to his family from the intimacy were more than possible. She did not imagine that her father had at present an idea of the kind. Mrs. Clay had freckles, and a projecting tooth, and a clumsy wrist, which he was continually making severe remarks upon in her absence; but she was young, and certainly altogether well-looking, and possessed, in an acute mind and assiduous pleasing manners, infinitely more dangerous attractions than any merely personal might have been. Anne was so impressed by the degree of their danger, that she could not excuse herself from trying to make it perceptible to her sister. She had little hope of success, but Elizabeth, who in the event of such a reverse would be

so much more to be pitied than herself, should never, she
thought, have reason to reproach her for giving no warning.

She spoke, and seemed only to offend. Elizabeth could
not conceive how such an absurd suspicion should occur to
her, and indignantly answered for each party's perfection
knowing their situation.

" Mrs. Clay," said she, warmly, " never forgets who she
is; and as I am rather better acquainted with her sentiments than you can be, I can assure you, that upon the
subject of marriage they are particularly nice, and that
she reprobates all inequality of condition and rank more
strongly than most people. And as to my father, I really
should not have thought that he who has kept himself single
so long for our sakes need be suspected now. If Mrs. Clay
were a very beautiful woman, I grant you it might be wrong to
have her so much with me; not that anything in the world,
I am sure, would induce my father to make a degrading match,
but he might be rendered unhappy. But poor Mrs. Clay, who
with all her merits, can never have been reckoned tolerably
pretty, I really think poor Mrs. Clay may be staying here in
perfect safety. One would imagine you had never heard my
father speak of her personal misfortunes, though I know you
must fifty times. That tooth of hers and those freckles.
Freckles do not disgust me so very much as they do him. I
have known a face not materially disfigured by a few, but he
abominates them. You must have heard him notice Mrs.
Clay's freckles."

" There is hardly any personal defect," replied Anne,
" which an agreeable manner might not gradually reconcile
one to."

" I think very differently," answered Elizabeth, shortly;
" an agreeable manner may set off handsome features, but
can never alter plain ones. However, at any rate, as I have
a great deal more at stake on this point than anybody else
can have, I think it rather unnecessary in you to be advising
me."

Anne had done; glad that it was over, and not absolutely
hopeless of doing good. Elizabeth, though resenting the
suspicion, might yet be made observant by it.

The last office of the four carriage-horses was to draw

Sir Walter, Miss Elliot, and Mrs. Clay to Bath. The party drove off in very good spirits; Sir Walter prepared with condescending bows for all the afflicted tenantry and cottagers who might have had a hint to show themselves, and Anne walked up at the same time in a sort of desolate tranquillity to the Lodge, where she was to spend the first week.

Her friend was not in better spirits than herself. Lady Russell felt this break-up of the family exceedingly. Their respectability was as dear to her as her own, and a daily intercourse had become precious by habit. It was painful to look upon their deserted grounds, and still worse to anticipate the new hands they were to fall into; and to escape the solitariness and the melancholy of so altered a village, and be out of the way when Admiral and Mrs. Croft first arrived, she had determined to make her own absence from home begin when she must give up Anne. Accordingly their removal was made together, and Anne was set down at Uppercross Cottage, in the first stage of Lady Russell's journey.

Uppercross was a moderate-sized village, which a few years back had been completely in the old English style, containing only two houses superior in appearance to those of the yeomen and labourers; the mansion of the squire, with its high walls, great gates, and old trees, substantial and unmodernised, and the compact, tight parsonage, enclosed in its own neat garden, with a vine and a pear-tree trained round its casements; but upon the marriage of the young 'squire, it had received the improvement of a farm-house, elevated into a cottage, for his residence, and Uppercross Cottage, with its veranda, French windows, and other prettinesses, was quite as likely to catch the traveller's eye as the more consistent and considerable aspect and premises of the Great House, about a quarter of a mile farther on.

Here Anne had often been staying. She knew the ways of Uppercross as well as those of Kellynch. The two families were so continually meeting, so much in the habit of running in and out of each other's house at all hours, that it was rather a surprise to her to find Mary alone; but being alone, her being unwell and out of spirits was almost a matter of course. Though better endowed than the elder sister, Mary had not Anne's understanding nor temper. While well, and happy, and properly attended to, she had great good humour and excellent spirits; but any indisposition sunk her completely. She had no resources for solitude; and, inheriting a considerable share of the Elliot self-importance, was very prone to add to every other distress that of fancying herself neglected and ill-used. In person, she was inferior to both sisters, and had, even in her bloom, only reached the dignity of being " a fine girl." She was now lying on the faded sofa of the pretty little drawing-room, the once elegant furniture of which had been gradually growing shabby under the influence of four summers and two children; and, on Anne's appearing, greeted her with—

" So you are come at last! I began to think I should never see you. I am so ill I can hardly speak. I have not seen a creature the whole morning! "

" I am sorry to find you unwell," replied Anne. " You sent me such a good account of yourself on Thursday."

" Yes, I made the best of it; I always do: but I was very far from well at the time; and I do not think I ever was so ill in my life as I have been all this morning: very unfit to be left alone, I am sure. Suppose I were to be seized of a sudden in some dreadful way, and not able to ring the bell! So Lady Russell would not get out. I do not think she has been in this house three times this summer."

Anne said what was proper, and enquired after her husband. " Oh! Charles is out shooting. I have not seen him since seven o'clock. He would go, though I told him how ill I was. He said he should not stay out long; but he has never come back, and now it is almost one. I assure you I have not seen a soul this whole long morning."

" You have had your little boys with you? "

" Yes, as long as I could bear their noise; but they are so unmanageable that they do me more harm than good. Little Charles does not mind a word I say, and Walter is growing quite as bad."

" Well, you will soon be better now," replied Anne, cheerfully. " You know I always cure you when I come. How are your neighbours at the Great House? "

" I can give you no account of them. I have not seen one

of them to-day, except Mr. Musgrove, who just stopped and spoke through the window, but without getting off his horse; and though I told him how ill I was, not one of them have been near me. It did not happen to suit the Miss Musgroves, I suppose, and they never put themselves out of their way."

"You will see them yet, perhaps, before the morning is gone. It is early."

"I never want them, I assure you. They talk and laugh a great deal too much for me. Oh! Anne, I am so very unwell! It was quite unkind of you not to come on Thursday."

"My dear Mary, recollect what a comfortable account you sent me of yourself! You wrote in the cheerfullest manner, and said you were perfectly well, and in no hurry for me; and that being the case, you must be aware that my wish would be to remain with Lady Russell to the last. and besides what I felt on her account, I have really been so busy, have had so much to do, that I could not very conveniently have left Kellynch sooner."

"Dear me! what can *you* possibly have to do?"

"A great many things, I assure you. More than I can recollect in a moment; but I can tell you some. I have been making a duplicate of the catalogue of my father's books and pictures. I have been several times in the garden with Mackenzie, trying to understand, and make him understand, which of Elizabeth's plants are for Lady Russell. I have had all my own little concerns to arrange, books and music to divide, and all my trunks to repack, from not having understood in time what was intended as to the waggons: and one thing I have had to do, Mary, of a more trying nature: going to almost every house in the parish, as a sort of take-leave. I was told that they wished it; but all these things took up a great deal of time."

"Oh, well!" and after a moment's pause, "but you have never asked me one word about our dinner at the Pooles yesterday."

"Did you go, then? I have made no enquiries, because I concluded you must have been obliged to give up the party."

"Oh, yes! I went. I was very well yesterday; nothing

at all the matter with me till this morning. It would have been strange if I had not gone."

"I am very glad you were well enough, and I hope you had a pleasant party."

"Nothing remarkable. One always knows beforehand what the dinner will be, and who will be there; and it is so very uncomfortable not having a carriage of one's own. Mr. and Mrs. Musgrove took me, and we were so crowded! They are both so very large, and take up so much room; and Mr. Musgrove always sits forward. So there was I crowded into the back seat with Henrietta and Louisa; and I think it very likely that my illness to-day may be owing to it."

A little farther perseverance in patience and forced cheerfulness on Anne's side produced nearly a cure on Mary's. She could soon sit upright on the sofa, and began to hope she might be able to leave it by dinner-time. Then, forgetting to think of it, she was at the other end of the room, beautifying a nosegay; then she ate her cold meat; and then she was well enough to propose a little walk.

"Where shall we go?" said she, when they were ready. "I suppose you will not like to call at the Great House before they have been to see you?"

"I have not the smallest objection on that account," replied Anne. "I should never think of standing on such ceremony with people I know so well as Mrs. and the Miss Musgroves."

"Oh! but they ought to call upon you as soon as possible. They ought to feel what is due to you as *my* sister. However, we may as well go and sit with them a little while, and when we have got that over, we can enjoy our walk."

Anne had always thought such a style of intercourse highly imprudent; but she had ceased to endeavour to check it, from believing that, though there were on each side continual subjects of offence, neither family could now do without it. To the Great House accordingly they went, to sit the full half hour in the old-fashioned square parlour, with a small carpet and shining floor, to which the present daughters of the house were gradually giving the proper air of confusion by a grand piano-forte and a harp, flower-stands, and little tables placed in every direction. Oh! could the originals of the portraits against the wainscot, could the gentlemen in brown velvet and the ladies in blue satin have seen what was going on, have been conscious of such an overthrow of all order and neatness! The portraits themselves seemed to be staring in astonishment.

The Musgroves, like their houses, were in a state of alteration, perhaps of improvement. The father and mother were in the old English style, and the young people in the new. Mr. and Mrs. Musgrove were a very good sort of people; friendly and hospitable, not much educated, and not at all elegant. Their children had more modern minds and manners. There was a numerous family; but the only two grown up, excepting Charles, were Henrietta and Louisa, young ladies of nineteen and twenty, who had brought from a school at Exeter all the usual stock of accomplishments, and were now, like thousands of other young ladies, living to be fashionable, happy, and merry. Their dress had every advantage, their faces were rather pretty, their spirits extremely good, their manners unembarrassed and pleasant; they were of consequence at home, and favourites abroad. Anne always contemplated them as some of the happiest creatures of her acquaintance: but still, saved as we all are, by some comfortable feeling of superiority from wishing for the possibility of exchange, she would not have given up her own more elegant and cultivated mind for all their enjoyments; and envied them nothing but that seemingly perfect good understanding and agreement together, that good-humoured mutual affection, of which she had known so little herself with either of her sisters.

They were received with great cordiality. Nothing seemed amiss on the side of the Great House family, which was generally, as Anne very well knew, the least to blame. The half hour was chatted away pleasantly enough; and she was not at all surprised, at the end of it, to have their walking party joined by both the Miss Musgroves, at Mary's particular invitation.

CHAPTER VI

ANNE had not wanted this visit to Uppercross to learn that a removal from one set of people to another, though at a distance of only three miles, will often include a total change of conversation, opinion, and idea. She had never been staying there before, without being struck by it, or without wishing that other Elliots could have her advantage in seeing how unknown, or unconsidered there, were the affairs which at Kellynch Hall were treated as of such general publicity and pervading interest; yet, with all this experience, she believed she must now submit to feel that another lesson, in the art of knowing our own nothingness beyond our own circle, was become necessary for her; for certainly, coming as she did, with a heart full of the subject which had been completely occupying both houses in Kellynch for many weeks, she had expected rather more curiosity and sympathy than she found in the separate, but very similar remark of Mr. and Mrs. Musgrove: "So, Miss Anne, Sir Walter and your sister are gone; and what part of Bath do you think they will settle in?" and this, without much waiting for an answer; or in the young ladies addition of, "I hope *we* shall be in Bath in the winter; but remember, papa, if we do go, we must be in a good situation: none of your Queen Squares for us!" or in the anxious supplement from Mary, of—"Upon my word, I shall be pretty well off, when you are all gone away to be happy at Bath!"

She could only resolve to avoid such self-delusion in future, and think with heightened gratitude of the extraordinary blessing of having one such truly sympathising friend as Lady Russell.

The Mr. Musgroves had their own game to guard and to destroy, their own horses, dogs, and newspapers to engage them, and the females were fully occupied in all the other common subjects of housekeeping, neighbours, dress, dancing and music. She acknowledged it to be very fitting, that every little social commonwealth should dictate its own matters of discourse; and hoped, ere long, to become a not unworthy member of the one she was now transplanted into. With the prospect of spending at least two months at Uppercross, it was highly incumbent on her to clothe her imagination, her memory, and all her ideas in as much of Uppercross as possible.

She had no dread of these two months. Mary was not so repulsive and unsisterly as Elizabeth, nor so inaccessible to all influence of hers; neither was there anything among the other component parts of the cottage inimical to comfort. She was always on friendly terms with her brother-in-law; and in the children, who loved her nearly as well, and respected her a great deal more than their mother, she had an object of interest, amusement, and wholesome exertion.

Charles Musgrove was civil and agreeable; in sense and temper he was undoubtedly superior to his wife, but not of powers, or conversation, or grace to make the past, as they were connected together, at all a dangerous contemplation; though, at the same time, Anne could believe, with Lady Russell, that a more equal match might have greatly improved him; and that a woman of real understanding might have given more consequence to his character, and more usefulness, rationality, and elegance to his habits and pursuits. As it was, he did nothing with much zeal, but sport; and his time was otherwise trifled away, without benefit from books or anything else. He had very good spirits, which never seemed much affected by his wife's occasional lowness, bore with her unreasonableness sometimes to Anne's admiration, and upon the whole, though there was very often a little disagreement (in which she had sometimes more share than she wished, being appealed to by both parties), they might pass for a happy couple. They were always perfectly agreed in the want of more money, and a strong inclination for a handsome present from his father; but here, as on most topics, he had the superiority, for while Mary thought it a great shame that such a present was not made, he always contended for his father's having many other uses for his money, and a right to spend it as he liked.

As to the management of their children, his theory was

much better than his wife's, and his practice not so bad, " I could manage them very well, if it were not for Mary's interference," was what Anne often heard him say, and had a good deal of faith in; but when listening in turn to Mary's reproach of, " Charles spoils the children so that I cannot get them into any order," she never had the smallest temptation to say, " Very true."

One of the least agreeable circumstances of her residence there was her being treated with too much confidence by all parties, and being too much in the secret of the complaints of each house. Known to have some influence with her sister, she was continually requested, or at least receiving hints to exert it, beyond what was practicable. " I wish you could persuade Mary not to be always fancying herself ill," was Charles's language; and, in an unhappy mood, thus spoke Mary: " I do believe if Charles were to see me dying, he would not think there was anything the matter with me. I am sure, Anne, if you would, you might persuade him that I really am very ill—a great deal worse than I ever own."

Mary's declaration was, " I hate sending the children to the Great House, though their grandmamma is always wanting to see them, for she humours and indulges them to such a degree, and gives them so much trash and sweet things, that they are sure to come back sick and cross for the rest of the day." And Mrs. Musgrove took the first opportunity of being alone with Anne, to say, " Oh! Miss Anne, I cannot help wishing Mrs. Charles had a little of your method with those children. They are quite different creatures with you! But to be sure, in general, they are so spoilt! It is a pity you cannot put your sister in the way of managing them. They are as fine healthy children as ever were seen, poor little dears! without partiality; but Mrs. Charles knows no more how they should be treated—! Bless me! how troublesome they are sometimes. I assure you, Miss Anne, it prevents my wishing to see them at our house so often as I otherwise should. I believe Mrs. Charles is not quite pleased with my not inviting them oftener; but you know it is very bad to have children with one that one is obliged to be checking every moment; ' don't do this,' and ' don't do that; ' or that one can only keep in tolerable order by more cake than is good for them."

She had this communication, moreover, from Mary. " Mrs. Musgrove thinks all her servants so steady, that it would be high treason to call it in question; but I am sure, without exaggeration, that her upper house-maid and laundry-maid, instead of being in their business, are gadding about the village all day long. I meet them wherever I go; and I declare I never go twice into my nursery without seeing something of them. If Jemima were not the trustiest, steadiest creature in the world, it would be enough to spoil her; for she tells me they are always tempting her to take a walk with them." And on Mrs. Musgrove's side it was, " I make a rule of never interfering in any of my daughter-in-law's concerns, for I know it would not do; but I shall tell *you*, Miss Anne, because you may be able to set things to rights, that I have no very good opinion of Mrs. Charles's nursery-maid: I hear strange stories of her; she is always upon the gad; and from my own knowledge, I can declare, she is such a fine-dressing lady, that she is enough to ruin any servants she comes near. Mrs. Charles quite swears by her, I know; but I just give you this hint, that you may be upon the watch; because, if you see anything amiss, you need not be afraid of mentioning it."

Again, it was Mary's complaint that Mrs. Musgrove was very apt not to give her the precedence that was her due, when they dined at the Great House with other families; and she did not see any reason why she was to be considered so much at home as to lose her place. And one day when Anne was walking with only the Miss Musgroves, one of them after talking of rank, people of rank, and jealousy of rank, said, " I have no scruple of observing to *you*, how nonsensical some persons are about their place, because all the world knows how easy and indifferent you are about it; but I wish anybody would give Mary a hint that it would be a great deal better if she were not so very tenacious, especially if she would not be always putting herself forward to take place of mamma. Nobody doubts her right to have precedence of mamma, but it would be more becoming in her not to be always insisting on it. It is not that mamma cares about it the least in the world, but I know it is taken notice of by many persons."

How was Anne to set all these matters to rights? She could do little more than listen patiently, soften every grievance, and excuse each to the other; give them all hints of the forbearance necessary between such near neighbours, and make those hints broadest which were meant for her sister's benefit.

In all other respects, her visit began and proceeded very well. Her own spirits improved by change of place and subject, by being removed three miles from Kellynch; Mary's ailments lessened by having a constant companion, and their daily intercourse with the other family, since there was neither superior affection, confidence nor employment in the cottage to be interrupted by it, was rather an advantage. It was certainly carried nearly as far as possible, for they met every morning, and hardly ever spent an evening asunder; but she believed they should not have done so well without the sight of Mr. and Mrs. Musgrove's respectable forms in the usual places, or without the talking, laughing, and singing of their daughters.

She played a great deal better than either of the Miss Musgroves, but having no voice, no knowledge of the harp, and no fond parents, to sit by and fancy themselves delighted, her performance was little thought of, only out of civility, or to refresh the others, as she was well aware. She knew that when she played she was giving pleasure only to herself; but this was no new sensation. Excepting one short period of her life, she had never, since the age of fourteen, never since the loss of her dear mother, known the happiness of being listened to, or encouraged by any just appreciation or real taste. In music she had been always used to feel alone in the world; and Mr. and Mrs. Musgrove's fond partiality for their own daughters' performance, and total indifference to any other person's, gave her much more pleasure for their sakes, than mortification for her own.

The party at the Great House was sometimes increased by other company. The neighbourhood was not large, but the Musgroves were visited by everybody, and had more dinner-parties, and more callers, more visitors by invitation and by chance, than any other family. They were more completely popular.

The girls were wild for dancing; and the evenings ended, occasionally, in an unpremeditated little ball. There was a family of cousins within a walk of Uppercross, in less affluent circumstances, who depended on the Musgroves for all their pleasures; they would come at any time, or help to play at anything, or dance anywhere; and Anne, very much preferring the office of musician to a more active post, played country dances to them by the hour together; a kindness which always recommended her musical powers to the notice of Mr. and Mrs. Musgrove more than anything else, and often drew this compliment—" Well done, Miss Anne! very well done, indeed! Lord bless me! how those little fingers of yours fly about! "

So passed the first three weeks. Michaelmas came; and now Anne's heart must be in Kellynch again. A beloved home made over to others; all the precious rooms and furniture, groves and prospects, beginning to own other eyes and other limbs! She could not think of much else on the 29th of September; and she had this sympathetic touch in the evening from Mary, who, on having occasion to note down the day of the month, exclaimed, " Dear me, is not this the day the Crofts were to come to Kellynch? I am glad I did not think of it before. How low it makes me! "

The Crofts took possession with true naval alertness, and were to be visited. Mary deplored the necessity for herself. " Nobody knew how much she should suffer. She should put it off as long as she could; " but was not easy till she had talked Charles into driving her over on an early day, and was in a very animated, comfortable state of imaginary agitation when she came back. Anne had very sincerely rejoiced in there being no means of her going. She wished, however, to see the Crofts, and was glad to be within when the visit was returned. They came: the master of the house was not at home, but the two sisters were together; and as it chanced that Mrs. Croft fell to the share of Anne, while the Admiral sat by Mary, and made himself very agreeable by his good-humoured notice of her little boys, she was well able to watch for a likeness, and if it failed her in the features, to catch it in the voice, or in the turn of sentiment and expression.

Mrs. Croft, though neither tall nor fat, had a squareness, uprightness, and vigour of form, which gave importance to her person. She had bright dark eyes, good teeth, and altogether an agreeable face; though her reddened and weather-beaten complexion, the consequence of her having been almost as much at sea as her husband, made her seem to have lived some years longer in the world than her real eight-and-thirty. Her manners were open, easy, and decided, like one who had no distrust of herself, and no doubts of what to do; without any approach to coarseness, however, or any want of good humour. Anne gave her credit, indeed, for feelings of great consideration towards herself, in all that related to Kellynch, and it pleased her: especially, as she had satisfied herself in the very first half minute, in the instant even of introduction, that there was not the smallest symptom of any knowledge or suspicion on Mrs. Croft's side to give a bias of any sort. She was quite easy on that head, and consequently full of strength and courage, till for a moment electrified by Mrs. Croft's suddenly saying—

" It was you, and not your sister, I find, that my brother had the pleasure of being acquainted with, when he was in this country."

Anne hoped she had outlived the age of blushing; but the age of emotion she certainly had not.

" Perhaps you may not have heard that he is married? " added Mrs. Croft.

She could now answer as she ought; and was happy to feel, when Mrs. Croft's next words explained it to be Mr. Wentworth of whom she spoke, that she had said nothing which might not do for either brother. She immediately felt how reasonable it was, that Mrs. Croft should be thinking and speaking of Edward, and not of Frederick; and with shame at her own forgetfulness, applied herself to the knowledge of their former neighbour's present state with proper interest.

The rest was all tranquillity; till, just as they were moving, she heard the Admiral say to Mary—

"We are expecting a brother of Mrs. Croft's here soon; I dare say you know him by name?"

He was cut short by the eager attacks of the little boys, clinging to him like an old friend, and declaring he should not go; and being too much engrossed by proposals of carrying them away in his coat pocket, etc., to have another moment for finishing or recollecting what he had begun, Anne was left to persuade herself, as well as she could, that the same brother must still be in question. She could not, however, reach such a degree of certainty as not to be anxious to hear whether anything had been said on the subject at the other house, where the Crofts had previously been calling.

The folks of Great House were to spend the evening of this day at the Cottage; and it being now too late in the year for such visits to be made on foot, the coach was beginning to be listened for, when the youngest Miss Musgrove walked in. That she was coming to apologise, and that they should have to spend the evening by themselves, was the first black idea; and Mary was quite ready to be affronted, when Louisa made all right by saying, that she only came on foot, to leave more room for the harp, which was bringing in the carriage.

"And I will tell you our reason," she added, "and all about it. I am come on to give you notice, that papa and mamma are out of spirits this evening, especially mamma; she is thinking so much of poor Richard! And we agreed it would be best to have the harp, for it seems to amuse her more than the piano-forte. I will tell you why she is out of spirits. When the Crofts called this morning (they called here afterwards, did not they?), they happened to say that her brother, Captain Wentworth, is just returned to England, or paid off, or something, and is coming to see them almost directly; and most unluckily it came into mamma's head, when they were gone, that Wentworth, or something very like it, was the name of poor Richard's captain, at one time; I do not know when or where, but a great while before he died, poor fellow! And upon looking over his letters and things, she found it was so, and is perfectly sure that this must be the very man, and her head is quite full of it, and of poor Richard! So we must all be as merry as we can, that she may not be dwelling upon such gloomy things."

The real circumstances of this pathetic piece of family history were, that the Musgroves had had the ill fortune of a very troublesome, hopeless son, and the good fortune to lose him before he reached his twentieth year; that he had been sent to sea because he was stupid and unmanageable on shore; that he had been very little cared for at any time by his family, though quite as much as he deserved; seldom heard of, and scarcely at all regretted, when the intelligence of his death abroad had worked its way to Uppercross, two years before.

He had, in fact, though his sisters were now doing all they could for him, by calling him " poor Richard," been nothing better than a thick-headed, unfeeling, unprofitable Dick Musgrove, who had never done anything to entitle himself to more than the abbreviation of his name, living or dead.

He had been several years at sea, and had, in the course of those removals to which all midshipmen are liable, and especially such midshipmen as every captain wishes to get rid of, been six months on board Captain Frederick Wentworth's frigate, the *Laconia*; and from the *Laconia* he had, under the influence of his captain, written the only two letters which his father and mother had ever received from him during the whole of his absence; that is to say, the only two disinterested letters: all the rest had been mere applications for money.

In each letter he had spoken well of his captain; but yet, so little were they in the habit of attending to such matters, so unobservant and incurious were they as to the names of men or ships, that it had made scarcely any impression at the time; and that Mrs. Musgrove should have been suddenly struck, this very day, with a recollection of the name of Wentworth, as connected with her son, seemed one of those extraordinary bursts of mind which do sometimes occur.

She had gone to her letters, and found it all as she supposed; and the re-perusal of these letters, after so long an interval, her poor son gone for ever, and all the strength of his faults forgotten, had affected her spirits exceedingly, and thrown her into greater grief for him than she had known on first hearing of his death. Mr. Musgrove was, in a lesser degree, affected likewise; and when they reached the cottage, they were evidently in want, first, of being listened to anew on this subject, and afterwards, of all the relief which cheerful companions could give.

To hear them talking so much of Captain Wentworth, repeating his name so often, puzzling over past years, and at last ascertaining that it *might*, that it probably *would*, turn out to be the very same Captain Wentworth whom they recollected meeting, once or twice, after their coming back from Clifton—a very fine young man—but they could not say whether it was seven or eight years ago, was a new sort of trial to Anne's nerves. She found, however, that it was one to which she must enure herself. Since he actually was expected in the country, she must teach herself to be insensible on such points. And not only did it appear that he was expected, and speedily, but the Musgroves, in their warm gratitude for the kindness he had shewn poor Dick, and very high respect for his character, stamped as it was by poor Dick's having been six months under his care, and mentioning him in strong, though not perfectly well-spelt praise, as " a fine dashing felow, only two perticular about the schoolmaster," were bent on introducing themselves, and seeking his acquaintance as soon as they could hear of his arrival.

The resolution of doing so helped to form the comfort of their evening.

CHAPTER VII

A very few days more, and Captain Wentworth was known to be at Kellynch, and Mr. Musgrove had called on him, and come back warm in his praise, and he was engaged with the Crofts to dine at Uppercross by the end of another week. It had been a great disappointment to Mr. Musgrove to find that no earlier day could be fixed, so impatient was he to shew his gratitude, by seeing Captain Wentworth under his own roof, and welcoming him to all that was strongest and best in his cellars. But a week must pass; only a week, in

Anne's reckoning, and then, she supposed, they must meet;
and soon she began to wish that she could feel secure even
for a week.

Captain Wentworth made a very early return to Mr.
Musgrove's civility, and she was all but calling there in the
same half hour.   She and Mary were actually setting forward
for the Great House, where, as she afterwards learnt, they
must inevitably have found him, when they were stopped
by the eldest boy's being at that moment brought home in
consequence of a bad fall.   The child's situation put the
visit entirely aside; but she could not hear of her escape
with indifference, even in the midst of the serious anxiety
which they afterwards felt on his account.

His collar-bone was found to be dislocated, and such
injury [received] in the back, as roused the most alarming
ideas. It was an afternoon of distress, and Anne had
everything to do at once; the apothecary to send for, the
father to have pursued and informed, the mother to support
and keep from hysterics, the servants to control, the youngest
child to banish, and the poor suffering one to attend and
soothe; besides sending, as soon as she recollected it, proper
notice to the other house, which brought her an accession
rather of frightened enquiring companions, than of very
useful assistants.

Her brother's return was the first comfort; he could take
best care of his wife; and the second blessing was the arrival
of the apothecary. Till he came and had examined the
child, their apprehensions were the worse for being vague;
they suspected great injury, but knew not where; but now
the collar-bone was soon replaced, and though Mr. Robinson
felt and felt, and rubbed, and looked grave, and spoke low
words both to the father and the aunt, still they were all to
hope the best, and to be able to part and eat their dinner in
tolerable ease of mind; and then it was, just before they
parted, that the two young aunts were able so far to digress
from their nephew's state, as to give the information of
Captain Wentworth's visit; staying five minutes behind
their father and mother, to endeavour to express how
perfectly delighted they were with him, how much handsomer, how infinitely more agreeable they thought him than

any individual among their male acquaintance, who had been at all a favourite before. How glad they had been to hear papa invite him to stay dinner, how sorry when he said it was quite out of his power, and how glad again when he had promised to reply to papa and mamma's farther pressing invitations to come and dine with them on the morrow— actually on the morrow; and he had promised it in so pleasant a manner, as if he felt all the motive of their attention just as he ought. And in short, he had looked and said everything with such exquisite grace, that they could assure them all, their heads were both turned by him; and off they ran, quite as full of glee as of love, and apparently more full of Captain Wentworth than of little Charles.

The same story and the same raptures were repeated, when the two girls came with their father, through the gloom of the evening, to make enquiries; and Mr. Musgrove, no longer under the first uneasiness about his heir, could add his confirmation and praise, and hope there would be now no occasion for putting Captain Wentworth off, and only be sorry to think that the cottage party, probably, would not like to leave the little boy, to give him the meeting. "Oh! no; as to leaving the little boy," both father and mother were in much too strong and recent alarm to bear the thought; and Anne, in the joy of the escape, could not help adding her warm protestations to theirs.

Charles Musgrove, indeed, afterwards, shewed more of inclination: "the child was going on so well, and he wished so much to be introduced to Captain Wentworth, that, perhaps, he might join them in the evening; he would not dine from home, but he might walk in for half an hour." But in this he was eagerly opposed by his wife, with "Oh! no, indeed, Charles, I cannot bear to have you go away. Only think, if anything should happen?"

The child had a good night, and was going on well the next day. It must be a work of time to ascertain that no injury had been done to the spine; but Mr. Robinson found nothing to increase alarm, and Charles Musgrove began, consequently, to feel no necessity for longer confinement. The child was to be kept in bed and amused as quietly as possible; but what was there for a father to do? This was quite a female case, and it would be highly absurd in him, who could be of no use at home, to shut himself up. His father very much wished him to meet Captain Wentworth, and there being no sufficient reason against it, he ought to go; and it ended in his making a bold, public declaration, when he came in from shooting, of his meaning to dress directly, and dine at the other house.

"Nothing can be going on better than the child," said he; "so I told my father, just now, that I would come, and he thought me quite right. Your sister being with you, my love, I have no scruple at all. You would not like to leave him yourself, but you see I can be of no use. Anne will send for me if anything is the matter."

Husbands and wives generally understand when opposition will be vain. Mary knew, from Charles's manner of speaking, that he was quite determined on going, and that it would be of no use to teaze him. She said nothing, therefore, till he was out of the room; but as soon as there was only Anne to hear—

"So you and I are to be left to shift by ourselves, with this poor sick child; and not a creature coming near us all the evening! I knew how it would be. This is always my luck. If there is anything disagreeable going on men are always sure to get out of it, and Charles is as bad as any of them. Very unfeeling! I must say it is very unfeeling of him to be running away from his poor little boy. Talks of his being going on so well! how does he know that he is going on well, or that there may not be a sudden change half an hour hence? I did not think Charles would have been so unfeeling. So here he is to go away and enjoy himself, and because I am the poor mother, I am not to be allowed to stir; and yet, I am sure, I am more unfit than anybody else to be about the child. My being the mother is the very reason why my feelings should not be tried. I am not at all equal to it. You saw how hysterical I was yesterday."

"But that was only the effect of the suddenness of your alarm—of the shock. You will not be hysterical again. I dare say we shall have nothing to distress us. I perfectly understand Mr. Robinson's directions, and have no fears; and, indeed, Mary, I cannot wonder at your husband.

Nursing does not belong to a man; it is not his province. A sick child is always the mother's property: her own feelings generally make it so."

" I hope I am as fond of my child as any mother, but I do not know that I am of any more use in the sick-room than Charles, for I cannot be always scolding and teazing a poor child when it is ill; and you saw, this morning, that if I told him to keep quiet, he was sure to begin kicking about. I have not nerves for the sort of thing."

" But could you be comfortable yourself, to be spending the whole evening away from the poor boy? "

"Yes; you see his papa can, and why should not I? Jemima is so careful; and she could send us word every hour how he was. I really think Charles might as well have told his father we would all come. I am not more alarmed about little Charles now than he is. I was dreadfully alarmed yesterday, but the case is very different to-day."

" Well, if you do not think it too late to give notice for yourself, suppose you were to go, as well as your husband. Leave little Charles to my care. Mr. and Mrs. Musgrove cannot think it wrong while I remain with him."

" Are you serious? " cried Mary, her eyes brightening. " Dear me! that's a very good thought, very good, indeed. To be sure, I may just as well go as not, for I am of no use at home—am I? and it only harasses me. You, who have not a mother's feelings, are a great deal the properest person. You can make little Charles do anything; he always minds you at a word. It will be a great deal better than leaving him with only Jemima. Oh! I will certainly go; I am sure I ought if I can, quite as much as Charles, for they want me excessively to be acquainted with Captain Wentworth, and I know you do not mind being left alone. An excellent thought of yours, indeed, Anne. I will go and tell Charles, and get ready directly. You can send for us, you know, at a moment's notice, if anything is the matter; but I dare say there will be nothing to alarm you. I should not go, you may be sure, if I did not feel quite at ease about my dear child."

The next moment she was tapping at her husband's dressing-room door, and as Anne followed her upstairs, she was in time for the whole conversation, which began with Mary's saying, in a tone of great exultation—

" I mean to go with you, Charles, for I am of no more use at home than you are. If I were to shut myself up for ever with the child, I should not be able to persuade him to do anything he did not like. Anne will stay; Anne undertakes to stay at home and take care of him. It is Anne's own proposal, and so I shall go with you, which will be a great deal better, for I have not dined at the other house since Tuesday."

" This is very kind of Anne," was her husband's answer, " and I should be very glad to have you go; but it seems rather hard that she should be left at home by herself, to nurse our sick child."

Anne was now at hand to take up her own cause, and the sincerity of her manner being soon sufficient to convince him, where conviction was at least very agreeable, he had no farther scruples as to her being left to dine alone, though he still wanted her to join them in the evening, when the child might be at rest for the night, and kindly urged her to let him come and fetch her, but she was quite unpersuadable; and this being the case, she had ere long the pleasure of seeing them set off together in high spirits. They were gone, she hoped, to be happy, however oddly constructed such happiness might seem; as for herself, she was left with as many sensations of comfort, as were, perhaps, ever likely to be hers. She knew herself to be of the first utility to the child; and what was it to her if Frederick Wentworth were only half a mile distant, making himself agreeable to others?

She would have liked to know how he felt as to a meeting. Perhaps indifferent, if indifference could exist under such circumstances. He must be either indifferent or unwilling. Had he wished ever to see her again, he need not have waited till this time; he would have done what she could not but believe that in his place she should have done long ago, when events had been early giving him the independence which alone had been wanting.

Her brother and sister came back delighted with their new acquaintance, and their visit in general. There had been music, singing, talking, laughing, all that was most agreeable; charming manners in Captain Wentworth, no shyness or reserve; they seemed all to know each other perfectly, and he was coming the very next morning to shoot with Charles. He was to come to breakfast, but not at the Cottage, though that had been proposed at first; but then he had been pressed to come to the Great House instead, and he seemed afraid of being in Mrs. Charles Musgrove's way, on account of the child, and therefore, somehow, they hardly knew how, it ended in Charles's being to meet him to breakfast at his father's.

Anne understood it. He wished to avoid seeing her. He had inquired after her, she found, slightly, as might suit a former slight acquaintance, seeming to acknowledge such as she had acknowledged, actuated, perhaps, by the same view of escaping introduction when they were to meet.

The morning hours of the Cottage were always later than those of the other house, and on the morrow the difference was so great that Mary and Anne were not more than beginning breakfast when Charles came in to say that they were just setting off, that he was come for his dogs, that his sisters were following with Captain Wentworth; his sisters meaning to visit Mary and the child, and Captain Wentworth proposing also to wait on her for a few minutes if not inconvenient; and though Charles had answered for the child's being in no such state as could make it inconvenient, Captain Wentworth would not be satisfied without his running on to give notice.

Mary, very much gratified by this attention, was delighted to receive him, while a thousand feelings rushed on Anne, of which this was the most consoling, that it would soon be over. And it was soon over. In two minutes after Charles's preparation, the others appeared; they were in the drawing-room. Her eye half met Captain Wentworth's, a bow, a courtsey passed; she heard his voice; he talked to Mary, said all that was right, said something to the Miss Musgroves, enough to mark an easy footing; the room seemed full, full of persons and voices, but a few minutes ended it. Charles shewed himself at the window, all was ready, their visitor had bowed and was gone, the Miss Musgroves were gone too, suddenly resolving to walk to the end of the village with the sportsmen; the room was cleared, and Anne might finish her breakfast as she could.

" It is over! it is over! " she repeated to herself again and again, in nervous gratitude. " The worst is over! "

Mary talked, but she could not attend. She had seen him. They had met. They had been once more in the same room.

Soon, however, she began to reason with herself, and try to be feeling less. Eight years, almost eight years had passed, since all had been given up. How absurd to be resuming the agitation which such an interval had banished into distance and indistinctness! What might not eight years do? Events of every description, changes, alienations, removals —all, all must be comprised in it, and oblivion of the past— how natural, how certain too! It included nearly a third part of her own life.

Alas! with all her reasonings she found, that to retentive feelings eight years may be little more than nothing.

Now, how were his sentiments to be read? Was this like wishing to avoid her? And the next moment she was hating herself for the folly which asked the question.

On one other question, which perhaps her utmost wisdom might not have prevented, she was soon spared all suspense; for, after the Miss Musgroves had returned and finished their visit at the Cottage, she had this spontaneous information from Mary:—

" Captain Wentworth is not very gallant by you, Anne, though he was so attentive to me. Henrietta asked him what he thought of you, when they went away, and he said, ' You were so altered he should not have known you again.' "

Mary had no feelings to make her respect her sister's in a common way, but she was perfectly unsuspicious of being inflicting any peculiar wound.

" Altered beyond his knowledge." Anne fully submitted, in silent, deep mortification. Doubtless it was so, and she could take no revenge, for he was not altered, or not for the worse. She had already acknowledged it to herself, and she could not think differently, let him think of her as he would. No: the years which had destroyed her youth and bloom had only given him a more glowing, manly, open look, in no respect lessening his personal advantages. She had seen the same Frederick Wentworth.

" So altered that he should not have known her again! "

These were words which could not but dwell with her. Yet she soon began to rejoice that she had heard them. They were of sobering tendency; they allayed agitation; they composed, and consequently must make her happier.

Frederick Wentworth had used such words, or something like them, but without an idea that they would be carried round to her. He had thought her wretchedly altered, and in the first moment of appeal, had spoken as he felt. He had not forgiven Anne Elliot. She had used him ill, deserted and disappointed him; and worse, she had shewn a feeble-ness of character in doing so, which his own decided, con-fident temper could not endure. She had given him up to oblige others. It had been the effect of over-persuasion. It had been weakness and timidity.

He had been most warmly attached to her, and had never seen a woman since whom he thought her equal; but, except from some natural sensation of curiosity, he had no desire of meeting her again. Her power with him was gone for ever.

It was now his object to marry. He was rich, and being turned on shore, fully intended to settle as soon as he could be properly tempted; actually looking round, ready to fall in love with all the speed which a clear head and quick taste could allow. He had a heart for either of the Miss Musgroves, if they could catch it; a heart, in short, for any pleasing young woman who came in his way, excepting Anne Elliot. This was his only secret exception, when he said to his sister, in answer to her suppositions:—

"Yes, here I am, Sophia, quite ready to make a foolish match. Anybody between fifteen and thirty may have me for asking. A little beauty, and a few smiles, and a few compliments to the navy, and I am a lost man. Should not this be enough for a sailor, who has had no society among women to make him nice?"

He said it, she knew, to be contradicted. His bright proud eye spoke the happy conviction that he was nice; and Anne Elliot was not out of his thoughts, when he more than seriously described the woman he should wish to meet with. "A strong mind, with sweetness of manner," made the first and the last of the description.

" That is the woman I want," said he. " Something a little inferior I shall of course put up with, but it must not be much. If I am a fool, I shall be a fool indeed, for I have thought on the subject more than most men."

CHAPTER VIII

FROM this time Captain Wentworth and Anne Elliot were repeatedly in the same circle. They were soon dining in company together at Mr. Musgrove's, for the little boy's state could no longer supply his aunt with a pretence for absenting herself; and this was but the beginning of other dinings and other meetings.

Whether former feelings were to be renewed must be brought to the proof; former times must undoubtedly be brought to the recollection of each; *they* could not but be reverted to; the year of their engagement could not but be named by him, in the little narratives or descriptions which conversation called forth. His profession qualified him, his disposition led him to talk; and " *That* was in the year six; " " *That* happened before I went to sea, in the year six," occurred in the course of the first evening they spent together: and though his voice did not falter, and though she had no reason to suppose his eye wandering towards her while he spoke, Anne felt the utter impossibility, from her knowledge of his mind, that he could be unvisited by remembrance any more than herself. There must be the same immediate association of thought, though she was very far from conceiving it to be of equal pain.

They had no conversation together, no intercourse but what the commonest civility required. Once so much to each other! Now nothing! There *had* been a time, when of all the large party now filling the drawing-room at Uppercross, they would have found it most difficult to cease to speak to one another. With the exception, perhaps, of Admiral and Mrs. Croft, who seemed particularly attached and happy (Anne could allow no other exception, even among the married couples), there could have been no two hearts so open, no tastes so similar, no feelings so in unison, no countenances so beloved. Now they were as strangers; nay, worse than strangers, for they could never become acquainted. It was a perpetual estrangement.

When he talked, she heard the same voice, and discerned the same mind. There was a very general ignorance of all naval matters throughout the party; and he was very much questioned, and especially by the two Miss Musgroves, who seemed hardly to have any eyes but for him, as to the manner of living on board, daily regulations, food, hours, etc.; and their surprise at his accounts, at learning the degree of accommodation and arrangement which was practicable, drew from him some pleasant ridicule, which reminded Anne of the early days when she too had been ignorant, and she too had been accused of supposing sailors to be living on board without anything to eat, or any cook to dress it if there were, or any servant to wait, or any knife and fork to use.

From thus listening and thinking, she was roused by a whisper of Mrs. Musgrove's, who, overcome by fond regrets, could not help saying—

"Ah! Miss Anne, if it had pleased Heaven to spare my poor son, I dare say he would have been just such another by this time."

Anne suppressed a smile, and listened kindly, while Mrs. Musgrove relieved her heart a little more; and for a few minutes, therefore, could not keep pace with the conversation of the others.

When she could let her attention take its natural course again, she found the Miss Musgroves just fetching the Navy List (their own navy list, the first that had ever been at Uppercross), and sitting down together to pore over it, with the professed view of finding out the ships which Captain Wentworth had commanded.

"Your first was the *Asp*, I remember; we will look for the *Asp*."

"You will not find her there. Quite worn out and broken up. I was the last man who commanded her. Hardly fit for service then. Reported fit for home service for a year or two, and so I was sent off to the West Indies."

The girls looked all amazement.

"The Admiralty," he continued, "entertain themselves now and then, with sending a few hundred men to sea in a ship not fit to be employed. But they have a great many to provide for; and among the thousands that may just as well go to the bottom as not, it is impossible for them to distinguish the very set who may be least missed."

"Phoo! phoo!" cried the Admiral, "what stuff these young fellows talk! Never was there a better sloop than the *Asp* in her day. For an old built sloop, you would not see her equal. Lucky fellow to get her! He knows there must have been twenty better men than himself applying for her at the same time. Lucky fellow to get anything so soon, with no more interest than his."

"I felt my luck, Admiral, I assure you," replied Captain Wentworth, seriously. "I was as well satisfied with my appointment as you can desire. It was a great object with me at that time to be at sea; a very great object, I wanted to be doing something."

"To be sure you did. What should a young fellow like you do ashore for half a year together? If a man has not a wife, he soon wants to be afloat again."

"But, Captain Wentworth," cried Louisa, "how vexed you must have been when you came to the *Asp*, to see what an old thing they had given you!"

"I knew pretty well what she was before that day," said he, smiling. "I had no more discoveries to make than you would have as to the fashion and strength of any old pelisse, which you had seen lent about among half your acquaintance ever since you could remember, and which at last, on some very wet day, is lent to yourself. Ah! she was a dear old *Asp* to me. She did all that I wanted. I knew she would. I knew that we should either go to the bottom together, or that she would be the making of me; and I never had two days of foul weather all the time I was at sea in her; and after taking privateers enough to be very entertaining, I had the good luck in my passage home, the next autumn, to fall in with the very French frigate I wanted. I brought her into Plymouth; and here was another instance of luck. We had not been six hours in the Sound, when a gale came on, which lasted four days and nights, and which would have done for poor old *Asp* in half the time; our touch with the Great Nation not having much improved our condition. Four-and-twenty hours later, and I should only have been a gallant Captain Wentworth, in a small paragraph at one corner of the newspapers; and being lost in only a sloop, nobody would have thought about me."

Anne's shudderings were to herself alone; but the Miss Musgroves could be as open as they were sincere, in their exclamations of pity and horror.

"And so then, I suppose," said Mrs. Musgrove, in a low voice, as if thinking aloud, "so then he went away to the *Laconia*, and there he met with our poor boy. Charles, my dear " (beckoning him to her), " do ask Captain Wentworth where it was he first met with your poor brother. I always forget."

"It was at Gibraltar, mother, I know. Dick had been left ill at Gibraltar, with a recommendation from his former captain to Captain Wentworth."

"Oh! but Charles, tell Captain Wentworth, he need not be afraid of mentioning poor Dick before me, for it would be rather a pleasure to hear him talked of by such a good friend."

Charles being somewhat more mindful of the probabilities of the case, only nodded in reply, and walked away.

The girls were now hunting for the *Laconia ;* and Captain Wentworth could not deny himself the pleasure of taking the precious volume into his own hands to save them the trouble, and once more read aloud the little statement of her name and rate, and present non-commissioned class, observing over it that she too had been one of the best friends man ever had.

"Ah, those were pleasant days when I had the *Laconia !* How fast I made money in her! A friend of mine and I had such a lovely cruise together off the Western Islands. Poor Harville, sister! You know how much he wanted money: worse than myself. He had a wife. Excellent fellow! I shall never forget his happiness. He felt it all, so much for her sake. I wished for him again the next summer, when I had still the same luck in the Mediterranean."

"And I am sure, sir," said Mrs. Musgrove, "it was a lucky

day for *us*, when you were put captain into that ship. *We* shall never forget what you did."

Her feelings made her speak low; and Captain Wentworth, hearing only in part, and probably not having Dick Musgrove at all near his thoughts, looked rather in suspense, and as if waiting for more.

" My brother," whispered one of the girls; " mamma is thinking of poor Richard."

" Poor dear fellow! " continued Mrs. Musgrove; " he was grown so steady, and such an excellent correspondent, while he was under your care! Ah! it would have been a happy thing, if he had never left you. I assure you, Captain Wentworth, we are very sorry he ever left you."

There was a momentary expression in Captain Wentworth's face at this speech, a certain glance of his bright eye, and curl of his handsome mouth, which convinced Anne, that instead of sharing in Mrs. Musgrove's kind wishes, as to her son, he had probably been at some pains to get rid of him; but it was too transient an indulgence of self-amusement to be detected by any who understood him less than herself; in another moment he was perfectly collected and serious, and almost instantly afterwards coming up to the sofa, on which she and Mrs. Musgrove were sitting, took a place by the latter, and entered into conversation with her, in a low voice, about her son, doing it with so much sympathy and natural grace, as shewed the kindest consideration for all that was real and unabsurd in the parent's feelings.

They were actually on the same sofa, for Mrs. Musgrove had most readily made room for him: they were divided only by Mrs. Musgrove. It was no insignificant barrier, indeed. Mrs. Musgrove was of a comfortable substantial size, infinitely more fitted by nature to express good cheer and good humour than tenderness and sentiment; and while the agitations of Anne's slender form, and pensive face, may be considered as very completely screened, Captain Wentworth should be allowed some credit for the self-command with which he attended to her large fat sighings over the destiny of a son, whom alive nobody had cared for.

Personal size and mental sorrow have certainly no necessary proportions. A large bulky figure has as good a right to be in deep affliction as the most graceful set of limbs in the world. But, fair or not fair, there are unbecoming conjunctions, which reason will patronise in vain—which taste cannot tolerate—which ridicule will seize.

The Admiral, after taking two or three refreshing turns about the room with his hands behind him, being called to order by his wife, now came up to Captain Wentworth, and without any observation of what he might be interrupting, thinking only of his own thoughts, began with—

" If you had been a week later at Lisbon, last spring, Frederick, you would have been asked to give a passage to Lady Mary Grierson and her daughters."

" Should I? I am glad I was not a week later then!"

The Admiral abused him for his want of gallantry. He defended himself; though professing that he would never willingly admit any ladies on board a ship of his, excepting for a ball, or a visit, which a few hours might comprehend.

" But, if I know myself," said he, " this is from no want of gallantry towards them. It is rather from feeling how impossible it is, with all one's efforts, and all one's sacrifices, to make the accommodations on board such as women ought to have. There can be no want of gallantry, Admiral, in rating the claims of women to every personal comfort *high*, and this is what I do. I hate to hear of women on board, or to see them on board; and no ship under my command shall ever convey a family of ladies anywhere, if I can help it."

This brought his sister upon him.

" Oh! Frederick! But I cannot believe it of you.—All idle refinement!—Women may be as comfortable on board as in the best house in England. I believe I have lived as much on board as most women, and I know nothing superior to the accommodations of a man-of-war. I declare I have not a comfort or an indulgence about me, even at Kellynch Hall " (with a kind bow to Anne), " beyond what I always had in most of the ships I have lived in; and they have been five altogether."

" Nothing to the purpose," replied her brother. " You were living with your husband, and were the only woman on board."

"But you, yourself, brought Mrs. Harville, her sister, her cousin, and the three children, round from Portsmouth to Plymouth. Where was this superfine, extraordinary sort of gallantry of yours then?"

"All merged in my friendship, Sophia. I would assist any brother officer's wife that I could, and I would bring anything of Harville's from the world's end, if he wanted it. But do not imagine that I did not feel it an evil in itself."

"Depend upon it, they were all perfectly comfortable."

"I might not like them the better for that, perhaps. Such a number of women and children have no *right* to be comfortable on board."

"My dear Frederick, you are talking quite idly. Pray, what would become of us poor sailors' wives, who often want to be conveyed to one port or another, after our husbands, if everybody had your feelings?"

"My feelings, you see, did not prevent my taking Mrs. Harville and all her family to Plymouth."

"But I hate to hear you talking so like a fine gentleman, and as if women were all fine ladies, instead of rational creatures. We none of us expect to be in smooth water all our days."

"Ah! my dear," said the Admiral, "when he has got a wife, he will sing a different tune. When he is married, if we have the good luck to live to another war, we shall see him do as you and I, and a great many others, have done. We shall have him very thankful to anybody that will bring him his wife."

"Ay, that we shall."

"Now I have done," cried Captain Wentworth. "When once married people begin to attack me with—'Oh! you will think very differently when you are married,' I can only say, 'No, I shall not;' and then they say again, 'Yes, you will,' and there is an end of it."

He got up and moved away.

"What a great traveller you must have been, ma'am!" said Mrs. Musgrove to Mrs. Croft.

"Pretty well, ma'am, in the fifteen years of my marriage; though many women have done more. I have crossed the Atlantic four times, and have been once to the East Indies and back again, and only once; besides being in different places about home: Cork, and Lisbon, and Gibraltar. But I never went beyond the Streights, and never was in the West Indies. We do not call Bermuda or Bahama, you know, the West Indies."

Mrs. Musgrove had not a word to say in dissent; she could not accuse herself of having ever called them anything in the whole course of her life.

"And I do assure you, ma'am," pursued Mrs. Croft, "that nothing can exceed the accommodations of a man-of-war, I speak, you know, of the higher rates. When you come to a frigate, of course, you are more confined; though any reasonable woman may be perfectly happy in one of them; and I can safely say, that the happiest part of my life has been spent on board a ship. While we were together, you know, there was nothing to be feared. Thank God! I have always been blessed with excellent health, and no climate disagrees with me. A little disordered always the first twenty-four hours of going to sea, but never knew what sickness was afterwards. The only time that I ever really suffered in body or mind, the only time that I ever fancied myself unwell, or had any ideas of danger—was the winter that I passed by myself at Deal, when the Admiral (*Captain* Croft then) was in the North Seas. I lived in perpetual fright at that time, and had all manner of imaginary complaints from not knowing what to do with myself, or when I should hear from him next; but as long as we could be together, nothing ever ailed me, and I never met with the smallest inconvenience."

"Ay, to be sure. Yes, indeed, oh yes! I am quite of your opinion, Mrs. Croft," was Mrs. Musgrove's hearty answer. "There is nothing so bad as a separation. I am quite of your opinion. *I* know what it is, for Mr. Musgrove always attends the assizes, and I am so glad when they are over, and he is safe back again."

The evening ended with dancing. On its being proposed, Anne offered her services, as usual; and though her eyes would sometimes fill with tears as she sat at the instrument, she was extremely glad to be employed, and desired nothing in return but to be unobserved.

It was a merry, joyous party, and no one seemed in higher
spirits that Captain Wentworth. She felt that he had everything to elevate him, which general attention and deference,
and especially the attention of all the young women, could do.
The Miss Hayters, the females of the family of cousins already
mentioned, were apparently admitted to the honour of being
in love with him; and as for Henrietta and Louisa, they both
seemed so entirely occupied by him, that nothing but the
continued appearance of the most perfect good-will between
themselves could have made it credible that they were not
decided rivals. If he were a little spoilt by such universal,
such eager admiration, who could wonder?

These were some of the thoughts which occupied Anne,
while her fingers were mechanically at work, proceeding
for half an hour together, equally without error, and without
consciousness. *Once* she felt that he was looking at herself,
observing her altered features, perhaps, trying to trace in
them the ruins of the face which had once charmed him;
and *once* she knew that he must have spoken of her; she was
hardly aware of it till she heard the answer; but then she was
sure of his having asked his partner whether Miss Elliot never
danced? The answer was, "Oh, no! never; she has quite
given up dancing. She had rather play. She is never tired
of playing." Once, too, he spoke to her. She had left the
instrument on the dancing being over, and he had sat down
to try to make out an air which he wished to give the Miss
Musgroves an idea of. Unintentionally she returned to that
part of the room; he saw her, and instantly rising, said, with
studied politeness—

"I beg your pardon, madam, this is your seat;" and
though she immediately drew back with a decided negative,
he was not to be induced to sit down again.

Anne did not wish for more of such looks and speeches.
His cold politeness, his ceremonious grace, were worse than
anything.

CHAPTER IX

CAPTAIN WENTWORTH was come to Kellynch as to a home, to stay as long as he liked, being as thoroughly the object of the Admiral's fraternal kindness as of his wife's. He had intended, on first arriving, to proceed very soon into Shropshire, and visit the brother settled in that country, but the attractions of Uppercross induced him to put this off. There was so much of friendliness, and of flattery, and of everything most bewitching in his reception there; the old were so hospitable, the young so agreeable, that he could not but resolve to remain where he was, and take all the charms and perfections of Edward's wife upon credit a little longer.

It was soon Uppercross with him almost every day. The Musgroves could hardly be more ready to invite than he to come, particularly in the morning, when he had no companion at home; for the Admiral and Mrs. Croft were generally out of doors together, interesting themselves in their new possessions, their grass, and their sheep, and dawdling about in a way not endurable to a third person, or driving out in a gig, lately added to their establishment.

Hitherto there had been but one opinion of Captain Wentworth among the Musgroves and their dependencies. It was unvarying, warm admiration everywhere; but this intimate footing was not more than established, when a certain Charles Hayter returned among them, to be a good deal disturbed by it, and to think Captain Wentworth very much in the way.

Charles Hayter was the eldest of all the cousins, and a very amiable, pleasing young man, between whom and Henrietta there had been a considerable appearance of attachment previous to Captain Wentworth's introduction. He was in orders; and having a curacy in the neighbourhood, where residence was not required, lived at his father's house, only two miles from Uppercross. A short absence from home had left his fair one unguarded by his attentions at this critical period, and when he came back he had the pain of finding very altered manners, and of seeing Captain Went worth.

Mrs. Musgrove and Mrs. Hayter were sisters. They had each had money, but their marriages had made a material difference in their degree of consequence. Mr. Hayter had some property of his own, but it was insignificant compared with Mr. Musgrove's; and while the Musgroves were in the first class of society in the country, the young Hayters would, from their parents' inferior, retired, and unpolished way of living, and their own defective education, have been hardly in any class at all, but for their connection with Uppercross, this eldest son of course excepted, who had chosen to be a scholar and a gentleman, and who was very superior in cultivation and manners to all the rest.

The two families had always been on excellent terms, there being no pride on one side, and no envy on the other, and only such a consciousness of superiority in the Miss Musgroves, as made them pleased to improve their cousins. Charles's attentions to Henrietta had been observed by her father and mother without any disapprobation. " It would not be a great match for her; but if Henrietta liked him,"— and Henrietta *did* seem to like him.

Henrietta fully thought so herself, before Captain Wentworth came; but from that time Cousin Charles had been very much forgotten.

Which of the two sisters was preferred by Captain Wentworth was as yet quite doubtful, as far as Anne's observation reached. Henrietta was perhaps the prettiest, Louisa had the higher spirits; and she knew not *now*, whether the more gentle or the more lively character were most likely to attract him.

Mr. and Mrs. Musgrove, either from seeing little, or from an entire confidence in the discretion of both their daughters, and of all the young men who came near them, seemed to leave everything to take its chance. There was not the smallest appearance of solicitude or remark about them in the Mansion-house; but it was different at the Cottage; the young couple there were more disposed to speculate and wonder; and Captain Wentworth had not been above four or five times in the Miss Musgroves' company, and

Charles Hayter had but just reappeared, when Anne had to listen to the opinions of her brother and sister, as to *which* was the one liked best. Charles gave it for Louisa, Mary for Henrietta, but quite agreeing that to have him marry either would be extremely delightful.

Charles " had never seen a pleasanter man in his life; and from what he had once heard Captain Wentworth himself say, was very sure that he had not made less than twenty thousand pounds by the war. Here was a fortune at once: besides which, there would be the chance of what might be done in any future war; and he was sure Captain Wentworth was as likely a man to distinguish himself as any officer in the navy. Oh! it would be a capital match for either of his sisters."

" Upon my word it would," replied Mary. " Dear me! If he should rise to any very great honours! If he should ever be made a baronet! ' Lady Wentworth ' sounds very well. That would be a noble thing, indeed, for Henrietta! She would take place of me then, and Henrietta would not dislike that. Sir Frederick and Lady Wentworth! It would be but a new creation, however, and I never think much of your new creations."

It suited Mary best to think Henrietta the one preferred on the very account of Charles Hayter, whose pretensions she wished to see put an end to. She looked down very decidedly upon the Hayters, and thought it would be quite a misfortune to have the existing connexion between the families renewed—very sad for herself and her children.

" You know," said she, " I cannot think him at all a fit match for Henrietta; and considering the alliances which the Musgroves have made, she has no right to throw herself away. I do not think any young woman has a right to make a choice that may be disagreeable and inconvenient to the *principal* part of her family, and be giving bad connexions to those who have not been used to them. And, pray, who is Charles Hayter? Nothing but a country curate. A most improper match for Miss Musgrove of Uppercross."

Her husband, however, would not agree with her here; for besides having a regard for his cousin, Charles Hayter was an eldest son, and he saw things as an eldest son himself.

"Now you are talking nonsense, Mary," was therefore his answer. "It would not be a *great* match for Henrietta, but Charles has a very fair chance, through the Spicers, of getting something from the Bishop in the course of a year or two; and you will please to remember, that he is the eldest son; whenever my uncle dies, he steps into very pretty property. The estate at Winthrop is not less than two hundred and fifty acres, besides the farm near Taunton, which is some of the best land in the country. I grant you, that any of them but Charles would be a very shocking match for Henrietta, and indeed it could not be; he is the only one that could be possible; but he is a very good-natured, good sort of a fellow; and whenever Winthrop comes into his hands, he will make a different sort of place of it, and live in a very different sort of way; and with that property he will never be a contemptible man—good freehold property. No, no; Henrietta might do worse than marry Charles Hayter; and if she has him, and Louisa can get Captain Wentworth, I shall be very well satisfied."

"Charles may say what he pleases," cried Mary to Anne, as soon as he was out of the room, "but it would be shocking to have Henrietta marry Charles Hayter: a very bad thing for *her*, and still worse for *me;* and therefore it is very much to be wished that Captain Wentworth may soon put him quite out of her head, and I have very little doubt that he has. She took hardly any notice of Charles Hayter yesterday. I wish you had been there to see her behaviour. And as to Captain Wentworth's liking Louisa as well as Henrietta, it is nonsense to say so; for he certainly *does* like Henrietta a great deal the best. But Charles is so positive! I wish you had been with us yesterday, for then you might have decided between us; and I am sure you would have thought as I did, unless you had been determined to give it against me."

A dinner at Mr. Musgrove's had been the occasion when all these things should have been seen by Anne; but she had staid at home, under the mixed plea of a headache of her own, and some return of indisposition in little Charles. She had thought only of avoiding Captain Wentworth; but an escape from being appealed to as umpire was now added to the advantages of a quiet evening.

As to Captain Wentworth's views, she deemed it of more consequence that he should know his own mind early enough not to be endangering the happiness of either sister, or impeaching his own honour, than that he should prefer Henrietta to Louisa, or Louisa to Henrietta. Either of them would, in all probability, make him an affectionate, good-humoured wife. With regard to Charles Hayter, she had delicacy which must be pained by any lightness of conduct in a well-meaning young woman, and a heart to sympathise in any of the sufferings it occasioned; but if Henrietta found herself mistaken in the nature of her feelings, the alteration could not be understood too soon.

Charles Hayter had met with much to disquiet and mortify him in his cousin's behaviour. She had too old a regard for him to be so wholly estranged as might in two meetings extinguish every past hope, and leave him nothing to do but to keep away from Uppercross: but there was such a change as became very alarming, when such a man as Captain Wentworth was to be regarded as the probable cause. He had been absent only two Sundays, and when they parted, had left her interested, even to the height of his wishes, in his prospect of soon quitting his present curacy, and obtaining that of Uppercross instead. It had then seemed the object nearest her heart, that Dr. Shirley, the rector, who for more than forty years had been zealously discharging all the duties of his office, but was now growing too infirm for many of them, should be quite fixed on engaging a curate; should make his curacy quite as good as he could afford, and should give Charles Hayter the promise of it. The advantage of his having to come only to Uppercross, instead of going six miles another way; of his having, in every respect, a better curacy; of his belonging to their dear Dr. Shirley; and of dear, good Dr. Shirley's being relieved from the duty which he could no longer get through without most injurious fatigue, had been a great deal, even to Louisa, but had been almost everything to Henrietta. When he came back, alas! the zeal of the business was gone by. Louisa could not listen at all to his account of a conversation which he had just held with Dr. Shirley: she was at the window, looking out for Captain Wentworth; and even Henrietta had at best only a divided attention to give, and seemed to have forgotten all the former doubt and solicitude of the negotiation.

"Well, I am very glad, indeed; but I always thought you would have it; I always thought you sure. It did not appear to me that—in short, you know, Dr. Shirley *must* have a curate, and you had secured his promise. Is he coming, Louisa?"

One morning, very soon after the dinner at the Musgroves, at which Anne had not been present, Captain Wentworth walked into the drawing-room at the Cottage, where were only herself and the little invalid Charles, who was lying on the sofa.

The surprise of finding himself almost alone with Anne Elliot deprived his manners of their usual composure: he started, and could only say, " I thought the Miss Musgroves had been here: Mrs. Musgrove told me I should find them here," before he walked to the window to recollect himself, and feel how he ought to behave.

" They are upstairs with my sister: they will be down in a few moments, I dare say," had been Anne's reply, in all the confusion that was natural; and if the child had not called her to come and do something for him, she would have been out of the room the next moment, and released Captain Wentworth as well as herself.

He continued at the window; and after calmly and politely saying, " I hope the little boy is better," was silent.

She was obliged to kneel down by the sofa, and remain there to satisfy her patient; and thus they continued a few minutes, when, to her very great satisfaction, she heard some other person crossing the little vestibule. She hoped, on turning her head, to see the master of the house; but it proved to be one much less calculated for making matters easy—Charles Hayter, probably not at all better pleased by the sight of Captain Wentworth, than Captain Wentworth had been by the sight of Anne.

She only attempted to say, " How do you do? Will not you sit down? The others will be here presently."

Captain Wentworth, however, came from his window, apparently not ill-disposed for conversation; but Charles Hayter soon put an end to his attempts, by seating himself near the table, and taking up the newspaper; and Captain Wentworth returned to his window.

Another minute brought another addition. The younger boy, a remarkable stout, forward child, of two years old, having got the door opened for him by some one without, made his determined appearance among them, and went straight to the sofa to see what was going on, and put in his claim to anything good that might be giving away.

There being nothing to be eat, he could only have some play; and as his aunt would not let him tease his sick brother, he began to fasten himself upon her, as she knelt, in such a way that, busy as she was about Charles, she could not shake him off. She spoke to him, ordered, intreated, and insisted in vain. Once she did contrive to push him away, but the boy had the greater pleasure in getting upon her back again directly.

"Walter," said she, "get down this moment. You are extremely troublesome. I am very angry with you."

"Walter," cried Charles Hayter, "why do you not do as you are bid? Do not you hear your aunt speak? Come to me, Walter; come to cousin Charles."

But not a bit did Walter stir.

In another moment, however, she found herself in the state of being released from him; some one was taking him from her, though he had bent down her head so much, that his little sturdy hands were unfastened from around her neck, and he was resolutely borne away, before she knew that Captain Wentworth had done it.

Her sensations on the discovery made her perfectly speechless. She could not even thank him. She could only hang over little Charles, with most disordered feelings. His kindness in stepping forward to her relief, the manner, the silence in which it had passed, the little particulars of the circumstance, with the conviction soon forced on her by the noise he was studiously making with the child, that he meant to avoid hearing her thanks, and rather sought to testify that her conversation was the last of his wants, produced such a confusion of varying, but very painful agitation, as she could not recover from, till enabled, by the entrance of Mary and the Miss Musgroves, to make over her little patient to their cares, and leave the room. She could not stay. It might have been an opportunity of watching the loves and jealousies of the four—they were now altogether; but she could stay for none of it. It was evident that Charles Hayter was not well inclined towards Captain Wentworth. She had a strong impression of his having said, in a vext tone of voice, after Captain Wentworth's interference, "You ought to have minded *me*, Walter; I told you not to tease your aunt;" and could comprehend his regretting that Captain Wentworth should do what he ought to have done himself. But neither Charles Hayter's feelings, nor anybody's feelings, could interest her, till she had a little better arranged her own. She was ashamed of herself, quite ashamed of being so nervous, so overcome by such a trifle; but so it was, and it required a long application of solitude and reflection to recover her.

CHAPTER X

OTHER opportunities of making her observations could not fail to occur. Anne had soon been in company with all the four together often enough to have an opinion, though too wise to acknowledge as much at home, where she knew it would have satisfied neither husband nor wife; for while she considered Louisa to be rather the favourite, she could not but think, as far as she might dare to judge from memory and experience, that Captain Wentworth was not in love with either. They were more in love with him; yet there it was not love. It was a little fever of admiration; but it might, probably must, end in love with some. Charles Hayter seemed aware of being slighted, and yet Henrietta had sometimes the air of being divided between them. Anne longed for the power of representing to them all what they were about, and of pointing out some of the evils they were exposing themselves to. She did not attribute guile to any. It was the highest satisfaction to her to believe Captain Wentworth not in the least aware of the pain he was occasioning. There was no triumph, no pitiful triumph in his manner. He had, probably, never heard, and never thought of any claims of Charles Hayter. He was only wrong in accepting the attentions (for accepting must be the word) of two young women at once.

After a short struggle, however, Charles Hayter seemed to quit the field. Three days had passed without his coming once to Uppercross; a most decided change. He had even refused one regular invitation to dinner; and having been found on the occasion by Mr. Musgrove with some large books before him, Mr. and Mrs. Musgrove were sure all could not be right, and talked, with grave faces, of his studying himself to death. It was Mary's hope and belief that he had received a positive dismissal from Henrietta, and her husband lived under the constant dependance of seeing him to-morrow. Anne could only feel that Charles Hayter was wise.

One morning, about this time, Charles Musgrove and Captain Wentworth being gone a-shooting together, as the sisters in the Cottage were sitting quietly at work, they were visited at the window by the sisters from the Mansion-house.

It was a very fine November day, and the Miss Musgroves came through the little grounds, and stopped for no other purpose than to say, that they were going to take a *long* walk, and therefore concluded Mary could not like to go with them; and when Mary immediately replied, with some jealousy at not being supposed a good walker, "Oh, yes! I should like to join you very much, I am very fond of a long walk;" Anne felt persuaded, by the looks of the two girls, that it was precisely what they did not wish, and admired again the sort of necessity which the family habits seemed to produce, of everything being to be communicated, and everything being to be done together, however undesired and inconvenient. She tried to dissuade Mary from going, but in vain; and that being the case, thought it best to accept the Miss Musgroves' much more cordial invitation to herself to go likewise, as she might be useful in turning back with her sister, and lessening the interference in any plan of their own.

" I cannot imagine why they should suppose I should not like a long walk," said Mary, as she went upstairs. " Everybody is always supposing that I am not a good walker; and yet they would not have been pleased if we had refused to join them. When people come in this manner on purpose to ask us, how can one say no? "

Just as they were setting off, the gentlemen returned. They had taken out a young dog, which had spoilt their sport, and sent them back early. Their time, and strength, and spirits, were, therefore, exactly ready for this walk, and they entered into it with pleasure. Could Anne have foreseen such a junction, she would have staid at home; but, from some feelings of interest and curiosity, she fancied now that it was too late to retract, and the whole six set forward together in the direction chosen by the Miss Musgroves, who evidently considered the walk as under their guidance.

Anne's object was, not to be in the way of anybody; and where the narrow paths across the fields made many separations necessary, to keep with her brother and sister. Her *pleasure* in the walk must arise from the exercise and the day, from the view of the last smiles of the year upon the tawny leaves, and withered hedges, and from repeating to herself some few of the thousand poetical descriptions extant of autumn, that season of peculiar and inexhaustible influence on the mind of taste and tenderness, that season which has drawn from every poet, worthy of being read, some attempt at description, or some lines of feeling. She occupied her mind as much as possible in such like musings and quotations; but it was not possible, that when within reach of Captain Wentworth's conversation with either of the Miss Musgroves, she should not try to hear it; yet she caught little very remarkable. It was mere lively chat, such as any young persons, on an intimate footing, might fall into. He was more engaged with Louisa, than with Henrietta. Louisa certainly put more forward for his notice than her sister. This distinction appeared to increase, and there was one speech of Louisa's which struck her. After one of the many praises of the day, which were continually bursting forth, Captain Wentworth added:—

" What glorious weather for the Admiral and my sister! They meant to take a long drive this morning; perhaps we may hail them from some of these hills. They talked of coming into this side of the country. I wonder whereabouts they will upset to-day. Oh! it does happen very often, I assure you; but my sister makes nothing of it; she would as lieve be tossed out as not."

"Ah! you make the most of it, I know," cried Louisa; "but if it were really so, I should do just the same in her place. If I loved a man as she loves the Admiral, I would always be with him, nothing should ever separate us, and I would rather be overturned by him, than driven safely by anybody else."

It was spoken with enthusiasm.

"Had you?" cried he, catching the same tone; "I honour you!" And there was silence between them for a little while.

Anne could not immediately fall into a quotation again. The sweet scenes of autumn were for a while put by, unless some tender sonnet, fraught with the apt analogy of the declining year, with declining happiness, and the images of youth, and hope, and spring, all gone together, blessed her memory. She roused herself to say, as they struck by order into another path, "Is not this one of the ways to Winthrop?" But nobody heard, or, at least, nobody answered her.

Winthrop, however, or its environs—for young men are sometimes to be met with, strolling about near home—was their destination; and after another half mile of gradual ascent through large enclosures, where the ploughs at work, and the fresh made path spoke the farmer counteracting the sweets of poetical despondence, and meaning to have spring again, they gained the summit of the most considerable hill, which parted Uppercross and Winthrop, and soon commanded a full view of the latter, at the foot of the hill on the other side.

Winthrop, without beauty and without dignity, was stretched before them an indifferent house, standing low, and hemmed in by the barns and buildings of a farmyard.

Mary exclaimed, "Bless me! here is Winthrop. I declare I had no idea! Well now, I think we had better turn back; I am excessively tired."

Henrietta, conscious and ashamed, and seeing no cousin Charles walking along any path, or leaning against any gate, was ready to do as Mary wished; but " No!" said Charles Musgrove, and " No, no!" cried Louisa, more eagerly, and taking her sister aside, seemed to be arguing the matter warmly.

Charles, in the meanwhile, was very decidedly declaring his resolution of calling on his aunt, now that he was so near; and very evidently, though more fearfully, trying to induce his wife to go too. But this was one of the points on which the lady shewed her strength; and when he recommended the advantage of resting herself a quarter of an hour at Winthrop, as she felt so tired, she resolutely answered, " Oh, no, indeed! walking up that hill again would do her more harm than any sitting down could do her good; " and in short, her look and manner declared, that go she would not.

After a little succession of these sort of debates and consultations, it was settled between Charles and his two sisters, that he and Henrietta should just run down for a few minutes, to see their aunt and cousins, while the rest of the party waited for them at the top of the hill. Louisa seemed the principal arranger of the plan; and, as she went a little way with them down the hill, still talking to Henrietta, Mary took the opportunity of looking scornfully around her, and saying to Captain Wentworth—

" It is very unpleasant having such connexions! But, I assure you, I have never been in the house above twice in my life."

She received no other answer than an artificial, assenting smile, followed by a contemptuous glance, as he turned away, which Anne perfectly knew the meaning of.

The brow of the hill, where they remained, was a cheerful spot: Louisa returned; and Mary, finding a comfortable seat for herself on the step of a stile, was very well satisfied so long as the others all stood about her; but when Louise drew Captain Wentworth away, to try for a gleaning of nuts in an adjoining hedge-row, and they were gone by degrees quite out of sight and sound, Mary was happy no longer: she quarrelled with her own seat, was sure Louisa had got a much better somewhere, and nothing could prevent her from going to look for a better also. She turned through the same gate, but could not see them. Anne found a nice seat for her, on a dry sunny bank, under the hedge-row, in which she had no doubt of their still being, in some spot or other. Mary sat down for a moment, but it would not do; she was sure Louisa had found a better seat somewhere else, and she would go on till she overtook her.

Anne, really tired herself, was glad to sit down; and she very soon heard Captain Wentworth and Louisa in the hedge-row behind her, as if making their way back along the rough, wild sort of channel, down the centre. They were speaking as they drew near. Louisa's voice was the first distinguished. She seemed to be in the middle of some eager speech. What Anne first heard was—

" And so, I made her go. I could not bear that she should be frightened from the visit by such nonsense. What! would I be turned back from doing a thing that I had determined to do, and that I knew to be right, by the airs and interference of such a person, or of any person, I may say? No, I have no idea of being so easily persuaded. When I have made up my mind, I have made it; and Henrietta seemed entirely to have made up hers to call at Winthrop to-day; and yet, she was as near giving it up out of nonsensical complaisance! "

" She would have turned back, then, but for you? "

" She would, indeed. I am almost ashamed to say it."

" Happy for her, to have such a mind as yours at hand! After the hints you gave just now, which did but confirm my own observations, the last time I was in company with him, I need not affect to have no comprehension of what is going on. I see that more than a mere dutiful morning visit to your aunt was in question; and woe betide him, and her too, when it comes to things of consequence, when they are placed in circumstances requiring fortitude and strength of mind, if she have not resolution enough to resist idle inter-ference in such a trifle as this. Your sister is an amiable creature; but *yours* is the character of decision and firmness, I see. If you value her conduct or happiness, infuse as much of your own spirit into her as you can. But this, no doubt, you have been always doing. It is the worst evil of too yielding and indecisive a character, that no influence over it can be depended on. You are never sure of a good impression being durable; everybody may sway it. Let those who would be happy be firm. Here is a nut," said he, catching one down from an upper bough, " to exemplify: a beautiful glossy nut, which, blessed with original strength, has outlived all the storms of autumn. Not a puncture, not a weak spot anywhere. This nut," he continued, with playful solemnity, " while so many of its brethren have fallen and been trodden under foot, is still in possession of all the happiness that a hazel nut can be supposed capable of." Then returning to his former earnest tone—" My first wish for all whom I am interested in, is that they should be firm. If Louisa Musgrove would be beautiful and happy in her November of life, she will cherish all her present powers of mind."

He had done, and was unanswered. It would have surprised Anne if Louisa could have readily answered such a speech: words of such interest, spoken with such serious warmth! She could imagine what Louisa was feeling. For herself, she feared to move, lest she should be seen. While she remained, a bush of low rambling holly protected her, and they were moving on. Before they were beyond her hearing, however, Louisa spoke again.

" Mary is good-natured enough in many respects," said she; " but she does sometimes provoke me excessively by her nonsense and pride—the Elliot pride. She has a great deal too much of the Elliot pride. We do so wish that Charles had married Anne instead. I suppose you know he wanted to marry Anne? "

After a moment's pause, Captain Wentworth said—

" Do you mean that she refused him? "

" Oh! yes; certainly."

" When did that happen? "

" I do not exactly know, for Henrietta and I were at school at the time; but I believe about a year before he married Mary. I wish she had accepted him. We should all have liked her a great deal better; and papa and mamma always think it was her great friend Lady Russell's doing that she did not. They think Charles might not be learned and bookish enough to please Lady Russell, and that, therefore, she persuaded Anne to refuse him."

The sounds were retreating, and Anne distinguished no

more. Her own emotions still kept her fixed. She had much to recover from before she could move. The listener's proverbial fate was not absolutely hers: she had heard no evil of herself, but she had heard a great deal of very painful import. She saw how her own character was considered by Captain Wentworth, and there had been just that degree of feeling and curiosity about her in his manner which must give her extreme agitation.

As soon as she could, she went after Mary, and having found, and walked back with her to their former station, by the stile, felt some comfort in their whole party being immediately afterwards collected, and once more in motion together. Her spirits wanted the solitude and silence which only numbers could give.

Charles and Henrietta returned, bringing, as may be conjectured, Charles Hayter with them. The minutiæ of the business Anne could not attempt to understand; even Captain Wentworth did not seem admitted to perfect confidence here; but that there had been a withdrawing on the gentleman's side, and a relenting on the lady's, and that they were now very glad to be together again, did not admit a doubt. Henrietta looked a little ashamed, but very well pleased;—Charles Hayter exceedingly happy: and they were devoted to each other almost from the first instant of their all setting forward for Uppercross.

Everything now marked out Louisa for Captain Wentworth: nothing could be plainer; and where many divisions were necessary, or even where they were not, they walked side by side nearly as much as the other two. In a long strip of meadow land, where there was ample space for all, they were thus divided, forming three distinct parties; and to that party of the three which boasted least animation, and least complaisance, Anne necessarily belonged. She joined Charles and Mary, and was tired enough to be very glad of Charles's other arm; but Charles, though in very good humour with her, was out of temper with his wife. Mary had shewn herself disobliging to him, and was now to reap the consequence, which consequence was his dropping her arm almost every moment to cut off the heads of some nettles in the hedge with his switch; and when Mary began to complain of it, and lament her being ill-used, according to custom, in being on the hedge side, while Anne was never incommoded on the other, he dropped the arms of both, to hunt after a weasel, which he had a momentary glance of, and they could hardly get him along at all.

This long meadow bordered a lane which their footpath, at the end of it, was to cross, and when the party had all reached the gate of exit, the carriage advancing in the same direction, which had been some time heard, was just coming up, and proved to be Admiral Croft's gig. He and his wife had taken their intended drive, and were returning home. Upon hearing how long a walk the young people had engaged in, they kindly offered a seat to any lady who might be particularly tired; it would save her full a mile, and they were going through Uppercross. The invitation was general and generally declined. The Miss Musgroves were not at all tired, and Mary was either offended by not being asked before any of the others, or what Louisa called the Elliot pride could not endure to make a third in a one-horse chaise.

The walking party had crossed the lane, and were surmounting an opposite stile, and the Admiral was putting his horse into motion again, when Captain Wentworth cleared the hedge in a moment, to say something to his sister. The something might be guessed by its effects.

"Miss Elliot, I am sure *you* are tired," cried Mrs. Croft. "Do let us have the pleasure of taking you home. Here is excellent room for three, I assure you. If we were all like you, I believe we might sit four. You must, indeed, you must."

Anne was still in the lane, and though instinctively beginning to decline, she was not allowed to proceed. The Admiral's kind urgency came in support of his wife's: they would not be refused: they compressed themselves into the smallest possible space to leave her a corner, and Captain Wentworth, without saying a word, turned to her, and quietly obliged her to be assisted into the carriage.

Yes; he had done it. She was in the carriage, and felt that he had placed her there, that his will and his hands had done it, that she owed it to his perception of her fatigue, and his resolution to give her rest. She was very much affected by the view of his disposition towards her, which all these things made apparent. This little circumstance seemed the completion of all that had gone before. She understood him. He could not forgive her, but he could not be unfeeling. Though condemning her for the past, and considering it with high and unjust resentment, though perfectly careless of her, and though becoming attached to another, still he could not see her suffer without the desire of giving her relief. It was a remainder of former sentiment; it was an impulse of pure, though unacknowledged, friendship; it was a proof of his own warm and amiable heart, which she could not contemplate without emotions so compounded of pleasure and pain, that she knew not which prevailed.

Her answers to the kindness and the remarks of her companions were at first unconsciously given. They had travelled half their way along the rough lane before she was quite awake to what they said. She then found them talking of " Frederick."

" He certainly means to have one or other of those two girls, Sophy," said the Admiral; " but there is no saying which. He has been running after them, too, long enough, one would think, to make up his mind. Ay, this comes of the peace. If it were war now, he would have settled it long ago. We sailors, Miss Elliot, cannot afford to make long courtships in time of war. How many days was it, my dear, between the first time of my seeing you and our sitting down together in our lodgings at North Yarmouth? "

" We had better not talk about it, my dear," replied Mrs. Croft, pleasantly; " for if Miss Elliot were to hear how soon we came to an understanding, she would never be persuaded that we could be happy together. I had known you by character, however, long before."

" Well, and I had heard of you as a very pretty girl, and what were we to wait for besides? I do not like having such things so long in hand. I wish Frederick would spread a little more canvas, and bring us home one of these young ladies to Kellynch. Then there would always be company for them. And very nice young ladies they both are; I hardly know one from the other."

"Very good humoured, unaffected girls, indeed," said Mrs. Croft, in a tone of calmer praise, such as made Anne suspect that her keener powers might not consider either of them as quite worthy of her brother; "and a very respectable family. One could not be connected with better people. My dear Admiral, that post! we shall certainly take that post."

But by coolly giving the reins a better direction herself they happily passed the danger; and by once afterwards judiciously putting out her hand they neither fell into a rut, nor ran foul of a dung-cart; and Anne, with some amusement at their style of driving, which she imagined no bad representation of the general guidance of their affairs, found herself safely deposited by them at the Cottage.

CHAPTER XI

The time now approached for Lady Russell's return: the day was even fixed; and Anne, being engaged to join her as soon as she was resettled, was looking forward to an early removal to Kellynch, and beginning to think how her own comfort was likely to be affected by it.

It would place her in the same village with Captain Wentworth, within half a mile of him; they would have to frequent the same church, and there must be intercourse between the two families. This was against her; but on the other hand, he spent so much of his time at Uppercross, that in removing thence she might be considered rather as leaving him behind, than as going towards him; and upon the whole, she believed she must, on this interesting question, be the gainer, almost as certainly as in her change of domestic society, in leaving poor Mary for Lady Russell.

She wished it might be possible for her to avoid ever seeing Captain Wentworth at the Hall: those rooms had witnessed former meetings which would be brought too painfully before her; but she was yet more anxious for the possibility of Lady Russell and Captain Wentworth never meeting anywhere. They did not like each other, and no renewal of acquaintance now could do any good; and were Lady Russell to see them together, she might think that he had too much self-possession, and she too little.

These points formed her chief solicitude in anticipating her removal from Uppercross, where she felt she had been stationed quite long enough. Her usefulness to little Charles would always give some sweetness to the memory of her two months' visit there, but he was gaining strength apace, and she had nothing else to stay for.

The conclusion of her visit, however, was diversified in a way which she had not at all imagined. Captain Wentworth, after being unseen and unheard of at Uppercross for two whole days, appeared again among them to justify himself by a relation of what had kept him away.

A letter from his friend, Captain Harville, having found him out at last, had brought intelligence of Captain Harville's being settled with his family at Lyme for the winter; of their being, therefore, quite unknowingly, within twenty miles of each other. Captain Harville had never been in good health since a severe wound which he received two years before, and Captain Wentworth's anxiety to see him had determined him to go immediately to Lyme. He had been there for four-and-twenty hours. His acquittal was complete, his friendship warmly honoured, a lively interest excited for his friend, and his description of the fine country about Lyme so feelingly attended to by the party, that an earnest desire to see Lyme themselves, and a project for going thither was the consequence.

The young people were all wild to see Lyme. Captain Wentworth talked of going there again himself, it was only seventeen miles from Uppercross; though November, the weather was by no means bad; and, in short, Louisa, who was the most eager of the eager, having formed the resolution to go, and besides the pleasure of doing as she liked, being now armed with the idea of merit in maintaining her own way, bore down all the wishes of her father and mother for putting it off till summer; and to Lyme they were to go — Charles, Mary, Anne, Henrietta, Louisa, and Captain Wentworth.

The first heedless scheme had been to go in the morning and return at night; but to this Mr. Musgrove, for the sake of his horses, woud not consent; and when it came to be rationally considered, a day in the middle of November would not leave much time for seeing a new place, after deducting seven hours, as the nature of the country required, for going and returning. They were, consequently, to stay the night there, and not to be expected back till the next day's dinner. This was felt to be a considerable amendment; and though they all met at the Great House at rather a early breakfast hour, and set off very punctually, it was so much past noon before the two carriages, Mr. Musgrove's coach containing the four ladies, and Charles's curricle, in which he drove Captain Wentworth, were descending the long hill into Lyme, and entering upon the still steeper street of the town itself, that it was very evident they would not have more than time for looking about them, before the light and warmth of the day were gone.

After securing accommodations, and ordering a dinner at one of the inns, the next thing to be done was unquestionably to walk directly down to the sea. They were come too late in the year for any amusement or variety which Lyme, as a public place, might offer. The rooms were shut up, the lodgers almost all gone, scarcely any family but of the residents left; and, as there is nothing to admire in the buildings themselves, the remarkable situation of the town, the principal street almost hurrying into the water, the walk to the Cobb, skirting round the pleasant little bay, which, in the season, is animated with bathing machines and company; the Cobb itself, its old wonders and new improvements, with the very beautiful line of cliffs stretching out to the east of the town, are what the stranger's eye will seek; and a very strange stranger it must be, who does not see charms in the immediate environs of Lyme, to make him wish to know it better. The scenes in its neighbourhood, Charmouth, with its high grounds and extensive sweeps of country, and still more, its sweet, retired bay, backed by dark cliffs, where fragments of low rock among the sands make it the happiest spot for watching the flow of the tide, for sitting in unwearied contemplation; the wooded varieties

of the cheerful village of Up Lyme; and, above all, Pinny,
with its green chasms between romantic rocks, where the
scattered forest trees and orchards of luxuriant growth,
declare that many a generation must have passed away since
the first partial falling of the cliff prepared the ground for
such a state, where a scene so wonderful and so lovely is
exhibited, as may more than equal any of the resembling
scenes of the far-famed Isle of Wight: these places must
be visited, and visited again to make the worth of Lyme
understood.

The party from Uppercross passing down by the now
deserted and melancholy looking rooms, and still descending,
soon found themselves on the sea-shore; and lingering only,
as all must linger and gaze on a first return to the sea, who
ever deserve to look on it at all, proceeded towards the Cobb,
equally their object in itself and on Captain Wentworth's
account: for in a small house, near the foot of an old pier of
unknown date, were the Harvilles settled. Captain Wentworth turned in to call on his friend; the others walked on,
and he was to join them on the Cobb.

They were by no means tired of wondering and admiring;
and not even Louisa seemed to feel that they had parted
with Captain Wentworth long, when they saw him coming
after them, with three companions, all well known already,
by description, to be Captain and Mrs. Harville, and a
Captain Benwick, who was staying with them.

Captain Benwick had some time ago been first lieutenant
of the *Laconia;* and the account which Captain Wentworth
had given of him, on his return from Lyme before, his warm
praise of him as an excellent young man and an officer,
whom he had always valued highly, which must have stamped
him well in the esteem of every listener, had been followed
by a little history of his private life, which rendered him
perfectly interesting in the eyes of all the ladies. He had
been engaged to Captain Harville's sister, and was now
mourning her loss. They had been a year or two waiting
for fortune and promotion. Fortune came, his prize-money
as lieutenant being great; promotion, too, came at *last;*
but Fanny Harville did not live to know it. She had died
the preceding summer while he was at sea. Captain Went-

worth believed it impossible for man to be more attached to woman than poor Benwick had been to Fanny Harville, or to be more deeply afflicted under the dreadful change. He considered his disposition as of the sort which must suffer heavily, uniting very strong feelings with quiet, serious, and retiring manners, and a decided taste for reading, and sedentary pursuits. To finish the interest of the story, the friendship between him and the Harvilles seemed, if possible, augmented by the event which closed all their views of alliance, and Captain Benwick was now living with them entirely. Captain Harville had taken his present house for half a year; his taste, and his health, and his fortune, all directing him to a residence unexpensive, and by the sea; and the grandeur of the country, and the retirement of Lyme in the winter, appeared exactly adapted to Captain Benwick's state of mind. The sympathy and good-will excited towards Captain Benwick was very great.

"And yet," said Anne to herself, as they now moved forward to meet the party, "he has not, perhaps, a more sorrowing heart than I have. I cannot believe his prospects so blighted for ever. He is younger than I am; younger in feeling, if not in fact; younger as a man. He will rally again, and be happy with another."

They all met, and were introduced. Captain Harville was a tall, dark man, with a sensible, benevolent countenance: a little lame; and, from strong features and want of health, looking much older than Captain Wentworth. Captain Benwick looked, and was, the youngest of the three, and, compared with either of them, a little man. He had a pleasing face and a melancholy air, just as he ought to have, and drew back from conversation.

Captain Harville, though not equalling Captain Wentworth in manners, was a perfect gentleman, unaffected, warm, and obliging. Mrs. Harville, a degree less polished than her husband, seemed, however, to have the same good feelings; and nothing could be more pleasant than their desire of considering the whole party as friends of their own, because the friends of Captain Wentworth, or more kindly hospitable than their entreaties for their all promising to dine with them. The dinner, already ordered at the inn, was at last, though unwillingly, accepted as an excuse; but they seemed almost hurt that Captain Wentworth should have brought any such party to Lyme, without considering it as a thing of course that they should dine with them.

There was so much attachment to Captain Wentworth in all this, and such a bewitching charm in a degree of hospitality so uncommon, so unlike the usual style of give-and-take invitations, and dinners of formality and display, that Anne felt her spirits not likely to be benefited by an increasing acquaintance among his brother-officers. " These. would have been all my friends," was her thought; and she had to struggle against a great tendency to lowness.

On quitting the Cobb, they all went in-doors with their new friends, and found rooms so small as none but those who invite from the heart could think capable of accommodating so many. Anne had a moment's astonishment on the subject herself; but it was soon lost in the pleasanter feelings which sprang from the sight of all the ingenious contrivances and nice arrangements of Captain Harville, to turn the actual space to the best possible account, to supply the deficiencies of lodging-house furniture, and defend the windows and doors against the winter storms to be expected. The varieties in the fitting-up of the rooms, where the common necessaries provided by the owner, in the common indifferent plight, were contrasted with some few articles of a rare species of wood, excellently worked up, and with something curious and valuable from all the distant countries Captain Harville had visited, were more than amusing to Anne: connected as it all was with his profession, the fruit of its labours, the effect of its influence on his habits, the picture of repose and domestic happiness it presented, made it to her a something more, or less, than gratification.

Captain Harville was no reader; but he had contrived excellent accommodations, and fashioned very pretty shelves, for a tolerable collection of well-bound volumes, the property of Captain Benwick. His lameness prevented him from taking much exercise; but a mind of usefulness and ingenuity seemed to furnish him with constant employment within. He drew, he varnished, he carpentered, he glued; he made toys for the children; he fashioned new netting-needles and pins with improvements; and if everything else was done, sat down to his large fishing-net at one corner of the room.

Anne thought she left great happiness behind her when they quitted the house; and Louisa, by whom she found herself walking, burst forth into raptures of admiration and delight on the character of the navy; their friendliness, their brotherliness, their openness, their uprightness; protesting that she was convinced of sailors having more worth and warmth than any other set of men in England; that they only knew how to live, and they only deserved to be respected and loved.

They went back to dress and dine; and so well had the scheme answered already, that nothing was found amiss; though its being " so entirely out of the season," and the " no thoroughfare of Lyme," and the " no expectation of company," had brought many apologies from the heads of the inn.

Anne found herself by this time growing so much more hardened to being in Captain Wentworth's company than she had at first imagined could ever be, that the sitting down to the same table with him now, and the interchange of the common civilities attending on it (they never got beyond), was become a mere nothing.

The nights were too dark for the ladies to meet again till the morrow, but Captain Harville had promised them a visit in the evening; and he came, bringing his friend also, which was more than had been expected, it having been agreed that Captain Benwick had all the appearance of being oppressed by the presence of so many strangers. He ventured among them again, however, though his spirits certainly did not seem fit for the mirth of the party in general.

While Captains Wentworth and Harville led the talk on one side of the room, and by recurring to former days, supplied anecdotes in abundance to occupy and entertain the others, it fell to Anne's lot to be placed rather apart with Captain Benwick; and a very good impulse of her nature obliged her to begin an acquaintance with him. He was shy, and disposed to abstraction; but the engaging mildness of her countenance, and gentleness of her manner, soon had their effect; and Anne was well repaid the first trouble of exertion. He was evidently a young man of considerable taste in reading, though principally in poetry; and besides the persuasion of having given him at least an evening's indulgence in the discussion of subjects, which his usual companions had probably no concern in, she had the hope of being of real use to him in some suggestions as to the duty and benefit of struggling against affliction, which had naturally grown out of their conversation. For, though shy, he did not seem reserved: it had rather the appearance of feelings glad to burst their usual restraints; and having talked of poetry, the richness of the present age, and gone through a brief comparison of opinion as to the first-rate poets, trying to ascertain whether *Marmion* or *The Lady of the Lake* were to be preferred, and how ranked the *Giaour* and *The Bride of Abydos*, and moreover, how the *Giaour* was to be pronounced, he showed himself so intimately acquainted with all the tenderest songs of the one poet, and all the impassioned descriptions of hopeless agony of the other; he repeated, with such tremulous feeling, the various lines which imaged a broken heart, or a mind destroyed by wretchedness, and looked so entirely as if he meant to be understood, that she ventured to hope he did not always read only poetry, and to say, that she thought it was the misfortune of poetry to be seldom safely enjoyed by those who enjoyed it completely; and that the strong feelings which alone could estimate it truly were the very feelings which ought to taste it but sparingly.

His looks shewing him not pained, but pleased with this allusion to his situation, she was emboldened to go on; and feeling in herself the right of seniority of mind, she ventured to recommend a larger allowance of prose in his daily study; and on being requested to particularise, mentioned such works of our best moralists, such collections of the finest letters, such memoirs of characters of worth and suffering, as occurred to her at the moment as calculated to rouse and fortify the mind by the highest precepts and the strongest examples of moral and religious endurances.

Captain Benwick listened attentively, and seemed grateful for the interest implied; and though with a shake of the head, and sighs which declared his little faith in the efficacy of any books on grief like his, noted down the names of those she recommended, and promised to procure and read them.

When the evening was over, Anne could not but be amused at the idea of her coming to Lyme to preach patience and resignation to a young man whom she had never seen before; nor could she help fearing, on more serious reflection, that, like many other great moralists and preachers, she had been eloquent on a point in which her own conduct would ill bear examination.

CHAPTER XII

ANNE and Henrietta, finding themselves the earliest of the party the next morning, agreed to stroll down to the sea before breakfast. They went to the sands, to watch the flowing of the tide, which a fine south-easterly breeze was bringing in with all the grandeur which so flat a shore admitted. They praised the morning; gloried in the sea; sympathised in the delight of the fresh-feeling breeze—and were silent; till Henrietta suddenly began again, with—

"Oh, yes! I am quite convinced that, with very few exceptions, the sea-air always does good. There can be no doubt of its having been of the greatest service to Dr. Shirley, after his illness, last spring twelvemonth. He declares himself, that coming to Lyme for a month did him more good than all the medicine he took; and that being by the sea always makes him feel young again. Now, I cannot help thinking it a pity that he does not live entirely by the sea. I do think he had better leave Uppercross entirely, and fix at Lyme. Do not you, Anne? Do not you agree with me, that it is the best thing he could do, both for himself and Mrs. Shirley? She has cousins here, you know, and many acquaintance, which would make it cheerful for her, and I am sure she would be glad to get to a place where she could have medical attendance at hand, in case of his having another seizure. Indeed, I think it quite melancholy to have such excellent people as Dr. and Mrs. Shirley, who have been doing

good all their lives, wearing out their last days in a place like
Uppercross, where, excepting our family, they seem shut out
from all the world. I wish his friends would propose it to
him. I really think they ought. And, as to procuring a
dispensation, there could be no difficulty at his time of life and
with his character. My only doubt is, whether anything
could persuade him to leave his parish. He is so very strict
and scrupulous in his notions; over-scrupulous I must say.
Do not you think, Anne, it is being over-scrupulous? Do
not you think it is quite a mistaken point of conscience,
when a clergyman sacrifices his health for the sake of duties
which may be just as well performed by another person?
And at Lyme, too, only seventeen miles off, he would be near
enough to hear if people thought there was anything to complain of."

Anne smiled more than once to herself during this speech,
and entered into the subject, as ready to do good by entering
into the feelings of a young lady as of a young man, though
here it was good of a lower standard, for what could be offered
but general acquiescence? She said all that was reasonable
and proper on the business; felt the claims of Dr. Shirley to
repose as she ought; saw how very desirable it was that he
should have some active, respectable young man as a resident
curate, and was even courteous enough to hint at the advantage of such resident curate's being married.

" I wish," said Henrietta, very well pleased with her companion, "I wish Lady Russell lived at Uppercross, and were
intimate with Dr. Shirley. I have always heard of Lady
Russell as a woman of the greatest influence with everybody!
I always look upon her as able to persuade a person to anything! I am afraid of her, as I told you before, quite afraid
of her, because she is so very clever; but I respect her amazingly, and wish we had such a neighbour at Uppercross."

Anne was amused by Henrietta's manner of being grateful,
and amused also that the course of events and the new
interests of Henrietta's views should have placed her friend
at all in favour with any of the Musgrove family; she had
only time, however, for a general answer, and a wish that
such another woman were at Uppercross, before all subjects
suddenly ceased, on seeing Louisa and Captain Wentworth

coming towards them. They came also for a stroll till breakfast was likely to be ready; but Louisa recollecting immediately afterwards that she had something to procure at a shop,
invited them all to go back with her into the town. They
were all at her disposal.

When they came to the steps, leading upwards from the
beach, a gentleman, at the same moment preparing to come
down, politely drew back, and stopped to give them way.
They ascended and passed him; and as they passed, Anne's
face caught his eye, and he looked at her with a degree of
earnest admiration which she could not be insensible of.
She was looking remarkably well; her very regular, very
pretty features, having the bloom and freshness of youth
restored by the fine wind which had been blowing on her
complexion, and by the animation of eye which it had also
produced. It was evident that the gentleman (completely
a gentleman in manner) admired her exceedingly. Captain
Wentworth looked round at her instantly in a way which
shewed his noticing of it. He gave her a momentary glance,
a glance of brightness, which seemed to say, " That man is
struck with you, and even I, at this moment, see something
like Anne Elliot again."

After attending Louisa through her business, and loitering
about a little longer, they returned to the inn; and Anne, in
passing afterwards quickly from her own chamber to their
dining-room, had nearly run against the very same gentleman, as he came out of an adjoining apartment. She had
before conjectured him to be a stranger like themselves, and
determined that a well-looking groom, who was strolling
about near the two inns as they came back, should be his
servant. Both master and man being in mourning assisted
the idea. It was now proved that he belonged to the same
inn as themselves; and this second meeting, short as it was,
also proved again, by the gentleman's looks, that he thought
hers very lovely, and by the readiness and propriety of his
apologies, that he was a man of exceedingly good manners.
He seemed about thirty, and though not handsome, had an
agreeable person. Anne felt that she should like to know
who he was.

They had nearly done breakfast, when the sound of a

carriage (almost the first they had heard since entering Lyme), drew half the party to the window. It was a gentleman's carriage, a curricle, but only coming round from the stable-yard to the front door; somebody must be going away. It was driven by a servant in mourning.

The word curricle made Charles Musgrove jump up that he might compare it with his own; the servant in mourning roused Anne's curiosity, and the whole six were collected to look, by the time the owner of the curricle was to be seen issuing from the door, amidst the bows and civilities of the household, and taking his seat, to drive off.

" Ah! " cried Captain Wentworth, instantly, and with half a glance at Anne, " it is the very man we passed."

The Miss Musgroves agreed to it; and having all kindly watched him as far up the hill as they could, they returned to the breakfast table. The waiter came into the room soon afterwards.

" Pray," said Captain Wentworth, immediately, " can you tell us the name of the gentleman who is just gone away? "

" Yes, sir, a Mr. Elliot, a gentleman of large fortune, came in last night from Sidmouth. Dare say you heard the carriage, sir, while you were at dinner; and going on now for Crewkherne, on his way to Bath and London."

" Elliot! " Many had looked on each other, and many had repeated the name, before all this had been got through, even by the smart rapidity of a waiter.

" Bless me! " cried Mary, " it must be our cousin; it must be our Mr. Elliot, it must, indeed! Charles, Anne, must not it? In mourning, you see, just as our Mr. Elliot must be. How very extraordinary! In the very same inn with us! Anne, must not it be our Mr. Elliot? my father's next heir? Pray, sir," turning to the waiter, " did not you hear, did not his servant say whether he belonged to the Kellynch family? "

" No, ma'am, he did not mention no particular family; but he said his master was a very rich gentleman, and would be a baronet some day."

" There! you see! " cried Mary in an ecstasy; " just as I said! Heir to Sir Walter Elliot! I was sure that would come out, if it was so. Depend upon it, that is a circumstance which his servants take care to publish, wherever he goes. But, Anne, only conceive how extraordinary! I wish I had looked at him more. I wish we had been aware in time who it was, that he might have been introduced to us. What a pity that we should not have been introduced to each other! Do you think he had the Elliot countenance? I hardly looked at him, I was looking at the horses; but I think he had something of the Elliot countenance. I wonder the arms did not strike me! Oh! the great-coat was hanging over the panel, and hid the arms, so it did; otherwise, I am sure, I should have observed them, and the livery too; if the servant had not been in mourning, one should have known him by the livery."

"Putting all these very extraordinary circumstances together," said Captain Wentworth, "we must consider it to be the arrangement of Providence that you should not be introduced to your cousin."

When she could command Mary's attention, Anne quietly tried to convince her that their father and Mr. Elliot had not, for many years, been on such terms as to make the power of attempting an introduction at all desirable.

At the same time, however, it was a secret gratification to herself to have seen her cousin, and to know that the future owner of Kellynch was undoubtedly a gentleman, and had an air of good sense. She would not, upon any account, mention her having met with him the second time; luckily Mary did not much attend to their having passed close by him in their early walk, but she would have felt quite ill-used by Anne's having actually run against him in the passage, and received his very polite excuses, while she had never been near him at all; no, that cousinly little interview must remain a perfect secret.

"Of course," said Mary, "you will mention our seeing Mr. Elliot the next time you write to Bath. I think my father certainly ought to hear of it; do mention all about him."

Anne avoided a direct reply, but it was just the circumstance which she considered as not merely unnecessary to be communicated, but as what ought to be suppressed. The offence which had been given her father, many years back, she knew; Elizabeth's particular share in it she suspected; and that Mr. Elliot's idea always produced irritation in both was beyond a doubt. Mary never wrote to Bath herself; all the toil of keeping up a slow and unsatisfactory correspondence with Elizabeth fell on Anne.

Breakfast had not been long over when they were joined by Captain and Mrs. Harville and Captain Benwick; with whom they had appointed to take their last walk about Lyme. They ought to be setting off for Uppercross by one, and in the meanwhile were to be all together, and out of doors as long as they could.

Anne found Captain Benwick getting near her, as soon as they were all fairly in the street. Their conversation the preceding evening did not disincline him to seek her again; and they walked together some time, talking as before of Mr. Scott and Lord Byron, and still as unable as before, and as unable as any other two readers, to think exactly alike of the merits of either, till something occasioned an almost general change amongst their party, and instead of Captain Benwick, she had Captain Harville by her side.

" Miss Elliot," said he, speaking rather low, " you have done a good deed in making that poor fellow talk so much. I wish he could have such company oftener. It is bad for him, I know, to be shut up as he is; but what can we do? We cannot part."

" No," said Anne, " that I can easily believe to be impossible; but in time, perhaps—we know what time does in every case of affliction, and you must remember, Captain Harville, that your friend may yet be called a young mourner—only last summer, I understand."

" Ay, true enough " (with a deep sigh), " only June."

" And not known to him, perhaps, so soon."

" Not till the first week in August, when he came home from the Cape, just made into the *Grappler*. I was at Plymouth dreading to hear of him; he sent in letters, but the *Grappler* was under orders for Portsmouth. There the news must follow him, but who was to tell it? not I. I would as soon have been run up to the yard-arm. Nobody could do it, but that good fellow " (pointing to Captain Wentworth). " The *Laconia* had come into Plymouth the week before;

no danger of her being sent to sea again. He stood his chance for the rest; wrote up for leave of absence, but without waiting the return, travelled night and day till he got to Portsmouth, rowed off to the *Grappler* that instant, and never left the poor fellow for a week. That's what he did, and nobody else could have saved poor James. You may think, Miss Elliot, whether he is dear to us!"

Anne did think on the question with perfect decision, and said as much in reply as her own feelings could accomplish, or as his seemed able to bear, for he was too much affected to renew the subject, and when he spoke again, it was of something totally different.

Mrs. Harville's giving it as her opinion that her husband would have quite walking enough by the time he reached home, determined the direction of all the party in what was to be their last walk; they would accompany them to their door, and then return and set off themselves. By all their calculations there was just time for this; but as they drew near the Cobb, there was such a general wish to walk along it once more, all were so inclined, and Louisa soon grew so determined, that the difference of a quarter of an hour, it was found, would be no difference at all; so with all the kind leave-taking, and all the kind interchange of invitations and promises which may be imagined, they parted from Captain and Mrs. Harville at their own door, and still accompanied by Captain Benwick, who seemed to cling to them to the last, proceeded to make the proper adieus to the Cobb.

Anne found Captain Benwick again drawing near her. Lord Byron's "dark blue seas" could not fail of being brought forward by their present view, and she gladly gave him all her attention as long as attention was possible. It was soon drawn, perforce, another way.

There was too much wind to make the high part of the new Cobb pleasant for the ladies, and they agreed to get down the steps to the lower, and all were contented to pass quietly and carefully down the steep flight, excepting Louisa; she must be jumped down them by Captain Wentworth. In all their walks he had had to jump her from the stiles; the sensation was delightful to her. The hardness of the pavement for her feet made him less willing upon the present occasion; he did it, however. She was safely down, and instantly to show her enjoyment, ran up the steps to be jumped down again. He advised her against it, thought the jar too great; but no, he reasoned and talked in vain, she smiled and said, " I am determined I will: " he put out his hands; she was too precipitate by half a second, she fell on the pavement on the Lower Cobb, and was taken up lifeless! There was no wound, no blood, no visible bruise; but her eyes were closed, she breathed not, her face was like death. The horror of that moment to all who stood around!

Captain Wentworth, who had caught her up, knelt with her in his arms, looking on her with a face as pallid as her own in an agony of silence. " She is dead! she is dead! " screamed Mary, catching hold of her husband, and contributing with his own horror to make him immoveable; and in another moment, Henrietta, sinking under the conviction, lost her senses too, and would have fallen on the steps but for Captain Benwick and Anne, who caught and supported her between them.

" Is there no one to help me? " were the first words which burst from Captain Wentworth, in a tone of despair, and as if all his own strength were gone.

" Go to him, go to him," cried Anne, " for heaven's sake go to him. I can support her myself. Leave me, and go to him. Rub her hands, rub her temples; here are salts: take them, take them."

Captain Benwick obeyed, and Charles at the same moment disengaging himself from his wife, they were both with him; and Louisa was raised up and supported more firmly between them, and everything was done that Anne had prompted, but in vain; while Captain Wentworth, staggering against the wall for his support, exclaimed in the bitterest agony—

" Oh God! her father and mother! "

" A surgeon! " said Anne.

He caught the word: it seemed to rouse him at once; and saying only—" True, true, a surgeon this instant," was darting away, when Anne eagerly suggested—

" Captain Benwick, would not it be better for Captain Benwick? He knows where a surgeon is to be found."

Every one capable of thinking felt the advantage of the

idea, and in a moment (it was all done in rapid moments) Captain Benwick had resigned the poor corpse-like figure entirely to the brother's care, and was off for the town with the utmost rapidity.

As to the wretched party left behind, it could scarcely be said which of the three, who were completely rational, was suffering most: Captain Wentworth, Anne, or Charles, who, really a very affectionate brother, hung over Louisa with sobs of grief, and could only turn his eyes from one sister to see the other in a state as insensible, or to witness the hysterical agitations of his wife, calling on him for help which he could not give.

Anne, attending with all the strength, and zeal, and thought, which instinct supplied, to Henrietta, still tried, at intervals, to suggest comfort to the others, tried to quiet Mary, to animate Charles, to assuage the feelings of Captain Wentworth. Both seemed to look to her for directions.

"Anne, Anne," cried Charles, "what is to be done next? What, in heaven's name, is to be done next?"

Captain Wentworth's eyes were also turned towards her.

"Had not she better be carried to the inn? Yes, I am sure: carry her gently to the inn."

"Yes, yes, to the inn," repeated Captain Wentworth, comparatively collected, and eager to be doing something. "I will carry her myself. Musgrove, take care of the others."

By this time the report of the accident had spread among the workmen and boatmen about the Cobb, and many were collected near them, to be useful if wanted; at anyrate, to enjoy the sight of a dead young lady, nay, two dead young ladies, for it proved twice as fine as the first report. To some of the best-looking of these good people Henrietta was consigned, for, though partially revived, she was quite helpless; and in this manner, Anne walking by her side, and Charles attending to his wife, they set forward, treading back, with feelings unutterable, the ground which so lately, so very lately, and so light of heart, they had passed along.

They were not off the Cobb before the Harvilles met them. Captain Benwick had been seen flying by their house, with a countenance which showed something to be wrong; and they had set off immediately, informed and directed as they passed, towards the spot. Shocked as Captain Harville was, he brought senses and nerves that could be instantly useful; and a look between him and his wife decided what was to be done. She must be taken to their house; all must go to their house; and wait the surgeon's arrival there. They would not listen to scruples: he was obeyed: they were all beneath his roof; and while Louisa, under Mrs. Harville's direction, was conveyed upstairs, and given possession of her own bed, assistance, cordials, restoratives were supplied by her husband to all who needed them.

Louisa had once opened her eyes, but soon closed them again, without apparent consciousness. This had been a proof of life, however, of service to her sister; and Henrietta, though perfectly incapable of being in the same room with Louisa, was kept, by the agitation of hope and fear, from a return of her own insensibility. Mary, too, was growing calmer.

The surgeon was with them almost before it had seemed possible. They were sick with horror, while he examined; but he was not hopeless. The head had received a severe contusion, but he had seen greater injuries recovered from; he was by no means hopeless; he spoke cheerfully.

That he did not regard it as a desperate case, that he did not say a few hours must end it, was at first felt beyond the hope of most; and the ecstacy of such a reprieve, the rejoicing, deep and silent, after a few fervent ejaculations of gratitude to Heaven had been offered, may be conceived.

The tone, the look, with which "Thank God!" was uttered by Captain Wentworth, Anne was sure could never be forgotten by her; nor the sight of him afterwards, as he sat near a table, leaning over it with folded arms, and face concealed, as if overpowered by the various feelings of his soul, and trying by prayer and reflection to calm them.

Louisa's limbs had escaped. There was no injury but to the head.

It now became necessary for the party to consider what was best to be done, as to their general situation. They were now able to speak to each other and consult. That Louisa must remain where she was, however distressing to her friends to be involving the Harvilles in such trouble, did not admit a doubt. Her removal was impossible. The Harvilles silenced all scruples, and, as much as they could, all gratitude. They had looked forward and arranged everything before the others began to reflect. Captain Benwick must give up his room to them and get a bed elsewhere; and the whole was settled. They were only concerned that the house could accommodate no more; and yet, perhaps, by " putting the children away in the maid's room, or swinging a cot somewhere," they could hardly bear to think of not finding room for two or three besides, supposing they might wish to stay; though, with regard to any attendance on Miss Musgrove, there need not be the least uneasiness in leaving her to Mrs. Harville's care entirely. Mrs. Harville was a very experienced nurse, and her nursery-maid, who had lived with her long, and gone about with her everywhere, was just such another. Between those two she could want no possible attendance by day or night. And all this was said with a truth and sincerity of feeling irresistible.

Charles, Henrietta, and Captain Wentworth were the three in consultation, and for a little while it was only an interchange of perplexity and terror. " Uppercross, the necessity of some one's going to Uppercross; the news to be conveyed; how it could be broken to Mr. and Mrs. Musgrove; the lateness of the morning; an hour already gone since they ought to have been off; the impossibility of being in tolerable time." At first they were capable of nothing more to the purpose than such exclamations; but after a while Captain Wentworth, exerting himself, said—

" We must be decided, and without the loss of another minute. Every minute is valuable. Some one must resolve on being off for Uppercross instantly. Musgrove, either you or I must go."

Charles agreed, but declared his resolution of not going away. He would be as little encumbrance as possible to Captain and Mrs. Harville; but as to leaving his sister in such a state, he neither ought nor would. So far it was decided; and Henrietta at first declared the same. She, however, was soon persuaded to think differently. The usefulness of her staying! She, who had not been able to remain in Louisa's room, or to look at her, without sufferings which made her worse than helpless! She was forced to acknowledge that she could do no good, yet was still unwilling to be away, till, touched by the thought of her father and mother, she gave it up; she consented, she was anxious to be at home.

The plan had reached this point, when Anne, coming quietly down from Louisa's room, could not but hear what followed, for the parlour door was open.

" Then it is settled, Musgrove," cried Captain Wentworth, " that you stay, and that I take care of your sister home. But as to the rest, as to the others, if one stays to assist Mrs. Harville, I think it need be only one. Mrs. Charles Musgrove will, of course, wish to get back to her children; but if Anne will stay, no one so proper, so capable as Anne."

She paused a moment to recover from the emotion of hearing herself so spoken of. The other two warmly agreed to what he said, and she then appeared.

" You will stay, I am sure; you will stay and nurse her," cried he, turning to her and speaking with a glow, and yet a gentleness, which seemed almost restoring the past. She coloured deeply, and he recollected himself and moved away. She expressed herself most willing, ready, happy to remain. " It was what she had been thinking of, and wishing to be allowed to do. A bed on the floor in Louisa's room would be sufficient for her, if Mrs. Harville would but think so."

One thing more, and all seemed arranged. Though it was rather desirable that Mr. and Mrs. Musgrove should be previously alarmed by some share of delay; yet the time required by the Uppercross horses to take them back, would be a dreadful extension of suspense; and Captain Wentworth proposed, and Charles Musgrove agreed, that it would be much better for him to take a chaise from the inn, and leave Mr. Musgrove's carriage and horses to be sent home the next morning early, when there could be the farther advantage of sending an account of Louisa's night.

Captain Wentworth now hurried off to get everything ready on his part, and to be soon followed by the two ladies. When the plan was made known to Mary, however, there was an end of all peace in it. She was so wretched, and so vehement, complained so much of injustice in being expected to go away instead of Anne: Anne, who was nothing to Louisa, while she was her sister, and had the best right to stay in Henrietta's stead! Why was not she to be as useful as Anne? And to go home without Charles, too, without her husband! No, it was too unkind. And in short, she said more than her husband could long withstand, and as none of the others could oppose when he gave way, there was no help for it: the change of Mary for Anne was inevitable.

Anne had never submitted more reluctantly to the jealous and ill-judging claims of Mary; but so it must be, and they set off for the town, Charles taking care of his sister, and Captain Benwick attending to her. She gave a moment's recollection, as they hurried along, to the little circumstances which the same spots had witnessed earlier in the morning. There she had listened to Henrietta's schemes for Dr. Shirley's leaving Uppercross; farther on, she had first seen Mr. Elliot; a moment seemed all that could now be given to any one but Louisa, or those who were wrapped up in her welfare.

Captain Benwick was most considerately attentive to her; and, united as they all seemed by the distress of the day, she felt an increasing degree of good-will towards him, and a pleasure even in thinking that it might, perhaps, be the occasion of continuing their acquaintance.

Captain Wentworth was on the watch for them, and a chaise and four in waiting, stationed for their convenience in the lowest part of the street; but his evident surprise and vexation at the substitution of one sister for the other, the change of his countenance, the astonishment, the expressions begun and suppressed, with which Charles was listened to, made but a mortifying reception of Anne; or must at least convince her that she was valued only as she could be useful to Louisa.

She endeavoured to be composed, and to be just. Without emulating the feelings of an Emma towards her Henry, she would have attended on Louisa with a zeal above the common claims of regard, for his sake; and she hoped he would not long be so unjust as to suppose she would shrink unnecessarily from the office of a friend.

In the meanwhile she was in the carriage. He had handed

them both in, and placed himself between them; and in this manner, under these circumstances, full of astonishment and emotion to Anne, she quitted Lyme. How the long stage would pass; how it was to affect their manners; what was to be their sort of intercourse, she could not foresee. It was all quite natural, however. He was devoted to Henrietta; always turning towards her; and when he spoke at all, always with the view of supporting her hopes and raising her spirits. In general, his voice and manner were studiously calm. To spare Henrietta from agitation seemed the governing principle. Once only, when she had been grieving over the last ill-judged, ill-fated walk to the Cobb, bitterly lamenting that it ever had been thought of, he burst forth, as if wholly overcome—

"Don't talk of it, don't talk of it," he cried. "Oh, God! that I had not given way to her at the fatal moment! Had I done as I ought! But so eager and so resolute! Dear, sweet Louisa!"

Anne wondered whether it ever occurred to him now, to question the justness of his own previous opinion as to the universal felicity and advantage of firmness of character; and whether it might not strike him that, like all other qualities of the mind, it should have its proportions and limits. She thought it could scarcely escape him to feel that a persuadable temper might sometimes be as much in favour of happiness as a very resolute character.

They got on fast. Anne was astonished to recognise the same hills and the same objects so soon. Their actual speed, heightened by some dread of the conclusion, made the road appear but half as long as on the day before. It was growing quite dusk, however, before they were in the neighbourhood of Uppercross, and there had been total silence among them for some time, Henrietta leaning back in the corner, with a shawl over her face, giving the hope of her having cried herself to sleep; when, as they were going up their last hill, Anne found herself all at once addressed by Captain Wentworth. In a low cautious voice, he said:—

"I have been considering what we had best do. She must not appear at first. She could not stand it. I have been thinking whether you had not better remain in the carriage with her, while I go in and break it to Mr. and Mrs. Musgrove. Do you think this a good plan?"

She did: he was satisfied, and said no more. But the remembrance of the appeal remained a pleasure to her, as a proof of friendship, and of deference for her judgment, a great pleasure; and when it became a sort of parting proof, its value did not lessen.

When the distressing communication at Uppercross was over, and he had seen the father and mother quite as composed as could be hoped, and the daughter all the better for being with them, he announced his intention of returning in the same carriage to Lyme; and when the horses were baited, he was off.

CHAPTER XIII

THE remainder of Anne's time at Uppercross, comprehending only two days, was spent entirely at the Mansion House; and she had the satisfaction of knowing herself extremely useful there, both as an immediate companion, and as assisting in all those arrangements for the future, which, in Mr. and Mrs. Musgrove's distressed state of spirits, would have been difficulties.

They had an early account from Lyme the next morning. Louisa was much the same. No symptoms worse than before had appeared. Charles came a few hours afterwards to bring a later and more particular account. He was tolerably cheerful. A speedy cure must not be hoped, but everything was going on as well as the nature of the case admitted. In speaking of the Harvilles, he seemed unable to satisfy his own sense of their kindness, especially of Mrs. Harville's exertions as a nurse. " She really left nothing for Mary to do. He and Mary had been persuaded to go early to their inn last night. Mary had been hysterical again this morning. When he came away, she was going to walk out with Captain Benwick, which he hoped would do her good. He almost wished she had been prevailed on to come home the day before;

but the truth was, that Mrs. Harville left nothing for anybody to do."

Charles was to return to Lyme the same afternoon, and his father had at first half a mind to go with him, but the ladies could not consent. It would be going only to multiply trouble to the others, and increase his own distress; and a much better scheme followed, and was acted upon. A chaise was sent for from Crewkherne, and Charles conveyed back a far more useful person in the old nursery-maid of the family, one who, having brought up all the children, and seen the very last, the lingering and long-petted Master Harry, sent to school after his brothers, was now living in her deserted nursery to mend stockings, and dress all the blains and bruises she could get near her, and who, consequently, was only too happy in being allowed to go and help nurse dear Miss Louisa. Vague wishes of getting Sarah thither had occurred before to Mrs. Musgrove and Henrietta; but without Anne, it would hardly have been resolved on, and found practicable so soon.

They were indebted, the next day, to Charles Hayter, for all the minute knowledge of Louisa, which it was so essential to obtain every twenty-four hours. He made it his business to go to Lyme, and his account was still encouraging. The intervals of sense and consciousness were believed to be stronger. Every report agreed in Captain Wentworth's appearing fixed in Lyme.

Anne was to leave them on the morrow, an event which they all dreaded. "What should they do without her? They were wretched comforters for one another." And so much was said in this way, that Anne thought she could not do better than impart among them the general inclination to which she was privy, and persuade them all to go to Lyme at once. She had little difficulty; it was soon determined that they would go: go to-morrow, fix themselves at the inn, or get into lodgings, as it suited, and there remain till dear Louisa could be moved. They must be taking off some trouble from the good people she was with: they might at least relieve Mrs. Harville from the care of her own children: and in short, they were so happy in the decision, that Anne was delighted with what she had done, and felt that she could not spend her last morning at Uppercross better than in assisting their preparations, and sending them off at an early hour, though her being left to the solitary range of the house was the consequence.

She was the last, excepting the little boys at the Cottage, she was the very last, the only remaining one of all that had filled and animated both houses, of all that had given Upper-cross its cheerful character. A few days had made a change indeed!

If Louisa recovered, it would all be well again. More than former happiness would be restored. There could not be a doubt, to her mind there was none, of what would follow her recovery. A few months hence and the [room now] so deserted, occupied but by her silent, pensive self, might be filled again with all that was happy and gay, all that was glowing and bright in prosperous love, all that was most unlike Anne Elliot!

An hour's complete leisure for such reflections as these, on a dark November day, a small thick rain almost blotting out the very few objects ever to be discerned from the windows, was enough to make the sound of Lady Russell's carriage exceedingly welcome; and yet, though desirous to be gone, she could not quit the Mansion House, or look an adieu to the Cottage, with its black, dripping and comfortless verandah, or even notice through the misty glasses the last humble tenements of the village, without a saddened heart. Scenes had passed in Uppercross which made it precious. It stood the record of many sensations of pain, once severe, but now softened; and of some instances of relenting feeling, some breathings of friendship and reconciliation, which could never be looked for again, and which could never cease to be dear. She left it all behind her, all but the recollection that such things had been.

Anne had never entered Kellynch since her quitting Lady Russell's house in September. It had not been necessary, and the few occasions of its being possible for her to go to the Hall she had contrived to evade and escape from. Her first return was to resume her place in the modern and elegant apartments of the Lodge, and to gladden the eyes of its mistress.

There was some anxiety mixed with Lady Russell's joy in

meeting her. She knew who had been frequenting Upper-cross. But happily, either Anne was improved in plump-ness and looks, or Lady Russell fancied her so; and Anne, in receiving her compliments on the occasion, had the amuse-ment of connecting them with the silent admiration of her cousin, and of hoping that she was to be blessed with a second spring of youth and beauty.

When they came to converse, she was soon sensible of some mental change. The subjects of which her heart had been full on leaving Kellynch, and which she had felt slighted, and been compelled to smother among the Musgroves, were now become but of secondary interest. She had lately lost sight even of her father, and sister, and Bath. Their concerns had been sunk under those of Uppercross; and when Lady Russell reverted to their former hopes and fears, and spoke her satisfaction in the house in Camden Place which had been taken, and her regret that Mrs. Clay should still be with them, Anne would have been ashamed to have it known how much more she was thinking of Lyme and Louisa Mus-grove, and all her acquaintance there; how much more interesting to her was the home and the friendship of the Harvilles and Captain Benwick, than her own father's house in Camden Place, or her own sister's intimacy with Mrs. Clay. She was actually forced to exert herself to meet Lady Russell with anything like the appearance of equal solicitude, on topics which had by nature the [first] claim on her.

There was a little awkwardness at first in their discourse on another subject. They must speak of the accident at Lyme. Lady Russell had not been arrived five minutes the day before, when a full account of the whole had burst on her; but still it must be talked of, she must make enquiries, she must regret the imprudence, lament the result, and Captain Wentworth's name must be mentioned by both. Anne was conscious of not doing it so well as Lady Russell. She could not speak the name, and look straight forward to Lady Russell's eye, till she had adopted the expedient of telling her briefly what she thought of the attachment between him and Louisa. When this was told, his name distressed her no longer.

Lady Russell had only to listen composedly, and wish them happy, but internally her heart revelled in angry pleasure, in pleased contempt, that the man who at twenty-three had seemed to understand somewhat of the value of an Anne Elliot, should, eight years afterwards, be charmed by a Louisa Musgrove.

The first three or four days passed most quietly, with no circumstance to mark them excepting the receipt of a note or two from Lyme, which found their way to Anne, she could not tell how, and brought a rather improving account of Louisa. At the end of that period, Lady Russell's politeness could repose no longer, and the fainter self-threatenings of the past became in a decided tone, " I must call on Mrs. Croft; I really must call upon her soon. Anne, have you courage to go with me and pay a visit in that house? It will be some trial to us both."

Anne did not shrink from it: on the contrary, she truly felt as she said, in observing—

" I think you are very likely to suffer the most of the two; your feelings are less reconciled to the change than mine. By remaining in the neighbourhood, I am become inured to it."

She could have said more on the subject, for she had in fact so high an opinion of the Crofts, and considered her father so very fortunate in his tenants, felt the parish to be so sure of a good example, and the poor of the best attention and relief, that however sorry and ashamed for the necessity of the removal, she could not but in conscience feel that they were gone who deserved not to stay, and that Kellynch Hall had passed into better hands than its owners. These convictions must unquestionably have their own pain, and severe was its kind; but they precluded that pain which Lady Russell would suffer in entering the house again, and returning through the well-known apartments.

In such moments Anne had no power of saying to herself, " These rooms ought to belong only to us. Oh, how fallen in their destination! How unworthily occupied! An ancient family to be so driven away! Strangers filling their place!" No, except when she thought of her mother, and remembered where she had been used to sit and preside, she had no sigh of that description to heave.

Mrs. Croft always met her with a kindness which gave her the pleasure of fancying herself a favourite, and on the present occasion, receiving her in that house, there was particular attention.

The sad accident at Lyme was soon the prevailing topic, and on comparing their latest accounts of the invalid, it appeared that each lady dated her intelligence from the same hour of yestermorn; that Captain Wentworth had been in Kellynch yesterday (the first time since the accident), had brought Anne the last note, which she had not been able to trace the exact steps of; had staid a few hours, and then returned again to Lyme, and without any present intention of quitting it any more. He had enquired after her, she found particularly; had expressed his hope of Miss Elliot's not being the worse for her exertions, and had spoken of those exertions as great. This was handsome, and gave her more pleasure than almost anything else could have done.

As to the sad catastrophe itself, it could be canvassed only in one style by a couple of steady, sensible women, whose judgments had to work on ascertained events; and it was perfectly decided that it had been the consequence of much thoughtlessness and much imprudence; that its effects were most alarming, and that it was frightful to think how long Miss Musgrove's recovery might yet be doubtful, and how liable she would still remain to suffer from the concussion hereafter! The Admiral wound it all up summarily by exclaiming—

"Ay, a very bad business, indeed. A new sort of way this, for a young fellow to be making love, by breaking his mistress's head, is not it, Miss Elliot? This is breaking a head and giving a plaster, truly!"

Admiral Croft's manners were not quite of the tone to suit Lady Russell, but they delighted Anne. His goodness of heart and simplicity of character were irresistible.

"Now, this must be very bad for you," said he, suddenly rousing from a little reverie, "to be coming and finding us here. I had not recollected it before, I declare, but it must be very bad. But now, do not stand upon ceremony. Get up and go over all the rooms in the house, if you like it."

"Another time, sir, I thank you; not now."

" Well, whenever it suits you. You can slip in from the shrubbery at any time; and there you will find we keep our umbrellas hanging up by that door. A good place is not it? But " (checking himself), " you will not think it a good place, for yours were always kept in the butler's room. Ay, so it always is, I believe. One man's ways may be as good as another's, but we all like our own best; and so you must judge for yourself, whether it would be better for you to go about the house or not."

Anne, finding she might decline it, did so very gratefully.

" We have made very few changes either," continued the Admiral, after thinking a moment. " Very few. We told you about the laundry-door at Uppercross. That has been a very great improvement. The wonder was, how any family upon earth could bear with the inconvenience of its opening as it did so long! You will tell Sir Walter what we have done, and that Mr. Shepherd thinks it the greatest improvement the house ever had. Indeed, I must do ourselves the justice to say, that the few alterations we have made have been all very much for the better. My wife should have the credit of them, however. I have done very little besides sending away some of the large looking-glasses from my dressing-room, which was your father's. A very good man, and very much the gentleman, I am sure; but I should think, Miss Elliot " (looking with serious reflection), " I should think he must be rather a dressy man for his time of life. Such a number of looking-glasses! oh, Lord! there was no getting away from one's self. So I got Sophy to lend me a hand, and we soon shifted their quarters; and now I am quite snug, with my little shaving-glass in one corner, and another great thing that I never go near."

Anne, amused in spite of herself, was rather distressed for an answer; and the Admiral, fearing he might not have been civil enough, took up the subject again, to say—

" The next time you write to your good father, Miss Elliot, pray give my compliments and Mrs. Croft's, and say that we are settled here quite to our liking, and have no fault at all to find with the place. The breakfast-room chimney smokes a little, I grant you, but it is only when the wind is due north and blows hard, which may not happen three times a winter.

And take it altogether, now that we have been into most of the houses hereabouts and can judge, there is not one that we like better than this. Pray say so, with my compliments. He will be glad to hear it."

Lady Russell and Mrs. Croft were very well pleased with each other: but the acquaintance which this visit began was fated not to proceed far at present; for when it was returned, the Crofts announced themselves to be going away for a few weeks, to visit their connexions in the north of the county, and probably might not be at home again before Lady Russell would be removing to Bath.

So ended all danger to Anne of meeting Captain Wentworth at Kellynch Hall, or of seeing him in company with her friend. Everything was safe enough, and she smiled over the many anxious feelings she had wasted on the subject.

CHAPTER XIV

THOUGH Charles and Mary had remained at Lyme much longer after Mr. and Mrs. Musgrove's going than Anne conceived they could have been at all wanted, they were yet the first of the family to be at home again; and as soon as possible after their return to Uppercross they drove over to the Lodge. They had left Louisa beginning to sit up; but her head, though clear, was exceedingly weak, and her nerves susceptible to the highest extreme of tenderness; and though she might be pronounced to be altogether doing very well, it was still impossible to say when she might be able to bear the removal home; and her father and mother, who must return in time to receive their younger children for the Christmas holidays, had hardly a hope of being allowed to bring her with them.

They had been all in lodgings together. Mrs. Musgrove had got Mrs. Harville's children away as much as she could, every possible supply from Uppercross had been furnished, to lighten the inconvenience to the Harvilles, while the Harvilles had been wanting them to come to dinner ever

day; and, in short, it seemed to have been only a struggle
on each side, as to which should be most disinterested and
hospitable.

Mary had had her evils; but upon the whole, as was
evident by her staying so long, she had found more to enjoy
than to suffer. Charles Hayter had been at Lyme oftener
than suited her; and when they dined with the Harvilles
there had been only a maid-servant to wait, and at first Mrs.
Harville had always given Mrs. Musgrove precedence; but
then she had received so very handsome an apology from
her on finding out whose daughter she was, and there had been
so much going on every day, there had been so many walks
between their lodgings and the Harvilles, and she had got
books from the library, and changed them so often, that
the balance had certainly been much in favour of Lyme.
She had been taken to Charmouth too, and she had bathed,
and she had gone to church, and there were a great many
more people to look at in the church at Lyme than at Uppercross; and all this, joined to the sense of being so very useful,
had made really an agreeable fortnight.

Anne inquired after Captain Benwick. Mary's face was
clouded directly. Charles laughed.

"Oh! Captain Benwick is very well, [I] believe, but he
is a very odd young man. I do not know what he would
be at. We asked him to come home with us for a day or
two: Charles undertook to give him some shooting, and he
seemed quite delighted, and, for my part, I thought it was
all settled, when, behold! on Tuesday night, he made a very
awkward sort of an excuse; 'he never shot,' and he had
'been quite misunderstood,' and he had promised this and
he had promised that, and the end of it was, I found, that he
did not mean to come. I suppose he was afraid of finding
it dull; but upon my word I should have thought we were
lively enough at the Cottage for such a heart-broken man as
Captain Benwick."

Charles laughed again, and said, "Now, Mary, you know
very well how it really was. It was all your doing" (turning
to Anne). "He fancied that if he went with us he should
find you close by: he fancied everybody to be living in
Uppercross; and when he discovered that Lady Russell

lived three miles off, his heart failed him, and he had not courage to come. That is the fact, upon my honour. Mary knows it is."

But Mary did not give into it very graciously, whether from not considering Captain Benwick entitled by birth and situation to be in love with an Elliot, or from not wanting to believe Anne a greater attraction to Uppercross than herself, must be left to be guessed. Anne's goodwill, however, was not to be lessened by what she heard. She boldly acknowledged herself flattered, and continued her enquiries.

" Oh! he talks of you," cried Charles, " in such terms——" Mary interrupted him. " I declare, Charles, I never heard him mention Anne twice all the time I was there. I declare, Anne, he never talks of you at all."

" No," admitted Charles, " I do not know that he ever does, in a general way; but, however, it is a very clear thing that he admires you exceedingly. His head is full of some books that he is reading upon your recommendation, and he wants to talk to you about them; he has found out something or other in one of them which he thinks—oh! I cannot pretend to remember it, but it was something very fine—I overheard him telling Henrietta all about it; and then ' Miss Elliot ' was spoken of in the highest terms! Now, Mary, I declare it was so, I heard it myself, and you were in the other room. ' Elegance, sweetness, beauty.' Oh! there was no end of Miss Elliot's charms."

" And I am sure," cried Mary, warmly, " it was very little to his credit if he did. Miss Harville only died last June. Such a heart is very little worth having, is it, Lady Russell? I am sure you will agree with me."

" I must see Captain Benwick before I decide," said Lady Russell, smiling.

" And that you are very likely to do very soon, I can tell you, ma'am," said Charles. " Though he had not nerves for coming away with us, and setting off again afterwards to pay a formal visit here, he will make his way over to Kellynch one day by himself, you may depend on it. I told him the distance and the road, and I told him of the church's being so very well worth seeing; for as he has a taste for those sort of things, I thought that would be a good excuse, and he listened with all his understanding and soul; and I am sure, from his manner, that you will have him calling here soon. So, I give you notice, Lady Russell."

"Any acquaintance of Anne's will be always welcome to me," was Lady Russell's kind answer.

"Oh! as to being Anne's acquaintance," said Mary, "I think he is rather my acquaintance, for I have been seeing him every day this last fortnight."

"Well, as your joint acquaintance, then, I shall be very happy to see Captain Benwick."

"You will not find anything very agreeable in him, I assure you, ma'am. He is one of the dullest young men that ever lived. He has walked with me, sometimes, from one end of the sands to the other, without saying a word. He is not at all a well-bred young man. I am sure you will not like him."

"There we differ, Mary," said Anne. "I think Lady Russell would like him. I think she would be so much pleased with his mind, that she would very soon see no deficiency in his manner."

"So do I, Anne," said Charles. "I am sure Lady Russell would like him. He is just Lady Russell's sort. Give him a book, and he will read all day long."

"Yes, that he will!" exclaimed Mary, tauntingly. "He will sit poring over his book, and not know when a person speaks to him, or when one drops one's scissors, or anything that happens. Do you think Lady Russell would like that?"

Lady Russell could not help laughing. "Upon my word," said she, "I should not have supposed that my opinion of any one could have admitted of such difference of conjecture, steady and matter of fact as I may call myself. I have really a curiosity to see the person who can give occasion to such directly opposite notions. I wish he may be induced to call here. And when he does, Mary, you may depend upon hearing my opinion; but I am determined not to judge him beforehand."

"You will not like him; I will answer for it."

Lady Russell began talking of something else. Mary spoke with animation of their meeting with, or rather missing Mr. Elliot so extraordinarily.

"He is a man," said Lady Russell, "whom I have no wish to see. His declining to be on cordial terms with the head of his family has left a very strong impression in his disfavour with me."

This decision checked Mary's eagerness, and stopped her short in the midst of the Elliot countenance.

With regard to Captain Wentworth, though Anne hazarded no enquiries, there was voluntary communication sufficient. His spirits had been greatly recovering lately, as might be expected. As Louisa improved, he had improved, and he was now quite a different creature from what he had been the first week. He had not seen Louisa; and was so extremely fearful of any ill consequence to her from an interview, that he did not press for it at all; and, on the contrary, seemed to have a plan of going away for a week or ten days, till her head was stronger. He had talked of going down to Plymouth for a week, and wanted to persuade Captain Benwick to go with him; but, as Charles maintained to the last, Captain Benwick seemed much more disposed to ride over to Kellynch.

There can be no doubt that Lady Russell and Anne were both occasionally thinking of Captain Benwick, from this time. Lady Russell could not hear the door-bell without feeling that it might be his herald; nor could Anne return from any stroll of solitary indulgence in her father's grounds, or any visit of charity in the village, without wondering whether she might see him or hear of him. Captain Benwick came not, however. He was either less disposed for it than Charles had imagined, or he was too shy; and after giving him a week's indulgence, Lady Russell determined him to be unworthy of the interest which he had been beginning to excite.

The Musgroves came back to receive their happy boys and girls from school, bringing with them Mrs. Harville's little children, to improve the noise of Uppercross, and lessen that of Lyme. Henrietta remained with Louisa, but all the rest of the family were again in their usual quarters.

Lady Russell and Anne paid their compliments to them once, when Anne could not but feel that Uppercross was already quite alive again. Though neither Henrietta, nor

Louisa, nor Charles Hayter, nor Captain Wentworth were
there, the room presented as strong a contrast as could be
wished to the last state she had seen it in.

Immediately surrounding Mrs. Musgrove were the little
Harvilles, whom she was sedulously guarding from the
tyranny of the two children from the Cottage, expressly
arrived to amuse them. On one side was a table occupied
by some chattering girls, cutting up silk and gold paper; and
on the other were tressels and trays, bending under the weight
of brawn and cold pies, where riotous boys were holding high
revel; the whole completed by a roaring Christmas fire,
which seemed determined to be heard in spite of all the noise
of the others. Charles and Mary also came in, of course,
during their visit, and Mr. Musgrove made a point of paying
his respects to Lady Russell, and sat down close to her for
ten minutes, talking with a very raised voice, but from the
clamour of the children on his knees, generally in vain. It
was a fine family-piece.

Anne, judging from her own temperament, would have
deemed such a domestic hurricane a bad restorative of the
nerves, which Louisa's illness must have so greatly shaken.
But Mrs. Musgrove, who got Anne near her on purpose to
thank her most cordially, again and again, for all her attentions to them, concluded a short recapitulation of what she
had suffered herself by observing, with a happy glance round
the room, that after all she had gone through, nothing was
so likely to do her good as a little quiet cheerfulness at home.

Louisa was now recovering apace. Her mother could even
think of her being able to join their party at home, before
her brothers and sisters went to school again. The Harvilles
had promised to come with her and stay at Uppercross whenever she returned. Captain Wentworth was gone for the
present, to see his brother in Shropshire.

"I hope I shall remember, in future," said Lady Russell,
as soon as they were reseated in the carriage, "not to call at
Uppercross in the Christmas holidays."

Everybody has their taste in noises as well as in other
matters; and sounds are quite innoxious or most distressing,
by their sort rather than their quantity. When Lady Russell
not long afterwards, was entering Bath on a wet afternoon,

and driving through the long course of streets from the Old
Bridge to Camden Place, amidst the dash of other carriages,
the heavy rumble of carts and drays, the bawling of newsmen,
muffin-men, and milkmen, and the ceaseless clink of pattens,
she made no complaint. No, these were noises which belonged to the winter pleasures; her spirits rose under their
influence; and like Mrs. Musgrove, she was feeling, though
not saying, that after being long in the country, nothing
could be so good for her as a little quiet cheerfulness.

Anne did not share these feelings. She persisted in a very
determined, though very silent disinclination for Bath;
caught the first dim view of the extensive buildings, smoking
in rain, without any wish of seeing them better; felt their
progress through the streets to be, however disagreeable, yet
too rapid; for who would be glad to see her when she arrived?
And looked back with fond regret to the bustles of Uppercross and the seclusion of Kellynch.

Elizabeth's last letter had communicated a piece of news
of some interest. Mr. Elliot was in Bath. He had called in
Camden Place; had called a second time, a third; had been
pointedly attentive. If Elizabeth and her father did not
deceive themselves, had been taking as much pains to seek
the acquaintance, and proclaim the value of the connexion,
as he had formerly taken pains to show neglect. This was
very wonderful if it were true; and Lady Russell was in a
state of very agreeable curiosity and perplexity about Mr.
Elliot, already recanting the sentiment she had so lately expressed to Mary, of his being " a man whom she had no wish
to see." She had a great wish to see him. If he really
sought to reconcile himself like a dutiful branch, he must be
forgiven for having dismembered himself from the paternal
tree.

Anne was not animated to an equal pitch by the circumstance, but she felt that she would rather see Mr. Elliot again
than not, which was more than she could say for many other
persons in Bath.

She was put down in Camden Place, and Lady Russell then
drove to her own lodgings in Rivers Street.

CHAPTER XV

SIR WALTER had taken a very good house in Camden Place, a lofty dignified situation, such as becomes a man of consequence; and both he and Elizabeth were settled there, much to their satisfaction.

Anne entered it with a sinking heart, anticipating an imprisonment of many months, and anxiously saying to herself, " Oh! when shall I leave you again? " A degree of unexpected cordiality, however, in the welcome she received, did her good. Her father and sister were glad to see her, for the sake of shewing her the house and furniture, and met her with kindness. Her making a fourth, when they sat down to dinner, was noticed as an advantage.

Mrs. Clay was very pleasant and very smiling, but her courtesies and smiles were more a matter of course. Anne had always felt that she would pretend what was proper on her arrival, but the complaisance of the others was unlooked for. They were evidently in excellent spirits, and she was soon to listen to the causes. They had no inclination to listen to her. After laying out for some compliments of being deeply regretted in their old neighbourhood, which Anne could not pay, they had only a few faint inquiries to make, before the talk must be all their own. Uppercross excited no interest, Kellynch very little: it was all Bath.

They had the pleasure of assuring her that Bath more than answered their expectations in every respect. Their house was undoubtedly the best in Camden Place, their drawing-rooms had many decided advantages over all the others which they had either seen or heard of, and the superiority was not less in the style of the fitting-up or the taste of the furniture. Their acquaintance was exceedingly sought after. Everybody was wanting to visit them. They had drawn back from many introductions, and still were perpetually having cards left by people of whom they knew nothing.

Here were funds of enjoyment! Could Anne wonder that

her father and sister were happy? She might not wonder, but she must sigh that her father should feel no degradation in his change, should see nothing to regret in the duties and dignity of the resident landholder, should find so much to be vain of in the littlenesses of a town; and she must sigh, and smile, and wonder too, as Elizabeth threw open the folding-doors, and walked with exultation from one drawing-room to the other, boasting of their space: at the possibility of that woman, who had been mistress of Kellynch Hall, finding extent to be proud of between two walls, perhaps thirty feet asunder.

But this was not all which they had to make them happy. They had Mr. Elliot too. Anne had a great deal to hear of Mr. Elliot. He was not only pardoned, they were delighted with him. He had been in Bath about a fortnight (he had passed through Bath in November, in his way to London, when the intelligence of Sir Walter's being settled there had of course reached him, though only twenty-four hours in the place, but he had not been able to avail himself of it); but he had now been a fortnight in Bath, and his first object on arriving had been to leave his card in Camden Place, following it up by such assiduous endeavours to meet, and when they did meet, by such great openness of conduct, such readiness to apologise for the past, such solicitude to be received as a relation again, that their former good understanding was completely re-established.

They had not a fault to find in him. He had explained away all the appearance of neglect on his own side. It had originated in misapprehension entirely. He had never had an idea of throwing himself off; he had feared that he was thrown off, but knew not why, and delicacy had kept him silent. Upon the hint of having spoken disrespectfully or carelessly of the family and the family honours, he was quite indignant. He, who had ever boasted of being an Elliot, and whose feelings, as to connexion, were only too strict to suit the unfeudal tone of the present day. He was astonished, indeed, but his character and general conduct must refute it. He could refer Sir Walter to all who knew him; and certainly, the pains he had been taking on this, the first opportunity of reconciliation, to be restored to the footing of a relation and heir-presumptive, was a strong proof of his opinions on the subject.

The circumstances of his marriage, too, were found to admit of much extenuation. This was an article not to be entered on by himself; but a very intimate friend of his, a Colonel Wallis, a highly respectable man, perfectly the gentleman (and not an ill-looking man, Sir Walter added), who was living in very good style in Marlborough Buildings, and had, at his own particular request, been admitted to their acquaintance through Mr. Elliot, had mentioned one or two things relative to the marriage, which made a material difference in the discredit of it.

Colonel Wallis had known Mr. Elliot long, had been well acquainted also with his wife, had perfectly understood the whole story. She was certainly not a woman of family, but well educated, accomplished, rich, and excessively in love with his friend. There had been the charm. She had sought him. Without that attraction, not all her money would have tempted Elliot, and Sir Walter was, moreover, assured of her having been a very fine woman. Here was a great deal to soften the business. A very fine woman with a large fortune, in love with him! Sir Walter seemed to admit it as complete apology; and though Elizabeth could not see the circumstance in quite so favourable a light, she allowed it to be a great extenuation.

Mr. Elliot had called repeatedly, had dined with them once, evidently delighted by the distinction of being asked, for they gave no dinners in general; delighted, in short, by every proof of cousinly notice, and placing his whole happiness in being on intimate terms in Camden Place.

Anne listened, but without quite understanding it. Allowances, large allowances, she knew, must be made for the ideas of those who spoke. She heard it all under embellishment. All that sounded extravagant or irrational in the progress of the reconciliation might have no origin but in the language of the relators. Still, however, she had the sensation of there being something more than immediately appeared, in Mr. Elliot's wishing, after an interval of so many years, to be well received by them. In a worldly view, he had nothing to gain by being on terms with Sir Walter; nothing to risk by a state of variance. In all probability he was already the richer of the two, and the Kellynch estate would as surely be his hereafter as the title. A sensible man, and he had looked like a *very* sensible man, why should it be an object to him? She could only offer one solution: it was, perhaps, for Elizabeth's sake. There might really have been a liking formerly, though convenience and accident had drawn him a different way; and now that he could afford to please himself, he might mean to pay his addresses to her. Elizabeth was certainly very handsome, with well-bred, elegant manners, and her character might never have been penetrated by Mr. Elliot, knowing her but in public, and when very young himself. How her temper and understanding might bear the investigation of his present keener time of life was another concern and rather a fearful one. Most earnestly did she wish that he might not be too nice, or too observant if Elizabeth were his object; and that Elizabeth was disposed to believe herself so, and that her friend, Mrs. Clay was encouraging the idea, seemed apparent by a glance or two between them, while Mr. Elliot's frequent visits were talked of.

Anne mentioned the glimpses she had had of him at Lyme, but without being much attended to. "Oh! yes, perhaps, it had been Mr. Elliot. They did not know. It might be him, perhaps." They could not listen to her description of him. They were describing him themselves; Sir Walter especially. He did justice to his very gentleman-like appearance, his air of elegance and fashion, his good-shaped face, his sensible eye; but, at the same time, "must lament his being very much under-hung, a defect which time seemed to have increased; nor could he pretend to say that the years had not altered almost every feature for the worse. Mr. Elliot appeared to think that he (Sir Walter) was looking exactly as he had done when they last parted;" but Sir Walter had "not been able to return the compliment entirely, which had embarrassed him. He did not mean to complain, however. Mr. Elliot was better to look at than most men, and he had no objection to being seen with him anywhere."

Mr. Elliot, and his friends in Marlborough Buildings, were talked of the whole evening. "Colonel Wallis had been so impatient to be introduced to them! and Mr. Elliot so anxious that he should!" and there was a Mrs. Wallis, at present known only to them by description, as she was in daily expectation of her confinement; but Mr. Elliot spoke of her as "a most charming woman, quite worthy of being known in Camden Place," and as soon as she recovered they were to be acquainted. Sir Walter thought much of Mrs. Wallis; she was said to be an excessively pretty woman, beautiful. "He longed to see her. He hoped she might make some amends for the many very plain faces he was continually passing in the streets. The worst of Bath was the number of its plain women. He did not mean to say that there were no pretty women, but the number of the plain was out of all proportion. He had frequently observed, as he walked, that one handsome face would be followed by thirty, or five-and-thirty frights; and once, as he had stood in a shop in Bond Street, he had counted eighty-seven women go by, one after another, without there being a tolerable face among them. It had been a frosty morning, to be sure, a sharp frost, which hardly one woman in a thousand could stand the test of. But still, there certainly were a dreadful multitude of ugly women in Bath; and as for the men! they were infinitely worse. Such scarecrows as the streets were full of! It was evident how little the women were used to the sight of anything tolerable, by the effect which a man of decent appearance produced. He had never walked anywhere arm-in-arm with Colonel Wallis (who was a fine military figure, though sandy-haired) without observing that every woman's eye was upon him; every woman's eye was sure to be upon Colonel Wallis." Modest Sir Walter! He was not allowed to escape, however. His daughter and Mrs. Clay united in hinting that Colonel Wallis's companion might have as good a figure as Colonel Wallis, and certainly was not sandy-haired.

"How is Mary looking?" said Sir Walter, in the height of his good humour. "The last time I saw her she had a red nose, but I hope that may not happen every day."

"Oh! no, that must have been quite accidental. In general she has been in very good health and very good looks since Michaelmas."

"If I thought it would not tempt her to go out in sharp

winds, and grow coarse, I would send her a new hat and pelisse."

Anne was considering whether she should venture to suggest that a gown, or a cap, would not be liable to any such misuse, when a knock at the door suspended everything. " A knock at the door! and so late! It was ten o'clock. Could it be Mr. Elliot? They knew he was to dine in Lansdown Crescent. It was possible that he might stop in his way home to ask them how they did. They could think of no one else. Mrs. Clay decidedly thought it Mr. Elliot's knock." Mrs. Clay was right. With all the state which a butler and foot-boy could give, Mr. Elliot was ushered into the room.

It was the same, the very same man, with no difference but of dress. Anne drew a little back, while the others received his compliments, and her sister his apologies for calling at so unusual an hour, but " he could not be so near without wishing to know that neither she nor her friend had taken cold the day before," etc., etc.; which was all as politely done, and as politely taken, as possible, but her part must follow then. Sir Walter talked of his youngest daughter; " Mr. Elliot must give him leave to present him to his youngest daughter " (there was no occasion for remembering Mary); and Anne, smiling and blushing, very becomingly shewed to Mr. Elliot the pretty features which he had by no means forgotten, and instantly saw, with amusement at his little start of surprise, that he had not been at all aware of who she was. He looked completely astonished, but not more astonished than pleased: his eyes brightened! and with the most perfect alacrity he welcomed the relationship, alluded to the past, and entreated to be received as an acquaintance already. He was quite as good-looking as he had appeared at Lyme, his countenance improved by speaking, and his manners were so exactly what they ought to be, so polished, so easy, so particularly agreeable, that she could compare them in excellence to only one person's manners. They were not the same, but they were, perhaps, equally good.

He sat down with them, and improved their conversation very much. There could be no doubt of his being a sensible man. Ten minutes were enough to certify that. His tone, his expressions, his choice of subject, his knowing where to stop: it was all the operation of a sensible, discerning mind. As soon as he could, he began to talk to her of Lyme, wanting to compare opinions respecting the place, but especially wanting to speak of the circumstance of their happening to be guests in the same inn at the same time; to give his own route, understand something of hers, and regret that he should have lost such an opportunity of paying his respects to her. She gave him a short account of her party and business at Lyme. His regret increased as he listened. He had spent his whole solitary evening in the room adjoining theirs; had heard voices, mirth continually; thought they must be a most delightful set of people, longed to be with them, but certainly without the smallest suspicion of his possessing the shadow of a right to introduce himself. If he had but asked who the party were! The name of Musgrove would have told him enough. " Well, it would serve to cure him of an absurd practice of never asking a question at an inn, which he had adopted, when quite a young man, on the principle of its being very ungenteel to be curious."

" The notions of a young man of one or two and twenty," said he, " as to what is necessary in manners to make him quite the thing, are more absurd, I believe, than those of any other set of beings in the world. The folly of the means they often employ is only to be equalled by the folly of what they have in view."

But he must not be addressing his reflections to Anne alone: he knew it; he was soon diffused again among the others, and it was only at intervals that he could return to Lyme.

His enquiries, however, produced at length an account of the scene she had been engaged in there, soon after his leaving the place. Having alluded to " an accident," he must hear the whole. When he questioned, Sir Walter and Elizabeth began to question also, but the difference in their manner of doing it could not be unfelt. She could only compare Mr. Elliot to Lady Russell, in the wish of really comprehending what had passed, and in the degree of concern for what she must have suffered in witnessing it.

He staid an hour with them. The elegant little clock on

the mantel-piece had struck "eleven with its silver sounds," and the watchman was beginning to be heard at a distance telling the same tale, before Mr. Elliot or any of them seemed to feel that he had been there long.

Anne could not have supposed it possible that her first evening in Camden Place could have pased so well.

CHAPTER XVI

THERE was one point which Anne, on returning to her family, would have been more thankful to ascertain even than Mr. Elliot's being in love with Elizabeth, which was, her father's not being in love with Mrs. Clay; and she was very far from easy about it, when she had been at home a few hours. On going down to breakfast the next morning, she found there had just been a decent pretence on the lady's side of meaning to leave them. She could imagine Mrs. Clay to have said, that "now Miss Anne was come, she could not suppose herself at all wanted;" for Elizabeth was replying in a sort of whisper, "That must not be any reason, indeed. I assure you I feel it none. She is nothing to me, compared with you;" and she was in full time to hear her father say, "My dear madam, this must not be. As yet, you have seen nothing of Bath. You have been here only to be useful. You must not run away from us now. You must stay to be acquainted with Mrs. Wallis, the beautiful Mrs. Wallis. To your fine mind, I well know the sight of beauty is a real gratification."

He spoke and looked so much in earnest, that Anne was not surprised to see Mrs. Clay stealing a glance at Elizabeth and herself. Her countenance, perhaps, might express some watchfulness; but the praise of the fine mind did not appear to excite a thought in her sister. The lady could not but yield to such joint entreaties, and promise to stay.

In the course of the same morning, Anne and her father chancing to be alone together, he began to compliment her on her improved looks; he thought her " less thin in her

person, in her cheeks; her skin, her complexion, greatly
improved; clearer, fresher. Had she been using anything
in particular?" "No, nothing." "Merely Gowland," he
supposed. "No, nothing at all." "Ha! he was surprised
at that;" and added, "certainly you cannot do better than
continue as you are; you cannot be better than well; or I
should recommend Gowland, the constant use of Gowland,
during the spring months. Mrs. Clay has been using it at
my recommendation, and you see what it has done for her.
You see how it has carried away her freckles."

If Elizabeth could but have heard this! Such personal
praise might have struck her, especially as it did not appear
to Anne that the freckles were at all lessened. But everything must take its chance. The evil of the marriage would
be much diminished, if Elizabeth were also to marry. As for
herself, she might always command a home with Lady Russell.

Lady Russell's composed mind and polite manners were
put to some trial on this point, in her intercourse in Camden
Place. The sight of Mrs. Clay in such favour, and of Anne
so overlooked, was a perpetual provocation to her there;
and vexed her as much when she was away, as a person in
Bath who drinks the water, gets all the new publications,
and has a very large acquaintance, has time to be vexed.

As Mr. Elliot became known to her, she grew more
charitable, or more indifferent, towards the others. His
manners were an immediate recommendation; and on
conversing with him she found the solid so fully supporting
the superficial, that she was at first, as she told Anne, almost
ready to exclaim. "Can this be Mr. Elliot?" and could not
seriously picture to herself a more agreeable or estimable
man. Everything united in him; good understanding,
correct opinions, knowledge of the world, and a warm heart.
He had strong feelings of family attachment and family
honour, without pride or weakness; he lived with the
liberality of a man of fortune, without display; he judged
for himself in everything essential, without defying public
opinion in any point of worldly decorum. He was steady,
observant, moderate, candid; never run away with by
spirits or by selfishness, which fancied itself strong feeling;
and yet, with a sensibility to what was amiable and lovely,

and a value for all the felicities of domestic life, which characters of fancied enthusiasm and violent agitation seldom really possess. She was sure that he had not been happy in marriage. Colonel Wallis said it, and Lady Russell saw it; but it had been no unhappiness to sour his mind, nor (she began pretty soon to suspect) to prevent his thinking of a second choice. Her satisfaction in Mr. Elliot outweighed all the plague of Mrs. Clay.

It was now some years since Anne had begun to learn that she and her excellent friend could sometimes think differently; and it did not surprise her, therefore, that Lady Russell should see nothing suspicious or inconsistent, nothing to require more motives than appeared, in Mr. Elliot's great desire of a reconciliation. In Lady Russell's view, it was perfectly natural that Mr. Elliot, at a mature time of life, should feel it a most desirable object, and what would very generally recommend him among all sensible people, to be on good terms with the head of his family; the simplest process in the world of time upon a head naturally clear, and only erring in the heyday of youth. Anne presumed, however, still to smile about it, and at last to mention " Elizabeth." Lady Russell listened, and looked, and made only this cautious reply:—" Elizabeth! very well; time will explain."

It was a reference to the future, which Anne, after a little observation, felt she must submit to. She could determine nothing at present. In that house Elizabeth must be first; and she was in the habit of such general observance as " Miss Elliot," that any particularity of attention seemed almost impossible. Mr. Elliot, too, it must be remembered, had not been a widower seven months. A little delay on his side might be very excusable. In fact, Anne could never see the crape round his hat, without fearing that she was the inexcusable one, in attributing to him such imaginations; for though his marriage had not been very happy, still it had existed so many years that she could not comprehend a very rapid recovery from the awful impression of its being dissolved.

However it might end, he was without any question their pleasantest acquaintance in Bath: she saw nobody equal

to him; and it was a great indulgence now and then to talk
to him about Lyme, which he seemed to have as lively a
wish to see again, and to see more of, as herself.   They went
through the particulars of their first meeting a great many
times.   He gave her to understand that he had looked at
her with some earnestness.   She knew it well; and she
remembered another person's look also.

They did not always think alike.   His value for rank and
connexion she perceived to be greater than hers.   It was
not merely complaisance, it must be a liking to the cause,
which made him enter warmly into her father and sister's
solicitudes on a subject which she thought unworthy to
excite them.   The Bath paper one morning announced the
arrival of the Dowager Viscountess Dalrymple, and her
daughter, the Honourable Miss Carteret; and all the comfort
of No. — Camden Place, was swept away for many days; for
the Dalrymples (in Anne's opinion, most unfortunately) were
cousins of the Elliots; and the agony was how to introduce
themselves properly.

Anne had never seen her father and sister before in contact
with nobility, and she must acknowledge herself disappointed.
She had hoped better things from their high ideas of their
own situation in life, and was reduced to form a wish which
she had never foreseen; a wish that they had more pride;
for " our cousins, Lady Dalrymple and Miss Carteret; "
" our cousins the Dalrymples," sounded in her ears all day
long.

Sir Walter had once been in company with the late
viscount, but had never seen any of the rest of the family;
and the difficulties of the case arose from there having been
a suspension of all intercourse by letters of ceremony, ever
since the death of that said late viscount, when, in consequence
of a dangerous illness of Sir Walter's at the same time, there
had been an unlucky omission at Kellynch.   No letter of
condolence had been sent to Ireland.   The neglect had been
visited on the head of the sinner; for when poor Lady Elliot
died herself, no letter of condolence was received at Kellynch,
and, consequently, there was but too much reason to apprehend that the Dalrymples considered the relationship as
closed.   How to have this anxious business set to rights, and

be admitted as cousins again, was the question: and it was a question which, in a more rational manner, neither Lady Russell nor Mr. Elliot thought unimportant. " Family connexions were always worth preserving, good company always worth seeking; Lady Dalrymple had taken a house, for three months, in Laura Place, and would be living in style. She had been at Bath the year before, and Lady Russell had heard her spoken of as a charming woman. It was very desirable that the connexion should be renewed, if it could be done, without any compromise of propriety on the side of the Elliots."

Sir Walter, however, would choose his own means, and at last wrote a very fine letter of ample explanation, regret, and entreaty, to his right honourable cousin. Neither Lady Russell nor Mr. Elliot could admire the letter; but it did all that was wanted, in bringing three lines of scrawl from the Dowager Viscountess. " She was very much honoured, and should be happy in their acquaintance." The toils of the business were over, the sweets began. They visited in Laura Place, they had the cards of Dowager Viscountess Dalrymple, and the Honourable Miss Carteret, to be arranged wherever they might be most visible: and " Our cousins in Laura Place,"—" Our cousins, Lady Dalrymple and Miss Carteret," were talked of to everybody.

Anne was ashamed. Had Lady Dalrymple and her daughter even been very agreeable, she would still have been ashamed of the agitation they created, but they were nothing. There was no superiority of manner, accomplishment, or understanding. Lady Dalrymple had acquired the name of " a charming woman," because she had a smile and a civil answer for everybody. Miss Carteret, with still less to say, was so plain and so awkward, that she would never have been tolerated in Camden Place but for her birth.

Lady Russell confessed that she had expected something better; but yet " it was an acquaintance worth having; " and when Anne ventured to speak her opinion of them to Mr. Elliot, he agreed to their being nothing in themselves, but still maintained that, as a family connexion, as good company, as those who would collect good company around them, they had their value. Anne smiled and said—

"My idea of good company, Mr. Elliot, is the company of clever, well-informed people, who have a great deal of conversation; that is what I call good company."

"You are mistaken," said he, gently, "that is not good company; that is the best. Good company requires only birth, education, and manners, and with regard to education is not very nice. Birth and good manners are essential; but a little learning is by no means a dangerous thing in good company; on the contrary, it will do very well. My cousin Anne shakes her head. She is not satisfied. She is fastidious. My dear cousin" (sitting down by her), "you have a better right to be fastidious than almost any other woman I know; but will it answer? Will it make you happy? Will it not be wiser to accept the society of these good ladies in Laura Place, and enjoy all the advantages of the connexion as far as possible? You may depend upon it, that they will move in the first set in Bath this winter, and as rank is rank, your being known to be related to them will have its use in fixing your family (our family let me say) in that degree of consideration which we must all wish for."

"Yes," sighed Anne, "we shall, indeed, be known to be related to them!" then recollecting herself, and not wishing to be answered, she added, "I certainly do think there has been by far too much trouble taken to procure the acquaintance. I suppose" (smiling) "I have more pride than any of you; but I confess it does vex me, that we should be so solicitous to have the relationship acknowledged, which we may be very sure is a matter of perfect indifference to them."

"Pardon me, my dear cousin, you are unjust to your own claims. In London, perhaps, in your present quiet style of living, it might be as you say; but in Bath, Sir Walter Elliot and his family will always be worth knowing: always acceptable as acquaintance."

"Well," said Anne, "I certainly am proud, too proud to enjoy a welcome which depends so entirely upon place."

"I love your indignation," said he; "it is very natural. But here you are in Bath, and the object is to be established here with all the credit and dignity which ought to belong to Sir Walter Elliot. You talk of being proud; I am called proud, I know, and I shall not wish to believe myself otherwise; for our pride, if investigated, would have the same object, I have no doubt, though the kind may seem a little different. In one point, I am sure, my dear cousin" (he continued, speaking lower, though there was no one else in the room), "in one point I am sure we must feel alike. We must feel that every addition to your father's society, among his equals or superiors, may be of use in diverting his thoughts from those who are beneath him."

He looked, as he spoke, to the seat which Mrs. Clay had been lately occupying: a sufficient explanation of what he particularly meant; and though Anne could not believe in their having the same sort of pride, she was pleased with him for not liking Mrs. Clay; and her conscience admitted that his wishing to promote her father's getting great acquaintance was more than excusable in the view of defeating her.

CHAPTER XVII

WHILE Sir Walter and Elizabeth were assiduously pushing their good fortune in Laura Place, Anne was renewing an acquaintance of a very different description.

She had called on her former governess, and had heard from her of there being an old schoolfellow in Bath, who had the two strong claims on her attention of past kindness and present suffering. Miss Hamilton, now Mrs. Smith, had shewn her kindness in one of those periods of her life when it had been most valuable. Anne had gone unhappy to school, grieving for the loss of a mother whom she had dearly loved, feeling her separation from home, and suffering as a girl of fourteen, of strong sensibility and not high spirits, must suffer at such a time; and Miss Hamilton, three years older than herself, but still, from the want of near relations and a settled home, remaining another year at school, had been useful and good to her in a way which had considerably lessened her misery, and could never be remembered with indifference.

Miss Hamilton had left school, had married not long afterwards, was said to have married a man of fortune, and this was all that Anne had known of her, till now that their governess's account brought her situation forward in a more decided but very different form.

She was a widow, and poor. Her husband had been extravagant; and at his death, about two years before, had left his affairs dreadfully involved. She had had difficulties of every sort to contend with, and in addition to these distresses had been afflicted with a severe rheumatic fever, which, finally settling in her legs, had made her for the present a cripple. She had come to Bath on that account, and was now in lodgings near the hot baths, living in a very humble way, unable even to afford herself the comfort of a servant, and of course almost excluded from society.

Their mutual friend answered for the satisfaction which a visit from Miss Elliot would give Mrs. Smith, and Anne therefore lost no time in going. She mentioned nothing of what she had heard, or what she intended, at home. It would excite no proper interest there. She only consulted Lady Russell, who entered thoroughly into her sentiments, and was most happy to convey her as near to Mrs. Smith's lodgings, in Westgate Buildings, as Anne chose to be taken.

The visit was paid, their acquaintance re-established, their interest in each other more than rekindled. The first ten minutes had its awkwardness and its emotion. Twelve years were gone since they had parted, and each presented a somewhat different person from what the other had imagined. Twelve years had changed Anne from the blooming, silent, unformed girl of fifteen, to the elegant little woman of seven-and-twenty, with every beauty excepting bloom, and with manners as consciously right as they were invariably gentle; and twelve years had transformed the fine-looking, well-grown Miss Hamilton, in all the glow of health and confidence of superiority, into a poor, infirm, helpless widow, receiving the visit of her former protegée as a favour; but all that was uncomfortable in the meeting had soon passed away, and left only the interesting charm of remembering former partialities and talking over old times.

Anne found in Mrs. Smith the good sense and agreeable manners which she had almost ventured to depend on, and a disposition to converse and be cheerful beyond her expectation. Neither the dissipations of the past—and she had lived very much in the world—nor the restrictions of the present, neither sickness nor sorrow seemed to have closed her heart or ruined her spirits.

In the course of a second visit she talked with great openness, and Anne's astonishment increased. She could scarcely imagine a more cheerless situation in itself than Mrs. Smith's. She had been very fond of her husband: she had buried him. She had been used to affluence: it was gone. She had no child to connect her with life and happiness again, no relations to assist in the arrangement of perplexed affairs, no health to make all the rest supportable. Her accommodations were limited to a noisy parlour, and a dark bedroom behind, with no possibility of moving from one to the other without assistance, which there was only one servant in the house to afford, and she never quitted the house but to be conveyed into the warm bath. Yet, in spite of all this, Anne had reason to believe that she had moments only of languor and depression to hours of occupation and enjoyment. How could it be? She watched, observed, reflected, and finally determined that this was not a case of fortitude or of resignation only. A submissive spirit might be patient, a strong understanding would supply resolution, but here was something more; here was that elasticity of mind, that disposition to be comforted, that power of turning readily from evil to good, and of finding employment which carried her out of herself, which was from nature alone. It was the choicest gift of Heaven; and Anne viewed her friend as one of those instances in which, by a merciful appointment, it seems designed to counterbalance almost every other want.

There had been a time, Mrs. Smith told her, when her spirits had nearly failed. She could not call herself an invalid now, compared with her state on first reaching Bath. Then she had, indeed, been a pitiable object; for she had caught cold on the journey, and had hardly taken possession of her lodgings before she was again confined to her bed, and suffering under severe and constant pain; and all this among

strangers, with the absolute necessity of having a regular
nurse, and finances at that moment particularly unfit to
meet any extraordinary expense. She had weathered it,
however, and could truly say that it had done her good.
It had increased her comforts by making her feel herself
to be in good hands. She had seen too much of the
world to expect sudden or disinterested attachment anywhere, but her illness had proved to her that her landlady
had a character to preserve, and would not use her ill; and
she had been particularly fortunate in her nurse, as a sister of
her landlady, a nurse by profession, and who had always a
home in that house when unemployed, chanced to be at
liberty just in time to attend her. "And she," said Mrs.
Smith, "besides nursing me most admirably, has really
proved an invaluable acquaintance. As soon as I could use
my hands she taught me to knit, which has been a great
amusement; and she put me in the way of making these
little thread-cases, pin-cushions, and card-racks, which you
always find me so busy about, and which supply me with the
means of doing a little good to one or two very poor families
in this neighbourhood. She has a large acquaintance, of
course professionally, among those who can afford to buy,
and she disposes of my merchandise. She always takes the
right time for applying. Everybody's heart is open, you
know, when they have recently escaped from severe pain,
or are recovering the blessing of health, and Nurse Rooke
thoroughly understands when to speak. She is a shrewd,
intelligent, sensible woman. Hers is a line for seeing human
nature; and she has a fund of good sense and observation,
which, as a companion, make her infinitely superior to
thousands of those who, having only received 'the best
education in the world,' know nothing worth attending to.
Call it gossip, if you will, but when Nurse Rooke has half an
hour's leisure to bestow on me, she is sure to have something
to relate that is entertaining and profitable: something that
makes one know one's species better. One likes to hear
what is going on, to be *au fait* as to the newest modes of being
trifling and silly. To me, who live so much alone, her
conversation, I assure you, is a treat"

Anne, far from wishing to cavil at the pleasure, replied,

" I can easily believe it. Women of that class have great opportunities, and if they are intelligent may be well worth listening to. Such varieties of human nature as they are in the habit of witnessing ! And it is not merely in its follies that they are well read; for they see it occasionally under every circumstance that can be most interesting or affecting. What instances must pass before them of ardent, disinterested, self-denying attachment, of heroism, fortitude, patience, resignation; of all the conflicts and all the sacrifices that ennoble us most. A sick chamber may often furnish the worth of volumes."

" Yes," said Mrs. Smith, more doubtingly, " sometimes it may, though I fear its lessons are not often in the elevated style you describe. Here and there, human nature may be great in times of trial; but, generally speaking, it is its weakness and not its strength that appears in a sick chamber: it is selfishness and impatience, rather than generosity and fortitude, that one hears of. There is so little real friendship in the world! and unfortunately " (speaking low and tremulously), " there are so many who forget to think seriously till it is almost too late."

Anne saw the misery of such feelings. The husband had not been what he ought, and the wife had been led among that part of mankind which made her think worse of the world than she hoped it deserved. It was but a passing emotion, however, with Mrs. Smith; she shook it off, and soon added in a different tone—

" I do not suppose the situation my friend Mrs. Rooke is in at present will furnish much either to interest or edify me. She is only nursing Mrs. Wallis of Marlborough Buildings; a mere pretty, silly, expensive, fashionable woman, I believe; and of course will have nothing to report but of lace and finery. I mean to make my profit of Mrs. Wallis, however. She has plenty of money, and I intend she shall buy all the high-priced things I have in hand now."

Anne had called several times on her friend, before the existence of such a person was known in Camden Place. At last, it became necessary to speak of her. Sir Walter, Elizabeth, and Mrs. Clay, returned one morning from Laura Place, with a sudden invitation from Lady Dalrymple for the same evening, and Anne was already engaged to spend that evening in Westgate Buildings. She was not sorry for the excuse. They were only asked, she was sure, because Lady Dalrymple, being kept at home by a bad cold, was glad to make use of the relationship which had been so pressed on her; and she declined on her own account with great alacrity —" She was engaged to spend the evening with an old schoolfellow." They were not much interested in anything relative to Anne; but still there were questions enough asked, to make it understood what this old schoolfellow was; and Elizabeth was disdainful, and Sir Walter severe.

" Westgate Buildings!" said he; " and who is Miss Anne Elliot to be visiting in Westgate Buildings? A Mrs. Smith. A widow Mrs. Smith; and who was her husband? One of the five thousand Mr. Smiths whose names are to be met with everywhere. And what is her attraction? That she is old and sickly. Upon my word, Miss Anne Elliot, you have the most extraordinary taste! Everything that revolts other people, low com' any, paltry rooms, foul air, disgusting associations, are inviting to you. But surely you may put off this old lady till to-morrow: she is not so near her end, I presume, but that she may hope to see another day. What is her age? Forty? "

" No, sir, she is not one-and-thirty; but I do not think I can put off my engagement, because it is the only evening for some time which will at once suit her and myself. She goes into the warm bath to-morrow; and for the rest of the week, you know, we are engaged."

" But what does Lady Russell think of this acquaintance? " asked Elizabeth.

" She sees nothing to blame in it," replied Anne; " on the contrary, she approves it, and has generally taken me when I have called on Mrs. Smith."

" Westgate Buildings must have been rather surprised by the appearance of a carriage drawn up near its pavement," observed Sir Walter. " Sir Henry Russell's widow, indeed, has no honours to distinguish her arms, but still it is a handsome equipage, and no doubt is well known to convey a Miss Elliot. A widow Mrs. Smith, lodging in Westgate Buildings! A poor widow, barely able to live, between thirty and forty;

a mere Mrs. Smith, an every-day Mrs. Smith, of all people and all names in the world, to be the chosen friend of Miss Anne Elliot, and to be preferred by her to her own family connexions among the nobility of England and Ireland! Mrs. Smith! Such a name!"

Mrs. Clay, who had been present while all this passed, now thought it advisable to leave the room, and Anne could have said much, and did long to say a little in defence of *her* friend's not very dissimilar claims to theirs, but her sense of personal respect to her father prevented her. She made no reply. She left it to himself to recollect, that Mrs. Smith was not the only widow in Bath between thirty and forty, with little to live on, and no sirname of dignity.

Anne kept her appointment, the others kept theirs, and of course she heard the next morning that they had had a delightful evening. She had been the only one of the set absent, for Sir Walter and Elizabeth had not only been quite at her ladyship's service themselves, but had actually been happy to be employed by her in collecting others, and had been at the trouble of inviting both Lady Russell and Mr. Elliot; and Mr. Elliot had made a point of leaving Colonel Wallis early, and Lady Russell had fresh arranged all her evening engagements, in order to wait on her. Anne had the whole history of all that such an evening could supply from Lady Russell. To her, its greatest interest must be, in having been very much talked of between her friend and Mr. Elliot; in having been wished for, regretted, and at the same time honoured for staying away in such a cause. Her kind, compassionate visits to this old schoolfellow, sick and reduced, seemed to have quite delighted Mr. Elliot. He thought her a most extraordinary young woman: in her temper, manners, mind, a model of female excellence. He could meet even Lady Russell in a discussion of her merits; and Anne could not be given to understand so much by her friend, could not know herself to be so highly rated by a sensible man, without many of those agreeable sensations which her friend meant to create.

Lady Russell was now perfectly decided in her opinion of Mr. Elliot. She was as much convinced of his meaning to gain Anne in time as of his deserving her, and was beginning to calculate the number of weeks which would free him from all the remaining restraints of widowhood, and leave him at liberty to exert his most open powers of pleasing. She would not speak to Anne with half the certainty she felt on the subject, she would venture on little more than hints of what might be hereafter, of a possible attachment on his side, of the desirableness of the alliance, supposing such an attachment to be real and returned. Anne heard her, and made no violent exclamations; she only smiled, blushed, and gently shook her head.

" I am no match-maker, as you well know," said Lady Russell, "being much too well aware of the uncertainty of all human events and calculations. I only mean that if Mr. Elliot should some time hence pay his addresses to you, and if you should be disposed to accept him, I think there would be every possibility of your being happy together. A most suitable connexion everybody must consider it, but I think it might be a very happy one."

" Mr. Elliot is an exceedingly agreeable man, and in many respects I think highly of him," said Anne; " but we should not suit."

Lady Russell let this pass, and only said in rejoinder, " I own that to be able to regard you as the future mistress of Kellynch, the future Lady Elliot, to look forward and see you occupying your dear mother's place, succeeding to all her rights, and all her popularity, as well as to all her virtues, would be the highest possible gratification to me. You are your mother's self in countenance and disposition; and if I might be allowed to fancy you such as she was, in situation, and name, and home, presiding and blessing in the same spot, and only superior to her in being more highly valued! My dearest Anne, it would give me more delight than is often felt at my time of life."

Anne was obliged to turn away, to rise, to walk to a distant table, and, leaning there in pretended employment, try to subdue the feelings this picture excited. For a few moments her imagination and her heart were bewitched. The idea of becoming what her mother had been; of having the precious name of " Lady Elliot " first revived in herself; of being restored to Kellynch, calling it her home again, her home for ever, was a charm which she could not immediately resist. Lady Russell said not another word, willing to leave the matter to its own operation; and believing that, could Mr. Elliot at that moment with propriety have spoken for himself!—she believed, in short, what Anne did not believe. The same image of Mr. Elliot speaking for himself brought Anne to composure again. The charm of Kellynch and of " Lady Elliot " all faded away. She never could accept him. And it was not only that her feelings were still adverse to any man save one; her judgment, on a serious consideration of the possibilities of such a case, was against Mr. Elliot.

Though they had now been acquainted a month, she could not be satisfied that she really knew his character. That he was a sensible man, an agreeable man, that he talked well, professed good opinions, seemed to judge properly and as a man of principle, this was all clear enough. He certainly knew what was right, nor could she fix on any one article of moral duty evidently transgressed; but yet she would have been afraid to answer for his conduct. She distrusted the past, if not the present. The names which occasionally dropt of former associates, the allusions to former practices and pursuits, suggested suspicions not favourable of what he had been. She saw that there had been bad habits; that Sunday travelling had been a common thing; that there had been a period of his life (and probably not a short one) when he had been, at least, careless on all serious matters; and, though he might now think very differently, who could answer for the true sentiments of a clever, cautious man, grown old enough to appreciate a fair character? How could it ever be ascertained that his mind was truly cleansed?

Mr. Elliot was rational, discreet, polished, but he was not open. There was never any burst of feeling, any warmth of indignation or delight, at the evil or good of others. This, to Anne, was a decided imperfection. Her early impressions were incurable. She prized the frank, the open-hearted, the eager character beyond all others. Warmth and enthusiasm did captivate her still. She felt that she could so much more depend upon the sincerity of those who sometimes looked or said a careless or a hasty thing, than of those whose presence of mind never varied, whose tongue never slipped.

Mr. Elliot was too generally agreeable. Various as were the tempers in her father's house, he pleased them all. He endured too well, stood too well with every body. He had spoken to her with some degree of openness of Mrs. Clay; had appeared completely to see what Mrs. Clay was about, and to hold her in contempt; and yet Mrs. Clay found him as agreeable as any body.

Lady Russell saw either less or more than her young friend, for she saw nothing to excite distrust. She could not imagine a man more exactly what he ought to be than Mr. Elliot; nor did she ever enjoy a sweeter feeling than the hope of seeing him receive the hand of her beloved Anne in Kellynch church, in the course of the following autumn.

CHAPTER XVIII

IT was the beginning of February; and Anne, having been a month in Bath, was growing very eager for news from Uppercross and Lyme. She wanted to hear much more than Mary communicated. It was three weeks since she had heard at all. She only knew that Henrietta was at home again; and that Louisa, though considered to be recovering fast, was still at Lyme; and she was thinking of them all very intently one evening, when a thicker letter than usual from Mary was delivered to her; and, to quicken the pleasure and surprise, with Admiral and Mrs. Croft's compliments.

The Crofts must be in Bath! A circumstance to interest her. They were people whom her heart turned to very naturally.

"What is this?" cried Sir Walter. "The Crofts arrived in Bath? The Crofts who rent Kellynch? What have they brought you?"

"A letter from Uppercross Cottage, sir."

"Oh! those letters are convenient passports. They

secure an introduction. I should have visited Admiral Croft, however, at any rate. I know what is due to my tenant."

Anne could listen no longer; she could not even have told how the poor Admiral's complexion escaped; her letter engrossed her. It had been begun several days back.

February 1st——.

"My Dear Anne,—I make no apology for my silence, because I know how little people think of letters in such a place as Bath. You must be a great deal too happy to care for Uppercross, which, as you well know, affords little to write about. We have had a very dull Christmas; Mr. and Mrs. Musgrove have not had one dinner-party all the holidays. I do not reckon the Hayters as anybody. The holidays, however, are over at last: I believe no children ever had such long ones. I am sure I had not. The house was cleared yesterday, except of the little Harvilles; but you will be surprised to hear that they have never gone home. Mrs. Harville must be an odd mother to part with them so long. I do not understand it. They are not at all nice children, in my opinion; but Mrs. Musgrove seems to like them quite as well, if not better, than her grandchildren. What dreadful weather we have had! It may not be felt in Bath, with your nice pavements; but in the country it is of some consequence. I have not had a creature call on me since the second week in January, except Charles Hayter, who has been calling much oftener than was welcome. Between ourselves, I think it a great pity Henrietta did not remain at Lyme as long as Louisa; it would have kept her a little out of his way. The carriage is gone to-day, to bring Louisa and the Harvilles to-morrow. We are not asked to dine with them, however, till the day after, Mrs. Musgrove is so afraid of her being fatigued by the journey, which is not very likely, considering the care that will be taken of her; and it would be much more convenient to me to dine there to-morrow. I am glad you find Mr. Elliot so agreeable, and wish I could be acquainted with him too; but I have my usual luck: I am always out of the way when anything desirable is going on; always the last of my family to be noticed. What an immense time Mrs. Clay has been staying with Elizabeth! Does she never mean to go away? But, perhaps, if she were to leave the room vacant, we might not be invited. Let me know what you think of this. I do not expect my children to be asked, you know. I can leave them at the Great House very well, for a month or six weeks. I have this moment heard that the Crofts are going to Bath almost immediately: they think the Admiral gouty. Charles heard it quite by chance: they have not had the civility to give me any notice, or offer to take anything. I do not think they improve at all as neighbours. We see nothing of them, and this is really an instance of gross inattention. Charles joins me in love, and everything proper. Yours affectionately,

"MARY M——.

"I am sorry to say that I am very far from well; and Jemima has just told me that the butcher says there is a bad sore-throat very much about. I dare say I shall catch it; and my sore-throats, you know, are always worse than anybody's."

So ended the first part, which had been afterwards put into an envelope, containing nearly as much more.

"I kept my letter open, that I might send you word how Louisa bore her journey, and now I am extremely glad I did, having a great deal to add. In the first place, I had a note from Mrs. Croft yesterday, offering to convey anything to you; a very kind, friendly note indeed, addressed to me, just as it ought; I shall therefore be able to make my letter as long as I like. The Admiral does not seem very ill, and I sincerely hope Bath will do him all the good he wants. I shall be truly glad to have them back again. Our neighbourhood cannot spare such a pleasant family. But now for Louisa. I have something to communicate that will astonish you not a little. She and the Harvilles came on Tuesday very safely, and in the evening we went to ask her how she did, when we were rather surprised not to find Captain

Benwick of the party, for he had been invited as well as the Harvilles; and what do you think was the reason? Neither more nor less than his being in love with Louisa, and not choosing to venture to Uppercross till he had had an answer from Mr. Musgrove; for it was all settled between him and her before she came away, and he had written to her father by Captain Harville. True, upon my honour! Are not you astonished? I shall be surprised at least if you ever received a hint of it, for I never did. Mrs. Musgrove protests solemnly that she knew nothing of the matter. We are all very well pleased, however; for though it is not equal to her marrying Captain Wentworth, it is infinitely better than Charles Hayter; and Mr. Musgrove has written his consent, and Captain Benwick is expected to-day. Mrs. Harville says her husband feels a good deal on his poor sister's account; but, however, Louisa is a great favourite with both. Indeed, Mrs. Harville and I quite agree that we love her the better for having nursed her. Charles wonders what Captain Wentworth will say; but if you remember, I never thought him attached to Louisa; I never could see anything of it. And this is the end, you see, of Captain Benwick's being supposed to be an admirer of yours. How Charles could take such a thing into his head was always incomprehensible to me. I hope he will be more agreeable now. Certainly not a great match for Louisa Musgrove, but a million times better than marrying among the Hayters."

Mary need not have feared her sister's being in any degree prepared for the news. She had never in her life been more astonished. Captain Benwick and Louisa Musgrove! It was almost too wonderful for belief, and it was with the greatest effort that she could remain in the room, preserve an air of calmness, and answer the common questions of the moment. Happily for her, they were not many. Sir Walter wanted to know whether the Crofts travelled with four horses, and whether they were likely to be situated in such a part of Bath as it might suit Miss Elliot and himself to visit in; but had little curiosity beyond.

"How is Mary?" said Elizabeth; and without waiting for an answer, "And pray what brings the Crofts to Bath?"

" They come on the Admiral's account. He is thought to be gouty."

" Gout and decrepitude! " said Sir Walter. " Poor old gentleman! "

" Have they any acquaintance here? " asked Elizabeth.

" I do not know; but I can hardly suppose that, at Admiral Croft's time of life, and in his profession, he should not have many acquaintance in such a place as this."

" I suspect," said Sir Walter, coolly, " that Admiral Croft will be best known in Bath as the renter of Kellynch Hall. Elizabeth, may we venture to present him and his wife in Laura Place? "

" Oh no! I think not. Situated as we are with Lady Dalrymple, cousins, we ought to be very careful not to embarrass her with acquaintance she might not approve. If we were not related it would not signify; but as cousins, she would feel scrupulous as to any proposal of ours. We had better leave the Crofts to find their own level. There are several odd-looking men walking about here, who, I am told, are sailors. The Crofts will associate with them."

This was Sir Walter and Elizabeth's share of interest in the letter; when Mrs. Clay had paid her tribute of more decent attention, in an enquiry after Mrs. Charles Musgrove and her fine little boys, Anne was at liberty.

In her own room she tried to comprehend it. Well might Charles wonder how Captain Wentworth would feel! Perhaps he had quitted the field, had given Louisa up, had ceased to love, had found he did not love her. She could not endure the idea of treachery or levity, or anything akin to ill usage between him and his friend. She could not endure that such a friendship as theirs should be severed unfairly.

Captain Benwick and Louisa Musgrove! The high-spirited, joyous-talking Louisa Musgrove, and the dejected, thinking, feeling, reading Captain Benwick, seemed each of them everything that would not suit the other. Their minds most dissimilar! Where could have been the attraction? The answer soon presented itself. It had been in situation. They had been thrown together several weeks; they had been living in the same small family party: since Henrietta's coming away, they must have been depending almost entirely on each other, and Louisa, just recovering from illness, had been in an interesting state, and Captain Benwick was not inconsolable. That was a point which Anne had not been able to avoid suspecting before; and instead of drawing the same conclusion as Mary, from the present course of events, they served only to confirm the idea of his having felt some dawning of tenderness toward herself. She did not mean, however, to derive much more from it to gratify her vanity than Mary might have allowed. She was persuaded that any tolerably pleasing young woman who had listened and seemed to feel for him would have received the same compliment. He had an affectionate heart. He must love somebody.

She saw no reason against their being happy. Louisa had fine naval fervour to begin with, and they would soon grow more alike. He would gain cheerfulness, and she would learn to be an enthusiast for Scott and Lord Byron; nay, that was probably learnt already; of course they had fallen in love over poetry. The idea of Louisa Musgrove turned into a person of literary taste and sentimental reflection was amusing, but she had no doubt of its being so. The day at Lyme, the fall from the Cobb, might influence her health, her nerves, her courage, her character to the end of her life, as thoroughly as it appeared to have influenced her fate.

The conclusion of the whole was, that if the woman who had been sensible of Captain Wentworth's merits could be allowed to prefer another man, there was nothing in the engagement to excite lasting wonder; and if Captain Wentworth lost no friend by it, certainly nothing to be regretted. No, it was not regret which made Anne's heart beat in spite of herself, and brought the colour into her cheeks when she thought of Captain Wentworth unshackled and free. She had some feelings which she was ashamed to investigate. They were too much like joy, senseless joy!

She longed to see the Crofts; but when the meeting took place, it was evident that no rumour of the news had yet reached them. The visit of ceremony was paid and returned; and Louisa Musgrove was mentioned, and Captain Benwick, too, without even half a smile.

The Crofts had placed themselves in lodgings in Gay

Street, perfectly to Sir Walter's satisfaction. He was not at all ashamed of the acquaintance, and did, in fact, think and talk a great deal more about the Admiral than the Admiral ever thought or talked about him.

The Crofts knew quite as many people in Bath as they wished for, and considered their intercourse with the Elliots as a mere matter of form, and not in the least likely to afford them any pleasure. They brought with them their country habit of being always together. He was ordered to walk to keep off the gout, and Mrs. Croft seemed to go shares with him in everything, and to walk for her life to do him good. Anne saw them wherever she went. Lady Russell took her out in her carriage almost every morning, and she never failed to think of them, and never failed to see them. Knowing their feelings as she did, it was a most attractive picture of happiness to her. She always watched them as long as she could, delighted to fancy she understood what they might be talking of, as they walked along in happy independence, or equally delighted to see the Admiral's hearty shake of the hand when he encountered an old friend, and observe their eagerness of conversation when occasionally forming into a little knot of the navy, Mrs. Croft looking as intelligent and keen as any of the officers around her.

Anne was too much engaged with Lady Russell to be often walking herself; but it so happened that one morning, about a week or ten days after the Crofts' arrival, it suited her best to leave her friend, or her friend's carriage, in the lower part of the town, and return alone to Camden Place, and in walking up Milsom Street she had the good fortune to meet with the Admiral. He was standing by himself, at a printshop window, with his hands behind him, in earnest contemplation of some print, and she not only might have passed him unseen, but was obliged to touch as well as address him before she could catch his notice. When he did perceive and acknowledge her, however, it was done with all his usual frankness and good-humour. " Ha! is it you? Thank you, thank you. This is treating me like a friend. Here I am, you see, staring at a picture. I can never get by this shop without stopping. But what a thing here is, by way of a boat! Do look at it. Did you ever see the like? What

queer fellows your fine painters must be, to think that anybody would venture their lives in such a shapeless old cockle-
shell as that? And yet here are two gentlemen stuck up in
it mightily at their ease, and looking about them at the rocks
and mountains, as if they were not to be upset the next
moment, which they certainly must be. I wonder where
that boat was built!" (laughing heartily); "I would not
venture over a horsepond in it. Well" (turning away),
"now, where are you bound? Can I go anywhere for you,
or with you? Can I be of any use?"

"None, I thank you, unless you will give me the pleasure
of your company the little way our road lies together. I am
going home."

"That I will, with all my heart, and farther too. Yes,
yes, we will have a snug walk together, and I have something
to tell you as we go along. There, take my arm; that's
right; I do not feel comfortable if I have not a woman there.
Lord! what a boat it is!" taking a last look at the picture,
as they began to be in motion.

"Did you say that you had something to tell me, sir?"

"Yes, I have, presently. But here comes a friend,
Captain Brigden; I shall only say, 'How d'ye do?' as we
pass, however. I shall not stop. 'How d'ye do?' Brigden
stares to see anybody with me but my wife. She, poor soul,
is tied by the leg. She has a blister on one of her heels, as
large as a three-shilling piece. If you look across the street,
you will see Admiral Brand coming down and his brother.
Shabby fellows, both of them! I am glad they are not on
this side of the way. Sophy cannot bear them. They
played me a pitiful trick once: got away some of my best
men. I will tell you the whole story another time. There
comes old Sir Archibald Drew and his grandson. Look, he
sees us; he kisses his hand to you; he takes you for my wife.
Ah! the peace has come too soon for that younker. Poor old
Sir Archibald! How do you like Bath, Miss Elliot? It
suits us very well. We are always meeting with some old
friend or other; the streets full of them every morning; sure
to have plenty of chat; and then we get away from them all,
and shut ourselves into our lodgings, and draw in our chairs,
and are as snug as if we were at Kellynch, ay, or as we used

to be even at North Yarmouth and Deal. We do not like our lodgings here the worse, I can tell you, for putting us in mind of those we first had at North Yarmouth. The wind blows through one of the cupboards just in the same way."

When they were got a little farther, Anne ventured to press again for what he had to communicate. She had hoped when clear of Milsom Street to have her curiosity gratified; but she was still obliged to wait, for the Admiral had made up his mind not to begin till they had gained the greater space and quiet of Belmont; and as she was not really Mrs. Croft, she must let him have his own way. As soon as they were fairly ascending Belmont, he began—

"Well, now you shall hear something that will surprise you. But first of all, you must tell me the name of the young lady I am going to talk about. That young lady, you know, that we have all been so concerned for. The Miss Musgrove that all this has been happening to. Her Christian name: I always forget her Christian name."

Anne had been ashamed to appear to comprehend so soon as she really did; but now she could safely suggest the name of " Louisa."

"Ay, ay, Miss Louisa Musgrove, that is the name. I wish young ladies had not such a number of fine Christian names. I should never be out if they were all Sophys, or something of that sort. Well, this Miss Louisa, we all thought, you know, was to marry Frederick. He was courting her week after week. The only wonder was, what they could be waiting for, till the business at Lyme came; then, indeed, it was clear enough that they must wait till her brain was set to right. But even then there was something odd in their way of going on. Instead of staying at Lyme, he went off to Plymouth, and then he went off to see Edward. When we came back from Minehead he was gone down to Edward's, and there he has been ever since. We have seen nothing of him since November. Even Sophy could not understand it. But now, the matter has taken the strangest turn of all; for this young lady, this same Miss Musgrove, instead of being to marry Frederick, is to marry James Benwick. You know James Benwick?"

"A little. I am a little acquainted with Captain Benwick."

" Well, she is to marry him. Nay, most likely they are married already, for I do not know what they should wait for."

" I thought Captain Benwick a very pleasing young man," said Anne, " and I understand that he bears an excellent character."

" Oh! yes, yes, there is not a word to be said against James Benwick. He is only a commander, it is true, made last summer, and these are bad times for getting on, but he has not another fault that I know of. An excellent, good-hearted fellow, I assure you; a very active, zealous officer, too, which is more than you would think for, perhaps, for that soft sort of manner does not do him justice."

" Indeed, you are mistaken there, sir; I should never augur want of spirit from Captain Benwick's manners. I thought them particularly pleasing, and I will answer for it, they would generally please."

" Well, well, ladies are the best judges; but James Benwick is rather too piano for me; and though very likely it is all our partiality, Sophy and I cannot help thinking Frederick's manners better than his. There is something about Frederick more to our taste."

Anne was caught. She had only meant to oppose the too common idea of spirit and gentleness being incompatible with each other, not at all to represent Captain Benwick's manners as the very best that could possibly be; and, after a little hesitation, she was beginning to say, " I was not entering into any comparison of the two friends; " but the Admiral interrupted her with—

" And the thing is certainly true. It is not a mere bit of gossip. We have it from Frederick himself. His sister had a letter from him yesterday, in which he tells us of it, and he had just had it in a letter from Harville, written upon the spot, from Uppercross. I fancy they are all at Uppercross."

This was an opportunity which Anne could not resist; she said, therefore, " I hope, Admiral, I hope there is nothing in the style of Captain Wentworth's letter to make you and Mrs. Croft particularly uneasy. It did certainly seem, last autumn, as if there were an attachment between him and Louisa Musgrove; but I hope it may be understood to have

worn out on each side equally, and without violence. I hope
his letter does not breathe the spirit of an ill-used man."

"Not at all, not at all: there is not an oath or a murmur
from beginning to end."

Anne looked down to hide her smile.

"No, no; Frederick is not a man to whine and complain;
he has too much spirit for that. If the girl likes another man
better, it is very fit she should have him."

"Certainly. But what I mean is, that I hope there is
nothing in Captain Wentworth's manner of writing, to make
you suppose he thinks himself ill-used by his friend, which
might appear, you know, without its being absolutely said. I
should be very sorry that such a friendship as has subsisted
between him and Captain Benwick should be destroyed, or
even wounded by a circumstance of this sort."

"Yes, yes, I understand you. But there is nothing at all
of that nature in the letter. He does not give the least fling at
Benwick; does not so much as say, ' I wonder at it. I have a
reason of my own for wondering at it.' No, you would not
guess, from his way of writing, that he had ever thought of
this Miss (what's her name?) for himself. He very handsomely hopes they will be happy together; and there is
nothing very unforgiving in that, I think."

Anne did not receive the perfect conviction which the
Admiral meant to convey, but it would have been useless to
press the enquiry farther. She therefore satisfied herself
with common-place remarks or quiet attention, and the
Admiral had it all his own way.

"Poor Frederick!" said he, at last. "Now he must begin
all over again with somebody else. I think we must get him
to Bath. Sophy must write, and beg him to come to Bath.
Here are pretty girls enough, I am sure. It would be of no
use to go to Uppercross again, for that other Miss Musgrove,
I find, is bespoke by her cousin, the young parson. Do not
you think, Miss Elliot, we had better try to get him to Bath?"

CHAPTER XIX

WHILE Admiral Croft was taking this walk with Anne, and expressing his wish of getting Captain Wentworth to Bath, Captain Wentworth was already on his way thither. Before Mrs. Croft had written, he was arrived, and the very next time Anne walked out, she saw him.

Mr. Elliot was attending his two cousins and Mrs. Clay. They were in Milsom Street. It began to rain, not much, but enough to make shelter desirable for women, and quite enough to make it very desirable for Miss Elliot to have the advantage of being conveyed home in Lady Dalrymple's carriage, which was seen waiting at a little distance: she, Anne, and Mrs. Clay, therefore, turned into Molland's, while Mr. Elliot stepped to Lady Dalrymple, to request her assistance. He soon joined them again, successful, of course; Lady Dalrymple would be most happy to take them home, and would call for them in a few minutes.

Her ladyship's carriage was a barouche, and did not hold more than four with any comfort. Miss Carteret was with her mother; consequently it was not reasonable to expect accommodation for all the three Camden Place ladies. There could be no doubt as to Miss Elliot. Whoever suffered inconvenience, she must suffer none, but it occupied a little time to settle the point of civility between the other two. The rain was a mere trifle, and Anne was most sincere in preferring a walk with Mr. Elliot. But the rain was also a mere trifle to Mrs. Clay; she would hardly allow it even to drop at all, and her boots were so thick! much thicker than Miss Anne's; and, in short, her civility rendered her quite as anxious to be left to walk with Mr. Elliot as Anne could be, and it was discussed between them with a generosity so polite and so determined, that the others were obliged to settle it for them; Miss Elliot maintaining that Mrs. Clay had a little cold already, and Mr. Elliot, deciding, on appeal, that his cousin Anne's boots were rather the thickest.

It was fixed, accordingly, that Mrs. Clay should be of the

party in the carriage; and they had just reached this point, when Anne, as she sat near the window, descried, most decidedly and distinctly, Captain Wentworth walking down the street.

Her start was perceptible only to herself; but she instantly felt that she was the greatest simpleton in the world, the most unaccountable and absurd! For a few minutes she saw nothing before her: it was all confusion. She was lost, and when she had scolded back her senses, she found the others still waiting for the carriage, and Mr. Elliot (always obliging) just setting off for Union Street on a commission of Mrs. Clay's.

She now felt a great inclination to go to the outer door; she wanted to see if it rained. Why was she to suspect herself of another motive? Captain Wentworth must be out of sight. She left her seat, she would go; one half of her should not be always so much wiser than the other half, or always suspecting the other of being worse than it was. She would see if it rained. She was sent back, however, in a moment, by the entrance of Captain Wentworth himself, among a party of gentlemen and ladies, evidently his acquaintance, and whom he must have joined a little below Milsom Street. He was more obviously struck and confused by the sight of her than she had ever observed before; he looked quite red. For the first time since their renewed acquaintance, she felt that she was betraying the least sensibility of the two. She had the advantage of him in the preparation of the last few moments. All the overpowering, blinding, bewildering, first effects of strong surprise were over with her. Still, however, she had enough to feel! It was agitation, pain, pleasure; a something between delight and misery.

He spoke to her, and then turned away. The character of his manner was embarrassment. She could not have called it either cold or friendly, or anything so certainly as embarrassed.

After a short interval, however, he came towards her, and spoke again. Mutual inquiries on common subjects passed: neither of them, probably, much the wiser for what they heard, and Anne continuing fully sensible of his being less at ease than formerly. They had by dint of being so very much together, got to speak to each other with a considerable portion of apparent indifference and calmness; but he could not do it now. Time had changed him, or Louisa had changed him. There was consciousness of some sort or other. He looked very well, not as if he had been suffering in health or spirits, and he talked of Uppercross, of the Musgroves, nay, even of Louisa, and had even a momentary look of his own arch significance as he named her; but yet it was Captain Wentworth not comfortable, not easy, not able to feign that he was.

It did not surprise, but it grieved Anne to observe that Elizabeth would not know him. She saw that he saw Elizabeth, that Elizabeth saw him, that there was complete internal recognition on each side; she was convinced that he was ready to be acknowledged as an acquaintance, expecting it, and she had the pain of seeing her sister turn away with unalterable coldness.

Lady Dalrymple's carriage, for which Miss Elliot was growing very impatient, now drew up; the servant came to announce it. It was beginning to rain again, and altogether there was a delay, and a bustle, and a talking, which must make all the little crowd in the shop understand that Lady Dalrymple was calling to convey Miss Elliot. At last Miss Elliot and her friend, unattended but by the servant (for there was no cousin returned), were walking off; and Captain Wentworth, watching them, turned again to Anne, and by manner, rather than words, was offering his services to her.

" I am much obliged to you," was her answer, " but I am not going with them. The carriage would not accommodate so many. I walk: I prefer walking."

" But it rains."

" Oh! very little. Nothing that I regard."

After a moment's pause, he said: " Though I came only yesterday, I have equipped myself properly for Bath already, you see " (pointing to a new umbrella); " I wish you would make use of it, if you are determined to walk; though I think it would be more prudent to let me get you a chair."

She was very much obliged to him, but declined it all,

repeating her conviction, that the rain would come to nothing at present, and adding, " I am only waiting for Mr. Elliot. He will be here in a moment, I am sure."

She had hardly spoken the words when Mr. Elliot walked in. Captain Wentworth recollected him perfectly. There was no difference between him and the man who had stood on the steps at Lyme, admiring Anne as she passed, except in the air and look, and manner of the privileged relation and friend. He came in with eagerness, appeared to see and think only of her, apologised for his stay, was grieved to have kept her waiting, and anxious to get her away without further loss of time, and before the rain increased; and in another moment they walked off together, her arm under his, a gentle and embarrassed glance, and a " Good morning to you ! " being all that she had time for, as she passed away.

As soon as they were out of sight, the ladies of Captain Wentworth's party began talking of them.

" Mr. Elliot does not dislike his cousin, I fancy? "

" Oh! no, that is clear enough. One can guess what will happen there. He is always with them; half lives in the family, I believe. What a very good-looking man ! "

" Yes, and Miss Atkinson, who dined with him once at the Wallises, says he is the most agreeable man she ever was in company with."

" She is pretty, I think; Anne Elliot; very pretty when one comes to look at her. It is not the fashion to say so, but I confess I admire her more than her sister."

" Oh! so do I."

" And so do I. No comparison. But the men are all wild after Miss Elliot. Anne is too delicate for them."

Anne would have been particularly obliged to her cousin if he would have walked by her side all the way to Camden Place without saying a word. She had never found it so difficult to listen to him, though nothing could exceed his solicitude and care, and though his subjects were principally such as were wont to be always interesting: praise, warm, just, and discriminating, of Lady Russell, and insinuations highly rational against Mrs. Clay. But just now she could think only of Captain Wentworth. She could not understand his present feelings, whether he were really suffering much from disappointment or not; and till that point were settled, she could not be quite herself.

She hoped to be wise and reasonable in time; but alas! alas! she must confess to herself that she was not wise yet.

Another circumstance very essential for her to know, was how long he meant to be in Bath; he had not mentioned it, or she could not recollect it. He might be only passing through. But it was more probable that he should be come to stay. In that case, so liable as every body was to meet every body in Bath, Lady Russell would in all likelihood see him somewhere. Would she recollect him? How would it all be?

She had already been obliged to tell Lady Russell that Louisa Musgrove was to marry Captain Benwick. It had cost her something to encounter Lady Russell's surprise; and now, if she were by any chance to be thrown into company with Captain Wentworth, her imperfect knowledge of the matter might add another shade of prejudice against him.

The following morning Anne was out with her friend, and for the first hour, in an incessant and fearful sort of watch for him in vain; but at last, in returning down Pulteney Street, she distinguished him on the right hand pavement at such a distance as to have him in view the greater part of the street. There were many other men about him, many groups walking the same way, but there was no mistaking him. She looked instinctively at Lady Russell, but not from any mad idea of her recognising him so soon as she did herself. No, it was not to be supposed that Lady Russell would perceive him till they were nearly opposite. She looked at her, however, from time to time, anxiously; and when the moment approached which must point him out, though not daring to look again (for her own countenance she knew was unfit to be seen), she was yet perfectly conscious of Lady Russell's eyes being turned exactly in the direction for him—of her being, in short, intently observing him. She could thoroughly comprehend the sort of fascination he must possess over Lady Russell's mind, the difficulty it must be for her to withdraw her eyes, the astonishment she must be feeling that eight or nine years should have passed

over him, and in foreign climes and in active service too,
without robbing him of one personal grace!

At last, Lady Russell drew back her head. " Now, how
would she speak of him?"

" You will wonder," said he, " what has been fixing my
eye so long; but I was looking after some window-curtains,
which Lady Alicia and Mrs. Frankland were telling me of
last night. They described the drawing-room window-
curtains of one of the houses on this side of the way, and
this part of the street, as being the handsomest and best
hung of any in Bath, but could not recollect the exact
number, and I have been trying to find out which it could be;
but I confess I can see no curtains hereabouts that answer
their description."

Anne sighed, and blushed, and smiled, in pity and disdain,
either at her friend or herself. The part which provoked
her most, was that in all this waste of foresight and caution,
she should have lost the right moment for seeing whether
he saw them.

A day or two passed without producing anything. The
theatre or the rooms, where he was most likely to be, were
not fashionable enough for the Elliots, whose evening amusements were solely in the elegant stupidity of private parties,
in which they were getting more and more engaged; and
Anne, wearied of such a state of stagnation, sick of knowing
nothing, and fancying herself stronger because her strength
was not tried, was quite impatient for the concert evening.
It was a concert for the benefit of a person patronised by
Lady Dalrymple. Of course they must attend. It was
really expected to be a good one, and Captain Wentworth
was very fond of music. If she could only have a few
minutes' conversation with him again, she fancied she should
be satisfied; and as to the power of addressing him, she felt
all over courage if the opportunity occurred. Elizabeth had
turned from him, Lady Russell overlooked him; her nerves
were strengthened by these circumstances; she felt that she
owed him attention.

She had once partly promised Mrs. Smith to spend the
evening with her; but in a short hurried call she excused
herself and put it off, with the more decided promise of a

longer visit on the morrow. Mrs. Smith gave a most good-humoured acquiescence.

"By all means," said she; "only tell me all about it, when you do come. Who is your party?"

Anne named them all. Mrs. Smith made no reply; but when she was leaving her said, and with an expression half serious, half arch, "Well, I heartily wish your concert may answer; and do not fail me to-morrow if you can come; for I begin to have a foreboding that I may not have many more visits from you."

Anne was startled and confused; but after standing in a moment's suspense, was obliged, and not sorry to be obliged, to hurry away.

CHAPTER XX

SIR WALTER, his two daughters, and Mrs. Clay, were the earliest of all their party at the rooms in the evening; and as Lady Dalrymple must be waited for, they took their station by one of the fires in the Octagon Room. But hardly were they so settled, when the door opened again, and Captain Wentworth walked in alone. Anne was the nearest to him, and making a little advance, she instantly spoke. He was preparing only to bow and pass on, but her gentle "How do you do?" brought him out of the straight line to stand near her, and make enquiries in return, in spite of the formidable father and sister in the background. Their being in the background was a support to Anne; she knew nothing of their looks, and felt equal to everything which she believed right to be done.

While they were speaking, a whispering between her father and Elizabeth caught her ear. She could not distinguish, but she must guess the subject; and on Captain Wentworth's making a distant bow, she comprehended that her father had judged so well as to give him that simple acknowledgment of acquaintance, and she was just in time by a side glance to see a slight courtsey from Elizabeth herself. This, though late, and reluctant, and ungracious, was yet better than nothing, and her spirits improved.

After talking, however, of the weather, and Bath, and the concert, their conversation began to flag, and so little was said at last, that she was expecting him to go every moment, but he did not; he seemed in no hurry to leave her; and presently with renewed spirit, with a little smile, a little glow, he said—

" I have hardly seen you since our day at Lyme. I am afraid you must have suffered from the shock, and the more from its not overpowering you at the time."

She assured him that she had not.

" It was a frightful hour," said he, " a frightful day!" and he passed his hand across his eyes, as if the remembrance were still too painful, but in a moment, half smiling again, added, " The day has produced some effects, however; has had some consequences which must be considered as the very reverse of frightful. When you had the presence of mind to suggest that Benwick would be the properest person to fetch a surgeon, you could have little idea of his being eventually one of those most concerned in her recovery."

" Certainly I could have none. But it appears—I should hope it would be a very happy match. There are on both sides good principles and good temper."

" Yes," said he, looking not exactly forward; " but there, I think, ends the resemblance. With all my soul I wish them happy, and rejoice over every circumstance in favour of it. They have no difficulties to contend with at home, no opposition, no caprice, no delays. The Musgroves are behaving like themselves, most honourably and kindly, only anxious with true parental hearts to promote their daughter's comfort. All this is much, very much in favour of their happiness; more than perhaps—"

He stopped. A sudden recollection seemed to occur, and to give him some taste of that emotion which was reddening Anne's cheeks and fixing her eyes on the ground. After clearing his throat, however, he proceeded thus—

" I confess that I do think there is a disparity, too great a disparity, and in a point no less essential than mind. I regard Louisa Musgrove as a very amiable, sweet-tempered girl, and not deficient in understanding, but Benwick is something more. He is a clever man, a reading man; and I confess, that I do consider his attaching himself to her with some surprise. Had it been the effect of gratitude, had he learnt to love her, because he believed her to be preferring him, it would have been another thing. But I have no reason to suppose it so. It seems, on the contrary, to have been a perfectly spontaneous, untaught feeling on his side, and this surprises me. A man like him, in his situation! with a heart pierced, wounded, almost broken! Fanny Harville was a very superior creature, and his attachment to her was indeed attachment. A man does not recover from such a devotion of the heart to such a woman! He ought not; he does not."

Either from the consciousness, however, that his friend had recovered, or from some other consciousness, he went no farther; and Anne who, in spite of the agitated voice in which the latter part had been uttered, and in spite of all the various noises of the room, the almost ceaseless slam of the door, and ceaseless buzz of persons walking through, had distinguished every word, was struck, gratified, confused, and beginning to breathe very quick, and feel an hundred things in a moment. It was impossible for her to enter on such a subject; and yet, after a pause, feeling the necessity of speaking, and having not the smallest wish for a total change, she only deviated so far as to say—

" You were a good while at Lyme, I think? "

" About a fortnight. I could not leave it till Louisa's doing well was quite ascertained. I had been too deeply concerned in the mischief to be soon at peace. It had been my doing, solely mine. She would not have been obstinate if I had not been weak. The country round Lyme is very fine. I walked and rode a great deal, and the more I saw, the more I found to admire."

" I should very much like to see Lyme again," said Anne.

" Indeed! I should not have supposed that you could have found anything in Lyme to inspire such a feeling. The horror and distress you were involved in, the stretch of mind, the wear of spirits! I should have thought your last impressions of Lyme must have been strong disgust."

" The last few hours were certainly very painful," replied Anne; " but when pain is over, the remembrance of it often becomes a pleasure. One does not love a place the less for having suffered in it, unless it has been all suffering, nothing but suffering, which was by no means the case at Lyme. We were only in anxiety and distress during the last two hours, and previously there had been a great deal of enjoyment. So much novelty and beauty! I have travelled so little, that every fresh place would be interesting to me; but there is real beauty at Lyme, and in short," with a faint blush at some recollections, " altogether my impressions of the place are very agreeable."

As she ceased, the entrance door opened again, and the very party appeared for whom they were waiting. " Lady Dalrymple, Lady Dalrymple!" was the rejoicing sound; and with all the eagerness compatible with anxious elegance, Sir Walter and his two ladies stepped forward to meet her. Lady Dalrymple and Miss Carteret, escorted by Mr. Elliot and Colonel Wallis, who had happened to arrive nearly at the same instant, advanced into the room. The others joined them, and it was a group in which Anne found herself also necessarily included. She was divided from Captain Wentworth. Their interesting, almost too interesting conversation, must be broken up for a time, but slight was the penance compared with the happiness which brought it on! She had learnt, in the last ten minutes, more of his feelings towards Louisa, more of all his feelings, than she dared to think of; and she gave herself up to the demands of the party, to the needful civilities of the moment, with exquisite, though agitated sensations. She was in good humour with all. She had received ideas which disposed her to be courteous and kind to all, and to pity every one, as being less happy than herself.

The delightful emotions were a little subdued, when on stepping back from the group, to be joined again by Captain Wentworth, she saw that he was gone. She was just in time to see him turn into the Concert Room. He was gone; he had disappeared, she felt a moment's regret. But " they should meet again. He would look for her, he would find her out long before the evening were over, and at present, perhaps, it was as well to be asunder. She was in need of a little interval for recollection."

Upon Lady Russell's appearance soon afterwards, the whole party was collected, and all that remained was to marshal themselves, and proceed into the Concert Room; and be of all the consequence in their power, draw as many eyes, excite as many whispers, and disturb as many people as they could.

Very, very happy were both Elizabeth and Anne Elliot as they walked in. Elizabeth arm-in-arm with Miss Carteret, and looking on the broad back of the dowager Viscountess Dalrymple before her, had nothing to wish for which did not seem within her reach; and Anne—but it would be an insult to the nature of Anne's felicity to draw any comparison between it and her sister's; the origin of one all selfish vanity, of the other all generous attachment.

Anne saw nothing, thought nothing of the brilliancy of the room. Her happiness was from within. Her eyes were bright, and her cheeks glowed; but she knew nothing about it. She was thinking only of the last half hour, and as they passed to their seats, her mind took a hasty range over it. His choice of subjects, his expressions, and still more his manner and look, had been such as she could see in only one light. His opinion of Louisa Musgrove's inferiority, an opinion which he had seemed solicitous to give, his wonder at Captain Benwick, his feelings as to a first, strong attachment; sentences begun which he could not finish, his half-averted eyes and more than half-expressive glance, all, all declared that he had a heart returning to her at least; that anger, resentment, avoidance, were no more; and that they were succeeded, not merely by friendship and regard, but by the tenderness of the past. Yes, some share of the tenderness of the past! She could not contemplate the change as implying less. He must love her.

These were thoughts, with their attendant visions, which occupied and flurried her too much to leave her any power of observation; and she passed along the room without having a glimpse of him, without even trying to discern him. When their places were determined on, and they were all properly arranged, she looked round to see if he should happen to be in the same part of the room, but he was not; her eye could not reach him; and the concert being just opening, she must consent for a time to be happy in an humbler way.

The party was divided and disposed of on two contiguous benches: Anne was among those on the foremost, and Mr. Elliot had manœuvred so well, with the assistance of his friend Colonel Wallis, as to have a seat by her. Miss Elliot, surrounded by her cousins, and the principal object of Colonel Wallis's gallantry, was quite contented.

Anne's mind was in a most favourable state for the entertainment of the evening; it was just occupation enough: she had feelings for the tender, spirits for the gay, attention for the scientific, and patience for the wearisome; and had never liked a concert better, at least during the first act. Towards the close of it, in the interval succeeding an Italian song, she explained the words of the song to Mr. Elliot. They had a concert bill between them.

"This," said she, "is nearly the sense, or rather the meaning of the words, for certainly the sense of an Italian love-song must not be talked of, but it is as nearly the meaning as I can give; for I do not pretend to understand the language. I am a very poor Italian scholar."

"Yes, yes, I see you are. I see you know nothing of the matter. You have only knowledge enough of the language to translate at sight these inverted, transposed, curtailed Italian lines, into clear, comprehensible, elegant English. You need not say anything more of your ignorance. Here is complete proof."

"I will not oppose such kind politeness; but I should be sorry to be examined by a real proficient."

"I have not had the pleasure of visiting in Camden Place so long," replied he, "without knowing something of Miss Anne Elliot; and I do regard her as one who is too modest for the world in general to be aware of half her accomplishments, and too highly accomplished for modesty to be natural in any other woman."

"For shame! for shame! this is too much of flattery. I forget what we are to have next," turning to the bill.

"Perhaps," said Mr. Elliot, speaking low, "I have had a

longer acquaintance with your character than you are aware of."

" Indeed! How so? You can have been acquainted with it only since I came to Bath, excepting as you might hear me previously spoken of in my own family."

" I knew you by report long before you came to Bath. I had heard you described by those who knew you intimately. I have been acquainted with you by character many years. Your person, your disposition, accomplishments, manner; they were all described, they were all present to me."

Mr. Elliot was not disappointed in the interest he hoped to raise. No one can withstand the charm of such a mystery. To have been described long ago to a recent acquaintance, by nameless people, is irresistible; and Anne was all curiosity. She wondered, and questioned him eagerly; but in vain. He delighted in being asked, but he would not tell.

" No, no, some time or other, perhaps, but not now. He would mention no names now; but such, he could assure her, had been the fact. He had many years ago received such a description of Miss Anne Elliot as had inspired him with the highest idea of her merit, and excited the warmest curiosity to know her."

Anne could think of no one so likely to have spoken with partiality of her many years ago as the Mr. Wentworth of Monkford, Captain Wentworth's brother. He might have been in Mr. Elliot's company, but she had not courage to ask the question.

" The name of Anne Elliot," said he, " has long had an interesting sound to me. Very long has it possessed a charm over my fancy; and, if I dared, I would breathe my wishes that the name might never change."

Such, she believed, were his words; but scarcely had she received their sound, than her attention was caught by other sounds immediately behind her, which rendered everything else trivial. Her father and Lady Dalrymple were speaking.

" A well-looking man," said Sir Walter, " a very well-looking man."

" A very fine young man, indeed!" said Lady Dalrymple. " More air than one often sees in Bath. Irish, I dare say?"

" No, I just know his name. A bowing acquaintance.

Wentworth: Captain Wentworth of the navy. His sister married my tenant in Somersetshire, the Croft, who rents Kellynch."

Before Sir Walter had reached this point, Anne's eyes had caught the right direction, and distinguished Captain Wentworth, standing among a cluster of men at a little distance. As her eyes fell on him, his seemed to be withdrawn from her. It had that appearance. It seemed as if she had been one moment too late; and as long as she dared observe, he did not look again; but the performance was recommencing, and she was forced to seem to restore her attention to the orchestra, and look straight forward.

When she could give another glance, he had moved away. He could not have come nearer to her if he would; she was so surrounded and shut in: but she would rather have caught his eye.

Mr. Elliot's speech, too, distressed her. She had no longer any inclination to talk to him. She wished him not so near her.

The first act was over. Now she hoped for some beneficial change; and, after a period of nothing-saying amongst the party, some of them did decide on going in quest of tea. Anne was one of the few who did not choose to move. She remained in her seat, and so did Lady Russell; but she had the pleasure of getting rid of Mr. Elliot; and she did not mean, whatever she might feel on Lady Russell's account, to shrink from conversation with Captain Wentworth, if he gave her the opportunity. She was persuaded by Lady Russell's countenance that she had seen him.

He did not come, however. Anne sometimes fancied she discerned him at a distance, but he never came. The anxious interval wore away unproductively. The others returned, the room filled again, benches were reclaimed and repossessed, and another hour of pleasure or of penance was to be [sat] out, another hour of music was to give delight or the gapes, as real or affected taste for it prevailed. To Anne it chiefly wore the prospect of an hour of agitation. She could not quit that room in peace without seeing Captain Wentworth once more, without the interchange of one friendly look.

In re-settling themselves there were now many changes,

the result of which was favourable for her. Colonel Wallis declined sitting down again, and Mr. Elliot was invited by Elizabeth and Miss Carteret, in a manner not to be refused, to sit between them; and by some other removals, and a little scheming of her own, Anne was enabled to place herself much nearer the end of the bench than she had been before, much more within reach of a passer-by. She could not do so, without comparing herself with Miss Larolles, the inimitable Miss Larolles; but still she did it, and not with much happier effect; though by what seemed prosperity in the shape of an early abdication in her next neighbours, she found herself at the very end of the bench before the concert closed.

Such was her situation, with a vacant space at hand, when Captain Wentworth was again in sight. She saw him not far off. He saw her too; yet he looked grave, and seemed irresolute, and only by very slow degrees came at last near enough to speak to her. She felt that something must be the matter. The change was indubitable. The difference between his present air and what it had been in the Octagon Room was strikingly great. Why was it? She thought of her father, of Lady Russell. Could there have been any unpleasant glances? He began by speaking of the concert gravely, more like the Captain Wentworth of Uppercross; owned himself disappointed, had expected better singing; and, in short, must confess that he should not be sorry when it was over. Anne replied, and spoke in defence of the performance so well, and yet in allowance for his feelings so pleasantly, that his countenance improved, and he replied again with almost a smile. They talked for a few minutes more; the improvement held; he even looked down towards the bench, as if he saw a place on it well worth occupying; when at that moment a touch on her shoulder obliged Anne to turn round. It came from Mr. Elliot. He begged her pardon, but she must be applied to, to explain Italian again. Miss Carteret was very anxious to have a general idea of what was next to be sung. Anne could not refuse; but never had she sacrificed to politeness with a more suffering spirit.

A few minutes, though as few as possible, were inevitably consumed; and when her own mistress again, when able to

turn and look as she had done before, she found herself
accosted by Captain Wentworth, in a reserved yet hurried
sort of farewell. " He must wish her good night; he was
going; he should get home as fast as he could."

" Is not this song worth staying for? " said Anne, suddenly
struck by an idea which made her yet more anxious to be
encouraging.

" No! " he replied, impressively, " there is nothing worth
my staying for; " and he was gone directly.

Jealousy of Mr. Elliot! It was the only intelligible motive.
Captain Wentworth jealous of her affection! Could she
have believed it a week ago; three hours ago! For a
moment the gratification was exquisite. But, alas! there
were very different thoughts to succeed. How was such
jealousy to be quieted? How was the truth to reach him?
How, in all the peculiar disadvantages of their respective
situations, would he ever learn her real sentiments? It was
misery to think of Mr. Elliot's attentions. Their evil was
incalculable.

CHAPTER XXI

ANNE recollected with pleasure the next morning her promise
of going to Mrs. Smith, meaning that it should engage her
from home at the time when Mr. Elliot would be most likely
to call, for to avoid Mr. Elliot was almost a first object.

She felt a great deal of good-will towards him. In spite of
the mischief of his attentions, she owed him gratitude and
regard, perhaps compassion. She could not help thinking
much of the extraordinary circumstances attending their
acquaintance, of the right which he seemed to have to
interest her, by everything in situation, by his own sentiments, by his early prepossession. It was altogether very
extraordinary; flattering, but painful. There was much to
regret. How she might have felt had there been no Captain
Wentworth in the case, was not worth enquiry; for there
was a Captain Wentworth; and be the conclusion of the

present suspense good or bad, her affection would be his for ever. Their union, she believed, could not divide her more from other men than their final separation.

Prettier musings of high-wrought love and eternal constancy could never have passed along the streets of Bath than Anne was sporting with from Camden Place to Westgate Buildings. It was almost enough to spread purification and perfume all the way.

She was sure of a pleasant reception; and her friend seemed this morning particularly obliged to her for coming, seemed hardly to have expected her, though it had been an appointment.

An account of the concert was immediately claimed; and Anne's recollections of the concert were quite happy enough to animate her features and make her rejoice to talk of it. All that she could tell she told most gladly, but the all was little for one who had been there, and unsatisfactory for such an enquirer as Mrs. Smith, who had already heard, through the short cut of a laundress and a waiter, rather more of the general success and produce of the evening than Anne could relate, and who now asked in vain for several particulars of the company. Everybody of any consequence or notoriety in Bath was well known by name to Mrs. Smith.

" The little Durands were there, I conclude," said she, " with their mouths open to catch the music, like unfledged sparrows ready to be fed. They never miss a concert."

" Yes; I did not see them myself, but I heard Mr. Elliot say they were in the room."

" The Ibbotsons, were they there? and the two new beauties, with the tall Irish officer, who is talked of for one of them? "

" I do not know. I do not think they were."

" Old Lady Mary Maclean? I need not ask after her. She never misses, I know; and you must have seen her. She must have been in your own circle; for as you went with Lady Dalrymple, you were in the seats of grandeur, round the orchestra, of course."

" No, that was what I dreaded. It would have been very unpleasant to me in every respect. But happily Lady Dalrymple always chooses to be farther off; and we were

exceedingly well placed, that is, for hearing; I must not say
for seeing, because I appear to have seen very little."

"Oh! you saw enough for your own amusement. I can
understand. There is a sort of domestic enjoyment to be
known even in a crowd, and this you had. You were a large
party in yourselves, and you wanted nothing beyond."

"But I ought to have looked about me more," said Anne,
conscious while she spoke that there had in fact been no want
of looking about, that the object only had been deficient.

"No, no; you were better employed. You need not tell
me that you had a pleasant evening. I see it in your eye. I
perfectly see how the hours passed: that you had always
something agreeable to listen to. In the intervals of the
concert it was conversation."

Anne half smiled and said, "Do you see that in my eye?"

"Yes, I do. Your countenance perfectly informs me that
you were in company last night with the person whom you
think the most agreeable in the world, the person who
interests you at this present time more than all the rest of
the world put together."

A blush overspread Anne's cheeks. She could say nothing.

"And such being the case," continued Mrs. Smith, after
a short pause, "I hope you believe that I do know how to
value your kindness in coming to me this morning. It is
really very good of you to come and sit with me, when you
must have so many pleasanter demands upon your time."

Anne heard nothing of this. She was still in the astonishment and confusion excited by her friend's penetration,
unable to imagine how any report of Captain Wentworth
could have reached her. After another short silence—

"Pray," said Mrs. Smith, "is Mr. Elliot aware of your
acquaintance with me? Does he know that I am in Bath?"

"Mr. Elliot!" repeated Anne, looking up surprised. A
moment's reflection showed her the mistake she had been
under. She caught it instantaneously; and recovering
courage with the feeling of safety, soon added, more composedly, "Are you acquainted with Mr. Elliot?"

"I have been a good deal acquainted with him," replied
Mrs. Smith, gravely, "but it seems worn out now. It is a
great while since we met."

" I was not at all aware of this. You never mentioned it before. Had I known it, I would have had the pleasure of talking to him about you."

" To confess the truth," said Mrs. Smith, assuming her usual air of cheerfulness, " that is exactly the pleasure I want you to have. I want you to talk about me to Mr. Elliot. I want your interest with him. He can be of essential service to me; and if you would have the goodness, my dear Miss Elliot, to make it an object to yourself, of course it is done."

" I should be extremely happy; I hope you cannot doubt my willingness to be of even the slightest use to you," replied Anne; " but I suspect that you are considering me as having a higher claim on Mr. Elliot, a greater right to influence him, than is really the case. I am sure you have, somehow or other, imbibed such a notion. You must consider me only as Mr. Elliot's relation. If in that light there is anything which you suppose his cousin might fairly ask of him, I beg you would not hesitate to employ me."

Mrs. Smith gave her a penetrating glance, and then, smiling, said—

" I have been a little premature, I perceive; I beg your pardon. I ought to have waited for official information. But now, my dear Miss Elliot, as an old friend, do give me a hint as to when I may speak. Next week? To be sure by next week I may be allowed to think it all settled, and build my own selfish schemes on Mr. Elliot's good fortune."

" No," replied Anne, " nor next week, nor next, nor next. I assure you that nothing of the sort you are thinking of will be settled any week. I am not going to marry Mr. Elliot. I should like to know why you imagine I am? "

Mrs. Smith looked at her again, looked earnestly, smiled, shook her head, and exclaimed—

" Now, how I do wish I understood you! How I do wish I knew what you were at! I have a great idea that you do not design to be cruel, when the right moment comes. Till it does come, you know, we women never mean to have any-body. It is a thing of course among us, that every man is refused, till he offers. But why should you be cruel? Let me plead for my—present friend I cannot call him, but for

my former friend.   Where can you look for a more suitable
match?   Where could you expect a more gentlemanlike,
agreeable man?   Let me recommend Mr. Elliot.   I am sure
you hear nothing but good of him from Colonel Wallis; and
who can know him better than Colonel Wallis? "

" My dear Mrs. Smith, Mr. Elliot's wife has not been dead
much above half a year.   He ought not to be supposed to be
paying his addresses to any one."

" Oh, if these are your only objections," cried Mrs. Smith,
archly, " Mr. Elliot is safe, and I shall give myself no more
trouble about him.   Do not forget me when you are married,
that's all.   Let him know me to be a friend of yours, and
then he will think little of the trouble required, which it is
very natural for him now, with so many affairs and engagements of his own, to avoid and get rid of as he can; very
natural, perhaps.   Ninety-nine out of a hundred would do
the same.   Of course, he cannot be aware of the importance
to me.   Well, my dear Miss Elliot, I hope and trust you will
be very happy.   Mr. Elliot has sense to understand the value
of such a woman.   Your peace will not be shipwrecked as
mine has been.   You are safe in all worldly matters, and safe
in his character.   He will not be led astray; he will not be
misled by others to his ruin."

" No," said Anne, " I can readily believe all that of my
cousin.   He seems to have a calm decided temper, not at all
open to dangerous impressions.   I consider him with great
respect.   I have no reason, from anything that has fallen
within my observation to do otherwise.   But I have not known
him long; and he is not a man, I think, to be known intimately soon.   Will not this manner of speaking of him, Mrs.
Smith, convince you that he is nothing to me?   Surely this
must be calm enough.   And, upon my word, he is nothing to
me.   Should he ever propose to me (which I have very little
reason to imagine he has any thought of doing), I shall not
accept him.   I assure you I shall not.   I assure you, Mr.
Elliot had not the share, which you have been supposing, in
whatever pleasure the concert of last night might afford:
not Mr. Elliot; it is not Mr. Elliot that——"

She stopped, regretting, with a deep blush, that she had
implied so much; but less would hardly have been sufficient.

Mrs. Smith would hardly have believed so soon in Mr. Elliot's failure, but from the perception of there being a somebody else. As it was, she instantly submitted, and with all the semblance of seeing nothing beyond; and Anne, eager to escape farther notice, was impatient to know why Mrs. Smith should have fancied she was to marry Mr. Elliot; where she could have received the idea, or from whom she could have heard it.

" Do tell me how it first came into your head? "

" It first came into my head," replied Mrs. Smith, " upon finding how much you were together, and feeling it to be the most probable thing in the world to be wished for by every-body belonging to either of you; and you may depend upon it, that all your acquaintance have disposed of you in the same way. But I never heard it spoken of till two days ago."

" And has it, indeed, been spoken of? "

" Did you observe the woman who opened the door to you when you called yesterday? "

" No. Was not it Mrs. Speed, as usual, or the maid? I observed no one in particular."

" It was my friend Mrs. Rooke; Nurse Rooke; who, by-the-bye, had a great curiosity to see you, and was delighted to be in the way to let you in. She came away from Marl-borough Buildings only on Sunday; and she it was who told me you were to marry Mr. Elliot. She had had it from Mrs. Wallis herself, which did not seem bad authority. She sat an hour with me on Monday evening, and gave me the whole history."

" The whole history! " repeated Anne, laughing. " She could not make a very long history, I think, of one such little article of unfounded news."

Mrs. Smith said nothing.

" But," continued Anne, presently, " though there is no truth in my having this claim on Mr. Elliot, I should be extremely happy to be of use to you, in any way that I could. Shall I mention to him your being in Bath? Shall I take any message? "

" No, I thank you: no, certainly not. In the warmth of the moment, and under a mistaken impression, I might, perhaps, have endeavoured to interest you in some circumstances; but not now. No, I thank you, I have nothing to trouble you with."

"I think you spoke of having known Mr. Elliot many years?"

"I did."

"Not before he married, I suppose?"

"Yes; he was not married when I knew him first."

"And—were you much acquainted?"

"Intimately."

"Indeed! Then do tell me what he was at that time of life. I have a great curiosity to know what Mr. Elliot was as a very young man. Was he at all such as he appears now?"

"I have not seen Mr. Elliot these three years," was Mrs. Smith's answer, given so gravely that it was impossible to pursue the subject farther; and Anne felt that she had gained nothing but an increase of curiosity. They were both silent: Mrs. Smith very thoughtful. At last—

"I beg your pardon, my dear Miss Elliot," she cried, in her natural tone of cordiality, "I beg your pardon for the short answers I have been giving you, but I have been uncertain what I ought to do. I have been doubting and considering as to what I ought to tell you. There were many things to be taken into the account. One hates to be officious, to be giving bad impressions, making mischief. Even the smooth surface of family-union seems worth preserving, though there may be nothing durable beneath. However, I have determined; I think I am right; I think you ought to be made acquainted with Mr. Elliot's real character. Though I fully believe that, at present, you have not the smallest intention of accepting him, there is no saying what may happen. You might, some time or other, be differently affected towards him. Hear the truth, therefore, now, while you are unprejudiced. Mr. Elliot is a man without heart or conscience; a designing, wary, cold-blooded being, who thinks only of himself; who, for his own interest or ease, would be guilty of any cruelty, or any treachery, that could be perpetrated without risk of his general character. He has no feeling for others. Those whom he has been the chief cause of leading into ruin, he can neglect and desert without the smallest compunction. He is totally beyond the reach of any sentiment of justice or compassion. Oh! he is black at heart; hollow and black!"

Anne's astonished air, and exclamation of wonder, made her pause, and in a calmer manner, she added—

"My expressions startle you. You must allow for an injured, angry woman. But I will try to command myself. I will not abuse him. I will only tell you what I have found him. Facts shall speak. He was the intimate friend of my dear husband, who trusted and loved him, and thought him as good as himself. The intimacy had been formed before our marriage. I found them most intimate friends; and I, too, became excessively pleased with Mr. Elliot, and entertained the highest opinion of him. At nineteen, you know, one does not think very seriously; but Mr. Elliot appeared to me quite as good as others, and much more agreeable than most others, and we were almost always together. We were principally in town, living in very good style. He was then the inferior in circumstances; he was then the poor one; he had chambers in the Temple, and it was as much as he could do to support the appearance of a gentleman. He had always a home with us whenever he chose it; he was always welcome; he was like a brother. My poor Charles, who had the finest, most generous spirit in the world, would have divided his last farthing with him; I know that his purse was open to him; I know that he often assisted him."

"This must have been about that very period of Mr. Elliot's life," said Anne, "which has always excited my particular curiosity. It must have been about the same time that he became known to my father and sister. I never knew him myself, I only heard of him; but there was a something in his conduct then, with regard to my father and sister, and afterwards in the circumstances of his marriage, which I never could quite reconcile with present times. It seemed to announce a different sort of man."

"I know it all, I know it all," cried Mrs. Smith. "He had been introduced to Sir Walter and your sister before I was acquainted with him, but I heard him speak of them for ever. I know he was invited and encouraged, and I know he did not choose to go. I can satisfy you, perhaps, on points which you would little expect; and as to his marriage, I knew all about it at the time. I was privy to all the fors and againsts; I was the friend to whom he confided his hopes and plans; and though I did not know his wife previously, her inferior situation in society, indeed, rendered that impossible, yet I knew her all her life afterwards, or at least till within the last two years of her life, and can answer any question you wish to put."

"Nay," said Anne, "I have no particular enquiry to make about her. I have always understood they were not a happy couple. But I should like to know why, at that time of his life, he should slight my father's acquaintance as he did. My father was certainly disposed to take very kind and proper notice of him. Why did Mr. Elliot draw back?"

"Mr. Elliot," replied Mrs. Smith, "at that period of his life had one object in view: to make his fortune, and by a rather quicker process than the law. He was determined to make it by marriage. He was determined, at least, not to mar it by an imprudent marriage; and I know it was his belief (whether justly or not, of course I cannot decide), that your father and sister, in their civilities and invitations, were designing a match between the heir and the young lady, and it was impossible that such a match should have answered his ideas of wealth and independence. That was his motive for drawing back, I can assure you. He told me the whole story. He had no concealments with me. It was curious, that having just left you behind me in Bath, my first and principal acquaintance on marrying should be your cousin; and that, through him, I should be continually hearing of your father and sister. He described one Miss Elliot, and I thought very affectionately of the other."

"Perhaps," cried Anne, struck by a sudden idea, "you sometimes spoke of me to Mr. Elliot?"

"To be sure I did; very often. I used to boast of my own Anne Elliot, and vouch for your being a very different creature from——"

She checked herself just in time.

"This accounts for something which Mr. Elliot said last night," cried Anne. "This explains it. I found he had been used to hear of me. I could not comprehend how. What wild imaginations one forms where dear self is concerned! How sure to be mistaken! But I beg your pardon; I have interrupted you. Mr. Elliot married then completely for money? The circumstance, probably, which first opened your eyes to his character?"

Mrs. Smith hesitated a little here. "Oh! those things are too common. When one lives in the world, a man or woman's marrying for money is too common to strike one as it ought. I was very young, and associated only with the young, and we were a thoughtless, gay set, without any strict rules of conduct. We lived for enjoyment. I think differently now; time and sickness and sorrow have given me other notions; but at that period, I must own I saw nothing reprehensible in what Mr. Elliot was doing. 'To do the best for himself' passed as a duty."

"But was not she a very low woman?"

"Yes; which I objected to, but he would not regard. Money, money, was all that he wanted. Her father was a grazier, her grandfather had been a butcher, but that was all nothing. She was a fine woman, had had a decent education, was brought forward by some cousins, thrown by chance into Mr. Elliot's company, and fell in love with him; and not a difficulty or a scruple was there on his side with respect to her birth. All his caution was spent in being secured of the real amount of her fortune, before he committed himself. Depend upon it, whatever esteem Mr. Elliot may have for his own situation in life now, as a young man he had not the smallest value for it. His chance of the Kellynch estate was something, but all the honour of the family he held as cheap as dirt. I have often heard him declare, that if baronetcies were saleable, anybody should have his for fifty pounds, arms and motto, name and livery included; but I will not pretend to repeat half that I used to hear him say on that subject. It would not be fair; and yet you ought to have proof, for what is all this but assertion, and you shall have proof."

"Indeed, my dear Mrs. Smith, I want none," cried Anne. "You have asserted nothing contradictory to what Mr. Elliot appeared to be some years ago. This is all in confirmation, rather, of what we used to hear and believe. I am more curious to know why he should be so different now."

" But for my satisfaction, if you will have the goodness to ring for Mary; stay: I am sure you will have the still greater goodness of going yourself into my bedroom, and bringing me the small inlaid box which you will find on the upper shelf of the closet."

Anne, seeing her friend to be earnestly bent on it, did as she was desired. The box was brought and placed before her, and Mrs. Smith, sighing over it as she unlocked it, said—

" This is full of papers belonging to him, to my husband; a small portion only of what I had to look over when I lost him. The letter I am looking for was one written by Mr. Elliot to him before our marriage, and happened to be saved; why, one can hardly imagine. But he was careless and immethodical, like other men, about those things; and when I came to examine his papers, I found it with others, still more trivial, from different people scattered here and there, while many letters and memorandums of real importance had been destroyed. Here it is; I would not burn it, because being even then very little satisfied with Mr. Elliot, I was determined to preserve every document of former intimacy. I have now another motive for being glad that I can produce it."

This was the letter, directed to " Charles Smith, Esq., Tunbridge Wells," and dated from London, as far back as July, 1803:—

" DEAR SMITH,—I have received yours. Your kindness almost overpowers me. I wish nature had made such hearts as [yours] more common, but I have lived three-and-twenty years in the world, and have seen none like it. At present, believe me, I have no need of your services, being in cash again. Give me joy: I have got rid of Sir Walter and Miss. They are gone back to Kellynch, and almost made me swear to visit them this summer; but my first visit to Kellynch will be with a surveyor, to tell me how to bring it with best advantage to the hammer. The baronet, nevertheless, is not unlikely to marry again; he is quite fool enough. If he does, however, they will leave me in peace, which may be a decent equivalent for the reversion. He is worse than last year.

" I wish I had any name but Elliot. I am sick of it. The name of Walter I can drop, thank God! and I desire you will never insult me with my second W. again, meaning, for the rest of my life, to be only yours truly,—WM. ELLIOT."

Such a letter could not be read without putting Anne in a glow; and Mrs. Smith, observing the high colour in her face, said—

" The language, I know, is highly disrespectful. Though I have forgot the exact terms, I have a perfect impression of the general meaning. But it shows you the man. Mark his professions to my poor husband. Can anything be stronger ? "

Anne could not immediately get over the shock and mortification of finding such words applied to her father. She was obliged to recollect that her seeing the letter was a violation of the laws of honour, that no one ought to be judged or to be known by such testimonies, that no private correspondence could bear the eye of others, before she could recover calmness enough to return the letter which she had been meditating over, and say—

" Thank you. This is full proof undoubtedly: proof of everything you were saying. But why be acquainted with us now ? "

" I can explain this too," cried Mrs. Smith, smiling.

" Can you really ? "

" Yes. I have shewn you Mr. Elliot as he was a dozen years ago, and I will shew him as he is now. I cannot produce written proof again, but I can give as authentic oral testimony as you can desire, of what he is now wanting, and what he is now doing. He is no hypocrite now. He truly wants to marry you. His present attentions to your family are very sincere: quite from the heart. I will give you my authority: his friend Colonel Wallis."

" Colonel Wallis! are you acquainted with him ? "

" No. It does not come to me in quite so direct a line as that; it takes a bend or two, but nothing of consequence. The stream is as good as at first; the little rubbish it collects in the turnings is easily moved away. Mr. Elliot talks unreservedly to Colonel Wallis of his views on you, which said Colonel Wallis, I imagine to be, in himself, a sensible, careful, discerning sort of character; but Colonel Wallis has a very pretty silly wife, to whom he tells things which he had better not, and he repeats it all to her. She in the overflowing spirits of her recovery, repeats it all to her nurse; and the nurse knowing my acquaintance with you, very naturally brings it all to me. On Monday evening, my good friend Mrs. Rooke let me thus much into the secrets of Marlborough Buildings. When I talked of a whole history, therefore, you see I was not romancing so much as you supposed."

" My dear Mrs. Smith, your authority is deficient. This will not do. Mr. Elliot's having any views on me will not in the least account for the efforts he made towards a reconciliation with my father. That was all prior to my coming to Bath. I found them on the most friendly terms when I arrived."

" I know you did; I know it all perfectly, but—"

" Indeed, Mrs. Smith, we must not expect to get real information in such a line. Facts or opinions which are to pass through the hands of so many, to be misconceived by folly in one, and ignorance in another, can hardly have much truth left."

" Only give me a hearing. You will soon be able to judge of the general credit due, by listening to some particulars which you can yourself immediately contradict or confirm. Nobody supposes that you were his first inducement. He had seen you, indeed, before he came to Bath, and admired you, but without knowing it to be you. So says my historian, at least. Is this true? Did he see you last summer or autumn ' somewhere down in the west,' to use her own words, without knowing it to be you? "

" He certainly did. So far it is very true. At Lyme. I happened to be at Lyme."

" Well," continued Mrs. Smith, triumphantly, " grant my friend the credit due to the establishment of the first point asserted. He saw you then at Lyme, and liked you so well as to be exceedingly pleased to meet with you again in Camden Place, as Miss Anne Elliot, and from that moment, I have no doubt, had a double motive in his visits there.

But there was another, and an earlier, which I will now explain. If there is anything in my story which you know to be either false or improbable, stop me. My account states, that your sister's friend, the lady now staying with you, whom I have heard you mention, came to Bath with Miss Elliot and Sir Walter as long ago as September (in short when they first came themselves), and has been staying there ever since; that she is a clever, insinuating, handsome woman, poor and plausible, and altogether such in situation and manner, as to give a general idea, among Sir Walter's acquaintance, of her meaning to be Lady Elliot, and as general a surprise that Miss Elliot should be, apparently, blind to the danger."

Here Mrs. Smith paused a moment; but Anne had not a word to say, and she continued—

" This was the light in which it appeared to those who knew the family, long before you returned to it; and Colonel Wallis had his eye upon your father enough to be sensible of it, though he did not then visit in Camden Place; but his regard for Mr. Elliot gave him an interest in watching all that was going on there, and when Mr. Elliot came to Bath for a day or two, as he happened to do a little before Christmas, Colonel Wallis made him acquainted with the appearance of things, and the reports beginning to prevail. Now you are to understand, that time had worked a very material change in Mr. Elliot's opinions as to the value of a baronetcy. Upon all points of blood and connexion he is a completely altered man. Having long had as much money as he could spend, nothing to wish for on the side of avarice or indulgence, he has been gradually learning to pin his happiness upon the consequence he is heir to. I thought it coming on before our acquaintance ceased, but it is now a confirmed feeling. He cannot bear the idea of not being Sir William. You may guess, therefore, that the news he heard from his friend could not be very agreeable, and you may guess what it produced; the resolution of coming back to Bath as soon as possible, and of fixing himself here for a time, with the view of renewing his former acquaintance, and recovering such a footing in the family as might give him the means of ascertaining the degree of his danger, and

of circumventing the lady if he found it material. This was
agreed upon between the two friends as the only thing to be
done; and Colonel Wallis was to assist in every way that
he could. He was to be introduced, and Mrs. Wallis was
to be introduced, and everybody was to be introduced.
Mr. Elliot came back accordingly; and on application was
forgiven, as you know, and re-admitted into the family;
and there it was his constant object, and his only object (till
your arrival added another motive), to watch Sir Walter and
Mrs. Clay. He omitted no opportunity of being with them,
threw himself in their way, called at all hours; but I need
not be particular on this subject. You can imagine what
an artful man would do; and with this guide, perhaps, may
recollect what you have seen him do."

" Yes," said Anne, " you tell me nothing which does not
accord with what I have known, or could imagine. There
is always something offensive in the details of cunning. The
manœuvres of selfishness and duplicity must ever be revolting, but I have heard nothing which really surprises me. I
know those who would be shocked by such a representation
of Mr. Elliot, who would have difficulty in believing it, but
I have never been satisfied. I have always wanted some
other motive for his conduct than appeared. I should like
to know his present opinion, as to the probability of the
event he has been in dread of; whether he considers the
danger to be lessening or not."

" Lessening, I understand," replied Mrs. Smith. " He
thinks Mrs. Clay afraid of him, aware that he sees through
her, and not daring to proceed as she might do in his absence.
But since he must be absent some time or other, I do not
perceive how he can ever be secure while she holds her present
influence. Mrs. Wallis has an amusing idea, as nurse tells
me, that it is to be put into the marriage articles when you
and Mr. Elliot marry, that your father is not to marry Mrs.
Clay. A scheme worthy of Mrs. Wallis's understanding, by
all accounts; but my sensible nurse Rooke sees the absurdity
of it. " Why, to be sure, ma'am,' said she, ' it would not
prevent his marrying anybody else.' And, indeed, to own
the truth, I do not think nurse, in her heart, is a very strenuous
opposer of Sir Walter's making a second match. She must

be allowed to be a favourer of matrimony, you know; and (since self will intrude) who can say that she may not have some flying visions of attending the next Lady Elliot, through Mrs. Wallis's recommendation? "

" I am very glad to know all this," said Anne, after a little thoughtfulness. " It will be more painful to me in some respects to be in company with him, but I shall know better what to do. My line of conduct will be more direct. Mr. Elliot is evidently a disingenuous, artificial, worldly man, who has had never any better principle to guide him than selfishness."

But Mr. Elliot was not yet done with. Mrs. Smith had been carried away from her first direction, and Anne had forgotten, in the interest of her own family concerns, how much had been originally implied against him; but her attention was now called to the explanation of those first hints, and she listened to a recital which, if it did not perfectly justify the unqualified bitterness of Mrs. Smith, proved him to have been very unfeeling in his conduct towards her; very deficient both in justice and compassion.

She learned that (the intimacy between them continuing unimpaired by Mr. Elliot's marriage) they had been as before always together, and Mr. Elliot had led his friend into expenses much beyond his fortune. Mrs. Smith did not want to take the blame to herself, and was most tender of throwing any on her husband; but Anne could collect that their income had never been equal to their style of living, and that from the first there had been a great deal of general and joint extravagance. From his wife's account of him she could discern Mr. Smith to have been a man of warm feelings, easy temper, careless habits, and not strong understanding; much more amiable than his friend, and very unlike him, led by him, and probably despised by him. Mr. Elliot, raised by his marriage to great affluence, and disposed to every gratification of pleasure and vanity which could be commanded without involving himself (for with all his self-indulgence he had become a prudent man), and beginning to be rich, just as his friend ought to have found himself to be poor, seemed to have had no concern at all for that friend's probable finances, but, on the contrary, had been prompting and encouraging expenses which could end only in ruin: and the Smiths accordingly had been ruined.

The husband had died just in time to be spared the full knowledge of it. They had previously known embarrassments enough to try the friendship of their friends, and to prove that Mr. Elliot's had better not be tried; but it was not till his death that the wretched state of his affairs was fully known. With a confidence in Mr. Elliot's regard, more creditable to his feelings than his judgment, Mr. Smith had appointed him the executor of his will; but Mr. Elliot would not act, and the difficulties and distresses which this refusal had heaped on her, in addition to the inevitable sufferings of her situation, had been such as could not be related without anguish of spirit, or listened to without corresponding indignation.

Anne was shewn some letters of his on the occasion, answers to urgent applications from Mrs. Smith, which all breathed the same stern resolution of not engaging in a fruitless trouble, and, under a cold civility, the same hard-hearted indifference to any of the evils it might bring on her. It was a dreadful picture of ingratitude and inhumanity; and Anne felt, at some moments, that no flagrant open crime could have been worse. She had a great deal to listen to; all the particulars of past sad scenes, all the minutiæ of distress upon distress, which in former conversations had been merely hinted at, were dwelt on now with a natural indulgence. Anne could perfectly comprehend the exquisite relief, and was only the more inclined to wonder at the composure of her friend's usual state of mind.

There was one circumstance in the history of her grievances of particular irritation. She had good reason to believe that some property of her husband in the West Indies, which had been for many years under a sort of sequestration for the payment of its own incumbrances, might be recoverable by proper measures; and this property, though not large, would be enough to make her comparatively rich. But there was nobody to stir in it. Mr. Elliot would do nothing, and she could do nothing herself, equally disabled from personal exertion by her state of bodily weakness, and from employing others by her want of money. She had no natural connexions to assist her even with their counsel, and she could not afford to purchase the assistance of the law. This was a cruel aggravation of actually streightened means. To feel that she ought to be in better circumstances, that a little trouble in the right place might do it, and to fear that delay might be even weakening her claims, was hard to bear.

It was on this point that she had hoped to engage Anne's good offices with Mr. Elliot. She had previously, in the anticipation of their marriage, been very apprehensive of losing her friend by it; but on being assured that he could have made no attempt of that nature, since he did not even know her to be in Bath, it immediately occurred, that something might be done in her favour by the influence of the woman he loved, and she had been hastily preparing to interest Anne's feelings as far as the observances due to Mr. Elliot's character would allow, when Anne's refutation of the supposed engagement changed the face of everything; and while it took from her the new-formed hope of succeeding in the object of her first anxiety, left her at least the comfort of telling the whole story her own way.

After listening to this full description of Mr. Elliot, Anne could not but express some surprise at Mrs. Smith's having spoken of him so favourably in the beginning of their conversation. "She had seemed to recommend and praise him!"

"My dear," was Mrs. Smith's reply, "there was nothing else to be done. I considered your marrying him as certain, though he might not yet have made the offer, and I could no more speak the truth of him, than if he had been your husband. My heart bled for you as I talked of happiness; and yet he is sensible, he is agreeable, and with such a woman as you, it was not absolutely hopeless. He was very unkind to his first wife. They were wretched together. But she was too ignorant and giddy for respect, and he had never loved her. I was willing to hope that you must fare better."

Anne could just acknowledge within herself such a possibility of having been induced to marry him, as made her shudder at the idea of the misery which must have followed. It was just possible that she might have been persuaded by Lady Russell! And under such a supposition, which would

have been most miserable, when time had disclosed all, too
late?

It was very desirable that Lady Russell should be no
longer deceived; and one of the concluding arrangements of
this important conference, which carried them through the
greater part of the morning, was, that Anne had full liberty to
communicate to her friend everything relative to Mrs. Smith,
in which his conduct was involved.

CHAPTER XXII

Anne went home to think over all that she had heard. In
one point, her feelings were relieved by this knowledge of Mr.
Elliot. There was no longer anything of tenderness due to
him. He stood as opposed to Captain Wentworth, in all his
own unwelcome obtrusiveness; and the evil of his attentions
last night, the irremediable mischief he might have done,
was considered with sensations unqualified, unperplexed.
Pity for him was all over. But this was the only point of
relief. In every other respect, in looking around her, or
penetrating forward, she saw more to distrust and to apprehend. She was concerned for the disappointment and pain
Lady Russell would be feeling; for the mortifications which
must be hanging over her father and sister, and had all the
distress of foreseeing many evils without knowing how to
avert any one of them. She was most thankful for her own
knowledge of him. She had never considered herself as
entitled to reward for not slighting an old friend like Mrs.
Smith, but here was a reward, indeed, springing from it!
Mrs. Smith had been able to tell her what no one else could
have done. Could the knowledge have been extended
through her family? But this was a vain idea. She must
talk to Lady Russell, tell her, consult with her, and having
done her best, wait the event with as much composure as
possible; and after all, her greatest want of composure would
be in that quarter of the mind which could not be opened to

Lady Russell; in that flow of anxieties and fears which must be all to herself.

She found, on reaching home, that she had, as she intended, escaped seeing Mr. Elliot; that he had called and paid them a long morning visit; but hardly had she congratulated herself, and felt safe, when she heard that he was coming again in the evening.

"I had not the smallest intention of asking him," said Elizabeth, with affected carelessness, "but he gave so many hints; so Mrs. Clay says, at least."

"Indeed, I do say it. I never saw any body in my life spell harder for an invitation. Poor man! I was really in pain for him; for your hard-hearted sister, Miss Anne, seems bent on cruelty."

"Oh!" cried Elizabeth, "I have been rather too much used to the game to be soon overcome by a gentleman's hints. However, when I found how excessively he was regretting that he should miss my father this morning, I gave way immediately, for I would never really omit an opportunity of bringing him and Sir Walter together. They appear to so much advantage in company with each other. Each behaving so pleasantly. Mr. Elliot looking up with so much respect."

"Quite delightful!" cried Mrs. Clay, not daring, however, to turn her eyes towards Anne. "Exactly like father and son! Dear Miss Elliot, may I not say father and son?"

"Oh! I lay no embargo on any body's words. If you will have such ideas! But, upon my word, I am scarcely sensible of his attentions being beyond those of other men."

"My dear Miss Elliot!" exclaimed Mrs. Clay, lifting up her hands and eyes, and sinking all the rest of her astonishment in a convenient silence.

"Well, my dear Penelope, you need not be so alarmed about him. I did invite him, you know. I sent him away with smiles. When I found he was really going to his friends at Thornberry Park for the whole day to-morrow, I had compassion on him."

Anne admired the good acting of the friend, in being able to shew such pleasure, as she did, in the expectation and in the actual arrival of the very person whose presence must really be interfering with her prime object. It was impossible but that Mrs. Clay must hate the sight of Mr. Elliot; and yet she could assume a most obliging, placid look, and appear quite satisfied with the curtailed license of devoting herself only half as much to Sir Walter as she would have done otherwise.

To Anne herself it was most distressing to see Mr. Elliot enter the room; and quite painful to have him approach and speak to her. She had been used before to feel that he could not be always quite sincere, but now she saw insincerity in everything. His attentive deference to her father, contrasted with his former language, was odious; and when she thought of his cruel conduct towards Mrs. Smith, she could hardly bear the sight of his present smiles and mildness, or the sound of his artificial good sentiments.

She meant to avoid any such alteration of manners as might provoke a remonstrance on his side. It was a great object with her to escape all enquiry or eclat; but it was her intention to be as decidedly cool to him as might be compatible with their relationship; and to retract, as quietly as she could, the few steps of unnecessary intimacy she had been gradually led along. She was accordingly more guarded, and more cool, than she had been the night before.

He wanted to animate her curiosity again as to how and where he could have heard her formerly praised; wanted very much to be gratified by more solicitation; but the charm was broken: he found that the heat and animation of a public room was necessary to kindle his modest cousin's vanity; he found, at least, that it was not to be done now, by any of those attempts which he could hazard among the too-commanding claims of the others. He little surmised that it was a subject acting now exactly against his interest, bringing immediately to her thoughts all those parts of his conduct which were least excusable.

She had some satisfaction in finding that he was really going out of Bath the next morning, going early, and that he would be gone the greater part of two days. He was invited again to Camden Place the very evening of his return; but from Thursday to Saturday evening his absence was certain. It was bad enough that a Mrs. Clay should be always before her; but that a deeper hypocrite should be added to their party, seemed the destruction of everything like peace and comfort. It was so humiliating to reflect on the constant deception practised on her father and Elizabeth; to consider the various sources of mortification preparing for them! Mrs. Clay's selfishness was not so complicate nor so revolting as his; and Anne would have compounded for the marriage at once, with all its evils, to be clear of Mr. Elliot's subtleties in endeavouring to prevent it.

On Friday morning she meant to go very early to Lady Russell, and accomplish the necessary communication; and she would have gone directly after breakfast, but that Mrs. Clay was also going out on some obliging purpose of saving her sister trouble, which determined her to wait till she might be safe from such a companion. She saw Mrs. Clay fairly off, therefore, before she began to talk of spending the morning in Rivers Street.

"Very well," said Elizabeth, "I have nothing to send but my love. Oh! you may as well take back that tiresome book she would lend me, and pretend I have read it through. I really cannot be plaguing myself for ever with all the new poems and states of the nation that come out. Lady Russell quite bores one with her new publications. You need not tell her so, but I thought her dress hideous the other night. I used to think she had some taste in dress, but I was ashamed of her at the concert. Something so formal and *arrangé* in her air! and she sits so upright! My best love, of course."

"And mine," added Sir Walter. "Kindest regards. And you may say, that I mean to call upon her soon. Make a civil message; but I shall only leave my card. Morning visits are never fair by women at her time of life, who make themselves up so little. If she would only wear rouge she would not be afraid of being seen; but last time I called, I observed the blinds were let down immediately."

While her father spoke, there was a knock at the door. Who could it be? Anne, remembering the preconcerted visits, at all hours, of Mr. Elliot, would have expected him, but for his known engagement seven miles off. After the usual period of suspense, the usual sounds of approach were heard, and " Mr. and Mrs. Charles Musgrove " were ushered into the room.

Surprise was the strongest emotion raised by their appearance; but Anne was really glad to see them; and the others were not so sorry but that they could put on a decent air of welcome; and as soon as it became clear that these, their nearest relations, were not arrived with any views of accommodation in that house, Sir Walter and Elizabeth were able to rise in cordiality, and do the honours of it very well. They were come to Bath for a few days with Mrs. Musgrove; and were at the White Hart. So much was pretty soon understood; but till Sir Walter and Elizabeth were walking Mary into the other drawing-room, and regaling themselves with her admiration, Anne could not draw upon Charles's brain for a regular history of their coming, or an explanation of some smiling hints of particular business, which had been ostentatiously dropped by Mary, as well as of some apparent confusion as to whom their party consisted of.

She then found that it consisted of Mrs. Musgrove, Henrietta, and Captain Harville, beside their two selves. He gave her a very plain, intelligible account of the whole; a narration in which she saw a great deal of most characteristic proceeding. The scheme had received its first impulse by Captain Harville's wanting to come to Bath on business. He had begun to talk of it a week ago; and by way of doing something, as shooting was over, Charles had proposed coming with him, and Mrs. Harville had seemed to like the idea of it very much, as an advantage to her husband; but Mary could not bear to be left, and had made herself so unhappy about it, that for a day or two everything seemed to be in suspense, or at an end. But then, it had been taken up by his father and mother. His mother had some old friends in Bath whom she wanted to see; it was thought a good opportunity for Henrietta to come and buy wedding-clothes for herself and her sister; and, in short, it ended in being his mother's party, that everything might be comfortable and easy to Captain Harville; and he and Mary were included in it by way of general convenience. They had arrived late the night before. Mrs. Harville, her children, and Captain Benwick, remained with Mr. Musgrove and Louisa at Uppercross.

Anne's only surprise was, that affairs should be in forwardness enough for Henrietta's wedding-clothes to be talked of. She had imagined such difficulties of fortune to exist there as must prevent the marriage from being near at hand; but she learned from Charles that, very recently (since Mary's last letter to herself), Charles Hayter had been applied to by a friend to hold a living for a youth who could not possibly claim it under many years; and that on the strength of this present income, with almost a certainty of something more permanent long before the term in question, the two families had consented to the young people's wishes, and that their marriage was likely to take place in a few months, quite as soon as Louisa's. "And a very good living it was," Charles added: "only five-and-twenty miles from Uppercross, and in a very fine country: fine part of Dorsetshire. In the centre of some of the best preserves in the kingdom, surrounded by three great proprietors, each more careful and jealous than the other; and to two of the three at least, Charles Hayter might get a special recommendation. Not that he will value it as he ought," he observed: "Charles is too cool about sporting. That's the worst of him."

"I am extremely glad, indeed," cried Anne; "particularly glad that this should happen; and that of two sisters who both deserve equally well, and who have always been such good friends, the pleasant prospects of one should not be dimming those of the other—that they should be so equal in their prosperity and comfort. I hope your father and mother are quite happy with regard to both."

"Oh yes! My father would be as well pleased if the gentlemen were richer, but he has no other fault to find. Money, you know, coming down with money—two daughters at once—it cannot be a very agreeable operation, and it streightens him as to many things. However, I do not mean to say they have not a right to it. It is very fit they should have daughters' shares; and I am sure he has always been a very kind, liberal father to me. Mary does not above half like Henrietta's match. She never did, you know. But she does not do him justice, nor think enough about Winthrop.

I cannot make her attend to the value of the property. It is a very fair match as times go; and I have liked Charles Hayter all my life, and I shall not leave off now."

"Such excellent parents as Mr. and Mrs. Musgrove," exclaimed Anne, "should be happy in their children's marriages. They do everything to confer happiness, I am sure. What a blessing to young people to be in such hands! Your father and mother seem totally free from all those ambitious feelings which have led to so much misconduct and misery, both in young and old. I hope you think Louisa perfectly recovered now?"

He answered rather hesitatingly, "Yes, I believe I do; very much recovered; but she is altered; there is no running or jumping about, no laughing or dancing; it is quite different. If one happens only to shut the door a little hard, she starts and wriggles like a young dab-chick in the water; and Benwick sits at her elbow, reading verses, or whispering to her, all day long."

Anne could not help laughing. "That cannot be much to your taste, I know," said she; "but I do believe him to be an excellent young man."

"To be sure he is: nobody doubts it; and I hope you do not think I am so illiberal as to want every man to have the same objects and pleasures as myself. I have a great value for Benwick; and when one can but get him to talk, he has plenty to say. His reading has done him no harm, for he has fought as well as read. He is a brave fellow. I got more acquainted with him last Monday than ever I did before. We had a famous set-to at rat-hunting all the morning in my father's great barns; and he played his part so well that I have liked him the better ever since."

Here they were interrupted by the absolute necessity of Charles's following the others to admire mirrors and china: but Anne had heard enough to understand the present state of Uppercross, and rejoice in its happiness; and though she sighed as she rejoiced, her sigh had none of the ill-will of envy in it. She would certainly have risen to their blessings if she could, but she did not want to lessen theirs.

The visit passed off altogether in high good humour. Mary was in excellent spirits, enjoying the gaiety and the change, and so well satisfied with the journey in her mother-in-law's carriage with four horses, and with her own complete independence of Camden Place, that she was exactly in a temper to admire everything as she ought, and enter most readily into all the superiorities of the house, as they were detailed to her. She had no demands on her father or sister, and her consequence was just enough increased by their handsome drawing-rooms.

Elizabeth was, for a short time, suffering a good deal. She felt that Mrs. Musgrove and all her party ought to be asked to dine with them; but she could not bear to have the difference of style, the reduction of servants, which a dinner must betray, witnessed by those who had been always so inferior to the Elliots of Kellynch. It was a struggle between propriety and vanity; but vanity got the better, and then Elizabeth was happy again. These were her internal persuasions: " Old-fashioned notions; country hospitality; we do not profess to give dinners; few people in Bath do; Lady Alicia never does; did not even ask her own sister's family, though they were here a month; and I daresay it would be very inconvenient to Mrs. Musgrove; put her quite out of her way. I am sure she would rather not come; she cannot feel easy with us. I will ask them all for an evening; that will be much better; that will be a novelty and a treat. They have not seen two such drawing-rooms before. They will be delighted to come to-morrow evening. It shall be a regular party, small, but most elegant." And this satisfied Elizabeth; and when the invitation was given to the two present, and promised for the absent, Mary was as completely satisfied. She was particularly asked to meet Mr. Elliot, and be introduced to Lady Dalrymple and Miss Carteret, who were fortunately already engaged to come; and she could not have received a more gratifying attention. Miss Elliot was to have the honour of calling on Mrs. Musgrove in the course of the morning; and Anne walked off with Charles and Mary, to go and see her and Henrietta directly.

Her plan of sitting with Lady Russell must give way for the present. They all three called in Rivers Street for a couple of minutes; but Anne convinced herself that a day's delay of the intended communication could be of no consequence, and hastened forward to the White Hart, to see again the friends and companions of the last autumn, with an eagerness of good-will which many associations contributed to form.

They found Mrs. Musgrove and her daughter within, and by themselves, and Anne had the kindest welcome from each. Henrietta was exactly in that state of recently-improved views, of fresh-formed happiness, which made her full of regard and interest for everybody she had ever liked before at all; and Mrs. Musgrove's real affection had been won by her usefulness when they were in distress. It was a heartiness, and a warmth, and a sincerity which Anne delighted in the more, from the sad want of such blessings at home. She was intreated to give them as much of her time as possible, invited for every day and all day long, or rather claimed as a part of the family; and, in return, she naturally fell into all her wonted ways of attention and assistance, and on Charles's leaving them together, was listening to Mrs. Musgrove's history of Louisa, and to Henrietta's of herself, giving opinions on business, and recommendations to shops; with intervals of every help which Mary required, from altering her ribbon to settling her accounts; from finding her keys, and assorting her trinkets, to trying to convince her that she was not ill-used by anybody; which Mary, well amused as she generally was, in her station at a window overlooking the entrance to the Pump Room, could not but have her moments of imagining.

A morning of thorough confusion was to be expected. A large party in an hotel ensured a quick-changing, unsettled scene. One five minutes brought a note, the next a parcel; and Anne had not been there half an hour, when their dining-room, spacious as it was, seemed more than half filled; a party of steady old friends were seated round Mrs. Musgrove, and Charles came back with Captains Harville and Wentworth. The appearance of the latter could not be more than the surprise of the moment. It was impossible for her to have forgotten to feel that this arrival of their common friends must be soon bringing them together again. Their last meeting had been most important in opening his feelings:

she had derived from it a delightful conviction; but she feared from his looks, that the same unfortunate persuasion, which had hastened him away from the Concert Room, still governed. He did not seem to want to be near enough for conversation.

She tried to be calm, and leave things to take their course, and tried to dwell much on this argument of rational dependance:—" Surely, if there be constant attachment on each side, our hearts must understand each other ere long. We are not boy and girl, to be captiously irritable, misled by every moment's inadvertence, and wantonly playing with our own happiness." And yet, a few minutes afterwards, she felt as if their being in company with each other, under their present circumstances, could only be exposing them to inadvertencies and misconstructions of the most mischievous kind.

" Anne," cried Mary, still at her window, " there is Mrs. Clay, I am sure, standing under the colonnade, and a gentleman with her. I saw them turn the corner from Bath Street just now. They seem deep in talk. Who is it? Come, and tell me. Good heavens! I recollect. It is Mr. Elliot himself."

" No," cried Anne, quickly, " it cannot be Mr. Elliot, I assure you. He was to leave Bath at nine this morning, and does not come back till to-morrow."

As she spoke, she felt that Captain Wentworth was looking at her, the consciousness of which vexed and embarrassed her, and made her regret that she had said so much, simple as it was.

Mary, resenting that she should be supposed not to know her own cousin, began talking very warmly about the family features, and protesting still more positively that it was Mr. Elliot, calling again upon Anne to come and look herself, but Anne did not mean to stir, and tried to be cool and unconcerned. Her distress returned, however, on perceiving smiles and intelligent glances pass between two or three of the lady visitors, as if they believed themselves quite in the secret. It was evident that the report concerning her had spread, and a short pause succeeded, which seemed to ensure that it would now spread farther.

" Do come, Anne," cried Mary, " come and look yourself.
You will be too late if you do not make haste. They are
parting; they are shaking hands. He is turning away.
Not know Mr. Elliot, indeed! You seem to have forgot
all about Lyme."

To pacify Mary, and perhaps screen her own embarrassment, Anne did move quietly to the window. She was just
in time to ascertain that it really was Mr. Elliot, which she
had never believed, before he disappeared on one side, as
Mrs. Clay walked quickly off on the other; and checking the
surprise which she could not but feel at such an appearance
of friendly conference between two persons of totally opposite
interests, she calmly said, " Yes, it is Mr. Elliot, certainly.
He has changed his hour of going, I suppose, that is all, or I
may be mistaken, I might not attend; " and walked back to
her chair, recomposed, and with the comfortable hope of
having acquitted herself well.

The visitors took their leave; and Charles, having civilly
seen them off, and then made a face at them, and abused them
for coming, began with—

" Well, mother, I have done something for you that you
will like. I have been to the theatre, and secured a box for
to-morrow night. A'n't I a good boy? I know you love a
play; and there is room for us all. It holds nine. I have
engaged Captain Wentworth. Anne will not be sorry to
join us, I am sure. We all like a play. Have not I done
well, mother? "

Mrs. Musgrove was good humouredly beginning to express
her perfect readiness for the play, if Henrietta and all the
others liked it, when Mary eagerly interrupted her by exclaiming—

" Good heavens! Charles, how can you think of such a
thing? Take a box for to-morrow night! Have you forgot
that we are engaged to Camden Place to-morrow night?
and that we were most particularly asked to meet Lady
Dalrymple and her daughter, and Mr. Elliot, all the principal
family connexions, on purpose to be introduced to them?
How can you be so forgetful? "

" Phoo! phoo! " replied Charles, " what's an evening
party? Never worth remembering. Your father might

have asked us to dinner, I think, if he had wanted to see us You may do as you like, but I shall go to the play."

" Oh! Charles, I declare it will be too abominable if you do, when you promised to go."

" No, I did not promise. I only smirked and bowed, and said the word ' happy.' There was no promise."

" But you must go, Charles. It would be unpardonable to fail. We were asked on purpose to be introduced. There was always such a great connexion between the Dalrymples and ourselves. Nothing ever happened on either side that was not announced immediately. We are quite near relations, you know; and Mr. Elliot too, whom you ought so particularly to be acquainted with! Every attention is due to Mr. Elliot. Consider, my father's heir: the future representative of the family."

" Don't talk to me about heirs and representatives," cried Charles. " I am not one of those who neglect the reigning power to bow to the rising sun. If I would not go for the sake of your father, I should think it scandalous to go for the sake of his heir. What is Mr. Elliot to me?" The careless expression was life to Anne, who saw that Captain Wentworth was all attention, looking and listening with his whole soul; and that the last words brought his enquiring eyes from Charles to herself.

Charles and Mary still talked on in the same style; he, half serious and half jesting, maintaining the scheme for the play, and she, invariably serious, most warmly opposing it, and not omitting to make it known that, however determined to go to Camden Place herself, she should not think herself very well used, if they went to the play without her. Mrs. Musgrove interposed.

" We had better put it off. Charles, you had much better go back and change the box for Tuesday. It would be a pity to be divided, and we should be losing Miss Anne too, if there is a party at her father's; and I am sure neither Henrietta nor I should care at all for the play if Miss Anne could not be with us."

Anne felt truly obliged to her for such kindness; and quite as much so for the opportunity it gave her of decidedly saying—

" If it depended only on my inclination, ma'am, the party at home (excepting on Mary's account) would not be the smallest impediment. I have no pleasure in the sort of meeting, and should be too happy to change it for a play, and with you. But it had better not be attempted, perhaps." She had spoken it; but she trembled when it was done, conscious that her words were listened to, and daring not even to try to observe their effect.

It was soon generally agreed that Tuesday should be the day; Charles only reserving the advantage of still teasing his wife, by persisting that he would go to the play to-morrow, if nobody else would.

Captain Wentworth left his seat, and walked to the fire-place; probably for the sake of walking away from it soon afterwards, and taking a station, with less barefaced design, by Anne.

" You have not been long enough in Bath," said he, " to enjoy the evening parties of the place."

" Oh! no. The usual character of them has nothing for me. I am no card-player."

" You were not formerly, I know. You did not use to like cards; but time makes many changes."

" I am not yet so much changed," cried Anne, and stopped, fearing she hardly knew what misconstruction. After waiting a few moments he said, and as if it were the result of immediate feeling, " It is a period, indeed! Eight years and a half is a period!"

Whether he would have proceeded farther was left to Anne's imagination to ponder over in a calmer hour; for while still hearing the sounds he had uttered, she was startled to other subjects by Henrietta, eager to make use of the present leisure for getting out, and calling on her companions to lose no time, lest somebody else should come in.

They were obliged to move. Anne talked of being perfectly ready, and tried to look it; but she felt that could Henrietta have known the regret and reluctance of her heart in quitting that chair, in preparing to quit the room, she would have found, in all her own sensations for her cousin, in the very security of his affection, wherewith to pity her.

Their preparations, however, were stopped short. Alarming sounds were heard; other visitors approached, and the door was thrown open for Sir Walter and Miss Elliot, whose entrance seemed to give a general chill. Anne felt an instant oppression, and wherever she looked saw symptoms of the same. The comfort, the freedom, the gaiety of the room was over, hushed into cold composure, determined silence, or insipid talk, to meet the heartless elegance of her father and sister. How mortifying to feel that it was so!

Her jealous eye was satisfied in one particular. Captain Wentworth was acknowledged again by each, by Elizabeth more graciously than before. She even addressed him once, and looked at him more than once. Elizabeth was, in fact, revolving a great measure. The sequel explained it. After the waste of a few minutes in saying the proper nothings, she began to give the invitation which was to comprise all the remaining dues of the Musgroves. "To-morrow evening, to meet a few friends: no formal party." It was all said very gracefully, and the cards with which she had provided herself, the "Miss Elliot at home," were laid on the table, with a courteous, comprehensive smile to all, and one smile and one card more decidedly for Captain Wentworth. The truth was, that Elizabeth had been long enough in Bath to understand the importance of a man of such an air and appearance as his. The past was nothing. The present was that Captain Wentworth would move about well in her drawing-room. The card was pointedly given, and Sir Walter and Elizabeth arose and disappeared.

The interruption had been short though severe, and ease and animation returned to most of those they left as the door shut them out, but not to Anne. She could think only of the invitation she had with such astonishment witnessed, and of the manner in which it had been received: a manner of doubtful meaning, of surprise rather than gratification, of polite acknowledgment rather than acceptance. She knew him: she saw disdain in his eyes, and could not venture to believe that he had determined to accept such an offering as an atonement for all the insolence of the past. Her spirits sank. He held the card in his hand after they were gone, as if deeply considering it.

"Only think of Elizabeth's including everybody!"

whispered Mary, very audibly. " I do not wonder Captain Wentworth is delighted! You see he cannot put the card out of his hand."

Anne caught his eye, saw his cheeks glow, and his mouth form itself into a momentary expression of contempt, and turned away, that she might neither see nor hear more to vex her.

The party separated. The gentlemen had their own pursuits, the ladies proceeded on their own business, and they met no more while Anne belonged to them. She was earnestly begged to return and dine, and give them all the rest of the day, but her spirits had been so long exerted that at present she felt unequal to [more,] and fit only for home, where she might be sure of being as silent as she chose.

Promising to be with them the whole of the following morning, therefore, she closed the fatigues of the present by a toilsome walk to Camden Place, there to spend the evening chiefly in listening to the busy arrangements of Elizabeth and Mrs. Clay for the morrow's party, the frequent enumeration of the persons invited, and the continually improving detail of all the embellishments which were to make it the most completely elegant of its kind in Bath, while harassing herself in secret with the never-ending question of whether Captain Wentworth would come or not? They were reckoning him as certain, but with her it was a gnawing solicitude never appeased for five minutes together. She generally thought he would come, because she generally thought he ought; but it was a case which she could not so shape into any positive act of duty or discretion, as inevitably to defy the suggestions of very opposite feelings.

She only roused herself from the broodings of this restless agitation, to let Mrs. Clay know that she had been seen with Mr. Elliot three hours after his being supposed to be out of Bath, for having watched in vain for some intimation of the interview from the lady herself, she determined to mention it, and it seemed to her that there was guilt in Mrs. Clay's face as she listened. It was transient: cleared away in an instant; but Anne could imagine she read there the consciousness of having, by some complication of mutual trick, or some overbearing authority of his, been obliged to attend (perhaps for half an hour) to his lectures and restrictions on her designs on Sir Walter. She exclaimed, however, with a very tolerable imitation of nature:—

"Oh, dear! very true. Only think, Miss Elliot, to my great surprise I met with Mr. Elliot in Bath Street. I was never more astonished. He turned back and walked with me to the Pump Yard. He had been prevented setting off for Thornberry, but I really forget by what; for I was in a hurry, and could not much attend, and I can only [answer] for his being determined not to be delayed in his return. He wanted to know how early he might be admitted to-morrow. He was full of 'to-morrow,' and it is very evident that I have been full of it too, ever since I entered the house and learned the extension of your plan and all that had happened, or my seeing him could never have gone so entirely out of my head."

CHAPTER XXIII

ONE day only had passed since Anne's conversation with Mrs. Smith; but a keener interest had succeeded, and she was now so little touched by Mr. Elliot's conduct, except by its effects in one quarter, that it became a matter of course the next morning still to defer her explanatory visit in Rivers Street. She had promised to be with the Musgroves from breakfast to dinner. Her faith was plighted, and Mr. Elliot's character, like the Sultaness Scheherazade's head, must live another day.

She could not keep her appointment punctually, however; the weather was unfavourable, and she had grieved over the rain on her friend's account, and felt it very much on her own, before she was able to attempt the walk. When she reached the White Hart, and made her way to the proper apartment, she found herself neither arriving quite in time, nor the first to arrive. The party before her were, Mrs. Musgrove talking to Mrs. Croft, and Captain Harville to Captain Wentworth; and she immediately heard that Mary and Henrietta, too impatient to wait, had gone out the moment it had cleared, but would be back again soon, and that the strictest injunctions had been left with Mrs. Musgrove to keep her there till they returned. She had only to submit, sit down, be outwardly composed, and feel herself plunged at once in all the agitations which she had merely laid her account of tasting a little before the morning closed. There was no delay, no waste of time. She was deep in the happiness of such misery, or the misery of such happiness, instantly. Two minutes after her entering the room, Captain Wentworth said—

" We will write the letter we were talking of, Harville, now, if you will give me materials."

Materials were all at hand, on a separate table; he went to it, and nearly turning his back on them all, was engrossed by writing.

Mrs. Musgrove was giving Mrs. Croft the history of her eldest daughter's engagement, and just in that inconvenient tone of voice which was perfectly audible while it pretended to be a whisper. Anne felt that she did not belong to the conversation, and yet, as Captain Harville seemed thoughtful and not disposed to talk, she could not avoid hearing many undesirable particulars; such as, " how Mr. Musgrove and my brother Hayter had met again and again to talk it over; what my brother Hayter had said one day, and what Mr. Musgrove had proposed the next, and what had occurred to my sister Hayter, and what the young people had wished, and what I said at first I never could consent to, but was afterwards persuaded to think might do very well," and a great deal in the same style of open-hearted communication: minutiæ which, even with every advantage of taste and delicacy, good Mrs. Musgrove could not give, could be properly interesting only to the principals. Mrs. Croft was attending with great good-humour, and whenever she spoke at all it was very sensibly. Anne hoped the gentlemen might each be too much self-occupied to hear.

" And so, ma'am, all these things considered," said Mrs. Musgrove, in her powerful whisper, " though we could have wished it different, yet, altogether, we did not think it fair to stand out any longer, for Charles Hayter was quite wild about it, and Henrietta was pretty near as bad; and so we thought they had better marry at once, and make the best of it, as many others have done before them. At any rate, said I, it will be better than a long engagement."

"That is precisely what I was going to observe," cried Mrs. Croft. "I would rather have young people settle on a small income at once, and have to struggle with a few difficulties together, than be involved in a long engagement. I always think that no mutual—"

"Oh! dear Mrs. Croft," cried Mrs. Musgrove, unable to let her finish her speech, "there is nothing I so abominate for young people as a long engagement. It is what I always protested against for my children. It is all very well, I used to say, for young people to be engaged, if there is a certainty of their being able to marry in six months, or even in twelve; but a long engagement!—"

"Yes, dear ma'am," said Mrs. Croft, "or an uncertain engagement, an engagement which may be long. To begin without knowing that at such a time there will be the means of marrying, I hold to be very unsafe and unwise, and what I think all parents should prevent as far as they can."

Anne found an unexpected interest here. She felt its application to herself, felt it in a nervous thrill all over her; and at the same moment that her eyes instinctively glanced towards the distant table, Captain Wentworth's pen ceased to move, his head was raised, pausing, listening, and he turned round the next instant to give a look, one quick, conscious look at her.

The two ladies continued to talk, to re-urge the same admitted truths, and enforce them with such examples of the ill effect of a contrary practice as had fallen within their observation, but Anne heard nothing distinctly; it was only a buzz of words in her ear, her mind was in confusion.

Captain Harville, who had in truth been hearing none of it, now left his seat, and moved to a window, and Anne seeming to watch him, though it was from thorough absence of mind, became gradually sensible that he was inviting her to join him where he stood. He looked at her with a smile, and a little motion of the head, which expressed, "Come to me, I have something to say;" and the unaffected, easy kindness of manner which denoted the feelings of an older acquaintance than he really was, strongly enforced the invitation. She roused herself and went to him. The window at which he stood was at the other end of the room from where the two ladies were sitting, and though nearer to Captain Wentworth's table, not very near. As she joined him, Captain Harville's countenance re-assumed the serious, thoughtful expression, which seemed its natural character.

"Look here," said he, unfolding a parcel in his hand, and displaying a small miniature painting; "do you know who that is?"

"Certainly: Captain Benwick."

"Yes, and you may guess who it is for. But" (in a deep tone), "it was not done for her. Miss Elliot, do you remember our walking together at Lyme, and grieving for him? I little thought then—but no matter. This was drawn at the Cape. He met with a clever young German artist at the Cape, and in compliance with a promise to my poor sister, sat to him, and was bringing it home for her; and I have now the charge of getting it properly set for another! It was a commission to me! But who else was there to employ? I hope I can allow for him. I am not sorry, indeed, to make it over to another. He undertakes it;" (looking towards Captain Wentworth,) "he is writing about it now." And with a quivering lip he wound up the whole by adding, "Poor Fanny! she would not have forgotten him so soon."

"No," replied Anne, in a low, feeling voice, "that I can easily believe."

"It was not in her nature. She doated on him."

"It would not be the nature of any woman who truly loved."

Captain Harville smiled, as much as to say, "Do you claim that for your sex?" and she answered the question, smiling also, "Yes. We certainly do not forget you so soon as you forget us. It is, perhaps, our fate rather than our merit. We cannot help ourselves. We live at home, quiet, confined, and our feelings prey upon us. You are forced on exertion. You have always a profession, pursuits, business of some sort or other, to take you back into the world immediately, and continual occupation and change soon weaken impressions."

"Granting your assertion that the world does all this so soon for men (which, however, I do not think I shall grant), it does not apply to Benwick. He has not been forced upon any exertion. The peace turned him on shore at the very moment, and he has been living with us, in our little family circle, ever since."

"True," said Anne, "very true; I did not recollect; but what shall we say now, Captain Harville? If the change be not from outward circumstances, it must be from within; it must be nature, man's nature, which has done the business for Captain Benwick."

"No, no, it is not man's nature. I will not allow it to be more man's nature than woman's to be inconstant and forget those they do love, or have loved. I believe the reverse. I believe in a true analogy between our bodily frames and our mental; and that as our bodies are the strongest, so are our feelings; capable of bearing most rough usage, and riding out the heaviest weather."

"Your feelings may be the strongest," replied Anne, "but the same spirit of analogy will authorise me to assert that ours are the most tender. Man is more robust than woman, but he is not longer lived; which exactly explains my view of the nature of their attachments. Nay, it would be too hard upon you, if it were otherwise. You have difficulties, and privations, and dangers enough to struggle with. You are always labouring and toiling, exposed to every risk and hardship. Your home, country, friends, all quitted. Neither time, nor health, nor life, to be called your own. It would be too hard, indeed" (with a faltering voice), "if woman's feelings were to be added to all this."

"We shall never agree upon this question," Captain Harville was beginning to say, when a slight noise called their attention to Captain Wentworth's hitherto perfectly quiet division of the room. It was nothing more than that his pen had fallen down; but Anne was startled at finding him nearer than she had supposed, and half inclined to suspect that the pen had only fallen because he had been occupied by them, striving to catch sounds, which yet she did not think he could have caught.

"Have you finished your letter?" said Captain Harville.

"Not quite, a few lines more. I shall have done in five minutes."

"There is no hurry on my side. I am only ready whenever you are. I am in very good anchorage here" (smiling at Anne), "well supplied, and want for nothing. No hurry for a signal at all. Well, Miss Elliot" (lowering his voice), "as I was saying, we shall never agree, I suppose, upon this point. No man and woman would, probably. But let me observe that all histories are against you—all stories, prose and verse. If I had such a memory as Benwick, I could bring you fifty quotations in a moment on my side the argument, and I do not think I ever opened a book in my life which had not something to say upon woman's inconstancy. Songs and proverbs, all talk of woman's fickleness. But, perhaps, you will say, these were all written by men."

"Perhaps I shall. Yes, yes, if you please, no reference to examples in books. Men have had every advantage of us in telling their own story. Education has been theirs in so much higher a degree; the pen has been in their hands. I will not allow books to prove anything."

"But how shall we prove anything?"

"We never shall. We never can expect to prove anything upon such a point. It is a difference of opinion which does not admit of proof. We each begin, probably, with a little bias towards our own sex; and upon that bias build every circumstance in favour of it which has occurred within our own circle; many of which circumstances (perhaps those very cases which strike us the most) may be precisely such as cannot be brought forward without betraying a confidence, or in some respect, saying what should not be said."

"Ah!" cried Captain Harville, in a tone of strong feeling, "if I could but make you comprehend what a man suffers when he takes a last look at his wife and children, and watches the boat that he has sent them off in, as long as it is in sight, and then turns away and says, 'God knows whether we ever meet again!' And then, if I could convey to you the glow of his soul when he does see them again; when, coming back after a twelvemonth's absence, perhaps, and obliged to put into another port, he calculates how soon it be possible to get them there, pretending to deceive himself, and saying, ' They cannot be here till such a day,' but all the while hoping for them twelve hours sooner, and seeing them arrive at last, as if Heaven had given them wings, by many hours sooner still! If I could explain to you all this, and all that a man can bear and do, and glories to do, for the sake of these treasures of his existence! I speak, you know, only of such men as have hearts!" pressing his own with emotion.

"Oh!" cried Anne, eagerly, "I hope I do justice to all that is felt by you, and by those who resemble you. God forbid that I should undervalue the warm and faithful feelings of any of my fellow-creatures! I should deserve utter contempt if I dared to suppose that true attachment and constancy were known only by woman. No, I believe you capable of everything great and good in your married lives. I believe you equal to every important exertion, and to every domestic forbearance, so long as—if I may be allowed the expression, so long as you have an object. I mean while the woman you love lives, and lives for you. All the privilege I claim for my own sex (it is not a very enviable one: you need not covet it), is that of loving longest, when existence or when hope is gone!"

She could not immediately have uttered another sentence; her heart was too full, her breath too much oppressed.

"You are a good soul," cried Captain Harville, putting his hand on her arm, quite affectionately. "There is no quarrelling with you. And when I think of Benwick, my tongue is tied."

Their attention was called towards the others. Mrs. Croft was taking leave.

"Here, Frederick, you and I part company, I believe," said she. "I am going home, and you have an engagement with your friend. To-night we may have the pleasure of all meeting again at your party" (turning to Anne). "We had your sister's card yesterday, and I understood Frederick had a card too, though I did not see it; and you are disengaged, Frederick, are you not, as well as ourselves?"

Captain Wentworth was folding up a letter in great haste, and either could not or would not answer fully.

"Yes," said he, "very true; here we separate, but

Harville and I shall soon be after you; that is, Harville,
if you are ready, I am in half a minute. I know you will
not be sorry to be off. I shall be at your service in half a
minute."

Mrs. Croft left them, and Captain Wentworth, having
sealed his letter with great rapidity, was indeed ready, and
had even a hurried, agitated air, which shewed impatience
to be gone. Anne knew not how to understand it. She
had the kindest " Good morning, God bless you ! " from
Captain Harville, but from him not a word, nor a look ! He
had passed out of the room without a look !

She had only time, however, to move closer to the table
where he had been writing, when footsteps were heard
returning; the door opened, it was himself. He begged
their pardon, but he had forgotten his gloves, and instantly
crossing the room to the writing table, and standing with
his back towards Mrs. Musgrove, he drew out a letter from
under the scattered paper, placed it before Anne with eyes
of glowing entreaty fixed on her for a time, and hastily
collecting his gloves, was again out of the room, almost
before Mrs. Musgrove was aware of his being in it: the work
of an instant !

The revolution which one instant had made in Anne was
almost beyond expression. The letter, with a direction
hardly legible, to " Miss A. E——," was evidently the one
which he had been folding so hastily. While supposed to
be writing only to Captain Benwick he had been also addressing her ! On the contents of that letter depended all which
this world could do for her. Anything was possible, anything
might be defied rather than suspense. Mrs. Musgrove had
little arrangements of her own at her own table; to their
protection she must trust, and, sinking into the chair which
he had occupied, succeeding to the very spot where he had
leaned and written, her eyes devoured the following words:

" I can listen no longer in silence. I must speak to you
by such means as are within my reach. You pierce my soul.
I am half agony, half hope. Tell me not that I am too late,
that such precious feelings are gone for ever. I offer myself
to you again with a heart even more your own than when

you almost broke it, eight years and a half ago. Dare not say that man forgets sooner than woman, that his love has an earlier death. I have loved none but you. Unjust I may have been, weak and resentful I have been, but never inconstant. You alone have brought me to Bath. For you alone, I think and plan. Have you not seen this? Can you fail to have understood my wishes? I had not waited even these ten days, could I have read your feelings, as I think you must have penetrated mine. I can hardly write. I am every instant hearing something which overpowers me. You sink your voice, but I can distinguish the tones of that voice when they would be lost on others. Too good, too excellent creature! You do us justice, indeed. You do believe that there is true attachment and constancy among men. Believe it to be most fervent, most undeviating, in

"F. W.

"I must go, uncertain of my fate; but I shall return hither, or follow your party, as soon as possible. A word, a look, will be enough to decide whether I enter your father's house this evening or never."

Such a letter was not to be soon recovered from. Half an hour's solitude and reflection might have tranquillised her; but the ten minutes only which now passed before she was interrupted, with all the restraints of her situation, could do nothing towards tranquillity. Every moment rather brought fresh agitation. It was an overpowering happiness. And before she was beyond the first stage of full sensation, Charles, Mary, and Henrietta, all came in.

The absolute necessity of seeming like herself produced then an immediate struggle; but after a while she could do no more. She began not to understand a word they said, and was obliged to plead indisposition and excuse herself. They could then see that she looked very ill, were shocked and concerned, and would not stir without her for the world. This was dreadful. Would they only have gone away, and left her in the quiet possession of that room it would have been her cure; but to have them all standing or waiting around her was distracting, and in desperation, she said she would go home.

" By all means, my dear," cried Mrs. Musgrove, " go home directly, and take care of yourself, that you may be fit for the evening. I wish Sarah was here to doctor you, but I am no doctor myself. Charles, ring and order a chair. She must not walk."

But the chair would never do. Worse than all! To lose the possibility of speaking two words to Captain Wentworth in the course of her quiet, solitary progress up the town (and she felt almost certain of meeting him) could not be borne. The chair was earnestly protested against, and Mrs. Musgrove, who thought only of one sort of illness, having assured herself with some anxiety, that there had been no fall in the case; that Anne had not at any time lately slipped down, and got a blow on her head; that she was perfectly convinced of having had no fall; could part with her cheerfully, and depend on finding her better at night.

Anxious to omit no precaution, Anne struggled, and said—

" I am afraid, ma'am, that it is not perfectly understood. Pray be so good as to mention to the other gentlemen that we hope to see your whole party this evening. I am afraid there has been some mistake; and I wish you particularly to assure Captain Harville and Captain Wentworth, that we hope to see them both."

" Oh; my dear, it is quite understood, I give you my word. Captain Harville has no thought but of going."

" Do you think so? But I am afraid; and I should be so very sorry. Will you promise me to mention it when you see them again? You will see them both again this morning, I dare say. Do promise me."

" To be sure I will, if you wish it. Charles, if you see Captain Harville anywhere, remember to give Miss Anne's message. But, indeed, my dear, you need not be uneasy. Captain Harville holds himself quite engaged, I'll answer for it; and Captain Wentworth the same, I dare say."

Anne could do no more; but her heart prophesied some mischance to damp the perfection of her felicity. It could not be very lasting, however. Even if he did not come to Camden Place himself, it would be in her power to send an intelligible sentence by Captain Harville. Another momentary vexation occurred. Charles, in his real concern **and**

good nature, would go home with her; there was no preventing him. This was almost cruel. But she could not be long
ungrateful; he was sacrificing an engagement at a gun-
smith's, to be of use to her, and she set off with him, with no
feeling but gratitude apparent.

They were in Union Street, when a quicker step behind, a
something of familiar sound, gave her two moments' preparation for the sight of Captain Wentworth. He joined them;
but, as if irresolute whether to join or to pass on, said nothing,
only looked. Anne could command herself enough to receive
that look, and not repulsively. The cheeks which had been
pale now glowed, and the movements which had hesitated
were decided. He walked by her side. Presently, struck
by a sudden thought, Charles said—

"Captain Wentworth, which way are you going? Only
to Gay Street, or farther up the town?"

"I hardly know," replied Captain Wentworth, surprised.

"Are you going as high as Belmont? Are you going near
Camden Place? Because, if you are, I shall have no scruple
in asking you to take my place, and give Anne your arm to
her father's door. She is rather done for this morning, and
must not go so far without help, and I ought to be at that
fellow's in the Market Place. He promised me the sight of a
capital gun he is just going to send off; said he would keep
it unpacked to the last possible moment, that I might see it;
and if I do not turn back now, I have no chance. By his
description, a good deal like the second sized double-barrel
of mine, which you shot with one day round Winthrop."

There could not be an objection. There could be only a
most proper alacrity, a most obliging compliance for public
view; and smiles reined in and spirits dancing in private
rapture. In half a minute Charles was at the bottom of
Union Street again, and the other two proceeding together:
and soon words enough had passed between them to decide
their direction towards the comparatively quiet and retired
gravel walk, where the power of conversation would make
the present hour a blessing indeed, and prepare it for all
the immortality which the happiest recollections of their own
future lives could bestow. There they exchanged again those
feelings and those promises which had once before seemed to

secure everything, but which had been followed by so many, many years of division and estrangement. There they returned again into the past, more exquisitely happy, perhaps in their re-union, than when it had been first projected; more tender, more tried, more fixed in a knowledge of each other's character, truth, and attachment; more equal to act, more justified in acting. And there, as they slowly paced the gradual ascent, heedless of every group around them, seeing neither sauntering politicians, bustling housekeepers, flirting girls, nor nursery-maids and children, they could indulge in those retrospections and acknowledgments, and especially in those explanations of what had directly preceded the present moment, which were so poignant and so ceaseless in interest. All the little variations of the last week were gone through; and of yesterday and to-day there could scarcely be an end.

She had not mistaken him. Jealousy of Mr. Elliot had been the retarding weight, the doubt, the torment. That had begun to operate in the very hour of first meeting her in Bath; that had returned, after a short suspension, to ruin the concert; and that had influenced him in everything he had said and done, or omitted to say and do, in the last four-and-twenty hours. It had been gradually yielding to the better hopes which her looks, or words, or actions occasionally encouraged; it had been vanquished at last by those sentiments and those tones which had reached him while she talked with Captain Harville; and under the irresistible governance of which he had seized a sheet of paper, and poured out his feelings.

Of what he had then written nothing was to be retracted or qualified. He persisted in having loved none but her. She had never been supplanted. He never even believed himself to see her equal. Thus much, indeed, he was obliged to acknowledge: that he had been constant unconsciously, nay unintentionally; that he had meant to forget her, and believed it to be done. He had imagined himself indifferent, when he had only been angry; and he had been unjust to her merits, because he had been a sufferer from them. Her character was now fixed on his mind as perfection itself, maintaining the loveliest medium of fortitude and gentleness; but he was obliged to acknowledge that only at Uppercross had he learnt to do her justice, and only at Lyme had he begun to understand himself. At Lyme he had received lessons of more than one sort. The passing admiration of Mr. Elliot had at least roused him, and the scenes on the Cobb and at the Captain Harville's had fixed her superiority.

In his preceding attempts to attach himself to Louisa Musgrove (the attempts of angry pride), he protested that he had for ever felt it to be impossible; that he had not cared, could not care, for Louisa; though till that day, till the leisure for reflection which followed it, he had not understood the perfect excellence of the mind with which Louisa's could so ill bear a comparison, or the perfect unrivalled hold it possessed over his own. There, he had learnt to distinguish between the steadiness of principle and the obstinacy of self-will, between the darings of heedlessness and the resolution of a collected mind. There he had seen everything to exalt in his estimation the woman he had lost; and there begun to deplore the pride, the folly, the madness of resentment, which had kept him from trying to regain her when thrown in his way.

From that period his penance had become severe. He had no sooner been free from the horror and remorse attending the first few days of Louisa's accident, no sooner begun to feel himself alive again, than he had began to feel himself, though alive, not at liberty.

" I found," said he, " that I was considered by Harville an engaged man! That neither Harville nor his wife entertained a doubt of our mutual attachment. I was startled and shocked. To a degree, I could contradict this instantly; but, when I began to reflect that others might have felt the same—her own family, nay, perhaps herself—I was no longer at my own disposal. I was hers in honour if she wished it. I had been unguarded. I had not thought seriously on this subject before. I had not considered that my excessive intimacy must have its danger of ill consequence in many ways; and that I had no right to be trying whether I could attach myself to either of the girls, at the risk of raising even an unpleasant report, were there no other ill effects. I had been grossly wrong, and must abide the consequences."

He found too late, in short, that he had entangled himself: and that precisely as he became fully satisfied of his not caring for Louisa at all, he must regard himself as bound to her, if her sentiments for him were what the Harvilles supposed. It determined him to leave Lyme, and await her complete recovery elsewhere. He would gladly weaken, by any fair means, whatever feelings or speculations concerning him might exist; and he went, therefore, to his brother's, meaning after a while to return to Kellynch, and act as circumstances might require.

"I was six weeks with Edward," said he, "and saw him happy. I could have no other pleasure. I deserved none. He enquired after you very particularly; asked even if you were personally altered, little suspecting that to my eye you could never alter."

Anne smiled, and let it pass. It was too pleasing a blunder for a reproach. It is something for a woman to be assured, in her eight-and-twentieth year, that she has not lost one charm of earlier youth: but the value of such homage was inexpressibly increased to Anne, by comparing it with former words, and feeling it to be the result, not the cause, of a revival of his warm attachment.

He had remained in Shropshire, lamenting the blindness of his own pride, and the blunders of his own calculations, till at once released from Louisa by the astonishing and felicitous intelligence of her engagement with Benwick.

"Here," said he, "ended the worst of my state; for now I could at least put myself in the way of happiness; I could exert myself; I could do something. But to be waiting so long in inaction, and waiting only for evil, had been dreadful. Within the first five minutes I said, 'I will be at Bath on Wednesday,' and I was. Was it unpardonable to think it worth my while to come? and to arrive with some degree of hope? You were single. It was possible that you might retain the feelings of the past, as I did: and one encouragement happened to be mine. I could never doubt that you would be loved and sought by others, but I knew to a certainty that you had refused one man, at least, of better pretensions than myself; and I could not help often saying, 'Was this for me?'"

Their first meeting in Milsom Street afforded much to be said, but the concert still more. That evening seemed to be made up of exquisite moments. The moment of her stepping forward in the Octagon Room to speak to him: the moment of Mr. Elliot's appearing and tearing her away, and one or two subsequent moments, marked by returning hope or increasing despondency, were dwelt on with energy.

"To see you," cried he, "in the midst of those who could not be my well-wishers; to see your cousin close by you, conversing and smiling, and feel all the horrible eligibilities and proprieties of the match! To consider it as the certain wish of every being who could hope to influence you! Even if your own feelings were reluctant or indifferent, to consider what powerful supports would be his! Was it not enough to make the fool of me which I appeared? How could I look on without agony? Was not the very sight of the friend who sat behind you, was not the recollection of what had been, the knowledge of her influence, the indelible, immovable impression of what persuasion had once done—was it not all against me?"

"You should have distinguished," replied Anne. "You should not have suspected me now; the case so different, and my age so different. If I was wrong in yielding to persuasion once, remember that it was to persuasion exerted on the side of safety, not of risk. When I yielded, I thought it was to duty, but no duty could be called in aid here. In marrying a man indifferent to me, all risk would have been incurred, and all duty violated."

"Perhaps I ought to have reasoned thus," he replied, "but I could not. I could not derive benefit from the late knowledge I had acquired of your character. I could not bring it into play; it was overwhelmed, buried, lost in those earlier feelings which I had been smarting under year after year. I could think of you only as one who had yielded, who had given me up, who had been influenced by any one rather than by me. I saw you with the very person who had guided you in that year of misery. I had no reason to believe her of less authority now. The force of habit was to be added."

" I should have thought," said Anne, " that my manner to yourself might have spared you much or all of this."

" No, no! your manner might be only the ease which your engagement to another man would give. I left you in this belief; and yet, I was determined to see you again. My spirits rallied with the morning, and I felt that I had still a motive for remaining here."

At last Anne was at home again, and happier than any one in that house could have conceived. All the surprise and suspense, and every other painful part of the morning dissipated by this conversation, she re-entered the house so happy as to be obliged to find an alloy in some momentary apprehensions of its being impossible to last. An interval of meditation, serious and grateful, was the best corrective of everything dangerous in such high-wrought felicity; and she went to her room, and grew steadfast and fearless in the thankfulness of her enjoyment.

The evening came, the drawing-rooms were lighted up, the company assembled. It was but a card party, it was but a mixture of those who had never met before, and those who met too often: a commonplace business, too numerous for intimacy, too small for variety; but Anne had never found an evening shorter. Glowing and lovely in sensibility and happiness, and more generally admired than she thought about or cared for, she had cheerful or forbearing feelings for every creature around her. Mr. Elliot was there; she avoided, but she could pity him. The Wallises, she had amusement in understanding them. Lady Dalrymple and Miss Carteret —they would soon be innoxious cousins to her. She cared not for Mrs. Clay, and had nothing to blush for in the public manners of her father and sister. With the [Musgroves] there was the happy chat of perfect ease; with Captain Harville, the kind-hearted intercourse of brother and sister; with Lady Russell, attempts at conversation, which a delicious consciousness cut short; with Admiral and Mrs. Croft, everything of peculiar cordiality and fervent interest, which the same consciousness sought to conceal; and with Captain Wentworth, some moments of communication continually occurring, and always the hope of more, and always the knowledge of his being there.

It was in one of these short meetings, each apparently occupied in admiring a fine display of greenhouse plants, that she said—

"I have been thinking over the past, and trying impartially to judge of the right and wrong, I mean with regard to myself; and I must believe that I was right, much as I suffered from it, that I was perfectly right in being guided by the friend whom you will love better than you do now. To me, she was in the place of a parent. Do not mistake me, however. I am not saying that she did not err in her advice. It was, perhaps, one of those cases in which advice is good or bad only as the event decides; and for myself, I certainly never should, in any circumstance of tolerable similarity, give such advice. But I mean, that I was right in submitting to her, and that if I had done otherwise, I should have suffered more in continuing the engagement than I did even in giving it up, because I should have suffered in my conscience. I have now, as far as such a sentiment is allowable in human nature, nothing to reproach myself with; and if I mistake not, a strong sense of duty is no bad part of a woman's portion."

He looked at her, looked at Lady Russell, and looking again at her, replied, as if in cool deliberation—

"Not yet, but there are hopes of her being forgiven in time. I trust to being in charity with her soon. But I too have been thinking over the past, and a question has suggested itself, whether there may not have been one person more my enemy even than that lady? My own self. Tell me if, when I returned to England, in the year eight, with a few thousand pounds, and was posted into the *Laconia*, if I had then written to you, would you have answered my letter? Would you, in short, have renewed the engagement then?"

"Would I?" was all her answer; but the accent was decisive enough.

"Good God!" he cried, "you would! It is not that I did not think of it, or desire it, as what could alone crown all my other success; but I was proud, too proud to ask again. I did not understand you. I shut my eyes, and would not understand you, or do you justice. This is a recollection, which ought to make me forgive every one sooner than myself. Six years of separation and suffering might have been spared. It is a sort of pain, too, which is new to me. I have been used to the gratification of believing myself to earn every blessing that I enjoyed. I have valued myself on honourable toils and just rewards. Like other great men under reverses," he added, with a smile, " I must endeavour to subdue my mind to my fortune. I must learn to brook being happier than I deserve."

CHAPTER XXIV

WHO can be in doubt of what followed? When any two young people take it into their heads to marry, they are pretty sure by perseverance to carry their point, be they ever so poor, or ever so imprudent, or ever so little likely to be necessary to each other's ultimate comfort. This may be bad morality to conclude with, but I believe it to be truth; and if such parties succeed, how should a Captain Wentworth and an Anne Elliot, with the advantage of maturity of mind, consciousness of right, and one independent fortune between them, fail of bearing down every opposition? They might, in fact, have borne down a great deal more than they met with, for there was little to distress them beyond the want of graciousness and warmth. Sir Walter made no objection, and Elizabeth did nothing worse than look cold and unconcerned. Captain Wentworth, with five-and-twenty thousand pounds, and as high in his profession as merit and activity could place him, was no longer nobody. He was now esteemed quite worthy to address the daughter of a foolish, spendthrift baronet, who had not had principle or sense enough to maintain himself in the situation in which Providence had placed him, and who could give his daughter at present but a small part of the share of ten thousand pounds which must be hers hereafter.

Sir Walter, indeed, though he had no affection for Anne, and no vanity flattered, to make him really happy on the occasion, was very far from thinking it a bad match for her.

On the contrary, when he saw more of Captain Wentworth, saw him repeatedly by daylight, and eyed him well, he was very much struck by his personal claims, and felt that his superiority of appearance might be not unfairly balanced against her superiority of rank; and all this, assisted by his well-sounding name, enabled Sir Walter, at last, to prepare his pen, with a very good grace, for the insertion of the marriage in the volume of honour.

The only one among them whose opposition of feeling could excite any serious anxiety was Lady Russell. Anne knew that Lady Russell must be suffering some pain in understanding and relinquishing Mr. Elliot, and be making some struggles to become truly acquainted with, and do justice to Captain Wentworth. This, however, was what Lady Russell had now to do. She must learn to feel that she had been mistaken with regard to both; that she had been unfairly influenced by appearances in each; that because Captain Wentworth's manners had not suited her own ideas, she had been too quick in suspecting them to indicate a character of dangerous impetuosity; and that because Mr. Elliot's manners had precisely pleased her in their propriety and correctness, their general politeness and suavity, she had been too quick in receiving them as the certain result of the most correct opinions and well-regulated mind. There was nothing less for Lady Russell to do, than to admit that she had been pretty completely wrong, and to take up a new set of opinions and of hopes.

There is a quickness of perception in some, a nicety in the discernment of character, a natural penetration, in short, which no experience in others can equal, and Lady Russell had been less gifted in this part of understanding than her young friend. But she was a very good woman, and if her second object was to be sensible and well-judging, her first was to see Anne happy. She loved Anne better than she loved her own abilities; and, when the awkwardness of the beginning was over, found little hardship in attaching herself as a mother to the man who was securing the happiness of her other child.

Of all the family, Mary was probably the one most immediately gratified by the circumstance. It was creditable to have a sister married, and she might flatter herself with having been greatly instrumental to the connexion, by keeping Anne with her in the autumn; and as her own sister must be better than her husband's sisters, it was very agreeable that Captain Wentworth should be a richer man than either Captain Benwick or Charles Hayter. She had something to suffer, perhaps, when they came into contact again, in seeing Anne restored to the rights of seniority, and the mistress of a very pretty landaulette; but she had a future to look forward to, of powerful consolation. Anne had no Uppercross Hall before her, no landed estate, no headship of a family; and if they could but keep Captain Wentworth from being made a baronet, she would not change situations with Anne.

It would be well for the eldest sister if she were equally satisfied with her situation, for a change is not very probable there. She had soon the mortification of seeing Mr. Elliot withdraw, and no one of proper condition has since presented himself to raise even the unfounded hopes which sunk with him.

The news of his cousin Anne's engagement burst on Mr. Elliot most unexpectedly. It deranged his best plan of domestic happiness, his best hope of keeping Sir Walter single by the watchfulness which a son-in-law's rights would have given. But, though discomfited and disappointed, he could still do something for his own interest and his own enjoyment. He soon quitted Bath; and on Mrs. Clay's quitting it soon afterwards, and being next heard of as established under his protection in London, it was evident how double a game he had been playing, and how determined he was to save himself from being cut out by one artful woman, at least.

Mrs. Clay's affections had overpowered her interest, and she had sacrificed, for the young man's sake, the possibility of scheming longer for Sir Walter. She has abilities, however, as well as affections; and it is now a doubtful point whether his cunning, or hers, may finally carry the day; whether, after preventing her from being the wife of Sir Walter, he may not be wheedled and caressed at last into making her the wife of Sir William.

It cannot be doubted that Sir Walter and Elizabeth were shocked and mortified by the loss of their companion, and the discovery of their deception in her. They had their great cousins, to be sure, to resort to for comfort; but they must long feel that to flatter and follow others, without being flattered and followed in turn, is but a state of half enjoyment.

Anne, satisfied at a very early period of Lady Russell's meaning to love Captain Wentworth as she ought, had no other alloy to the happiness of her prospects than what arose from the consciousness of having no relations to bestow on him which a man of sense could value. There she felt her own inferiority keenly. The disproportion in their fortune was nothing; it did not give her a moment's regret; but to have no family to receive and estimate him properly, nothing of respectability, of harmony, of good will, to offer in return for all the worth and all the prompt welcome which met her in his brothers and sisters, was a source of as lively pain as her mind could well be sensible of under circumstances of otherwise strong felicity. She had but two friends in the world to add to his list, Lady Russell and Mrs. Smith. To those, however, he was very well disposed to attach himself Lady Russell, in spite of all her former transgressions, he could now value from his heart. While he was not obliged to say that he believed her to have been right in originally dividing them, he was ready to say almost everything else in her favour, and as for Mrs. Smith, she had claims of various kinds to recommend her quickly and permanently.

Her recent good offices by Anne had been enough in themselves, and their marriage, instead of depriving her of one friend, secured her two. She was their earliest visitor in their settled life, and Captain Wentworth, by putting her in the way of recovering her husband's property in the West Indies, by writing for her, acting for her, and seeing her through all the petty difficulties of the case with the activity and exertion of a fearless man and a determined friend, fully requited the services which she had rendered, or ever meant to render, to his wife.

Mrs. Smith's enjoyments were not spoiled by this improvement of income, with some improvement of health, and the acquisition of such friends to be often with, for her cheerfulness and mental alacrity did not fail her; and while these prime supplies of good remained, she might have bid defiance even to greater accessions of worldly prosperity. She might have been absolutely rich and perfectly healthy, and yet be happy. Her spring of felicity was in the glow of her spirits, as her friend Anne's was in the warmth of her heart. Anne was tenderness itself, and she had the full worth of it in Captain Wentworth's affection. His profession was all that could ever make her friends wish that tenderness less, the dread of a future war all that could dim her sunshine. She gloried in being a sailor's wife, but she must pay the tax of quick alarm for belonging to that profession which is, if possible, more distinguished in its domestic virtues than in its national importance.

THE END

EMMA

Emma Woodhouse, handsome, clever, and rich, with a comfortable home and happy disposition, seemed to unite some of the best blessings of existence; and had lived nearly twenty-one years in the world with very little to distress or vex her.

She was the youngest of the two daughters of a most affectionate, indulgent father; and had, in consequence of her sister's marriage, been mistress of his house from a very early period. Her mother had died too long ago for her to have more than an indistinct remembrance of her caresses; and her place had been supplied by an excellent woman as governess, who had fallen little short of a mother in affection.

Sixteen years had Miss Taylor been in Mr Woodhouse's family, less as a governess than a friend, very fond of both daughters, but particularly of Emma. Between *them* it was more the intimacy of sisters. Even before Miss Taylor had ceased to hold the nominal office of governess, the mildness of her temper had hardly allowed her to impose any restraint; and the shadow of authority being now long passed away, they had been living together as friend and friend very mutually attached, and Emma doing just what she liked; highly esteeming Miss Taylor's judgment, but directed chiefly by her own.

The real evils, indeed, of Emma's situation were the power of having rather too much her own way, and a disposition to think a little too well of herself: these were the disadvantages which threatened alloy to her many enjoyments. The danger, however, was at present so unperceived, that they did not by any means rank as misfortunes with her.

Sorrow came—a gentle sorrow—but not at all in the shape of any disagreeable consciousness. Miss Taylor married. It was Miss Taylor's loss which first brought grief. It was on the wedding day of this beloved friend that Emma first sat in mournful thought of any continuance. The wedding over, and the bride people gone, her father and herself were left to dine together, with no prospect of a third to cheer a long evening. Her father composed himself to sleep after dinner, as usual, and she had then only to sit and think of what she had lost.

The event had every promise of happiness for her friend. Mr Weston was a man of unexceptionable character, easy fortune, suitable age, and pleasant manners; and there was some satisfaction in considering with what self-denying, generous friendship she had always wished and promoted the match; but it was a black morning's work for her. The want of Miss Taylor would be felt every hour of every day. She recalled her past kindness—the kindness, the affection of sixteen years—how she had taught and how she had played with her from five years old—how she had devoted all her powers to attach and amuse her in health—and how nursed her through the various illnesses of childhood. A large debt of gratitude was owing here; but the intercourse of the last seven years, the equal footing and perfect unreserve which had soon followed Isabella's marriage, on their being left to each other, was yet a dearer, tenderer recollection. It had been a friend and companion such as few possessed: intelligent, well-informed, useful, gentle, knowing all the ways of the family, interested in all its concerns, and peculiarly interested in herself, in every pleasure, every scheme of hers—one to whom she could speak every thought as it arose, and who had such an affection for her as could never find fault.

How was she to bear the change? It was true that her friend was going only half a mile from them; but Emma was aware that great must be the difference between a Mrs Weston, only half a mile from them, and a Miss Taylor in the house; and with all her advantages, natural and domestic, she was now in great danger of suffering from intellectual solitude. She dearly loved her father, but he was no companion for her. He could not meet her in conversation, rational or playful.

The evil of the actual disparity in their ages (and Mr Woodhouse had not married early) was much increased by his constitution and habits; for having been a valetudinarian all his life, without activity of mind or body, he was a much older man in ways than in years; and though everywhere beloved for the friendliness of his heart and his amiable temper, his talents could not have recommended him at any time.

Her sister, though comparatively but little removed by matrimony, being settled in London, only sixteen miles off, was much beyond her daily reach; and many a long October and November evening must be struggled through at Hartfield, before Christmas brought the next visit from Isabella and her husband, and their little children, to fill the house, and give her pleasant society again.

Highbury, the large and populous village almost amounting to a town, to which Hartfield, in spite of its separate lawn, and shrubberies, and name, did really belong, afforded her no equals. The Woodhouses were first in consequence there. All looked up to them. She had many acquaintances in the place, for her father was universally civil, but not one among them who could be accepted in lieu of Miss Taylor for even half a day. It was a melancholy change; and Emma could not but sigh over it, and wish for impossible things, till her father awoke, and made it necessary to be cheerful. His spirits required support. He was a nervous man, easily depressed; fond of everybody that he was used to, and hating to part with them; hating change of every kind. Matrimony, as the origin of change, was always disagreeable; and he was by no means yet reconciled to his own daughter's marrying, nor could ever speak of her but with compassion, though it had been entirely a match of affection, when he was now obliged to part with Miss Taylor too; and from his habits of gentle selfishness, and of being never able to suppose that other people could feel differently from himself, he was very much disposed to think Miss Taylor had done as sad a thing for herself as for them, and would have been a great deal happier if she had spent all the rest of her life at Hartfield. Emma smiled and chatted as cheerfully as she could, to keep him from such thoughts; but when tea came, it was impossible for him not to say exactly as he had said at dinner:

'Poor Miss Taylor! I wish she were here again. What a pity it is that Mr Weston ever thought of her!'

'I cannot agree with you, papa; you know I cannot. Mr Weston is such a good-humoured, pleasant, excellent man, that he thoroughly deserves a good wife; and you would not have had Miss Taylor live with us for ever, and bear all my odd humours, when she might have a house of her own?'

'A house of her own! but where is the advantage of a house of her own? This is three times as large; and you have never any odd humours, my dear.'

'How often we shall be going to see them, and they coming to see us! We shall be always meeting! *We* must begin; we must go and pay our wedding-visit very soon.'

'My dear, how am I to get so far? Randalls is such a distance. I could not walk half so far.'

'No, papa; nobody thought of your walking. We must go in the carriage, to be sure.'

'The carriage! But James will not like to put the horses to for such a little way; and where are the poor horses to be while we are paying our visit?'

'They are to be put into Mr Weston's stable, papa. You know

we have settled all that already. We talked it all over with Mr Weston last night. And as for James, you may be very sure he will always like going to Randalls, because of his daughter's being housemaid there. I only doubt whether he will ever take us anywhere else. That was your doing, papa. You got Hannah that good place. Nobody thought of Hannah till you mentioned her—James is so obliged to you! '

' I am very glad I did think of her. It was very lucky, for I would not have had poor James think himself slighted upon any account; and I am sure she will make a very good servant; she is a civil, pretty-spoken girl; I have a great opinion of her. Whenever I see her, she always curtseys and asks me how I do, in a very pretty manner; and when you have had her here to do needlework, I observe she always turns the lock of the door the right way, and never bangs it. I am sure she will be an excellent servant; and it will be a great comfort to poor Miss Taylor to have somebody about that she is used to see. Whenever James goes over to see his daughter, you know, she will be hearing of us. He will be able to tell her how we all are.'

Emma spared no exertions to maintain this happier flow of ideas, and hoped, by the help of backgammon, to get her father tolerably through the evening, and be attacked by no regrets but her own. The backgammon-table was placed; but a visitor immediately afterwards walked in and made it unnecessary.

Mr Knightley, a sensible man about seven or eight-and-thirty, was not only a very old and intimate friend of the family, but particularly connected with it, as the elder brother of Isabella's husband. He lived about a mile from Highbury, was a frequent visitor, and always welcome, and at this time more welcome than usual, as coming directly from their mutual connections in London. He had returned to a late dinner after some days' absence, and now walked up to Hartfield to say that all were well in Brunswick Square. It was a happy circumstance, and animated Mr Woodhouse for some time. Mr Knightley had a cheerful manner, which always did him good; and his many inquiries after ' poor Isabella ' and her children were answered most satisfactorily. When this was over, Mr Woodhouse gratefully observed:

' It is very kind of you, Mr Knightley, to come out at this late hour to call upon us. I am afraid you must have had a shocking walk.'

'Not at all, sir. It is a beautiful moonlight night; and so mild that I must draw back from your great fire.'

4

'But you must have found it very damp and dirty. I wish you may not catch cold.'

'Dirty, sir! Look at my shoes. Not a speck on them.'

'Well, that is quite surprising, for we have had a vast deal of rain here. It rained dreadfully hard for half an hour while we were at breakfast. I wanted them to put off the wedding.'

'By the bye, I have not wished you joy. Being pretty well aware of what sort of joy you must both be feeling, I have been in no hurry with my congratulations; but I hope it all went off tolerably well. How did you all behave? Who cried most?'

'Ah! poor Miss Taylor! 'tis a sad business.'

'Poor Mr and Miss Woodhouse, if you please; but I cannot possibly say "poor Miss Taylor." I have a great regard for you and Emma; but when it comes to the question of dependence or independence! at any rate, it must be better to have only one to please than two.'

'Especially when *one* of those two is such a fanciful, troublesome creature!' said Emma playfully. 'That is what you have in your head, I know—and what you would certainly say if my father were not by.'

'I believe it is very true, my dear, indeed,' said Mr Woodhouse, with a sigh. 'I am afraid I am sometimes very fanciful and troublesome.'

'My dearest papa! You do not think I could mean *you*, or suppose Mr Knightley to mean *you*. What a horrible idea! Oh, no! I meant only myself. Mr Knightley loves to find fault with me, you know—in a joke—it is all a joke. We always say what we like to one another.'

Mr Knightley, in fact, was one of the few people who could see faults in Emma Woodhouse, and the only one who ever told her of them; and though this was not particularly agreeable to Emma herself, she knew it would be so much less so to her father, that she would not have him really suspect such a circumstance as her not being thought perfect by everybody.

'Emma knows I never flatter her,' said Mr Knightley, 'but I meant no reflection on anybody. Miss Taylor has been used to have two persons to please; she will now have but one. The chances are that she must be a gainer.'

'Well,' said Emma, willing to let it pass, 'you want to hear about the wedding; and I shall be happy to tell you, for we all behaved charmingly. Everybody was punctual, everybody in their best looks: not a tear, and hardly a long face to be seen.

Oh, no; we all felt that we were going to be only half a mile apart, and were sure of meeting every day.'

'Dear Emma bears everything so well,' said her father. 'But, Mr Knightley, she is really very sorry to lose poor Miss Taylor, and I am sure she *will* miss her more than she thinks for.'

Emma turned away her head, divided between tears and smiles.

'It is impossible that Emma should not miss such a companion,' said Mr Knightley. 'We should not like her so well as we do, sir, if we could suppose it: but she knows how much the marriage is to Miss Taylor's advantage; she knows how very acceptable it must be, at Miss Taylor's time of life, to be settled in a home of her own, and how important to her to be secure of a comfortable provision, and therefore cannot allow herself to feel so much pain as pleasure. Every friend of Miss Taylor must be glad to have her so happily married.'

'And you have forgotten one matter of joy to me,' said Emma, 'and a very considerable one—that I made the match myself. I made the match, you know, four years ago; and to have it take place, and be proved in the right, when so many people said Mr Weston would never marry again, may comfort me for anything.'

Mr Knightley shook his head at her. Her father fondly replied, 'Ah! my dear, I wish you would not make matches and foretell things, for whatever you say always comes to pass. Pray do not make any more matches.'

'I promise you to make none for myself, papa; but I must, indeed, for other people. It is the greatest amusement in the world! And after such success, you know! Everybody said that Mr Weston would never marry again. Oh dear, no! Mr Weston who had been a widower so long, and who seemed so perfectly comfortable without a wife, so constantly occupied either in his business in town or among his friends here, always acceptable wherever he went, always cheerful—Mr Weston need not spend a single evening in the year alone if he did not like it. Oh no! Mr Weston certainly would never marry again. Some people even talked of a promise to his wife on her deathbed, and others of the son and the uncle not letting him. All manner of solemn nonsense was talked on the subject, but I believed none of it. Ever since the day (about four years ago) that Miss Taylor and I met with him in Broadway Lane, when, because it began to mizzle, he darted away with so much gallantry, and borrowed two umbrellas for us from Farmer Mitchell's, I made up my mind on the subject. I planned the match from that hour; and when such success has blessed me in this instance, dear papa, you cannot think that I shall leave off match-making.'

'I do not understand what you mean by "success,"' said Mr Knightley. 'Success supposes endeavour. Your time has been properly and delicately spent, if you have been endeavouring for the last four years to bring about this marriage. A worthy employment for a young lady's mind! but if, which I rather imagine, your making the match, as you call it, means only your planning it, your saying to yourself one idle day, "I think it would be a very good thing for Miss Taylor if Mr Weston were to marry her," and saying it again to yourself every now and then afterwards—why do you talk of success? where is your merit? What are you proud of? You made a lucky guess; and *that* is all that can be said.'

'And have you never known the pleasure and triumph of a lucky guess? I pity you. I thought you cleverer; for, depend upon it, a lucky guess is never merely luck. There is always some talent in it. And as to my poor word "success," which you quarrel with, I do not know that I am so entirely without any claim to it. You have drawn two pretty pictures; but I think there may be a third—a something between the do-nothing and the do-all. If I had not promoted Mr Weston's visits here, and given many little encouragements, and smoothed many little matters, it might not have come to anything after all. I think you must know Hartfield enough to comprehend that.'

'A straightforward, open-hearted man like Weston, and a rational, unaffected woman like Miss Taylor, may be safely left to manage their own concerns. You are more likely to have done harm to yourself, than good to them, by interference.'

'Emma never thinks of herself, if she can do good to others,' rejoined Mr Woodhouse, understanding but in part. 'But, my dear, pray do not make any more matches; they are silly things, and break up one's family circle grievously.'

'Only one more, papa; only for Mr Elton. Poor Mr Elton! You like Mr Elton, papa; I must look about for a wife for him. There is nobody in Highbury who deserves him—and he has been here a whole year, and has fitted up his house so comfortably, that it would be a shame to have him single any longer; and I thought when he was joining their hands to-day, he looked so very much as if he would like to have the same kind office done for him! I think very well of Mr Elton, and this is the only way I have of doing him a service.'

'Mr Elton is a very pretty young man, to be sure, and a very good young man, and I have great regard for him. But if you want to show him any attention, my dear, ask him to come and dine with us some day. That will be a much better thing. I dare say Mr Knightley will be so kind as to meet him.'

'With a great deal of pleasure, sir, at any time,' said Mr Knightley, laughing: 'and I agree with you entirely that it will be a much better thing. Invite him to dinner, Emma, and help him to the best of the fish and the chicken, but leave him to choose his own wife. Depend upon it, a man of six or seven-and-twenty can take care of himself.'

2

MR WESTON was a native of Highbury, and born of a respectable family, which for the last two or three generations had been rising into gentility and property. He had received a good education, but, on succeeding early in life to a small independence, had become indisposed for any of the more homely pursuits in which his brothers were engaged; and had satisfied an active, cheerful mind and social temper by entering into the militia of his county, then embodied.

Captain Weston was a general favourite; and when the chances of his military life had introduced him to Miss Churchill, of a great Yorkshire family, and Miss Churchill fell in love with him, nobody was surprised, except her brother and his wife, who had never seen him, and who were full of pride and importance, which the connection would offend.

Miss Churchill, however, being of age, and with the full command of her fortune—though her fortune bore no proportion to the family estate—was not to be dissuaded from the marriage, and it took place, to the infinite mortification of Mr and Mrs Churchill, who threw her off with due decorum. It was an unsuitable connection, and did not produce much happiness. Mrs Weston ought to have found more in it, for she had a husband whose warm heart and sweet temper made him think everything due to her in return for the great goodness of being in love with him; but though she had one sort of spirit, she had not the best. She had resolution enough to pursue her own will in spite of her brother, but not enough to refrain from unreasonable regrets at that brother's unreasonable anger, nor from missing the luxuries of her former home. They lived beyond their income, but still it was nothing in comparison of Enscombe: she did not cease to love her husband; but she wanted at once to be the wife of Captain Weston, and Miss Churchill of Enscombe.

Captain Weston, who had been considered, especially by the Churchills, as making such an amazing match, was proved to have much the worst of the bargain; for when his wife died, after a three years' marriage, he was rather a poorer man than at first, and with a child to maintain. From the expense of the child, however, he was soon relieved. The boy had, with the additional softening claim of a lingering illness of his mother's, been the means of a sort of reconciliation; and Mr and Mrs Churchill, having no children of their own, nor any other young creature of equal kindred to care for, offered to take the whole charge of the little Frank soon after her decease. Some scruples and some reluctance the widower-father may be supposed to have felt; but as they were overcome by other considerations, the child was given up to the care and the wealth of the Churchills, and he had only his own comfort to seek, and his own situation to improve as he could.

A complete change of life became desirable. He quitted the militia and engaged in trade, having brothers already established in a good way in London, which afforded him a favourable opening. It was a concern which brought just employment enough. He had still a small house in Highbury, where most of his leisure days were spent; and between useful occupation and the pleasures of society, the next eighteen or twenty years of his life passed cheerfully away. He had, by that time, realised an easy competence—enough to secure the purchase of a little estate adjoining Highbury, which he had always longed for—enough to marry a woman as portionless even as Miss Taylor, and to live according to the wishes of his own friendly and social disposition.

It was now some time since Miss Taylor had begun to influence his schemes; but as it was not the tyrannic influence of youth on youth, it had not shaken his determination of never settling till he could purchase Randalls, and the sale of Randalls was long looked forward to; but he had gone steadily on, with these objects in view, till they were accomplished. He had made his fortune, bought his house, and obtained his wife; and was beginning a new period of existence, with every probability of greater happiness than in any yet passed through. He had never been an unhappy man; his own temper had secured him from that, even in his first marriage; but his second must show him how delightful a well-judging and truly amiable woman

9

could be, and must give him the pleasantest proof of its being a great deal better to choose than to be chosen, to excite gratitude than to feel it.

He had only himself to please in his choice; his fortune was his own; for as to Frank, it was more than being tacitly brought up as his uncle's heir, it had become so avowed an adoption as to have him assume the name of Churchill on coming of age. It was most unlikely, therefore, that he should ever want his father's assistance. His father had no apprehension of it. The aunt was a capricious woman, and governed her husband entirely; but it was not in Mr Weston's nature to imagine that any caprice could be strong enough to affect one so dear, and, as he believed, so deservedly dear. He saw his son every year in London, and was proud of him; and his fond report of him as a very fine young man had made Highbury feel a sort of pride in him too. He was looked on as sufficiently belonging to the place to make his merits and prospects a kind of common concern.

Mr Frank Churchill was one of the boasts of Highbury, and a lively curiosity to see him prevailed, though the compliment was so little returned that he had never been there in his life. His coming to visit his father had been often talked of but never achieved.

Now, upon his father's marriage, it was very generally proposed, as a most proper attention, that the visit should take place. There was not a dissentient voice on the subject, either when Mrs Perry drank tea with Mrs and Miss Bates, or when Mrs and Miss Bates returned the visit. Now was the time for Mr Frank Churchill to come among them; and the hope strengthened when it was understood that he had written to his new mother on the occasion. For a few days, every morning visit in Highbury included some mention of the handsome letter Mrs Weston had received. ' I suppose you have heard of the handsome letter Mr Frank Churchill has written to Mrs Weston? I understand it was a very handsome letter, indeed. Mr Woodhouse told me of it. Mr Woodhouse saw the letter, and he says he never saw a handsomer letter in his life.'

It was, indeed, a highly-prized letter. Mrs Weston had, of course, formed a very favourable idea of the young man; and such a pleasing attention was an irresistible proof of his great good sense, and a most welcome addition to every source and every expression of congratulation which her marriage had already secured. She felt herself a most fortunate woman; and she had lived long enough to know how fortunate she might well be thought, where the only regret was for a partial separation from friends whose friendship for her had never cooled, and who could ill bear to part with her.

She knew that at times she must be missed; and could not think, without pain, of Emma's losing a single pleasure, or suffering an hour's ennui from the want of her companionableness: but dear Emma was of no feeble character; she was more equal to her situation than most girls would have been, and had sense, and energy, and spirits that might be hoped would bear her well and happily through its little difficulties and privations. And then there was such comfort in the very easy distance of Randalls from Hartfield, so convenient for even solitary female walking, and in Mr Weston's disposition and circumstances, which would make the approaching season no hindrance to their spending half the evenings in the week together.

Her situation was altogether the subject of hours of gratitude to Mrs Weston, and of moments only of regret; and her satisfaction—her more than satisfaction—her cheerful enjoyment, was so just and so apparent, that Emma, well as she knew her father, was sometimes taken by surprise at his being still able to pity 'poor Miss Taylor,' when they left her at Randalls in the centre of every domestic comfort, or saw her go away in the evening attended by her pleasant husband to a carriage of her own. But never did she go without Mr Woodhouse's giving a gentle sigh, and saying:

' Ah, poor Miss Taylor! She would be very glad to stay.'

There was no recovering Miss Taylor—nor much likelihood of ceasing to pity her; but a few weeks brought some alleviation to Mr Woodhouse. The compliments of his neighbours were over; he was no longer teased by being wished joy of so sorrowful an event; and the wedding-cake, which had been a great distress to him, was all eaten up. His own stomach could bear nothing rich, and he could never believe other people to be different from himself. What was unwholesome to him he regarded as unfit for anybody; and he had, therefore, earnestly tried to dissuade them from having any wedding-cake at all, and when that proved vain, as earnestly tried to prevent anybody's eating it. He had been at the pains of consulting Mr Perry, the apothecary, on the subject. Mr Perry was an intelligent, gentlemanlike man, whose frequent visits were one of the comforts of Mr Woodhouse's life; and, upon being applied to, he could not but acknowledge (though it seemed rather against the bias of inclination) that wedding-cake might certainly disagree with many—

perhaps with most people, unless taken moderately. With such an opinion, in confirmation of his own, Mr Woodhouse hoped to influence every visitor of the newly-married pair; but still the cake was eaten; and there was no rest for his benevolent nerves till it was all gone.

There was a strange rumour in Highbury of all the little Perrys being seen with a slice of Mrs Weston's wedding-cake in their hands; but Mr Woodhouse would never believe it.

3

MR WOODHOUSE was fond of society in his own way. He liked very much to have his friends come and see him; and from various united causes, from his long residence at Hartfield, and his good nature, from his fortune, his house, and his daughter, he could command the visits of his own little circle, in a great measure, as he liked. He had not much intercourse with any families beyond that circle; his horror of late hours, and large dinner-parties, made him unfit for any acquaintance but such as would visit him on his own terms. Fortunately for him, Highbury, including Randalls in the same parish, and Donwell Abbey in the parish adjoining, the seat of Mr Knightley, comprehended many such. Not unfrequently, through Emma's persuasion, he had some of the chosen and the best to dine with him: but evening parties were what he preferred; and, unless he fancied himself at any time unequal to company, there was scarcely an evening in the week in which Emma could not make up a card-table for him.

Real, long-standing regard brought the Westons and Mr Knightley; and by Mr Elton, a young man living alone without liking it, the privilege of exchanging any vacant evening of his own blank solitude for the elegancies and society of Mr Woodhouse's drawing-room, and the smiles of his lovely daughter, was in no danger of being thrown away.

After these came a second set: among the most come-at-able of whom were Mrs and Miss Bates, and Mrs Goddard, three ladies almost always at the service of an invitation from Hartfield, and who were fetched and carried home so often, that Mr Woodhouse thought it no hardship for either James or the horses. Had it taken place only once a year, it would have been a grievance.

Mrs Bates, the widow of a former vicar of Highbury, was a

very old lady, almost past everything but tea and quadrille. She lived with her single daughter in a very small way, and was considered with all the regard and respect which a harmless old lady, under such untoward circumstances, can excite. Her daughter enjoyed a most uncommon degree of popularity for a woman neither young, handsome, rich, nor married. Miss Bates stood in the very worst predicament in the world for having much of the public favour; and she had no intellectual superiority to make atonement to herself, or frighten those who might hate her into outward respect. She had never boasted either beauty or cleverness. Her youth had passed without distinction, and her middle of life was devoted to the care of a failing mother, and the endeavour to make a small income go as far as possible. And yet she was a happy woman, and a woman whom no one named without goodwill. It was her own universal goodwill and contented temper which worked such wonders. She loved everybody, was interested in everybody's happiness, quicksighted to everybody's merits; thought herself a most fortunate creature, and surrounded with blessings in such an excellent mother, and so many good neighbours and friends, and a home that wanted for nothing. The simplicity and cheerfulness of her nature, her contented and grateful spirit, were a recommendation to everybody, and a mine of felicity to herself. She was a great talker upon little matters, which exactly suited Mr Woodhouse, full of trivial communications and harmless gossip.

Mrs Goddard was the mistress of a school—not of a seminary, or an establishment, or anything which professed, in long sentences of refined nonsense, to combine liberal acquirements with elegant morality, upon new principles and new systems—and where young ladies for enormous pay might be screwed out of health and into vanity—but a real, honest, old-fashioned boarding-school, where a reasonable quantity of accomplishments were sold at a reasonable price, and where girls might be sent to be out of the way, and scramble themselves into a little education, without any danger of coming back prodigies. Mrs Goddard's school was in high repute—and very deservedly; for Highbury was reckoned a particularly healthy spot: she had an ample house and garden, gave the children plenty of wholesome food, let them run about a great deal in the summer, and in winter dressed their chilblains with her own hands. It was no wonder that a train of twenty young couples now walked after her to church. She was a plain, motherly kind of woman, who had worked hard in her youth, and now thought herself entitled to the occasional holiday of a tea-visit; and having formerly owed much to Mr Woodhouse's kindness, felt his particular claim on her to leave her neat parlour, hung round with fancy work, whenever she could, and win or lose a few sixpences by his fireside.

These were the ladies whom Emma found herself very frequently able to collect; and happy was she, for her father's sake, in the power; though, as far as she was herself concerned, it was no remedy for the absence of Mrs Weston. She was delighted to see her father look comfortable, and very much pleased with herself for contriving things so well; but the quiet prosings of three such women made her feel that every evening so spent was indeed one of the long evenings she had fearfully anticipated.

As she sat one morning, looking forward to exactly such a close of the present day, a note was brought from Mrs Goddard requesting, in most respectful terms, to be allowed to bring Miss Smith with her: a most welcome request; for Miss Smith was a girl of seventeen, whom Emma knew very well by sight, and had long felt an interest in, on account of her beauty. A very gracious invitation was returned, and the evening no longer dreaded by the fair mistress of the mansion.

Harriet Smith was the natural daughter of somebody. Somebody had placed her, several years back, at Mrs Goddard's school, and somebody had lately raised her from the condition of scholar to that of parlour boarder. This was all that was generally known of her history. She had no visible friends, but what had been acquired at Highbury, and was now just returned from a long visit in the country to some young ladies who had been at school there with her.

She was a very pretty girl, and her beauty happened to be of a sort which Emma particularly admired. She was short, plump, and fair, with a fine bloom, blue eyes, light hair, regular features, and a look of great sweetness; and, before the end of the evening, Emma was as much pleased with her manners as her person, and quite determined to continue the acquaintance.

She was not struck by anything remarkably clever in Miss Smith's conversation, but she found her altogether very engaging—not inconveniently shy, not unwilling to talk—and yet so far from pushing, showing so proper and becoming a deference, seeming so pleasantly grateful for being admitted to Hartfield, and so artlessly impressed by the appearance of everything in so superior a style to what she had been used to, that she must have good sense, and deserve encouragement. Encouragement should be given. Those soft blue eyes, and all those natural graces, should not be wasted on the inferior society of Highbury and its connections. The acquaintance she had already formed were unworthy of her. The friends from whom she had just parted, though very good sort of people, must be doing her harm. They were a family of the name of Martin, whom Emma well knew by character, as renting a large farm of Mr Knightley, and residing in the parish of Donwell—very creditably, she believed; she knew Mr Knightley thought highly of them; but they must be coarse and unpolished, and very unfit to be the intimates of a girl who wanted only a little more knowledge and elegance to be quite perfect. *She* would notice her; she would improve her; she would detach her from her bad acquaintance, and introduce her into good society; she would form her opinions and her manners. It would be an interesting, and certainly a very kind undertaking; highly becoming her own situation in life, her leisure, and powers.

She was so busy in admiring those soft blue eyes, in talking and listening, and forming all these schemes in the in-betweens, that the evening flew away at a very unusual rate; and the supper-table, which always closed such parties, and for which she had been used to sit and watch the due time, was all set out and ready, and moved forwards to the fire, before she was aware. With an alacrity beyond the common impulse of a spirit which yet was never indifferent to the credit of doing everything well and attentively, with the real good-will of a mind delighted with its own ideas, did she then do all the honours of the meal, and help and recommend the minced chicken and scalloped oysters, with an urgency which she knew would be acceptable to the early hours and civil scruples of their guests.

Upon such occasions poor Mr Woodhouse's feelings were in sad warfare. He loved to have the cloth laid, because it had been the fashion of his youth, but his conviction of suppers being very unwholesome made him rather sorry to see anything put on it; and while his hospitality would have welcomed his visitors to everything, his care for their health made him grieve that they would eat.

Such another small basin of thin gruel as his own was all that he could, with thorough self-approbation, recommend; though he might constrain himself, while the ladies were comfortably clearing the nicer things, to say:

' Mrs Bates, let me propose your venturing on one of these eggs. An egg boiled very soft is not unwholesome. Serle under-

15

stands boiling an egg better than anybody. I would not recommend an egg boiled by anybody else—but you need not be afraid, they are very small, you see—one of our small eggs will not hurt you. Miss Bates, let Emma help you to a *little* bit of tart—a *very* little bit. Ours are all apple-tarts. You need not be afraid of unwholesome preserves here. I do not advise the custard. Mrs Goddard, what say you to *half* a glass of wine? A *small* half-glass, put into a tumbler of water? I do not think it could disagree with you.'

Emma allowed her father to talk—but supplied her visitors in a much more satisfactory style; and on the present evening had particular pleasure in sending them away happy. The happiness of Miss Smith was quite equal to her intentions. Miss Woodhouse was so great a personage in Highbury, that the prospect of the introduction had given as much panic as pleasure; but the humble, grateful little girl went off with highly gratified feelings, delighted with the affability with which Miss Woodhouse had treated her all the evening, and actually shaken hands with her at last!

4

HARRIET SMITH's intimacy at Hartfield was soon a settled thing. Quick and decided in her ways, Emma lost no time in inviting, encouraging, and telling her to come very often; and as their acquaintance increased, so did their satisfaction in each other. As a walking companion, Emma had very early foreseen how useful she might find her. In that respect Mrs Weston's loss had been important. Her father never went beyond the shrubbery, where two divisions of the ground sufficed him for his long walk, or his short, as the year varied; and since Mrs Weston's marriage her exercise had been too much confined. She had ventured once alone to Randalls, but it was not pleasant; and a Harriet Smith, therefore, one whom she could summon at any time to a walk, would be a valuable addition to her privileges. But in every respect, as she saw more of her, she approved her, and was confirmed in all her kind designs.

Harriet certainly was not clever, but she had a sweet, docile, grateful disposition, was totally free from conceit, and only desiring to be guided by any one she looked up to. Her early attachment to herself was very amiable; and her inclination for good company, and power of appreciating what was elegant and clever, showed that there was no want of taste, though strength of understanding must not be expected. Altogether she was quite convinced of Harriet Smith's being exactly the young friend she wanted—exactly the something which her home required. Such a friend as Mrs Weston was out of the question. Two such could never be granted. Two such she did not want. It was quite a different sort of thing, a sentiment distinct and independent. Mrs Weston was the object of a regard which had its basis in gratitude and esteem. Harriet would be loved as one to whom she could be useful. For Mrs Weston there was nothing to be done; for Harriet everything.

Her first attempts at usefulness were in an endeavour to find out who were the parents; but Harriet could not tell. She was ready to tell everything in her power, but on this subject questions were vain. Emma was obliged to fancy what she liked; but she could never believe that in the same situation *she* should not have discovered the truth. Harriet had no penetration. She had been satisfied to hear and believe just what Mrs Goddard chose to tell her; and looked no farther.

Mrs Goddard and the teachers, and the girls, and the affairs of the school in general, formed naturally a great part of the conversation—and but for her acquaintance with the Martins of Abbey Mill Farm, it must have been the whole. But the Martins occupied her thoughts a good deal; she had spent two very happy months with them, and now loved to talk of the pleasures of her visit, and describe the many comforts and wonders of the place. Emma encouraged her talkativeness, amused by such a picture of another set of beings, and enjoying the youthful simplicity which could speak with so much exultation of Mrs Martin's having ' *two* parlours, two very good parlours, indeed; one of them quite as large as Mrs Goddard's drawing-room; and of her having an upper maid who had lived five-and-twenty years with her; and of their having eight cows, two of them Alderneys, and one a little Welsh cow, a very pretty little Welsh cow, indeed; and of Mrs Martin's saying, as she was so fond of it, it should be called *her* cow; and of their having a very handsome summer-house in their garden, where some day next year they were all to drink tea; a very handsome summer-house, large enough to hold a dozen people.'

For some time she was amused, without thinking beyond the immediate cause; but as she came to understand the family better, other feelings arose. She had taken up a wrong idea, fancying it was a mother and daughter, a son and son's wife, who all lived together; but when it appeared that the Mr Martin, who bore a part in the narrative, and was always mentioned with approbation for his great good-nature in doing something or other, was a single man—that there was no young Mrs Martin, no wife in the case—she did suspect danger to her poor little friend from all this hospitality and kindness, and that, if she were not taken care of, she might be required to sink herself for ever.

With this inspiriting notion, her questions increased in number and meaning; and she particularly led Harriet to talk more of Mr Martin, and there was evidently no dislike to it. Harriet was very ready to speak of the share he had had in their moonlight walks and merry evening games; and dwelt a good deal upon his being so very good-humoured and obliging. 'He had gone three miles round one day in order to bring her some walnuts, because she had said how fond she was of them, and in everything else he was so very obliging. He had his shepherd's son into the parlour one night on purpose to sing to her. She was very fond of singing. He could sing a little himself. She believed he was very clever, and understood everything. He had a very fine flock, and, while she was with them, he had been bid more for his wool than anybody in the country. She believed everybody spoke well of him. His mother and sisters were very fond of him. Mrs Martin had told her one day (and there was a blush as she said it) that it was impossible for anybody to be a better son, and therefore she was sure, whenever he married, he would make a good husband. Not that she *wanted* him to marry. She was in no hurry at all.'

'Well done, Mrs Martin!' thought Emma. 'You know what you are about.'

'And when she had come away, Mrs Martin was so very kind as to send Mrs Goddard a beautiful goose—the finest goose Mrs Goddard had ever seen. Mrs Goddard had dressed it on a Sunday, and asked all the three teachers, Miss Nash, and Miss Prince, and Miss Richardson, to sup with her.'

'Mr Martin, I suppose, is not a man of information beyond the line of his own business? He does not read?'

'Oh, yes!—that is, no—I do not know—but I believe he has read a good deal—but not what you would think anything of. He reads the Agricultural Reports, and some other books that lay in one of the window seats—but he reads all *them* to himself. But sometimes of an evening, before we went to cards, he would read something aloud out of the *Elegant Extracts*, very entertaining. And I know he has read the *Vicar of Wakefield*. He never read the *Romance of the Forest*, nor the *Children of the Abbey*. He had never heard of such books before I mentioned them, but he is determined to get them now as soon as ever he can.'

The next question was:

'What sort of looking man is Mr Martin?'

'Oh! not handsome—not at all handsome. I thought him very plain at first, but I do not think him so plain now. One does not, you know, after a time. But did you never see him? He is in Highbury every now and then, and he is sure to ride through every week in his way to Kingston. He has passed you very often.'

'That may be, and I may have seen him fifty times, but without having any idea of his name. A young farmer, whether on horseback or on foot, is the very last sort of person to raise my curiosity. The yeomanry are precisely the order of people with whom I feel I can have nothing to do. A degree or two lower, and a creditable appearance might interest me; I might hope to be useful to their families in some way or other. But a farmer can need none of my help, and is, therefore, in one sense, as much above my notice, as in every other he is below it.'

'To be sure. Oh, yes! it is not likely you should ever have observed him; but he knows you very well indeed—I mean by sight.'

'I have no doubt of his being a very respectable young man. I know, indeed, that he is so, and, as such, wish him well. What do you imagine his age to be?'

'He was four-and-twenty the 8th of last June, and my birth-day is the 23rd—just a fortnight and a day's difference—which is very odd.'

'Only four-and-twenty. That is too young to settle. His mother is perfectly right not to be in a hurry. They seem very comfortable as they are, and if she were to take any pains to marry him, she would probably repent it. Six years hence, if he could meet with a good sort of young woman in the same rank as his own, with a little money, it might be very desirable.'

'Six years hence! dear Miss Woodhouse, he would be thirty years old!'

'Well, and that is as early as most men can afford to marry, who are not born to an independence. Mr Martin, I imagine, has his fortune entirely to make—cannot be at all beforehand with the world. Whatever money he might come into when his father died, whatever his share of the family property, it is, I dare say, all afloat, all employed in his stock, and so forth;

19

and though, with diligence and good luck, he may be rich in time, it is next to impossible that he should have realised anything yet.'

'To be sure, so it is. But they live very comfortably. They have no indoors man, else they do not want for anything; and Mrs Martin talks of taking a boy another year.'

'I wish you may not get into a scrape, Harriet, whenever he does marry—I mean, as to being acquainted with his wife; for though his sisters, from a superior education, are not to be altogether objected to, it does not follow that he might marry anybody at all fit for you to notice. The misfortune of your birth ought to make you particularly careful as to your associates. There can be no doubt of your being a gentleman's daughter, and you must support your claim to that station by everything within your own power, or there will be plenty of people who would take pleasure in degrading you.'

'Yes, to be sure, I suppose there are. But while I visit at Hartfield, and you are so kind to me, Miss Woodhouse, I am not afraid of what anybody can do.'

'You understand the force of influence pretty well, Harriet; but I would have you so firmly established in good society, as to be independent even of Hartfield and Miss Woodhouse. I want to see you permanently well connected, and to that end it will be advisable to have as few odd acquaintance as may be; and, therefore, I say, that if you should still be in this country when Mr Martin marries, I wish you may not be drawn in by your intimacy with the sisters, to be acquainted with the wife, who will probably be some mere farmer's daughter, without education.'

'To be sure. Yes. Not that I think Mr Martin would ever marry anybody but what had had some education, and been very well brought up. However, I do not mean to set up my opinion against yours—and I am sure I shall not wish for the acquaintance of his wife. I shall always have a great regard for the Miss Martins, especially Elizabeth, and should be very sorry to give them up, for they are quite as well educated as me. But if he marries a very ignorant vulgar woman, certainly I had better not visit her, if I can help it.'

Emma watched her through the fluctuations of this speech, and saw no alarming symptoms of love. The young man had been the first admirer, but she trusted there was no other hold, and that there would be no serious difficulty, on Harriet's side, to oppose any friendly arrangement of her own.

They met Mr Martin the very next day, as they were walking on the Donwell road. He was on foot, and after looking very respectfully at her, looked with most unfeigned satisfaction at her companion. Emma was not sorry to have such an opportunity of survey; and walking a few yards forward, while they talked together, soon made her quick eye sufficiently acquainted with Mr Robert Martin. His appearance was very neat, and he looked like a sensible young man, but his person had no other advantage: and when he came to be contrasted with gentlemen, she thought he must lose all the ground he had gained in Harriet's inclination. Harriet was not insensible of manner; she had voluntarily noticed her father's gentleness with admiration as well as wonder. Mr Martin looked as if he did not know what manner was.

They remained but a few minutes together, as Miss Woodhouse must not be kept waiting; and Harriet then came running to her with a smiling face, and in a flutter of spirits, which Miss Woodhouse hoped very soon to compose.

' Only think of our happening to meet him! How very odd. It was quite a chance, he said, that he had not gone round by Randalls. He did not think we ever walked this road. He thought we walked towards Randalls most days. He has not been able to get the *Romance of the Forest* yet. He was so busy the last time he was at Kingston that he quite forgot it, but he goes again to-morrow. So very odd we should happen to meet! Well, Miss Woodhouse, is he like what you expected? What do you think of him? Do you think him so very plain? '

' He is very plain, undoubtedly; remarkably plain; but that is nothing compared with his entire want of gentility. I had no right to expect much, and I did not expect much; but I had no idea that he could be so very clownish, so totally without air. I had imagined him, I confess, a degree or two nearer gentility.'

' To be sure,' said Harriet, in a mortified voice, ' he is not so genteel as real gentlemen.'

' I think, Harriet, since your acquaintance with us, you have been repeatedly in the company of some such very real gentlemen, that you must yourself be struck with the difference in Mr Martin. At Hartfield, you have had very good specimens of well-educated, well-bred men. I should be surprised if, after seeing them, you could be in company with Mr Martin again without perceiving him to be a very inferior creature—and rather wondering at yourself for having ever thought him at all agreeable before. Do not you begin to feel that now? Were not you struck? I am sure you must have been struck by his awkward look and abrupt manner, and the uncouthness of a voice which I heard to be wholly unmodulated as I stood here.'

' Certainly, he is not like Mr Knightley. He has not such a fine air and way of walking as Mr Knightley. I see the difference plain enough. But Mr Knightley is so very fine a man!'

' Mr Knightley's air is so remarkably good that it is not fair to compare Mr Martin with *him*. You might not see one in a hundred with *gentleman* so plainly written as in Mr Knightley. But he is not the only gentleman you have been lately used to. What say you to Mr Weston and Mr Elton? Compare Mr Martin with either of *them*. Compare their manner of carrying themselves, of walking, of speaking, of being silent. You must see the difference.'

' Oh, yes, there is a great difference. But Mr Weston is almost an old man. Mr Weston must be between forty and fifty.'

' Which makes his good manners the more valuable. The older a person grows, Harriet, the more important it is that their manners should not be bad; the more glaring and disgusting any loudness, or coarseness, or awkwardness becomes. What is passable in youth is detestable in later age. Mr Martin is now awkward and abrupt; what will he be at Mr Weston's time of life?'

' There is no saying, indeed,' replied Harriet, rather solemnly.

' But there may be pretty good guessing. He will be a completely gross, vulgar farmer, totally inattentive to appearances, and thinking of nothing but profit and loss.'

' Will he, indeed? that will be very bad.'

' How much his business engrosses him already, is very plain from the circumstance of his forgetting to inquire for the book you recommended. He was a great deal too full of the market to think of anything else—which is just as it should be for a thriving man. What has he to do with books? And I have no doubt that he *will* thrive, and be a very rich man in time; and his being illiterate and coarse need not disturb *us*.'

' I wonder he did not remember the book,' was all Harriet's answer, and spoken with a degree of grave displeasure which Emma thought might be safely left to itself. She, therefore, said no more for some time. Her next beginning was:

' In one respect, perhaps, Mr Elton's manners are superior to Mr Knightley's or Mr Weston's. They have more gentleness. They might be more safely held up as a pattern. There is an openness, a quickness, almost a bluntness in Mr Weston, which everybody likes in *him*, because there is so much good humour with it— but that would not do to be copied. Neither would Mr Knightley's downright, decided, commanding sort of manner, though it suits *him* very well: his figure, and look, and situation in life seem to allow it; but if any young man were to set about copying him, he would not be sufferable. On the contrary, I think a young man might be very safely recommended to take Mr Elton as a model. Mr Elton is good-humoured, cheerful, obliging, and gentle. He seems to me to be grown particularly gentle of late. I do not know whether he has any design of ingratiating himself with either of us, Harriet, by additional softness, but it strikes me that his manners are softer than they used to be. If he means anything, it must be to please you. Did not I tell you what he said of you the other day? '

She then repeated some warm personal praise which she had drawn from Mr Elton, and now did full justice to; and Harriet blushed and smiled, and said she had always thought Mr Elton very agreeable.

Mr Elton was the very person fixed on by Emma for driving the young farmer out of Harriet's head. She thought it would be an excellent match; and only too palpably desirable, natural, and probable, for her to have much merit in planning it. She feared it was what everybody else must think of and predict. It was not likely, however, that anybody should have equalled her in the date of the plan, as it had entered her brain during the very first evening of Harriet's coming to Hartfield. The longer she considered it, the greater was her sense of its expediency. Mr Elton's situation was most suitable, quite the gentleman himself, and without low connections; at the same time, not of any family that could fairly object to the doubtful birth of Harriet. He had a comfortable home for her, and Emma imagined a very sufficient income; for though the vicarage of Highbury was not large, he was known to have some independent property; and she thought very highly of him as a good-humoured, well-meaning, respectable young man, without any deficiency of useful understanding or knowledge of the world.

She had already satisfied herself that he thought Harriet a beautiful girl, which she trusted, with such frequent meetings at Hartfield, was foundation enough on his side; and on Harriet's there could be little doubt that the idea of being preferred by him would have all the usual weight and efficacy. And he was really a very pleasing young man, a young man whom any woman not fastidious might like. He was reckoned very handsome; his person much admired in general, though not by her, there being a want of elegance of feature which she could not dispense with:

but the girl who could be gratified by a Robert Martin's riding about the country to get walnuts for her might very well be conquered by Mr Elton's admiration.

5

'I DO not know what your opinion may be, Mrs Weston,' said Mr Knightley, ' of this great intimacy between Emma and Harriet Smith, but I think it a bad thing.'

' A bad thing! Do you really think it a bad thing? why so? '

' I think they will neither of them do the other any good.'

- 'You surprise me! Emma must do Harriet good; and by supplying her with a new object of interest, Harriet may be said to do Emma good. I have been seeing their intimacy with the greatest pleasure. How very differently we feel! Not think they will do each other any good! This will certainly be the beginning of one of our quarrels about Emma, Mr Knightley.'

' Perhaps you think I am come on purpose to quarrel with you, knowing Weston to be out, and that you must still fight your own battle.'

' Mr Weston would undoubtedly support me, if he were here, for he thinks exactly as I do on the subject. We were speaking of it only yesterday, and agreeing how fortunate it was for Emma that there should be such a girl in Highbury for her to associate with. Mr Knightley, I shall not allow you to be a fair judge in this case. You are so much used to live alone, that you do not know the value of a companion; and, perhaps, no man can be a good judge of the comfort a woman feels in the society of one of her own sex, after being used to it all her life. I can imagine your objection to Harriet Smith. She is not the superior young woman which Emma's friends ought to be. But, on the other hand, as Emma wants to see her better informed, it will be an inducement to her to read more herself. They will read together. She means it, I know.'

' Emma has been meaning to read more ever since she was twelve years old. I have seen a great many lists of her drawing-up, at various times, of books that she meant to read regularly through—and very good lists they were, very well chosen, and very neatly arranged—sometimes alphabetically, and sometimes by some other rule. The list she drew up when only fourteen— I remember thinking it did her judgment so much credit, that I preserved it some time, and I dare say she may have made out a very good list now. But I have done with expecting any course of steady reading from Emma. She will never submit to anything requiring industry and patience, and a subjection of the fancy to the understanding. Where Miss Taylor failed to stimulate, I may safely affirm that Harriet Smith will do nothing. You never could persuade her to read half so much as you wished. You know you could not.'

'I dare say,' replied Mrs Weston smiling, 'that I thought so *then*; but since we have parted, I can never remember Emma omitting to do anything I wished.'

'There is hardly any desiring to refresh such a memory as *that*,' said Mr Knightley feelingly; and for a moment or two he had done. 'But I,' he soon added, 'who have had no such charm thrown over my sense, must still see, hear, and remember. Emma is spoiled by being the cleverest of her family. At ten years old she had the misfortune of being able to answer questions which puzzled her sister at seventeen. She was always quick and assured; Isabella slow and diffident. And ever since she was twelve, Emma has been mistress of the house and of you all. In her mother she lost the only person able to cope with her. She inherits her mother's talents, and must have been under subjection to her.'

'I should have been sorry, Mr Knightley, to be dependent on *your* recommendation, had I quitted Mr Woodhouse's family and wanted another situation; I do not think you would have spoken a good word for me to anybody. I am sure you always thought me unfit for the office I held.'

'Yes,' said he, smiling. 'You are better placed *here*—very fit for a wife, but not at all for a governess. But you were preparing yourself to be an excellent wife all the time you were at Hartfield. You might not give Emma such a complete education as your powers would seem to promise; but you were receiving a very good education from *her*, on the very material matrimonial point of submitting your own will, and doing as you were bid; and if Weston had asked me to recommend him a wife, I should certainly have named Miss Taylor.'

'Thank you. There will be very little merit in making a good wife to such a man as Mr Weston.'

'Why, to own the truth, I am afraid you are rather thrown away, and that with every disposition to bear, there will be nothing to be borne. We will not despair, however. Weston may grow cross from the wantonness of comfort, or his son may plague him.'

'I hope not *that*. It is not likely. No, Mr Knightley, do not foretell vexation from that quarter.'

'Not I, indeed. I only name possibilities. I do not pretend to Emma's genius for foretelling and guessing. I hope, with all my heart, the young man may be a Weston in merit, and a Churchill in fortune. But Harriet Smith—I have not half done about Harriet Smith. I think her the very worst sort of companion that Emma could possibly have. She knows nothing herself, and looks upon Emma as knowing everything. She is a flatterer in all her ways; and so much the worse, because undesigned. Her ignorance is hourly flattery. How can Emma imagine she has anything to learn herself while Harriet is presenting such a delightful inferiority? And as for Harriet, I will venture to say that *she* cannot gain by the acquaintance. Hartfield will only put her out of conceit with all the other places she belongs to. She will grow just refined enough to be uncomfortable with those among whom birth and circumstances have placed her home. I am much mistaken if Emma's doctrines give any strength of mind, or tend at all to make a girl adapt herself rationally to the varieties of her situation in life. They only give a little polish.'

'I either depend more upon Emma's good sense than you do, or am more anxious for her present comfort; for I cannot lament the acquaintance. How well she looked last night!'

'Oh, you would rather talk of her person than her mind, would you? Very well; I shall not attempt to deny Emma's being pretty.'

'Pretty! say beautiful rather. Can you imagine anything nearer perfect beauty than Emma altogether—face and figure?'

'I don't know what I could imagine, but I confess that I have seldom seen a face or figure more pleasing to me than hers. But I am a partial old friend.'

'Such an eye!—the true hazel eye—and so brilliant! regular features, open countenance, with a complexion—oh, what a bloom of full health, and such a pretty height and size! such a firm and upright figure! There is health not merely in her bloom, but in her air, her head, her glance. One hears sometimes of a child being " the picture of health; " now, Emma always gives me the idea of being the complete picture of grown-up health. She is loveliness itself. Mr Knightley, is not she?'

'I have not a fault to find with her person,' he replied. 'I think her all you describe. I love to look at her; and I will add this praise, that I do not think her personally vain. Considering how very handsome she is, she appears to be little occupied with it; her vanity lies another way. Mrs Weston, I am not to be talked out of my dislike of her intimacy with Harriet Smith, or my dread of its doing them both harm.'

'And I, Mr Knightley, am equally stout in my confidence of its not doing them any harm. With all dear Emma's little faults, she is an excellent creature. Where shall we see a better daughter, or a kinder sister, or a truer friend? No, no; she has qualities which may be trusted; she will never lead any one really wrong; she will make no lasting blunder; where Emma errs once, she is in the right a hundred times.'

'Very well; I will not plague you any more. Emma shall be an angel, and I will keep my spleen to myself till Christmas brings John and Isabella. John loves Emma with a reasonable, and therefore not a blind affection, and Isabella always thinks as he does, except when he is not quite frightened enough about the children. I am sure of having their opinions with me.'

'I know that you all love her really too well to be unjust or unkind; but excuse me, Mr Knightley, if I take the liberty (I consider myself, you know, as having somewhat of the privilege of speech that Emma's mother might have had) the liberty of hinting that I do not think any possible good can arise from Harriet Smith's intimacy being made a matter of much discussion among you. Pray excuse me; our supposing any little inconvenience may be apprehended from the intimacy, it cannot be expected that Emma, accountable to nobody but her father, who perfectly approves the acquaintance, should put an end to it, so long as it is a source of pleasure to herself. It has been so many years my province to give advice, that you cannot be surprised, Mr Knightley, at this little remains of office.'

'Not at all,' cried he; 'I am much obliged to you for it. It is very good advice, and it shall have a better fate than your advice has often found; for it shall be attended to.'

'Mrs John Knightley is easily alarmed, and might be made unhappy about her sister.'

'Be satisfied,' said he, 'I will not raise any outcry. I will keep my ill humour to myself. I have a very sincere interest in Emma. Isabella does not seem more my sister; has never excited a greater interest; perhaps, hardly so great. There is an anxiety, a curiosity in what one feels for Emma. I wonder what will become of her.'

'So do I,' said Mrs Weston gently, 'very much.'

'She always declares she will never marry, which, of course, means just nothing at all. But I have no idea that she has yet ever seen a man she cared for. It would not be a bad thing for her to be very much in love with a proper object. I should like to see Emma in love, and in some doubt of a return; it would do her good. But there is nobody hereabouts to attach her; and she goes so seldom from home.'

'There does, indeed, seem as little to tempt her to break her resolution at present,' said Mrs Weston, 'as can well be; and while she is so happy at Hartfield, I cannot wish her to be forming any attachment which would be creating such difficulties on poor Mr Woodhouse's account. I do not recommend matrimony at present to Emma, though I mean no slight to the estate, I assure you.'

Part of her meaning was to conceal some favourite thoughts of her own and Mr Weston's on the subject as much as possible. There were wishes at Randalls respecting Emma's destiny, but it was not desirable to have them suspected; and the quiet transition which Mr Knightley soon afterwards made to 'What does Weston think of the weather?—shall we have rain?'—convinced her that he had nothing more to say or surmise about Hartfield.

6

EMMA could not feel a doubt of having given Harriet's fancy a proper direction, and raised the gratitude of her young vanity to a very good purpose; for she found her decidedly more sensible than before of Mr Elton's being a remarkably handsome man, with most agreeable manners; and as she had no hesitation in following up the assurance of his admiration by agreeable hints, she was soon pretty confident of creating as much liking on Harriet's side as there could be any occasion for. She was quite convinced of Mr Elton's being in the fairest way of falling in love, if not in love already. She had no scruple with regard to him. He talked of Harriet; and praised her so warmly that she could not suppose anything wanting which a little time would not add. His perception of the striking improvement of Harriet's manner, since her introduction at Hartfield, was not one of the least agreeable proofs of his growing attachment.

'You have given Miss Smith all that she required,' said he; 'you have made her graceful and easy. She was a beautiful creature when she came to you; but, in my opinion, the attractions you have added are infinitely superior to what she received from nature.'

'I am glad you think I have been useful to her; but Harriet

only wanted drawing out, and receiving a few, very few hints. She had all the natural grace of sweetness of temper and artlessness in herself. I have done very little.'

'If it were admissible to contradict a lady——' said the gallant Mr Elton.

'I have, perhaps, given her a little more decision of character —have taught her to think on points which had not fallen in her way before.'

'Exactly so; that is what principally strikes me. So much superadded decision of character! Skilful has been the hand!'

'Great has been the pleasure, I am sure. I never met with a disposition more truly amiable.'

'I have no doubt of it.' And it was spoken with a sort of sighing animation which had a vast deal of the lover. She was not less pleased, another day, with the manner in which he seconded a sudden wish of hers—to have Harriet's picture.

'Did you ever have your likeness taken, Harriet?' said she; 'did you ever sit for your picture?'

Harriet was on the point of leaving the room, and only stopped to say, with a very interesting naïveté—

'Oh dear, no—never.'

No sooner was she out of sight than Emma exclaimed:

'What an exquisite possession a good picture of her would be! I would give any money for it. I almost long to attempt her likeness myself. You do not know it, I dare say, but two or three years ago I had a great passion for taking likenesses, and attempted several of my friends, and was thought to have a tolerable eye in general; but, from one cause or another, I gave it up in disgust. But really, I could almost venture if Harriet would sit to me. It would be such a delight to have her picture!'

'Let me entreat you,' cried Mr Elton; 'it would indeed be a delight; let me entreat you, Miss Woodhouse, to exercise so charming a talent in favour of your friend. I know what your drawings are. How could you suppose me ignorant? Is not this room rich in specimens of your landscapes and flowers! and has not Mrs Weston some inimitable figure pieces in her drawing-room at Randalls?'

Yes, good man! thought Emma, but what has all that to do with taking likenesses? You know nothing of drawing. Don't pretend to be in raptures about mine. Keep your raptures for Harriet's face. 'Well, if you give me such kind encouragement, Mr Elton, I believe I shall try what I can do. Harriet's features are very delicate, which makes a likeness difficult; and yet, there is 'a peculiarity in the shape of the eye, and the lines about the mouth, which one ought to catch.'

' Exactly so—the shape of the eye and the lines about the mouth—I have not a doubt of your success. Pray, pray attempt it. As you will do it, it will indeed, to use your own words, be an exquisite possession.'

' But I am afraid, Mr Elton, Harriet will not like to sit; she thinks so little of her own beauty. Did not you observe her manner of answering me? How completely it meant " Why should my picture be drawn." '

' Oh, yes, I observed it, I assure you. It was not lost on me. But still I cannot imagine she would not be persuaded.'

Harriet was soon back again, and the proposal almost immediately made; and she had no scruples which could stand many minutes against the earnest pressing of both the others. Emma wished to go to work directly, and therefore produced the portfolio containing her various attempts at portraits, for not one of them had ever been finished, that they might decide together on the best size for Harriet. Her many beginnings were displayed. Miniatures, half-lengths, whole-lengths, pencil, crayon, and watercolours had been all tried in turn. She had always wanted to do everything, and had made more progress, both in drawing and music, than many might have done with so little labour as she would ever submit to. She played and sang, and drew in almost every style; but steadiness had always been wanting; and in nothing had she approached the degree of excellence which she would have been glad to command, and ought not to have failed of. She was not much deceived as to her own skill, either as an artist or a musician; but she was not unwilling to have others deceived, or sorry to know her reputation for accomplishment often higher than it deserved.

There was merit in every drawing—in the least finished, perhaps the most. Her style was spirited; but had there been much less, or had there been ten times more, the delight and admiration of her two companions would have been the same. They were both in ecstasies. A likeness pleases everybody; and Miss Woodhouse's performances must be capital.

' No great variety of faces for you,' said Emma. ' I had only my own family to study from. There is my father—another of my father—but the idea of sitting for his picture made him so nervous, that I could only take him by stealth, neither of them very like, therefore. Mrs Weston again, and again, and again, you see. Dear Mrs Weston—always my kindest friend on every occasion. She would sit whenever I asked her. There is my sister; and really quite her own little elegant figure—and the face not unlike. I should have made a good likeness of her, if she would have sat longer; but she was in such a hurry to have me draw her four children that she would not be quiet. Then, here comes all my attempts at three of those four children—there they are, Henry, and John, and Bella, from one end of the sheet to the other, and any one of them might do for any one of the rest. She was so eager to have them drawn that I could not refuse; but there is no making children of three or four years old stand still, you know; nor can it be very easy to take any likeness of them, beyond the hair and complexion, unless they are coarser featured than any mamma's children ever were. Here is my sketch of the fourth, who was a baby. I took him as he was sleeping on the sofa, and it is as strong a likeness of his cockade as you would wish to see. He had nestled down his head most conveniently: that's very like. I am rather proud of little George. The corner of the sofa is very good. Then here is my last,'—unclosing a pretty sketch of a gentleman in small size, whole length— my last and my best—my brother, Mr John Knightley. This did not want much of being finished, when I put it away in a pet, and vowed I would never take another likeness. I could not help being provoked; for, after all my pains, and when I had really made a very good likeness of it—(Mrs Weston and I were quite agreed in thinking it very like)—only too handsome—too flattering—but that was a fault on the right side—after all this, came poor dear Isabella's cold approbation of "Yes, it was a little like; but, to be sure, it did not do him justice." We had had a great deal of trouble in persuading him to sit at all. It was made a great favour of; and altogether it was more than I could bear; and so I never would finish it, to have it apologised over as an unfavourable likeness, to every morning visitor in Brunswick Square; and, as I said, I did then forswear ever drawing anybody again. But, for Harriet's sake, or rather for my own, and as there are no husbands and wives in the case at present, I will break my resolution now.'

Mr Elton seemed very properly struck and delighted by the idea, and was repeating, 'No husbands and wives in the case at present indeed, as you observe. Exactly so. No husbands and wives,' with so interesting a consciousness, that Emma began to consider whether she had not better leave them together at once. But as she wanted to be drawing, the declaration must wait a little longer.

She had soon fixed on the size and sort of portrait. It was to be a whole-length in water-colours, like Mr John Knightley's, and was destined, if she could please herself, to hold a very honourable station over the mantelpiece.

The sitting began; and Harriet, smiling and blushing, and afraid of not keeping her attitude and countenance, presented a very sweet mixture of youthful expression to the steady eyes of the artist. But there was no doing anything, with Mr Elton fidgeting behind her, and watching every touch. She gave him credit for stationing himself where he might gaze and gaze again without offence; but was really obliged to put an end to it, and request him to place himself elsewhere. It then occurred to her to employ him in reading.

' If he would be so good as to read to them, it would be a kindness indeed! It would amuse away the difficulties of her part, and lessen the irksomeness of Miss Smith's.'

Mr Elton was only too happy. Harriet listened, and Emma drew in peace. She must allow him to be still frequently coming to look; anything less would certainly have been too little in a lover; and he was ready at the smallest intermission of the pencil to jump up and see the progress, and be charmed. There was no being displeased with such an encourager, for his admiration made him discern a likeness almost before it was possible. She could not respect his eyes, but his love and his complaisance were unexceptionable.

The sitting was altogether very satisfactory: she was quite enough pleased with the first day's sketch to wish to go on. There was no want of likeness; she had been fortunate in the attitude; and as she meant to throw in a little improvement to the figure, to give a little more height, and considerably more elegance, she had great confidence of its being in every way a pretty drawing at last, and of its filling its destined place with credit to them both, a standing memorial of the beauty of one, the skill of the other, and the friendship of both; with as many other agreeable associations as Mr Elton's very promising attachment was likely to add.

Harriet was to sit again the next day; and Mr Elton, just as he ought, entreated for the permission of attending and reading to them again.

' By all means. We shall be most happy to consider you as one of the party.'

The same civilities and courtesies, the same success and satisfaction, took place on the morrow, and accompanied the whole progress of the picture, which was rapid and happy. Everybody who saw it was pleased, but Mr Elton was in continual raptures, and defended it through every criticism.

'Miss Woodhouse has given her friend the only beauty she wanted,' observed Mrs Weston to him, not in the least suspecting that she was addressing a lover.

'The expression of the eye is most correct, but Miss Smith has not those eyebrows and eyelashes. It is the fault of her face that she has them not.'

'Do you think so?' replied he. 'I cannot agree with you. It appears to me a most perfect resemblance in every feature. I never saw such a likeness in my life. We must allow for the effect of shade you know.'

'You have made her too tall, Emma,' said Mr Knightley.

.Emma knew that she had, but would not own it; and Mr Elton warmly added:

'Oh no—certainly not too tall—not in the least too tall. Consider, she is sitting down, which naturally presents a different—which in short gives exactly the idea—and the proportions must be preserved, you know. Proportions, fore-shortening—oh no! it gives one exactly the idea of such a height as Miss Smith's—exactly so, indeed.'

'It is very pretty,' said Mr Woodhouse. 'So prettily done! Just as your drawings always are, my dear. I do not know anybody who draws so well as you do. The only thing I do not thoroughly like is, that she seems to be sitting out-of-doors, with only a little shawl over her shoulders; and it makes one think she must catch cold.'

'But, my dear papa, it is supposed to be summer; a warm day in summer. Look at the tree.'

'But it is never safe to sit out-of-doors, my dear.'

'You, sir, may say anything,' cried Mr Elton, 'but I must confess that I regard it as a most happy thought the placing of Miss Smith out of doors; and the tree is touched with such inimitable spirit! Any other situation would have been much less in character. The *naïveté* of Miss Smith's manners—and altogether—oh, it is most admirable! I cannot keep my eyes from it. I never saw such a likeness.'

The next thing wanted was to get the picture framed; and here were a few difficulties. It must be done directly; it must be done in London; the order must go through the hands of some intelligent person whose taste could be depended on; and Isabella, the usual doer of all commissions, must not be applied to, because it was December, and Mr Woodhouse could not bear the idea of her stirring out of her house in the fogs of December. But no sooner was the distress known to Mr Elton than it was removed. His gallantry was always on the alert. ' Might he be trusted with the commission, what infinite pleasure should he have in executing it! he could ride to London at any time. It was impossible to say how much he should be gratified by being employed on such an errand.'

' He was too good!—she could not endure the thought!—she would not give him such a troublesome office for the world '—brought on the desired repetition of entreaties and assurances—and a very few minutes settled the business.

Mr Elton was to take the drawing to London, choose the frame, and give the directions; and Emma thought she could so pack it as to ensure its safety without much incommoding him, while he seemed mostly fearful of not being incommoded enough.

' What a precious deposit! ' said he, with a tender sigh, as he received it.

' This man is almost too gallant to be in love,' thought Emma. ' I should say so, but that I suppose there may be a hundred different ways of being in love. He is an excellent young man, and will suit Harriet exactly; it will be an " exactly so," as he says himself; but he does sigh and languish, and study for compliments rather more than I could endure as a principal. I come in for a pretty good share as a second. But it is his gratitude on Harriet's account.'

7

THE very day of Mr Elton's going to London produced a fresh occasion for Emma's services towards her friend. Harriet had been at Hartfield, as usual, soon after breakfast; and, after a time, had gone home to return again to dinner; she returned, and sooner than had been talked of, and with an agitated, hurried look, announcing something extraordinary to have happened which she was longing to tell. Half a minute brought it all out. She had heard, as soon as she got back to Mrs Goddard's, that Mr Martin had been there an hour before, and finding she was not at home, nor particularly expected, had left a little parcel for her from one of his sisters, and gone away; and, on opening this parcel, she had actually found, besides the two songs which she had lent Elizabeth to copy, a letter to herself; and this letter was from him—from Mr Martin—and contained a direct proposal of marriage. 'Who could have thought it? She was so surprised she did not know what to do. Yes, quite a proposal of marriage; and a very good letter, at least she thought so. And he wrote as if he really loved her very much—but she did not know—and so, she was come as fast as she could to ask Miss Woodhouse what she should do.' Emma was half ashamed of her friend for seeming so pleased and so doubtful.

'Upon my word,' she cried, 'the young man is determined not to lose anything for want of asking. He will connect himself well if he can.'

'Will you read the letter?' cried Harriet. 'Pray do, I'd rather you would.'

Emma was not sorry to be pressed. She read, and was surprised. The style of the letter was much above her expectation. There were not merely no grammatical errors, but as a composition it would not have disgraced a gentleman; the language, though plain, was strong and unaffected, and the sentiments it conveyed very much to the credit of the writer. It was short, but expressed good sense, warm attachment, liberality, propriety, even delicacy of feeling. She paused over it, while Harriet stood anxiously watching for her opinion, with a 'Well, well,' and was at last forced to add, 'Is it a good letter? or is it too short?'

'Yes, indeed, a very good letter,' replied Emma, rather slowly; 'so good a letter, Harriet, that, everything considered, I think one of his sisters must have helped him. I can hardly imagine the young man whom I saw talking with you the other day could express himself so well, if left quite to his own powers, and yet it is not the style of a woman; no, certainly, it is too strong and concise; not diffuse enough for a woman. No doubt he is a sensible man, and I suppose may have a natural talent for—thinks strongly and clearly—and when he takes a pen in hand, his thoughts naturally find proper words. It is so with some men. Yes, I understand the sort of mind. Vigorous, decided, with sentiments to a certain point not coarse. A better written letter, Harriet (returning it) than I had expected.'

'Well,' said the still waiting Harriet; 'well—and—and what shall I do?'

'What shall you do! in what respect? Do you mean with regard to this letter?'

'Yes.'

'But what are you in doubt of? You must answer it of course, and speedily.'

' Yes. But what shall I say? Dear Miss Woodhouse, do advise me.'

' Oh, no, no; the letter had much better be all your own. You will express yourself very properly, I am sure. There is no danger of your not being intelligible, which is the first thing. Your meaning must be unequivocal; no doubts or demurs; and such expressions of gratitude and concern for the pain you are inflicting as propriety requires, will present themselves unbidden to *your* mind, I am persuaded. *You* need not be prompted to write with the appearance of sorrow for his disappointment.'

' You think I ought to refuse him then?' said Harriet, looking down.

' Ought to refuse him! My dear Harriet, what do you mean? Are you in any doubt as to that? I thought—but I beg your pardon, perhaps I have been under a mistake. I certainly have been misunderstanding you, if you feel in doubt as to the *purport* of your answer. I had imagined you were consulting me only as to the wording of it.'

Harriet was silent. With a little reserve of manner, Emma continued:

' You mean to return a favourable answer, I collect.'

' No, I do not; that is, I do not mean—what shall I do? What would you advise me to do? Pray, dear Miss Woodhouse, tell me what I ought to do.'

' I shall not give you any advice, Harriet. I will have nothing to do with it. This is a point which you must settle with your own feelings.'

' I had no notion that he liked me so very much,' said Harriet, contemplating the letter. For a little while Emma persevered in her silence; but, beginning to apprehend the bewitching flattery of that letter might be too powerful, she thought it best to say:

' I lay it down as a general rule, Harriet, that if a woman *doubts* as to whether she would accept a man or not, she certainly ought to refuse him. If she can hesitate as to " Yes," she ought to say " No," directly. It is not a state to be safely entered into with doubtful feelings, with half a heart. I thought it my duty as a friend, and older than yourself, to say thus much to you. But do not imagine that I want to influence you.'

' Oh, no, I am sure you are a great deal too kind to— but if you would just advise me what I had best do—no, no, I do not mean that—as you say, one's mind ought to be quite made up— one should not be hesitating—it is a very serious thing. It will

be safer to say " No," perhaps. Do you think I had better say
" No? " '

'Not for the world,' said Emma, smiling graciously, ' would
I advise you either way. You must be the best judge of your own
happiness. If you prefer Mr Martin to every other person, if you
think him the most agreeable man you have ever been in company
with, why should you hesitate? You blush, Harriet. Does anybody else occur to you at this moment under such a definition?
Harriet, Harriet, do not deceive yourself; do not be run away
with by gratitude and compassion. At this moment whom are
you thinking of? '

The symptoms were favourable. Instead of answering, Harriet
turned away confused, and stood thoughtfully by the fire; and
though the letter was still in her hand, it was now mechanically
twisted about without regard. Emma waited the result with impatience, but not without strong hopes. At last, with some hesitation, Harriet said:

'Miss Woodhouse, as you will not give me your opinion, I
must do as well as I can by myself; and I have now quite determined, and really almost made up my mind to refuse Mr Martin.
Do you think I am right? '

'Perfectly, perfectly right, my dearest Harriet; you are doing
just what you ought. While you were at all in suspense, I kept
my feelings to myself, but now that you are so completely decided,
I have no hesitation in approving. Dear Harriet, I give myself
joy of this. It would have grieved me to lose your acquaintance,
which must have been the consequence of your marrying Mr
Martin. While you were in the smallest degree wavering, I said
nothing about it, because I would not influence; but it would
have been the loss of a friend to me. I could not have visited
Mrs Robert Martin, of Abbey Hill Farm. Now I am secure of
you for ever.'

Harriet had not surmised her own danger, but the idea of it
struck her forcibly.

'You could not have visited me! ' she cried, looking aghast.
'No, to be sure you could not; but I never thought of that before. That would have been too dreadful! What an escape!
Dear Miss Woodhouse, I would not give up the pleasure
and honour of being intimate with you for anything in the
world.'

'Indeed, Harriet, it would have been a severe pang to lose you;
but it must have been. You would have thrown yourself out of
all good society. I must have given you up.'

'Dear me! How should I ever have borne it? It would have killed me never to come to Hartfield any more.'

'Dear, affectionate creature! *You* banished to Abbey Mill Farm! *You* confined to the society of the illiterate and vulgar all your life! I wonder how the young man could have the assurance to ask it. He must have a pretty good opinion of himself.'

'I do not think he is conceited, either, in general,' said Harriet, her conscience opposing such censure; 'at least, he is very good-natured, and I shall always feel much obliged to him, and have a great regard for—but that is quite a different thing from—and you know, though he may like me, it does not follow that I should —and, certainly, I must confess that since my visiting here, I have seen people—and if one comes to compare them, person and manners, there is no comparison at all, *one* is so very hand-some and agreeable. However, I do really think Mr Martin a very amiable young man, and have a great opinion of him; and his being so much attached to me, and his writing such a letter; but as to leaving you, it is what I would not do upon any con-sideration.

'Thank you, thank you, my own sweet little friend. We will not be parted. A woman is not to marry a man merely because she is asked, or because he is attached to her, and can write a tolerable letter.'

'Oh, no; and it is but a short letter too.'

Emma felt the bad taste of her friend, but let it pass with a 'Very true: and it would be a small consolation to her, for the clownish manner which might be offending her every hour of the day, to know that her husband could write a good letter.'

'Oh yes, very. Nobody cares for a letter; the thing. is, to be always happy with pleasant companions. I am quite determined to refuse him. But how shall I do? What shall I say?'

Emma assured her there would be no difficulty in the answer, and advised its being written directly, which was agreed to, in the hope of her assistance; and though Emma continued to pro-test against any assistance being wanted, it was, in fact, given in the formation of every sentence. The looking over his letter again, in replying to it, had such a softening tendency, that it was particularly necessary to brace her up with a few decisive expressions; and she was so very much concerned at the idea of making him unhappy, and thought so much of what his mother and sisters would think and say, and was so anxious that they should not fancy her ungrateful, that Emma believed, if the young man had come in her way at that moment, he would have been accepted after all.

This letter, however, was written, and sealed, and sent. The business was finished, and Harriet safe. She was rather low all the evening; but Emma could allow for her amiable regrets, and sometimes relieved them by speaking of her own affection, sometimes by bringing forward the idea of Mr Elton.

'I shall never be invited to Abbey Mill again,' was said in rather a sorrowful tone.

'Nor, if you were, could I ever bear to part with you, my Harriet. You are a great deal too necessary at Hartfield to be spared to Abbey Mill.'

'And I am sure I should never want to go there; for I am never happy but at Hartfield.'

Some time afterwards it was, 'I think Mrs Goddard would be very much surprised if she knew what had happened. I am sure Miss Nash would; for Miss Nash thinks her own sister very well married, and it is only a linen-draper.'

'One should be sorry to see greater pride or refinement in the teacher of a school, Harriet. I dare say Miss Nash would envy you such an opportunity as this of being married. Even this conquest would appear valuable in her eyes. As to anything superior for you, I suppose she is quite in the dark. The attentions of a certain person can hardly be among the tittle-tattle of Highbury yet. Hitherto I fancy you and I are the only people to whom his looks and manners have explained themselves.'

Harriet blushed and smiled, and said something about wondering that people should like her so much. The idea of Mr Elton was certainly cheering; but still, after a time, she was tenderhearted again towards the rejected Mr Martin.

'Now he has got my letter,' said she softly. 'I wonder what they are all doing—whether his sisters know—if he is unhappy, they will be unhappy too. I hope he will not mind it so very much.'

'Let us think of those among our absent friends who are more cheerfully employed,' cried Emma. 'At this moment, perhaps, Mr Elton is showing your picture to his mother and sisters, telling how much more beautiful is the original, and after being asked for it five or six times, allowing them to hear your name—your own dear name.'

'My picture! But he has left my picture in Bond Street.'

'Has he so! Then I know nothing of Mr Elton. No, my dear little modest Harriet, depend upon it, the picture will not be in Bond Street till just before he mounts his horse to-morrow. It is his companion all this evening, his solace, his delight. It opens his designs to his family, it introduces you among them, it diffuses through the party those pleasantest feelings of our nature—eager curiosity and warm prepossession. How cheerful, how animated, how auspicious, how busy their imaginations all are!'

Harriet smiled again, and her smiles grew stronger.

8

HARRIET slept at Hartfield that night. For some weeks past she had been spending more than half her time there, and gradually getting to have a bedroom appropriated to herself; and Emma judged it best in every respect, safest and kindest, to keep her with them as much as possible just at present. She was obliged to go the next morning for an hour or two to Mrs Goddard's, but it was then to be settled that she should return to Hartfield, to make a regular visit of some days.

While she was gone, Mr Knightley called, and sat some time with Mr Woodhouse and Emma, till Mr Woodhouse, who had previously made up his mind to walk out, was persuaded by his daughter not to defer it, and was induced by the entreaties of both, though against the scruples of his own civilities, to leave Mr Knightley for that purpose. Mr Knightley, who had nothing of ceremony about him, was offering, by his short, decided answers, an amusing contrast to the protracted apologies and civil hesitations of the other.

'Well, I believe, if you will excuse me, Mr Knightley, if you will not consider me as doing a very rude thing, I shall take Emma's advice and go out for a quarter of an hour. As the sun is out, I believe I had better take my three turns while I can. I treat you without ceremony, Mr Knightley. We invalids think we are privileged people.'

'My dear sir, do not make a stranger of me.'

'I leave an excellent substitute in my daughter. Emma will be happy to entertain you. And therefore I think I will beg your excuse, and take my three turns—my winter walk.'

'You cannot do better, sir.'

'I would ask for the pleasure of your company, Mr Knightley, but I am a very slow walker, and my pace would be tedious to you; and, besides, you have another long walk before you, to Donwell Abbey.'

'Thank you, sir, thank you; I am going this moment myself;

and I think the sooner *you* go the better. I will fetch your great-coat and open the garden door for you.'

Mr Woodhouse at last was off; but Mr Knightley, instead of being immediately off likewise, sat down again, seemingly inclined for more chat. He began speaking of Harriet, and speaking of her with more voluntary praise than Emma had ever heard before.

' I cannot rate her beauty as you do,' said he; ' but she is a pretty little creature, and I am inclined to think very well of her disposition. Her character depends upon those she is with; but in good hands she will turn out a valuable woman.'

' I am glad you think so; and the good hands, I hope, may not be wanting.'

' Come,' said he, ' you are anxious for a compliment, so I will tell you that you have improved her. You have cured her of her schoolgirl's giggle; she really does you credit.'

' Thank you. I should be mortified, indeed, if I did not believe I had been of some use; but it is not everybody who will bestow praise where they may. *You* do not often overpower me with it.'

' You are expecting her again, you say, this morning?'

' Almost every moment. She has been gone longer already than she intended.'

' Something has happened to delay her; some visitors, perhaps.'

' Highbury gossips! Tiresome wretches!'

' Harriet may not consider everybody tiresome that you would.'

Emma knew this was too true for contradiction, and, therefore, said nothing. He presently added, with a smile:

' I do not pretend to fix on times or places, but I must tell you that I have good reason to believe your little friend will soon hear of something to her advantage.'

' Indeed! how so? of what sort?'

' A very serious sort, I assure you,' still smiling.

' Very serious! I can think of but one thing—who is in love with her? Who makes you their confidant?'

Emma was more than half in hopes of Mr Elton's having dropped a hint. Mr Knightley was a sort of general friend and adviser, and she knew Mr Elton looked up to him.

' I have reason to think,' he replied, ' that Harriet Smith will soon have an offer of marriage, and from a most unexceptionable quarter—Robert Martin is the man. Her visit to Abbey Mill, this summer, seems to have done his business. He is desperately in love, and means to marry her.'

' He is very obliging,' said Emma; ' but is he sure that Harriet means to marry him?'

'Well, well, means to make her an offer, then. Will that do? He came to the Abbey two evenings ago, on purpose to consult me about it. He knows I have a thorough regard for him and all his family, and, I believe, considers me as one of his best friends. He came to ask me whether I thought it would be imprudent in him to settle so early; whether I thought her too young—in short, whether I approved his choice altogether; having some apprehension, perhaps, of her being considered (especially since *your* making so much of her) as in a line of society above him. I was very much pleased with all that he said. I never hear better sense from any one than Robert Martin. He always speaks to the purpose; open, straightforward, and very well judging. He told me everything; his circumstances and plans, and what they all proposed doing in the event of his marriage. He is an excellent young man, both as son and brother. I had no hesitation in advising him to marry. He proved to me that he could afford it, and that being the case, I was convinced he could not do better. I praised the fair lady too, and altogether sent him away very happy. If he had never esteemed my opinion before, he would have thought highly of me then; and I dare say, left the house thinking me the best friend and counsellor man ever had. This happened the night before last. Now, as we may fairly suppose, he would not allow much time to pass before he spoke to the lady, and as he does not appear to have spoken yesterday, it is not unlikely that he should be at Mrs Goddard's to-day; and she may be detained by a visitor, without thinking him at all a tiresome wretch.'

'Pray, Mr Knightley,' said Emma, who had been smiling to herself through a great part of this speech, 'how do you know that Mr Martin did not speak yesterday?'

'Certainly,' replied he, surprised, 'I do not absolutely know it, but it may be inferred. Was not she the whole day with you?'

'Come,' said she, 'I will tell you something in return for what you have told me. He did speak yesterday—that is, he wrote, and was refused.'

This was obliged to be repeated before it could be believed; and Mr Knightley actually looked red with surprise and displeasure, as he stood up, in tall indignation, and said:

'Then she is a greater simpleton than I ever believed her. What is the foolish girl about?'

'Oh, to be sure,' cried Emma, 'it is always incomprehensible to a man, that a woman should ever refuse an offer of marriage.

A man always imagines a woman to be ready for anybody who asks her.'

' Nonsense! a man does not imagine any such thing. But what is the meaning of this? Harriet Smith refuse Robert Martin! Madness, if it is so; but I hope you are mistaken.'

' I saw her answer!—nothing could be clearer.'

' You saw her answer!—you wrote her answer too. Emma, this is your doing. You persuaded her to refuse him.'

' And if I did (which, however, I am far from allowing), I should not feel that I had done wrong. Mr Martin is a very respectable young man, but I cannot admit him to be Harriet's equal; and am rather surprised, indeed, that he should have ventured to address her. By your account he does seem to have had some scruples. It is a pity that they were ever got over.'

' Not Harriet's equal!' exclaimed Mr Knightley, loudly and warmly; and with calmer asperity added, a few moments afterwards, ' No, he is not her equal, indeed, for he is as much her superior in sense as in situation. Emma, your infatuation about that girl blinds you. What are Harriet Smith's claims, either of birth, nature, or education, to any connection higher than Robert Martin? She is the natural daughter of nobody knows whom, with probably no settled provision at all, and certainly no respectable relations. She is known only as parlour boarder at a common school. She is not a sensible girl, nor a girl of any information. She has been taught nothing useful, and is too young and too simple to have acquired anything herself. At her age she can have no experience; and, with her little wit, is not very likely ever to have any that can avail her. She is pretty, and she is good tempered, and that is all. My only scruple in advising the match was on his account, as being beneath his deserts, and a bad connection for him. I felt that, as to fortune, in all probability he might do much better, and that, as to a rational companion or a useful helpmate, he could not do worse. But I could not reason so to a man in love, and was willing to trust to there being no harm in her; to her having that sort of disposition, which, in good hands like his, might be easily led aright, and turn out very well. The advantage of the match I felt to be all on her side; and had not the smallest doubt (nor have I now) that there would be a general cry out upon her extreme good luck. Even *your* satisfaction I made sure of. It crossed my mind immediately that you would not regret your friend leaving Highbury, for the sake of her being settled so well. I remember saying to myself, " Even Emma, with all her partiality for Harriet, will think this a good match." '

' I cannot help wondering at your knowing so little of Emma as to say any such thing. What! think a farmer (and with all his sense and all his merit Mr Martin is nothing more) a good match for my intimate friend! Not regret her leaving Highbury, for the sake of marrying a man whom I could never admit as an acquaintance of my own! I wonder you should think it possible for me to have such feelings. I assure you mine are very different. I must think your statement by no means fair. You are not just to Harriet's claims. They would be estimated very differently by others as well as myself; Mr Martin may be the richest of the two, but he is undoubtedly her inferior as to rank in society. The sphere in which she moves is much above his. It would be a degradation.'

' A degradation to illegitimacy and ignorance to be married to a respectable, intelligent, gentleman-farmer! '

' As to the circumstances of her birth, though in a legal sense she may be called Nobody, it will not hold in common sense. She is not to pay for the offence of others, by being held below the level of those with whom she is brought up. There can scarcely be a doubt that her father is a gentleman—and a gentleman of fortune. Her allowance is very liberal; nothing has ever been grudged for her improvement or comfort. That she is a gentleman's daughter is indubitable to me; that she associates with gentlemen's daughters, no one, I apprehend, will deny. She is superior to Mr Robert Martin.'

' Whoever might be her parents,' said Mr Knightley, ' whoever may have had the charge of her, it does not appear to have been any part of their plan to introduce her into what you would call good society. After receiving a very indifferent education, she is left in Mrs Goddard's hands to shift as she can—to move, in short, in Mrs Goddard's line, to have Mrs Goddard's acquaintance. Her friends evidently thought this good enough for her; and it *was* good enough. She desired nothing better herself. Till you chose to turn her into a friend, her mind had no distaste for her own sex, nor any ambition beyond it. She was as happy as possible with the Martins in the summer. She had no sense of superiority then. If she has it now, you have given it. You have been no friend to Harriet Smith, Emma. Robert Martin would never have proceeded so far, if he had not felt persuaded of her not being disinclined to him. I know him well. He has too much real feeling to address any woman on the hap-hazard of selfish passion. And as to conceit, he is the furthest from it of any man I know. Depend upon it, he had encouragement.'

It was most convenient to Emma not to make a direct reply to this assertion; she chose rather to take up her own line of the subject again.

'You are a very warm friend to Mr Martin; but, as I said before, are unjust to Harriet. Harriet's claims to marry well are not so contemptible as you represent them. She is not a clever girl, but she has better sense than you are aware of, and does not deserve to have her understanding spoken of so slightingly. Waiving that point, however, and supposing her to be, as you describe her, only pretty and good-natured, let me tell you, that in the degree she possesses them, they are not trivial recommendations to the world in general, for she is, in fact, a beautiful girl, and must be thought so by ninety-nine people out of a hundred; and till it appears that men are much more philosophic on the subject of beauty than they are generally supposed, till they do fall in love with well-informed minds instead of handsome faces, a girl, with such loveliness as Harriet, had a certainty of being admired and sought after, of having the power of choosing from among many, consequently a claim to be nice. Her good nature, too, is not so very slight a claim, comprehending, as it does, real, thorough sweetness of temper and manner, a very humble opinion of herself, and a great readiness to be pleased with other people. I am very much mistaken if your sex in general would not think such beauty, and such temper, the highest claim a woman could possess.'

'Upon my word, Emma, to hear you abusing the reason you have, is almost enough to make me think so too. Better be without sense than misapply it as you do.'

'To be sure,' cried she playfully. 'I know *that* is the feeling of you all. I know that such a girl as Harriet is exactly what every man delights in—what at once bewitches his senses and satisfies his judgment. Oh, Harriet may pick and choose. Were you, yourself, ever to marry, she is the very woman for you. And is she, at seventeen, just entering into life, just beginning to be known, to be wondered at because she does not accept the first offer she receives? No—pray, let her have time to look about her.'

'I have always thought it a very foolish intimacy,' said Mr Knightley presently, ' though I have kept my thoughts to myself; but I now perceive that it will be a very unfortunate one for Harriet. You will puff her up with such ideas of her own beauty, and of what she has a claim to, that, in a little while, nobody within her reach will be good enough for her. Vanity working on a weak head produces every sort of mischief. Nothing so easy as for a young lady to raise her expectations too high. Miss Harriet Smith may not find offers of marriage flow in so fast, though she is a very pretty girl. Men of sense, whatever you may choose to say, do not want silly wives. Men of family would not be very fond of connecting themselves with a girl of such obscurity—and most prudent men would be afraid of the inconvenience and disgrace they might be involved in, when the mystery of her parentage came to be revealed. Let her marry Robert Martin, and she is safe, respectable, and happy for ever; but if you encourage her to expect to marry greatly, and teach her to be satisfied with nothing less than a man of consequence and large fortune, she may be a parlour boarder at Mrs Goddard's all the rest of her life—or, at least (for Harriet Smith is a girl who will marry somebody or other) till she grow desperate, and is glad to catch at the old writing-master's son.'

'We think so very differently on this point, Mr Knightley, that there can be no use in canvassing it. We shall only be making each other more angry. But as to my *letting* her marry Robert Martin, it is impossible; she has refused him, and so decidedly, I think, as must prevent any second application. She must abide by the evil of having refused him, whatever it may be; and as to the refusal itself, I will not pretend to say that I might not influence her a little; but I assure you there was very little for me or for anybody to do. His appearance is so much against him, and his manner so bad, that if she ever were disposed to favour him, she is not now. I can imagine, that, before she had seen anybody superior, she might tolerate him. He was the brother of her friends, and he took pains to please her; and altogether, having seen nobody better (that must have been his great assistant), she might not, while she was at Abbey Mill, find him disagreeable. But the case is altered now. She knows now what gentlemen are; and nothing but a gentleman in education and manner has any chance with Harriet.'

'Nonsense, arrant nonsense, as ever was talked!' cried Mr Knightley. 'Robert Martin's manners have sense, sincerity, and good humour to recommend them; and his mind has more true gentility than Harriet Smith could understand.'

Emma made no answer, and tried to look cheerfully unconcerned, but was really feeling uncomfortable, and wanting him very much to be gone. She did not repent what she had done; she still thought herself a better judge of such a point of female right and refinement than he could be; but yet she had a sort of habitual respect for his judgment in general, which made her dislike having it so loudly against her; and to have him sitting just opposite to her in angry state was very disagreeable. Some minutes passed in this unpleasant silence, with only one attempt on Emma's side to talk of the weather, but he made no answer. He was thinking. The result of his thoughts appeared at last in these words:

' Robert Martin has no great loss—if he can but think so; and I hope it will not be long before he does. Your views for Harriet are best known to yourself; but as you make no secret of your love of match-making, it is fair to suppose that views, and plans, and projects you have; and as a friend I shall just hint to you, that if Elton is the man, I think it will be all labour in vain.'

Emma laughed and disclaimed. He continued:

' Depend upon it, Elton will not do. Elton is a very good sort of man, and a very respectable vicar of Highbury, but not at all likely to make an imprudent match. He knows the value of a good income as well as anybody. Elton may talk sentimentally, but he will act rationally. He is as well acquainted with his own claims as you can be with Harriet's. He knows that he is a very handsome young man, and a great favourite wherever he goes; and from his general way of talking in unreserved moments, when there are only men present, I am convinced that he does not mean to throw himself away. I have heard him speak with great animation of a large family of young ladies that his sisters are intimate with, who have all twenty thousand pounds apiece.'

' I am very much obliged to you,' said Emma, laughing again. ' If I had set my heart on Mr Elton's marrying Harriet, it would have been very kind to open my eyes; but at present I only want to keep Harriet to myself. I have done with match-making, indeed. I could never hope to equal my own doings at Randalls. I shall leave off while I am well.'

' Good morning to you,' said he, rising, and walking off abruptly. He was very much vexed. He felt the disappointment of the young man, and was mortified to have been the means of promoting it, by the sanction he had given; and the part which, he was persuaded, Emma had taken in the affair was provoking him exceedingly.

Emma remained in a state of vexation too; but there was more indistinctness in the causes of hers than in his. She did not always feel so absolutely satisfied with herself, so entirely convinced that her opinions were right and her adversary's wrong, as Mr Knightley. He walked off in more complete self-approbation than he left for her. She was not so materially cast down, however, but that a little time and the return of Harriet were very adequate restoratives. Harriet's staying away so long was beginning to make her uneasy. The possibility of the young man's coming to Mrs Goddard's that morning, and meeting with Harriet and pleading his own cause, gave alarming ideas. The dread of such a failure, after all, became the prominent uneasiness; and when Harriet appeared, and in very good spirits, and without having any such reason to give for her long absence, she felt a satisfaction which settled her with her own mind, and convinced her that, let Mr Knightley think or say what he would, she had done nothing which woman's friendship and woman's feelings would not justify.

He had frightened her a little about Mr Elton; but when she considered that Mr Knightley could not have observed him as she had done, neither with the interest nor (she must be allowed to tell herself, in spite of Mr Knightley's pretensions) with the skill of such an observer on such a question as herself, that he had spoken it hastily and in anger, she was able to believe, that he had rather said what he wished resentfully to be true, than what he knew anything about. He certainly might have heard Mr Elton speak with more unreserve than she had ever done, and Mr Elton might not be of an imprudent, inconsiderate disposition, as to money matters; he might naturally be rather attentive than otherwise to them; but then, Mr Knightley did not make due allowance for the influence of a strong passion, at war with all interested motives. Mr Knightley saw no such passion, and of course thought nothing of its effects; but she saw too much of it to feel a doubt of its overcoming any hesitations that a reasonable prudence might originally suggest; and more than a reasonable, becoming degree of prudence, she was very sure did not belong to Mr Elton.

Harriet's cheerful look and manner established hers; she came back, not to think of Mr Martin, but to talk of Mr Elton. Miss Nash had been telling her something, which she repeated immediately with great delight. Mr Perry had been to Mrs Goddard's to attend a sick child, and Miss Nash had seen him; and he had told Miss Nash that as he was coming back yesterday from Clayton Park he had met Mr Elton, and found, to his great surprise, that Mr Elton was actually on his road to London, and not meaning to return till the morrow, though it was the whist club night, which he had been never known to miss before; and Mr Perry had remonstrated with him about it, and told him how shabby it was in him, their best player, to absent himself, and tried very much to persuade him to put off his journey only one day; but it would not do; Mr Elton had been determined to go on, and had said in a *very particular* way indeed, that he was going on business which he would not put off for any inducement in the world; and something about a very enviable commission, and being the bearer of something exceedingly precious. Mr Perry could not quite understand him, but he was very sure there must be a *lady* in the case, and he told him so; and Mr Elton only looked very conscious and smiling, and rode off in great spirits. Miss Nash had told her all this, and had talked a great deal more about Mr Elton; and said, looking so very significantly at her, ' that she did not pretend to understand what his business might be, but she only knew that any woman whom Mr Elton could prefer, she should think the luckiest woman in the world; for, beyond a doubt, Mr Elton had not his equal for beauty or agreeableness.'

9

Mr Knightley might quarrel with her, but Emma could not quarrel with herself. He was so much displeased, that it was longer than usual before he came to Hartfield again; and when they did meet, his grave looks showed that she was not forgiven. She was sorry but could not repent. On the contrary, her plans and proceedings were more and more justified, and endeared to her by the general appearances of the next few days.

The Picture, elegantly framed, came safely to hand soon after Mr Elton's return, and being hung over the mantelpiece of the common sitting-room, he got up to look at it, and sighed out his half sentences of admiration, just as he ought; and as for Harriet's feelings, they were vividly forming themselves into as strong and steady an attachment as her youth and sort of mind admitted. Emma was soon perfectly satisfied of Mr Martin's being no otherwise remembered, than as he furnished a contrast with Mr Elton, of the utmost advantage to the latter.

Her views of improving her little friend's mind, by a great deal of useful reading and conversation, had never yet led to more than a few first chapters, and the intention of going on to-morrow. It was much easier to chat than to study; much pleasanter to let her imagination range and work at Harriet's fortune, than to be labouring to enlarge her comprehension, or exercise it on sober facts; and the only literary pursuit which engaged Harriet at present, the only mental provision she was making for the evening of life, was the collection and transcribing all the riddles of every sort that she could meet with, into a thin quarto of hot-pressed paper, made up by her friend, and ornamented with cyphers and trophies.

In this age of literature, such collections on a very grand scale are not uncommon. Miss Nash, head-teacher at Mrs Goddard's, had written out at least three hundred; and Harriet, who had taken the first hint of it from her, hoped, with Miss Woodhouse's help, to get a great many more. Emma assisted with her invention, memory, and taste; and as Harriet wrote a very pretty hand, it was likely to be an arrangement of the first order, in form as well as quantity.

Mr. Woodhouse was almost as much interested in the business as the girls, and tried very often to recollect something worth their putting in. ' So many clever riddles as there used to be when he was young—he wondered he could not remember them; but he hoped he should in time.' And it always ended in ' Kitty, a fair but frozen maid.'

His good friend Perry, too, whom he had spoken to on the subject, did not at present recollect anything of the riddle kind; but he had desired Perry to be upon the watch, and as he went about so much, something, he thought, might come from that quarter.

It was by no means his daughter's wish that the intellects of Highbury in general should be put under requisition. Mr Elton was the only one whose assistance she asked. He was invited to contribute any really good enigmas, charades or conundrums, that he might recollect; and she had the pleasure of seeing him most intently at work with his recollections; and at the same time, as she could perceive, most earnestly careful that nothing ungallant, nothing that did not breathe a compliment to the sex, should pass his lips. They owed to him their two or three politest puzzles; and the joy and exultation with which at last he recalled, and rather sentimentally recited, that well known charade:

> My first doth affliction denote,
>   Which my second is destin'd to feel;
> And my whole is the best antidote
>   That affliction to soften and heal,

made her quite sorry to acknowledge that they had transcribed it some pages ago already.

' Why will not you write one yourself for us, Mr Elton? '
said she; ' that is the only security for its freshness; and nothing
could be easier to you.'

' Oh, no, he had never written, hardly ever, anything of the
kind in his life. The stupidest fellow! He was afraid not even
Miss Woodhouse '—he stopped a moment—' or Miss Smith could
inspire him.'

The very next day, however, produced some proof of inspira-
tion. He called for a few moments, just to leave a piece of paper
on the table containing, as he said, a charade which a friend of his
had addressed to a young lady, the object of his admiration; but
which, from his manner, Emma was immediately convinced must
be his own.

' I do not offer it for Miss Smith's collection,' said he. "Being
my friend's, I have no right to expose it in any degree to the
public eye, but perhaps you may not dislike looking at it.'

The speech was more to Emma than to Harriet, which Emma
could understand. There was deep consciousness about him, and
he found it easier to meet her eyes than her friend's. He was
gone the next moment; after another moment's pause:

' Take it,' said Emma, smiling, and pushing the paper towards
Harriet—' it is for you. Take your own.'

But Harriet was in a tremor, and could not touch it; and Emma, never loath to be first, was obliged to examine it herself.

To Miss ———

CHARADE

My first displays the wealth and pomp of kings,
  Lords of the earth! their luxury and ease.
Another view of man, my second brings,
  Behold him there, the monarch of the seas!

But ah! united, what reverse we have!
  Man's boasted power and freedom, all are flown:
Lord of the earth and sea, he bends a slave,
  And woman, lovely woman, reigns alone.

Thy ready wit the word will soon supply,
May its approval beam in that soft eye!

She cast her eye over it, pondered, caught the meaning, read
it through again to be quite certain, and quite mistress of the

lines, and then passing it to Harriet, sat happily smiling, and saying to herself, while Harriet was puzzling over the paper in all the confusion of hope and dullness, 'Very well, Mr Elton, very well, indeed. I have read worse charades. *Courtship*—a very good hint. I give you credit for it. This is feeling your way. This is saying very plainly—" Pray, Miss Smith, give me leave to pay my addresses to you. Approve my charade and my attentions in the same glance."

May its approval beam in that soft eye!

Harriet exactly. Soft is the very word for her eye—of all epithets, the justest that could be given.

Thy ready wit the word will soon supply.

Humph—Harriet's ready wit. All the better. A man must be very much in love indeed, to describe her so. Ah! Mr Knightley, I wish you had the benefit of this; I think this would convince you. For once in your life you would be obliged to own yourself mistaken. An excellent charade, indeed, and very much to the purpose. Things must come to a crisis soon now.'

She was obliged to break off from these very pleasant observations, which were otherwise of a sort to run into great length, by the eagerness of Harriet's wondering questions.

'What can it be, Miss Woodhouse? —what can it be? I have not an idea—I cannot guess it in the least. What can it possibly be? Do try to find it out, Miss Woodhouse. Do help me. I never saw anything so hard. Is it kingdom? I wonder who the friend was—and who could be the young lady. Do you think it is a good one? Can it be woman?

And woman, lovely woman, reigns alone.

Can it be Neptune?

Behold him there, the monarch of the seas!

Or a trident? or a mermaid? or a shark? Oh, no; shark is only one syllable. It must be very clever, or he would not have brought it. Oh, Miss Woodhouse, do you think we shall ever find it out?'

'Mermaids and sharks! Nonsense! My dear Harriet, what are you thinking of? Where would be the use of his bringing us a charade made by a friend upon a mermaid or a shark? Give me the paper and listen.

" For Miss————," read Miss Smith,

> My first displays the wealth and pomp of kings,
>   Lords of the earth! their luxury and ease.

That is *court*.

> Another view of man, my second brings;
>   Behold him there, the monarch of the seas!

That is *ship*—plain as it can be. Now for the cream.

> But ah! united (*courtship*, you know), what reverse
>   we have!
> Man's boasted power and freedom, all are flown:
> Lord of the earth and sea, he bends a slave,
> And woman, lovely woman, reigns alone.

A very proper compliment! and then follows the application which I think, my dear Harriet, you cannot find much difficulty in comprehending. Read it in comfort to yourself. There can be no doubt of its being written for you and to you.'

Harriet could not long resist so delightful a persuasion. She read the concluding lines, and was all flutter and happiness. She could not speak. But she was not wanted to speak. It was enough for her to feel. Emma spoke for her.

'There is so pointed and so particular a meaning in this compliment,' said she, ' that I cannot have a doubt as to Mr Elton's intentions. You are his object—and you will soon receive the completest proof of it. I thought it must be so. I thought I could not be so deceived; but now it is clear; the state of his mind is as clear and decided as my wishes on the subject have been ever since I knew you. Yes, Harriet, just so long have I been wanting the very circumstance to happen which has happened. I could never tell whether an attachment between you and Mr Elton were most desirable or most natural. Its probability and its eligibility have really so equalled each other! I am very happy. I congratulate you, my dear Harriet, with all my heart. This is an attachment which a woman may well feel proud in creating. This is a connection which offers nothing but good. It will give you everything that you want—consideration, independence, a proper home—it will fix you in the centre of all your real friends, close to Hartfield and to me, and confirm our intimacy for ever. This, Harriet, is an alliance which can never raise a blush in either of us.'

'Dear Miss Woodhouse!' and 'Dear Miss Woodhouse!' was all that Harriet, with many tender embraces, could articulate at first; but when they did arrive at something more like conversation, it was sufficiently clear to her friend that she saw, felt, anticipated, and remembered just as she ought. Mr Elton's superiority had very ample acknowledgment.

'Whatever you say is always right,' cried Harriet, 'and therefore I suppose, and believe, and hope it must be so; but otherwise I could not have imagined it. It is so much beyond anything I deserve. Mr Elton, who might marry anybody! There cannot be two opinions about *him*. He is so very superior. Only think of those sweet verses—" To Miss——." Dear me, how clever! Could it really be meant for me?'

'I cannot make a question, or listen to a question about that. It is a certainty. Receive it on my judgment. It is a sort of prologue to the play, a motto to the chapter; and will be soon followed by matter-of-fact prose.'

'It is a sort of thing which nobody could have expected. I am sure, a month ago, I had no more idea myself. The strangest things do take place!'

'When Miss Smiths and Mr Eltons get acquainted—they do indeed—and really it is strange; it is out of the common course that what is so evidently, so palpably desirable—what courts the pre-arrangement of other people—should so immediately shape itself into the proper form. You and Mr Elton are by situation called together; you belong to one another by every circumstance of your respective homes. Your marrying will be equal to the match at Randalls. There does seem to be something in the air of Hartfield which gives love exactly the right direction, and sends it into the very channel where it ought to flow.

The course of true love never did run smooth—

A Hartfield edition of Shakespeare would have a long note on that passage.'

'That Mr Elton should really be in love with me—me, of all people, who did not know him, to speak to him at Michaelmas. And he, the very handsomest man that ever was, and a man that everybody looks up to, quite like Mr Knightley. His company so sought after, that everybody says he need not eat a single meal by himself if he does not choose it; that he has more invitations than there are days in the week. And so excellent in the Church! Miss Nash has put down all the texts he has ever preached from since he came to Highbury. Dear me! When I look back to the first time I saw him! How little did I think! The two Abbots and I ran into the front room, and peeped through the blind when we heard he was going by, and Miss Nash came and scolded us away, and stayed to look through herself; however, she called me back presently, and let me look too, which was very good-natured. And how beautiful we thought he looked! He was arm-in-arm with Mr Cole.'

'This is an alliance which, whoever—whatever your friends may be, must be agreeable to them, provided, at least, they have common sense; and we are not to be addressing our conduct to fools. If they are anxious to see you *happily* married, here is a man whose amiable character gives every assurance of it; if they wish to have you settled in the same country and circle which they have chosen to place you in, here it will be accomplished; and if their only object is that you should, in the common phrase, be *well* married, here is the comfortable fortune, the respectable establishment, the rise in the world which must satisfy them.'

'Yes, very true. How nicely you talk! I love to hear you. You understand everything. You and Mr Elton are one as clever as the other. This charade! If I had studied a twelvemonth, I could never have made anything like it.'

'I thought he meant to try his skill, by his manner of declining it yesterday.'

'I do think it is, without exception, the best charade I ever read.'

'I never read one more to the purpose, certainly.'

'It is as long again as almost all we have had before.'

'I do not consider its length as particularly in its favour. Such things in general cannot be too short.'

Harriet was too intent on the lines to hear. The most satisfactory comparisons were rising in her mind.

'It is one thing,' said she presently, her cheeks in a glow, 'to have very good sense in a common way, like everybody else, and if there is anything to say, to sit down and write a letter, and say just what you must, in a short way; and another to write verses and charades like this.'

Emma could not have desired a more spirited rejection of Mr Martin's prose.

'Such sweet lines!' continued Harriet, 'these two last! But

how shall I ever be able to return the paper, or say I have found it out? Oh, Miss Woodhouse, what can we do about that?'

'Leave it to me. You do nothing. He will be here this evening, I dare say, and then I will give it him back, and some nonsense or other will pass between us, and you shall not be committed. Your soft eyes shall choose their own time for beaming. Trust to me.'

'Oh, Miss Woodhouse, what a pity that I must not write this beautiful charade into my book; I am sure I have not got one half so good.'

'Leave out the two last lines, and there is no reason why you should not write it into your book.'

'Oh, but those two lines are—— '

'The best of all. Granted—for private enjoyment; and for private enjoyment keep them. They are not at all the less written, you know, because you divide them. The couplet does not cease to be, nor does its meaning change. But take it away, and all *appropriation* ceases, and a very pretty gallant charade remains, fit for any collection. Depend upon it, he would not like to have his charade slighted much better than his passion. A poet in love must be encouraged in both capacities, or neither. Give me the book. I will write it down, and then there can be no possible reflection on you.'

Harriet submitted, though her mind could hardly separate the parts, so as to feel quite sure that her friend were not writing down a declaration of love. It seemed too precious an offering for any degree of publicity.

'I shall never let that book go out of my own hands,' said she.

'Very well,' replied Emma, 'a most natural feeling, and the longer it lasts, the better I shall be pleased. But here is my father coming; you will not object to my reading the charade to him. It will be giving him so much pleasure. He loves anything of the sort, and especially anything that pays woman a compliment. He has the tenderest spirit of gallantry towards us all. You must let me read it to him.'

Harriet looked grave.

'My dear Harriet, you must not refine too much upon this charade. You will betray your feelings improperly, if you are too conscious and too quick, and appear to affix more meaning or even quite all the meaning which may be affixed to it. Do not be overpowered by such a little tribute of admiration. If he had been anxious for secrecy, he would not have left the paper while I was by, but he rather pushed it towards me than towards you. Do not let us be too solemn on the business He has encouragement enough to proceed, without our sighing out our souls over this charade.'

'Oh, no; I hope I shall not be ridiculous about it. Do as you please.'

Mr Woodhouse came in, and very soon led to the subject again, by the recurrence of his very frequent inquiry of 'Well, my dears, how does your book go on? Have you got anything fresh?'

'Yes, papa; we have something to read you, something quite fresh. A piece of paper was found on the table this morning (dropped, we suppose, by a fairy) containing a very pretty charade, and we have just copied it in.'

She read it to him, just as he liked to have anything read, slowly and distinctly, and two or three times over, with explanations of every part as she proceeded; and he was very much pleased, and, as she had foreseen, especially struck with the complimentary conclusion.

'Aye, that's very just, indeed; that's very properly said. Very true. "Woman, lovely woman." It is such a pretty charade, my dear, that I can easily guess what fairy brought it. Nobody could have written so prettily but you, Emma.'

Emma only nodded and smiled. After a little thinking, and a very tender sigh, he added:

'Ah, it is no difficulty to see who you take after. Your dear mother was so clever at all those things. If I had but her memory. But I can remember nothing; not even that particular riddle which you have heard me mention; I can only recollect the first stanza; and there are several:

> Kitty, a fair but frozen maid,
>   Kindled a flame I yet deplore;
> The hoodwink'd boy I called to aid,
> Though of his near approach afraid,
>   So fatal to my suit before.

And that is all that I can recollect of it; but it is very clever all the way through. But I think, my dear, you said you had got it.'

'Yes, papa, it is written out in our second page. We copied it from the *Elegant Extracts*. It was Garrick's, you know.'

'Aye, very true—I wish I could recollect more of it:

> Kitty, a fair but frozen maid.

The name makes me think of poor Isabella; for she was very near being christened Catherine, after her grandmamma. I hope we shall have her here next week. Have you thought, my dear, where you shall put her, and what room there will be for the children?'

'Oh, yes; she will have her own room of course; the room she always has; and there is the nursery for the children—just as usual, you know. Why should there be any change?'

'I do not know, my dear; but it is so long since she was here— not since last Easter, and then only for a few days. Mr John Knightley's being a lawyer is very inconvenient. Poor Isabella! she is sadly taken away from us all; and how sorry she will be, when she comes, not to see Miss Taylor here.'

'She will not be surprised, papa, at least.'

'I do not know, my dear. I am sure I was very much surprised when I first heard she was going to be married.'

'We must ask Mr and Mrs Weston to dine with us, while Isabella is here.'

'Yes, my dear, if there is time. But' (in a very depressed tone) 'she is coming for only one week. There will not be time for anything.'

'It is unfortunate that they cannot stay longer, but it seems a case of necessity. Mr John Knightley must be in town again on the 28th; and we ought to be thankful, papa, that we are to have the whole of the time they can give to the country, that two or three days are not to be taken out for the Abbey. Mr Knightley promises to give up his claim this Christmas, though you know it is longer since they were with him than with us.'

'It would be very hard, indeed, my dear, if poor Isabella were to be anywhere but at Hartfield.'

Mr Woodhouse could never allow for Mr Knightley's claims on his brother, or anybody's claims on Isabella, except his own. He sat musing a little while, and then said:

'But I do not see why poor Isabella should be obliged to go back so soon, though he does. I think, Emma, I shall try and persuade her to stay longer with us. She and the children might stay very well.'

'Ah, papa, that is what you never have been able to accomplish, and I do not think you ever will. Isabella cannot bear to stay behind her husband.'

This was too true for contradiction. Unwelcome as it was, Mr Woodhouse could only give a submissive sigh; and as Emma saw his spirits affected by the idea of his daughter's attachment to her husband, she immediately led to such a branch of the subject as must raise them.

'Harriet must give us as much of her company as she can while my brother and sister are here. I am sure she will be pleased with the children. We are very proud of the children, are not we, papa? I wonder which she will think the handsomest, Henry or John?'

'Aye, I wonder which she will. Poor little dears, how glad they will be to come. They are very fond of being at Hartfield, Harriet.'

'I dare say they are, sir. I am sure I do not know who is not.'

'Henry is a fine boy, but John is very like his mamma. Henry is the eldest; he was named after me, not after his father. John, the second, is named after his father. Some people are surprised, I believe, that the eldest was not, but Isabella would have him called Henry, which I thought very pretty of her. And he is a very clever boy, indeed. They are all remarkably clever; and they have so many pretty ways. They will come and stand by my chair and say, " Grandpapa, can you give me a bit of string? " and once Henry asked me for a knife, but I told him knives were only made for grandpapas. I think their father is too rough with them very often.'

'He appears rough to you,' said Emma, 'because you are so very gentle yourself; but if you could compare him with other papas, you would not think him rough. He wishes his boys to be active and hardy; and if they misbehave, can give them a sharp word now and then; but he is an affectionate father—certainly Mr John Knightley is an affectionate father. The children are all fond of him.'

'And then their uncle comes in and tosses them up to the ceiling in a very frightful way.'

'But they like it, papa; there is nothing they like so much. It is such enjoyment to them, that if their uncle did not lay down the rule of their taking turns, whichever began would never give way to the other.'

'Well, I cannot understand it.'

'That is the case with us all, papa. One half of the world cannot understand the pleasures of the other.'

Later in the morning, and just as the girls were going to separate, in preparation for the regular four o'clock dinner, the hero of this inimitable charade walked in again. Harriet turned away; but Emma could receive him with the usual smile, and her quick eye soon discerned in his the consciousness of having made a push, of having thrown a die; and she imagined he was come to see how it might turn up. His ostensible reason, however, was to ask whether Mr Woodhouse's party could be made up in the evening without him, or whether he should be in the smallest degree necessary at Hartfield. If he were, everything else must give way; but otherwise his friend Cole had been saying so much about his dining with him—had made such a point of it—that he had promised him conditionally to come.

Emma thanked him, but could not allow of his disappointing his friend on their account; her father was sure of his rubber. He re-urged—she re-declined; and he seemed then about to make his bow, when, taking the paper from the table, she returned it.

'Oh, here is the charade you were so obliging as to leave with us; thank you for the sight of it. We admired it so much that I have ventured to write it into Miss Smith's collection. Your friend will not take it amiss, I hope. Of course, I have not transcribed beyond the first eight lines.'

Mr Elton certainly did not very well know what to say. He looked rather doubtingly—rather confused; said something about 'honour,'—glanced at Emma and at Harriet, and then, seeing the book open on the table, took it up, and examined it very attentively. With the view of passing off an awkward moment, Emma smilingly said:

'You must make my apologies to your friend; but so good a charade must not be confined to one or two. He may be sure of every woman's approbation while he writes with such gallantry.'

'I have no hesitation in saying,' replied Mr Elton, though hesitating a good deal while he spoke—' I have no hesitation in saying—at least if my friend feels at all as *I* do—I have not the smallest doubt that, could he see his little effusion honoured as *I* see it (looking at the book again and replacing it on the table), he would consider it as the proudest moment of his life.'

After this speech he was gone as soon as possible. Emma could not think it too soon; for with all his good and agreeable qualities there was a sort of parade in his speeches which was very apt to incline her to laugh. She ran away to indulge the inclination, leaving the tender and the sublime of pleasure to Harriet's share.

THOUGH now the middle of December, there had yet been no weather to prevent the young ladies from tolerably regular exercise; and on the morrow, Emma had a charitable visit to pay to a poor sick family who liveᴅ a little way out of Highbury.

Their road to this detached cottage was down Vicarage Lane, a lane leading at right angles from the broad, though irregular, main street of the place; and, as may be inferred, containing the blessed abode of Mr Elton. A few inferior dwellings were first to be passed, and then, about a quarter of a mile down the lane, rose the vicarage, an old and not very good house, almost as close to the road as it could be. It had no advantage of situation; but had been very much smartened up by the present proprietor; and, such as it was, there could be no possibility of the two friends passing it without a slackened pace and observing eyes. Emma's remark was:

'There it is. There go you and your riddle book one of these days.' Harriet's was:

'Oh, what a sweet house! How very beautiful! There are the yellow curtains that Miss Nash admires so much.'

'I do not often walk this way *now*,' said Emma, as they proceeded, ' but *then* there will be an inducement, and I shall gradually get intimately acquainted with all the hedges, gates, pools, and pollards, of this part of Highbury.'

Harriet, she found, had never in her life been within side the vicarage; and her curiosity to see it was so extreme, that, considering exteriors and probabilities, Emma could only class it as a proof of love, with Mr Elton's seeing ready wit in her.

'I wish we could contrive it,' said she; 'but I cannot think of any tolerable pretence for going in; no servant that I want to inquire about of his housekeeper—no message from my father.'

She pondered, but could think of nothing. After a mutual silence of some minutes, Harriet thus began again:

'I do so wonder, Miss Woodhouse, that you should not be married, or going to be married—so charming as you are.'

Emma laughed, and replied:

'My being charming, Harriet, is not quite enough to induce me to marry; I must find other people charming—one other person at least. And I am not only not going to be married at present, but have very little intention of ever marrying at all.'

'Ah, so you say, but I cannot believe it.'

'I must see somebody very superior to any one I have seen yet, to be tempted; Mr Elton, you know' (recollecting herself) 'is out of the question; and I do *not* wish to see any such person. I would rather not be tempted. I cannot really change for the better. If I were to marry, I must expect to repent it.'

'Dear me!—it is so odd to hear a woman talk so!'

'I have none of the usual inducements of women to marry. Were I to fall in love, indeed, it would be a different thing; but I never have been in love; it is not my way, or my nature; and I do not think I ever shall. And, without love, I am sure I should be a fool to change such a situation as mine. Fortune I do not want; employment I do not want; consequence I do not want; I believe few married women are half as much mistress of their husband's house as I am of Hartfield; and never, never could I expect to be so truly beloved and important; so always first and always right in any man's eyes as I am in my father's.'

'But then, to be an old maid at last, like Miss Bates!'

'That is as formidable an image as you could present, Harriet; and if I thought I should ever be like Miss Bates—so silly, so satisfied, so smiling, so prosing, so undistinguishing, and unfastidious, and so apt to tell everything relative to everybody about me, I would marry to-morrow. But between *us*, I am convinced there never can be any likeness, except in being unmarried.'

'But still, you will be an old maid—and that's so dreadful!'

'Never mind, Harriet, I shall not be a poor old maid; and it is poverty only which makes celibacy contemptible to a generous public! A single woman with a very narrow income must be a ridiculous, disagreeable old maid! the proper sport of boys and girls; but a single woman of good fortune is always respectable, and may be as sensible and pleasant as anybody else! And the distinction is not quite so much against the candour and common sense of the world as appears at first; for a very narrow income has a tendency to contract the mind, and sour the temper. Those who can barely live, and who live perforce in a very small, and generally very inferior, society, may well be illiberal and cross. This does not apply, however, to Miss Bates; she is only too good-natured and too silly to suit me; but, in general, she is very much to the taste of everybody, though single, and though poor. Poverty certainly has not contracted her mind; I really believe, if she had only a shilling in the world, she would be very likely to give away sixpence of it; and nobody is afraid of her—that is a great charm.'

'Dear me! but what shall you do? How shall you employ yourself when you grow old?'

'If I know myself, Harriet, mine is an active, busy mind, with a great many independent resources; and I do not perceive why I should be more in want of employment at forty or fifty than one-and-twenty. Woman's usual occupations of eye, and hand, and mind, will be as open to me then as they are now, or with no important variation. If I draw less, I shall read more; if I give up music, I shall take to carpet-work. And as for objects of interest, objects for the affections, which is, in truth, the great point of inferiority, the want of which is really the great evil to be avoided in *not* marrying, I shall be very well off, with all the children of a sister I love so much to care about. There will be enough of them in all probability, to supply every sort of sensation that declining life can need. There will be enough for every hope and every fear; and though my attachment to none can equal that of a parent, it suits my ideas of comfort better than what is warmer and blinder. My nephews and nieces: I shall often have a niece with me.'

'Do you know Miss Bates's niece? That is, I know you must have seen her a hundred times—but are you acquainted?'

'Oh, yes; we are always forced to be acquainted whenever she comes to Highbury. By the bye, *that* is almost enough to put one out of conceit with a niece. Heaven forbid, at least, that I should ever bore people half so much about all the Knightleys together as she does about Jane Fairfax. One is sick of the very name of Jane Fairfax. Every letter from her is read forty times over; her compliments to all friends go round and round again; and if she does but send her aunt the pattern of a stomacher, or knit a pair of garters for her grandmother, one hears of nothing else for a month. I wish Jane Fairfax very well, but she tires me to death.'

They were now approaching the cottage, and all idle topics were superseded. Emma was very compassionate; and the distresses of the poor were as sure of relief from her personal attention and kindness, her counsel and her patience, as from her purse. She understood their ways, could allow for their ignorance and their temptations, had no romantic expectations of extraordinary virtue from those for whom education had done so little, entered into their troubles with ready sympathy, and always gave her assistance with as much intelligence as goodwill. In the present instance it was sickness and poverty together which she came to visit; and after remaining there as long as she could give comfort or advice, she quitted the cottage with such an impression of the scene as made her say to Harriet, as they walked away:

'These are the sights, Harriet, to do one good. How trifling they make everything else appear! I feel now as if I could think of nothing but these poor creatures all the rest of the day; and yet who can say how soon it may all vanish from my mind?'

'Very true,' said Harriet. 'Poor creatures! one can think of nothing else.'

'And really, I do not think the impression will soon be over,' said Emma, as she crossed the low hedge, and tottering footstep which ended the narrow slippery path through the cottage garden, and brought them into the lane again. 'I do not think it will,' stopping to look once more at all the outward wretchedness of the place, and recall the still greater within.

'Oh, dear no,' said her companion.

They walked on. The lane made a slight bend; and when that bend was passed, Mr Elton was immediately in sight and so near as to give Emma time only to say further:

'Ah, Harriet, here come a very sudden trial of our stability in good thoughts. Well' (smiling), 'I hope it may be allowed that if compassion has produced exertion and relief to the sufferers, it has done all that is truly important. If we feel for the wretched enough to do all we can for them, the rest is empty sympathy, only distressing to ourselves.'

Harriet could just answer, 'Oh, dear, yes,' before the gentleman joined them. The wants and sufferings of the poor family, however, were the first subject on meeting. He had been going to call on them. His visit he would now defer; but they had a very interesting parley about what could be done and should be done. Mr Elton then turned back to accompany them.

'To fall in with each other on such an errand as this,' thought Emma; 'to meet in a charitable scheme; this will bring a great increase of love on each side. I should not wonder if it were to bring on the declaration. It must, if I were not here. I wish I were anywhere else.'

Anxious to separate herself from them as far as she could, she soon afterwards took possession of a narrow footpath, a little raised on one side of the lane, leaving them together in the main road. But she had not been there two minutes when she found that Harriet's habits of dependence and imitation were bringing her up too, and that, in short, they would both be soon after her. This would not do; she immediately stopped, under pretence of having some alteration to make in the lacing of her half-boot, and stooping down in complete occupation of the footpath, begged them to have the goodness to walk on, and she would follow in half a minute. They did as they were desired; and by the time she judged it reasonable to have done with her boot, she had the comfort of further delay in her power, being over-taken by a child from the cottage, setting out, according to orders, with her pitcher, to fetch broth from Hartfield. To walk by the side of this child, and talk to and question her, was the most natural thing in the world, or would have been the most natural, had she been acting just then without design; and by this means the others were still able to keep ahead, without any obligation of waiting for her. She gained on them, however, involuntarily; the child's pace was quick, and theirs rather slow; and she was the more concerned at it, from their being evidently in a conver-sation which interested them. Mr Elton was speaking with ani-mation, Harriet listening with a very pleased attention; and Emma having sent the child on, was beginning to think how she might draw back a little more, when they both looked around, and she was obliged to join them.

Mr Elton was still talking, still engaged in some interesting detail; and Emma experienced some disappointment when she found that he was only giving his fair companion an account of the yesterday's party at his friend Cole's, and that she was come in herself for the Stilton cheese, the North Wiltshire, the butter, the celery, the beetroot, and all the dessert.

'This would soon have led to something better, of course,' was her consoling reflection; 'anything interests between those who love; and anything will serve as introduction to what is near the heart. If I could but have kept longer away.'

They now walked on together quietly till within view of the vicarage pales, when a sudden resolution of at least getting Har-riet into the house, made her again find something very much amiss about her boot, and fall behind to arrange it once more. She then broke the lace off short, and dexterously throwing it into a ditch, was presently obliged to entreat them to stop, and acknowledge her inability to put herself to rights so as to be able to walk home in tolerable comfort.

'Part of my lace is gone,' said she, 'and I do not know how I am to contrive. I really am a most troublesome companion to you both, but I hope I am not often so ill-equipped. Mr Elton, I must beg leave to stop at your house, and ask your housekeeper for a bit of ribband or string, or anything just to keep my boot on.'

Mr Elton looked all happiness at this proposition; and nothing could exceed his alertness and attention in conducting them into his house, and endeavouring to make everything appear to advantage. The room they were taken into was the one he chiefly occupied, and looking forwards; behind it was another with which it immediately communicated; the door between them was open, and Emma passed into it with the housekeeper, to receive her assistance in the most comfortable manner. She was obliged to leave the door ajar as she found it; but she fully intended that Mr Elton should close it. It was not closed, however, it still remained ajar; but by engaging the housekeeper in incessant conversation, she hoped to make it practicable for him to choose his own subject in the adjoining room. For ten minutes she could hear nothing but herself. It could be protracted no longer. She was then obliged to be finished, and make her appearance.

The lovers were standing together at one of the windows. It had a most favourable aspect; and, for half a minute, Emma felt the glory of having schemed successfully. But it would not do; he had not come to the point. He had been most agreeable, most delightful; he had told Harriet that he had seen them go by, and had purposely followed them; other little gallantries and allusions had been dropped, but nothing serious.'

'Cautious, very cautious,' thought Emma; 'he advances inch by inch, and will hazard nothing till be believes himself secure.'

Still, however, though everything had not been accomplished by her ingenious device, she could not but flatter herself that it had been the occasion of much present enjoyment to both, and must be leading them forward to the great event.

II

MR ELTON must now be left to himself. It was no longer in Emma's power to superintend his happiness, or quicken his measures. The coming of her sister's family was so very near at hand, that first in anticipation, and then in reality, it became henceforth her prime object of interest; and during the ten days of their stay at Hartfield it was not to be expected—she did not herself expect—that anything beyond occasional, fortuitous assistance could be afforded by her to the lovers. They might advance rapidly if they would, however; they must advance somehow or other, whether they would or no. She hardly wished to have more leisure for them. There are people, who, the more you do for them, the less they will do for themselves.

Mr and Mrs John Knightley, from having been longer than usual absent from Surrey, were exciting, of course, rather more than the usual interest. Till this year, every long vacation since their marriage had been divided between Hartfield and Donwell Abbey; but all the holidays of this autumn had been given to sea-bathing for the children; and it was therefore many months since they had been seen in a regular way by their Surrey connections, or seen at all by Mr Woodhouse, who could not be induced to get so far as London, even for poor Isabella's sake; and who, consequently, was now most nervously and apprehensively happy in forestalling this too short visit.

He thought much of the evils of the journey for her, and not a little of the fatigues of his own horses and coachman, who were to bring some of the party the last half of the way; but his alarms were needless, the sixteen miles being happily accomplished, and Mr and Mrs John Knightley, their five children, and a competent number of nursery-maids, all reaching Hartfield in safety. The bustle and joy of such an arrival, the many to be talked to, welcomed, encouraged, and variously dispersed and disposed of, produced a noise and confusion which his nerves could not have borne under any other cause, nor have endured much longer even for this; but the ways of Hartfield and the feelings of her father were so respected by Mrs John Knightley, that in spite of maternal solicitude for the immediate enjoyment of her little ones, and for their having instantly all the liberty and attendance, all the eating and drinking, and sleeping and playing, which they could possibly wish for, without the smallest delay, the children were never allowed to be long a disturbance to him, either in themselves or in any restless attendance on them.

Mrs John Knightley was a pretty, elegant little woman, of gentle, quiet manners, and a disposition remarkably amiable and affectionate, wrapped up in her family, a devoted wife, a doting mother, and so tenderly attached to her father and sister that, but for these higher ties, a warmer love might have seemed impossible. She could never see a fault in any of them. She was not a woman of strong understanding, or any quickness; and with this resemblance of her father, she inherited also much of his constitution; was delicate in her own health, over careful of that of her children, had many fears, and many nerves, and was as fond of her own Mr Wingfield in town as her father could be of Mr Perry. They were alike, too, in a general benevolence of temper, and a strong habit of regard for every old acquaintance.

Mr John Knightley was a tall, gentlemanlike, and very clever man, rising in his profession; domestic and respectable in his private character; but with reserved manners which prevented him being generally pleasing; and capable of being sometimes out of humour. He was not an ill-tempered man, not so often unreasonably cross as to deserve such a reproach; but his temper was not his great perfection; and, indeed, with such a worshipping wife, it was hardly possible that any natural defects in it should not be increased. The extreme sweetness of her temper must hurt his. He had all the clearness and quickness of mind which she wanted; and he could sometimes act an ungracious, or say a severe thing. He was not a great favourite with his fair sister-in-law. Nothing wrong in him escaped her. She was quick in feeling the little injuries to Isabella, which Isabella never felt herself. Perhaps she might have passed over more had his manners been flattering to Isabella's sister, but they were only those of a calmly kind brother and friend, without praise and without blindness; but hardly any degree of personal compliment could have made her regardless of that greatest fault of all in her eyes which he sometimes fell into, the want of respectful forbearance towards her father. There he had not always the patience that could have been wished. Mr Woodhouse's peculiarities and fidgetiness were sometimes provoking him to a rational remonstrance or sharp retort equally ill-bestowed. It did not often happen; for Mr John Knightley had really a great regard for his father-in-law, and generally a strong sense of what was due to him: but it was too often for Emma's charity, especially as there was all the pain of apprehension frequently to be endured, though the offence came not. The beginning, however, of every visit displayed none but the properest feelings, and this being of necessity so short might be hoped to pass away in unsullied cordiality. They had not been long seated and composed when Mr Woodhouse, with a melancholy shake of the head and a sigh, called his daughter's attention to the sad change at Hartfield since she had been there last.

'Ah, my dear,' said he, 'poor Miss Taylor! It is a grievous business.' '

'Oh, yes, sir,' cried she, with ready sympathy, 'how you must miss her! And dear Emma too. What a dreadful loss to you both! I have been so grieved for you. I could not imagine how you could possibly do without her. It is a sad change, indeed; but I hope she is pretty well, sir.'

'Pretty well, my dear—I hope—pretty well. I do not know but that the place agrees with her tolerably.'

Mr John Knightley here asked Emma, quietly, whether there were any doubts of the air of Randalls.

'Oh, no, none in the least. I never saw Mrs Weston better in my life—never looking so well. Papa is only speaking his own regret.'

'Very much to the honour of both,' was the handsome reply.

'And do you see her, sir, tolerably often?' asked Isabella, in the plaintive tone which just suited her father.

Mr Woodhouse hesitated. 'Not near so often, my dear, as I could wish.'

'Oh, papa, we have missed seeing them but one entire day since they married. Either in the morning or evening of every day, excepting one, have we seen either Mr Weston or Mrs Weston, and generally both, either at Randalls or here; and, as you may suppose, Isabella, most frequently here. They are very, very kind in their visits. Mr Weston is really as kind as herself. Papa, if you speak in that melancholy way, you will be giving Isabella a false idea of us all. Everybody must be aware that Miss Taylor must be missed; but everybody ought also to be assured that Mr and Mrs Weston do really prevent our missing her by any means to the extent we ourselves anticipated—which is the exact truth.'

'Just as it should be,' said Mr John Knightley, 'and just as I hoped it was from your letters. Her wish of showing you attention could not be doubted, and his being a disengaged and social man makes it all easy. I have been always telling you, my love, that I had no idea of the change being so very material to Hartfield as you apprehended; and now you have Emma's account, I hope you will be satisfied.'

'Why, to be sure,' said Mr Woodhouse—'yes, certainly. I cannot deny that Mrs Weston—poor Mrs Weston—does come and see us pretty often; but then, she is always obliged to go away again.'

'It would be very hard upon Mr Weston if she did not, papa. You quite forget poor Mr Weston.'

'I think, indeed,' said John Knightley, pleasantly, 'that Mr Weston has some little claim. You and I, Emma, will venture to take the part of the poor husband. I being a husband, and you not being a wife, the claims of the man may very likely strike us with equal force. As for Isabella, she has been married long enough to see the convenience of putting all the Mr Westons aside as much as she can.'

' Me, my love? ' cried his wife, hearing and understanding only in part. ' Are you talking about me? I am sure nobody ought to be, or can be, a greater advocate for matrimony than I am; and if it had not been for the misery of her leaving Hartfield, I should never have thought of Miss Taylor but as the most fortunate woman in the world; and as to slighting Mr Weston —that excellent Mr Weston—I think there is nothing he does not deserve. I believe he is one of the very best-tempered men that ever existed. Excepting yourself and your brother, I do not know his equal for temper. I shall never forget his flying Henry's kite for him that very windy day last Easter; and ever since his particular kindness last September twelvemonth in writing that note, at twelve o'clock at night, on purpose to assure me that there was no scarlet fever at Cobham, I have been convinced there could not be a more feeling heart nor a better man in existence. If anybody can deserve him, it must be Miss Taylor.'

' Where is the young man? ' said John Knightley. ' Has he been here on this occasion, or has he not? '

' He has not been here yet,' replied Emma. ' There was a strong expectation of his coming soon after the marriage, but it ended in nothing; and I have not heard him mentioned lately.'

' But you should tell them of the letter, my dear,' said her father. ' He wrote a letter to poor Mrs Weston, to congratulate her, and a very proper, handsome letter it was. She showed it to me. I thought it very well done of him, indeed. Whether it was his own idea, you know, one cannot tell. He is but young, and his uncle, perhaps——'

' My dear papa, he is three-and-twenty. You forget how time passes.'

' Three-and-twenty! is he indeed? Well, I could not have thought it; and he was but two years old when he lost his poor mother. Well, time does fly, indeed! and my memory is very bad. However, it was an exceeding good, pretty letter, and gave Mr and Mrs Weston a great deal of pleasure. I remember it was written from Weymouth, and dated Sept. 28th, and began " My dear Madam," but I forget how it went on; and it was signed " F. C. Weston Churchill." I remember that perfectly.'

' How very pleasing and proper of him! ' cried the good-hearted Mrs John Knightley. ' I have no doubt of his being a most amiable young man. But how sad it is that he should not live at home with his father! There is something so shocking in a child's being taken away from his parents and natural home.

I never could comprehend how Mr Weston could part with him. To give up one's child. I really never could think well of anybody who proposed such a thing to anybody else.'

'Nobody ever did think well of the Churchills, I fancy,' observed Mr John Knightley coolly. ' But you need not imagine Mr Weston to have felt what you would feel in giving up Henry or John. Mr Weston is rather an easy cheerful-tempered man, than a man of strong feelings; he takes things as he finds them, and makes enjoyment of them somehow or other, depending, I suspect, much more upon what is called *society* for his comforts, that is, upon the power of eating and drinking and playing whist with his neighbours five times a week, than upon family affection, or anything that home affords.'

Emma could not like what bordered on a reflection on Mr Weston, and had half a mind to take it up; but she struggled, and let it pass. She would keep the peace if possible; and there was something honourable and valuable in the strong domestic habits, the all-sufficiency of home to himself, whence resulted her brother's disposition to look down on the common rate of social intercourse, and those to whom it was important. It had a high claim to forbearance.

12

MR KNIGHTLEY was to dine with them, rather against the inclination of Mr Woodhouse, who did not like that any one should share with him in Isabella's first day. Emma's sense of right, however, had decided it; and, besides the consideration of what was due to each brother, she had particular pleasure, from the circumstance of the late disagreement between Mr Knightley and herself, in procuring him the proper invitation.

She hoped they might now become friends again. She thought it was time to make up. Making up, indeed, would not do. *She* certainly had not been in the wrong, and *he* would never own that he had. Concession must be out of the question; but it was time to appear to forget that they had ever quarrelled; and she hoped it might rather assist the restoration of friendship, that when he came into the room she had one of the children with her—the youngest, a nice little girl about eight months old, who was now making her first visit to Hartfield, and very happy to be danced about in her aunt's arms. It did assist; for though he began with grave looks and short questions, he was soon led on to talk of them all in the usual way, and to take the child out of her arms with all the unceremoniousness of perfect amity. Emma felt they were friends again; and the conviction giving her at first great satisfaction, and then a little sauciness, she could not help saying, as he was admiring the baby:

'What a comfort it is that we think alike about our nephews and nieces! As to men and women, our opinions are sometimes very different; but with regard to these children I observe we never disagree.'

'If you were as much guided by nature in your estimate of men and women, and as little under the power of fancy and whim in your dealings with them, as you are where these children are concerned, we might always think alike.'

'To be sure—our discordances must always arise from my being in the wrong.'

'Yes,' said he, smiling, 'and reason good. I was sixteen years old when you were born.'

'A material difference, then,' she replied; 'and no doubt you were much my superior in judgment at that period of our lives; but does not the lapse of one-and-twenty years bring our understandings a good deal nearer?'

'Yes, a good deal *nearer*.'

'But still, not near enough to give me a chance of being right, if we think differently.'

'I have still the advantage of you by sixteen years' experience, and by not being a pretty young woman and a spoiled child. Come, my dear Emma, let us be friends, and say no more about it. Tell your aunt, little Emma, that she ought to set you a better example than to be renewing old grievances, and that if she were not wrong, before, she is now.'

'That's true,' she cried, 'very true. Little Emma, grow up a better woman than your aunt. Be infinitely cleverer, and not half so conceited. Now, Mr Knightley, a word or two more, and I have done. As far as good intentions went, we were *both* right, and I must say that no effects on my side of the argument have yet proved wrong. I only want to know that Mr Martin is not very, very bitterly disappointed.'

'A man cannot be more so,' was his short, full answer.

'Ah! Indeed I am very sorry. Come, shake hands with me.'

This had just taken place, and with great cordiality, when John Knightley made his appearance; and, 'How d'ye do, George?' and 'John, how are you!' succeeded in the true English style, burying under a calmness that seemed all but indifference the real attachment which would have led either of them, if requisite, to do everything for the good of the other.

The evening was quiet and conversable, as Mr Woodhouse declined cards entirely, for the sake of comfortable talk with his dear Isabella, and the little party made two natural divisions; on one side he and his daughter; on the other the two Mr Knightleys; their subjects totally distinct, or very rarely mixing, and Emma only occasionally joining in one or the other.

The brothers talked of their own concerns and pursuits, but principally of those of the elder, whose temper was by much the most communicative, and who was always the greater talker. As a magistrate, he had generally some point of law to consult John about, or, at least, some curious anecdote to give; and as a farmer, as keeping in hand the home farm at Donwell, he had to tell what every field was to bear next year, and to give all such local information as could not fail of being interesting to a brother whose home it had equally been the longest part of his life, and whose attachments were strong. The plan of a drain, the change of a fence, the felling of a tree, and the destination of every acre of wheat, turnips, or spring corn, was entered into with as much equality of interest by John as his cooler manners rendered possible; and if his willing brother ever left him anything to inquire about, his inquiries even approached a tone of eagerness.

While they were thus comfortably occupied, Mr Woodhouse was enjoying a full flow of happy regrets and fearful affection with his daughter.

'My poor dear Isabella,' said he, fondly taking her hand, and interrupting, for a few moments, her busy labours for some one of her five children, 'how long it is, how terribly long since you were here! And how tired you must be after your journey! You must go to bed early, my dear—and I recommend a little gruel to you before you go. You and I will have a nice basin of gruel together. My dear Emma, suppose we all have a little gruel.'

Emma could not suppose any such thing, knowing as she did, that both the Mr Knightleys were as unpersuadable on that article as herself—and two basins only were ordered. After a little more discourse in praise of gruel, with some wondering at its not being taken every evening by everybody, he proceeded to say, with an air of grave reflection:

'It was an awkward business, my dear, your spending the autumn at Southend instead of coming here. I never had much opinion of the sea air.'

'Mr Wingfield most strenuously recommended it, sir, or we should not have gone. He recommended it for all the children, but particularly for the weakness in little Bella's throat—both sea air and bathing.'

'Ah, my dear, but Perry had many doubts about the sea doing her any good; and as to myself, I have been long perfectly convinced, though perhaps I never told you so before, that the sea is very rarely of use to anybody. I am sure it almost killed me once.'

'Come, come,' cried Emma, feeling this to be an unsafe subject, 'I must beg you not to talk of the sea. It makes me envious and miserable; I who have never seen it! Southend is prohibited, if you please. My dear Isabella, I have not heard you make one inquiry about Mr Perry yet; and he never forgets you.'

'Oh, good Mr Perry, how is he, sir?'

'Why, pretty well; but not quite well. Poor Perry is bilious, and he has no time to take care of himself; he tells me he has not time to take care of himself—which is very sad—but he is always wanted all round the country. I suppose there is not a man in such practice anywhere. But then there is not so clever a man anywhere.'

'And Mrs Perry and the children, how are they? Do the children grow? I have a great regard for Mr Perry. I hope he will be calling soon. He will be so pleased to see my little ones.'

'I hope he will be here to-morrow, for I have a question or two to ask him about myself of some consequence. And, my dear, whenever he comes, you had better let him look at little Bella's throat.'

'Oh, my dear sir, her throat is so much better that I have hardly any uneasiness about it. Either bathing has been of the greatest service to her, or else it is to be attributed to an excellent embrocation of Mr Wingfield's, which we have been applying at times ever since August.'

'It is not very likely, my dear, that bathing should have been of use to her; and if I had known you were wanting an embrocation, I would have spoken to—'

'You seem to me to have forgotten Mrs and Miss Bates,' said Emma; 'I have not heard one inquiry after them.'

'Oh! the good Bateses. I am quite ashamed of myself, but you mention them in most of your letters. I hope they are quite well. Good old Mrs Bates! I will call upon her to-morrow, and take my children. They are always so pleased to see my children.

And that excellent Miss Bates!—such thorough worthy people! How are they, sir?'

'Why, pretty well, my dear, upon the whole. But poor Mrs Bates had a bad cold about a month ago.'

'How sorry I am! but colds were never so prevalent as they have been this autumn. Mr Wingfield told me that he has never known them more general or heavy, except when it has been quite an influenza.'

'That has been a good deal the case, my dear, but not to the degree you mention. Perry says that colds have been very general, but not so heavy as he has very often known them in November. Perry does not call it altogether a sickly season.'

'No, I do not know that Mr Wingfield considers it *very* sickly, except—— '

'Ah, my poor dear child, the truth is, that in London it is always a sickly season. Nobody is healthy in London. Nobody can be. It is a dreadful thing to have you forced to live there—so far off!—and the air so bad.'

'No, indeed, *we* are not at all in a bad air. Our part of London is very superior to most others. You must not confound us with London in general, my dear sir. The neighbourhood of Brunswick Square is very different from almost all the rest. We are so very airy! I should be unwilling, I own, to live in any other part of the town; there is hardly any other that I could be satisfied to have my children in; but *we* are so remarkably airy! Mr Wingfield thinks the vicinity of Brunswick Square decidedly the most favourable as to air.'

'Ah, my dear, it is not like Hartfield. You make the best of it—but after you have been a week at Hartfield, you are all of you different creatures; you do not look like the same. Now I cannot say that I think you are any of you looking well at present.'

'I am sorry to hear you say so, sir; but I assure you, excepting those little nervous headaches and palpitations which I am never entirely free from anywhere, I am quite well myself; and if the children were rather pale before they went to bed, it was only because they were a little more tired than usual, from their journey and the happiness of coming. I hope you will think better of their looks to-morrow; for I assure you Mr Wingfield told me, that he did not believe he had ever sent us off altogether, in such good case. I trust, at least, that you do not think Mr Knightley looking ill,' turning her eyes with affectionate anxiety towards her husband.

75

'Middling, my dear; I cannot compliment you. I think Mr John Knightley very far from looking well.'

'What is the matter, sir? Did you speak to me!' cried Mr John Knightley, hearing his own name.

'I am sorry to find, my love, that my father does not think you looking well; but I hope it is only from being a little fatigued. I could have wished, however, as you know, that you had seen Mr Wingfield before you left home.'

'My dear Isabella,' exclaimed he hastily, 'pray do not concern yourself about my looks. Be satisfied with doctoring and coddling yourself and the children, and let me look as I choose.'

'I did not thoroughly understand what you were telling your brother,' cried Emma, 'about your friend Mr Graham's intending to have a bailiff from Scotland to look after his new estate. But will it answer? Will not the old prejudice be too strong?'

And she talked in this way so long and successfully that, when forced to give her attention again to her father and sister, she had nothing worse to hear than Isabella's kind inquiry after Jane Fairfax; and Jane Fairfax, though no great favourite with her in general, she was, at that moment, very happy to assist in praising.

'That sweet, amiable Jane Fairfax!' said Mrs John Knightley. 'It is so long since I have seen her, except now and then for a moment accidentally in town. What happiness it must be to her good old grandmother and excellent aunt, when she comes to visit them! I always regret excessively, on dear Emma's account, that she cannot be more at Highbury; but now their daughter is married, I suppose Colonel and Mrs Campbell will not be able to part with her at all. She would be such a delightful companion for Emma.'

Mr Woodhouse agreed to it all, but added:

'Our little friend Harriet Smith, however, is just such another pretty kind of young person. You will like Harriet. Emma could not have a better companion than Harriet.'

'I am most happy to hear it; but only Jane Fairfax one knows to be so very accomplished and superior, and exactly Emma's age.'

This topic was discussed very happily, and others succeeded of similar moment, and passed away with similar harmony; but the evening did not close without a little return of agitation. The gruel came, and supplied a great deal to be said—much praise and many comments—undoubting decision of its wholesomeness for every constitution, and pretty severe philippics upon the many houses where it was never met with tolerable; but, unfortunately, among the failures which the daughter had to instance, the most recent, and therefore most prominent, was in her own cook at Southend, a young woman hired for the time, who never had been able to understand what she meant by a basin of nice smooth gruel, thin, but not too thin. Often as she had wished for and ordered it, she had never been able to get anything tolerable. Here was a dangerous opening.

'Ah,' said Mr Woodhouse, shaking his head, and fixing his eye on her with tender concern. The ejaculation in Emma's ear expressed, 'Ah, there is no end of the sad consequences of your going to Southend. It does not bear talking of.' And for a little while she hoped he would not talk of it, and that a silent rumination might suffice to restore him to the relish of his own smooth gruel. After an interval of some minutes, however, he began with:

'I shall always be very sorry that you went to the sea this autumn, instead of coming here.'

'But why should you be sorry, sir? I assure you it did the children a great deal of good.'

'And, moreover, if you must go to the sea, it had better not have been to Southend. Southend is an unhealthy place. Perry was surprised to hear you had fixed upon Southend.'

'I know there is such an idea with many people, but indeed it is quite a mistake, sir. We all had our health perfectly well there, never found the least inconvenience from the mud, and Mr Wingfield says it is entirely a mistake to suppose the place unhealthy; and I am sure he may be depended on, for he thoroughly understands the nature of the air, and his own brother and family have been there repeatedly.'

'You should have gone to Cromer, my dear, if you went anywhere. Perry was a week at Cromer once, and he holds it to be the best of all the sea bathing places. A fine open sea, he says, and very pure air. And, by what I understand, you might have had lodgings there quite away from the sea—a quarter of a mile off—very comfortable. You should have consulted Perry.'

'But, my dear sir, the difference of the journey; only consider how great it would have been. A hundred miles, perhaps, instead of forty.'

'Ah, my dear, as Perry says, where health is at stake nothing else should be considered; and if one is to travel, there is not much to choose between forty miles and a hundred. Better not move at all, better stay in London altogether, than travel forty miles to get into a worse air. This is just what Perry said. It seemed to him a very ill-judged measure.'

Emma's attempts to stop her father had been vain; and when he had reached such a point as this, she could not wonder at her brother-in-law's breaking out.

'Mr Perry,' said he, in a voice of very strong displeasure, 'would do as well to keep his opinion till it is asked for. Why does he make it any business of his to wonder at what I do?—at my taking my family to one part of the coast or another? I may be allowed, I hope, the use of my judgment as well as Mr Perry. I want his directions no more than his drugs.' He paused, and growing cooler in a moment, added, with only sarcastic dryness, 'If Mr Perry can tell me how to convey a wife and five children a distance of a hundred and thirty miles with no greater expense or inconvenience than a distance of forty, I should be as willing to prefer Cromer to Southend as he could himself.'

'True, true,' cried Mr Knightley, with most ready interposition—'very true. That's a consideration, indeed. But, John, as to what I was telling you of my idea of moving the path to Langham, of turning it more to the right that it may not cut through the home meadows, I cannot conceive any difficulty. I should not attempt it, if it were to be the means of inconvenience to the Highbury people, but if you call to mind exactly the present line of the path—the only way of proving it, however, will be to turn to our maps. I shall see you at the Abbey to-morrow morning, I hope, and then we will look them over, and you shall give me your opinion.'

Mr Woodhouse was rather agitated by such harsh reflections on his friend Perry, to whom he had in fact, though unconsciously, been attributing many of his own feelings and expressions; but the soothing attentions of his daughters gradually removed the present evil, and the immediate alertness of one brother, and better recollections of the other, prevented any renewal of it.

13

THERE could hardly be a happier creature in the world than Mrs John Knightley, in this short visit to Hartfield, going about every morning among her old acquaintance with her five children, and talking over what she had done every evening with her father and sister. She had nothing to wish otherwise, but that the days did not pass so swiftly. It was a delightful visit—perfect, in being much too short.

In general their evenings were less engaged with friends than their mornings; but one complete dinner engagement, and out of the house too, there was no avoiding, though at Christmas. Mr Weston would take no denial; they must all dine at Randalls one day; even Mr Woodhouse was persuaded to think it a possible thing in preference to a division of the party.

How they were all to be conveyed, he would have made a difficulty if he could, but as his son and daughter's carriage and horses were actually at Hartfield, he was not able to make more than a simple question on that head; it hardly amounted to a doubt, nor did it occupy Emma long to convince him that they might in one of the carriages find room for Harriet also.

Harriet, Mr Elton, and Mr Knightley, their own especial set, were the only persons invited to meet them—the hours were to be early as well as the numbers few; Mr Woodhouse's habits and inclinations being consulted in everything.

The evening before this great event (for it was a very great event that Mr Woodhouse should dine out on the 24th of December) had been spent by Harriet at Hartfield, and she had gone home so much indisposed with a cold, that, but for her own earnest wish of being nursed by Mrs Goddard, Emma could not have allowed her to leave the house. Emma called on her the next day, and found her doom already signed with regard to Randalls. She was very feverish and had a bad sore throat; Mrs Goddard was full of care and affection, Mr Perry was talked of, and Harriet herself was too ill and low to resist the authority which excluded her from this delightful engagement, though she could not speak of her loss without many tears.

Emma sat with her as long as she could, to attend her in Mrs Goddard's unavoidable absences, and raise her spirits by representing how much Mr Elton's would be depressed when he knew her state; and left her at last tolerably comfortable, in the sweet dependence of his having a most comfortless visit, and of their all missing her very much. She had not advanced many yards from Mrs Goddard's door, when she was met by Mr Elton himself, evidently coming towards it, and as they walked on slowly together in conversation about the invalid—of whom he, on the rumour of considerable illness, had been going to inquire, that he might carry some report of her to Hartfield—they were overtaken by Mr John Knightley, returning from the daily visit to Donwell, with his two eldest boys, whose healthy glowing faces showed all the benefit of a country run, and seemed to ensure a quick despatch of the roast mutton and rice pudding they were hastening home for. They joined company and proceeded together. Emma was just describing the nature of her friend's complaint—' a throat very much inflamed, with a great deal of heat about her, a quick low pulse, etc., and she was sorry to find from Mrs Goddard that Harriet was liable to very bad sore throats, and had often alarmed her with them.' Mr Elton looked all alarm on the occasion, as he exclaimed:

' A sore throat!—I hope not infectious. I hope not of a putrid infectious sort. Has Perry seen her? Indeed you should take care of yourself as well as of your friend. Let me entreat you to run no risks. Why does not Perry see her? '

Emma, who was not really at all frightened herself, tranquillised this excess of apprehension by assurances of Mrs Goddard's experience and care; but as there must still remain a degree of uneasiness which she could not wish to reason away, which she would rather feed and assist than not, she added soon afterwards— as if quite another subject:

' It is so cold, so very cold, and looks and feels so very much like snow, that if it were to any other place or with any other party, I should really try not to go out to-day, and dissuade my father from venturing; but as he has made up his mind, and does not seem to feel the cold himself, I do not like to interfere, as I know it would be so great a disappointment to Mr and Mrs Weston. But upon my word, Mr Elton, in your case, I should certainly excuse myself. You appear to me a little hoarse already; and when you consider what demand of voice and what fatigues to-morrow will bring, I think it would be no more than common prudence to stay at home and take care of yourself to-night.'

Mr Elton looked as if he did not very well know what answer to make; which was exactly the case; for though very much gratified by the kind care of such a fair lady, and not liking to resist any advice of hers, he had not really the least inclination to give up the visit; but Emma, too eager and busy in her own previous conceptions and views to hear him impartially, or see him with clear vision, was very well satisfied with his muttering acknowledgment of its being ' very cold, certainly very cold,' and walked on, rejoicing in having extricated himself from Randalls, and secured him the power of sending to inquire after Harriet every hour of the evening.'

' You do quite right,' said she; ' we will make your apologies to Mr and Mrs Weston.'

80

But hardly had she so spoken, when she found her brother was civilly offering a seat in his carriage, if the weather were Mr Elton's only objection, and Mr Elton actually accepting the offer with much prompt satisfaction. It was a done thing; Mr Elton was to go, and never had his broad handsome face expressed more pleasure than at this moment; never had his smile been stronger, nor his eyes more exulting than when he next looked at her.

'Well,' said she to herself, 'this is most strange! After I had got him off so well, to choose to go into company, and leave Harriet ill behind! Most strange indeed! But there is, I believe, in many men, especially single men, such an inclination—such a passion for dining out; a dinner engagement is so high in the class of their pleasures, their employments, their dignities, almost their duties, that anything gives way to it, and this must be the case with Mr Elton—a most valuable, amiable, pleasing young man undoubtedly, and very much in love with Harriet; but still he cannot refuse an invitation, he must dine out wherever he is asked. What a strange thing love is! he can see ready wit in Harriet, but will not dine alone for her.'

Soon afterwards Mr Elton quitted them, and she could not but do him the justice of feeling that there was a great deal of sentiment in his manner of naming Harriet at parting; in the tone of his voice, while assuring her that he should call at Mrs Goddard's for news of her fair friend, the last thing before he prepared for the happiness of meeting her again, when he hoped to be able to give a better report; and he sighed and smiled himself off in a way that left the balance of approbation much in his favour.

After a few minutes of entire silence between them, John Knightley began with:

'I never in my life saw a man more intent on being agreeable than Mr Elton. It is downright labour to him where ladies are concerned. With men he can be rational and unaffected, but when he has ladies to please, every feature works.'

'Mr Elton's manners are not perfect,' replied Emma; 'but where there is a wish to please, one ought to overlook, and one does overlook a great deal. Where a man does his best with only moderate powers, he will have the advantage over negligent superiority. There is such perfect good temper and goodwill in Mr Elton, as one cannot but value.'

'Yes,' said Mr John Knightley presently, with some slyness, 'he seems to have a great deal of goodwill towards *you*.'

'Me!' she replied, with a smile of astonishment; 'are you imagining me to be Mr Elton's object?'

'Such an imagination has crossed me, I own, Emma; and if it never occurred to you before, you may as well take it into consideration now.'

'Mr Elton in love with me! What an idea!'

'I do not say it is so; but you will do well to consider whether it is so or not, and to regulate your behaviour accordingly. I think your manners to him encouraging. I speak as a friend, Emma. You had better look about you, and ascertain what you do, and what you mean to do.'

'I thank you; but I assure you, you are quite mistaken. Mr Elton and I are very good friends, and nothing more;' and she walked on, amusing herself in the consideration of the blunders which often arise from a partial knowledge of circumstances, of the mistakes which people of high pretensions to judgment are for ever falling into; and not very well pleased with her brother for imagining her blind and ignorant, and in want of counsel. He said no more.

Mr Woodhouse had so completely made up his mind to the visit, that in spite of the increasing coldness, he seemed to have no idea of shrinking from it, and set forward at last most punctually with his eldest daughter in his own carriage, with less apparent consciousness of the weather than either of the others; too full of the wonder of his own going, and the pleasure it was to afford at Randalls, to see that it was cold, and too well wrapped up to feel it. The cold, however, was severe; and by the time the second carriage was in motion, a few flakes of snow vere finding their way down, and the sky had the appearance of being so overcharged as to want only a milder air to produce a very white world in a very short time.

Emma soon saw that her companion was not in the happiest humour. The preparing and the going abroad in such weather, with the sacrifice of his children after dinner, were evils, were disagreeables at least, which Mr John Knightley did not by any means like; he anticipated nothing in the visit that could be at all worth the purchase; and the whole of their drive to the vicarage was spent by him in expressing his discontent.

'A man,' said he, 'must have a very good opinion of himself when he asks people to leave their own fireside, and encounter such a day as this, for the sake of coming to see him. He must think himself a most agreeable fellow; I could not do such a thing. It is the greatest absurdity—actually snowing at this moment! The folly of not allowing people to be comfortable at home, and the folly of people's not staying comfortably at home when they can! If we were obliged to go out such an evening as this, by any call of duty or business, what a hardship we should deem it; and here are we, probably with rather thinner clothing than usual, setting forward voluntarily, without excuse, in defiance of the voice of nature, which tells man, in everything given to his view or his feelings, to stay at home himself, and keep all under shelter that he can; here are we setting forward to spend five dull hours in another man's house, with nothing to say or to hear that was not said and heard yesterday, and may not be said and heard again to-morrow. Going in dismal weather, to return probably in worse; four horses and four servants taken out for nothing but to convey five idle, shivering creatures into colder rooms and worse company than they might have had at home.'

Emma did not find herself equal to give the pleased assent, which no doubt he was in the habit of receiving, to emulate the ' Very true, my love,' which must have been usually administered by his travelling companion; but she had resolution enough to refrain from making any answer at all. She could not be complying; she dreaded being quarrelsome; her heroism reached only to silence. She allowed him to talk, and arranged the glasses, and wrapped herself up without opening her lips.

They arrived, the carriage turned, the step was let down, and Mr Elton, spruce, black, and smiling, was with them instantly. Emma thought with pleasure of some change of subject. Mr Elton was all obligation and cheerfulness; he was so very cheerful in his civilities indeed, that she began to think he must have received a different account of Harriet from what had reached her. She had sent while dressing and the answer had been, ' Much the same—not better.'

' *My* report from Mrs Goddard's ' said she, presently, ' was not so pleasant as I had hoped; " not better," was *my* answer.'

His face lengthened immediately, and his voice was the voice of sentiment as he answered:

' Oh no—I am grieved to find—I was on the point of telling you, that when I called at Mrs Goddard's door, which I did the very last thing before I returned to dress, I was told that Miss Smith was not better, by no means better, rather worse. Very much grieved and concerned—I had flattered myself that she must be better after such a cordial as I knew had been given her in the morning.'

Emma smiled and answered: ' My visit was of use to the nervous part of her complaint, I hope; but not even I can charm away a sore throat; it is a most severe cold, indeed. Mr Perry has been with her, as you probably heard.'

' Yes—I imagined—that is—I did not—— '

' He has been used to her in these complaints, and I hope to-morrow morning will bring us both a more comfortable report. But it is impossible not to feel uneasiness. Such a sad loss to our party to-day! '

' Dreadful! Exactly so, indeed. She will be missed every moment.'

This was very proper; the sigh which accompanied it was really estimable; but it should have lasted longer. Emma was rather in dismay when only half a minute afterwards he began to speak of other things, and in a voice of the greatest alacrity and enjoyment.

' What an excellent device,' said he, ' the use of a sheep-skin for carriages. How very comfortable they make it; impossible to feel cold with such precautions. The contrivances of modern days, indeed, have rendered a gentleman's carriage perfectly complete. One is so fenced and guarded from the weather that not a breath of air can find its way unpermitted. Weather becomes absolutely of no consequence. It is a very cold afternoon— but in this carriage we know nothing of the matter. Ha! snows a little, I see.'

' Yes,' said John Knightley, ' and I think we shall have a good deal of it.'

' Christmas weather,' observed Mr Elton. ' Quite seasonable; and extremely fortunate we may think ourselves that it did not begin yesterday, and prevent this day's party, which it might very possibly have done, for Mr Woodhouse would hardly have ventured had there been much snow on the ground; but now it is of no consequence. This is quite the season, indeed, for friendly meetings. At Christmas everybody invites their friends about them, and people think little of even the worst weather. I was snowed up at a friend's house once for a week. Nothing could be pleasanter. I went for only one night, and could not get away till that very day sennight.'

Mr John Knightley looked as if he did not comprehend the pleasure, but said only, coolly:

' I cannot wish to be snowed up a week at Randalls.'

At another time Emma might have been amused, but she was too much astonished now at Mr Elton's spirits for other feelings.

Harriet seemed quite forgotten in the expectation of a pleasant party.

'We are sure of excellent fires,' continued he, 'and everything in the greatest comfort. Charming people Mr and Mrs Weston; Mrs Weston indeed is much beyond praise, and he is exactly what one values, so hospitable, and so fond of society; it will be a small party, but where small parties are select, they are, perhaps, the most agreeable of any. Mr Weston's dining-room does not accommodate more than ten comfortably; and, for my part, I would rather, under such circumstances, fall short by two than exceed by two. I think you will agree with me (turning with a soft air to Emma), I think I shall certainly have your approbation, though Mr Knightley, perhaps, from being used to the large parties of London, may not quite enter into our feelings.'

'I know nothing of the large parties of London, sir—I never dine with anybody.'

'Indeed! (in a tone of wonder and pity) 'I had no idea that the law had been so great a slavery. Well, sir, the time must come when you will be paid for all this, when you will have little labour and great enjoyment.'

'My first enjoyment,' replied John Knightley, as they passed through the sweep-gate, 'will be to find myself safe at Hartfield again.'

14

SOME change of countenance was necessary for each gentleman as they walked into Mrs Weston's drawing-room; Mr Elton must compose his joyous looks, and Mr John Knightley disperse his ill humour. Mr Elton must smile less, and Mr John Knightley more, to fit them for the place. Emma only might be as nature prompted, and show herself just as happy as she was. To her, it was real enjoyment to be with the Westons. Mr Weston was a great favourite, and there was not a creature in the world to whom she spoke with such unreserve as to his wife; not any one, to whom she related with such conviction of being listened to, and understood, of being always interesting and always intelligible, the little affairs, arrangements, perplexities, and pleasures of her father and herself. She could tell nothing of Hartfield, in which Mrs Weston had not a lively concern; and half an hour's uninterrupted communication of all those little matters on which the daily happiness of private life depends, was one of the first gratifications of each.

This was a pleasure which perhaps the whole day's visit might not afford, which certainly did not belong to the present half hour; but the very sight of Mrs Weston, her smile, her touch, her voice, was grateful to Emma, and she determined to think as little as possibile of Mr Elton's oddities, or of anything else unpleasant, and enjoy all that was enjoyable to the utmost.

The misfortune of Harriet's cold had been pretty well gone through before her arrival. Mr Woodhouse had been safely seated long enough to give the history of it, besides all the history of his own and Isabella's coming, and of Emma's being to follow; and had, indeed, just got to the end of his satisfaction that James should come and see his daughter, when the others appeared, and Mrs Weston, who had been almost wholly engrossed by her attentions to him, was able to turn away and welcome her dear Emma.

Emma's project of forgetting Mr Elton for a while made her rather sorry to find, when they had all taken their places, that he was close to her. The difficulty was great of driving his strange sensibility towards Harriet from her mind, while he not only sat at her elbow, but was continually obtruding his happy countenance on her notice, and solicitously addressing her upon every occasion. Instead of forgetting him, his behaviour was such that she could not avoid the internal suggestion of 'Can it really be as my brother imagined? can it be possible for this man to be beginning to transfer his affections from Harriet to me?—Absurd and insufferable!' Yet he would be so anxious for her being perfectly warm, would be so interested about her father, and so delighted with Mrs Weston; and, at last, would begin admiring her drawings with so much zeal and so little knowledge, as seemed terribly like a would-be lover, and made it some effort with her to preserve her good manners. For her own sake she could not be rude; and for Harriet's in the hope that all would yet turn out right, she was even positively civil; but it was an effort, especially as something was going on amongst the others, in the most overpowering period of Mr Elton's nonsense, which she particularly wished to listen to. She heard enough to know that Mr Weston was giving some information about his son; she heard the words 'my son,' and 'Frank,' and 'my son,' repeated several times over; and, from a few other half-syllables, very much suspected that he was announcing an early visit from his son; but before she could quiet Mr Elton, the subject was so completely past, that any reviving question from her would have been awkward.

Now it so happened, that, in spite of Emma's resolution of never marrying, there was something in the name, in the idea, of Mr Frank Churchill, which always interested her. She had frequently thought—especially since his father's marriage with Miss Taylor—that if she *were* to marry, he was the very person to suit her in age, character and condition. He seemed by this connection between the families, quite to belong to her. She could not but suppose it to be a match that everybody who knew them must think of. That Mr and Mrs Weston did think of it, she was very strongly persuaded; and though not meaning to be induced by him, or by anybody else, to give up a situation which she believed more replete with good than any she could change it for, she had a great curiosity to see him, a decided intention of finding him pleasant, of being liked by him to a certain degree, and a sort of pleasure in the idea of their being coupled in their friends' imaginations.

With such sensations, Mr Elton's civilities were dreadfully ill-timed; but she had the comfort of appearing very polite, while feeling very cross; and of thinking that the rest of the visit could not possibly pass without bringing forward the same information again, or the substance of it, from the open-hearted Mr Weston. So it proved; for, when happily released from Mr Elton, and seated by Mr Weston at dinner, he made use of the very first interval in the cares of hospitality, the very first leisure from the saddle of mutton, to say to her:

' We want only two more to be just the right number. I should like to see two more here—your pretty little friend, Miss Smith, and my son—and then I should say we were quite complete. I believe you did not hear me telling the others in the drawing-room that we are expecting Frank. I had a letter from him this morning, and he will be with us within a fortnight.'

Emma spoke with a very proper degree of pleasure, and fully assented to his proposition, of Mr Frank Churchill and Miss Smith making their party quite complete.

' He has been wanting to come to us,' continued Mr Weston, 'ever since September; every letter has been full of it; but he cannot command his own time. He has those to please who must be pleased, and who (between ourselves) are sometimes to be pleased only by a good many sacrifices. But now I have no doubt of seeing him here about the second week in January.'

' What a very great pleasure it will be to you! and Mrs Weston is so anxious to be acquainted with him, that she must be almost as happy as yourself.'

'Yes, she would be, but that she thinks there will be another put-off. She does not depend upon his coming so much as I do; but she does not know the parties so well as I do. The case, you see, is—(but this is quite between ourselves; I did not mention a syllable of it in the other room. There are secrets in all families, you know)—the case is, that a party of friends are invited to pay a visit at Enscombe in January, and that Frank's coming depends upon their being put off. If they are not put off, he cannot stir. But I know they will, because it is a family that a certain lady, of some consequence at Enscombe, had a particular dislike to; and though it is thought necessary to invite them once in two or three years, they always are put off when it comes to the point. I have not the smallest doubt of the issue. I am as confident of seeing Frank here before the middle of January, as I am of being here myself; but your good friend there (nodding towards the upper end of the table) has so few vagaries herself, and has been so little used to them at Hartfield, that she cannot calculate on their effects, as I have been long in the practice of doing.'

'I am sorry there should be anything like doubt in the case,' replied Emma; 'but am disposed to side with you, Mr Weston. If you think he will come, I shall think so too; for you know Enscombe.'

'Yes—I have some right to that knowledge; though I have never been at the place in my life. She is an odd woman! But I never allow myself to speak ill of her, on Frank's account; for I do believe her to be very fond of him. I used to think she was not capable of being fond of anybody except herself; but she has always been kind to him (in her way—allowing for little whims and caprices, and expecting everything to be as she likes). And it is no small credit, in my opinion, to him, that he should excite such an affection; for, though I would not say it to anybody else, she has no more heart than a stone to people in general, and the devil of a temper.'

Emma liked the subject so well, that she began upon it to Mrs Weston, very soon after their moving into the drawing-room, wishing her joy—yet observing that she knew the first meeting must be rather alarming. Mrs Weston agreed to it; but added that she should be very glad to be secure of undergoing the anxiety of a first meeting at the time talked of; 'for I cannot depend upon his coming. I cannot be so sanguine as Mr Weston. I am very much afraid that it will all end in nothing. Mr Weston, I dare say, has been telling you exactly how the matter stands?'

'Yes; it seems to depend upon nothing but the ill humour of Mrs Churchill, which I imagine to be the most certain thing in the world.'

'My Emma!' replied Mrs Weston, smiling, 'what is the certainty of caprice?' Then turning to Isabella, who had not been attending before—'You must know, my dear Mrs Knightley, that we are by no means so sure of seeing Mr Frank Churchill, in my opinion, as his father thinks. It depends entirely upon his aunt's spirits and pleasure; in short, upon her temper. To you—to my two daughters—I may venture on the truth. Mrs Churchill rules at Enscombe, and is a very odd-tempered woman; and his coming now depends upon her being willing to spare him.'

'Oh, Mrs Churchill! everybody knows Mrs Churchill,' replied Isabella, 'and I am sure I never think of that poor young man without the greatest compassion. To be constantly living with an ill-tempered person must be dreadful. It is what we happily have never known anything of; but, it must be a life of misery. What a blessing that she never had any children! Poor little creatures, how unhappy she would have made them!'

Emma wished she had been alone with Mrs Weston. She should then have heard more. Mrs Weston would speak to her with a degree of unreserve which she would not hazard with Isabella; and she really believed, would scarcely try to conceal anything relative to the Churchills from her, excepting those views on the young man, of which her own imagination had already given her such instinctive knowledge. But at present there was nothing more to be said. Mr Woodhouse very soon followed them into the drawing-room. To be sitting long after dinner was a confinement that he could not endure. Neither wine nor conversation was anything to him; and gladly did he move to those with whom he was always comfortable.

While he talked to Isabella, however, Emma found an opportunity of saying:

'And so you do not consider this visit from your son as by any means certain. I am sorry for it. The introduction must be unpleasant, whenever it takes place; and the sooner it could be over the better.'

'Yes; and every delay makes one more apprehensive of other delays. Even if this family, the Braithwaites, are put off, I am still afraid that some excuse may be found for disappointing us. I cannot bear to imagine any reluctance on his side; but I am sure there is a great wish on the Churchills' to keep him to them-

selves. There is jealousy. They are jealous even of his regard
for his father. In short, I can feel no dependence on his coming,
and I wish Mr Weston were less sanguine.'

'He ought to come,' said Emma. 'If he could stay only a
couple of days, he ought to come; and one can hardly conceive
a young man's not having it in his power to do as much as that.
A young *woman*, if she fall into bad hands, may be teased, and kept
at a distance form those she wants to be with; but one cannot
comprehend a young *man's* being under such restraint as not to
be able to spend a week with his father, if he likes to.'

'One ought to be at Enscombe, and know the ways of the
family, before one decides upon what he can do,' replied Mrs
Weston. 'One ought to use the same caution, perhaps, in
judging of the conduct of any one individual of any one family;
but Enscombe, I believe, certainly must not be judged by general rules; *she* is so very unreasonable; and everything gives
way to her.'

'But she is so fond of the nephew; he is so very great a favourite. Now, according to my idea of Mrs Churchill, it would be
most natural, that while she makes no sacrifice for the comfort
of the husband, to whom she owes everything, while she exer-
cises incessant caprice towards *him*, she should frequently be
governed by the nephew, to whom she owes nothing at all.'

'My dearest Emma, do not pretend, with your sweet temper,
to understand a bad one, or to lay down rules for it; you must
let it go its own way. I have no doubt of his having, at times,
considerable influence; but it may be perfectly impossible for
him to know beforehand *when* it will be.'

Emma listened, and then coolly said, 'I shall not be satisfied
unless he comes.'

'He may have a great deal of influence on some points,' continued Mrs Weston, 'and on others, very little; and among those,
on which she is beyond his reach, it is but too likely may be
this very circumstance of his coming away from them to visit us.'

15

MR WOODHOUSE was soon ready for his tea; and when he
had drank his tea, he was quite ready to go home, and it
was as much as his three companions could do, to entertain away
his notice of the lateness of the hour, before the other gentlemen
appeared. Mr Weston was chatty and convivial, and no friend

to early separations of any sort; but at last the drawing-room party did receive an augmentation. Mr Elton, in very good spirits, was one of the first to walk in. Mrs Weston and Emma were sitting together on a sofa. He joined them immediately, and with scarcely an invitation, seated himself between them.

Emma, in good spirits too, from the amusement afforded her mind by the expectation of Mr Frank Churchill, was willing to forget his late improprieties, and be as well satisfied with him as before, and on his making Harriet his very first subject, was ready to listen with most friendly smiles.

He professed himself extremely anxious about her fair friend —her fair, lovely, amiable friend. 'Did she know?—had she heard anything about her since their being at Randalls?—he felt much anxiety—he must confess that the nature of her complaint alarmed him considerably.' And in this style he talked on for some time very properly, not much attending to any answer, but altogether sufficiently awake to the terror of a bad sore throat; and Emma was quite in charity with him.

But at last there seemed a perverse turn; it seemed all at once as if he were more afraid of its being a bad sore throat on her account than on Harriet's—more anxious that she should escape the infection, than that there should be no infection in the complaint. He began with great earnestness to entreat her to refrain from visiting the sick-chamber again, for the present, to entreat her to *promise him* not to venture into such hazard till he had seen Mr Perry and learnt his opinion, and though she tried to laugh it off and bring the subject back into its proper course, there was no putting an end to his extreme solicitude about her. She was vexed. It did appear—there was no concealing it—exactly like the pretence of being in love with her instead of Harriet; an inconstancy, if real, the most contemptible and abominable! and she had difficulty in behaving with temper. He turned to Mrs Weston to implore her assistance; 'Would not she give him her support?—would not she add her persuasions to his, to induce Miss Woodhouse not to go to Mrs Goddard's till it were certain that Miss Smith's disorder had no infection? He could not be satisfied without a promise—would not she give him her influence in procuring it?'

'So scrupulous for others,' he continued, 'and yet so careless for herself! She wanted me to nurse my cold by staying at home to-day, and yet will not promise to avoid the danger of catching an ulcerated sore throat herself. Is this fair, Mrs Weston? Judge between us. Have not I some right to complain? I am sure of your kind support and aid.'

Emma saw Mrs Weston's surprise, and felt that it must be great, at an address which, in words and manner, was assuming to himself the right of first interest in her; and as for herself, she was too much provoked and offended to have the power of directly saying anything to the purpose. She could only give him a look; but it was such a look as she thought must restore him to his senses, and then left the sofa, removing to a seat by her sister, and giving her all her attention.

She had not time to know how Mr Elton took the reproof, so rapidly did another subject succeed; for Mr John Knightley now came into the room from examining the weather, and opened on them all with the information of the ground being covered with snow, and of its still snowing fast, with a strong drifting wind; concluding with these words to Mr Woodhouse:

' This will prove a spirited beginning of your winter engagements, sir. Something new for your coachman and horses to be making their way through a storm of snow.'

Poor Mr Woodhouse was silent from consternation; but everybody else had something to say; everybody was either surprised, or not surprised, and had some question to ask, or some comfort to offer. Mrs Weston and Emma tried earnestly to cheer him and turn his attention from his son-in-law, who was pursuing his triumph rather unfeelingly.

' I admired your resolution very much, sir,' said he, 'in venturing out in such weather, for of course you saw there would be snow very soon. Everybody must have seen the snow coming on. I admired your spirit; and I dare say we shall get home very well. Another hour or two's snow can hardly make the road impassable; and we are two carriages; if *one* is blown over in the bleak part of the common field there will be the other at hand. I dare say we shall be all safe at Hartfield before midnight.'

Mr Weston, with triumph of a different sort, was confessing that he had known it to be snowing some time, but had not said a word, lest it should make Mr Woodhouse uncomfortable, and be an excuse for his hurrying away. As to there being any quantity of snow fallen or likely to fall to impede their return, that was a mere joke; he was afraid they would find no difficulty. He wished the road might be impassable, that he might be able to keep them all at Randalls; and with the utmost goodwill was sure that accommodation might be found for everybody, calling on his wife to agree with him, that, with a little contrivance, everybody might be lodged, which she hardly knew how to do, from the consciousness of there being but two spare rooms in the house.

'What is to be done, my dear Emma? what is to be done?' was Mr Woodhouse's first exclamation, and all that he could say for some time. To her he looked for comfort; and her assurances of safety, her representation of the excellence of the horses, and of James, and of their having so many friends about them, revived him a little.

His eldest daughter's alarm was equal to his own. The horror of being blocked up at Randalls, while her children were at Hartfield, was full in her imagination; and fancying the road to be now just passable for adventurous people, but in a state that admitted no delay, she was eager to have it settled, that her father and Emma should remain at Randalls, while she and her husband set forward instantly, through all the possible accumulations of drifted snow that might impede them.

'You had better order the carriage directly, my love,' said she; 'I dare say we shall be able to get along, if we set off directly; and if we do come to anything very bad, I can get out and walk. I am not at all afraid. I should not mind walking half the way. I could change my shoes, you know, the moment I got home; and it is not the sort of thing that gives me cold.'

'Indeed!' replied he. 'Then, my dear Isabella, it is the most extraordinary sort of thing in the world, for in general everything does give you cold. Walk home! you are prettily shod for walking home, I dare say. It will be bad enough for the horses.'

Isabella turned to Mrs Weston for her approbation of the plan. Mrs Weston could only approve. Isabella then went to Emma; but Emma could not so entirely give up the hope of their being all able to get away; and they were still discussing the point, when Mr Knightley, who had left the room immediately after his brother's first report of the snow, came back again, and told them that he had been out-of-doors to examine, and could answer for there not being the smallest difficulty in their getting home, whenever they liked it, either now or an hour hence. He had gone beyond the sweep—some way along the Highbury Road—the snow was nowhere above half an inch deep—in many places hardly enough to whiten the ground; a very few flakes were falling at present, but the clouds were parting, and there was every appearance of its being soon over. He had seen the coachmen, and they both agreed with him in there being nothing to apprehend.

To Isabella the relief of such tidings was very great, and they were scarcely less acceptable to Emma on her father's account, who was immediately set as much at ease on the subject as his nervous constitution allowed; but the alarm that had been raised could not be appeased, so as to admit of any comfort for him while he continued at Randalls. He was satisfied of there being no present danger in returning home, but no assurances could convince him that it was safe to stay; and while the others were variously urging and recommending, Mr Knightley and Emma settled it in a few brief sentences: thus:

' Your father will not be easy; why do not you go? '

' I am ready, if the others are.'

' Shall I ring the bell? '

' Yes, do.'

And the bell was rung, and the carriages spoken for. A few minutes more. and Emma hoped to see one troublesome companion deposited in his own house, to get sober and cool, and the other recover his temper and happiness when this visit of hardship were over.

The carriage came; and Mr Woodhouse, always the first object on such occasions, was carefully attended to his own by Mr Knightley and Mr Weston; but not all that either could say could prevent some renewal of alarm at the sight of the snow which had actually fallen, and the discovery of a much darker night than he had been prepared for. ' He was afraid they should have a very bad drive. He was afraid poor Isabella would not like it. And there would be poor Emma in the carriage behind. He did not know what they had best do. They must keep as much together as they could;' and James was talked to, and given a charge to go very slow, and wait for the other carriage.

Isabella stepped in after her father; John Knightley forgetting that he did not belong to their party, stept in after his wife very naturally; so that Emma found, on being escorted and followed into the second carriage by Mr Elton, that the door was to be lawfully shut on them, and that they were to have a *tête-à-tête* drive. It would not have been the awkwardness of a moment, it would have been rather a pleasure, previous to the suspicions of this very day; she could have talked to him of Harriet, and the three-quarters of a mile would have seemed but one. But now, she would rather it had not happened. She believed he had been drinking too much of Mr Weston's good wine, and felt sure that he would want to be talking nonsense.

To restrain him as much as might be, by her own manners,

she was immediately preparing to speak, with exquisite calmness and gravity, of the weather and the night; but scarcely had she begun, scarcely had they passed the sweep-gate and joined the other carriage, than she found her subject cut up—her hand seized—her attention demanded, and Mr Elton actually making violent love to her: availing himself of the precious opportunity, declaring sentiments which must be already well known, hoping —fearing—adoring—ready to die if she refused him; but flattering himself that his ardent attachment and unequalled love and unexampled passion could not fail of having some effect, and, in short, very much resolved on being seriously accepted as soon as possible. It really was so. Without scruple—without apology—without much apparent diffidence, Mr Elton, the lover of Harriet, was professing himself *her* lover. She tried to stop him; but vainly; he would go on, and say it all. Angry as she was, the thought of the moment made her resolve to restrain herself when she did speak. She felt that half this folly must be drunkenness, and therefore could hope that it might belong only to the passing hour. Accordingly, with a mixture of the serious and the playful, which she hoped would best suit his half-and-half state, she replied:

'I am very much astonished, Mr Elton. This to *me*! You forget yourself; you take me for my friend; any message to Miss Smith I shall be happy to deliver; but no more of this to *me*, if you please.'

'Miss Smith! message to Miss Smith! What could she possibly mean?' And he repeated her words with such assurance of accent, such boastful pretence of amazement, that she could not help replying with quickness:

'Mr Elton, this is the most extraordinary conduct! and I can account for it only in one way; you are not yourself, or you could not speak either to me or of Harriet in such a manner. Command yourself enough to say no more, and I will endeavour to forget it.'

But Mr Elton had only drunk wine enough to elevate his spirits, not at all to confuse his intellects. He perfectly knew his own meaning; and having warmly protested against her suspicion as most injurious, and slightly touched upon his respect for Miss Smith as her friend, but acknowledging his wonder that Miss Smith should be mentioned at all, he resumed the subject of his own passion, and was very urgent for a favourable answer.

As she thought less of his inebriety, she thought more of his

95

inconstancy and presumption, and with fewer struggles for politeness, replied:

' It is impossible for me to doubt any longer. You have made
yourself too clear. Mr Elton, my astonishment is much beyond
anything I can express. After such behaviour as I have witnessed
during the last month, to Miss Smith—such attentions as I have
been in the daily habit of observing—to be addressing me in this
manner: this is an unsteadiness of character, indeed, which I had
not supposed possible. Believe me, sir, I am far, very far, from
gratified in being the object of such professions.'

' Good Heaven!' cried Mr Elton, ' what can be the meaning
of this? Miss Smith! I never thought of Miss Smith in the whole
course of my existence; never paid her any attentions, but as
your friend; never cared whether she were dead or alive, but
as your friend. If she has fancied otherwise, her own wishes have
misled her, and I am very sorry, extremely sorry. But, Miss
Smith, indeed! Oh, Miss Woodhouse, who can think of Miss
Smith when Miss Woodhouse is near? No, upon my honour,
there is no unsteadiness of character. I have thought only of
you. I protest against having paid the smallest attention to any
one else. Everything that I have said or done, for many weeks
past, has been with the sole view of marking my adoration of
yourself. You cannot really seriously doubt it. No ' (in an accent
meant to be insinuating), ' I am sure you have seen and understood me.'

It would be impossible to say what Emma felt on hearing this;
which of all her unpleasant sensations was uppermost. She was
too completely overpowered to be immediately able to reply;
and two moments of silence being ample encouragement for Mr
Elton's sanguine state of mind, he tried to take her hand again,
as he joyously exclaimed:

' Charming Miss Woodhouse! allow me to interpret this interesting silence. It confesses that you have long understood me.'

' No, sir,' cried Emma, ' it confesses no such thing. So far
from having long understood you I have been in a most complete
error with respect to your views, till this moment. As to myself,
I am very sorry that you should have been giving way to any
feelings. Nothing could be further from my wishes—your attachment to my friend Harriet—your pursuit of her (pursuit it appeared) gave me great pleasure, and I have been very earnestly
wishing you success; but had I supposed that she were not
your attraction to Hartfield, I should certainly have thought
you judged ill in making your visits so frequent. Am I to believe

that you have never sought to recommend yourself particularly to Miss Smith—that you have never thought seriously of her?'

'Never, madam,' cried he, affronted in his turn; 'never, I assure you. *I* think seriously of Miss Smith! Miss Smith is a very good sort of girl: and I should be happy to see her respectably settled. I wish her extremely well; and, no doubt, there are men who might not object to—— Everybody has their level; but as for myself, I am not, I think, quite so much at a loss. I need not so totally despair of an equal alliance as to be addressing myself to Miss Smith! No, madam, my visits to Hartfield have been for yourself only; and the encouragement I received——'

'Encouragement! I give you encouragement! Sir, you have been entirely mistaken in supposing it. I have seen you only as the admirer of my friend. In no other light could you have been more to me than a common acquaintance. I am exceedingly sorry; but it is well that the mistake ends where it does. Had the same behaviour continued, Miss Smith might have been led into a misconception of your views; not being aware, probably, any more than myself, of the very great inequality which you are so sensible of. But, as it is, the disappointment is single, and, I trust, will not be lasting. I have no thoughts of matrimony at present.'

He was too angry to say another word, her manner too decided to invite supplication; and in this state of swelling resentment, and mutually deep mortification, they had to continue together a few minutes longer, for the fears of Mr Woodhouse had confined them to a foot-pace. If there had not been so much anger, there would have been desperate awkwardness; but their straightforward emotions left no room for the little zigzags of embarrassment. Without knowing when the carriage turned into Vicarage Lane, or when it stopped, they found themselves, all at once, at the door of his house; and he was out before another syllable passed. Emma then felt it indispensable to wish him a good night. The compliment was just returned, coldly and proudly; and, under indescribable irritation of spirits, she was then conveyed to Hartfield.

There she was welcomed, with the utmost delight, by her father, who had been trembling for the dangers of a solitary drive from Vicarage Lane—turning a corner which he could never bear to think of—and in strange hands—a mere common coachman—no James; and there it seemed as if her return only were wanted to make everything go well: for Mr John

Knightley, ashamed of his ill humour, was now all kindness and attention; and so particularly solicitous for the comfort of her father, as to seem—if not quite ready to join him in a basin of gruel—perfectly sensible of its being exceedingly wholesome; and the day was concluding in peace and comfort to all their little party, except herself. But her mind had never been in such perturbation; and it needed a very strong effort to appear attentive and cheerful till the usual hour of separating allowed her the relief of quiet reflection.

16

THE hair was curled, and the maid sent away, and Emma sat down to think and be miserable. It was a wretched business indeed. Such an overthrow of everything she had been wishing for. Such a development of everything most unwelcome! Such a blow for Harriet—that was the worst of all. Every part of it brought pain and humiliation of some sort or other; but, compared with the evil to Harriet, all was light; and she would gladly have submitted to feel yet more mistaken—more in error —more disgraced by misjudgment than she actually was, could the effects of her blunders have been confined to herself.

' If I had not persuaded Harriet into liking the man, I could have borne anything. He might have doubled his presumption to me—but poor Harriet! '

How she could have been so deceived! He protested that he had never thought seriously of Harriet—never! She looked back as well as she could; but it was all confusion. She had taken up the idea, she supposed, and made everything bend to it. His manners, however, must have been unmarked, wavering, dubious, or she could not have been so misled.

The picture! How eager he had been about the picture! and the charade! and an hundred other circumstances; how clearly they had seemed to point at Harriet! To be sure, the charade, with its ' ready wit '—but then, the ' soft eyes '—in fact, it suited neither; it was a jumble without taste or truth. Who could have seen through such thick-headed nonsense?

Certainly she had often, especially of late, thought his manners to herself unnecessarily gallant; but it had passed as his way, as a mere error of judgment, of knowledge, of taste, as one proof, among others, that he had not always lived in the best society; that, with all the gentleness of his address, true elegance was sometimes wanting; but, till this very day, she had never for an instant suspected it to mean anything but grateful respect to her as Harriet's friend.

To Mr John Knightley was she indebted for her first idea on the subject, for the first start of its possibility. There was no denying that those brothers had penetration. She remembered what Mr Knightley had once said to her about Mr Elton, the caution he had given, the conviction he had professed that Mr Elton would never marry indiscreetly; and blushed to think how much truer a knowledge of his character had been there shown than any she had reached herself. It was dreadfully mortifying; but Mr Elton was proving himself, in many respects, the very reverse of what she had meant and believed him—proud, assuming, conceited; very full of his own claims, and little concerned about the feelings of others.

Contrary to the usual course of things, Mr Elton's wanting to pay his addresses to her had sunk him in her opinion. His professions and his proposals did him no service. She thought nothing of his attachment, and was insulted by his hopes. He wanted to marry well, and having the arrogance to raise his eyes to her, pretended to be in love; but she was perfectly easy as to his not suffering any disappointment that need be cared for. There had been no real affection either in his language or manners. Sighs and fine words had been given in abundance; but she would hardly devise any set of expressions, or fancy any tone of voice, less allied with real love. She need not trouble herself to pity him. He only wanted to aggrandise and enrich himself; and if Miss Woodhouse of Hartfield, the heiress of thirty thousand pounds, were not quite so easily obtained as he had fancied, he would soon try for Miss Somebody-else with twenty, or with ten.

But, that she should talk of encouragement, should consider her as aware of his views, accepting his attentions, meaning, in short, to marry him—should suppose himself her equal in connection or mind—look down upon her friend, so well understanding the gradations of rank below him, and be so blind to what rose above, as to fancy himself showing no presumption in addressing her!—it was most provoking.

Perhaps it was not fair to expect him to feel how very much he was her inferior in talent, and all the elegancies of mind. The very want of such equality might prevent his perception of it; but he must know that in fortune and consequence she was greatly his superior. He must know that the Woodhouses had been settled for several generations at Hartfield, the younger branch of a very ancient family, and that the Eltons were nobody. The landed property of Hartfield certainly was inconsiderable, being but a sort of notch in the Donwell Abbey estate, to which all the rest of Highbury belonged; but their fortune, from other sources, was such as to make them scarcely secondary to Donwell Abbey itself, in every other kind of consequence; and the Woodhouses had long held a high place in the consideration of the neighbourhood which Mr Elton had first entered not two years ago, to make his way as he could, without any alliances but in trade, or anything to recommend him to notice but his situation and his civility. But he had fancied her in love with him; that evidently must have been his dependence; and after raving a little about the seeming incongruity of gentle manners and a conceited head, Emma was obliged, in common honesty, to stop and admit that her own behaviour to him had been so complaisant and obliging, so full of courtesy and attention, as (supposing her real motive unperceived) might warrant a man of ordinary observation and delicacy, like Mr Elton, in fancying himself a very decided favourite. If *she* had so misinterpreted his feelings, she had little right to wonder that *he*, with self-interest to blind him, should have mistaken hers.

The first error, and the worst, lay at her door. It was foolish, it was wrong, to take so active a part in bringing any two people together. It was adventuring too far, assuming too much, making light of what ought to be serious—a trick of what ought to be simple. She was quite concerned and ashamed, and resolved to do such things no more.

'Here have I,' said she, 'actually talked poor Harriet into being very much attached to this man. She might never have thought of him but for me; and certainly never would have thought of him with hope, if I had not assured her of his attachment, for she is as modest and humble as I used to think him. Oh that I had been satisfied with persuading her not to accept young Martin. There I was quite right: that was well done of me; but there I should have stopped, and left the rest to time and chance. I was introducing her into good company, and giving her the opportunity of pleasing some one worth having; I ought not to have attempted more. But now, poor girl! her peace is cut up for some time. I have been but half a friend to her! and if she were *not* to feel this disappointment so very much, I am sure I have not an idea of anybody else who would be at all desirable for her. William Coxe—oh no, I could not endure William Coxe—a pert young lawyer.'

She stopped to blush and laugh at her own relapse, and then resumed a more serious, more dispiriting cogitation upon what had been, and might be, and must be. The distressing explanation she had to make to Harriet, and all that poor Harriet would be suffering, with the awkwardness of future meetings, the difficulties of continuing or discontinuing the acquaintance, of subduing feelings, concealing resentment, and avoiding éclat, were enough to occupy her in most unmirthful reflections some time longer, and she went to bed at last with nothing settled but the conviction of her having blundered most dreadfully.

To youth and natural cheerfulness like Emma's, though under temporary gloom at night, the return of day will hardly fail to bring return of spirits. The youth and cheerfulness of morning are in happy analogy, and of powerful operation; and if the distress be not poignant enough to keep the eyes unclosed, they will be sure to open to sensations of softened pain and brighter hope.

Emma got up on the morrow more disposed for comfort than she had gone to bed; more ready to see alleviations of the evil before her, and to depend on getting tolerably out of it.

It was a great consolation that Mr Elton should not be really in love with her, or so particularly amiable as to make it shocking to disappoint him; that Harriet's nature should not be of that superior sort in which the feelings are most acute and retentive; and that there could be no necessity for anybody's knowing what had passed except the three principals, and especially for her father's being given a moment's uneasiness about it.

These were very cheering thoughts· and the sight of a great deal of snow on the ground did her further service, for anything was welcome that might justify their all three being quite asunder at present.

The weather was most favourable for her; though Christmas Day, she could not go to church. Mr Woodhouse would have been miserable had his daughter attempted it, and she was therefore safe from either exciting or receiving unpleasant and most unsuitable ideas. The ground covered with snow, and the atmosphere in that unsettled taste between frost and thaw which is, of all others, the most unfriendly for exercise, every morning beginning in rain or snow, and every evening setting in to freeze, she was for many days a most honourable prisoner. No intercourse with Harriet possible but by note; no church for her on Sunday any more than on Christmas Day; and no need to find excuses for Mr Elton's absenting himself.

It was weather which might fairly confine everybody at home; and though she hoped and believed him to be really taking comfort in some society or other, it was very pleasant to have her father so well satisfied with his being all alone in his own house, too wise to stir out; and to hear him say to Mr Knightley, whom no weather could keep entirely from them:

'Ah, Mr Knightley, why do not you stay at home like poor Mr Elton?'

These days of confinement would have been, but for her private perplexities, remarkably comfortable, as such seclusion exactly suited her brother, whose feelings must always be of great importance to his companions; and he had, besides, so thoroughly cleared off his ill humour at Randalls, that his amiableness never failed him during the rest of his stay at Hartfield. He was always agreeable and obliging, and speaking pleasantly of everybody. But with all the hopes of cheerfulness, and all the present comfort of delay, there was still such an evil hanging over her in the hour of explanation with Harriet, as made it impossible for Emma to be ever perfectly at ease.

17

Mr and Mrs John Knightley were not detained long at Hartfield. The weather soon improved enough for those to move who must move; and Mr Woodhouse having, as usual, tried to persuade his daughter to stay behind with all her children, was obliged to see the whole party set off, and return to his lamentations over the destiny of poor Isabella—which poor Isabella, passing her life with those she doted on, full of their merits, blind to their faults, and always innocently busy, might have been a model of right feminine happiness.

The evening of the very day on which they went brought a note from Mr Elton to Mr Woodhouse, a long, civil, ceremonious note, to say, with Mr Elton's best compliments, 'that he was proposing to leave Highbury the following morning in his way to Bath; where, in compliance with the pressing entreaties of some friends, he had engaged to spend a few weeks; and very much regretted the impossibility he was under, from various circumstances of weather and business, of taking a personal leave of Mr Woodhouse, of whose friendly civilities he should ever retain a grateful sense; and had Mr Woodhouse any commands, should be happy to attend to them.'

Emma was most agreeably surprised. Mr Elton's absence just at this time was the very thing to be desired. She admired him for contriving it, though not able to give him much credit for the manner in which it was announced. Resentment could not have been more plainly spoken than in a civility to her father, from which she was so pointedly excluded. She had not even a share in his opening compliments. Her name was not mentioned; and there was so striking a change in all this, and such an ill-judged solemnity of leave-taking in his graceful acknowledgments, as she thought, at first, could not escape her father's suspicion.

It did, however. Her father was quite taken up with the surprise of so sudden a journey, and his fears that Mr Elton might never get safely to the end of it, and saw nothing extraordinary in his language. It was a very useful note, for it supplied them with fresh matter for thought and conversation during the rest of their lonely evening. Mr Woodhouse talked over his alarms, and Emma was in spirits to persuade them away with all her usual promptitude.

She now resolved to keep Harriet no longer in the dark. He had reason to believe her nearly recovered from her cold, and it was desirable that she should have as much time as possible for getting the better of her other complaint before the gentleman's return. She went to Mrs Goddard's, accordingly, the very next day, to undergo the necessary penance of communication; and a severe one it was. She had to destroy all the hopes which she had been so industriously feeding, to appear in the ungracious character of the one preferred, and acknowledge herself grossly mistaken and misjudging in all her ideas on one subject, all her observations, all her convictions, all her prophecies for the last six weeks.

The confession completely renewed her first shame, and the sight of Harriet's tears made her think that she should never be in charity with herself again.

Harriet bore the intelligence very well, blaming nobody, and in everything testifying such an ingenuousness of disposition and lowly opinion of herself as must appear with particular advantage at that moment to her friend.

Emma was in the humour to value simplicity and modesty to the utmost; and all that was amiable, all that ought to be attaching, seemed on Harriet's side, not her own. Harriet did not consider herself as having anything to complain of. The affection of such a man as Mr Elton would have been too great a distinction. She never could have deserved him; and nobody but so partial and kind a friend as Miss Woodhouse would have thought it possible.

Her tears fell abundantly; but her grief was so truly artless, that no dignity could have made it more respectable in Emma's eyes; and she listened to her, and tried to console her with all her heart and understanding—really for the time convinced that Harriet was the superior creature of the two, and that to resemble her would be more for her own welfare and happiness than all that genius or intelligence could do.

It was rather too late in the day to set about being simple-minded and ignorant; but she left her with every previous resolution confirmed of being humble and discreet, and repressing imagination all the rest of her life. Her second duty now, inferior only to her father's claims, was to promote Harriet's comfort, and endeavour to prove her own affection in some better method than by match-making. She got her to Hartfield, and showed her the most unvarying kindness, striving to occupy and amuse her, and by books and conversation to drive Mr Elton from her thoughts.

Time, she knew, must be allowed for this being thoroughly done; and she could suppose herself but an indifferent judge of such matters in general, and very inadequate to sympathise in an attachment to Mr Elton in particular; but it seemed to her reasonable that at Harriet's age, and with the entire extinction of all hope, such a progress might be made towards a state of composure by the time of Mr Elton's return, as to allow them all to meet again in the common routine of acquaintance, without any danger of betraying sentiments or increasing them.

Harriet did think him all perfection, and maintain the non-existence of anybody equal to him in person or goodness, and did, in truth, prove herself more resolutely in love than Emma had foreseen; but yet it appeared to her so natural, so inevitable to strive against an inclination of that sort *unrequited*, that she could not comprehend its continuing very long in equal force.

If Mr Elton, on his return, made his own indifference as evident and indubitable as she could not doubt he would anxiously do, she could not imagine Harriet's persisting to place her happiness in the sight or the recollection of him.

Their being fixed, so absolutely fixed, in the same place, was bad for each, for all three. Not one of them had the power of removal, or of effecting any material change of society. They must encounter each other, and make the best of it.

Harriet was further unfortunate in the tone of her companions at Mrs Goddard's, Mr Elton being the adoration of all the teachers and great girls in the school; and it must be at Hartfield only that she could have any chance of hearing him spoken of with cooling moderation or repellant truth. Where the wound had been given, there must the cure be found, if anywhere; and Emma felt that till she saw her in the way of cure, there could be no true peace for herself.

18

Mr Frank Churchill did not come. When the time proposed drew near, Mrs Weston's fears were justified in the arrival of a letter of excuse. For the present, he could not be spared, to his 'very great mortification and regret; but still he looked forward with the hope of coming to Randalls at no distant period.'

Mrs Weston was exceedingly disappointed—much more disappointed, in fact, than her husband, though her dependence on seeing the young man had been so much more sober; but a sanguine temper, though for ever expecting more good than occurs, does not always pay for its hopes by any proportionate depression. It soon flies over the present failure, and begins to hope again. For half an hour Mr Weston was surprised and sorry; but then he began to perceive that Frank's coming two or three months later would be a much better plan, better time of year, better weather; and that he would be able, without any doubt, to stay considerably longer with them than if he had come sooner.

These feelings rapidly restored his comfort, while Mrs Weston, of a more apprehensive disposition, foresaw nothing but a repetition of excuses and delays; and after all her concern for what her husband was to suffer, suffered a great deal more herself.

Emma was not, at this time, in a state of spirits to care really about Mr Frank Churchill's not coming, except as a disappointment at Randalls. The acquaintance, at present, had no charm for her. She wanted rather to be quiet and out of temptation; but still, as it was desirable that she should appear, in general, like her usual self, she took care to express as much interest in the circumstance, and enter as warmly into Mr and Mrs Weston's disappointment as might naturally belong to their friendship.

She was the first to announce it to Mr Knightley; and exclaimed quite as much as was necessary (or, being acting a part, perhaps rather more), at the conduct of the Churchills in keeping him away. She then proceeded to say a good deal more than she felt of the advantage of such an addition to their confined society in Surrey; the pleasure of looking at somebody new; the gala-day to Highbury entire, which the sight of him would have made; and ending with reflections on the Churchills again, found herself directly involved in a disagreement with Mr Knightley; and, to her great amusement, perceived that she was taking the other side of the question from her real opinion, and making use of Mrs Weston's arguments against herself.

'The Churchills are very likely in fault,' said Mr Knightley coolly; 'but I dare say he might come if he would.'

'I do not know why you should say so. He wishes exceedingly to come; but his uncle and aunt will not spare him.'

'I cannot believe that he has not the power of coming, if he made a point of it. It is too unlikely for me to believe it without proof.'

'How odd you are! What has Mr Frank Churchill done, to make you suppose him such an unnatural creature?'

'I am not supposing him at all an unnatural creature, in suspecting that he may have learnt to be above his connections, and to care very little for anything but his own pleasure, from living with those who have always set him the example of it. It is a great deal more natural than one could wish, that a young man, brought up by those who are proud, luxurious, and selfish, should be proud, luxurious, and selfish too. If Frank Churchill had wanted to see his father, he would have contrived it between September and January. A man at his age—what is he? three or four-and-twenty—cannot be without the means of doing as much as that. It is impossible.'

'That's easily said, and easily felt by you, who have always been your own master. You are the worst judge in the world, Mr Knightley, of the difficulties of dependence. You do not know what it is to have tempers to manage.'

'It is not to be conceived that a man of three or four-and-twenty should not have liberty of mind or limb to that amount. He cannot want money, he cannot want leisure. We know, on the contrary, that he has so much of both, that he is glad to get rid of them at the idlest haunts in the kingdom. We hear of him for ever at some watering-place or other; a little while ago he was at Weymouth. This proves that he can leave the Churchills.'

' Yes, sometimes he can.'

' And those times are, whenever he thinks it worth his while; whenever there is any temptation of pleasure.'

' It is very unfair to judge of anybody's conduct without an intimate knowledge of their situation. Nobody, who has not been in the interior of a family, can say what the difficulties of any individual of that family may be. We ought to be acquainted with Enscombe, and with Mrs Churchill's temper before we pretend to decide upon what her nephew can do. He may, at times, be able to do a great deal more than he can at others.'

' There is one thing, Emma, which a man can always do, if he chooses, and that is, his duty; not by manœuvring and finessing, but by vigour and resolution. It is Frank Churchill's duty to pay this attention to his father. He knows it to be so, by his promises and messages; but if he wished to do it, it might be done. A man who felt rightly would say at once, simply and resolutely, to Mrs Churchill: " Every sacrifice of mere pleasure you will always find me ready to make to your convenience; but I must go and see my father immediately. I know he would be hurt by my failing in such a mark of respect to him on the present occasion. I shall, therefore, set off to-morrow." If he would say so to her at once in the tone of decision becoming a man, there would be no opposition made to his going.'

' No,' said Emma, laughing; ' but perhaps there might be some made to his coming back again. Such language for a young man entirely dependent to use! Nobody but you, Mr Knightley, would imagine it possible; but you have not an idea of what is requisite in situations directly opposite to your own. Mr Frank Churchill to be making such a speech as that to the uncle and aunt who have brought him up, and are to provide for him! standing up in the middle of the room, I suppose, and speaking as loud as he could! How can you imagine such conduct practicable?'

' Depend upon it, Emma, a sensible man would find no difficulty in it. He would feel himself in the right; and the declaration, made, of course, as a man of sense would make it, in a proper manner, would do him more good, raise him higher, fix his interest stronger with the people he depended on, than all that a line of shifts and expedients can ever do. Respect would be added to affection. They would feel that they could trust him; that the nephew who had done rightly by his father would do rightly by them; for they know as well as he does, as well as all the world must know, that he ought to pay this visit to his father; and while meanly exerting their power to delay it, are in their hearts not thinking the better of him for submitting to their whims. Respect for right conduct is felt by everybody: if he would act in this sort of manner on principle, consistently, regularly, their little minds would bend to his.'

'I rather doubt that. You are very fond of bending little minds; but where little minds belong to rich people in authority, I think they have a knack of swelling out till they are quite as unmanageable as great ones. I can imagine that if you, as you are, Mr Knightley, were to be transported and placed all at once in Mr Frank Churchill's situation, you would be able to say and do just what you have been recommending for him; and it might have a very good effect. The Churchills might not have a word to say in return; but then you would have no habits of early obedience and long observance to break through. To him who has, it might not be so easy to burst forth at once into perfect independence, and set all their claims on his gratitude and regard at naught. He may have as strong a sense of what would be right as you can have, without being so equal, under particular circumstances, to act up to it.'

'Then it would not be so strong a sense. If it failed to produce equal exertion, it could not be an equal conviction.'

'Oh the difference of situation and habit! I wish you would try to understand what an amiable young man may be likely to feel in directly opposing those whom, as child and boy, he has been looking up to all his life.'

'Your amiable young man is a very weak young man, if this be the first occasion of his carrying through a resolution to do right against the will of others. It ought to have been a habit with him, by this time, of following his duty, instead of consulting expediency. I can allow for the fears of the child, but not of the man. As he became rational, he ought to have roused himself, and shaken off all that was unworthy in their authority. He ought to have opposed the first attempt on their side to make him slight his father. Had he begun as he ought, there would have been no difficulty now.'

'We shall never agree about him,' cried Emma; 'but that is nothing extraordinary. I have not the least idea of his being a weak young man; I feel sure that he is not. Mr Weston would not be blind to folly, though in his own son; but he is very likely to have a more yielding, complying, mild disposition than would suit your notions of man's perfection. I dare say he has; and though it may cut him off from some advantages, it will secure him many others.'

'Yes; all the advantages of sitting still when he ought to move, and of leading a life of mere idle pleasure, and fancying himself extremely expert in finding excuses for it. He can sit down and write a fine flourishing letter, full of professions and falsehoods, and persuade himself that he has hit upon the very best method in the world of preserving peace at home, and preventing his father's having any right to complain. His letters disgust me.'

'Your feelings are singular. They seem to satisfy everybody else.'

'I suspect they do not satisfy Mrs Weston. They hardly can satisfy a woman of her good sense and quick feelings: standing in a mother's place, but without a mother's affection to blind her. It is on her account that attention to Randalls is doubly due, and she must doubly feel the omission. Had she been a person of consequence herself he would have come, I dare say; and it would not have signified whether he did or no. Can you think your friend behindhand in these sort of considerations? Do you suppose she does not often say all this to herself? No, Emma; your amiable young man can be amiable only in French, not in English. He may be very "amiable," have very good manners, and be very agreeable; but he can have no English delicacy towards the feelings of other people—nothing really amiable about him.'

'You seem determined to think ill of him.'

'Me! not at all,' replied Mr Knightley, rather displeased; 'I do not want to think ill of him. I should be as ready to acknowledge his merits as any other man; but I hear of none, except what are merely personal—that he is well-grown and good-looking, with smooth, plausible manners.'

'Well, if he have nothing else to recommend him, he will be a treasure at Highbury. We do not often look upon fine young men, well-bred and agreeable. We must not be nice, and ask for all the virtues into the bargain. Cannot you imagine, Mr Knightley, what a *sensation* his coming will produce? There will be but one subject throughout the parishes of Donwell and Highbury; but one interest—one object of curiosity; it will be all Mr Frank Churchill; we shall think and speak of nobody else.'

'You will excuse my being so much overpowered. If I find him conversable, I shall be glad of his acquaintance; but if he is only a chattering coxcomb, he will not occupy much of my time or thoughts.'

'My idea of him is, that he can adapt his conversation to the taste of everybody, and has the power as well as the wish of being universally agreeable. To you, he will talk of farming; to me, of drawing or music; and so on to everybody, having that general information on all subjects which will enable him to follow the lead, or take the lead, just as propriety may require, and to speak extremely well on each; that is my idea of him.'

'And mine,' said Mr Knightley warmly, 'is, that if he turn out anything like it, he will be the most insufferable fellow breathing! What! at three-and-twenty to be the king of his company—the great man—the practised politician, who is to read everybody's character, and make everybody's talents conduce to the display of his own superiority; to be dispensing his flatteries around, that he may make all appear like fools compared with himself! My dear Emma, your own good sense could not endure such a puppy when it came to the point.'

'I will say no more about him,' cried Emma—'you turn everything to evil. We are both prejudiced! you against, I for him; and we have no chance of agreeing till he is really here.'

'Prejudiced! I am not prejudiced.'

'But I am very much, and without being at all ashamed of it. My love for Mr and Mrs Weston gives me a decided prejudice in his favour.'

'He is a person I never think of from one month's end to another,' said Mr Knightley, with a degree of vexation, which made Emma immediately talk of something else, though she could not comprehend why he should be angry.

To take a dislike to a young man, only because he appeared to be of a different disposition from himself, was unworthy the real liberality of mind which she was always used to acknowledge in him; for, with all the high opinion of himself which she had often laid to his charge, she had never before for a moment supposed it could make him unjust to the merit of another.

19

EMMA and Harriet had been walking together one morning, and, in Emma's opinion, had been talking enough of Mr Elton for that day. She could not think that Harriet's solace or her own sins required more; and she was therefore industriously getting rid of the subject as they returned, but it burst out again when she thought she had succeeded, and after speaking some time of what the poor must suffer in winter, and receiving no other answer than a very plaintive—'Mr Elton is so good to the poor!' she found something else must be done.

They were just approaching the house where lived Mrs and Miss Bates. She determined to call upon them, and seek safety in numbers. There was always sufficient reason for such an attention; Mrs and Miss Bates loved to be called on; and she knew she was considered by the very few who presumed ever to see imperfection in her, as rather negligent in that respect, and as not contributing what she ought to the stock of their scanty comforts.

She had had many a hint from Mr Knightley, and some from her own heart, as to her deficiency, but none were equal to counteract the persuasion of its being very disagreeable—a waste of time—tiresome women—and all the horror of being in danger of falling in with the second rate and third rate of Highbury, who were calling on them for ever, and therefore she seldom went near them. But now she made the sudden resolution of not passing their door without going in; observing, as she proposed it to Harriet, that, as well as she could calculate, they were just now quite safe from any letter from Jane Fairfax.

The house belonged to people in business. Mrs and Miss Bates occupied the drawing-room floor; and there, in the very moderate-sized apartment, which was everything to them, the visitors were most cordially and even gratefully welcomed; the quiet neat old lady, who with her knitting was seated in the warmest corner, wanting even to give up her place to Miss Woodhouse, and her more active, talking daughter almost ready to overpower them with care and kindness, thanks for their visit, solicitude for their shoes, anxious inquiries after Mr Woodhouse's health, cheerful communications about her mother's, and sweet-cake from the beaufet: 'Mrs Cole had just been there, just called in for ten minutes, and had been so good as to sit an hour with them, and *she* had taken a piece of cake, and been so kind as to say she liked it very much; and, therefore, she hoped Miss Woodhouse and Miss Smith would do them the favour to eat a piece too.'

The mention of the Coles was sure to be followed by that of Mr Elton. There was intimacy between them, and Mr Cole had heard from Mr Elton since his going away. Emma knew what was coming: they must have the letter over again, and settle

how long he had been gone, and how much he was engaged in
company, and what a favourite he was wherever he went, and
how full the Master of the Ceremonies' ball had been; and she
went through it very well, with all the interest and all the commendation that could be requisite, and always putting forward
to prevent Harriet's being obliged to say a word.

This she had been prepared for when she entered the house;
but meant, having once talked him handsomely over, to be no
further incommodated by any troublesome topic, and to wander at large amongst all the Mistresses and Misses of Highbury,
and their card-parties. She had not been prepared of have Jane
Fairfax succeed Mr Elton; but he was actually hurried off by
Miss Bates; she jumped away from him at last abruptly to the
Coles, to usher in a letter from her niece.

'Oh yes—Mr Elton, I understand—certainly as to dancing—
Mrs Cole was telling me that dancing at the rooms at Bath was—
Mrs Cole was so kind as to sit some time with us, talking of Jane;
for as soon as she came in she began inquiring after her, Jane is
so very great a favourite there. Whenever she is with us, Mrs
Cole does not know how to show her kindness enough; and I
must say that Jane deserves it as much as anybody can. And so
she began inquiring after her directly, saying, "I know you cannot have heard from Jane lately, because it is not her time for
writing;" and when I immediately said, "But indeed we have,
we had a letter this very morning," I do not know that I ever
saw anybody more surprised. 'Have you, upon your honour?'
said she; "well, that is quite unexpected. Do let me hear what
she says." '

Emma's politeness was at hand directly, to say, with smiling
interest:

'Have you heard from Miss Fairfax so lately? I am extremely
happy. I hope she is well?'

'Thank you. You are so kind!' replied the happily deceived
aunt, while eagerly hunting for the letter. 'Oh, here it is. I
was sure it could not be far off; but I had put my huswife upon
it, you see, without being aware, and so it was quite hid; but
I had it in my hand so very lately that I was almost sure it must
be on the table. I was reading it to Mrs Cole, and, since she
went away, I was reading it again to my mother, for it is such
a pleasure to her—a letter from Jane—that she can never hear
it often enough; so I knew it could not be far off, and here it is,
only just under my huswife—and since you are so kind as to
wish to hear what she says—but, first of all, I really must, in jus-

tice to Jane, apologise for her writing so short a letter—only two pages, you see, hardly two, and in general she fills the whole paper and crosses half. My mother often wonders that I can make it out so well. She often says, when the letter is first opened, " Well, Hetty, now I think you will be put to it to make out all that checker-work "—don't you, ma'am? And then I tell her, I am sure she would contrive to make it out herself, if she had nobody to do it for her, every word of it—I am sure she would pore over it till she had made out every word. And, indeed, though my mother's eyes are not so good as they were, she can see amazingly well still, thank God! with the help of spectacles. It is such a blessing! My mother's are really very good indeed. Jane often says, when she is here, " I am sure, grandmamma, you must have had very strong eyes to see as you do, and so much fine work as you have done too! I only wish my eyes may last me as well." '

All this, spoken extremely fast, obliged Miss Bates to stop for breath; and Emma said something very civil about the excellence of Miss Fairfax's handwriting.

' You are extremely kind,' replied Miss Bates, highly gratified; ' you, who are such a judge, and write so beautifully yourself. I am sure there is nobody's praise that could give us so much pleasure as Miss Woodhouse's. My mother does not hear; she is a little deaf, you know. Ma'am,' addressing her, ' do you hear what Miss Woodhouse is so obliging to say about Jane's handwriting? '

And Emma had the advantage of hearing her own silly compliment repeated twice over before the good old lady could comprehend it. She was pondering, in the meanwhile, upon the possibility, without seeming very rude, of making her escape from Jane Fairfax's letter, and had almost resolved on hurrying away directly, under some slight excuse, when Miss Bates turned to her again and seized her attention.

' My mother's deafness is very trifling, you see, just nothing at all. By only raising my voice, and saying anything two or three times over, she is sure to hear; but then she is used to my voice. But it is very remarkable that she should always hear Jane better than she does me. Jane speaks so distinct! However, she will not find her grandmamma at all deafer than she was two years ago; which is saying a great deal at my mother's time of life; and it really is full two years, you know, since she was here. We never were so long without seeing her before; and, as I was telling Mrs Cole, we shall hardly know how to make enough of her now.'

'Are you expecting Miss Fairfax here soon?'

'Oh, yes; next week.'

'Indeed! that must be a very great pleasure.'

'Thank you. You are very kind. Yes, next week. Everybody is so surprised; and everybody says the same obliging things. I am sure she will be as happy to see her friends at Highbury as they can be to see her. Yes, Friday or Saturday; she cannot say which, because Colonel Campbell will be wanting the carriage himself one of those days. So very good of them to send her the whole way! But they always do, you know. Oh, yes, Friday or Saturday next. That is what she writes about. That is the reason of her writing out of rule, as we call it; for, in the common course, we should not have heard from her before next Tuesday or Wednesday.'

'Yes, so I imagined. I was afraid there could be little chance of my hearing anything of Miss Fairfax to-day.'

'So obliging of you! No, we should not have heard, if it had not been for this particular circumstance, of her being to come here so soon. My mother is so delighted! for she is to be three months with us at least. Three months, she says so, positively, as I am going to have the pleasure of reading to you. The case is, you see, that the Campbells are going to Ireland. Mrs Dixon has persuaded her father and mother to come over and see her directly. They had not intended to go over till the summer, but she is so impatient to see them again; for till she married, last October, she was never away from them so much as a week, which must make it very strange to be in different kingdoms, I was going to say, but, however, different countries, and so she wrote a very urgent letter to her mother, or her father—I declare I do not know which it was, but we shall see presently in Jane's letter—wrote in Mr Dixon's name as well as her own, to press their coming over directly; and they would give them the meeting in Dublin, and take them back to their country-seat, Baly-craig—a beautiful place, I fancy. Jane has heard a great deal of its beauty—from Mr Dixon I mean—I do not know that she ever heard about it from anybody else— but it was very natural, you know, that he should like to speak of his own place while he was paying his addresses—and as Jane used to be very often walking out with them—for Colonel and Mrs Campbell were very particular about their daughter's not walking out often with only Mr Dixon, for which I do not at all blame them; of course she heard everything he might be telling Miss Campbell about his own home in Ireland; and I think she wrote us word that he had shown them some drawings of the place, views that he had taken himself. He is a most amiable, charming young man, I believe. Jane was quite longing to go to Ireland, from his account of things.'

At this moment, an ingenious and animating suspicion entering Emma's brain with regard to Jane Fairfax, this charming Mr Dixon, and the not going to Ireland, she said, with the insidious design of further discovery:

'You must feel it very fortunate that Miss Fairfax should be allowed to come to you at such a time. Considering the very particular friendship between her and Mrs Dixon you could hardly have expected her to be excused from accompanying Colonel and Mrs Campbell.'

'Very true, very true, indeed. The very thing that we have always been rather afraid of; for we should not have liked to have her at such a distance from us, for months together—not able to come if anything was to happen; but you see everything turns out for the best. They want her (Mr and Mrs Dixon) excessively to come over with Colonel and Mrs Campbell; quite depend upon it; nothing can be more kind or pressing than their *joint* invitation, Jane says, as you will hear presently. Mr Dixon does not seem in the least backward in any attention. He is a most charming young man. Ever since the service he rendered Jane at Weymouth, when they were out in that party on the water, and she, by the sudden whirling round of something or other among the sails, would have been dashed into the sea at once, and actually was all but gone, if he had not with the greatest presence of mind caught hold of her habit—I can never think of it without trembling! But ever since we had the history of that day, I have been so fond of Mr Dixon!'

'But, in spite of all her friends' urgency, and her own wish of seeing Ireland, Miss Fairfax prefers devoting the time to you and Mrs Bates?'

'Yes—entirely her own doing, entirely her own choice; and Colonel and Mrs Campbell think she does quite right, just what they should recommend; and indeed they particularly *wish* her to try her native air, as she has not been quite so well as usual lately.'

'I am concerned to hear of it. I think they judge wisely; but Mrs Dixon must be very much disappointed. Mrs Dixon, I understand, has no remarkable degree of personal beauty—is not, by any means, to be compared with Miss Fairfax?'

'Oh, no. You are very obliging to say such things, but certainly not; there is no comparison between them. Miss Campbell always was absolutely plain, but extremely elegant and amiable.'

'Yes, that of course.'

'Jane caught a bad cold, poor thing! so long ago as the 7th of November (as I am going to read to you), and has never been well since. A long time, is not it, for a cold to hang upon her? She never mentioned it before, because she would not alarm us. Just like her! so considerate! But, however, she is so far from well, that her kind friends the Campbells think she had better come home, and try an air that always agrees with her: and they have no doubt that three or four months at Highbury will entirely cure her; and it is certainly a great deal better that she should come here than go to Ireland, if she is unwell. Nobody could nurse her as we should do.'

'It appears to me the most desirable arrangement in the world.'

'And so she is to come to us next Friday or Saturday, and the Campbells leave town in their way to Holyhead the Monday following, as you will find from Jane's letter. So sudden! You may guess, dear Miss Woodhouse, what a flurry it has thrown me in. If it was not for the drawback of her illness—but I am afraid we must expect to see her grown thin, and looking very poorly. I must tell you what an unlucky thing happened to me as to that. I always make a point of reading Jane's letters through to myself first, before I read them aloud to my mother, you know, for fear of there being anything in them to distress her. Jane desired me to do it, so I always do! and so I began to-day with my usual caution: but no sooner did I come to the mention of her being unwell, than I burst out, quite frightened, with "Bless me! poor Jane is ill!" which my mother, being on the watch, heard distinctly, and was sadly alarmed at. However, when I read on, I found it was not near so bad as I had fancied at first; and I make so light of it now to her that she does not think much about it: but I cannot imagine how I could be so off my guard. If Jane does not get well soon, we will call in Mr Perry. The expense shall not be thought of; and though he is so liberal and so fond of Jane, that I dare say he would not mean to charge anything for attendance, we could not suffer it to be so, you know. He has a wife and family to maintain, and is not to be giving away his time. Well, now I have just given you a hint of what Jane writes about, we will turn to her letter, and I am sure she tells her own story a great deal better than I can tell it for her.'

' I am afraid we must be running away,' said Emma, glancing at Harriet, and beginning to rise, ' my father will be expecting us. I had no intention, I thought I had no power, of staying more than five minutes, when I first entered the house. I merely called because I would not pass the door without inquiring after Mrs Bates; but I have been so pleasantly detained. Now, however, we must wish you and Mrs Bates good morning.'

And not all that could be urged to detain her succeeded. She regained the street, happy in this, that though much had been forced on her against her will; though she had, in fact, heard the whole substance of Jane Fairfax's letter, she had been able to escape the letter itself.

20

JANE FAIRFAX was an orphan, the only child of Mrs Bates's youngest daughter.

The marriage of Lieut. Fairfax of the —— regiment of infantry, and Miss Jane Bates, had had its day of fame and pleasure, hope and interest; but nothing now remained of it save the melancholy remembrance of him dying in action abroad, of his widow sinking under consumption and grief soon afterwards, and this girl.

By birth she belonged to Highbury; and when, at three years old, on losing her mother she became the property, the charge, the consolation, the fondling of her grandmother and aunt, there had seemed every probability of her being permanently fixed there; of her being taught only what very limited means could command, and growing up with no advantages of connection or improvement, to be engrafted on what nature had given her in a pleasing person, good understanding, and warm-hearted, well-meaning relations.

But the compassionate feelings of a friend of her father gave a change to her destiny. This was Colonel Campbell, who had very highly regarded Fairfax, as an excellent officer and most deserving young man; and further had been indebted to him for such attentions, during a severe camp-fever, as he believed had saved his life. These were claims which he did not learn to overlook, though some years passed away from the death of poor Fairfax before his own return to England put anything in his power. When he did return, he sought out the child and took notice of her. He was a married man, with only one living child, a girl, about Jane's age; and Jane became their guest, paying them long visits and growing a favourite with all, and before she was nine years old, his daughter's great fondness for her, and his own wish of being a real friend, united to produce an offer from Colonel Campbell of undertaking the whole charge of her education. It was accepted; and from that period Jane had belonged to Colonel Campbell's family, and had lived with them entirely, only visting her grandmother from time to time.

The plan was that she should be brought up for educating others; the very few hundred pounds which she inherited from her father making independence impossible. To provide for her otherwise was out of Colonel Campbell's power; for though his income, by pay and appointments, was handsome, his fortune was moderate, and must be all his daughter's; but, by giving her an education, he hoped to be supplying the means of respectable subsistence hereafter.

Such was Jane Fairfax's history. She had fallen into good hands, known nothing but kindness from the Campbells, and been given an excellent education. Living constantly with right-minded and well-informed people, her heart and understanding had received every advantage of discipline and culture; and Colonel Campbell's residence being in London, every lighter talent had been done full justice to, by the attendance of first-rate masters. Her disposition and abilities were equally worthy of all that friendship could do; and at eighteen or nineteen she was, as far as such an early age can be qualified for the care of children, fully competent to the office of instruction herself; but she was too much beloved to be parted with. Neither father nor mother could promote, and the daughter could not endure it. The evil day was put off. It was easy to decide that she was still too young; and Jane remained with them, sharing as another daughter, in all the rational pleasures of an elegant society, and a judicious mixture of home and amusement, with only the drawback of the future—the sobering suggestions of her own good understanding—to remind her that all this might soon be over.

The affection of the whole family, the warm attachment of Miss Campbell in particular, was the more honourable to each party from the circumstance of Jane's decided superiority, both in beauty and acquirements. That nature had given it in feature could not be unseen by the young woman, nor could her higher powers of mind be unfelt by the parents. They continued together with unabated regard, however, till the marriage of Miss Campbell, who, by that chance, that luck which so often defies anticipation in matrimonial affairs, giving attraction to what is moderate rather than to what is superior, engaged the affections of Mr Dixon, a young man, rich and agreeable, almost as soon as they were acquainted; and was eligibly and happily settled, while Jane Fairfax had yet her bread to earn.

This event had very lately taken place; too lately for anything to be yet attempted by her less fortunate friend towards entering on her path of duty, though she had now reached the age which her own judgment had fixed on for beginning. She had long resolved that one-and-twenty should be the period. With the fortitude of a devoted noviciate, she had resolved at one-and-twenty to complete the sacrifice, and retire from all the pleasures of life, of rational intercourse, equal society, peace and hope, to penance and mortification for ever.

The good sense of Colonel and Mrs Campbell could not op-pose such a resolution, though their feelings did. As long as they lived, no exertions would be necessary, their home might be hers for ever; and for their own comfort they would have retained her wholly; but this would be selfishness: what must be at last had better be soon. Perhaps they began to feel it might have been kinder and wiser to have resisted the temptation of any delay, and spared her from a taste of such enjoyments of ease and leisure as must now be relinquished. Still, however, affection was glad to catch at any reasonable excuse for not hurrying on the wretched moment. She had never been quite well since the time of their daughter's marriage; and till she should have completely recovered her usual strength, they must forbid her engaging in duties which, so far from being compatible with a weakened frame and varying spirits, seemed, under the most favourable circumstances, to require something more than human perfection of body and mind to be discharged with tolerable comfort.

With regard to her not accompanying them to Ireland, her account to her aunt contained nothing but truth, though there might be some truths not told. It was her own choice to give the time of their absence to Highbury; to spend, perhaps, her last months of perfect liberty with those kind relations to whom she was so very dear; and the Campbells, whatever might be their motive or motives, whether single, or double, or treble, gave the arrangement their ready sanction, and said that they depended more on a few months spent in her native air, for the recovery of her health, than on anything else. Certain it was that she was to come, and that Highbury, instead of welcoming that perfect novelty which had been so long promised it—Mr Frank Churchill—must put up for the present with Jane Fairfax, who could bring only the freshness of a two years' absence.

Emma was sorry to have to pay civilities to a person she did not like through three long months—to be always doing more than she wished, and less than she ought! Why she did not like Jane Fairfax might be a difficult question to answer; Mr Knightley had once told her it was because she saw in her the really accomplished young woman which she wanted to be thought herself; and though the accusation had been eagerly refuted at the time, there were moments of self-examination in which her conscience could not quite acquit her. But ' she could never get acquainted with her; she did not know how it was, but there was such coldness and reserve; such apparent indifference whether she pleased or not; and then, her aunt was such an eternal talker! and she was made such a fuss with by everybody! and it had been always imagined that they were to be intimate; because their ages were the same, everybody had supposed they must be so fond of each other.' These were her reasons; she had no better.

It was a dislike so little just—every imputed fault was so magnified by fancy—that she never saw Jane Fairfax, the first time after any considerable absence, without feeling that she had injured her; and now, when the due visit was paid on her arrival, after a two years' interval, she was particularly struck with the very appearance and manners which for those two whole years she had been depreciating. Jane Fairfax was very elegant, remarkably elegant, and she had herself the highest value for elegance. Her height was pretty, just such as almost everybody would think tall, and nobody could think very tall; her figure particularly graceful: her size a most becoming medium, between fat and thin, though a slight appearance of ill health seemed to point out the likeliest evil of the two. Emma could not but feel all this; and then, her face—her features—there was more beauty in them all together than she had remembered; it was not regular, but it was very pleasing beauty. Her eyes, a deep gray, with dark eyelashes and eyebrows, had never been denied their praise; but the skin, which she had been used to cavil at, as wanting colour, had a clearness and delicacy which really needed no fuller bloom. It was a style of beauty of which elegance was the reigning character, and as such, she must, in honour, by all her principles, admire it; elegance which, whether of person or of mind, she saw so little in Highbury. There, not to be vulgar, was distinction and merit.

In short, she sat, during the first visit, looking at Jane Fairfax with twofold complacency—the sense of pleasure and the sense of rendering justice, and was determining that she would dislike her no longer. When she took in her history, indeed, her situation, as well as her beauty; when she considered what all this elegance was destined to, what she was going to sink from, how she was going to live, it seemed impossible to feel anything but compassion and respect; especially, if to every well-known particular, entitling her to interest, were added the highly probable circumstance of an attachment to Mr Dixon, which she had so naturally started to herself. In that case, nothing could be more pitiable or more honourable than the sacrifices she had resolved on. Emma was very willing now to acquit her of having seduced Mr Dixon's affections from his wife, or of anything mischievous which her imagination had suggested at first. If it were love, it might be simple, single, successless love on her side alone. She might have been unconsciously sucking in the sad poison, while a sharer of his conversation with her friend; and from the best, the purest of motives, might now be denying herself this visit to Ireland, and resolving to divide herself effectually from him and his connections by soon beginning her career of laborious duty.

Upon the whole, Emma left her with such softened, charitable feelings, as made her look around in walking home, and lament that Highbury afforded no young man worthy of giving her independence—nobody that she could wish to scheme about for her.

These were charming feelings, but not lasting. Before she had committed herself by any public profession of eternal friendship for Jane Fairfax, or done more towards a recantation of past prejudices and errors, than saying to Mr Knightley, ' She certainly is handsome: she is better than handsome! ' Jane had spent an evening at Hartfield with her grandmother and aunt, and everything was relapsing much into its usual state. Former provocations reappeared. The aunt was as tiresome as ever; more tiresome, because anxiety for her health was now added to admiration of her powers; and they had to listen to the description of exactly how little bread and butter she ate for breakfast, and how small a slice of mutton for dinner, as well as to see exhibitions of new caps and new workbags for her mother and herself; and Jane's offences rose again. They had music: Emma was obliged to play; and the thanks and praise which necessarily followed appeared to her an affection of candour, an air of greatness, meaning only to show off in higher style her own very superior performance. She was, besides, which was the worst of all, so cold, so cautious! There was no getting at her real opinion. Wrapt up in a cloak of politeness, she seemed determined to hazard nothing. She was disgustingly, was suspiciously reserved.

If anything could be more, where all was most, she was more reserved on the subject of Weymouth and the Dixons than anything. She seemed bent on giving no real insight into Mr Dixon's character, or her own value for his company, or opinion of the suitableness of the match. It was all general approbation and smoothness; nothing delineated or distinguished. It did her no service, however. Her caution was thrown away. Emma saw its artifice, and returned to her first surmises. There probably *was* something more to conceal than her own preference; Mr Dixon, perhaps, had been very near changing one friend for the other, or been fixed only to Miss Campbell, for the sake of the future twelve thousand pounds.

The like reserve prevailed on other topics. She and Mr Frank Churchill had been at Weymouth at the same time. It was known that they were a little acquainted, but not a syllable of real information could Emma procure as to what he truly was. 'Was he handsome?' 'She believed he was reckoned a very fine young man.' 'Was he agreeable?' 'He was generally thought so.' 'Did he appear a sensible young man; a young man of information?' 'At a watering-place, or in a common London acquaintance, it was difficult to decide on such points. Manners were all that could be safely judged of, under a much longer knowledge than they had yet had of Mr Churchill. She believed everybody found his manners pleasing.' Emma could not forgive her.

21

EMMA could not forgive her; but as neither provocation nor resentment were discerned by Mr Knightley, who had been of the party, and had seen only proper attention and pleasing behaviour on each side, he was expressing the next morning, being

at Hartfield again on business with Mr Woodhouse, his approbation of the whole; not so openly as he might have done had
her father been out of the room, but speaking plain enough to be
very intelligible to Emma. He had been used to think her unjust
to Jane, and had now great pleasure in marking an improvement.

'A very pleasant evening,' he began, as soon as Mr Woodhouse had been talked into what was necessary, told that he understood, and the papers swept away—'particularly pleasant. You
and Miss Fairfax gave us some very good music. I do not know
a more luxurious state, sir, sitting at one's ease to be entertained
a whole evening by two such young women; sometimes with
music and sometimes with conversation. I am sure Miss Fairfax
must have found the evening pleasant, Emma. You left nothing
undone. I was glad you made her play so much, for having no
instrument at her grandmother's, it must have been a real indulgence.'

'I am happy you approved,' said Emma, smiling; 'but I
hope I am not often deficient in what is due to guests at
Hartfield.'

'No, my dear,' said her father instantly; '*that* I am sure you
are not. There is nobody half so attentive and civil as you are.
If anything you are too attentive. The muffin last night—if
it had been handed round once, I think it would have been
enough.'

'No,' said Mr Knightley, nearly at the same time; 'you are
not often deficient; not often deficient, either in manner or comprehension. I think you understand me, therefore.'

An arch look expressed—'I understand you well enough';
but she said only, 'Miss Fairfax is reserved.'

'I always told you she was—a little; but you will soon overcome all that part of her reserve which ought to be overcome,
all that has its foundation in diffidence. What arises from
discretion must be honoured.'

'You think her diffident. I do not see it.'

'My dear Emma,' said he, moving from his chair into one close
by her, 'you are not going to tell me, I hope, that you had not a
pleasant evening?'

'Oh no; I was pleased with my own perseverance in asking
questions; and amused to think how little information I obtained.'

'I am disappointed,' was his only answer.

'I hope everybody had a pleasant evening,' said Mr Woodhouse, in his quiet way. ' I had. Once, I felt the fire rather too much; but then I moved back my chair a little, a very little, and it did not disturb me. Miss Bates was very chatty and good-humoured, as she always is, though she speaks rather too quick. However, she is very agreeable, and Mrs Bates, too, in a different way. I like old friends; and Miss Jane Fairfax is a very pretty sort of young lady; a very pretty and a very well-behaved young lady indeed. She must have found the evening agreeable, Mr Knightley, because she had Emma.'

' True, sir; and Emma, because she had Miss Fairfax.'

Emma saw his anxiety, and wishing to appease it, at least for the present, said, and with a sincerity which no one could question:

' She is a sort of elegant creature that one cannot keep one's eyes from. I am always watching her to admire; and I do pity her from my heart.'

Mr Knightley looked as if he were more gratified than he cared to express; and before he could make any reply, Mr Wood-house, whose thoughts were on the Bates's, said:

' It is a great pity that their circumstances should be so confined! a great pity indeed! and I have often wished—but it is so little one can venture to do—small, trifling presents, of anything uncommon. Now, we have killed a porker, and Emma thinks of sending them a loin or a leg; it is very small and delicate—Hartfield pork is not like any other pork—but still it is pork—and, my dear Emma, unless one could be sure of their making it into steaks, nicely fried, as ours are fried, without the smallest grease, and not roast it, for no stomach can bear roast pork—I think we had better send the leg—do not you think so, my dear?'

' My dear papa, I sent the whole hind-quarter. I knew you would wish it. There will be the leg to be salted, you know, which is so very nice, and the loin to be dressed directly, in any manner they like.'

' That's right, my dear—very right. I had not thought of it .before, but that is the best way. They must not over-salt the leg; and then, if it is not over-salted, and if it is very thoroughly boiled, just as Serle boils ours, and eaten very moderately of, with a boiled turnip, and a little carrot or parsnip, I do not consider it unwholesome.'

' Emma,' said Mr Knightley presently, ' I have a piece of news for you. You like news—and I heard an article in my way hither that I think will interest you.'

'News! Oh yes, I always like news. What is it? why do you smile so? where did you hear it? at Randalls?'

He had time only to say:

'No, not at Randalls; I have not been near Randalls'—when the door was thrown open, and Miss Bates and Miss Fairfax walked into the room. Full of thanks, and full of news, Miss Bates knew not which to give quickest. Mr Knightley soon saw that he had lost his moment, and that not another syllable of communication could rest with him.

'Oh, my dear sir, how are you this morning? My dear Miss Woodhouse—I come quite overpowered. Such a beautiful hind-quarter of pork! You are too bountiful! Have you heard the news? Mr Elton is going to be married.'

Emma had not had time even to think of Mr Elton, and she was so completely surprised, that she could not avoid a little start, and a little blush, at the sound.

'There is my news—I thought it would interest you,' said Mr Knightley, with a smile, which implied a conviction of some part of what had passed between them.

'But where could *you* hear it?' cried Miss Bates. 'Where could you possibly hear it, Mr Knightley? For it is not five minutes since I received Mrs Cole's note—no, it cannot be more than five—or at least ten—for I had got my bonnet and spencer on, just ready to come out—I was only gone down to Patty again about the pork—Jane was standing in the passage (were not you, Jane?) for my mother was so afraid that we had not any salting-pan large enough. So I said I would go down and see, and Jane said, "Shall I go down instead? for I think you have a little cold, and Patty has been washing the kitchen." "Oh, my dear"—said I—well, and just then came the note. A Miss Hawkins—that's all I know. A Miss Hawkins of Bath. But, Mr Knightley, how could you possibly have heard it? for the very moment Mr Cole told Mrs Cole of it, she sat down and wrote to me. A Miss Hawkins——'

'I was with Mr Cole on business an hour and a half ago. He had just read Elton's letter as I was shown in, and handed it to me directly.'

'Well! that is quite—I suppose there never was a piece of news more generally interesting. My dear sir, you really are too bountiful. My mother desires her very best compliments and regards, and a thousand thanks, and says you really quite oppress her.'

'We consider our Hartfield pork,' replied Mr Woodhouse—

'indeed, it certainly is, so very superior to all other pork, that Emma and I cannot have a greater pleasure than——'

'Oh, my dear sir, as my mother says, our friends are only too good to us. If ever there were people who, without having great wealth themselves, had everything they could wish for, I am sure it is us. We may well say, that "our lot is cast in a goodly heritage." Well, Mr Knightley, and so you actually saw the letter—well——'

'It was short—merely to announce—but cheerful, exulting, of course.' Here was a sly glance at Emma. 'He had been so fortunate as to—I forget the precise words—one has no business to remember them. The information was, as you state, that he was going to be married to a Miss Hawkins. By his style I should imagine it just settled.'

'Mr Elton going to be married!' said Emma, as soon as she could speak. 'He will have everybody's wishes for his happiness.'

'He is very young to settle,' was Mr Woodhouse's observation. 'He had better not be in a hurry. He seemed to me very well off as he was. We were always glad to see him at Hartfield.'

'A new neighbour for us all, Miss Woodhouse!' said Miss Bates joyfully; 'my mother is so pleased! she says she cannot bear to have the poor old Vicarage without a mistress. This is great news, indeed. Jane, you have never seen Mr Elton; no wonder that you have such a curiosity to see him.'

Jane's curiosity did not appear of that absorbing nature as wholly to occupy her.

'No, I have never seen Mr Elton,' she replied, starting on this appeal: 'is he—is he a tall man?'

'Who shall answer that question?' cried Emma. 'My father would say, "Yes"; Mr Knightley, "No"; and Miss Bates and I, that he is just the happy medium. When you have been here a little longer, Miss Fairfax, you will understand that Mr Elton is the standard of perfection in Highbury, both in person and mind.'

'Very true, Miss Woodhouse, so she will. He is the very best young man; but, my dear Jane, if you remember, I told you yesterday he was precisely the height of Mr Perry. Miss Hawkins? I dare say, an excellent young woman. His extreme attention to my mother—wanting her to sit in the vicarage-pew, that she might hear the better, for my mother is a little deaf, you know—it is not much, but she does not hear quite quick. Jane says that Colonel Campbell is a little deaf. He fancied bathing might be good for it—the warm bath—but she says it did him no lasting benefit. Colonel Campbell, you know, is quite our angel. And Mr Dixon seems a very charming young man, quite worthy of him. It is such a happiness when good people get together—and they always do. Now, here will be Mr Elton and Miss Hawkins; and there are the Coles, such very good people; and the Perrys—I suppose there never was a happier or a better couple than Mr and Mrs Perry. I say, sir,' turning to Mr Woodhouse, ' I think there are few places with such society as Highbury. I always say, we are quite blessed in our neighbours. My dear sir, if there is one thing my mother loves better than another, it is pork—a roast loin of pork——'

' As to who, or what, Miss Hawkins is, or how long he has been acquainted with her,' said Emma, ' nothing, I suppose, can be known. One feels that it cannot be a very long acquaintance. He has been gone only four weeks.'

Nobody had any information to give; and, after a few more wanderings, Emma said:

' You are silent, Miss Fairfax—but I hope you mean to take an interest in this news. You, who have been hearing and seeing so much of late on these subjects, who must have been so deep in the business on Miss Campbell's account—we shall not excuse your being indifferent about Mr Elton and Miss Hawkins.'

' When I have seen Mr Elton,' replied Jane, ' I dare say I shall be interested—but I believe it requires *that* with me. And as it is some months since Miss Campbell married, the impression may be a little worn off.'

' Yes, he has been gone just four weeks, as you observe, Miss Woodhouse,' said Miss Bates, ' four weeks yesterday. A Miss Hawkins! Well, I had always rather fancied it would be some young lady hereabouts; not that I ever—Mrs Cole once whispered to me—but I immediately said: " No, Mr Elton is a most worthy young man—but—— " In short, I do not think I am particularly quick at those sort of discoveries. I do not pretend to it. What is before me, I see. At the same time, nobody could wonder if Mr Elton should have aspired—Miss Woodhouse lets me chatter on, so good-humouredly. She knows I would not offend for the world. How does Miss Smith do? She seems quite recovered now. Have you heard from Mrs John Knightley lately? Oh, those dear little children. Jane, do you know I always fancy Mr Dixon like Mr John Knightley. I mean in person—tall, and with that sort of look— and not very talkative.'

'Quite wrong, my dear aunt; there is no likeness at all.'

'Very odd! but one never does form a just idea of anybody beforehand. One takes up a notion and runs away with it. Mr Dixon, you see, is not, strictly speaking handsome.'

'Handsome! Oh no—far from it—certainly plain. I told you he was plain.'

'My dear, you said that Miss Campbell would not allow him to be plain, and that you yourself——'

'Oh, as for me, my judgment is worth nothing. Where I have a regard, I always think a person well-looking. But I gave what I believed the general opinion, when I called him plain.'

'Well, my dear Jane. I believe we must be running away. The weather does not look well, and grandmamma will be uneasy. You are too obliging, my dear Miss Woodhouse; but we really must take leave. This has been a most agreeable piece of news indeed. I shall just go round by Mrs Cole's; but I shall not stop three minutes; and, Jane, you had better go home directly—I would not have you out in a shower. We think she is the better for Highbury already. Thank you—we do indeed. I shall not attempt calling on Mrs Goddard, for I really do not think she cares for anything but *boiled* pork; when we dress the leg it will be another thing. Good morning to you, my dear sir. Oh, Mr Knightley is coming too. Well, that is so very—I am sure if Jane is tired, you will be so kind as to give her your arm. Mr Elton and Miss Hawkins! Good morning to you.'

Emma, alone with her father, had half her attention wanted by him, while he lamented that young people would be in such a hurry to marry—and to marry strangers too—and the other half she could give to her own view of the subject. It was to herself an amusing and a very welcome piece of news, as proving that Mr Elton could not have suffered long; but she was sorry for Harriet—Harriet must feel it—and all that she could hope was, by giving the first information herself, to save her from hearing it abruptly from others. It was now about the time that she was likely to call. If she were to meet Miss Bates in her way! and upon its beginning to rain, Emma was obliged to expect that the weather would be detaining her at Mrs Goddard's, and that the intelligence would undoubtedly rush upon her without preparation.

The shower was heavy, but short; and it had not been over five minutes, when in came Harriet, with just the heated, agitated look which hurrying thither with a full heart was likely to give; and the 'Oh, Miss Woodhouse, what do you think has happened?' which instantly burst forth, had all the evidence of corresponding perturbation. As the blow was given, Emma felt that she could not now show greater kindness than in listening; and Harriet, unchecked, ran eagerly through what she had to tell. 'She had set out from Mrs Goddard's half an hour ago—she had been afraid it would rain—she had been afraid it would pour down every moment—but she thought she might get to Hartfield first—she had hurried on as fast as possible; but then, as she was passing by the house where a young woman was making up a gown for her, she thought she would just step in and see how it went on; and though she did not seem to stay half a moment there, soon after she came out it began to rain, and she did not know what to do; so she ran on directly, as fast as she could, and took shelter at Ford's.' Ford's was the principal woollen-draper, linen-draper, and haberdasher's shop united—the shop first in size and fashion in the place. 'And so there she had set, without an idea of anything in the world, full ten minutes perhaps—when, all of a sudden, who should come in—to be sure it was so very odd! but they always dealt at Ford's—who should come in, but Elizabeth Martin and her brother! Dear Miss Woodhouse! only think. I thought I should have fainted. I did not know what to do. I was sitting near the door—Elizabeth saw me directly; but he did not; he was busy with the umbrella. I am sure she saw me, but she looked away directly, and took no notice; and they both went to quite the farther end of the shop; and I kept sitting near the door. Oh dear, I was so miserable! I am sure I must have been as white as my gown. I could not go away, you know, because of the rain; but I did so wish myself anywhere in the world but there. Oh dear, Miss Woodhouse! Well, at last, I fancy, he looked round and saw me; for instead of going on with her buyings, they began whispering to one another. I am sure they were talking of me; and I could not help thinking that he was persuading her to speak to me—(do you think he was, Miss Woodhouse?)—for presently she came forward—came quite up to me, and asked me how I did, and seemed ready to shake hands, if I would. She did not do any of it in the same way that she used: I could see she was altered; but, however, she seemed to *try* to be very friendly, and we shook hands, and stood talking some time; but I know no more what I said—I was in such a tremble! I remember she said she was sorry we never met now, which I thought almost too kind! Dear Miss Woodhouse, I was absolutely miserable! By that time, it was beginning to hold up, and I was determined that nothing should stop me from getting away—and then—only think! I found he was coming up towards me too—slowly, you know, and as if he did not quite know what to do; and so he came and spoke, and I answered—and I stood for a minute, feeling dreadfully, you know, one can't tell how; and then I took courage, and said it did not rain, and I must go; and so off I set; and I had not got three yards from the door, when he came after me, only to say, if I was going to Hartfield, he thought I had much better go round by Mr Cole's stables, for I should find the near way quite floated by this rain. Oh dear, I thought it would have been the death of me! So I said I was very much obliged to him: you know I could not do less; and then he went back to Elizabeth, and I came round by the stables—I believe I did—but I hardly knew where I was, or anything about it. Oh, Miss Woodhouse, I would rather have done anything than have had it happen; and yet, you know, there was a sort of satisfaction in seeing him behave so pleasantly and so kindly. And Elizabeth, too. Oh, Miss Woodhouse, do talk to me, and make me comfortable again.'

Very sincerely did Emma wish to do so; but it was not immediately in her power. She was obliged to stop and think. She was not thoroughly comfortable herself. The young man's conduct, and his sister's, seemed the result of real feeling, and she could not but pity them. As Harriet described it, there had been an interesting mixture of wounded affection and genuine delicacy in their behaviour; but she had believed them to be well-meaning, worthy people before; and what difference did this make in the evils of the connection? It was folly to be disturbed by it. Of course, he must be sorry to lose her—they must be all sorry—ambition, as well as love, had probably been mortified. They might all have hoped to rise by Harriet's acquaintance; and besides, what was the value of Harriet's description? So easily pleased— so little discerning—what signified her praise!

She exerted herself, and did try to make her comfortable, by considering all that had passed as a mere trifle, and quite unworthy of being dwelt on.

'It might be distressing for the moment,' said she, 'but you seem to have behaved extremely well; and it is over, and may never—can never, as a first meeting—occur again, and therefore you need not think about it.'

Harriet said, 'Very true,' and she 'would not think about it'; but still she talked of it—still she could talk of nothing else; and Emma, at last, in order to put the Martins out of her head, was obliged to hurry on the news, which she had meant to give with so much tender caution, hardly knowing herself whether to rejoice or be angry, ashamed, or only amused, at such a state of mind in poor Harriet—such a conclusion of Mr Elton's importance with her!

Mr Elton's rights, however, gradually revived. Though she did not feel the first intelligence as she might have done the day before, or an hour before, its interest soon increased; and before their first conversation was over, she had talked herself into all the sensations of curiosity, wonder, and regret, pain and pleasure, as to this fortunate Miss Hawkins, which could conduce to place the Martins under proper subordination in her fancy.

Emma learned to be rather glad that there had been such a meeting. It had been serviceable in deadening the first shock, without retaining any influence to alarm. As Harriet now lived, the Martins could not get at her, without seeking her where hitherto they had wanted either the courage or the condescension to seek her; for since her refusal of the brother, the sisters never had been at Mrs Goddard's; and a twelvemonth might pass without their being thrown together again, with any necessity, or even any power of speech.

22

HUMAN nature is so well disposed towards those who are in interesting situations, that a young person, who either marries or dies, is sure of being kindly spoken of.

A week had not passed since Miss Hawkins's name was first mentioned in Highbury, before she was, by some means or other, discovered to have every recommendation of person and mind—to be handsome, elegant, highly accomplished, and perfectly amiable; and when Mr Elton himself arrived to triumph in his happy prospects, and circulate the fame of her merits, there was very little more for him to do than to tell her Christian name, and say whose music she principally played.

Mr Elton returned, a very happy man. He had gone away rejected and mortified, disappointed in a very sanguine hope, after a series of what appeared to him strong encouragement; and not only losing the right lady, but finding himself debased to the level of a very wrong one. He had gone away deeply offended, he came back engaged to another; and to another as superior, of course, to the first, as under such circumstances what is gained always is to what is lost. He came back gay and self-satisfied, eager and busy, caring nothing for Miss Woodhouse, and defying Miss Smith.

The charming Augusta Hawkins, in addition to all the usual advantages of perfect beauty and merit, was in possession of an independent fortune, of so many thousands as would always be called ten—a point of some dignity, as well as some convenience. The story told well: he had not thrown himself away—he had gained a woman of £ 10,000, or thereabouts, and he had gained her with such delightful rapidity; the first hour of introduction had been so very soon followed by distinguishing notice; the history which he had to give Mrs Cole of the rise and progress of the affair was so glorious; the steps so quick, from the accidental rencontre, to the dinner at Mr Green's, and the party at Mrs Brown's—smiles and blushes rising in importance—with consciousness and agitation richly scattered; the lady had been so easily impressed—so sweetly disposed—had, in short, to use a most intelligible phrase, been so very ready to have him, that vanity and prudence were equally contented.

He had caught both substance and shadow, both fortune and affection, and was just the happy man he ought to be; talking only of himself and his own concerns—expecting to be congratulated—ready to be laughed at—and, with cordial, fearless smiles, now addressing all the young ladies of the place, to whom, a few weeks ago, he would have been more cautiously gallant.

The wedding was no distant event, as the parties had only themselves to please, and nothing but the necessary preparations to wait for; and when he set out for Bath again, there was a general expectation, which a certain glance of Mrs Cole's did not seem to contradict, that when he next entered Highbury he would bring his bride.

During his present short stay, Emma had barely seen him; but just enough to feel that the first meeting was over, and to give her the impression of his not being improved by the mixture of pique and pretension now spread over his air. She was, in fact, beginning very much to wonder that she had ever thought him pleasing at all; and his sight was so inseparably connected with some very disagreeable feelings, that, except in a moral light, as a penance, a lesson, a source of profitable humiliation to her own mind, she would have been thankful to be assured of never seeing him again. She wished him very well; but he gave her pain; and his welfare twenty miles off would administer most satisfaction.

The pain of his continued residence in Highbury, however, must certainly be lessened by his marriage. Many vain solicitudes would be prevented—many awkwardnesses smoothed by it. A *Mrs Elton* would be an excuse for any change of intercourse; former intimacy might sink without remark. It would be almost beginning their life of civility again.

Of the lady individually, Emma thought very little. She was good enough for Mr Elton, no doubt; accomplished enough for Highbury—handsome enough—to look plain, probably, by Harriet's side. As to connection, there Emma was perfectly easy; persuaded that, after all his own vaunted claims and disdain of Harriet, he had done nothing. On that article, truth seemed attainable. *What* she was, must be uncertain; but *who* she was, might be found out; and setting aside the £10,000 it did not appear that she was at all Harriet's superior. She brought no name, no blood, no alliance. Miss Hawkins was the youngest of the two daughters of a Bristol—merchant, of course, he must be called; but, as the whole of the profits of his mercantile life appeared so very moderate, it was not unfair to guess the dignity of his line of trade had been very moderate also. Part of every winter she had been used to spend in Bath; but Bristol was her home, the very heart of Bristol; for though the father and mother had died some years ago, an uncle remained—in the law line: nothing more distinctly honourable was hazarded of him, than that he was in the law line; and with him the daughter had lived. Emma guessed him to be the drudge of some attorney, and too stupid to rise. And all the grandeur of the connection seemed dependent on the elder sister, who was *very well married*, to a gentleman in a *great way*, near Bristol, who kept two carriages! That was the wind-up of the history; that was the glory of Miss Hawkins.

Could she but have given Harriet her feelings about it all! She had talked her into love; but, alas! she was not so easily to be talked out of it. The charm of an object to occupy the many vacancies of Harriet's mind was not to be talked away. He might be superseded by another; he certainly would, indeed; nothing could be clearer; even a Robert Martin would have been sufficient; but nothing else, she feared, would cure her. Harriet was one of those, who, having once begun, would be always in love. And now, poor girl, she was considerably worse from this reappearance of Mr Elton—she was always having a glimpse of him somewhere or other. Emma saw him only once; but two or three times every day Harriet was sure *just* to meet with him, or *just* to miss him, *just* to hear his voice, or see his shoulder, *just* to have something occur to preserve him in her fancy, in all the favouring warmth of surprise and conjecture. She was, moreover, perpetually hearing about him; for, excepting when at Hartfield, she was always among those who saw no fault in Mr Elton, and found nothing so interesting as the discussion of his concerns; and every report, therefore, every guess—all that had already occurred, all that might occur in the arrangement of his affairs, comprehending income, servants, and furniture—was continually in agitation around her. Her regard was receiving strength by invariable praise of him, and her regrets kept alive, and feelings irritated by ceaseless repetitions of Miss Hawkins's happiness, and continual observation of how much he seemed attached! his air as he walked by the house, the very sitting of his hat, being all in proof of how much he was in love.

Had it been allowable entertainment, had there been no pain to her friend, or reproach to herself, in the waverings of Harriet's mind, Emma would have been amused by its variations. Sometimes Mr Elton predominated, sometimes the Martins; and each was occasionally useful as a check to the other. Mr Elton's engagement had been the cure of the agitation of meeting Mr Martin. The unhappiness produced by the knowledge of that engagement had been a little put aside by Elizabeth Martin's calling at Mrs Goddard's a few days afterwards. Harriet had not been at home; but a note had been prepared and left for her, written in the very style to touch—a small mixture of reproach with a great deal of kindness; and till Mr Elton himself appeared, she had been much occupied by it, continually pondering over what could be done in return, and wishing to do more than she dared to confess. But Mr Elton, in person, had driven away all such cares. While he stayed, the Martins were forgotten; and on the very morning of his setting off for Bath again, Emma, to dissipate some of the distress it occasioned, judged it best for her to return Elizabeth Martin's visit.

How that visit was to be acknowledged, what would be necessary, and what might be safest, had been a point of some doubtful consideration. Absolute neglect of the mother and sisters, when invited to come, would be ingratitude. It must not be; and yet the danger of a renewal of the acquaintance!

After much thinking, she could determine on nothing better than Harriet's returning the visit; but in a way that, if they had understanding, should convince them that it was to be only a formal acquaintance. She meant to take her in the carriage, leave her at the Abbey Mill, while she drove a little farther, and call for her again so soon as to allow no time for insidious applications or dangerous recurrences to the past, and give the most decided proof of what degree of intimacy was chosen for the future.

She could think of nothing better; and though there was something in it which her own heart could not approve—something of ingratitude, merely glossed over—it must be done, or what would become of Harriet?

23

SMALL heart had Harriet for visiting. Only half an hour before her friend called for her at Mrs Goddard's, her evil stars had led her to the very spot where, at that moment, a trunk, directed to *The Rev. Philip Elton, White Hart, Bath,* was to be seen under the operation of being lifted into the butcher's cart, which was to convey it to where the coaches passed; and everything in this world, except that trunk and the direction, was consequently a blank.

She went, however; and when they reached the farm, and she was to be put down, at the end of the broad, neat gravel-walk, which led between espalier apple-trees to the front door, the sight of everything which had given her so much pleasure the autumn before was beginning to revive a little local agitation; and when they parted, Emma observed her to be looking around with a sort of fearful curiosity, which determined her not to allow the visit to exceed the proposed quarter of an hour. She went on herself, to give that portion of time to an old servant who was married, and settled in Donwell.

The quarter of an hour brought her punctually to the white gate again; and Miss Smith receiving her summons, was with her without delay, and unattended by any alarming young man. She came solitarily down the gravel-walk—a Miss Martin just appearing at the door, and parting with her seemingly with ceremonious civility.

Harriet could not very soon give an intelligible account. She was feeling too much; but at last Emma collected from her enough to understand the sort of meeting, and the sort of pain it was creating. She had seen only Mrs Martin and the two girls. They had received her doubtingly, if not coolly; and nothing beyond the merest commonplace had been talked almost all the time— till just at last, when Mrs Martin's saying all of a sudden, that she thought Miss Smith was grown, had brought on a more interesting subject, and a warmer manner. In that very room she had been measured last September with her two friends. There were the pencilled marks and memorandums in the wainscot by the window. *He* had done it. They all seemed to remember the day, the hour, the party, the occasion—to feel the same consciousness, the same regrets—to be ready to return to the same good understanding; and they were just growing again like themselves (Harriet, as Emma must suspect, as ready as the best of them to be cordial and happy) when the carriage reappeared, and all was over. The style of the visit, and the shortness of it, were then felt to be decisive. Fourteen minutes to be given to those with whom she had thankfully passed six weeks not six months ago! Emma could not but picture it all, and feel how justly they might resent, how naturally Harriet must suffer. It was a bad business. She would have given a great deal, or endured a great deal, to have had the Martins in a higher rank of life. They were so deserving, that a *little* higher should have been enough; but as it was, how could she have done otherwise? Impossibile! She could not repent. They must be separated; but there was a great deal of pain in the process—so much to herself at this time, that she soon felt the necessity of a little consolation, and resolved on going home by way of Randalls to procure it. Her mind was quite sick of Mr Elton and the Martins. The refreshment of Randalls was absolutely necessary.

It was a good scheme; but on driving to the door they heard that neither 'master nor mistress was at home'; they had both been out some time; the man believed they were gone to Hartfield.

'This is too bad!' cried Emma, as they turned away. 'And now we shall just miss them; too provoking. I do not know when I have been so disappointed.' And she leaned back in the corner, to indulge her murmurs, or to reason them away; probably a little of both—such being the commonplace process of a not ill-disposed mind. Presently the carriage stopped: she looked up; it was stopped by Mr and Mrs Weston, who were standing to speak to her. There was instant pleasure in the sight of them, and still greater pleasure was conveyed in sound; for Mr Weston immediately accosted her with:

'How d'ye do? how d'ye do? We have been sitting with your father—glad to see him so well. Frank comes to-morrow—I had a letter this morning —we see him to-morrow by dinner-time to a certainty—he is at Oxford to-day, and he comes for a whole fortnight—I knew it would be so. If he had come at Christmas he could not have stayed three days. I was always glad he did not come at Christmas; now we are going to have just the right weather for him—fine, dry, settled weather. We shall enjoy him completely; everything has turned out exactly as we could wish.'

There was no resisting such news, no possibility of avoiding the influence of such a happy face as Mr Weston's, confirmed as it all was by the words and the countenance of his wife, fewer and quieter, but not less to the purpose. To know that *she* thought his coming certain was enough to make Emma consider it so, and sincerely did she rejoice in their joy. It was a most delightful re-animation of exhausted spirits. The worn-out past was sunk in the freshness of what was coming; and in the rapidity of half a moment's thought she hoped Mr Elton would now be talked of no more.

Mr Weston gave her the history of the engagements at Enscombe, which allowed his son to answer for having an entire fortnight at his command, as well as the route and the method of his journey; and she listened, and smiled, and congratulated.

' I shall soon bring him over to Hartfield,' said he, at the conclusion.

Emma could imagine she saw a touch of the arm at this speech, from his wife.

' We had better move on, Mr Weston,' said she; ' we are detaining the girls.'

' Well, well, I am ready; ' and turning again to Emma—' but you must not be expecting such a *very* fine young man; you have only had *my* account, you know; I dare say he is really nothing extraordinary,' though his own sparkling eyes at the moment were speaking a very different conviction.

Emma could look perfectly unconscious and innocent, and answer in a manner that appropriated nothing.

' Think of me to-morrow, my dear Emma, about four o'clock,' was Mrs Weston's parting injunction, spoken with some anxiety, and meant only for her.

' Four o'clock! depend upon it, he will be here by three,' was Mr Weston's quick amendment; and so ended a most satisfactory meeting. Emma's spirits were mounted quite up to happiness. Everything wore a different air. James and his horses seemed not half so sluggish as before. When she looked at the hedges, she thought the elder, at least, must soon be coming out; and when she turned round to Harriet she saw something like a look of spring, a tender smile even there.

' Will Mr Frank Churchill pass through Bath as well as Oxford?' was a question, however, which did not augur much.

But neither geography nor tranquillity could come all at once; and Emma was now in a humour to resolve that they should both come in time.

The morning of the interesting day arrived, and Mrs Weston's faithful pupil did not forget either at ten, or eleven, or twelve o'clock, that she was to think of her at four.

'My dear, dear anxious friend,' said she, in mental soliloquy, while walking downstairs from her own room, 'always over-careful for everybody's comfort but your own; I see you now in all your little fidgets, going again and again into his room, to be sure that all is right.' The clock struck twelve as she passed through the hall. ''Tis twelve; I shall not forget to think of you four hours hence; and by this to-morrow, perhaps, or a little later, I may be thinking of the possibility of their all calling here. I am sure they will bring him soon.'

She opened the parlour door, and saw two gentlemen sitting with her father—Mr Weston and his son. They had been arrived only a few minutes; and Mr Weston had scarcely finished his explanation of Frank's being a day before his time, and her father was yet in the midst of his very civil welcome and congratulations, when she appeared, to have her share of surprise, introduction, and pleasure.

The Frank Churchill so long talked of, so high in interest, was actually before her. He was presented to her, and she did not think too much had been said in his praise. He was a *very* good-looking young man—height, air, address, all were unexceptionable, and his countenance had a great deal of the spirit and liveliness of his father's—he looked quick and sensible. She felt immediately that she should like him; and there was a well-bred ease of manner, and a readiness to talk, which convinced her that he came intending to be acquainted with her, and that acquainted they soon must be.

He had reached Randalls the evening before. She was pleased with the eagerness to arrive which had made him alter his plan, and travel earlier, later, and quicker, that he might gain half a day.

'I told you yesterday,' cried Mr Weston, with exultation, 'I told you all that he would be here before the time named. I remembered what I used to do myself. One cannot creep upon a journey; one cannot help getting on faster than one has planned: and the pleasure of coming in upon one's friends before the look-out begins is worth a great deal more than any little exertion it needs.'

' It is a great pleasure where one can indulge in it,' said the
young man, ' though there are not many houses that I should
presume on so far; but in coming *home* I felt I might do anything.'

The word *home* made his father look on him with fresh complacency. Emma was directly sure that he knew how to make himself agreeable; the conviction was strengthened by what followed.
He was very much pleased with Randalls, thought it a most
admirably-arranged house, would hardly allow it even to be
very small, admired the situation, the walk to Highbury, Highbury itself, Hartfield still more, and professed himself to have
always felt the sort of interest in the country, which none but
one's *own* country gives, and the greatest curiosity to visit it.
That he should never have been able to indulge so amiable a
feeling before passed suspiciously through Emma's brain; but
still if it were a falsehood, it was a pleasant one, and pleasantly
handled. His manner had no air of study or exaggeration. He
did really look and speak as if in a state of no common enjoyment.

Their subjects, in general, were such as belong to an opening
acquaintance. On his side were the inquiries —' Was she a
horse-woman? Pleasant rides? Pleasant walks? Had they a large
neighbourhood? Highbury, perhaps, afforded society enough?
There were several very pretty houses in and about it. Balls—had
they balls? Was it a musical society?'

But when satisfied on all these points, and their acquaintance
proportionately advanced, he contrived to find an opportunity,
while their two fathers were engaged with each other, of introducing his mother-in-law, and speaking of her with so much handsome praise, so much warm admiration, so much gratitude for
the happiness she secured to his father, and her very kind reception of himself, as was an additional proof of his knowing how
to please—and of his certainly thinking it worth while to try to
please her. He did not advance a word of praise beyond what
she knew to be thoroughly deserved by Mrs Weston; but, undoubtedly, he could know very little of the matter. He understood
what would be welcome; he could be sure of little else. ' His
father's marriage,' he said, ' had been the wisest measure: every
friend must rejoice in it; and the family from whom he had
received such a blessing must be ever considered as having con-
ferred the highest obligations on him.'

He got as near as he could to thanking her for Miss Taylor's
merits, without seeming quite to forget that, in the common
course of things, it was to be rather supposed that Miss Taylor
had formed Miss Woodhouse's character, than Miss Woodhouse

Miss Taylor's. And at last, as if resolved to qualify his opinion completely for travelling round to its object, he wound it all up with astonishment at the youth and beauty of her person.

'Elegant, agreeable manners, I was prepared for,' said he; 'but I confess that, considering everything, I had not expected more than a very tolerably well-looking woman of a certain age; I did not know that I was to find a pretty young woman in Mrs Weston.'

'You cannot see too much perfection in Mrs Weston, for my feelings,' said Emma; 'were you to guess her to be *eighteen*, I should listen with pleasure; but *she* would be ready to quarrel with you for using such words. Don't let her imagine that you have spoken of her as a pretty young woman.'

'I hope I should know better,' he replied; 'no, depend upon it' (with a gallant bow), 'that in addressing Mrs Weston, I should understand whom I might praise without any danger of being thought extravagant in my terms.'

Emma wondered whether the same suspicion of what might be expected from their knowing each other, which had taken strong possession of her mind, had ever crossed his, and whether his compliments were to be considered as marks of acquiescence or proofs of defiance. She must see more of him to understand his ways; at present she only felt they were agreeable.

She had no doubt of what Mr Weston was often thinking about. His quick eye she detected again and again glancing towards them with a happy expression; and even when he might have determined not to look she was confident that he was often listening.

Her own father's perfect exemption from any thought of the kind, the entire deficiency in him of all such sort of penetration or suspicion, was a most comfortable circumstance. Happily he was not further from approving matrimony than from foreseeing it. Though always objecting to every marriage that was arranged, he never suffered beforehand from the apprehension of any; it seemed as if he could not think so ill of any two persons' understanding as to suppose they meant to marry till it were proved against them. She blessed the favouring blindness. He could now, without the drawback of a single unpleasant surmise, without a glance forward at any possible treachery in his guest, give way to all his natural kind-hearted civility, in solicitous inquiries after Mr Frank Churchill's accommodation on his journey, through the sad evils of sleeping two nights on the road, and express very genuine unmixed anxiety to know that he had certainly escaped catching cold—which, however, he could not allow him to feel quite assured of himself, till after another night.

A reasonable visit paid, Mr Weston began to move. 'He must be going. He had business at the Crown about his hay, and a great many errands for Mrs Weston at Ford's; but he need not hurry anybody else.' His son, too well bred to hear the hint, rose immediately also, saying:

'As you are going farther on business, sir, I will take the opportunity of paying a visit, which must be paid some day or other, and therefore may as well be paid now. I have the honour of being acquainted with a neighbour of yours' (turning to Emma), 'a lady residing in or near Highbury; a family of the name of Fairfax. I shall have no difficulty, I suppose, in finding the house; though Fairfax, I believe, is not the proper name— I should rather say Barnes or Bates. Do you know any family of that name?'

'To be sure we do,' cried his father; 'Mrs Bates—we passed her house—I saw Miss Bates at the window. True, true, you are acquainted with Miss Fairfax; I remember you knew her at Weymouth, and a fine girl she is. Call upon her, by all means.'

'There is no necessity for my calling this morning,' said the young man; 'another day would do as well; but there was that degree of acquaintance at Weymouth, which——'

'Oh, go to-day, go to-day. Do not defer it. What is right to be done cannot be done too soon. And, besides, I must give you a hint, Frank—any want of attention to her *here* should be carefully avoided. You saw her with the Campbells, when she was the equal of everybody she mixed with, but here she is with a poor old grandmother, who has barely enough to live on. If you do not call early it will be a slight.'

The son looked convinced.

'I have heard her speak of the acquaintance,' said Emma; 'she is a very elegant young woman.'

He agreed to it, but with so quiet a 'Yes,' as inclined her almost to doubt his real concurrence; and yet there must be a very distinct sort of elegance for the fashionable world if Jane Fairfax could be thought only ordinarily gifted with it.

'If you were never particularly struck by her manners before,' said she, 'I think you will to-day. You will see her to advantage; see her and hear her—no, I am afraid you will not hear her at all, for she has an aunt who never holds her tongue.'

'You are acquainted with Miss Jane Fairfax, sir, are you?'

said Mr Woodhouse, always the last to make his way in conversation; ' then give me leave to assure you that you will find her a very agreeable young lady. She is staying here on a visit to her grandmamma and aunt, very worthy people; I have known them all my life. They will be extremely glad to see you, I am sure; and one of my servants shall go with you to show you the way.'

' My dear sir, upon no account in the world; my father can direct me.'

' But your father is not going so far; he is only going to the Crown, quite on the other side of the street, and there are a great many houses; you might be very much at a loss, and it is a very dirty walk, unless you keep on the footpath; but my coachman can tell you where you had best cross the street.'

Mr Frank Churchill still declined it, looking as serious as he could: and his father gave his hearty support, by calling out: ' My good friend, this is quite unnecessary; Frank knows a puddle of water when he sees it, and as to Mrs Bates's, he may get there from the Crown in a hop, step, and jump.'

They were permitted to go alone; and with a cordial nod from one, and a graceful bow from the other, the two gentlemen took leave. Emma remained very well pleased with this beginning of the acquaintance, and could now engage to think of them all at Randalls any hour of the day, with full confidence in their comfort.

24

THE next morning brought Mr Frank Churchill again. He came with Mrs Weston, to whom and to Highbury he seemed to take very cordially. He had been sitting with her, it appeared, most companionably at home, till her usual hour of exercise: and on being desired to choose their walk, immediately fixed on Highbury. ' He did not doubt there being very pleasant walks in every direction, but if left to him, he should always choose the same. Highbury, that airy, cheerful, happy-looking Highbury, would be his constant attraction.' Highbury, with Mrs Weston, stood for Hartfield; and she trusted to its bearing the same construction with him. They walked thither directly.

Emma had hardly expected them: for Mr Weston, who had called in for half a minute, in order to hear that his son was very handsome, knew nothing of their plans; and it was an agreeable surprise to her, therefore, to perceive them walking up to the house together, arm in arm. She was wanting to see him again; and especially to see him in company with Mrs Weston, upon his behaviour to whom her opinion of him was to depend. If he were deficient there, nothing should make amends for it. But on seeing them together she became perfectly satisfied. It was not merely in fine words or hyperbolical compliment that he paid his duty; nothing could be more proper or pleasing than his whole manner to her—nothing could more agreeably denote his wish of considering her as a friend, and securing her affection. And there was time enough for Emma to form a reasonable judgment, as their visit included all the rest of the morning. They were all three walking about together for an hour or two— first round the shrubberies of Hartfield, and afterwards in Highbury. He was delighted with everything; admired Hartfield sufficiently for Mr Woodhouse's ear; and when their going farther was resolved on, confessed his wish to be made acquainted with the whole village, and found matter of commendation and interest much oftener than Emma could have supposed.

Some of the objects of his curiosity spoke very amiable feelings. He begged to be shown the house which his father had lived in so long, and which had been the home of his father's father, and on recollecting that an old woman who had nursed him was still living, walked in quest of her cottage, from one end of the street to the other; and though in some points of pursuit or observation there was no positive merit, they showed altogether a good will towards Highbury in general, which must be very like a merit to those he was with.

Emma watched, and decided that with such feelings as were now shown it could not be fairly supposed that he had been ever voluntarily absenting himself; that he had not been acting a part, or making a parade of insincere professions; and that Mr Knightley certainly had not done him justice.

Their first pause was at the Crown Inn, an inconsiderable house, though the principal one of the sort, where a couple of pair of post-horses were kept, more for the convenience of the neighbourhood than from any run on the road; and his companions had not expected to be detained by any interest excited there; but in passing it they gave the history of the large room visibly added. It had been built many years ago for a ball-room, and while the neighbourhood had been in a particularly populous, dancing state, had been occasionally used as such; but such brilliant days had long passed away; and now the highest purpose for which it was ever wanted was to accommodate a whist-club, established among the gentlemen and half gentlemen of the place. He was immediately interested. Its character as a ball-room caught him; and instead of passing on, he stopped for several minutes at the two superior sashed windows which were open, to look in and contemplate its capabilities, and lament that its original purpose should have ceased. He saw no fault in the room; he would acknowledge none which they suggested. No; it was long enough, broad enough, handsome enough. It would hold the very number for comfort. They ought to have balls there at least every fortnight through the winter. Why had not Miss Woodhouse revived the former good old days of the room? She who could do anything in Highbury! The want of proper families in the place, and the conviction that none beyond the place and its immediate environs could be tempted to attend, were mentioned: but he was not satisfied. He could not be persuaded that so many good-looking houses as he saw around him could not furnish numbers enough for such a meeting; and even when particulars were given and families described, he was still unwilling to admit that the inconvenience of such a mixture would be anything, or that there would be the smallest difficulty in everybody's returning into their proper place the next morning. He argued like a young man very much bent on dancing; and Emma was rather surprised to see the constitution of the Weston prevail so decidedly against the habits of the Churchills. He seemed to have all the life and spirit, cheerful feelings, and social inclinations of his father, and nothing of the pride or reserve of Enscombe. Of pride, indeed, there was, perhaps, scarcely enough; his indifference to a confusion of rank bordered too much on inelegance of mind. He could be no judge, however, of the evil he was holding cheap. It was but an effusion of lively spirits.

At last he was persuaded to move on from the front of the Crown; and being now almost facing the house where the Bates lodged, Emma recollected his intended visit the day before, and asked him if he had paid it.

'Yes, oh yes!' he replied; 'I was just going to mention it. A very successful visit. I saw all the three ladies; and felt very much obliged to you for your preparatory hint. If the talking aunt had taken me quite by surprise, it must have been the death of me. As it was, I was only betrayed into paying a most unreasonable visit. Ten minutes would have been all that was necessary, perhaps all that was proper; and I had told my father I should certainly be at home before him, but there was no getting away, no pause; and, to my utter astonishment, I found, when he (finding me nowhere else) joined me there at last, that I had been actually sitting with them very nearly three quarters of an hour. The good lady had not given me the possibility of escape before.'

'And how did you think Miss Fairfax looking?'

'Ill, very ill—that is, if a young lady can ever be allowed to look ill; but the expression is hardly admissible, Mrs Weston, is it? Ladies can never look ill; and seriously, Miss Fairfax is naturally so pale as almost always to give the appearance of ill health— a most deplorable want of complexion.'

Emma would not agree to this, and began a warm defence of Miss Fairfax's complexion. 'It was certainly never brilliant, but she would not allow it to have a sickly hue in general, and there was a softness and delicacy in her skin which gave peculiar elegance to the character of her face.' He listened with all due deference; acknowledged that he had heard many people say the same; but yet he must confess that to him nothing could make amends for the want of the fine glow of health. Where features were indifferent, a fine complexion gave beauty to them all; and where they were good, the effect was—fortunately he need not attempt to describe what the effect was.

'Well,' said Emma, 'there is no disputing about taste. At least you admire her, except her complexion.'

He shook his head and laughed. 'I cannot separate Miss Fairfax and her complexion.'

'Did you see her often at Weymouth? Were you often in the same society?'

At this moment they were approaching Ford's, and he hastily exclaimed: 'Ha! this must be the very shop that everybody attends every day of their lives, as my father informs me. He comes to Highbury himself, he says, six days out of the seven, and has always business at Ford's. If it be not inconvenient to you, pray let us go in, that I may prove myself to belong to the place— to be a true citizen of Highbury. I must buy something at Ford's. It will be taking out my freedom. I dare say they sell gloves.'

'Oh yes, gloves and everything. I do admire your patriotism. You will be adored in Highbury. You were very popular before you came, because you were Mr Weston's son; but lay out half a guinea at Ford's, and your popularity will stand upon your own virtues.'

They went in; and while the sleek, well-tied parcels of 'Men's

145

Beavers' and 'York Tan' were bringing down and displaying on the counter, he said: 'But I beg your pardon, Miss Woodhouse; you were speaking to me, you were saying something at the very moment of this burst of my *amor patriæ*. Do not let me lose it. I assure you the utmost stretch of public fame would not make me amends for the loss of any happiness in private life.'

'I merely asked, whether you had known much of Miss Fairfax and her party at Weymouth?'

'And now that I understand your question I must pronounce it to be a very unfair one. It is always the lady's right to decide on the degree of acquaintance. Miss Fairfax must already have given her account. I shall not commit myself by claiming more than she may choose to allow.'

'Upon my word, you answer as discreetly as she could do herself. But her account of everything leaves so much to be guessed; she is so very reserved, so very unwilling to give the least information about anybody, that I really think you may say what you like of your acquaintance with her.'

'May I, indeed? Then I will speak the truth, and nothing suits me so well. I met her frequently at Weymouth. I had known the Campbells a little in town; and at Weymouth we were very much in the same set. Col. Campbell is a very agreeable man, and Mrs Campbell a friendly warm-hearted woman. I like them all.'

'You know Miss Fairfax's situation in life, I conclude—what she is destined to be?'

'Yes '—(rather hesitatingly)—' I believe I do.'

'You get upon delicate subjects, Emma,' said Mrs Weston, smiling; 'remember that I am here. Mr Frank Churchill hardly knows what to say when you speak of Miss Fairfax's situation in life. I will move a little farther off.'

'I certainly do forget to think of *her*,' said Emma, 'as having ever been anything but my friend and my dearest friend.'

He looked as if he fully understood and honoured such a sentiment.

When the gloves were bought, and they had quitted the shop again—' Did you ever hear the young lady we were speaking of play?' said Frank Churchill.

'Ever hear her?' repeated Emma. 'You forget how much she belongs to Highbury. I have heard her every year of our lives since we both began. She plays charmingly.'

'You think so, do you? I wanted the opinion of some one who would really judge. She appeared to me to play well, that is, with considerable taste, but I know nothing of the matter myself. I am excessively fond of music, but without the smallest skill or right of judging of anybody's performance. I have been used to hear hers admired; and I remember one proof of her being thought to play well: a man, a very musical man, and in love with another woman—engaged to her—on the point of marriage —would yet never ask that other woman to sit down to the instrument, if the lady in question could sit down instead —never seemed to like to hear one if he could hear the other. That, I thought, in a man of known musical talent, was some proof.'

'Proof, indeed!' said Emma, highly amused. 'Mr Dixon is very musical, is he? We shall know more about them all, in half an hour, from you, than Miss Fairfax would have vouchsafed in half a year.'

'Yes, Mr Dixon and Miss Campbell were the persons; and I thought it a very strong proof.'

'Certainly, very strong it was; to own the truth, a great deal stronger than, if *I* had been Miss Campbell, would have been at all agreeable to me. I could not excuse a man's having more music than love—more ear than eye—a more acute sensibility to fine sounds than to my feelings. How did Miss Campbell appear to like it?'

'It was her very particular friend, you know.'

'Poor comfort!' said Emma, laughing. 'One would rather have a stranger preferred than one's very particular friend, with a stranger it might not recur again, but the misery of having a very particular friend always at hand, to do everything better than one does oneself. Poor Mrs Dixon! Well, I am glad she is gone to settle in Ireland!'

'You are right. It was not very flattering to Miss Campbell; but she really did not seem to feel it.'

'So much the better, or so much the worse; I do not know which. But be it sweetness, or be it stupidity in her—quickness of friendship, or dullness of feeling—there was one person, I think, who must have felt it—Miss Fairfax herself. *She* must have felt the improper and dangerous distinction.'

'As to that—I do not——'

'Oh, do not imagine that I expect an account of Miss Fairfax's sensations from you, or from anybody else. They are known to no human being, I guess, but herself; but if she continued to play whenever she was asked by Mr Dixon, one may guess what one chooses.'

'There appeared such a perfectly good understanding among them all——' he began rather quickly, but checking himself, added: 'however, it is impossible for me to say on what terms they really were—how it might all be behind the scenes. I can only say that there was smoothness outwardly. But you, who have known Miss Fairfax from a child, must be a better judge of her character, and of how she is likely to conduct herself in critical situations, than I can be.'

'I have known her from a child, undoubtedly; we have been children and women together; and it is natural to suppose that we should be intimate—that we should have taken to each other whenever she visited her friends. But we never did. I hardly know how it has happened; a little, perhaps, from that wickedness on my side which was prone to take disgust towards a girl so idolised and so cried up as she always was, by her aunt and grandmother, and all their set. And then, her reserve! I never could attach myself to any one so completely reserved.'

'It is a most repulsive quality, indeed,' said he. 'Oftentimes very convenient, no doubt, but never pleasing. There is safety in reserve, but no attraction. One cannot love a reserved person.'

'Not till the reserve ceases towards oneself; and then the attraction may be the greater. But I must be more in want of a friend, or an agreeable companion, than I have yet been, to take the trouble of conquering anybody's reserve to procure one. Intimacy between Miss Fairfax and me is quite out of the question. I have no reason to think ill of her—not the least —except that such extreme and perpetual cautiousness of word and manner, such a dread of giving a distinct idea about anybody, is apt to suggest suspicions of there being something to conceal.'

He perfectly agreed with her; and after walking together so long, and thinking so much alike, Emma felt herself so well acquainted with him that she could hardly believe it to be only their second meeting. He was not exactly what she had expected; less of the man of the world in some of his notions, less of the spoiled child of fortune, therefore better than she had expected. His ideas seemed more moderate—his feelings warmer. She was particularly struck by his manner of considering Mr Elton's house, which, as well as the church, he would go and look at, and would not join them in finding much fault with. No, he could not believe it a bad house; not such a house as a man was to be pitied for having. If it were to be shared with the woman he loved, he could not think any man to be pitied for having that house. There must be ample room in it for every real comfort. The man must be a blockhead who wanted more.

Mrs Weston laughed, and said he did not know what he was talking about. Used only to a large house himself, and without ever thinking how many advantages and accommodations were attached to its size, he could be no judge of the privations inevitably belonging to a small one. But Emma, in her own mind, determined that he *did* know what he was talking about, and that he showed a very amiable inclination to settle early in life, and to marry from worthy motives. He might not be aware of the inroads on domestic peace to be occasioned by no housekeeper's room, or a bad butler's pantry; but no doubt he did perfectly feel that Enscombe could not make him happy, and that whenever he were attached he would willingly give up much of wealth to be allowed an early establishment.

25

EMMA'S very good opinion of Frank Churchill was a little shaken the following day by hearing that he was gone off to London, merely to have his hair cut. A sudden freak seemed to have seized him at breakfast, and he had sent for a chaise and set off, intending to return to dinner, but with no more important view that appeared than having his hair cut. There was certainly no harm in his travelling sixteen miles twice over on such an errand; but there was an air of foppery and nonsense in it which she could not approve. It did not accord with the rationality of plan, the moderation in expense, or even the unselfish warmth of heart, which she had believed herself to discern in him yesterday. Vanity, extravagance, love of change, restlessness of temper, which must be doing something, good or bad; heedlessness as to the pleasure of his father and Mrs Weston, indifference as to how his conduct might appear in general; he became liable to all these charges. His father only called him a coxcomb, and thought it a very good story; but that Mrs Weston did not like it was clear enough by her passing it over as quickly as possible, and making no other comment than that ' all young people would have their little whims.'

With the exception of this little blot, Emma found that his visit hitherto had given her friend only good ideas of him. Mrs Weston was very ready to say how attentive and pleasant a companion he made himself—how much she saw to like in his disposition altogether. He appeared to have a very open temper—certainly a very cheerful and lively one; she could observe nothing wrong in his notions—a great deal decidedly right; he spoke of his uncle with warm regard—was fond of talking of him; said he would be the best man in the world if he were left to himself; and though there was no being attached to the aunt, he acknowledged her kindness with gratitude, and seemed to mean always to speak of her with respect. This was all very promising; and but for such an unfortunate fancy for having his hair cut, there was nothing to denote him unworthy of the distinguished honour which her imagination had given him; the honour, if not of being really in love with her, of being at least very near it, and saved only by her own indifference—(for still her resolution held of never marrying)—the honour, in short, of being marked out for her by all their joint acquaintance.

Mr Weston, on his side, added a virtue to the account which must have some weight. He gave her to understand that Frank admired her extremely—thought her very beautiful and very charming; and with so much to be said for him altogether, she found she must not judge him harshly: as Mrs Weston observed: ' All young people would have their little whims.'

There was one person among his new acquaintance in Surrey not so leniently disposed. In general, he was judged, throughout the parishes of Donwell and Highbury with great candour; liberal allowances were made for the little excesses of such a handsome young man—one who smiled so often and bowed so well; but there was one spirit among them not to be softened, from its power of censure, by bows or smiles—Mr Knightley. The circumstance was told him at Hartfield; for the moment he was silent; but Emma heard him almost immediately afterwards say to himself, over a newspaper he held in his hand: ' Hum! just the trifling, silly fellow I took him for.' She had half a mind to resent; but an instant's observation convinced her that it was really said only to relieve his own feelings, and not meant to provoke; and therefore she let it pass.

Although in one instance the bearers of not good tidings, Mr and Mrs Weston's visit this morning was in another respect particularly opportune. Something occurred while they were at Hartfield to make Emma want their advice; and, which was still more lucky, she wanted exactly the advice they gave.

This was the occurrence:—The Coles had been settled some years in Highbury, and were very good sort of people, friendly, liberal, and unpretending; but, on the other hand, they were of low origin, in trade, and only moderately genteel. On their first coming into the country they had lived in proportion to their income, quietly, keeping little company, and that little unexpensively; but the last year or two had brought them a considerable increase of means—the house in town had yielded greater profits, and fortune in general had smiled on them. With their wealth their views increased; their want of a larger house, their inclination for more company. They added to their house, to their number of servants, to their expenses of every sort; and by this time were, in fortune and style of living, second only to the family at Hartfield. Their love of society, and their new dining-room, prepared everybody for their keeping dinner-company; and a few parties, chiefly among the single men, had already taken place. The regular and best families Emma could hardly suppose they would presume to invite—neither Donwell, nor Hartfield, nor Randalls. Nothing should tempt *her* to go, if they did; and she regretted that her father's known habits would be giving her refusal less meaning than she could wish. The Coles were very respectable in their way, but they ought to be taught that it was not for them to arrange the terms on which the superior families would visit them. This lesson, she very much feared, they would receive only from herself; she had little hope of Mr Knightley, none of Mr Weston.

But she had made up her mind how to meet this presumption so many weeks before it appeared, that when the insult came at last it found her very differently affected. Donwell and Randalls had received their invitation, and none had come for her father and herself; and Mrs Weston's accounting for it with, ' I suppose they will not take the liberty with you; they know you do not dine out,' was not quite sufficient. She felt that she should like to have had the power of refusal; and afterwards, as the idea of the party to be assembled there, consisting precisely of those whose society was dearest to her, occurred again and again, she did not know that she might not have been tempted to accept. Harriet was to be there in the evening, and the Bateses. They had been speaking of it as they walked about Highbury the day before, and Frank Churchill had most earnestly lamented her absence. Might not the evening end in a dance? had been a question of his. The bare possibility of it acted as a further irritation on her spirits; and her being left in solitary grandeur, even supposing the omission to be intended as a compliment, was but poor comfort.

It was the arrival of this very invitation, while the Westons were at Hartfield, which made their presence so acceptable; for though her first remark on reading it was, that 'Of course it must be declined,' she so very soon proceeded to ask them what they advised her to do, that their advice for her going was most prompt and successful.

She owned that, considering everything, she was not absolutely without inclination for the party. The Coles expressed themselves so properly—there was so much real attention in the manner of it—so much consideration for her father. 'They would have solicited the honour earlier, but had been waiting the arrival of a folding-screen from London, which they hoped might keep Mr Woodhouse from any draught of air, and, therefore, induce him the more readily to give them the honour of his company.' Upon the whole, she was very persuadable; and it being chiefly settled among themselves how it might be done without neglecting his comfort—how certainly Mrs Goddard, if not Mrs Bates, might be depended on for bearing him company—Mr Woodhouse was to be talked into an acquiescence of his daughter's going out to dinner on a day now near at hand, and spending the whole evening away from him. As for *his* going, Emma did not wish him to think it possible; the hours would be too late, and the party too numerous. He was soon pretty well resigned.

'I am not fond of dinner-visiting,' said he; 'I never was. No more is Emma. Late hours do not agree with us. I am sorry Mr and Mrs Cole should have done it. I think it would be much better if they would come in one afternoon next summer and take their tea with us; take us in their afternoon walk, which they might do, as our hours are so reasonable, and yet get home without being out in the damp of the evening. The dews of a summer evening are what I would not expose anybody to. However, as they are so very desirous to have dear Emma dine with them, and as you will both be there, and Mr Knightley too, to take care of her, I cannot wish to prevent it, provided the weather be what it ought, neither damp, nor cold, nor windy.' Then turning to Mrs Weston, with a look of gentle reproach—'Ah, Miss Taylor, if you had not married, you would have stayed at home with me.'

'Well, sir,' cried Mr Weston, 'as I took Miss Taylor away, it is incumbent on me to supply her place, if I can; and I will step to Mrs Goddard in a moment, if you wish it.'

But the idea of anything to be done in a *moment* was increasing, not lessening, Mr Woodhouse's agitation. The ladies knew better how to allay it. Mr Weston must be quiet, and everything deliberately arranged.

With this treatment Mr Woodhouse was soon composed enough for talking as usual. 'He should be happy to see Mrs Goddard. He had a great regard for Mrs Goddard; and Emma should write a line and invite her. James could take the note. But first of all there must be an answer written to Mrs Cole.'

'You will make my excuses, my dear, as civilly as possible. You will say that I am quite an invalid, and go nowhere, and therefore must decline their obliging invitation; beginning with my *compliments*, of course. But you will do everything right. I need not tell you what is to be done. We must remember to let James know that the carriage will be wanted on Tuesday. I shall have no fears for you with him. We have never been there above once since the new approach was made; but still I have no doubt that James will take you very safely; and when you get there you must tell him, at what time you would have him come for you again; and you had better name an early hour. You will not like staying late. You will get very tired when tea is over.'

'But you would not wish me to come away before I am tired, papa?'

'Oh no, my love; but you will soon be tired. There will be a great many people talking at once. You will not like the noise.'

'But, my dear sir,' cried Mr Weston, 'if Emma comes away early it will be breaking up the party.'

'And no great harm if it does,' said Mr Woodhouse. 'The sooner every party breaks up the better.'

'But you do not consider how it may appear to the Coles. Emma's going away directly after tea might be giving offence. They are good-natured people, and think little of their own claims; but still they must feel that anybody's hurrying away is no great compliment; and Miss Woodhouse's doing it would be more thought of than any other person's in the room. You would not wish to disappoint and mortify the Coles, I am sure, sir; friendly, good sort of people as ever lived, and who have been your neighbours these *ten* years.'

'No, upon no account in the world, Mr Weston, I am much obliged to you for reminding me. I should be extremely sorry to be giving them any pain. I know what worthy people they are. Perry tells me that Mr Cole never touches malt liquor. You would not think it to look at him, but he is bilious—Mr Cole is very bilious. No, I would not be the means of giving them any pain. My dear Emma, we must consider this. I am sure rather than run the risk of hurting Mr and Mrs Cole you would stay a little longer than you might wish. You will not regard being tired. You will be perfectly safe, you know, among your friends.'

' Oh yes, papa. I have no fears at all for myself; and I should have no scruples of staying as late as Mrs Weston, but on your account. I am only afraid of your sitting up for me. I am not afraid of your not being exceedingly comfortable with Mrs Goddard. She loves piquet, you know; but when she is gone home I am afraid you will be sitting up by yourself, instead of going to bed at your usual time; and the idea of that would entirely destroy my comfort. You must promise me not to sit up.'

He did, on the condition of some promises on her side; such as that, if she came home cold, she would be sure to warm herself thoroughly; if hungry, that she would take something to eat; that her own maid should sit up for her; and that Serle and the butler should see that everything were safe in the house as usual.

26

FRANK CHURCHILL came back again; and if he kept his father's dinner waiting it was not known at Hartfield; for Mrs Weston was too anxious for his being a favourite with Mr Woodhouse, to betray any imperfection which could be concealed.

He came back, had had his hair cut, and laughed at himself with a very good grace, but without seeming really at all ashamed of what he had done. He had no reason to wish his hair longer to conceal any confusion of face; no reason to wish the money unspent to improve his spirits. He was quite as undaunted and as lively as ever; and, after seeing him, Emma thus moralised to herself:

' I do not know whether it ought to be so, but certainly silly things do cease to be silly if they are done by sensible people in an impudent way. Wickedness is always wickedness, but folly is not always folly. It depends upon the character of those who handle it. Mr Knightley, he is not a trifling, silly young man. If he were, he would have done this differently. He would either have gloried in the achievement, or been ashamed of it. There would have been either the ostentation of a coxcomb, or the evasions of a mind too weak to defend its own vanities. No, I am perfectly sure that he is not trifling or silly.'

With Tuesday came the agreeable prospect of seeing him again, and for a longer time than hitherto; of judging of his general manners, and, by inference, of the meaning of his manners towards herself; of guessing how soon it might be necessary for her to throw coldness into her air; and of fancying what the observations of all those might be, who were now seeing them together for the first time.

She meant to be very happy, in spite of the scene being laid at Mr Cole's; and without being able to forget that among the failings of Mr Elton, even in the days of his favour, none had disturbed her more than his propensity to dine with Mr Cole.

Her father's comfort was amply secured, Mrs Bates as well as Mrs Goddard being able to come; and her last pleasing duty, before she left the house, was to pay her respects to them as they sat together after dinner; and while her father was fondly noticing the beauty of her dress, to make the two ladies all the amends in her power, by helping them to large slices of cake and full glasses of wine, for whatever unwilling self-denial his care of their constitution might have obliged them to practise during the meal. She had provided a plentiful dinner for them; she wished she could know that they had been allowed to eat it.

She followed another carriage to Mr Cole's door; and was pleased to see that it was Mr Knightley's; for Mr Knightley, keeping no horses, having little spare money and a great deal of health, activity, and independence, was too apt, in Emma's opinion, to get about as he could, and not use his carriage so often as became the owner of Donwell Abbey. She had an opportunity now of speaking her approbation while warm from her heart, for he stopped to hand her out.

' This is coming as you should do,' said she; ' like a gentleman. I am quite glad to see you.'

He thanked her, observing, ' How lucky that we should arrive at the same moment; for, if we had met first in the drawing-room, I doubt whether you would have discerned me to be more of a gentleman than usual. You might not have distinguished how I came by my look or manner.'

' Yes I should; I am sure I should. There is always a look of consciousness or bustle when people come in a way which they know to be beneath them. You think you carry it off very well, I dare say; but with you it is a sort of bravado, an air of affected unconcern; I always observe it whenever I meet you under those circumstances. *Now* you have nothing to try for. You are not afraid of being supposed ashamed. You are not striving to look taller than anybody else. *Now* I shall be very happy to walk into the same room with you.'

'Nonsensical girl!' was his reply, but not at all in anger.

Emma had as much reason to be satisfied with the rest of the party as with Mr Knightley. She was received with a cordial respect which could not but please, and given all the consequence she could wish for. When the Westons arrived, the kindest looks of love, the strongest of admiration, were for her, from both husband and wife; the son approached her with a cheerful eagerness, which marked her as his peculiar object, and at dinner she found him seated by her; and, as she firmly believed, not without some dexterity on his side.

The party was rather large, as it included one other family—a proper unobjectionable country family, whom the Coles had the advantage of naming among their acquaintance—and the male part of Mr Cox's family, the lawyer of Highbury. The less worthy females were to come in the evening, with Miss Bates, Miss Fairfax, and Miss Smith; but already, at dinner, they were too numerous for any subject of conversation to be general; and, while politics and Mr Elton were talked over, Emma could fairly surrender all her attention to the pleasantness of her neighbour. The first remote sound to which she felt herself obliged to attend was the name of Jane Fairfax. Mrs Cole seemed to be relating something of her that was expected to be very interesting. She listened, and found it well worth listening to. That very dear part of Emma, her fancy, received an amusing supply. Mrs Cole was telling that she had been calling on Miss Bates; and as soon as she entered the room, had been struck by the sight of a pianoforte, a very elegant looking instrument; not a grand, but a large-sized square pianoforte: and the substance of the story, the end of all the dialogue which ensued of surprise, and inquiry, and congratulations on her side, and explanations on Miss Bates's, was that this pianoforte had arrived from Broadwood's the day before, to the great astonishment of both aunt and niece, entirely unexpected; that, at first, by Miss Bates's account, Jane herself was quite at a loss, quite bewildered to think who could possibly have ordered it; but now they were both perfectly satisfied that it could be from only one quarter—of course it must be from Colonel Campbell.

'One can suppose nothing else,' added Mrs Cole; 'and I was only surprised that there could ever have been a doubt.

But Jane, it seems, had a letter from them very lately, and not a word was said about it. She knows their ways best; but I should not consider their silence as any reason for their not meaning to make the present. They might choose to surprise her.'

Mrs Cole had many to agree with her; everybody who spoke on the subject was equally convinced that it must come from Colonel Campbell, and equally rejoiced that such a present had been made; and there were enough ready to speak to allow Emma to think her own way, and still listen to Mrs Cole.

'I declare, I do not know when I have heard anything that has given me more satisfaction. It always has quite hurt me that Jane Fairfax, who plays so delightfully, should not have an instrument. It seemed quite a shame, especially considering how many houses there are where fine instruments are absolutely thrown away. This is like giving ourselves a slap, to be sure; and it was but yesterday I was telling Mr Cole I really was ashamed to look at our new grand pianoforte in the drawing-room, while I do not know one note from another, and our little girls, who are but just beginning, perhaps may never make anything of it; and there is poor Jane Fairfax, who is mistress of music, has not anything of the nature of an instrument, not even the pitifullest old spinnet in the world, to amuse herself with. I was saying this to Mr Cole but yesterday, and he quite agreed with me; only he is so particularly fond of music that he could not help indulging himself in the purchase, hoping that some of our good neighbours might be so obliging occasionally to put it to a better use than we can; and that really is the reason why the instrument was bought—or else I am sure we ought to be ashamed of it. We are in great hopes that Miss Woodhouse may be prevailed with to try it this evening.'

Miss Woodhouse made the proper acquiescence; and finding that nothing more was to be entrapped from any communication of Mrs Cole's, turned to Frank Churchill.

'Why do you smile?' said she.

'Nay, why do you?'

'Me! I suppose I smile for pleasure at Colonel Campbell's being so rich and so liberal. It is a handsome present.'

'Very.'

'I rather wonder that it was never made before.'

'Perhaps Miss Fairfax has never been staying here so long before.'

'Or that he did not give her the use of their own instrument, which must now be shut up in London, untouched by anybody.'

'That is a grand pianoforte, and he might think it too large for Mrs Bates's house.'

'You may *say* what you choose, but your countenance testifies that your *thoughts* on this subject are very much like mine.'

'I do not know. I rather believe you are giving me more credit for acuteness than I deserve. I smile because you smile, and shall probably suspect whatever I find you suspect; but at present I do not see what there is to question. If Colonel Campbell is not the person, who can be?'

'What do you say to Mrs Dixon?'

'Mrs Dixon! very true, indeed. I had not thought of Mrs Dixon. She must know, as well as her father, how acceptable an instrument would be; and perhaps the mode of it, the mystery, the surprise, is more like a young woman's scheme than an elderly man's. It is Mrs Dixon, I dare say. I told you that your suspicions would guide mine.'

'If so, you must extend your suspicions, and comprehend *Mr* Dixon in them.'

'Mr Dixon, very well. Yes. I immediately perceive that it must be the joint present of Mr and Mrs Dixon. We were speaking the other day, you know, of his being so warm an admirer of her performance.'

'Yes, and what you told me on that head confirmed an idea which I had entertained before. I do not mean to reflect upon the good intentions of either Mr Dixon or Miss Fairfax; but I cannot help suspecting either that, after making his proposals to her friend, he had the misfortune to fall in love with *her*, or that he became conscious of a little attachment on her side. One might guess twenty things without guessing exactly the right; but I am sure there must be a particular cause for her choosing to come to Highbury, instead of going with the Campbells to Ireland. Here, she must be leading a life of privation and penance; there it would have been all enjoyment. As to the pretence of trying her native air, I look upon that as a mere excuse. In the summer it might have passed; but what can anybody's native air do for them in the months of January, February, and March? Good fires and carriages would be much more to the purpose in most cases of delicate health, and I dare say in hers. I do not require you to adopt all my suspicions, though you make so noble a profession of doing it, but I honestly tell you what they are.'

'And, upon my word, they have an air of great probability. Mr Dixon's preference of her music to her friend's I can answer for being very decided.'

'And then, he saved her life. Did you ever hear of that? A water party; and by some accident she was falling overboard. He caught her.'

'He did. I was there—one of the party.'

'Were you really? Well! But you observed nothing, of course, for it seems to be a new idea to you. If I had been there, I think I should have made some discoveries.'

'I dare say you would; but I, simple I, saw nothing but the fact, that Miss Fairfax was nearly dashed from the vessel, and that Mr Dixon caught her—it was the work of a moment. And though the consequent shock and alarm was very great, and much more durable—indeed I believe it was half an hour before any of us were comfortable again—yet that was too general a sensation for anything of peculiar anxiety to be observable. I do not mean to say, however, that you might not have made discoveries.'

The conversation was here interrupted. They were called on to share in the awkwardness of a rather long interval between the courses, and obliged to be as formal and as orderly as the others; but when the table was again safely covered, when every corner dish was placed exactly right, and occupation and ease were generally restored, Emma said:

'The arrival of this pianoforte is decisive with me. I wanted to know a little more, and this tells me quite enough. Depend upon it, we shall soon hear that it is a present from Mr and Mrs Dixon.'

'And if the Dixons should absolutely deny all knowledge of it, we must conclude it to come from the Campbells.'

'No, I am sure it is not from the Campbells. Miss Fairfax knows it is not from the Campbells, or they would have been guessed at first. She would not have been puzzled had she dared fix on them. I may not have convinced you, perhaps, but I am perfectly convinced myself that Mr Dixon is a principal in the business.'

'Indeed you injure me if you suppose me unconvinced. Your reasonings carry my judgment along with them entirely. At first, while I supposed you satisfied that Colonel Campbell was the giver, I saw it only as paternal kindness, and thought it the most natural thing in the world. But when you mentioned Mrs Dixon, I felt how much more probable that it should be the tribute of warm female friendship. And now I can see it in no other light than as an offering of love.'

There was no occasion to press the matter further. The conviction seemed real; he looked as if he felt it. She said no more—other subjects took their turn, and the rest of the dinner passed away; the dessert succeeded, the children came in, and were talked to and admired amid the usual rate of conversation; a few clever things said, a few downright silly, but by much the larger proportion neither the one nor the other—nothing worse than everyday remarks, dull repetitions, old news, and heavy jokes.

The ladies had not been long in the drawing-room before the other ladies, in their different divisions, arrived. Emma watched the entrée of her own particular little friend; and if she could not exult in her dignity and grace she could not only love the blooming sweetness and the artless manner, but could most heartily rejoice in that light, cheerful, unsentimental disposition which allowed her so many alleviations of pleasure in the midst of the pangs of disappointed affection. There she sat—and who would have guessed how many tears she had been lately shedding? To be in company, nicely dressed herself, and seeing others nicely dressed, to sit and smile and look pretty and say nothing, was enough for the happiness of the present hour. Jane Fairfax did look and move superior; but Emma suspected she might have been glad to change feelings with Harriet—very glad to have purchased the mortification of having loved—yes, of having loved even Mr Elton in vain by the surrender of all the dangerous pleasure of knowing herself beloved by the husband of her friend.

In so large a party it was not necessary that Emma should approach her. She did not wish to speak of the pianoforte, she felt too much in the secret herself to think the appearance of curiosity or interest fair, and therefore purposely kept at a distance; but by the others the subject was almost immediately introduced, and she saw the blush of consciousness with which congratulations were received, the blush of guilt which accompanied the name of ' my excellent friend, Colonel Campbell.'

Mrs Weston, kind-hearted and musical, was particularly interested by the circumstance, and Emma could not help being amused at her perseverance in dwelling on the subject; and having so much to ask and to say as to tone, touch, and pedal, totally unsuspicious of that wish of saying as little about it as possible, which she plainly read in the fair heroine's countenance.

They were soon joined by some of the gentlemen; and the very first of the early was Frank Churchill. In he walked, the first and the handsomest; and after paying his compliments, *en passant* to Miss Bates and her niece, made his way directly to the opposite side of the circle, where sat Miss Woodhouse; and till he could find a seat by her would not sit at all. Emma divined what everybody present must be thinking. She was his object, and everybody must perceive it. She introduced him to her friend Miss Smith, and, at convenient moments afterwards, heard what each thought of the other. ' He had never seen so lovely a face, and was delighted with her *naïveté*.' And she—' only to be sure it was paying him too great a compliment, but she did think there were some looks a little like Mr Elton.' Emma restrained her indignation, and only turned from her in silence.

Smiles of intelligence passed between her and the gentleman on first glancing towards Miss Fairfax; but it was most prudent to avoid speech. He told her that he had been impatient to leave the dining-room—hated sitting long—was always the first to move when he could—that his father, Mr Knightley, Mr Cox, and Mr Cole, were left very busy over parish business—that as long as he had stayed, however, it had been pleasant enough, as he had found them in general a set of gentlemanlike, sensible men; and spoke so handsomely of Highbury altogether—thought it so abundant in agreeable families—that Emma began to feel she had been used to despise the place rather too much. She questioned him as to the society in Yorkshire, the extent of the neighbourhood about Enscombe, and the sort; and could make out from his answers that, as far as Enscombe was concerned, there was very little going on, that their visitings were among a range of great families, none very near; and that even when days were fixed, and invitations accepted, it was an even chance that Mrs Churchill were not in health and spirits for going; that they made a point of visiting no fresh person; and that, though he had his separate engagements, it was not without difficulty, without considerable address, *at times*, that he could get away, or introduce an acquaintance for a night.

She saw that Enscombe could not satisfy, and that Highbury, taken at its best, might reasonably please a young man who had more retirement at home than he liked. His importance at Enscombe was very evident. He did not boast, but it naturally betrayed itself, that he had persuaded his aunt where his uncle could do nothing, and on her laughing and noticing it, he owned that he believed (excepting one or two points) he could *with time* persuade her to anything. One of those points on which his influence failed he then mentioned. He had wanted very much to go abroad—had been very eager indeed to be allowed to travel—but she would not hear of it. This had happened the year before. *Now*, he said, he was beginning to have no longer the same wish.

The unpersuadable point, which he did not mention, Emma guessed to be good behaviour to his father.

'I have made a most wretched discovery,' said he, after a short pause. 'I have been here a week to-morrow—half my time. I never knew days fly so fast. A week to-morrow! and I have hardly begun to enjoy myself. But just got acquainted with Mrs Weston, and others. I hate the recollection.'

'Perhaps you may now begin to regret that you spent one whole day, out of so few, in having your hair cut.'

'No,' said he, smiling, 'that is no subject of regret at all. I have no pleasure in seeing my friends, unless I can believe myself fit to be seen.'

The rest of the gentlemen being now in the room, Emma found herself obliged to turn from him for a few minutes, and listen to Mr Cole. When Mr Cole had moved away, and her attention could be restored as before, she saw Frank Churchill looking intently across the room at Miss Fairfax, who was sitting exactly opposite.

'What is the matter?' said she.

He started. 'Thank you for rousing me,' he replied. 'I believe I have been very rude; but really Miss Fairfax has done her hair in so odd a way—so very odd a way—that I cannot keep my eyes from her. I never saw anything so *outré*! Those curls! This must be a fancy of her own. I see nobody else looking like her. I must go and ask her whether it is an Irish fashion. Shall I? Yes, I will—I declare I will; and you shall see how she takes it—whether she colours.'

He was gone immediately; and Emma soon saw him standing before Miss Fairfax, and talking to her; but as to its effect on the young lady, as he had improvidently placed himself exactly between them, exactly in front of Miss Fairfax, she could absolutely distinguish nothing.

Before he could return to his chair it was taken by Mrs Weston.

'This is the luxury of a large party,' said she; 'one can get near everybody, and say everything. My dear Emma, I am longing to talk to you. I have been making discoveries and forming plans, just like yourself, and I must tell them while the idea is fresh. Do you know how Miss Bates and her niece came here?'

'How! They were invited, were not they?'

'Oh yes—but how they were conveyed hither? the manner of their coming?'

'They walked, I conclude. How else could they come?'

'Very true. Well, a little while ago it occurred to me how very sad it would be to have Jane Fairfax walking home again, late at night, and cold as the nights are now. And as I looked at her, though I never saw her appear to more advantage, it struck me that she was heated, and would therefore be particularly liable to take cold. Poor girl! I could not bear the idea of it; so, as soon as Mr Weston came into the room, and I could get at him, I spoke to him about the carriage. You may guess how readily he came into my wishes; and having his approbation, I made my way directly to Miss Bates, to assure her that the carriage would be at her service before it took us home; for I thought it would be making her comfortable at once. Good soul! she was as grateful as possibile, you may be sure. " Nobody was ever so fortunate as herself! "—but with many, many thanks— " there was no occasion to trouble us, for Mr Knightley's carriage had brought, and was to take them home again." I was quite surprised—very glad, I am sure; but really quite surprised. Such a very kind attention—and so thoughtful an attention! the sort of thing that so few men would think of. And, in short, from knowing his usual ways, I am very much inclined to think that it was for their accommodation the carriage was used at all. I do suspect he would not have had a pair of horses for himself, and that it was only as an excuse for assisting them.'

'Very likely,' said Emma, 'nothing more likely. I know no man more likely than Mr Knightley to do the sort of thing— to do anything really good-natured, useful, considerate, or benevolent. He is not a gallant man, but he is a very humane one; and this, considering Jane Fairfax's ill health, would appear a case of humanity to him; and for an act of unostentatious kindness there is nobody whom I would fix on more than on Mr Knightley. I know he had horses to-day, for we arrived together; and I laughed at him about it, but he said not a word that could betray.'

'Well,' said Mrs Weston, smiling, 'you give him credit for more simple, disinterested benevolence in this instance than I do; for while Miss Bates was speaking, a suspicion darted into my head, and I have never been able to get it out again. The more I think of it, the more probable it appears. In short, I have made a match between Mr Knightley and Jane Fairfax.

See the consequence of keeping you company! What do you say to it? '

' Mr Knightley and Jane Fairfax! ' exclaimed Emma. ' Dear Mrs Weston, how could you think of such a thing? Mr Knightley! Mr Knightley must not marry! You would not have little Henry cut out from Donwell? Oh no, no; Henry must have Donwell. I cannot at all consent to Mr Knightley's marrying; and I am sure it is not at all likely; I am amazed that you should think of such a thing.'

' My dear Emma, I have told you what led me to think of it. I do not want the match—I do not want to injure dear little Henry—but the idea has been given me by circumstances; and if Mr Knightley really wished to marry, you would not have him refrain on Henry's account, a boy of six years old, who knows nothing of the matter? '

' Yes, I would. I could not bear to have Henry supplanted. Mr Knightley marry! No, I have never had such an idea, and I cannot adopt it now. And Jane Fairfax, too, of all women! '

' Nay, she has always been a first favourite with him, as you very well know.'

' But the imprudence of such a match! '

' I am not speaking of its prudence—merely its probability.'

' I see no probability in it, unless you have any better foundation than what you mention. His good nature, his humanity, as I tell you, would be quite enough to account for the horses. He has a great regard for the Bateses, you know, independent of Jane Fairfax—and is always glad to show them attention. My dear Mrs Weston, do not take to match making. You do it very ill. Jane Fairfax mistress of the Abbey? Oh no, no—every feeling revolts. For his own sake, I would not have him do so mad a thing.'

' Imprudent, if you please—but not mad. Excepting inequality of fortune, and perhaps a little disparity of age, I can see nothing unsuitable.'

' But Mr Knightley does not want to marry. I am sure he has not the least idea of it. Do not put it into his head. Why should he marry? He is as happy as possible by himself; with his farm, and his sheep, and his library, and all the parish to manage; and he is extremely fond of his brother's children. He has no occasion to marry, either to fill up his time or his heart.'

' My dear Emma, as long as he thinks so, it is so; but if he really loves Jane Fairfax—— '

' Nonsense! He does not care about Jane Fairfax. In the way

of love, I am sure he does not. He would do any good to her, or her family; but——'

'Well,' said Mrs Weston, laughing, 'perhaps the greatest good he could do them would be to give Jane such a respectable home.'

'If it would be good to her I am sure it would be evil to himself—a very shameful and degrading connection. How would he bear to have Miss Bates belonging to him? To have her haunting the Abbey, and thanking him all day long for his great kindness in marrying Jane? "So very kind and obliging! But he always had been such a very kind neighbour." And then fly off, through half a sentence, to her mother's old petticoat. "Not that it was such a very old petticoat either—for still it would last a great while—and, indeed, she must thankfully say that their petticoats were all very strong." '

'For shame, Emma! Do not mimic her. You divert me against my conscience. And, upon my word, I do not think Mr Knightley would be much disturbed by Miss Bates. Little things do not irritate him. She might talk on; and if he wanted to say anything himself, he would only talk louder, and drown her voice. But the question is not, whether it would be a bad connection for him, but whether he wishes it; and I think he does. I have heard him speak, and so must you, so very highly of Jane Fairfax! The interest he takes in her—his anxiety about her health—his concern that she should have no happier prospect! I have heard him express himself so warmly on those points. Such an admirer of her performance on the pianoforte, and of her voice. I have heard him say that he could listen to her for ever. Oh! and I had almost forgotten one idea that occurred to me—this pianoforte that has been sent here by somebody—though we have all been so well satisfied to consider it a present from the Campbells, may it not be from Mr Knightley? I cannot help suspecting him. I think he is just the person to do it, even without being in love.'

'Then it can be no argument to prove that he is in love. But I do not think it is at all a likely thing for him to do. Mr Knightley does nothing mysteriously.'

'I have heard him lamenting her having no instrument, repeatedly; oftener than I should suppose such a circumstance would in the common course of things occur to him.'

'Very well; and if he had intended to give her one, he would have told her so.'

'There might be scruples of delicacy, my dear Emma. I have

a very strong notion that it comes from him. I am sure he was particularly silent when Mrs Cole told us of it at dinner.'

'You take up an idea, Mrs Weston, and run away with it, as you have many a time reproached me with doing. I see no sign of attachment. I believe nothing of the pianoforte, and proof only shall convince me that Mr Knightley has any thought of marrying Jane Fairfax.'

They combated the point some time longer in the same way, Emma rather gaining ground over the mind of her friend; for Mrs Weston was the most used of the two to yield; till a little bustle in the room showed them that tea was over, and the instrument in preparation; and at the same moment, Mr Cole approaching to entreat Miss Woodhouse would do them the honour of trying it. Frank Churchill, of whom, in the eagerness of her conversation with Mrs Weston, she had been seeing nothing, except that he had found a seat by Miss Fairfax, followed Mr Cole, to add his very pressing entreaties; and as, in every respect, it suited Emma best to lead, she gave a very proper compliance.

She knew the limitation of her own powers too well to attempt more than she could perform with credit; she wanted neither taste nor spirit in the little things which are generally acceptable, and could accompany her own voice well. One accompaniment to her song took her agreeably by surprise; a second, slightly, but correctly taken by Frank Churchill. Her pardon was duly begged at the close of the song, and everything usual followed. He was accused of having a delightful voice, and a perfect knowledge of music, which was properly denied; and that he knew nothing of the matter, and had no voice at all, roundly asserted. They sang together once more: and Emma would then resign her place to Miss Fairfax, whose performance, both vocal and instrumental, she never could attempt to conceal from herself, was infinitely superior to her own.

With mixed feelings she seated herself at a little distance from the numbers round the instrument, to listen. Frank Churchill sang again. They had sung together once or twice, it appeared, at Weymouth. But the sight of Mr Knightley among the most attentive soon drew away half Emma's mind; and she fell into a train of thinking on the subject of Mrs Weston's suspicions, to which the sweet sounds of the united voices gave only momentary interruptions. Her objections to Mr Knightley's marrying did not in the least subside. She could see nothing but evil in it. It would be a great disappointment to Mr John Knightley, consequently to Isabella. A real injury to the children—a most mortifying change and material loss to them all—a very great deduction from her father's daily comfort—and, as to herself, she could not at all endure the idea of Jane Fairfax at Donwell Abbey. A Mrs Knightley for them all to give way to! No—Mr Knightley must never marry. Little Henry must remain the heir of Donwell.

Presently Mr Knightley looked back, and came and sat down by her. They talked at first only of the performance. His admiration was certainly very warm; yet she thought, but for Mrs Weston, it would not have struck her. As a sort of touchstone, however, she began to speak of his kindness in conveying the aunt and niece; and though his answer was in the spirit of cutting the matter short, she believed it to indicate only his disinclination to dwell on any kindness of his own.

' I often feel concern,' said she, ' that I dare not make *our* carriage more useful on such occasions. It is not that I am without the wish; but you know how impossible my father would deem it that James should put to for such a purpose.'

' Quite out of the question, quite out of the question,' he replied; ' but you must often wish it, I am sure.' And he smiled with such seeming pleasure at the conviction, that she must proceed another step.

' This present from the Campbells,' said she—' this pianoforte is very kindly given.'

' Yes,' he replied, and without the smallest apparent embarrassment. ' But they would have done better had they given her notice of it. Surprises are foolish things. The pleasure is not enhanced, and the inconvenience is often considerable. I should have expected better judgment in Colonel Campbell.'

From that moment Emma could have taken her oath that Mr Knightley had had no concern in giving the instrument. But whether he were entirely free from peculiar attachment—whether there were no actual preference—remained a little longer doubtful. Towards the end of Jane's second song her voice grew thick.

' That will do,' said he, when it was finished, thinking aloud; ' you have sung quite enough for one evening; now be quiet.'

Another song, however, was begged for. ' One more; they would not fatigue Miss Fairfax on any account, and would only ask for one more.' And Frank Churchill was heard to say, ' I think you could manage this without effort; the first part is so very trifling. The strength of the song falls on the second.'

Mr Knightley grew angry.

'That fellow,' said he, indignantly, 'thinks of nothing but showing off his own voice. This must not be.' And touching Miss Bates, who at that moment passed near, 'Miss Bates, are you mad, to let your niece sing herself hoarse in this manner? Go, and interfere. They have no mercy on her.'

Miss Bates, in her real anxiety for Jane, could hardly stay even to be grateful, before she stepped forward and put an end to all further singing. Here ceased the concert part of the evening, for Miss Woodhouse and Miss Fairfax were the only young lady performers; but soon (within five minutes) the proposal of dancing—originating nobody exactly knew where—was so effectually promoted by Mr and Mrs Cole that everything was rapidly clearing away, to give proper space. Mrs Weston, capital in her country-dances, was seated, and beginning an irresistible waltz; and Frank Churchill, coming up with most becoming gallantry to Emma, had secured her hand, and led her up to the top.

White waiting till the other young people could pair themselves off, Emma found time, in spite of the compliments she was receiving on her voice and her taste, to look about, and see what became of Mr Knightley. This would be a trial. He was no dancer in general. If he were to be very alert in engaging Jane Fairfax now it might augur something. There was no immediate appearance. No; he was talking to Mrs Cole—he was looking on unconcerned; Jane was asked by somebody else, and he was still talking to Mrs Cole.

Emma had no longer an alarm for Henry; his interest was yet safe; and she led off the dance with genuine spirit and enjoyment. Not more than five couple could be mustered; but the rarity and the suddenness of it made it very delightful, and she found herself well matched in a partner. They were a couple worth looking at.

Two dances, unfortunately, were all that could be allowed. It was growing late, and Miss Bates became anxious to get home, on her mother's account. After some attempts, therefore, to be permitted to begin again, they were obliged to thank Mrs Weston, look sorrowful, and have done.

'Perhaps it is as well,' said Frank Churchill, as he attended Emma to her carriage. 'I must have asked Miss Fairfax, and her languid dancing would not have agreed with me after yours.'

Emma did not repent her condescension in going to the Coles. The visit afforded her many pleasant recollections the next day, and all that she might be supposed to have lost on the side of dignified seclusion must be amply repaid in the splendour of popularity. She must have delighted the Coles—worthy people; who deserved to be made happy! and left a name behind her that would not soon die away.

Perfect happiness, even in memory, is not common; and there were two points on which she was not quite easy. She doubted whether she had not transgressed the duty of woman by woman, in betraying her suspicions of Jane Fairfax's feelings to Frank Churchill. It was hardly right; but it had been so strong an idea that it would escape her, and his submission to all that she told was a compliment to her penetration, which made it difficult for her to be quite certain that she ought to have held her tongue.

The other circumstance of regret related also to Jane Fairfax, and there she had no doubt. She did unfeignedly and unequivocally regret the inferiority of her own playing and singing. She did most heartily grieve over the idleness of her childhood; and sat down and practised vigorously an hour and a half.

She was then interrupted by Harriet's coming in; and if Harriet's praise could have satisfied her, she might soon have been comforted.

'Oh, if I could but play as well as you and Miss Fairfax!'

'Don't class us together, Harriet. My playing is no more like hers than a lamp is like sunshine.'

'O dear, I think you play the best of the two. I think you play quite as well as she does. I am sure I had much rather hear you. Everybody last night said how well you played.'

'Those who knew anything about it must have felt the difference. The truth is, Harriet, that my playing is just good enough to be praised, but Jane Fairfax's is much beyond it.'

'Well, I always shall think that you play quite as well as she does, or that if there is any difference nobody would ever find it out. Mr Cole said how much taste you had; and Mr Frank Churchill talked a great deal about your taste, and that he valued taste much more than execution.'

'Ah, but Jane Fairfax has them both, Harriet.'

'Are you sure? I saw she had execution, but I did not know

she had any taste. Nobody talked about it; and I hate Italian singing: there is no understanding a word of it. Besides, if she does play so very well, you know, it is no more than she is obliged to do, because she will have to teach. The Coxes were wondering last night whether she would get into any great family. How did you think the Coxes looked?'

'Just as they always do—very vulgar.'

'They told me something,' said Harriet, rather hesitatingly, 'but it is nothing of any consequence.'

Emma was obliged to ask what they had told her, though fearful of its producing Mr Elton.

'They told me that Mr Martin dined with them last Saturday.'

'Oh!'

'He came to their father upon some business, and he asked him to stay to dinner.'

'Oh!'

'They talked a great deal about him, especially Anne Cox. I do not know what she meant, but she asked me if I thought I should go and stay there again next summer.'

'She meant to be impertinently curious, just as such an Anne Cox should be.'

'She said he was very agreeable the day he dined there. He sat by her at dinner. Miss Nash thinks either of the Coxes would be very glad to marry him.'

'Very likely: I think they are, without exception, the most vulgar girls in Highbury.'

Harriet had business at Ford's. Emma thought it most prudent to go with her. Another accidental meeting with the Martins was possible, and in her present state, would be dangerous.

Harriet, tempted by everything, and swayed by half a word, was always very long at a purchase; and while she was still hanging over muslins and changing her mind Emma went to the door for amusement. Much could not be hoped from the traffic of even the busiest part of Highbury: Mr Perry walking hastily by; Mr William Cox letting himself in at the office-door; Mr Cole's carriage horses returning from exercise; or a stray letter-boy on an obstinate mule, were the liveliest objects she could presume to expect; and when her eyes fell only on the butcher with his tray, a tidy old woman travelling homewards from shop with her full basket, two curs quarrelling over a dirty bone, and a string of dawdling children round the baker's little bow-window eyeing the gingerbread, she knew she had no reason to complain, and was amused enough; quite enough still to stand at the door.

A mind lively and at ease can do with seeing nothing, and can see nothing that does not answer.

She looked down the Randalls Road. The scene enlarged: two persons appeared: Mrs Weston and her son-in-law. They were walking into Highbury—to Hartfield of course; they were stopping, however, in the first place at Mrs Bates's, whose house was a little nearer Randalls than Ford's, and had all but knocked when Emma caught their eye. Immediately they crossed the road and came forward to her; and the agreeableness of yesterday's engagement seemed to give fresh pleasure to the present meeting. Mrs Weston informed her that she was going to call on the Bateses, in order to hear the new instrument.

'For my companion tells me,' said she, 'that I absolutely promised Miss Bates last night that I would come this morning. I was not aware of it myself. I did not know that I had fixed a day; but as he says I did I am going now.'

'And while Mrs Weston pays her visit, I may be allowed, I hope,' said Frank Churchill, 'to join your party and wait for her at Hartfield, if you are going home.'

Mrs Weston was disappointed.

'I thought you meant to go with me. They would be very much pleased.'

'Me! I should be quite in the way. But, perhaps, I may be equally in the way here. Miss Woodhouse looks as if she did not want me. My aunt always sends me off when she is shopping. She says I fidget her to death; and Miss Woodhouse looks as if she could almost say the same. What am I to do?'

'I am here on no business of my own,' said Emma, 'I am only waiting for my friend. She will probably have soon done, and then we shall go home. But you had better go with Mrs Weston and hear the instrument.'

'Well, if you advise it. But' (with a smile) 'if Colonel Campbell should have employed a careless friend, and if it should prove to have an indifferent tone, what shall I say? I shall be no support to Mrs Weston. She might do very well by herself. A disagreeable truth would be palatable through her lips, but I am the wretchedest being in the world at a civil falsehood.'

'I do not believe any such thing,' replied Emma; 'I am persuaded that you can be as insincere as your neighbours, when it is necessary; but there is no reason to suppose the instrument is indifferent. Quite otherwise, indeed, if I understood Miss Fairfax's opinion last night.'

'Do come with me,' said Mrs Weston, 'if it be not very disagreeable to you. It need not detain us long. We will go to Hartfield afterwards. We will follow them to Hartfield. I really wish you to call with me: it will be felt so great an attention—and I always thought you meant it.'

He could say no more; and, with the hope of Hartfield to reward him, returned with Mrs Weston to Mrs Bates's door. Emma watched them in, and then joined Harriet at the interesting counter, trying, with all the force of her own mind, to convince her that if she wanted plain muslin, it was of no use to look at figured; and that a blue ribbon, be it ever so beautiful, would still never match her yellow pattern. At last it was all settled, even to the destination of the parcel.

'Should I send it to Mrs Goddard's, ma'am?' asked Mrs Ford. 'Yes—no—yes, to Mrs Goddard's. Only my pattern gown is at Hartfield. No, you shall send it to Hartfield, if you please. But then Mrs Goddard will want to see it. And I could take the pattern gown home any day. But I shall want the ribbon directly; so it had better go to Hartfield—at least the ribbon. You could make it into two parcels, Mrs Ford, could not you?'

'It is not worth while, Harriet, to give Mrs Ford the trouble of two parcels.'

'No more it is.'

'No trouble in the world, ma'am,' said the obliging Mrs Ford.

'Oh, but indeed I would much rather have it only in one. Then, if you please, you shall send it all to Mrs Goddard's—I do not know—no, I think, Miss Woodhouse, I may just as well have it sent to Hartfield, and take it home with me at night. What do you advise?'

'That you do not give another half-second to the subject. To Hartfield, if you please, Mrs Ford.'

'Aye, that will be much best,' said Harriet, quite satisfied; 'I should not at all like to have it sent to Mrs Goddard's.'

Voices approached the shop, or rather, one voice and two ladies; Mrs Weston and Miss Bates met them at the door.

'My dear Miss Woodhouse,' said the latter, 'I am just run across to entreat the favour of you to come and sit down with us a little while, and give us your opinion of our new instrument—you and Miss Smith. How do you do, Miss Smith? Very well, I thank you. And I begged Mrs Weston to come with me, that I might be sure of succeeding.'

'I hope Mrs Bates and Miss Fairfax are—— '

'Very well, I am much obliged to you. My mother is delight-

fully well; and Jane caught no cold last night. How is Mr
Woodhouse? I am so glad to hear such a good account. Mrs
Weston told me you were here. " Oh, then," said I, " I must
run across; I am sure Miss Woodhouse will allow me just to
run across and entreat her to come in: my mother will be so
very happy to see her; and now we are such a nice party, she
cannot refuse." " Aye, pray do," said Mr Frank Churchill,
" Miss Woodhouse's opinion of the instrument will be worth
having." " But," said I, " I shall be more sure of succeeding if one
of you will go with me." " Oh," said he, " wait half a minute,
till I have finished my job; " for, would you believe it, Miss
Woodhouse, there he is, in the most obliging manner in the world,
fastening in the rivet of my mother's spectacles. The rivet came
out, you know, this morning; so very obliging! For my mother
had no use of her spectacles—could not put them on. And, by
the bye, everybody ought to have two pair of spectacles; they
should indeed. Jane said so. I meant to take them over to John
Saunders the first thing I did, but something or other hindered
me all the morning; first one thing, then another, there is no
saying what: you know. At one time Patty came to say she
·thought the kitchen chimney wanted sweeping. " Oh," said I,
" Patty, do not come with your bad news to me. Here is the rivet
of your mistress's spectacles out." Then the baked apples came
home; Mrs Wallis sent them by her boy; they are extremely
civil and obliging to us, the Wallises, always. I have heard some
people say that Mrs Wallis can be uncivil and give a very rude
answer; but we have never known anything but the greatest
attention from them. And it cannot be for the value of out custom now, for what is our consumption of bread, you know?
only three of us. Besides, dear Jane at present—and she really
eats nothing—makes such a shocking breakfast, you would be
quite frightened if you saw it. I dare not let my mother know
how little she eats; so I say one thing, and then I say another,
and it passes off. But about the middle of the day she gets hungry, and there is nothing she likes so well as these baked apples,
and they are extremely wholesome; for I took the opportunity
the other day of asking Mr Perry; I happened to meet him in
the street. Not that I had any doubt before. I have so often
heard Mr Woodhouse recommend a baked apple. I believe it
is the only way that Mr Woodhouse thinks the fruit thoroughly
wholescme. We have apples dumplings, however, very often.
Patty makes an excellent apple-dumpling. Well, Mrs Weston,
you have prevailed, I hope, and these ladies will oblige us.'

Emma would be ' very happy to wait on Mrs Bates,' etc., and they did at last move out of the shop, with no further delay from Miss Bates than—

' How do you do, Mrs Ford? I beg your pardon; I did not see you before. I hear you have a charming collection of new ribbons from town. Jane came back delighted yesterday. Thank ye, the gloves do very well—only a little too large about the wrist; but Jane is taking them in.'

' What was I talking of? ' said she, beginning again when they were all in the street.

Emma wondered on what, of all the medley, she would fix.

' I declare I cannot recollect what I was talking of. Oh, my mother's spectacles! So very obliging of Mr Frank Churchill! " Oh," said he, " I do think I can fasten the rivet; I like a job of this kind excessively." Which, you know, showed him to be so very—Indeed I must say that, much as I had heard of him before, and much as I had expected, he very far exceeds anything—I do congratulate you, Mrs Weston, most warmly. He seems everything the fondest parent could—" Oh! " said he, " I can fasten the rivet. I like a job of that sort excessively." I never shall forget his manner. And when I brought out the baked apples from the closet, and hoped our friends would be so very obliging as to take some, " Oh! " said he directly, "there is nothing in the way of fruit half so good, and these are the finest-looking home-baked apples I ever saw in my life." That, you know, was so very—And I am sure, by his manner, it was no compliment. Indeed they are very delightful apples, and Mrs Wallis does them full justice, only we do not have them baked more than twice, and Mr Woodhouse made us promise to have them done three times; but Miss Woodhouse will be so good as not to mention it. The apples themselves are the very finest sort for baking, beyond a doubt; all from Donwell—some of Mr Knightley's most liberal supply. He sends us a sack every year; and certainly there never was such a keeping apple anywhere as one of his trees—I believe there is two of them. My mother says the orchard was always famous in her younger days. But I was really quite shocked the other day; for Mr Knightley called one morning, and Jane was eating these apples, and we talked about them, and said how much she enjoyed them, and he asked whether we were not got to the end of our stock. " I am sure you must be," said he, " and I will send you another supply; for I have a great many more than I can ever use. William Larkins let me keep a larger quantity than usual this year.

I will send you some more, before they get good for nothing."
So I begged he would not—for really as to ours being gone, I
could not absolutely say that we had a great many left—it was
half a dozen indeed; but they should be all kept for Jane; and
I could not at all bear that he should be sending us more, so liberal as he had been already; and Jane said the same. And
when he was gone she almost quarrelled with me—no, I should
not say quarrelled, for we never had quarrel in our lives—but
she was quite distressed that I had owned the apples were so nearly gone; she wished I had made him believe we had a great many
left. " Oh," said I, " my dear, I did say as much as I could."
However, the very same evening, William Larkins came over with
a large basket of apples, the same sort of apples, a bushel at least,
and I was very much obliged, and went down and spoke to William Larkins, and said everything, as you may suppose. William
Larkins is such an old acquaintance! I am always glad to see
him. But, however, I found afterwards from Patty that William
said it was all the apples of *that* sort his master had; he had
brought them all—and now his master had not one left to bake or
boil. William did not seem to mind it himself, he was so pleased to
think his master had sold so many; for William, you know, thinks
more of his master's profit than anything; but Mrs Hodges,
he said, was quite displeased at their being all sent away. She
could not bear that her master should not be able to have another
apple-tart this spring. He told Patty this, but bid her not mind it,
and be sure not to say anything to us about it, for Mrs Hodges
would be cross sometimes and as long as so many sacks were sold
it did not signify who ate the remainder. And so Patty told me,
and I was excessively shocked indeed! I would not have Mr
Knightley know anything about it for the world! He would be
so very—I wanted to keep it from Jane's knowledge; but, unluckily, I had mentioned it before I was aware.'

Miss Bates had just done as Patty opened the door; and her
visitors walked upstairs, without having any regular narration
to attend to, pursued only by the sounds of her desultory good-
will.

' Pray, take care, Mrs Weston, there is a step at the turning.
Pray, take care, Miss Woodhouse, ours is rather a dark staircase
—rather darker and narrower than one could wish. Miss Smith,
pray take care. Miss Woodhouse, I am quite concerned, I am
sure you hit your foot. Miss Smith, the step at the turning.'

THE appearance of the little sitting-room as they entered was tranquillity itself; Mrs Bates, deprived of her usual employment, slumbering on one side of the fire, Frank Churchill, at a table, near her, most deedily occupied about her spectacles, and Jane Fairfax, standing with her back to them, intent on her pianoforte.

Busy as he was, however, the young man was yet able to show a most happy countenance on seeing Emma again.

'This is a pleasure,' said he, in rather a low voice, 'coming at least ten minutes earlier than I had calculated. You find me trying to be useful; tell me if you think I shall succeed.'

'What!' said Mrs Weston, 'have you not finished it yet? You would not earn a very good livelihood as a working silversmith at this rate.'

'I have not been working uninterruptedly,' he replied, 'I have been assisting Miss Fairfax in trying to make her instrument stand steadily; it was not quite firm; an unevenness in the floor, I believe. You see we have been wedging one leg with paper. This was very kind of you to be persuaded to come. I was almost afraid you would be hurrying home.'

He contrived that she should be seated by him; and was sufficiently employed in looking out the best baked apple for her, and trying to make her help or advise him in his work, till Jane Fairfax was quite ready to sit down to the pianoforte again. That she was not immediately ready Emma did suspect to arise from the state of her nerves; she had not yet possessed the instrument long enough to touch it without emotion; she must reason herself into the power of performance; and Emma could not but pity such feelings, whatever their origin, and could not but resolve never to expose them to her neighbour again.

At last Jane began, and though the first bars were feebly given, the powers of the instrument were gradually done full justice to. Mrs Weston had been delighted before, and was delighted again; Emma joined her in all her praise; and the pianoforte, with every proper discrimination, was pronounced to be altogether of the highest promise.

'Whoever Colonel Campbell might employ,' said Frank Churchill, with a smile at Emma, 'the person has not chosen ill. I heard a good deal of Colonel Campbell's taste at Weymouth; and the softness of the upper notes I am sure is exactly what he and *all that party* would particularly prize. I dare say, Miss Fairfax, that he either gave his friend very minute directions, or wrote to Broadwood himself. Do not you think so?'

Jane did not look round. She was not obliged to hear. Mrs Weston had been speaking to her at the same moment.

'It is not fair,' said Emma, in a whisper; 'mine was a random guess. Do not distress her.'

He shook his head with a smile, and looked as if he had very little doubt and very little mercy. Soon afterwards he began again:

'How much your friends in Ireland must be enjoying your pleasure on this occasion, Miss Fairfax. I dare say they often think of you, and wonder which will be the day, the precise day, of the instrument's coming to hand. Do you imagine Colonel Campbell knows the business to be going forward just at this time? Do you imagine it to be the consequence of an immediate commission from him, or that he may have sent only a general direction, an order indefinite as to time, to depend upon contingencies and conveniences?'

He paused. She could not but hear; she could not avoid answering:

'Till I have a letter from Colonel Campbell,' said she, in a voice of forced calmness, 'I can imagine nothing with any confidence. It must be all conjecture.'

'Conjecture! aye, sometimes one conjectures right, and sometimes one conjectures wrong. I wish I could conjecture how soon I shall make this rivet quite firm. What nonsense one talks, Miss Woodhouse, when hard at work, if one talks at all; your real workmen, I suppose, hold their tongues; but we, gentlemen labourers, if we get hold of a word—Miss Fairfax said something about conjecturing. There, it is done. I have the pleasure, madam' (to Mrs Bates), 'of restoring your spectacles, healed for the present.'

He was very warmly thanked both by mother and daughter; to escape a little from the latter he went to the pianoforte, and begged Miss Fairfax, who was still sitting at it, to play something more.

'If you are very kind,' said he, 'it will be one of the waltzes we danced last night; let me live them over again. You did not enjoy them as I did: you appeared tired the whole time. I believe you were glad we danced no longer; but I would have given worlds—all the worlds one ever has to give—for another half-hour.'

She played.

' What felicity it is to hear a tune again which *has* made one happy! If I mistake not, that was danced at Weymouth.'

She looked up at him for a moment, coloured deeply, and played something else. He took some music from a chair near the pianoforte, and turning to Emma, said:

' Here is something quite new to me. Do you know it? Cramer. And here are a new set of Irish melodies. That, from such a quarter, one might expect. This was all sent with the instrument. Very thoughtful of Colonel Campbell, was not it? He knew Miss Fairfax could have no music here. I honour that part of the attention particularly; it shows it to have been so thoroughly from the heart. Nothing hastily done, nothing incomplete. True affection only could have prompted it.'

Emma wished he would be less pointed, yet could not help being amused, and, when, on glancing her eye towards Jane Fairfax, she caught the remains of a smile; when she saw that, with all the deep blush of consciousness, there had been a smile of secret delight, she had less scruple in the amusement, and much less compunction with respect to her. This amiable, upright, perfect Jane Fairfax, was apparently cherishing very reprehensible feelings.

He brought all the music to her, and they looked it over together. Emma took the opportunity of whispering:

' You speak too plain. She must understand you.'

' I hope she does. I would have her understand me. I am not in the least ashamed of my meaning.'

' But, really, I am half ashamed, and wish I had never taken up the idea.'

' I am very glad you did, and that you communicated it to me. I have now a key to all her odd looks and ways. Leave shame to her. If she does wrong, she ought to feel it.'

' She is not entirely without it, I think.'

' I do not see much sign of it. She is playing "Robin Adair" at this moment—*his* favourite.'

Shortly afterwards Miss Bates, passing near the window, descried Mr Knightley on horseback not far off.

' Mr Knightley, I declare! I must speak to him, if possible, just to thank him. I will not open the window here; it would give you all cold; but I can go into my mother's room, you know. I dare say he will come in when he knows who is here. Quite delightful to have you all meet so! Our little room so honoured!'

She was in the adjoining chamber while she still spoke, and, opening the casement there, immediately called Mr Knightley's attention, and every syllable of their conversation was as distinctly heard by the others as if it had passed within the same apartment.

'How d'ye do? How d'ye do? Very well, I thank you. So obliged to you for the carriage last night. We were just in time; my mother just ready for us. Pray come in; do come in. You will find some friends here.'

So began Miss Bates; and Mr Knightley seemed determined to be heard in his turn, for most resolutely and commandingly did he say:

'How is your niece, Miss Bates? I want to inquire after you all, but particularly your niece. How is Miss Fairfax? I hope she caught no cold last night? How is she to-day? Tell me how Miss Fairfax is.'

And Miss Bates was obliged to give a direct answer before he would hear her in anything else. The listeners were amused; and Mrs Weston gave Emma a look of particular meaning. But Emma still shook her head in steady scepticism.

'So obliged to you! so very much obliged to you for the carriage,' resumed Miss Bates.

He cut her short with—

'I am going to Kingston. Can I do anything for you?'

'Oh, dear! Kingston—are you? Mrs Cole was saying the other day she wanted something from Kingston.'

'Mrs Cole has servants to send; can I do anything for *you*?'

'No, I thank you. But do come in. Who do you think is here? Miss Woodhouse and Miss Smith; so kind as to call to hear the new pianoforte. Do put up your horse at the "Crown," and come in.'

'Well,' said he, in a deliberating manner, 'for five minutes, perhaps.'

'And here is Mrs Weston and Mr Frank Churchill too! Quite delightful! so many friends!'

'No, not now, I thank you. I could not stay two minutes. I must get on to Kingston as fast as I can.'

'Oh, do come in! They will be so very happy to see you.'

'No, no; your room is full enough! I will call another day and hear the pianoforte.'

'Well, I am so sorry! Oh, Mr Knightley, what a delightful party last night! how extremely pleasant! Did you ever see such dancing? Was not it delightful? Miss Woodhouse and Mr Frank Churchill; I never saw anything equal to it.'

'Oh, very delightful, indeed! I can say nothing less, for I suppose Miss Woodhouse and Mr Frank Churchill are hearing everything that passes. And' (raising his voice still more) 'I do not see why Miss Fairfax should not be mentioned too. I think Miss Fairfax dances very well; and Mrs Weston is the very best country-dance player, without exception, in England. Now, if your friends have my gratitude, they will say something pretty loud about you and me in return; but I cannot stay to hear it.'

'Oh, Mr Knightley, one moment more; something of consequence—so shocked! Jane and I are both so shocked about the apples!'

'What is the matter now?'

'To think of your sending us all your store apples! You said you had a great many, and now you have not one left. We really are so shocked! Mrs Hodges may well be angry. William Larkins mentioned it here. You should not have done it, indeed you should not. Ah, he is off! He never can bear to be thanked. But I thought he would have stayed now, and it would have been a pity not to have mentioned—well' (returning to the room), 'I have not been able to succeed. Mr Knightley cannot stop. He is going to Kingston. He asked me if he could do anything——'

'Yes,' said Jane, 'we heard his kind offers; we heard everything.'

'Oh, yes, my dear, I dare say you might; because, you know, the door was open, and the window was open, and Mr Knightley spoke loud. You must have heard everything, to be sure. "Can I do anything for you at Kingston?" said he; so I just mentioned—Oh, Miss Woodhouse, must you be going? You seem but just come; so very obliging of you.'

Emma found it really time to be at home; the visit had already lasted long; and, on examining watches, so much of the morning was perceived to be gone, that Mrs Weston and her companion, taking leave also, could allow themselves only to walk with the two young ladies to Hartfield gates before they set off for Randalls.

IT may be possible to do without dancing entirely. Instances have been known of young people passing many, many months successively without being at any ball of any description, and no material injury accrue either to body or mind; but when a beginning is made—when the felicities of rapid motion have once been, though slightly, felt—it must be a very heavy set that does not ask for more.

Frank Churchill had danced once at Highbury, and longed to dance again; and the last half-hour of an evening which Mr Woodhouse was persuaded to spend with his daughter at Randalls was passed by the two young people in schemes on the subject. Frank's was the first idea, and his the greatest zeal in pursuing it; for the lady was the best judge of the difficulties, and the most solicitous for accommodation and appearance. But still she had inclination enough for showing people again how delightfully Mr Frank Churchill and Miss Woodhouse danced —for doing that in which she need not blush to compare herself with Jane Fairfax—and even for simple dancing itself, without any of the wicked aids of vanity—to assist him first in pacing out the room they were in to see what it could be made to hold— and then in taking the dimensions of the other parlour, in the hope of discovering, in spite of all that Mr Weston could say of their exactly equal size, that it was a little the largest.

His first proposition and request, that the dance begun at Mr Cole's should be finished there—that the same party should be collected, and the same musician engaged—met with the readiest acquiescence. Mr Weston entered into the idea with thorough enjoyment, and Mrs Weston most willingly undertook to play as long as they could wish to dance; and the interesting employment had followed, of reckoning up exactly who there would be, and portioning out the indispensable division of space to every couple.

'You and Miss Smith and Miss Fairfax will be three, and the two Miss Coxes five,' had been repeated many times over. 'And there will be the two Gilberts, young Cox, my father, and myself, besides Mr Knightley. Yes, that will be quite enough for pleasure. You and Miss Smith and Miss Fairfax will be three, and the two Miss Coxes five, and for five couple there will be plenty of room.'

But soon it came to be on one side:

'But will there be good room for five couple? I really do not think there will.'

On another:

'And, after all, five couple are not enough to make it worth while to stand up. Five couple are nothing when one thinks seriously about it. It will not do to *invite* five couple. It can be allowable only as the thought of the moment.'

Somebody said that *Miss* Gilbert was expected at her brother's, and must be invited with the rest. Somebody else believed *Mrs* Gilbert would have danced the other evening if she had been asked. A word was put in for a second young Cox! and at last, Mr Weston naming one family of cousins who must be included, and another of very old acquaintance who could not be left out, it became a certainty that the five couple would be at least ten, and a very interesting speculation in what possible manner they could be disposed of.

The doors of the two rooms were just opposite each other. 'Might not they use both rooms, and dance across the passage?' It seemed the best scheme; and yet it was not so good but that many of them wanted a better. Emma said it would be awkward; Mrs Weston was in distress about the supper; and Mr Woodhouse opposed it earnestly on the score of health. It made him so very unhappy, indeed, that it could not be persevered in.

'Oh, no,' said he, 'it would be the extreme of imprudence. I could not bear it for Emma! Emma is not strong. She would catch a dreadful cold. So would poor little Harriet. So you would all. Mrs Weston, you would be quite laid up, do not let them talk of such a wild thing; pray do not let them talk of it. That young man' (speaking lower) 'is very thoughtless. Do not tell his father, but that young man is not quite the thing. He has been opening the doors very often this evening, and keeping them open very inconsiderately. He does not think of the draught. I do not mean to set you against him, but indeed he is not quite the thing.'

Mrs Weston was sorry for such a charge. She knew the importance of it, and said everything in her power to do it away. Every door was now closed, the passage plan given up, and the first scheme, of dancing only in the room they were in, resorted to again; and with such goodwill on Frank Churchill's part, that the space which a quarter of an hour before had been deemed barely sufficient for five couple was now endeavoured to be made out quite enough for ten.

'We were too magnificent,' said he. 'We allowed unnecessary room. Ten couple may stand here very well.'

Emma demurred. 'It would be a crowd—a sad crowd; and what could be worse than dancing without space to turn in?'

'Very true,' he gravely replied; 'it was very bad.' But still he went on measuring, and still he ended with:

'I think there will be very tolerable room for ten couple.'

'No, no,' said she, 'you are quite unreasonable. It would be dreadful to be standing so close. Nothing can be further from pleasure than to be dancing in a crowd—and a crowd in a little room.'

'There is no denying it,' he replied. 'I agree with you exactly. A crowd in a little room—Miss Woodhouse, you have the art of giving pictures in a few words. Exquisite, quite exquisite! Still, however, having proceeded so far, one is unwilling to give the matter up. It would be a disappointment to my father—and altogether—I do not know that—I am rather of opinion that ten couple might stand here very well.'

Emma perceived that the nature of his gallantry was a little self-willed, and that he would rather oppose than lose the pleasure of dancing with her; but she took the compliment, and forgave the rest. Had she intended ever to *marry* him, it might have been worth while to pause and consider, and try to understand the value of his preference, and the character of his temper; but for all the purposes of their acquaintance he was quite amiable enough.

Before the middle of the next day he was at Hartfield; and he entered the room with such an agreeable smile as certified the continuance of the scheme. It soon appeared that he came to announce an improvement.

'Well, Miss Woodhouse,' he almost immediately began, 'your inclination for dancing has not been quite frightened away, I hope, by the terrors of my father's little rooms. I bring a new proposal on the subject: a thought of my father's, which waits only your approbation to be acted upon. May I hope for the honour of your hand for the two first dances of this little projected ball, to be given, not at Randalls, but at the Crown Inn?'

'The Crown!'

'Yes; if you and Mr Woodhouse see no objection, and I trust you cannot, my father hopes his friends will be so kind as to visit him there. Better accommodations he can promise them, and not a less grateful welcome than at Randalls. It is his own idea. Mrs Weston sees no objection to it, provided you are satisfied. This is what we all feel. Oh, you were perfectly right! Ten couple, in either of the Randalls rooms, would have been insufferable—dreadful! I felt how right you were the whole time, but was too anxious for securing *anything* to like to yield. Is not it a good exchange? You consent—I hope you consent?'

'It appears to me a plan that nobody can object to, if Mr and Mrs Weston do not. I think it admirable; and, as far as I can answer for myself, shall be most happy—it seems the only improvement that could be. Papa, do you not think it an excellent improvement?'

She was obliged to repeat and explain it before it was fully comprehended; and then, being quite new, further representations were necessary to make it acceptable.

'No; he thought it very far from an improvement—a very bad plan—much worse than the other. A room at an inn was always damp and dangerous, never properly aired, or fit to be inhabited. If they must dance, they had better dance at Randalls. He had never been in the room at the Crown in his life—did not know the people who kept it by sight. Oh no—a very bad plan. They would catch worse colds at the Crown than anywhere.'

'I was going to observe, sir,' said Frank Churchill, 'that one of the great recommendations of this change would be the very little danger of anybody's catching cold—so much less danger at the Crown than at Randalls! Mr Perry might have reasons to regret the alteration, but nobody else could.'

'Sir,' said Mr Woodhouse, rather warmly, 'you are very much mistaken if you suppose Mr Perry to be that sort of character. Mr Perry is extremely concerned when any of us are ill. But I do not understand how the room at the Crown can be safer for you than your father's house.'

'From the very circumstance of its being larger, sir. We shall have no occasion to open the windows at all—not once the whole evening; and it is that dreadful habit of opening the windows, letting in cold air upon heated bodies, which (as you well know, sir) does the mischief.'

'Open the windows! but surely, Mr Churchill, nobody would think of opening the windows at Randalls. Nobody could be so imprudent! I never heard of such a thing. Dancing with open windows! I am sure neither your father nor Mrs Weston (poor Miss Taylor that was) would suffer it.'

'Ah! sir—but a thoughtless young person will sometimes step

behind a window-curtain, and throw up a sash, without its being suspected. I have often known it done myself.'

'Have you, indeed, sir! Bless me! I never should have supposed it. But I live out of the world, and am often astonished at what I hear. However, this does make a difference; and perhaps, when we come to talk it over—but these sort of things require a good deal of consideration. One cannot resolve upon them in a hurry. If Mr and Mrs Weston will be so obliging as to call here one morning we may talk it over, and see what can be done.'

'But, unfortunately, sir, my time is so limited——'

'Oh,' interrupted Emma, 'there will be plenty of time for talking everything over. There is no hurry at all. If it can be contrived to be at the Crown, papa, it will be very convenient for the horses. They will be so near their own stable.'

'So they will, my dear. That is a great thing. Not that James ever complains; but it is right to spare our horses when we can. If I could be sure of the rooms being thoroughly aired—but is Mrs Stokes to be trusted? I doubt it. I do not know her, even by sight.'

'I can answer for everything of that nature, sir, because it will be under Mrs Weston's care. Mrs Weston undertakes to direct the whole.'

'There, papa! now you must be satisfied—our own dear Mrs Weston, who is carefulness itself. Do not you remember what Mr Perry said, so many years ago, when I had the measles? "If *Miss Taylor* undertakes to wrap Miss Emma up, you need not have any fears, sir." How often have I heard you speak of it as such a compliment to her!'

'Aye, very true, Mr Perry did say so. I shall never forget it. Poor little Emma! You were very bad with the measles, that is, you would have been very bad, but for Perry's great attentions. He came four times a day for a week. He said, from the first, it was a very good sort—which was our great comfort; but the measles are a dreadful complaint. I hope whenever poor Isabella's little ones have the measles she will send for Perry.'

'My father and Mrs Weston are at the Crown at this moment,' said Frank Churchill, 'examining the capabilities of the house. I left them there and came on to Hartfield, impatient for your opinion, and hoping you might be persuaded to join them and give your advice on the spot. I was desired to say so from both. It would be the greatest pleasure to them if you could allow me to attend you there. They can do nothing satisfactorily without you.'

Emma was most happy to be called to such a council: and, her father engaging to think it all over while she was gone, the two young people went off together without delay for the Crown. There were Mr and Mrs Weston; delighted to see her and receive her approbation, very busy and very happy in their different way: she, in some little distress; and he, finding everything perfect.

'Emma,' said she, 'this paper is worse than I expected. Look! in places you see it is dreadfully dirty: and the wainscot is more yellow and forlorn than anything I could have imagined.'

'My dear, you are too particular,' said her husband. 'What does all that signify? You will see nothing of it by candle-light. It will be as clean as Randalls by candle-light. We never see anything of it on our club-nights.'

The ladies here probably exchanged looks which meant, 'Men never know when things are dirty or not;' and the gentlemen perhaps thought each to himself, 'Women will have their little nonsenses and needless cares.'

One perplexity, however, arose, which the gentlemen did not disdain· it regarded a supper-room. At the time of the ball-room's being built suppers had not been in question; and a small card-room adjoining was the only addition. What was to be done? This card-room would be wanted as a card-room now; or, if cards were conveniently voted unnecessary by their four selves, still was it not too small for any comfortable supper? Another room of much better size might be secured for the purpose; bit it was at the other end of the house, and a long awkward passage must be gone through to get at it. This made a difficulty. Mrs Weston was afraid of draughts for the young people in that passage; and neither Emma nor the gentlemen could tolerate the prospect of being miserably crowded at supper.

Mrs Weston proposed having no regular supper; merely sandwiches, etc., set out in the little room; but that was scouted as a wretched suggestion. A private dance without sitting down to supper, was pronounced an infamous fraud upon the rights of men and women; and Mrs Weston must not speak of it again. She then took another line of expediency, and looking into the doubtful room, observed:

'I do not think it *is* so very small. We shall not be many, you know.'

And Mr Weston at the same time, walking briskly with long steps through the passage, was calling out:

'You talk a great deal of the length of this passage, my dear. It is a mere nothing after all; and not the least draught from the stairs.'

'I wish,' said Mrs Weston, 'one could know which arrangement our guests in general would like best. To do what would be most generally pleasing must be our object—if one could but tell what that would be.'

'Yes, very true,' cried Frank, 'very true. You want your neighbours' opinions. I do not wonder at you. If one could ascertain what the chief of them—the Coles, for instance, they are not far off. Shall I call upon them? Or Miss Bates? She is still nearer. And I do not know whether Miss Bates is not as likely to understand the inclinations of the rest of the people as anybody. I think we do want a larger council. Suppose I go and invite Miss Bates to join us?'

'Well—if you please,' said Mrs Weston, rather hesitating. 'If you think she will be of any use.'

'You will get nothing to the purpose from Miss Bates,' said Emma; 'she will be all delight and gratitude, but she will tell you nothing. She will not even listen to your questions. I see no advantage in consulting Miss Bates.'

'But she is so amusing, so extremely amusing! I am very fond of hearing Miss Bates talk. And I need not bring the whole family, you know.'

Here Mr Weston joined them, and on hearing what was proposed gave it his decided approbation.

'Aye, do, Frank; go and fetch Miss Bates, and let us end the matter at once. She will enjoy the scheme, I am sure; and I do not know a properer person for showing us how to do away difficulties. Fetch Miss Bates. We are growing a little too nice. She is a standing lesson of how to be happy. But fetch them both. Invite them both.'

'Both, sir? Can the old lady——?'

'The old lady! No, the young lady, to be sure! I shall think you a great blockhead, Frank, if you bring the aunt without the niece.'

'Oh! I beg your pardon, sir. I did not immediately recollect. Undoubtedly, if you wish it, I will endeavour to persuade them both.' And away he ran.

Long before he reappeared, attending the short, neat, brisk-moving aunt, and her elegant niece—Mrs Weston, like a sweet-tempered woman and a good wife, had examined the passage again, and found the evils of it much less than she had supposed before—indeed, very trifling; and here ended the difficulties of decision. All the rest, in speculation at least, was perfectly smooth. All the minor arrangements of table and chair, lights and music, tea and supper, made themselves; or were left as mere trifles, to be settled at any time between Mrs Weston and Mrs Stokes. Everybody invited was certainly to come; Frank had already written to Enscombe to propose staying a few days beyond his fortnight, which could not possibly be refused. And a delightful dance it was to be.

Most cordially, when Miss Bates arrived, did she agree that it must. As a counsellor she was not wanted; but as an approver (a much safer character) she was truly welcome. Her approbation, at once general and minute, warm and incessant, could not but please; and for another half-hour they were all walking to and fro between the different rooms, some suggesting, some attending, and all in happy enjoyment of the future. The party did not break up without Emma's being positively secured for the two first dances by the hero of the evening, nor without her overhearing Mr Weston whisper to his wife, ' He has asked her, my dear. That's right. I knew he would! '

30

ONE thing only was wanting to make the prospect of the ball completely satisfactory to Emma—its being fixed for a day within the granted term of Frank Churchill's stay in Surrey; for, in spite of Mr Weston's confidence, she could not think it so very impossible that the Churchills might not allow their nephew to remain a day beyond his fortnight. But this was not judged feasible. The preparations must take their time, nothing could be properly ready till the third week were entered on, and for a few days they must be planning, proceeding, and hoping in uncertainty, at the risk—in her opinion, the great risk—of its being all in vain.

Enscombe, however, was gracious—gracious in fact, if not in word. His wish of staying longer evidently did not please; but it was not opposed. All was safe and prosperous; and as the removal of one solicitude generally makes way for another, Emma being now certain of her ball, began to adopt as the next vexation Mr Knightley's provoking indifference about it. Either because he did not dance himself, or because the plan had been formed without his being consulted, he seemed resolved that it should not interest him, determined against its exciting any present curiosity, or affording him any future amusement. To her voluntary communications Emma could get no more approving reply than:

'Very well. If the Westons think it worth while to be at all this trouble for a few hours of noisy entertainment, I have nothing to say against it, but that they shall not choose pleasures for me. Oh, yes! I must be there; I could not refuse; and I will keep as much awake as I can; but I would rather be at home, looking over William Larkins's week's account; much rather, I confess. Pleasure in seeing dancing! not I, indeed—I never look at it—I do not know who does. Fine dancing, I believe, like virtue, must be its own reward. Those who are standing by are usually thinking of something very different.'

This Emma felt was aimed at her; and it made her quite angry. It was not in compliment to Jane Fairfax, however, that he was so indifferent, or so indignant; he was not guided by *her* feelings in reprobating the ball, for *she* enjoyed the thought of it to an extraordinary degree. It made her animated—open-hearted; she voluntarily said:

'Oh! Miss Woodhouse, I hope nothing may happen to prevent the ball! What a disappointment it would be! I do look forward to it, I own, with *very* great pleasure.'

It was not to oblige Jane Fairfax, therefore, that he would have preferred the society of William Larkins. No!—she was more and more convinced that Mrs Weston was quite mistaken in that surmise. There was a great deal of friendly and of compassionate attachment on his side— but no love.

Alas! there was soon no leisure for quarrelling with Mr Knightley. Two days of joyful security were immediately followed by the overthrow of everything. A letter arrived from Mr Churchill to urge his nephew's instant return. Mrs Churchill was unwell—far too unwell to do without him; she had been in a very suffering state (so said her husband) when writing to her nephew two days before, though from her usual unwillingness to give pain, and constant habit of never thinking of herself, she had not mentioned it; but now she was too ill to trifle, and must entreat him to set off for Enscombe without delay.

The substance of this letter was forwarded to Emma, in a note from Mrs Weston, instantly. As to his going, it was inevitable. He must be gone within a few hours, though without feeling any real alarm for his aunt, to lessen his repugnance. He knew her illnesses; they never occurred but for her own convenience.

Mrs Weston added, 'that he could only allow himself time to hurry to Highbury, after breakfast, and take leave of the few friends there whom he could suppose to feel any interest in him; and that he might be expected at Hartfield very soon.'

This wretched note was the finale of Emma's breakfast. When once it had been read there was no doing anything but lament and exclaim. The loss of the ball—the loss of the young man—and all that the young man might be feeling! It was too wretched! Such a delightful evening as it would have been! Everybody so happy! and she and her partner the happiest! 'I said it would be so,' was the only consolation.

Her father's feelings were quite distinct. He thought principally of Mrs Churchill's illness, and wanted to know how she was treated; and as for the ball, it was shocking to have dear Emma disappointed; but they would all be safer at home.

Emma was ready for her visitor some time before he appeared; but if this reflected at all upon his impatience, his sorrowful look and total want of spirits when he did come might redeem him. He felt the going away almost too much to speak of it. His dejection was most evident. He sat really lost in thought for the first few minutes; and when rousing himself it was only to say:

'Of all horrid things leave-taking is the worst.'

'But you will come again,' said Emma. 'This will not be your only visit to Randalls.'

'Ah!'—(shaking his head)—'the uncertainty of when I may be able to return! I shall try for it with zeal! It will be the object of all my thoughts and cares! and if my uncle and aunt go to town this spring—but I am afraid—they did not stir last spring—I am afraid it is a custom gone for ever.'

'Our poor ball must be quite given up.'

'Ah! that ball! why did we wait for anything?—why not seize the pleasure at once? How often is happiness destroyed by preparation, foolish preparation! You told us it would be so. Oh! Miss Woodhouse, why are you always so right?'

'Indeed, I am very sorry to be right in this instance. I would much rather have been merry than wise.'

'If I can come again, we are still to have our ball. My father depends on it. Do not forget your engagement.'

Emma looked graciously.

'Such a fortnight as it has been!' he continued; 'every day more precious and more delightful than the day before! every day making me less fit to bear any other place. Happy those who can remain at Highbury!'

'As you do us ample justice now,' said Emma, laughing, 'I will venture to ask whether you did not come a little doubtfully at first? Do not we rather surpass your expectations? I am sure we do. I am sure you did not much expect to like us. You would not have been so long in coming if you had had a pleasant idea of Highbury.'

He laughed rather consciously; and though denying the sentiment, Emma was convinced that it had been so.

'And you must be off this very morning?'

'Yes; my father is to join me here: we shall walk back together, and I must be off immediately. I am almost afraid that every moment will bring him.'

'Not five minutes to spare even for your friends Miss Fairfax and Miss Bates? How unlucky! Miss Bates's powerful, argumentative mind might have strengthened yours.'

'Yes—I *have* called there; passing the door, I thought it better. It was a right thing to do. I went in for three minutes, and was detained by Miss Bates's being absent. She was out; and I felt it impossible not to wait till she came in. She is a woman that one may, that one *must* laugh at; but that one would not wish to slight. It was better to pay my visit, then—— '

He hesitated, got up, walked to a window.

'In short,' said he, 'perhaps, Miss Woodhouse—I think you can hardly be quite without suspicion—— '

He looked at her, as if wanting to read her thoughts. She hardly knew what to say. It seemed like the forerunner of something absolutely serious, which she did not wish. Forcing herself to speak, therefore, in the hope of putting it by, she calmly said:

'You are quite in the right; it was most natural to pay your visit, then—— '

He was silent. She believed he was looking at her; probably reflecting on what she had said, and trying to understand the manner. She heard him sigh. It was natural for him to feel that he had *cause* to sigh. He could not believe her to be encouraging him. A few awkward moments passed, and he sat down again; and in a more determined manner said:

'It was something to feel that all the rest of my time might be given to Hartfield. My regard for Hartfield is most warm—— '

He stopped again, rose again, and seemed quite embarrassed. He was more in love with her than Emma had supposed; and who can say how it might have ended, if his father had not made his appearance? Mr Woodhouse soon followed; and the necessity of exertion made him composed.

A very few minutes more, however, completed the present trial. Mr Weston, always alert when business was to be done, and as incapable of procrastinating any evil that was inevitable as of foreseeing any that was doubtful, said: ' It was time to go; ' and the young man, though he might and did sigh, could not but agree, and rise to take leave.

' I shall hear about you all,' said he; ' that is my chief consolation. I shall hear of everything that is going on among you. I have engaged Mrs Weston to correspond with me. She has been so kind as to promise it. Oh! the blessing of a female correspondent, when one is really interested in the absent! she will tell me everything. In her letters I shall be at dear Highbury again.'

A very friendly shake of the hand, a very earnest ' Good-bye,' closed the speech, and the door had soon shut out Frank Churchill. Short had been the notice—short their meeting; he was gone; and Emma felt so sorry to part, and foresaw so great a loss to their little society from his absence as to begin to be afraid of being too sorry, and feeling it too much.

It was a sad change. They had been meeting almost every day since his arrival. Certainly his being at Randalls had given great spirit to the last two weeks—indescribable spirit; the idea, the expectation of seeing him which every morning had brought, the assurance of his attentions, his liveliness, his manners! It had been a very happy fortnight, and forlorn must be the sinking from it into the common course of Hartfield days. To complete every other recommendation, he had *almost* told her that he loved her. What strength or what constancy of affection he might be subject to was another point; but at present she could not doubt his having a decidedly warm admiration, a conscious preference of herself; and this persuasion, joined to all the rest, made her think that she *must* be a little in love with him, in spite of every previous determination against it.

' I certainly must,' said she. ' This sensation of listlessness, weariness, stupidity, this disinclination to sit down and employ myself, this feeling of everything's being dull and insipid about the house! I must be in love; I should be the oddest creature in the world if I were not—for a few weeks at least. Well, evil to some is always good to others. I shall have many fellow-mourners for the ball, if not for Frank Churchill; but Mr Knightley will be happy. He may spend the evening with his dear William Larkins now if he likes.'

Mr Knightley, however, showed no triumphant happiness. He could not say that he was sorry on his own account; his very cheerful look would have contradicted him if he had; but he said, and very steadily, that he was sorry for the disappointment of the others, and with considerable kindness added:

'You, Emma, who have so few opportunities of dancing, you are really out of luck; you are very much out of luck!'

It was some days before she saw Jane Fairfax, to judge of her honest regret in this woeful change; but when they did meet her composure was odious. She had been particularly unwell, however, suffering from headache to a degree which made her aunt declare that, had the ball taken place, she did not think Jane could have attended it; and it was charity to impute some of her unbecoming indifference to the languor of ill-health.

31

EMMA continued to entertain no doubt of her being in love. Her ideas only varied as to the how much. At first she thought it was a good deal; and afterwards but little. She had great pleasure in hearing Frank Churchill talked of; and for his sake, greater pleasure than ever in seeing Mr and Mrs Weston; she was very often thinking of him, and quite impatient for a letter, that she might know how he was, how were his spirits, how was his aunt, and what was the chance of his coming to Randalls again this spring. But, on the other hand, she could not admit herself to be unhappy, nor, after the first morning, to be less disposed for employment than usual; she was still busy and cheerful; and, pleasing as he was, she could yet imagine him to have faults; and further, though thinking of him so much, and, as she sat drawing or working, forming a thousand amusing schemes for the progress and close of their attachment, fancying interesting dialogues, and inventing elegant letters; the conclusion of every imaginary declaration on his side was that she *refused him*. Their affection was always to subside into friendship. Everything tender and charming was to mark their parting; but still they were to part. When she became sensible of this, it struck her that she could not be very much in love; for, in spite of her previous and fixed determination never to quit her father, never to marry, a strong attachment certainly must produce more of a struggle than she could foresee in her own feelings.

'I do not find myself making any use of the word *sacrifice*,' said she. ' In not one of all my clever replies, my delicate negatives, is there any allusion to making a sacrifice. I do suspect that he is not really necessary to my happiness. So much the better. I certainly will not persuade myself to feel more than I do. I am quite enough in love. I should be sorry to be more.'

Upon the whole, she was equally contented with her view of his feelings.

' *He* is undoubtedly very much in love—everything denotes it— very much in love indeed!—and when he comes again, if his affection continue, I must be on my guard not to encourage it. It would be most inexcusable to do otherwise, as my own mind is quite made up. Not that I imagine he can think I have been encouraging him hitherto. No; if he had believed me at all to share his feelings he would not have been so wretched. Could he have thought himself encouraged, his looks and language at parting would have been different. Still, however, I must be on my guard. This is in the supposition of his attachment continuing what it now is; but I do not know that I expect it will; I do not look upon him to be quite the sort of man—I do not altogether build upon his steadiness or constancy. His feelings are warm, but I can imagine them rather changeable. Every consideration of the subject, in short, makes me thankful that my happiness is not more deeply involved. I shall do very well again after a little while—and then, it will be a good thing over; for they say everybody is in love once in their lives, and I shall have been let off easily.'

When his letter to Mrs Weston arrived, Emma had the perusal of it; and she read it with a degree of pleasure and admiration which made her at first shake her head over her own sensations, and think she had undervalued their strength. It was a long, well written letter, giving the particulars of his journey and of his feelings, expressing all the affection, gratitude, and respect which was natural and honourable, and describing everything exterior and local that could be supposed attractive, with spirit and precision. No suspicious flourishes now of apology or concern; it was the language of real feeling towards Mrs Weston; and the transition from Highbury to Enscombe, the contrast between the places in some of the first blessings of social life, was just enough touched on to show how keenly it was felt, and how much more might have been said but for the restraints of propriety. The charm of her own name was not wanting. *Miss Woodhouse* appeared more than once, and never without a something of pleasing connection, either a compliment to her taste, or a remembrance of what she had said; and in the very last time of its meeting her eye, unadorned as it was by any such broad wreath of gallantry, she yet could discern the effect of her influence, and acknowledge the greatest compliment perhaps of all conveyed. Compressed into the very lowest vacant corner were these words—'I had not a spare moment on Tuesday, as you know, for Miss Woodhouse's beautiful little friend. Pray make my excuses and adieus to her.' This, Emma could not doubt, was all for herself. Harriet was remembered only from being *her* friend. His information and prospects, as to Enscombe, were neither worse nor better than had been anticipated; Mrs Churchill was recovering, and he dared not yet, even in his own imagination, fix a time for coming to Randalls again.

Gratifying, however, and stimulative as was the letter in the material part, its sentiments, she yet found, when it was folded up and returned to Mrs Weston, that it had not added any lasting warmth—that she could still do without the writer, and that he must learn to do without her. Her intentions were unchanged. Her resolution of refusal only grew more interesting by the addition of a scheme for his subsequent consolation and happiness. His recollection of Harriet, and the words which clothed it—the 'beautiful little friend,'—suggested to her the idea of Harriet's succeeding her in his affections. Was it impossible? No. Harriet undoubtedly was greatly his inferior in understanding; but he had been very much struck with the loveliness of her face and the warm simplicity of her manner; and all the probabilities of circumstance and connection were in her favour. For Harriet it would be advantageous and delightful indeed.

'I must not dwell upon it,' said she; 'I must not think of it. I know the danger of indulging such speculations. But stranger things have happened; and when we cease to care for each other as we do now, it will be the means of confirming us in that sort of true disinterested friendship which I can already look forward to with pleasure.'

It was well to have a comfort in store on Harriet's behalf, though it might be wise to let the fancy touch it seldom; for evil in that quarter was at hand. As Frank Churchill's arrival had succeeded Mr Elton's engagement in the conversation of Highbury, as the latest interest had entirely borne down the first, so now, upon Frank Churchill's disappearance, Mr Elton's concerns were assuming the most irresistible form. His wedding-day was named. He would soon be among them again—Mr Elton and his bride. There was hardly time to talk over the first letter from Enscombe before ' Mr Elton and his bride ' was in everybody's mouth, and Frank Churchill was forgotten. Emma grew sick at the sound. She had had three weeks of happy exemption from Mr Elton; and Harriet's mind, she had been willing to hope, had been lately gaining strength. With Mr Weston's ball in view, at least, there had been a great deal of insensibility to other things; but it was now too evident that she had not attained such a state of composure as could stand against the actual approach—new carriage, bell-ringing, and all.

Poor Harriet was in a flutter of spirits which required all the reasonings, and soothings, and attentions of every kind that Emma could give. Emma felt that she could not do too much for her, that Harriet had a right to all her ingenuity and all her patience; but it was heavy work to be for ever convincing without producing any effect; for ever agreed to, without being able to make their opinions the same. Harriet listened submissively, and said: ' It was very true; it was just as Miss Woodhouse described—it was not worth while to think about them—and she would not think about them any longer.' But no change of subject could avail, and the next half-hour saw her as anxious and restless about the Eltons as before. At last Emma attacked her on another ground.

' Your allowing yourself to be so occupied and so unhappy about Mr Elton's marrying, Harriet, is the strongest reproach you can make *me*. You could not give me a greater reproof for the mistake I fell into. It was all my doing, I know. I have not forgotten it, I assure you. Deceived myself, I did very miserably deceive you; and it will be a painful reflection to me for ever. Do not imagine me in danger of forgetting it.'

Harriet felt this too much to utter more than a few words of eager exclamation. Emma continued:

' I have not said, exert yourself, Harriet, for my sake; think less, talk less of Mr Elton for my sake; because, for your own sake rather, I would wish it to be done, for the sake of what is more important than my comfort—a habit of self-command in you, a consideration of what is your duty, an attention to propriety, an endeavour to avoid the suspicions of others, to save your health and credit, and restore your tranquillity. These are the motives which I have been pressing on you. They are very important, and sorry I am that you cannot feel them sufficiently to act upon them. My being saved from pain is a very secondary consideration. I want you to save yourself from greater pain. Perhaps I may sometimes have felt that Harriet would not forget what was due—or rather, what would be kind by me.'

This appeal to her affections did more than all the rest. The idea of wanting gratitude and consideration for Miss Woodhouse, whom she really loved extremely, made her wretched for a while; and when the violence of grief was comforted away, still remained powerful enough to prompt to what was right, and support her in it very tolerably.

'You, who have been the best friend I ever had in my life! Want gratitude to you! Nobody is equal to you! I care for nobody as I do for you! Oh, Miss Woodhouse, how ungrateful I have been!'

Such expressions, assisted as they were by everything that look and manner could do, made Emma feel that she had never loved Harriet so well, nor valued her affection so highly before.

'There is no charm equal to tenderness of heart,' said she afterwards to herself. 'There is nothing to be compared to it. Warmth and tenderness of heart, with an affectionate, open manner, will beat all the clearness of head in the world, for attraction: I am sure it will. It is tenderness of heart which makes my dear father so generally beloved—which gives Isabella all her popularity. I have it not; but I know how to prize and respect it. Harriet is my superior in all the charm and all the felicity it gives. Dear Harriet! I would not change you for the clearest-headed, longest-sighted, best-judging female breathing. Oh, the coldness of a Jane Fairfax! Harriet is worth a hundred such; and for a wife—a sensible man's wife—it is invaluable. I mention no names; but happy the man who changes Emma for Harriet!'

32

Mrs Elton was first seen at church: but though devotion might be interrupted, curiosity could not be satisfied by a bride in a pew, and it must be left for the visits in form which were then to be paid, to settle whether she were very pretty indeed, or only rather pretty, or not pretty at all.

Emma had feelings, less of curiosity than of pride or propriety, to make her resolve on not being the last to pay her respects: and she made a point of Harriet's going with her, that the worst of the business might be gone through as soon as possible.

She could not enter the house again, could not be in the same room to which she had with such vain artifice retreated three months ago, to lace up her boot, without *recollecting*. A thousand vexatious thoughts would recur. Compliments, charades, and horrible blunders; and it was not to be supposed that poor Harriet should not be recollecting too; but she behaved very well, and was only rather pale and silent. The visit was of course short! and there was so much embarrassment and occupation of mind to shorten it that Emma would not allow herself entirely to form an opinion of the lady, and on no account to give one, beyond the nothing-meaning terms of being 'elegantly dressed, and very pleasing.'

She did not really like her. She would not be in a hurry to find fault, but she suspected that there was no elegance; ease, but not elegance. She was almost sure that for a young woman, a stranger, a bride, there was too much ease. Her person was rather good; her face not unpretty; but neither feature nor air, nor voice, nor manner were elegant. Emma thought, at least, it would turn out so.

As for Mr Elton, his manners did not appear—but no, she would not permit a hasty or a witty word from herself about his manners. It was an awkward ceremony at any time to be receiving wedding visits; and a man had need be all grace to acquit himself well through it. The woman was better off; she might have the assistance of fine clothes, and the privilege of bashfulness; but the man had only his own good sense to depend on: and when she considered how peculiarly unlucky poor Mr Elton was in being in the same room at once with the woman he had just married, the woman he had wanted to marry, and the woman whom he had been expected to marry, she must allow him to have the right to look as little wise, and to be as much affectedly, and as little really, easy as could be.

'Well, Miss Woodhouse,' said Harriet, when they had quitted the house, and after waiting in vain for her friend to begin; 'well, Miss Woodhouse' (with a gentle sigh), 'what do you think of her? Is not she very charming?'

There was a little hesitation in Emma's answer.

'Oh! yes—very—a very pleasing young woman.'

'I think her beautiful, quite beautiful.'

'Very nicely dressed, indeed; a remarkably elegant gown.'

'I am not at all surprised that he should have fallen in love.'

'Oh! no; there is nothing to surprise one at all; a pretty fortune, and she came in his way.'

'I dare say,' returned Harriet, sighing again, 'I dare say she was very much attached to him.'

'Perhaps she might; but it is not every man's fate to marry the woman who loves him best. Miss Hawkins, perhaps, wanted a home, and thought this the best offer she was likely to have.'

'Yes,' said Harriet earnestly, 'and well she might; nobody could ever have a better. Well, I wish them happy with all my heart. And now, Miss Woodhouse, I do not think I shall mind seeing them again. He is just as superior as ever; but being married, you know, it is quite a different thing. No, indeed, Miss Woodhouse, you need not be afraid; I can sit and admire him now without any great misery. To know that he has not thrown himself away is such a comfort! She does seem a charming young woman, just what he deserves. Happy creature! He called her "Augusta." How delightful!'

When the visit was returned, Emma made up her mind. She could then see more and judge better. From Harriet's happening not to be at Hartfield, and her father's being present to engage Mr Elton, she had a quarter of an hour of the lady's conversation to herself, and could composedly attend to her; and the quarter of an hour quite convinced her that Mrs Elton was a vain woman, extremely well satisfied with herself, and thinking much of her own importance; that she meant to shine and be very superior, but with manners which had been formed in a bad school; pert and familiar; that all her notions were drawn from one set of people, and one style of living; that, if not foolish, she was ignorant, and that her society would certainly do Mr Elton no good.

Harriet would have been a better match. If not wise or refined herself, she would have connected him with those who were; but Miss Hawkins, it might be fairly supposed, from her easy conceit, had been the best of her own set. The rich brother-in-law, near Bristol, was the pride of the alliance, and his place and his carriages were the pride of him.

The very first subject, after being seated, was Maple Grove, 'My brother, Mr Suckling's seat'; a comparison of Hartfield to Maple Grove. The grounds of Hartfield were small, but neat and pretty; and the house was modern and well-built. Mrs Elton seemed most favourably impressed by the size of the room, the entrance, and all that she could see or imagine. 'Very like Maple Grove indeed! She was quite struck by the likeness! That room was the very shape and size of the morning-room at Maple Grove; her sister's favourite room.' Mr Elton was appealed to. 'Was not it astonishingly like? She could really almost fancy herself at Maple Grove.

'And the staircase. You know, as I came in, I observed how very like the staircase was; placed exactly in the same part of the house. I really could not help exclaiming! I assure you, Miss Woodhouse, it is very delightful to me to be reminded of a place I am so extremely partial to as Maple Grove. I have spent so many happy months there!' (with a little sigh of sentiment.) 'A charming place, undoubtedly. Everybody who sees it is struck by its beauty; but to me it has been quite a home. Whenever you are transplanted, like me, Miss Woodhouse, you will understand how very delightful it is to meet with anything at all like what one has left behind. I always say this is quite one of the evils of matrimony.'

Emma made as slight a reply as she could; but it was fully sufficient for Mrs Elton, who only wanted to be talking herself.

'So extremely like Maple Grove! And it is not merely the house; the grounds, I assure you, as far as I could observe, are strikingly like. The laurels at Maple Grove are in the same profusion as here, and stand very much in the same way—just across the lawn; and I had a glimpse of a fine large tree, with a bench round it, which put me so exactly in mind! My brother and sister will be enchanted with this place. People who have extensive grounds themselves are always pleased with anything in the same style.'

Emma doubted the truth of this sentiment. She had a great idea that people who had extensive grounds themselves cared very little for the extensive grounds of anybody else; but it was not worth while to attack an error so double-dyed, and therefore only said in reply:

'When you have seen more of this country I am afraid you will think you have over-rated Hartfield. Surrey is full of beauties.'

'Oh! yes, I am quite aware of that. It is the garden of England, you know. Surrey is the garden of England.'

'Yes; but we must not rest our claims on that distinction. Many counties, I believe, are called the garden of England, as well as Surrey.'

'No, I fancy not,' replied Mrs Elton, with a most satisfied smile. 'I never heard any county but Surrey called so.'

Emma was silenced.

'My brother and sister have promised us a visit in the spring, or summer at farthest,' continued Mrs Elton; 'and that will be our time for exploring. While they are with us we shall explore a great deal, I dare say. They will have their barouche-landau, of course, which holds four perfectly; and therefore, without saying anything of *our* carriage, we should be able to explore the different beauties extremely well. They would hardly come in their chaise, I think, at that season of the year. Indeed, when the time draws on, I shall decidedly recommend their bringing the barouche-landau; it will be so very much preferable. When people come into a beautiful country of this sort, you know, Miss Woodhouse, one naturally wishes them to see as much as possible; and Mr Suckling is extremely fond of exploring. We explored to King's-Weston twice last summer, in that way, most delightfully, just after their first having the barouche-landau. You have many parties of that kind here, I suppose, Miss Woodhouse, every summer?'

'No; not immediately here. We are rather out of distance of the very striking beauties which attract the sort of parties you speak of; and we are a very quiet set of people, I believe; more disposed to stay at home than engage in schemes of pleasure.'

'Ah! there is nothing like staying at home for real comfort. Nobody can be more devoted to home than I am. I was quite a proverb for it at Maple Grove. Many a time has Selina said, when she has been going to Bristol, "I really cannot get this girl to move from the house. I absolutely must go in by myself, though I hate being stuck up in the barouche-landau without a companion: but Augusta, I believe, with her own good will, would never stir beyond the park paling." Many a time has she said so; and yet I am no advocate for entire seclusion. I think, on the contrary, when people shut themselves up entirely from society, it is a very bad thing; and that it is much more advisable to mix in the world in a proper degree, without living in it either too much or too little. I perfectly understand your situation however, Miss Woodhouse' (looking towards Mr Woodhouse), 'your father's state of health must be a great drawback. Why does not he try Bath? Indeed he should. Let me recommend Bath to you. I assure you I have no doubt of its doing Mr Woodhouse good.'

'My father tried it more than once, formerly, but without receiving any benefit; and Mr Perry, whose name, I dare say, is not unknown to you, does not conceive it would be at all more likely to be useful now.'

'Ah! that's a great pity; for I assure you, Miss Woodhouse, where the waters do agree, it is quite wonderful the relief they give. In my Bath life I have seen such instances of it! And it is so cheerful a place that it could not fail of being of use to Mr Woodhouse's spirits, which, I understand, are sometimes much depressed. And as to its recommendations to *you*, I fancy I need not take much pains to dwell on them. The advantages of Bath to the young are pretty generally understood. It would be a charming introduction for you, who have lived so secluded a life: and I could immediately secure you some of the best society in the place. A line from me would bring you a little host of acquaintance; and my particular friend Mrs Partridge, the lady I have always resided with when in Bath, would be most happy to show you any attentions, and would be the very person for you to go into public with.'

It was as much as Emma could bear, without being impolite! The idea of her being indebted to Mrs Elton for what was called an *introduction*—of her going into public under the auspices of a friend of Mrs Elton's—probably some vulgar dashing widow who, with the help of a boarder, just made a shift to live! The dignity of Miss Woodhouse, of Hartfield, was sunk indeed!

She restrained herself, however, from any of the reproofs she could have given, and only thanked Mrs Elton coolly; 'but their going to Bath was quite out of the question; and she was not perfectly convinced that the place might suit her better than her father.' And then, to prevent further outrage and indignation, changed the subject directly.'

'I do not ask whether you are musical, Mrs Elton. Upon these occasions a lady's character generally precedes her; and Highbury has long known that you are a superior performer.'

'Oh! no, indeed; I must protest against any such idea. A superior performer! very far from it, I assure you: consider from how partial a quarter your information came. I am dotingly fond of music—passionately fond; and my friends say I am not entirely devoid of taste; but as to anything else, upon my honour my performance is *mediocre* to the last degree. You, Miss Woodhouse, I well know, play delightfully. I assure you it has been the greatest satisfaction, comfort, and delight to me to hear what a musical society I am got into. I absolutely cannot do without music: it is a necessary of life to me; and having always been used to a very musical society, both at Maple Grove and in Bath, it would have been a most serious sacrifice. I honestly said as much to Mr E. when he was speaking of my future home, and expressing his fears lest the retirement of it should be disagreeable; and the inferiority of the house too—knowing what I had been accustomed to—of course he was not wholly without apprehension. When he was speaking of it in that way, I honestly said that *the world* I could give up—parties, balls, plays—for I had no fear of retirement. Blessed with so many resources within myself, the world was not necessary to *me*. I could do very well without it. To those who had no resources it was a different thing; but my resources made me quite independent. And as to smaller-sized rooms than I had been used to, I really could not give it a thought. I hoped I was perfectly equal to any sacrifice of that description. Certainly, I had been accustomed to every luxury at Maple Grove; but I did assure him that two carriages were not necessary to my happiness, nor were spacious apartments. "But," said I, "to be quite honest, I do not think I can live without something of a musical society. I condition for nothing else; but, without music, life would be a blank to me."'

'We cannot suppose,' said Emma, smiling, 'that Mr Elton would hesitate to assure you of there being a *very* musical society in Highbury; and I hope you will not find he has outstepped the truth more than may be pardoned, in consideration of the motive.'

'No, indeed, I have no doubts at all on that head. I am delighted to find myself in such a circle: I hope we shall have many sweet little concerts together. I think, Miss Woodhouse, you and I must establish a musical club, and have regular weekly meetings at your house, or ours. Will not it be a good plan? If *we* exert ourselves, I think we shall not be long in want of allies. Something of that nature would be particularly desirable for *me*, as an inducement to keep me in practice; for married women, you know—there is a sad story against them, in general. They are but too apt to give up music.'

'But you, who are so extremely fond of it—there can be no danger, surely?'

'I should hope not; but really when I look around among my acquaintance, I tremble. Selina has entirely given up music —never touches the instrument, though she played sweetly. And the same may be said of Mrs Jeffreys—Clara Partridge that was—and of the two Milmans, now Mrs Bird and Mrs James Cooper; and of more than I can enumerate. Upon my word, it is enough to put one in a fright. I used to be quite angry with Selina; but, really, I begin now to comprehend that a married woman has many things to call her attention. I believe I was half an hour this morning shut up with my housekeeper.'

'But everything of that kind,' said Emma, 'will soon be in so regular a train——'

'Well,' said Mrs Elton, laughing, 'we shall see.'

Emma, finding her so determined upon neglecting her music, had nothing more to say; and, after a moment's pause, Mrs Elton chose another subject.

'We have been calling at Randalls,' said she, 'and found them both at home; and very pleasant people they seem to be. I like them extremely. Mr Weston seems an excellent creature— quite a first-rate favourite with me already, I assure you. And *she* appears so truly good—there is something so motherly and kind-hearted about her, that it wins upon one directly. She was your governess, I think?'

Emma was almost too much astonished to answer; but Mrs Elton hardly waited for the affirmative before she went on:

'Having understood as much, I was rather astonished to find her so very ladylike. But she is really quite the gentlewoman.'

'Mrs Weston's manners,' said Emma, 'were always particularly good. Their propriety, simplicity, and elegance would make them the safest model for any young women.'

'And who do you think came in while we were there?'

Emma was quite at a loss. The tone implied some old acquaintance, and how could she possibly guess?

'Knightley!' continued Mrs Elton; 'Knightley himself! Was 'not it lucky? For, not being within when he called the other day, I had never seen him before; and of course, as so particular a friend of Mr E.'s, I had a great curiosity. "My friend Knightley" had been so often mentioned, that I was really impatient to see him; and I must do my *caro sposo* the justice to say that he need not be ashamed of his friend. Knightley is quite the gentleman; I like him very much. Decidedly, I think, a very gentlemanlike man.'

Happily, it was now time to be gone. They were off, and Emma could breathe.

'Insufferable woman!' was her immediate exclamation. 'Worse than I had supposed. Absolutely insufferable! Knightley! I could not have believed it. Knightley!—never seen him

in her life before, and call him Knightley! and discover that he
is a gentleman. A little upstart, vulgar being, with her Mr E.
and her *caro sposa*, and her resources, and all her airs of pert pre-
tention and underbred finery. Actually to discover that Mr Knightley is a gentleman! I doubt whether he will return the compliment, and discover her to be a lady. I could not have believed
it! And to propose that she and I should unite to form a musical
club! One would fancy we were bosom friends! And Mrs Weston!
Astonished that the person who had brought me up should
be a gentle-woman! Worse and worse! I never met with her
equal. Much beyond my hopes! Harriet is disgraced by any
comparison. Oh! what would Frank Churchill say to her if he
were here? How angry and how diverted he would be! Ah!
there I am thinking of him directly. Always the first person to
be thought of! How I catch myself out! Frank Churchill comes
as regularly into my mind——!'

All this ran so glibly through her thoughts, that by the time
her father had arranged himself, after the bustle of the Eltons'
departure, and was ready to speak, she was very tolerably capable of attending.

'Well, my dear,' he deliberately began, 'considering we never
saw her before, she seems a very pretty sort of young lady; and
I dare say she was very much pleased with you. She speaks a
little too quick. A little quickness of voice there is which rather
hurts the ear. But I believe I am nice; I do not like strange
voices; and nobody speaks like you and poor Miss Taylor. However, she seems a very obliging, pretty-behaved young lady,
and no doubt will make him a very good wife. Though I think
he had better not have married. I made the best excuses I could
for not having been able to wait on him and Mrs Elton on this
happy occasion: I said that I hoped I *should* in the course of the
summer. But I ought to have gone before. Not to wait upon
a bride is very remiss. Ah! it shows what a sad invalid I am!
But I do not like the corner into Vicarage Lane.'

'I dare say your apologies were accepted, sir. Mr Elton knows
you.'

'Yes; but a young lady—a bride—I ought to have paid my
respects to her, if possible. It was being very deficient.'

'But, my dear papa, you are no friend to matrimony; and
therefore why should you be so anxious to pay your respects to
a *bride*? It ought to be no recommendation to *you*. It is encouraging people to marry if you make so much of them.'

'No, my dear, I never encouraged anybody to marry, but I

would always wish to pay every proper attention to a lady—and a bride especially, is never to be neglected. More is avowedly due to *her*. A bride, you know, my dear, is always the first in company, let the others be who they may.'

' Well, papa, if this is not encouragement to marry, I do not know what is. And I should never have expected you to be lending your sanction to such vanity-baits for poor young ladies.'

' My dear, you do not understand me. This is a matter of mere common politeness and good-breeding, and has nothing to do with any encouragement to people to marry.'

Emma had done. Her father was growing nervous, and could not understand *her*. Her mind returned to Mrs Elton's offences, and long, very long, did they occupy her.

33

EMMA was not required, by any subsequent discovery, to retract her ill opinion of Mrs Elton. Her observation had been pretty correct. Such as Mrs Elton appeared to her on this second interview, such she appeared whenever they met again: self-important, presuming, familiar, ignorant, and ill-bred. She had a little beauty and a little accomplishment, but so little judgment that she thought herself coming with superior knowledge of the world, to enliven and improve a country neighbourhood; and conceived Miss Hawkins to have held such a place in society as Mrs Elton's consequence only could surpass.

There was no reason to suppose Mr Elton thought at all differently from his wife. He seemed not merely happy with her, but proud. He had the air of congratulating himself on having brought such a woman to Highbury, as not even Miss Woodhouse could equal; and the greater part of her new acquaintance, disposed to commend, or not in the habit of judging, following the lead of Miss Bates's goodwill, of taking it for granted that the bride must be as clever and as agreeable as she professed herself, were very well satisfied; so that Mrs Elton's praise passed from one mouth to another as it ought to do, unimpeded by Miss Woodhouse, who readily continued her first contribution, and talked with a good grace of her being ' very pleasant, and very elegantly dressed.'

In one respect Mrs Elton grew even worse than she had appeared at first. Her feelings altered towards Emma. Offended, probably, by the little encouragement which her proposals of intimacy met with, she drew back, in her turn, and gradually became much more cold and distant; and thought the effect was agreeable, the ill-will which produced it was necessarily increasing Emma's dislike. Her manners, too—and Mr Elton's—were unpleasant towards Harriet. They were sneering and negligent. Emma hoped it must rapidly work Harriet's cure; but the sensations which could prompt such behaviour sunk them both very much. It was not to be doubted that poor Harriet's attachment had been an offering to conjugal unreserve, and her own share in the story, under a colouring the least favourable to her, and the most soothing to him, had in all likelihood been given also. She was, of course, the object of their joint dislike. When they had nothing else to say, it must be always easy to begin abusing Miss Woodhouse; and the enmity which they dared not show in open disrespect to her found a broader vent in contemptuous treatment of Harriet.

Mrs Elton took a great fancy to Jane Fairfax; and from the first. Not merely when a state of warfare with one young lady might be supposed to recommend the other, but from the very first; and she was not satisfied with expressing a natural and reasonable admiration, but without solicitation, or plea, or privilege, she must be wanting to assist and befriend her. Before Emma had forfeited her confidence, and about the third time of their meeting, she heard all Mrs Elton's knight-errantry on the subject.

'Jane Fairfax is absolutely charming, Miss Woodhouse.' I quite rave about Jane Fairfax. A sweet, interesting creature. So mild and ladylike—and with such talents! I assure you I think she has very extraordinary talents! I do not scruple to say that she plays extremely well. I know enough of music to speak decidedly on that point. Oh! she is absolutely charming! You will laugh at my warmth, but, upon my word, I talk of nothing but Jane Fairfax—and her situation is so calculated to affect one! Miss Woodhouse, we must exert ourselves and endeavour to do something for her. We must bring her forward. Such talents as hers must not be suffered to remain unknown. I dare say you have heard those charming lines of the poet:

> Full many a flower is born to blush unseen
> And waste its fragrance on the desert air.

We must not allow them to be verified in sweet Jane Fairfax.'

' I cannot think there is any danger of it,' was Emma's calm answer: 'and when you are better acquainted with Miss Fairfax's situation, and understand what her home has been, with Colonel and Mrs Campbell, I have no idea that you will suppose her talents can be unknown.'

'Oh! but, dear Miss Woodhouse, she is now in such retirement, such obscurity, so thrown away. Whatever advantages she may have enjoyed with the Campbells are so palpably at an end! And I think she feels it. I am sure she does. She is very timid and silent. One can see that she feels the want of encouragement. I like her the better for it. I must confess it is a recommendation to me. I am a great advocate for timidity—and I am sure one does not often meet with it. But in those who are not at all inferior, it is extremely prepossessing. Oh! I assure you, Jane Fairfax is a very delightful character, and interests me more than I can express.'

'You appear to feel a great deal; but I am not aware how you or any of Miss Fairfax's acquaintance here, any of those who have known her longer than yourself, can show her any other attention than——'

'My dear Miss Woodhouse, a vast deal may be done by those who dare to act. You and I need not be afraid. If *we* set the example, many will follow it as far as they can; though all have not our situations. *We* have carriages to fetch and convey her home; and *we* live in a style which could not make the addition of Jane Fairfax at any time the least inconvenient. I should be extremely displeased if Wright were to send up such a dinner as could make me regret having asked *more* than Jane Fairfax to partake of it. I have no idea of that sort of thing. It is not likely that I *should*, considering what I have been used to. My greatest danger, perhaps, in housekeeping, may be quite the other way, in doing too much, and being too careless of expense. Maple Grove will probably be my model more than it ought to be—for we do not at all affect to equal my brother, Mr Suckling, in income. However, my resolution is taken as to noticing Jane Fairfax. I shall certainly have her very often at my house, shall introduce her wherever I can, shall have musical parties to draw out her talents, and shall be constantly on the watch for an eligible situation. My acquaintance is so very extensive, that I have little doubt of hearing of something to suit her shortly. I shall introduce her, of course, very particularly to my brother and sister when they come to us. I am sure they will like her extremely; and when she gets a little acquainted with them, her fears will completely wear off, for there really is nothing in the manners of either but what is highly conciliating. I shall have her very often, indeed, while they are with me; and I dare say we shall sometimes find a seat for her in the barouche-landau in some of our exploring parties.'

' Poor Jane Fairfax,' thought Emma, ' you have not deserved this. You may have done wrong with regard to Mr Dixon; but this is a punishment beyond what you can have merited. The kindness and protection of Mrs Elton!—" Jane Fairfax and Jane Fairfax! " Heavens! let me not suppose that she dares go about Emma Woodhouseing me! But, upon my honour, there seems no limits to the licentiousness of that woman's tongue!'

Emma had not to listen to such paradings again—to any so exclusively addressed to herself—so disgustingly decorated with a ' dear Miss Woodhouse.' The change on Mrs Elton's side soon afterwards appeared, and she was left in peace—neither forced to be the very particular friend of Mrs Elton nor, under Mrs Elton's guidance, the very active patroness of Jane Fairfax, and only sharing with others in a general way, in knowing what was felt, what was meditated, what was done.

She looked on with some amusement. Miss Bates's gratitude for Mrs Elton's attentions to Jane was in the first style of guileless simplicity and warmth. She was quite one of her worthies—the most amiable, affable, delightful woman—just as accomplished and condescending as Mrs Elton meant to be considered. Emma's only surprise was that Jane Fairfax should accept those attentions, and tolerate Mrs Elton as she seemed to do. She heard of her walking with the Eltons, sitting with the Eltons, spending a day with the Eltons! This was astonishing! She could not have believed it possible that the taste or the pride of Miss Fairfax could endure such society and friendship as the Vicarage had to offer.

' She is a riddle, quite a riddle,' said she. ' To choose to remain here month after month, under privations of every sort. And now to choose the mortification of Mrs Elton's notice, and the penury of her conversation, rather than return to the superior companions who have always loved her with such real, generous affection.'

Jane had come to Highbury professedly for three months; the Campbells were gone to Ireland for three months; but now the Campbells had promised their daughter to stay at least till Midsummer, and fresh invitations had arrived for her to join them there. According to Miss Bates—it all came from her—Mrs Dixon had written most pressingly. Would Jane but go, means were to be found, servants sent, friends contrived—no travelling difficulty allowed to exist; but still she had declined it.

' She must have some motive, more powerful than appears,

for refusing this invitation,' was Emma's conclusion. 'She must be under some sort of penance, inflicted either by the Campbells or herself. There is great fear, great caution, great resolution somewhere. She is *not* to be with the *Dixons*. The decree is issued by somebody. But why must she consent to be with the Eltons? Here is quite a separate puzzle.'

Upon her speaking her wonder aloud on that part of the subject, before the few who knew her opinion of Mrs Elton, Mrs Weston ventured this apology for Jane.

'We cannot suppose that she has any great enjoyment at the Vicarage, my dear Emma—but it is better than being always at home. Her aunt is a good creature; but, as a constant companion, must be very tiresome. We must consider what Miss Fairfax quits, before we condemn her taste for what she goes to.'

'You are right, Mrs Weston,' said Mr Knightley warmly; 'Miss Fairfax is as capable as any of us of forming a just opinion of Mrs Elton. Could she have chosen with whom to associate, she would not have chosen her. But' (with reproachful smile at Emma) 'she receives attentions from Mrs Elton, which nobody else pays her.'

Emma felt that Mrs Weston was giving her a momentary glance, and she was herself struck by his warmth. With a faint blush, she presently replied:

'Such attentions as Mrs Elton's, I should have imagined, would rather disgust than gratify Miss Fairfax. Mrs Elton's invitations I should have imagined anything but inviting.'

'I should not wonder,' said Mrs Weston, 'if Miss Fairfax were to have been drawn on beyond her own inclination, by her aunt's eagerness in accepting Mrs Elton's civilities for her. Poor Miss Bates may very likely have committed her niece, and hurried her into a greater appearance of intimacy than her own good sense would have dictated, in spite of the very natural wish of a little change.'

Both felt rather anxious to hear him speak again; and, after a few minutes' silence, he said:

'Another thing must be taken into consideration too—Mrs Elton does not talk to Miss Fairfax as she speaks *of* her. We all know the difference between the pronouns he or she and thou, the plainest spoken amongst us; we all feel the influence of a something beyond common civility in our personal intercourse with each other—a something more early implanted. We cannot give anybody the disagreeable hints that we may have been very full of the hour before. We feel things differently. And besides the operation of this, as a general principle, you may be sure that Miss Fairfax awes Mrs Elton by her superiority both of mind and manner; and that, face to face, Mrs Elton treats her with all the respect which she has a claim to. Such a woman as Jane Fairfax probably never fell in Mrs Elton's way before— and no degree of vanity can prevent her acknowledging her own comparative littleness in action, if not in consciousness.'

'I know how highly you think of Jane Fairfax,' said Emma. Little Henry was in her thoughts, and a mixture of alarm and delicacy made her irresolute what else to say.

'Yes,' he replied, 'anybody may know how highly I think of her.'

'And yet,' said Emma, beginning hastily, and with an arch look, but soon stopping—it was better, however, to know the worst at once—she hurried on, 'and yet, perhaps, you may hardly be aware yourself how highly it is. The extent of your admiration may take you by surprise some day or other.'

Mr Knightley was hard at work upon the lower buttons of his thick leather gaiters, and either the exertion of getting them together, or some other cause, brought the colour into his face, as he answered:

'Oh! are you there? But you are miserably behindhand. Mr Cole gave me a hint of it six weeks ago.'

He stopped. Emma felt her foot pressed by Mrs Weston, and did not herself know what to think. In a moment he went on:

'That will never be, however, I can assure you. Miss Fairfax, I dare say, would not have me if I were to ask her; and I am very sure I shall never ask her.'

Emma returned her friend's pressure with interest; and was pleased enough to exclaim:

'You are not vain, Mr Knightley. I will say that for you.'

He seemed hardly to hear her; he was thoughtful, and, in a manner which showed him not pleased, soon afterwards said:

'So you have been settling that I should marry Jane Fairfax?'

'No, indeed, I have not. You have scolded me too much for match-making for me to presume to take such a liberty with you. What I said just now meant nothing. One says those sort of things, of course, without any idea of a serious meaning. Oh! no; upon my word I have not the smallest wish for your marrying Jane Fairfax, or Jane anybody. You would not come in and sit with us in this comfortable way if you were married.'

Mr Knightley was thoughtful again. The result of his reverie was—'No, Emma, I do not think the extent of my admiration for her will ever take me by surprise. I never had a thought of her in that way, I assure you.'

And soon afterwards, 'Jane Fairfax is a very charming young woman—but not even Jane Fairfax is perfect. She has a fault. She has not the open temper which a man would wish for in a wife.'

Emma could not but rejoice to hear that she had a fault.

'Well,' said she, 'and you soon silenced Mr Cole, I suppose?'

'Yes, very soon. He gave me a quiet hint; I told him he was mistaken; he asked my pardon, and said no more. Cole does not want to be wiser or wittier than his neighbours.'

'In that respect how unlike dear Mrs Elton, who wants to be wiser and wittier than all the world! I wonder how she speaks of the Coles—what she calls them. How can she find any appellation for them, deep enough in familiar vulgarity? She calls you Knightley; what can she do for Mr Cole? And so I am not to be surprised that Jane Fairfax accepts her civilities, and consents to be with her. Mrs Weston, your argument weighs most with me. I can much more readily enter into the temptation of getting away from Miss Bates, than I can believe in the triumph of Miss Fairfax's mind over Mrs Elton. I have no faith in Mrs Elton's acknowledging herself the inferior in thought, word, or deed; or in her being under any restraint beyond her own scanty rule of good breeding. I cannot imagine that she will not be continually insulting her visitor with praise, encouragement, and offers of service; that she will not be continually detailing her magnificent intentions, from the procuring her a permanent situation to the including her in those delightful exploring parties, which are to take place in the barouche-landau.'

'Jane Fairfax has feeling,' said Mr Knightley; 'I do not accuse her of want of feeling. Her sensibilities, I suspect, are strong, and her temper excellent in its power of forbearance, patience, self-control; but it wants openness. She is reserved; more reserved, I think, than she used to be: and I love an open temper. No; till Cole alluded to my supposed attachment, it had never entered my head. I saw Jane Fairfax, and conversed with her, with admiration and pleasure always; but with no thought beyond.'

'Well, Mrs Weston,' said Emma triumphantly, when he left them, 'what do you say now to Mr Knightley's marrying Jane Fairfax?'

'Why, really, dear Emma, I say that he is so very much occupied by the idea of *not* being in love with her, that I should not wonder if it were to end in his being so at last. Do not beat me.'

34

EVERYBODY in and about Highbury, who had ever visited Mr Elton, was disposed to pay him attention on his marriage. Dinner parties and evening parties were made for him and his lady; and invitations flowed in so fast that she had soon the pleasure of apprehending they were never to have a disengaged day.

'I see how it is,' said she; 'I see what a life I am to lead among you. Upon my word we shall be absolutely dissipated.' We really seem quite the fashion. If this is living in the country, it is nothing very formidable. From Monday next to Saturday I assure you we have not a disengaged day! A woman with fewer resources than I have need not have been at a loss.'

No invitation came amiss to her. Her Bath habits made evening parties perfectly natural to her, and Maple Grove had given her a taste for dinners. She was a little shocked at the want of two drawing-rooms, at the poor attempt at rout-cakes, and there being no ice in the Highbury card-parties. Mrs Bates, Mrs Perry, Mrs Goddard, and others, were a good deal behindhand in knowledge of the world, but *she* would soon show them how everything ought to be arranged. In the course of the spring she must return their civilities by one very superior party; in which her card-tables should be set out with their separate candles and unbroken packs in the true style, and more waiters engaged for the evening than their own establishment could furnish, to carry round the refreshments at exactly the proper hour, and in the proper order.

Emma, in the meanwhile, could not be satisfied without a dinner at Hartfield for the Eltons. They must not do less than others, or she should be exposed to odious suspicion, and imagined capable of pitiful resentment. A dinner there must be. After Emma had talked about it for ten minutes, Mr Woodhouse felt no unwillingness, and only made the usual stipulation of not sitting at the bottom of the table himself, with the usual regular difficulty of deciding who should do it for him.

The persons to be invited required little thought. Besides the Eltons, it must be the Westons and Mr Knightley; so far it was all of course: and it was hardly less inevitable that poor little

Harriet must be asked to make the eighth; but this invitation was not given with equal satisfaction, and, on many accounts, Emma was particularly pleased by Harriet's begging to be allowed to decline it. ' She would rather not be in *his* company more than she could help. She was not yet quite able to see him and his charming happy wife together, without feeling uncomfortable. If Miss Woodhouse would not be displeased, she would rather stay at home.' It was precisely what Emma would have wished, had she deemed it possible enough for wishing. She was delighted with the fortitude of her little friend—for fortitude she knew it was in her to give up being in company, and stay at home; and she could now invite the very person whom she really wanted to make the eighth, Jane Fairfax. Since her last conversation with Mrs Weston and Mr Knightley, she was more conscience-stricken about Jane Fairfax than she had often been. Mr Knightley's words dwelt with her. He had said that Jane Fairfax received attentions from Mrs Elton which nobody else paid her.

' This is very true,' said she, ' at least as far as related to me, which was all that was meant, and it is very shameful. Of the same age, and always knowing her, I ought to have been more her friend. She will never like me now. I have neglected her too long. But I will show her greater attention than I have done.'

Every invitation was successful. They were all disengaged and all happy. The preparatory interest of this dinner, however, was not yet over. A circumstance rather unlucky occurred. The two eldest little Knightleys were engaged to pay their grandpapa and aunt a visit of some weeks in the spring and their papa now proposed bringing them, and staying one whole day at Hartfield— which one day would be the very day of this party. His professional engagements did not allow of his being put off, but both father and daughter were disturbed by its happening so. Mr Woodhouse considered eight persons at dinner together as the utmost that his nerves could bear—and here would be a ninth— and Emma apprehended that it would be a ninth very much out of humour, at not being able to come even to Hartfield for forty-eight hours, without falling in with a dinner party.

She comforted her father better than she could comfort herself, by representing that though he certainly would make them nine, yet he always said so little, that the increase of noise would be very immaterial. She thought it in reality a sad exchange for herself, to have him, with his grave looks and recluctant conversation, opposed to her instead of his brother.

The event was more favourable to Mr Woodhouse than to Emma. John Knightley came; but Mr Weston was unexpectedly summoned to town, and must be absent on the very day. He might be able to join them in the evening, but certainly not to dinner. Mr Woodhouse was quite at ease; and the seeing him so, with the arrival of the little boys, and the philosophic composure of her brother on hearing his fate, removed the chief of even Emma's vexation.

The day came, the party were punctually assembled, and Mr John Knightley seemed early to devote himself to the business of being agreeable. Instead of drawing his brother off to a window while they waited for dinner, he was talking to Miss Fairfax. Mrs Elton, as elegant as lace and pearls could make her, he looked at in silence—wanting only to observe enough for Isabella's information—but Miss Fairfax was an old acquaintance and a quiet girl, and he could talk to her. He had met her before breakfast as he was returning from a walk with his little boys, when it had been just beginning to rain. It was natural to have some civil hopes on the subject, and he said:

'I hope you did not venture far, Miss Fairfax, this morning, or I am sure you must have been wet. *We* scarcely got home in time. I hope you turned directly.'

'I went only to the post office,' said she, 'and reached home before the rain was much. It is my daily errand. I always fetch the letters when I am here. It saves trouble, and is a something to get me out. A walk before breakfast does me good.'

'Not a walk in the rain, I should imagine.'

'No; but it did not absolutely rain when I set out.'

Mr John Knightley smiled, and replied:

'That is to say, you chose to have your walk, for you were not six yards from your own door when I had the pleasure of meeting you; and Henry and John had seen more drops than they could count long before. The post office has a great charm at one period of our lives. When you have lived to my age, you will begin to think letters are never worth going through the rain for.'

There was a little blush, and then this answer:

'I must not hope to be ever situated as you are, in the midst of every dearest connection, and therefore I cannot expect that simply growing older should make me indifferent about letters.'

'Indifferent! Oh, no—I never conceived you could become indifferent. Letters are no matter of indifference; they are generally a very positive curse.'

'You are speaking of letters of business; mine are letters of friendship.'

'I have often thought them the worst of the two,' replied he coolly. 'Business you know, may bring money, but friendship hardly ever does.'

'Ah! you are not serious now. I know Mr John Knightley too well—I am very sure he understands the value of friendship as well as anybody. I can easily believe that letters are very little to you, much less than to me; but it is not your being ten years older than myself which makes the difference; it is not age, but situation. You have everybody dearest to you always at hand, I, probably, never shall again; and therefore, till I have outlived all my affections, a post office, I think, must always have power to draw me out, in worse weather than to-day.'

'When I talked of your being altered by time, by the progress of years,' said John Knightley, ' I meant to imply the change of situation which time usually brings. I consider one as including the other. Time will generally lessen the interest of every attachment not within the daily circle—but that is not the change I had in view for you. As an old friend, you will allow me to hope, Miss Fairfax, that ten years hence, you may have as many concentrated objects as I have.'

It was kindly said, and very far from giving offence. A pleasant ' thank you ' seemed meant to laugh it off; but a blush, a quivering lip, a tear in the eye, showed that it was felt beyond a laugh. Her attention was now claimed by Mr Woodhouse, who being, according to his custom on such occasions, making the circle of his guests, and paying his particular compliments to the ladies, was ending with her—and with all his mildest urbanity, said:

'I am very sorry to hear, Miss Fairfax, of your being out this morning in the rain. Young ladies should take care of themselves. Young ladies are delicate plants. They should take care of their health and their complexion. My dear, did you change your stockings?'

'Yes, sir, I did indeed; and I am very much obliged by your kind solicitude about me.'

'My dear Miss Fairfax, young ladies are very sure to be cared for. I hope your good grandmamma and aunt are well. They are some of my very old friends. I wish my health allowed me to be a better neighbour. You do us a great deal of honour to-day, I am sure. My daughter and I are both highly sensible of your goodness, and have the greatest satisfaction in seeing you at Hartfield.'

The kind-hearted, polite old man might then sit down and feel that he had done his duty, and made every fair lady welcome and easy.

By this time the walk in the rain had reached Mrs Elton, and her remonstrances now opened upon Jane.

' My dear Jane, what is this I hear? Going to the post office in the rain! This must not be, I assure you. You sad girl, how could you do such a thing? It is a sign I was not there to take care of you.'

Jane very patiently assured her that she had not caught any cold.

' Oh! do not tell *me*. You really are a very sad girl, and do not know how to take care of yourself. To the post office indeed! Mrs Weston, did you ever hear the like? You and I must positively exert our authority.'

' My advice,' said Mrs Weston, kindly and persuasively, ' I certainly do feel tempted to give. Miss Fairfax, you must not run such risks. Liable as you have been to severe colds, indeed you ought to be particularly careful, especially at this time of year. The spring I always think requires more than common care. Better wait an hour or two, or even half a day for your letters, than run the risk of bringing on your cough again. Now do not you feel that you had? Yes, I am sure you are much too reasonable. You look as if you would not do such a thing again.'

' Oh! she *shall not* do such a thing again,' eagerly rejoined Mrs Elton. ' We will not allow her to do such a thing again '—and nodding significantly—' there must be some arrangement made, there must indeed. I shall speak to Mr E. The man who fetches our letters every morning (one of our men, I forget his name) shall inquire for yours too and bring them to you. That will obviate all difficulties, you know; and from *us* I really think, my dear Jane, you can have no scruple to accept such an accommodation.'

' You are extremely kind,' said Jane; ' but I cannot give up my early walk. I am advised to be out-of-doors as much as I can; I must walk somewhere, and the post office is an object; and, upon my word, I have scarcely ever had a bad morning before.'

' My dear Jane, say no more about it. The thing is determined, that is' (laughing affectedly) ' as far as I can presume to determine anything without the concurrence of my lord and master. You know, Mrs Weston, you and I must be cautious how we express ourselves. But I do flatter myself, my dear Jane, that my influence is not entirely worn out. If I meet with no insuperable difficulties, therefore, consider that point as settled.'

'Excuse me,' said Jane earnestly, 'I cannot by any means consent to such an arrangement, so needlessly troublesome to your servant. If the errand were not a pleasure to me, it could be done, as it always is when I am not here, by my grand-mamma's——'

'Oh! my dear; but so much as Patty has to do! And it is a kindness to employ our men.'

Jane looked as if she did not mean to be conquered; but, instead of answering, she began speaking again to Mr John Knightley.

'The post office is a wonderful establishment!' said she. 'The regularity and despatch of it! If one thinks of all that it has to do, and all that it does so well, it is really astonishing!'

'It is certainly very well regulated.'

'So seldom that any negligence or blunder appears! So seldom that a letter, among the thousands that are constantly passing about the kingdom, is ever carried wrong—and not one in a million, I suppose, actually lost! And when one considers the variety of hands, and of bad hands too, that are to be deciphered, it increases the wonder.'

'The clerks grow expert from habit. They must begin with some quickness of sight and hand, and exercise improves them. If you want any further explanation,' continued he, smiling, 'they are paid for it. That is the key to a great deal of capacity. The public pays and must be served well.'

The varieties of handwriting were further talked of, and the usual observations made.

'I have heard it asserted,' said John Knightley, 'that the same sort of handwriting often prevails in a family; and where the same master teaches, it is natural enough. But for that reason, I should imagine the likeness must be chiefly confined to the females, for boys have very little teaching after an early age, and scramble into any hand they can get. Isabella and Emma, I think, do write very much alike. I have not always known their writing apart.'

'Yes,' said his brother hesitatingly; 'there is a likeness. I know what you mean—but Emma's hand is the strongest.'

'Isabella and Emma both write beautifully,' said Mr Wood-house; 'and always did. And so does poor Mrs Weston '—with half a sigh and half a smile at her.

'I never saw any gentleman's handwriting '—Emma began, looking also at Mrs Weston; but stopped, on perceiving that Mrs

Weston was attending to some one else—and the pause gave her time to reflect. ' Now, how am I going to introduce him? Am I unequal to speaking his name at once before all these people? Is it necessary for me to use any roundabout phrase? Your Yorkshire friend—your correspondent in Yorkshire—that would be the way, I suppose, if I were very bad. No, I can pronounce his name without the smallest distress. I certainly get better and better. Now for it.'

Mrs Weston was disengaged, and Emma began again—' Mr Frank Churchill writes one of the best gentleman's hands I ever saw.'

' I do not admire it,' said Mr Knightley. ' It is too small—wants strength. It is like a woman's writing.'

This was not submitted to by either lady. They vindicated him against the base aspersion. ' No, it by no means wanted strength—it was not a large hand, but very clear, and certainly strong. Had not Mrs Weston any letter about her to produce? ' No, she had heard from him very lately, but having answered the letter, had put it away.

' If we were in the other room,' said Emma—' If I had my writing-desk, I am sure I could produce a specimen. I have a note of his. Do not you remember, Mrs Weston, employing him to write for you one day? '

' He chose to say he was employed.'

' Well, well, I have that note; and can show it after dinner to convince Mr Knightley.'

' Oh! when a gallant young man, like Mr Frank Churchill,' said Mr Knightley dryly, ' writes to a fair lady like Miss Woodhouse, he will, of course, put forth his best.'

Dinner was on table. Mrs Elton, before she could be spoken to, was ready; and before Mr Woodhouse had reached her, with his request to be allowed to hand her into the dining-parlour, was saying:

' Must I go first? I really am ashamed of always leading the way.'

Jane's solicitude about fetching her own letters had not escaped Emma. She had heard and seen it all; and felt some curiosity to know whether the wet walk of this morning had produced any. She suspected that it *had*; that it would not have been so resolutely encountered but in full expectation of hearing from some one very dear, and that it had not been in vain. She thought there was an air of greater happiness than usual—a glow both of complexion and spirits.

She could have made an inquiry or two, as to the expedition and the expense of the Irish mails—it was at her tongue's end—but she abstained. She was quite determined not to utter a word that should hurt Jane Fairfax's feelings: and they followed the other ladies out of the room, arm-in-arm, with an appearance of goodwill highly becoming to the beauty and grace of each.

35

WHEN the ladies returned to the drawing-room after dinner, Emma found it hardly possible to prevent their making two distinct parties; with so much perseverance in judging and behaving ill did Mrs Elton engross Jane Fairfax and slight herself. She and Mrs Weston were obliged to be almost always either talking together or silent together. Mrs Elton left them no choice. If Jane repressed her for a little time she soon began again; and though much that passed between them was in a half-whisper, especially on Mrs Elton's side, there was no avoiding a knowledge of their principal subjects: the post office—catching cold—fetching letters—and friendship, were long under discussion; and to them succeeded one which must be at least equally unpleasant to Jane—inquiries whether she had yet heard of any situation likely to suit her, and professions of Mrs Elton's meditated activity.

'Here is April come,' said she; 'I get quite anxious about you. June will soon be here.'

'But I have never fixed on June or any other month—merely looked forward to the summer in general.'

'But have you really heard of nothing?'

'I have not even made any inquiry; I do not wish to make any yet.'

'Oh! my dear, we cannot begin too early; you are not aware of the difficulty of procuring exactly the desirable thing.'

'I not aware!' said Jane, shaking her head; 'dear Mrs Elton, who can have thought of it as I have done?'

'But you have not seen so much of the world as I have. You do not know how many candidates there always are for the *first* situations. I saw a vast deal of that in the neighbourhood round Maple Grove. A cousin of Mr Suckling, Mrs Bragge, had such an infinity of applications; everybody was anxious to be in her family, for she moves in the first circle. Wax-candles in the school-room! You may imagine how desirable! Of all houses in the kingdom, Mrs Bragge's is the one I would most wish to see you in.'

'Colonel and Mrs Campbell are to be in town again by mid-summer,' said Jane, 'and I must spend some time with them; I am sure they will want it—afterwards I may probably be glad to dispose of myself. But I would not wish you to take the trouble of making any inquiries at present.'

'Trouble! ay, I know your scruples. You are afraid of giving me trouble; but I assure you, my dear Jane, the Campbells can hardly be more interested about you than I am. I shall write to Mrs Partridge in a day or two, and shall give her a strict charge to be on the look-out for anything eligible.'

'Thank you, but I would rather you did not mention the subject to her; till the time draws nearer, I do not wish to be giving anybody trouble.'

'But, my dear child, the time *is* drawing near; here is April, and June, or say even July, is very near, with such business to accomplish before us. Your inexperience really amuses me! A situation such as you deserve, and your friends would require for you, is no everyday occurrence, is not obtained at a moment's notice; indeed, indeed, we must begin inquiring directly.'

'Excuse me, ma'am, but this is by no means my intention; I make no inquiry myself, and should be sorry to have any made by my friends. When I am quite determined as to the time, I am not at all afraid of being long unemployed. There are places in town, offices, where inquiry would soon produce something —offices for the sale, not quite of human flesh, but of human intellect!'

'Oh! my dear, human flesh! You quite shock me; if you mean a fling at the slave trade, I assure you Mr Suckling was always rather a friend to the abolition.'

'I did not mean—I was not thinking of the slave-trade,' replied Jane; 'governess-trade, I assure you, was all that I had in view; widely different, certainly, as to the guilt of those who carry it on; but as to the greater misery of the victims, I do not know where it lies. But I only mean to say that there are advertising offices, and that by applying to them I should have no doubt of very soon meeting with something that would do.'

'Something that would do!' repeated Mrs Elton. 'Ay, *that* may suit your humble ideas of yourself; I know what a modest creature you are; but it will not satisfy your friends to have you taking up with anything that may offer, any inferior common-place situation, in a family not moving in a certain circle, or able to command the elegancies of life.'

'You are very obliging; but as to all that I am very indifferent;

221

it would be no object to me to be with the rich; my mortifications, I think, would only be the greater; I should suffer more from comparison. A gentleman's family is all that I should condition for.'

' I know you, I know you; you would take up with anything; but I shall be a little more nice, and I am sure the good Campbells will be quite on my side; with your superior talents, you have a right to move in the first circle. Your musical knowledge alone would entitle you to name your own terms, have as many rooms as you like, and mix in the family as much as you chose— that is— I do not know—if you knew the harp, you might do all that, I am very sure; but you sing as well as play; yes, I really believe you might, even without the harp, stipulate for what you chose; and you must and shall be delightfully, honourably, and comfortably settled before the Campbells or I have any rest.'

' You may well class the delight, the honour, and the comfort of such a situation together,' said Jane, ' they are pretty sure to be equal; however, I am very serious in not wishing anything to be attempted at present for me. I am exceedingly obliged to you, Mrs Elton; I am obliged to anybody who feels for me, but I am quite serious in wishing nothing to be done till the summer. For two or three months longer I shall remain where I am, and as I am.'

' And I am quite serious too, I assure you,' replied Mrs Elton gaily, ' in resolving to be always on the watch, and employing my friends to watch also, that nothing really unexceptionable may pass us.'

In this style she ran on; never thoroughly stopped by anything till Mr Woodhouse came into the room; her vanity had then a change of object, and Emma heard her saying in the same half-whisper to Jane:

' Here comes this dear old beau of mine, I protest! Only think of his gallantry in coming away before the other men! what a dear creature he is! I assure you I like him excessively. I admire all that quaint, old-fashioned politeness; it is much more to my taste than modern ease; modern ease often disgusts me. But this good old Mr Woodhouse, I wish you had heard his gallant speeches to me at dinner. Oh! I assure you I began to think my *caro sposo* would be absolutely jealous. I fancy I am rather a favourite; he took notice of my gown. How do you like it? Selina's choice—handsome, I think, but I do not know whether it is not over-trimmed; I have the greatest dislike to the idea of being over-trimmed; quite a horror of finery. I must put on a few ornaments *now*, because it is expected of me. A bride, you know, must appear like a bride, but my natural taste is all for simplicity; a simple style of dress is so infinitely preferable to finery. But I am quite in the minority, I believe; few people seem to value simplicity of dress—show and finery are everything. I have some notion of putting such a trimming as this to my white and silver poplin. Do you think it will look well? '

The whole party were but just re-assembled in the drawing-room, when Mr Weston made his appearance among them. He had returned to a late dinner, and walked to Hartfield as soon as it was over. He had been too much expected by the best judges, for surprise—but there was great joy. Mr Woodhouse was almost as glad to see him now, as he would have been sorry to see him before. John Knightley only was in mute astonishment. That a man who might have spent his evening quietly at home after a day of business in London should set off again, and walk half a mile to another man's house for the sake of being in mixed company till bed-time, of finishing his day in the efforts of civility and the noise of numbers, was a circumstance to strike him deeply. A man who had been in motion since eight o'clock in the morning, and might now have been still—who had been long talking, and might have been silent—who had been in more than one crowd, and might have been alone! Such a man to quit the tranquillity and independence of his own fireside, and on the evening of a cold sleety April day rush out again into the world! Could he, by a touch of his finger, have instantly taken back his wife, there would have been a motive; but his coming would probably prolong rather than break up the party. John Knightley looked at him with amazement, then shrugged his shoulders, and said, ' I could not have believed it even of *him*.'

Mr Weston, meanwhile, perfectly unsuspicious of the indignation he was exciting, happy and cheerful as usual, and with all the right of being principal talker, which a day spent anywhere from home confers, was making himself agreeable among the rest; and having satisfied the inquiries of his wife as to his dinner, convincing her that none of all her careful directions to the servants had been forgotten, and spread abroad what public news he had heard, was proceeding to a family communication, which, though principally addressed to Mrs Weston, he had not the smallest doubt of being highly interesting to everybody in the room. He gave her a letter—it was from Frank, and to herself; he had met with it in his way, and had taken the liberty of opening it.

'Read it, read it,' said he—'it will give you pleasure; only a few lines—will not take you long; read it to Emma.'

The two ladies looked over it together; and he sat smiling and talking to them the whole time, in a voice a little subdued, but very audible to everybody.

'Well, he is coming, you see; good news, I think. Well, what do you say to it? I always told you he would be here again soon, did not I? Anne, my dear, did not I always tell you so, and you would not believe me? In town next week, you see—at the latest, I dare say; for *she* is as impatient as the black gentleman when anything is to be done; most likely they will be there to-morrow or Saturday. As to her illness, all nothing, of course. But it is an excellent thing to have Frank among us again, so near the town. They will stay a good while when they do come, and he will be half his time with us. This is precisely what I wanted. Well, pretty good news, is not it? Have you finished it? Has Emma read it all? Put it up, put it up; we will have a good talk about it some other time, but it will not do now. I shall only just mention the circumstance to the others in a common way.'

Mrs Weston was most comfortably pleased on the occasion. Her looks and words had nothing to restrain them. She was happy, she knew she was happy, and knew she ought to be happy. Her congratulations were warm and open; but Emma could not speak so fluently. *She* was a little occupied in weighing her own feelings, and trying to understand the degree of her agitation, which she rather thought was considerable.

Mr Weston, however, too eager to be very observant, too communicative to want others to talk, was very well satisfied with what she did say, and soon moved away to make the rest of his friends happy, by a partial communication of what the whole room must have overheard already.

It was well that he took everybody's joy for granted, or he might not have thought either Mr Woodhouse or Mr Knightley particularly delighted. They were the first entitled, after Mrs Weston and Emma, to be made happy. From them he would have proceeded to Miss Fairfax; but she was so deep in conversation with John Knightley, that it would have been too positive an interruption; and, finding himself close to Mrs Elton, and her attention disengaged, he necessarily began on the subject with her.

36

'I HOPE I shall soon have the pleasure of introducing my son to you,' said Mr Weston.

Mrs Elton, very willing to suppose a particular compliment intended her by such a hope, smiled most graciously.

'You have heard of a certain Frank Churchill, I presume,' he continued, 'and know him to be my son, though he does not bear my name.'

'Oh, yes, and I shall be very happy in his acquaintance. I am sure Mr Elton will lose no time in calling on him; and we shall both have great pleasure in seeing him at the Vicarage.'

'You are very obliging. Frank will be extremely happy, I am sure. He is to be in town next week, if not sooner. We have notice of it in a letter to-day. I met the letters in my way this morning, and seeing my son's hand, presumed to open it, though it was not directed to me—it was to Mrs Weston. She is his principal correspondent, I assure you. I hardly ever get a letter.'

'And so you absolutely opened what was directed to her! Oh, Mr Weston' (laughing affectedly), 'I must protest against that. A most dangerous precedent indeed! I beg you will not let your neighbours follow your example. Upon my word, if this is what I am to expect, we married women must begin to exert ourselves. Oh, Mr Weston, I could not have believed it of you!'

'Ay, we men are sad fellows. You must take care of yourself, Mrs Elton. This letter tells us— it is a short letter, written in a hurry, merely to give us notice —it tells us that they are all coming up to town directly, on Mrs Churchill's account! she has not been well the whole winter, and thinks Enscombe too cold for her; so they are all to move southward without loss of time.'

'Indeed! from Yorkshire, I think. Enscombe is in Yorkshire?'

'Yes, they are about 190 miles from London: a considerable journey.'

'Yes, upon my word, very considerable. Sixty-five miles farther than from Maple Grove to London. But what is distance, Mr Weston, to people of large fortune? You would be amazed to hear how my brother, Mr Suckling, sometimes flies about. You will hardly believe me, but twice in one week he and Mr Bragge went to London and back again with four horses.'

'The evil of the distance from Enscombe,' said Mr Weston,

' is that Mrs Churchill, *as we understand*, has not been able to leave the sofa for a week together. In Frank's last letter she complained, he said, of being too weak to get into her conservatory without having both his arm and his uncle's. This, you know, speaks a great degree of weakness; but now she is so impatient to be in town, that she means to sleep only two nights on the road—so Frank writes word. Certainly, delicate ladies have very extraordinary constitutions, Mrs Elton; you must grant me that.'

' No, indeed, I shall grant you nothing. I always take the part of my own sex; I do, indeed. I give you notice, you will find me a formidable antagonist on that point. I always stand up for women; and I assure you, if you knew how Selina feels with respect to sleeping at an inn, you would not wonder at Mrs Churchill's making incredible exertions to avoid it. Selina says it is quite horror to her; and I believe I have caught a little of her nicety. She always travels with her own sheets; an excellent precaution. Does Mrs Churchill do the same?'

' Depend upon it, Mrs Churchill does everything that any other fine lady ever did. Mrs Churchill will not be second to any lady in the land for—'

Mrs Elton eagerly interposed with:

' Oh, Mr Weston, do not mistake me. Selina is no fine lady, I assure you. Do not run away with such an idea.'

' Is not she? Then she is no rule for Mrs Churchill, who is as thorough a fine lady as anybody ever beheld.'

Mrs Elton began to think she had been wrong in disclaiming so warmly. It was by no means her object to have it believed that her sister was *not* a fine lady; perhaps there was want of spirit in the pretence of it; and she was considering in what way she had best retract, when Mr Weston went on:

' Mrs Churchill is not much in my good graces, as you may suspect; but this is quite between ourselves. She is very fond of Frank, and therefore I would not speak ill of her. Besides, she is out of health now; but *that* indeed, by her own account, she has always been. I would not say so to everybody, Mrs Elton; but I have not much faith in Mrs Churchill's illness.'

' If she is really ill, why not go to Bath, Mr Weston? To Bath, or to Clifton?'

' She has taken it into her head that Enscombe is too cold for her. The fact is, I suppose, that she is tired of Enscombe. She has now been a longer time stationary there than she ever was before, and she begins to want change. It is a retired place. A fine place, but very retired.'

'Ay, like Maple Grove, I dare say. Nothing can stand more retired from the road than Maple Grove. Such an immense plantation all round it! You seem shut out from everything—in the most complete retirement. And Mrs Churchill probably has not health or spirits like Selina to enjoy that sort of seclusion. Or, perhaps, she may not have resources enough in herself to be qualified for a country life. I always say a woman cannot have too many resources, and I feel very thankful that I have so many myself as to be quite independent of society.'

'Frank was here in February for a fortnight.'

'So I remember to have heard. He will find an *addition* to the society of Highbury when he comes again; that is, if I may presume to call myself an addition. But perhaps he may never have heard of there being such a creature in the world.'

This was too loud a call for a compliment to be passed by, and Mr Weston, with a very good grace, immediately exclaimed:

'My dear madam! Nobody but yourself could imagine such a thing possible. Not heard of you! I believe Mrs Weston's letters lately have been full of very little else than Mrs Elton.'

He had done his duty, and could return to his son.

'When Frank left us,' continued he, 'it was quite uncertain when we might see him again, which makes this day's news doubly welcome. It has been completely unexpected. That is, *I* always had a strong persuasion he would be here again soon; I was sure something favourable would turn up—but nobody believed me. He and Mrs Weston were both dreadfully desponding. "How could he contrive to come? And how could it be supposed that his uncle and aunt would spare him again?" and so forth. I always felt that something would happen in our favour, and so it has, you see. I have observed, Mrs Elton, in the course of my life, that if things are going untowardly one month, they are sure to mend the next.'

'Very true, Mr Weston, perfectly true. It is just what I used to say to a certain gentleman in company in the days of courtship, when, because things did not go quite right—did not proceed with all the rapidity, which suited his feelings—he was apt to be in despair, and exclaim that he was sure at this rate it would be *May* before Hymen's saffron robe would be put on for us! Oh! the pains I have been at to dispel those gloomy ideas, and give him cheerfuller views! The carriage—we had disappointments about the carriage—one morning, I remember, he came to me quite in despair.'

She was stopped by a slight fit of coughing, and Mr Weston instantly seized the opportunity of going on:

' You were mentioning May. May is the very month which Mrs Churchill is ordered, or has ordered herself to spend in some warmer place than Enscombe—in short, to spend in London; so that we have the agreeable prospect of frequent visits from Frank, the whole spring—precisely the season of the year which one should have chosen for it: days almost at the longest: weather genial and pleasant, always inviting one out, and never too hot for exercise. When he was here before, we made the best of it: but there was a good deal of wet, damp, cheerless weather; there always is in February, you know; and we could not do half that we-intended. Now will be the time. This will be complete enjoyment; and I do not know, Mrs Elton, whether the uncertainty of our meetings, the sort of constant expectation there will be of his coming in to-day or to-morrow, and at any hour, may not be more friendly to happiness than having him actually in the house. I think it is so. I think it is the state of mind which gives most spirit and delight. I hope you will be pleased with my son; but you must not expect a prodigy. He is generally thought a fine young man, but do not expect a prodigy. Mrs Weston's partiality for him is very great, and, as you may suppose, most gratifying to me. She thinks nobody equal to him.'

' And I assure you, Mr Weston, I have very little doubt that my opinion will be decidedly in his favour. I have heard so much in praise of Mr Frank Churchill. At the same time, it is fair to observe, that I am one of those who always judge for themselves, and are by no means implicitly guided by others. I give you notice, that as I find your son, so I shall judge of him. I am no flatterer.'

Mr Weston was musing.

' I hope,' said he presently, ' I have not been severe upon poor Mrs Churchill. If she is ill, I should be sorry to do her injustice; but there are some traits in her character which make it difficult for me to speak of her with the forbearance I could wish. You cannot be ignorant, Mrs Elton, of my connection with the family, nor of the treatment I have met with; and, between ourselves, the whole blame of it is to be laid to her. She was the instigator. Frank's mother would never have been slighted as she was but for her. Mr Churchill has pride; but his pride is nothing to his wife's; his is a quiet, indolent, gentleman-like sort of pride, that would harm nobody, and only make himself a little helpless and tiresome; but her pride is arrogance and insolence. And what inclines one less to bear, she has no fair pretence of family or blood. She was nobody when he married her, barely the daughter of a gentleman; but ever since her being turned into a Churchill, she has out-Churchill'd them all in high and mighty claims; but in herself, I assure you, she is an upstart.'

'Only think! well, that must be infinitely provoking! I have quite a horror of upstarts. Maple Grove has given me a thorough disgust to people of that sort; for there is a family in that neighbourhood who are such an annoyance to my brother and sister from the airs they give themselves! Your description of Mrs Churchill made me think of them directly. People of the name of Tupman, very lately settled there, and encumbered with many low connections, but giving themselves immense airs, and expecting to be on a footing with the old-established families. A year and a half is the very utmost that they can have lived at West Hall; and how they got their fortune nobody knows. They came from Birmingham, which is not a place to promise much, you know, Mr Weston. One has not great hopes from Birmingham. I always say there is something direful in the sound; but nothing more is positively known of the Tupmans, though a good many things, I assure you, are suspected; and yet by their manners they evidently think themselves equal even to my brother, Mr Suckling, who happens to be one of their nearest neighbours. It is infinitely too bad. Mr Suckling, who has been eleven years a resident at Maple Grove, and whose father had it before him—I believe, at least—I am almost sure that old Mr Suckling had completed the purchase before his death.'

They were interrupted. Tea was carrying round, and Mr Weston, having said all that he wanted, soon took the opportunity of walking away.

After tea, Mr and Mrs Weston, and Mr Elton, sat down with Mr Woodhouse to cards. The remaining five were left to their own powers, and Emma doubted their getting on very well; for Mr Knightley seemed little disposed for conservation; Mrs Elton was wanting notice, which nobody had inclination to pay, and she was herself in a worry of spirits which would have made her prefer being silent.

Mr John Knightley proved more talkative than his brother. He was to leave them early the next day; and he soon began with:

'Well, Emma, I do not believe I have anything more to say about the boys; but you have your sister's letter, and everything is down at full length there, we may be sure. My charge would be much more concise than hers, and probably not much in the same spirit; all that I have to recommend being comprised in— Do not spoil them, and do not physic them.'

' I rather hope to satisfy you both,' said Emma; ' for I shall do all in my power to make them happy, which will be enough for Isabella; and happiness must preclude false indulgence and physic.'

' And if you find them troublesome, you must send them home again.'

' That is very likely. You think so, do not you? '

' I hope I am aware that they may be too noisy for your father; or even may be some encumbrance to you, if your visiting engagements continue to increase as much as they have done lately.'

' Increase! '

' Certainly; you must be sensible that the last half-year has made a great difference in your way of life.'

' Difference! No, indeed, I am not.'

' There can be no doubt of your being much more engaged with company than you used to be. Witness this very time. Here am I come down for only one day, and you are engaged with a dinner-party! When did it happen before, or anything like it? Your neighbourhood is increasing, and you mix more with it. A little while ago, every letter to Isabella brought an account of fresh gaieties; dinners at Mr Cole's, or balls at the Crown. The difference which Randalls, Randalls alone, makes in your goings on is very great.'

' Yes,' said his brother quickly, ' it is Randalls that does it all.'

' Very well; and as Randalls, I suppose, is not likely to have less influence than heretofore, it strikes me as a possible thing, Emma, that Henry and John may be sometimes in the way. And if they are, I only beg you to send them home.'

' No,' cried Mr Knightley; ' that need not be the consequence. Let them be sent to Donwell. I shall certainly be at leisure.'

' Upon my word,' exclaimed Emma, ' you amuse me! I should like to know how many of all my numerous engagements take place without your being of the party; and why I am to be supposed in danger of wanting leisure to attend to the little boys. These amazing engagements of mine—what have they been? Dining once with the Coles, and having a ball talked of, which never took place. I can understand you '—(nodding at Mr John Knightley)—' your good fortune in meeting with so many of your friends at once here delights you too much to pass unnoticed. But you' (turning to Mr Knightley), 'who know how very, very seldom I am ever two hours from Hartfield—why you should foresee such a series of dissipation for me, I cannot imagine. And as to my dear little boys, I must say, that if Aunt Emma has not time for them, I do not think they would fare much better with Uncle Knightley, who is absent from home about five hours where she is absent one; and who, when he is at home, is either reading to himself or settling his accounts.'

Mr Knightley seemed to be trying not to smile; and succeeded without difficulty, upon Mrs Elton's beginning to talk to him.

37

A VERY little quiet reflection was enough to satisfy Emma as to the nature of her agitation on hearing this news of Frank Churchill. She was soon convinced that it was not for herself she was feeling at all apprehensive or embarrassed—it was for him. Her own attachment had really subsided into a mere nothing—it was not worth thinking of; but if he, who had undoubtedly been always so much the most in love of the two, were to be returning with the same warmth of sentiment which he had taken away, it would be very distressing. If a separation of two months should not have cooled him, there were dangers and evils before her: caution for him and for herself would be necessary. She did not mean to have her own affections entangled again, and it would be incumbent on her to avoid any encouragement of his.

She wished she might be able to keep him from an absolute declaration. That would be so very painful a conclusion of their present acquaintance; and yet she could not help rather anticipating something decisive. She felt as if the spring would not pass without bringing a crisis, an event, a something to alter her present composed and tranquil state.

It was not very long, though rather longer than Mr Weston had foreseen, before she had the power of forming some opinion of Frank Churchill's feelings. The Enscombe family were not in town quite so soon as had been imagined, but he was at Highbury very soon afterwards. He rode down for a couple of hours; he could not yet do more; but as he came from Randalls immediately to Hartfield, she could then exercise all her quick observation, and speedily determine how he was influenced, and how she must act. They met with the utmost friendliness. There could be no doubt of his great pleasure in seeing her. But she had an almost instant doubt of his caring for her as he had done, of his feeling the same tenderness in the same degree. She watched him well. It was a clear thing he was less in love than he had been. Absence, with the conviction probably of her indifference, had produced this very natural and very desirable effect.

He was in high spirits; as ready to talk and laugh as ever; and seemed delighted to speak of his former visit, and recur to old stories; and he was not without agitation. It was not in his calmness that she read his comparative difference. He was not calm; his spirits were evidently fluttered; there was restlessness about him. Lively as he was, it seemed a liveliness that did not satisfy himself; but what decided her belief on the subject, was his staying only a quarter of an hour, and hurrying away to make other calls in Highbury. ' He had seen a group of old acquaintance in the street as he passed—he had not stopped, he would not stop for more than a word—but he had the vanity to think they would be disappointed if he did not call; and, much as he wished to stay longer at Hartfield, he must hurry off.'

She had no doubt as to his being less in love, but neither his agitated spirits nor his hurrying away seemed like a perfect cure; and she was rather inclined to think it implied a dread of her returning power, and a discreet resolution of not trusting himself with her long.

This was the only visit from Frank Churchill in the course of ten days. He was often hoping, intending to come; but was always prevented. His aunt could not bear to have him leave her. Such was his own account at Randalls. If he were quite sincere, if he really tried to come, it was to be inferred that Mrs Churchill's removal to London had been of no service to the wilful or nervous part of her disorder. That she was really ill was very certain; he had declared himself convinced of it, at Randalls. Though much might he fancy, he could not doubt, when he looked back, that she was in a weaker state of health than she had been half a year ago. He did not believe it to proceed from anything that care and medicine might not remove, or at least that she might not have many years of existence before her; but he could not be prevailed on, by all his father's doubts, to say that her complaints were merely imaginary, or that she was as strong as ever.

It soon appeared that London was not the place for her. She could not endure its noise. Her nerves were under continual irritation and suffering; and by the ten days' end, her nephew's letter to Randalls communicated a change of plan. They were going to remove immediately to Richmond. Mrs Churchill had been recommended to the medical skill of an eminent person there, and had otherwise a fancy for the place. A ready-furnished house in a favourite spot was engaged, and much benefit expected from the change.

Emma heard that Frank wrote in the highest spirits of this arrangement, and seemed most fully to appreciate the blessing of having two months before him of such near neighbourhood to many dear friends; for the house was taken for May and June. She was told that now he wrote with the greatest confidence of being often with them, almost as often as he could even wish.

Emma saw how Mr Weston understood these joyous prospects. He was considering her as the source of all the happiness they offered. She hoped it was not so. Two months must bring it to the proof.

Mr Weston's own happiness was indisputable. He was quite delighted. It was the very circumstance he could have wished for. Now, it would be really having Frank in their neighbourhood. What were nine miles to a young man? An hour's ride. He would be always coming over. The difference in that respect of Richmond and London was enough to make the whole difference of seeing him always and seeing him never. Sixteen miles—nay, eighteen—it must be full eighteen to Manchester Street—was a serious obstacle. Were he ever able to get away, the day would be spent in coming and returning. There was no comfort in having him in London; he might as well be at Enscombe; but Richmond was the very distance for easy intercourse. Better than nearer!

One good thing was immediately brought to a certainty by this removal—the ball at the Crown. It had not been forgotten before; but it had been soon acknowledged vain to attempt to fix a day. Now, however, it was absolutely to be; every preparation was resumed; and very soon after the Churchills had removed to Richmond, a few lines from Frank, to say that his aunt felt already much better for the change, and that he had no doubt of being able to join them for twenty-four hours at any given time, induced them to name as early a day as possible.

Mr Weston's ball was to be a real thing. A very few to-morrows stood between the young people of Highbury and happiness.

Mr Woodhouse was resigned. The time of year lightened the evil to him. May was better for everything than February. Mrs

233

Bates was engaged to spend the evening at Hartfield; James had due notice, and he sanguinely hoped that neither dear little Henry nor dear little John would have anything the matter with them while dear Emma were gone.

38

No misfortune occurred again to prevent the ball. The day approached, the day arrived; and, after a morning of some anxious watching, Frank Churchill, in all the certainty of his own self, reached Randalls before dinner; and everything was safe. No second meeting had there yet been between him and Emma. The room at the Crown was to witness it; but it would be better than a common meeting in a crowd. Mr Weston had been so very earnest in his entreaties for her early attendance, for her arriving there as soon as possible after themselves, for the purpose of taking her opinion as to the propriety and comfort of the rooms before any other persons came, that she could not refuse him, and therefore must spend some quiet interval in the young man's company. She was to convey Harriet, and they drove to the Crown in good time, the Randalls' party just sufficiently before them.

Frank Churchill seemed to have been on the watch; and though he did not say much, his eyes declared that he meant to have a delightful evening. They all walked about together, to see that everything was as it should be; and within a few minutes were joined by the contents of another carriage, which Emma could not hear the sound of at first without great surprise. 'So unreasonably early!' she was going to exclaim; but she presently found that it was a family of old friends, who were coming, like herself, by particular desire, to help Mr Weston's judgment; and they were so very closely followed by another carriage of cousins, who had been entreated to come early with the same distinguishing earnestness, on the same errand, that it seemed as if half the company might soon be collected together for the purpose of preparatory inspection.

Emma perceived that her taste was not the only taste on which Mr Weston depended, and felt that to be the favourite and intimate of a man who had so many intimates and confidantes, was not the very first distinction in the scale of vanity. She liked his open manners, but a little less of open-heartedness would have made him a higher character. General benevolence, but not general friendship, made a man what he ought to be. She could fancy such a man.

The whole party walked about, and looked, and praised again; and then, having nothing else to do, formed a sort of half-circle round the fire, to observe in their various modes, till other subjects were started, that, though *May*, a fire in the evening was still very pleasant.

Emma found that it was not Mr Weston's fault that the number of privy counsellors was not yet larger. They had stopped at Mrs Bates's door to offer the use of their carriage, but the aunt and niece were to be brought by the Eltons.

Frank was standing by her, but not steadily; there was a restlessness, which showed a mind not at ease. He was looking about, he was going to the door, he was watching for the sound of other carriages—impatient to begin, or afraid of being always near her.

Mrs Elton was spoken of. ' I think she must be here soon,' said he. ' I have a great curiosity to see Mrs Elton, I have heard so much of her. It cannot be long, I think, before she comes.'

A carriage was heard. He was on the move immediately; but coming back, said:

' I am forgetting that I am not acquainted with her. I have never seen either Mr or Mrs Elton. I have no business to put myself forward.'

Mr and Mrs Elton appeared; and all the smiles and the proprieties passed.

' But Miss Bates and Miss Fairfax! ' said Mr Weston, looking about. ' We thought you were to bring them.'

The mistake had been slight. The carriage was sent for them now. Emma longed to know what Frank's first opinion of Mrs Elton might be; how he was affected by the studied elegance of her dress, and her smiles of graciousness. He was immediately qualifying himself to form an opinion, by giving her very proper attention, after the introduction had passed.

In a few minutes the carriage returned. Somebody talked of rain. ' I will see that there are umbrellas, sir,' said Frank to his father: ' Miss Bates must not be forgotten; ' and away he went. Mr Weston was following: but Mrs Elton detained him, to gratify him by her opinion of his son; and so briskly did she begin, that the young man himself, though by no means moving slowly, could hardly be out of hearing.

' A very fine young man, indeed, Mr Weston. You know I candidly told you I should form my own opinion; and I am happy to say that I am extremely pleased with him. You may believe me. I never compliment. I think him a very handsome young man, and his manners are precisely what I like and approve—so truly the gentleman, without the least conceit or puppyism. You must know I have a vast dislike to puppies—quite a horror of them. They were never tolerated at Maple Grove. Neither Mr Suckling nor me had ever any patience with them; and we used sometimes to say very cutting things. Selina, who is mild almost to a fault, bore with them much better.'

While she talked of his son, Mr Weston's attention was chained; but when she got to Maple Grove, he could recollect that there were ladies just arriving to be attended to, and with happy smiles must hurry away.

Mrs Elton turned to Mrs Weston. ' I have no doubt of its being our carriage with Miss Bates and Jane. Our coachman and horses are so extremely expeditious! I believe we drive faster than anybody. What a pleasure it is to send one's carriage for a friend! I understand you were so kind as to offer, but another time it will be quite unnecessary. You may be very sure I shall always take care of *them*.'

Miss Bates and Miss Fairfax, escorted by the two gentlemen, walked into the room; and Mrs Elton seemed to think it as much her duty as Mrs Weston's to receive them. Her gestures and movements might be understood by any one who looked on like Emma; but her words, everybody's words, were soon lost under the incessant flow of Miss Bates, who came in talking, and had not finished her speech under many minutes after her being admitted into the circle at the fire. As the door opened she was heard:

' So very obliging of you! No rain at all. Nothing to signify. I do not care for myself. Quite thick shoes. And Jane declares— Well! ' (as soon as she was within the door), ' Well! This is brilliant indeed! This is admirable! Excellently contrived, upon my word. Nothing wanting. Could not have imagined it. So well lighted up! Jane, Jane, look! did you ever see anything ——? Oh! Mr Weston, you must really have had Aladdin's lamp. Good Mrs Stokes would not know her own room again. I saw her as I came in; she was standing in the entrance. "Oh! Mrs Stokes," said I—but I had not time for more.' She was now met by Mrs Weston. ' Very well, I thank you, ma'am. I hope you are quite well. Very happy to hear it. So afraid you might have a headache! seeing you pass by so often, and knowing how much trouble you must have. Delighted to hear it indeed! Ah! dear Mrs Elton, so obliged to you for the carriage; excellent time; Jane and I quite ready. Did not keep the horses a moment. Most comfortable carriage. Oh! and I am sure our thanks are due to you, Mrs Weston, on that score. Mrs Elton had most kindly sent Jane a note, or we should have been. But two such offers in one day! Never were such neighbours. I said to my mother, "Upon my word, ma'am—— " Thank you, my mother is remarkably well. Gone to Mr Woodhouse's. I made her take her shawl—for the evenings are not warm—her large new shawl, Mrs Dixon's wedding present. So kind of her to think of my mother! Bought at Weymouth, you know; Mr Dixon's choice. There were three others, Jane says, which they hesitated about some time. Colonel Campbell rather preferred an olive. My dear Jane, are you sure you did not wet your feet! It was but a drop or two, but I am so afraid; but Mr Frank Churchill was so extremely—and there was a mat to step upon. I shall never forget his extreme politeness. Oh! Mr Frank Churchill, I must tell you my mother's spectacles have never been in fault since; the rivet never came out again. My mother often talks of your good nature; does not she, Jane? Do not we often talk of Mr Frank Churchill? Ah! here's Miss Woodhouse. Dear Miss Woodhouse, how do you do? Very well, I thank you, quite well. This is meeting quite in fairy land. Such a transformation! Must not compliment, I know ' (eyeing Emma most complacently)—' that would be rude; but upon my word, Miss Woodhouse, you do look—how do you like Jane's hair? You are a judge. She did it all herself. Quite wonderful how she does her hair! No hairdresser from London, I think, could —Ah! Dr Hughes, I declare—and Mrs Hughes. Must go and speak to Dr and Mrs Hughes for a moment. How do you do? How do you do? Very well, I thank you. This is delightful, is not it? Where's dear Mr Richard? Oh! there he is. Don't disturb him. Much better employed talking to the young ladies. How do you do, Mr Richard? I saw you the other day as you rode through the town. Mrs Otway, I protest, and good Mr Otway, and Miss Otway, and Miss Caroline. Such a host of friends! and Mr George and Mr Arthur! How do you do? How do you all do? Quite well, I am much obliged to you. Never better. Don't I hear another carriage? Who can this be? very likely the worthy Coles. Upon my word, this is charming, to be standing about among such friends! and such a noble fire! I am quite roasted. No coffee, I thank you, for me; never take coffee. A little tea, if you please, sir, by-and-by; no hurry. Oh! here it comes. Everything is so good!'

Frank Churchill returned to his station by Emma; and as soon as Miss Bates was quiet, she found herself necessarily overhearing the discourse of Mrs Elton and Miss Fairfax, who were standing a little way behind her. He was thoughtful. Whether he were overhearing too she could not determine. After a good many compliments to Jane on her dress and look—compliments very quietly and properly taken—Mrs Elton was evidently wanting to be complimented herself—and it was, ' How do you like my gown? How do you like my trimming? How has Wright done my hair? ' with many other relative questions, all answered with patient politeness. Mrs Elton then said:

' Nobody can think less of dress in general than I do: but upon such an occasion as this, when everybody's eyes are so much upon me, and in compliment to the Westons, who I have no doubt are giving this ball chiefly to do me honour. I would not wish to be inferior to others; and I see very few pearls in the room except mine. So Frank Churchill is a capital dancer, I understand. We shall see if our styles suit. A fine young man certainly is Frank Churchill. I like him very well.'

At this moment Frank began talking so vigorously, that Emma could not but imagine he had overheard his own praises, and did not want to hear more; and the voices of the ladies were drowned for a while, till another suspension brought Mrs Elton's tones again distinctly forward. Mr Elton had just joined them, and his wife was exclaiming:

' Oh! you have found us out at last, have you, in our seclusion? I was this moment telling Jane, I thought you would begin to be impatient for tidings of us.'

' Jane! ' repeated Frank Churchill, with a look of surprise and displeasure. ' That is easy; but Miss Fairfax does not disapprove it, I suppose.'

' How do you like Mrs Elton? ' said Emma, in a whisper.

' Not at all.'

' You are ungrateful.'

' Ungrateful! What do you mean? ' Then changing from a frown to a smile: ' No, do not tell me—I do not want to know what you mean. Where is my father? When are we to begin dancing? '

Emma could hardly understand him; he seemed in an odd humour. He walked off to find his father, but was quickly back again with both Mr and Mrs Weston. He had met with them in a little perplexity, which must be laid before Emma. It had just occurred to Mrs Weston that Mrs Elton must be asked to begin the ball; that she would expect it; which interfered with all their wishes of giving Emma that distinction. Emma heard the sad truth with fortitude.

'And what are we to do for a proper partner for her?' said Mr Weston. 'She will think Frank ought to ask her.'

Frank turned instantly to Emma, to claim her former promise; and boasted himself an engaged man, which his father looked his most perfect approbation of—and it then appeared that Mrs Weston was wanting *him* to dance with Mrs Elton himself, and that their business was to help to persuade him into it, which was done pretty soon. Mr Weston and Mrs Elton led the way; Mr Frank Churchill and Miss Woodhouse followed. Emma must submit to stand second to Mrs Elton though she had always considered the ball as peculiarly for her. It was almost enough to make her think of marrying.

Mrs Elton had undoubtedly the advantage, at this time, in vanity completely gratified; for though she had intended to begin with Frank Churchill, she could not lose by the change. Mr Weston might be his son's superior. In spite of this little rub, however, Emma was smiling with enjoyment, delighted to see the respectable length of the set as it was forming, and to feel that she had so many hours of unusual festivity before her. She was more disturbed by Mr Knightley's not dancing than by anything else. There he was, among the standers-by, where he ought not to be; he ought to be dancing, not classing himself with the husbands, and fathers, and whist-players, who were pretending to feel an interest in the dance till their rubbers were made up,—so young as he looked! He could not have appeared to greater advantage perhaps anywhere, than where he had placed himself. His tall, firm, upright figure, among the bulky forms and stooping shoulders of the elderly men, was such as Emma felt must draw everybody's eyes; and, excepting her own partner, there was not one among the whole row of young men who could be compared with him. He moved a few steps nearer, and those few steps were enough to prove in how gentlemanlike a manner, with what natural grace, he must have danced, would he but take the trouble. Whenever she caught his eye, she forced him to smile; but in general he was looking grave. She wished he could love a ball-room better, and could like Frank Churchill better. He seemed often observing her. She must not flatter herself that he thought of her dancing; but if he were criticising her behaviour, she did not feel afraid. There was nothing like flirtation between her and her partner. They seemed more like cheerful easy friends than lovers. That Frank Churchill thought less of her than he had done was indubitable.

The ball proceeded pleasantly. The anxious cares, the incessant attentions of Mrs Weston were not thrown away. Everybody seemed happy; and the praise of being a delightful ball, which is seldom bestowed till after a ball has ceased to be, was repeatedly given in the very beginning of the existence of this. Of very important, very recordable events, it was not more productive than such meetings usually are. There was one, however, which Emma thought something of. The two last dances before supper were begun, and Harriet had no partner—the only young lady sitting down; and so equal had been hitherto the number of dancers, that how there could be any one disengaged was the wonder. But Emma's wonder lessened soon afterwards, on seeing Mr Elton sauntering about. He would not ask Harriet to dance, if it were possible to be avoided; she was sure he would not—and she was expecting him every moment to escape into the card-room.

Escape, however, was not his plan. He came to the part of the room where the sitters-by were collected, spoke to some, and walked about in front of them, as if to show his liberty, and his resolution of maintaining it. He did not omit being sometimes directly before Miss Smith, or speaking to those who were close to her. Emma saw it. She was not yet dancing; she was working her way up from the bottom, and had therefore leisure to look round, and by only turning her head a little she saw it all. When she was half way up the set, the whole group were exactly behind her, and she would no longer allow her eyes to watch; but Mr Elton was so near, that she heard every syllable of a dialogue which just then took place between him and Mrs Weston; and she perceived that his wife, who was standing immediately above her, was not only listening also, but even encouraging him by significant glances. The kind-hearted, gentle Mrs Weston had left her seat to join him and say, ' Do not you dance, Mr Elton? ' to which his prompt reply was, ' Most readily, Mrs Weston, if you will dance with me.'

' Me! oh! no—I would get you a better partner than myself. I am no dancer.'

' If Mrs Gilbert wishes to dance,' said he, ' I shall have great pleasure, I am sure; for, though beginning to feel myself rather an old married man, and that my dancing days are over, it would give me very great pleasure at any time to stand up with an old friend like Mrs Gilbert.

'Mrs Gilbert does not mean to dance, but there is a young lady disengaged whom I should be very glad to see dancing—Miss Smith.'

'Miss Smith—oh!—I had not observed. You are extremely obliging—and if I were not an old married—but my dancing days are over, Mrs Weston. You will excuse me. Anything else I should be most happy to do, at your command—but my dancing days are over.'

Mrs Weston said no more; and Emma could imagine with what surprise and mortification she must be returning to her seat. This was Mr Elton! the amiable, obliging, gentle Mr Elton. She looked round for a moment; he had joined Mr Knightley at a little distance, and was arranging himself for settled conversation, while smiles of high glee passed between him and his wife. She would not look again. Her heart was in a glow, and she feared her face might be as hot.

In another moment a happier sight caught her—Mr Knightley leading Harriet to the set! Never had she been more surprised, seldom more delighted, than at that instant. She was all pleasure and gratitude, both for Harriet and herself, and longed to be thanking him; and though too distant for speech, her countenance said much, as soon as she could catch his eye again.

His dancing proved to be just what she had believed it, extremely good; and Harriet would have seemed almost too lucky, if it had not been for the cruel state of things before, and for the very complete enjoyment and very high sense of the distinction which her happy features announced. It was not thrown away on her; she bounded higher than ever, flew farther down the middle, and was in a continual course of smiles.

Mr Elton had retreated into the card-room, looking (Emma trusted) very foolish. She did not think he was quite so hardened as his wife, though growing very like her; *she* spoke some of her feelings, by observing audibly to her partner:

'Knightley has taken pity on poor little Miss Smith! Very good-natured, I declare.'

Supper was announced. The move began; and Miss Bates might be heard from that moment without interruption, till her being seated at table and taking up her spoon.

'Jane, Jane, my dear Jane, where are you? Here is your tippet. Mrs Weston begs you to put on your tippet. She says she is afraid there will be draughts in the passage, though every-

thing has been done—one door nailed up—quantities of matting
—my dear Jane, indeed you must. Mr Churchill, oh! you are
too obliging. How well you put it on—so gratified! Excellent
dancing indeed. Yes, my dear, I ran home, as I said I should,
to help grandmamma to bed, and got back again, and nobody
missed me. I set off without saying a word, just as I told you.
Grandmamma was quite well, had a charming evening with Mr
Woodhouse, a vast deal of chat, and backgammon. Tea was
made downstairs, biscuits and baked apples, and wine before
she came away: amazing luck in some of her throws: and she
inquired a great deal about you, how you were amused, and
who were your partners. " Oh! " said I, " I shall not forestall
Jane; I left her dancing with Mr George Otway; she will love
to tell you all about it herself to-morrow: her first partner was
Mr Elton; I do not know who will ask her next, perhaps Mr
William Cox." My dear sir, you are too obliging. Is there
nobody you would not rather? I am not helpless. Sir, you are
most kind. Upon my word, Jane on one arm, and me on the
other. Stop, stop, let us stand a little back, Mrs Elton is going;
dear Mrs Elton, how elegant she looks—beautiful lace. Now we
all follow in her train. Quite the queen of the evening! Well,
here we are at the passage. Two steps, Jane, take care of the
two steps. Oh, no, there is but one. Well, I was persuaded there
were two. How very odd! I was convinced there were two, and
there is but one. I never saw anything equal to the comfort and
style—candles everywhere. I was telling you of your grandmamma, Jane—there was a little disappointment. The baked
apples and biscuits, excellent in their way, you know; but there
was a delicate fricassee of sweetbread and some asparagus brought
in at first, and good Mr Woodhouse, not thinking the asparagus
quite boiled enough, sent it all out again. Now there is nothing
grandmamma loves better than sweetbread and asparagus—so
she was rather disappointed; but we agreed we would not speak
of it to anybody, for fear of its getting round to dear Miss Woodhouse, who would be so very much concerned. Well, this is
brilliant! I am all amazement!—could not have supposed anything—such elegance and profusion! I have seen nothing like it
since—Well, where shall we sit? Where shall we sit? Anywhere,
so that Jane is not in a draught. Where I sit is of no consequence.
Oh! do you recommend this side? Well, I am sure, Mr Churchill
—only it seems too good—but just as you please. What you
direct in this house cannot be wrong. Dear Jane, how shall we
ever recollect half the dishes for grandmamma? Soup too! Bless

me! I should not be helped so soon, but it smells most excellent, and I cannot help beginning.'

Emma had no opportunity of speaking to Mr Knightley till after supper; but, when they were all in the ball-room again, her eyes invited him irresistibly to come to her and be thanked. He was warm in his reprobation of Mr Elton's conduct; it had been unpardonable rudeness; and Mrs Elton's looks also received the due share of censure.

'They aimed at wounding more than Harriet,' said he. 'Emma, why is it that they are your enemies?'

He looked with smiling penetration; and, on receiving no answer, added, '*She* ought not to be angry with you, I suspect, whatever he may be. To that surmise, you say nothing, of course: but confess, Emma, that you did want him to marry Harriet.'

'I did,' replied Emma, 'and they cannot forgive me.'

He shook his head; but there was a smile of indulgence with it, and he only said:

'I shall not scold you. I leave you to your own reflections.'

'Can you trust me with such flatterers? Does my vain spirit ever tell me I am wrong?'

'Not your vain spirit, but your serious spirit. If one leads you wrong, I am sure the other tells you of it.'

'I do own myself to have been completely mistaken in Mr Elton. There is a littleness about him which you discovered, and which I did not: and I was fully convinced of his being in love with Harriet. It was through a series of strange blunders!'

'And, in return for your acknowledging so much, I will do you the justice to say, that you would have chosen for him better than he has chosen for himself. Harriet Smith has some first-rate qualities, which Mrs Elton is totally without. An unpretending, single-minded, artless girl—infinitely to be preferred by any man of sense and taste to such a woman as Mrs Elton. I found Harriet more conversable than I expected.'

Emma was extremely gratified. They were interrupted by the bustle of Mr Weston calling on everybody to begin dancing again.

'Come, Miss Woodhouse, Miss Otway, Miss Fairfax, what are you all doing? Come, Emma, set your companions the example. Everybody is lazy! Everybody is asleep!'

'I am ready,' said Emma, 'whenever I am wanted.'

'Whom are you going to dance with?' asked Mr Knightley.

She hesitated a moment, and then replied, ' With you, if you will ask me.'

' Will you? ' said he, offering his hand.

' Indeed, I will. You have shown that you can dance, and you know we are not really so much brother and sister as to make it at all improper.'

' Brother and sister!—no, indeed.'

39

THIS little explanation with Mr Knightley gave Emma considerable pleasure. It was one of the agreeable recollections of the ball, which she walked about the lawn the next morning to enjoy. She was extremely glad that they had come to so good an understanding respecting the Eltons, and that their opinions of both husband and wife were so much alike; and his praise of Harriet, his concession in her favour, was peculiarly gratifying. The impertinence of the Eltons, which for a few moments had threatened to ruin the rest of her evening, had been the occasion of some of its highest satisfactions; and she looked forward to another happy result—the cure of Harriet's infatuation. From Harriet's manner of speaking of the circumstance before they quitted the ball-room she had strong hopes. It seemed as if her eyes were suddenly opened, and she were enabled to see that Mr Elton was not the superior creature she had believed him. The fever was over, and Emma could harbour little fear of the pulse being quickened again by injurious courtesy. She depended on the evil feelings of the Eltons for supplying all the discipline of pointed neglect that could be further requisite. Harriet rational, Frank Churchill not too much in love, and Mr Knightley not wanting to quarrel with her, how very happy a summer must be before her.

She was not to see Frank Churchill this morning. He had told her that he could not allow himself the pleasure of stopping at Hartfield, as he was to be home by the middle of the day. She did not regret it.

Having arranged all these matters, looked them through, and put them all to rights, she was just turning to the house, with spirits freshened up for the demands of the two little boys, as well as of their grandpapa, when the great iron sweep-gate opened, and two persons entered whom she had never less expected to see together—Frank Churchill, with Harriet leaning on his arm—actually Harriet! A moment sufficed to convince her that something extraordinary had happened. Harriet looked white and frightened, and he was trying to cheer her. The iron gates and the front-door were not twenty yards asunder—they were all three soon in the hall; and Harriet immediately sinking into a chair, fainted away.

A young lady who faints must be recovered; questions must be answered, and surprises be explained. Such events are very interesting; but the suspense of them cannot last long. A few minutes made Emma acquainted with the whole.

Miss Smith, and Miss Bickerton, another parlour boarder at Mrs Goddard's, who had been also at the ball, had walked out together, and taken a road—the Richmond Road, which, though apparently public enough for safety, had led them into alarm. About half a mile beyond Highbury, making a sudden turn, and deeply shaded by elms on each side, it became for a considerable stretch very retired; and when the young ladies had advanced some way into it, they had suddenly perceived, at a small distance before them, on a broader patch of greensward by the side, a party of gipsies. A child on the watch came towards them to beg; and Miss Bickerton, excessively frightened, gave a great scream, and calling on Harriet to follow her, ran up a steep bank, cleared a slight hedge at the top, and made the best of her way by a short cut back to Highbury. But poor Harriet could not follow. She had suffered very much from cramp after dancing, and her first attempt to mount the bank brought on such a return of it as made her absolutely powerless; and in this state, and exceedingly terrified, she had been obliged to remain.

How the trampers might have behaved, had the young ladies been more courageous, must be doubtful; but such an invitation for attack could not be resisted; and Harriet was soon assailed by half a dozen children, headed by a stout woman, and a great boy, all clamorous, and impertinent in look, though not absolutely in word. More and more frightened, she immediately promised them money, and taking out her purse gave them a shilling, and begged them not to want more, or to use her ill. She was then able to walk, though but slowly, and was moving away—but her terror and her purse were too tempting; and she was followed, or rather surrounded, by the whole gang, demanding more.

In this state Frank Churchill had found her, she trembling and conditioning, they loud and insolent. By a most fortunate chance, his leaving Highbury had been delayed so as to bring him to her assistance at this critical moment. The pleasantness of the morning had induced him to walk forward, and leave his horses to meet him by another road, a mile or two beyond Highbury; and happening to have borrowed a pair of scissors the night before of Miss Bates, and to have forgotten to restore them, he had been obliged to stop at her door, and go in for a few minutes; he was therefore later than he had intended; and being on foot, was unseen by the whole party till almost close to them. The terror which the woman and boy had been creating in Harriet was then their own portion. He had left them completely frightened; and Harriet eagerly clinging to him, and hardly able to speak, had just strength enough to reach Hartfield, before her spirits were quite overcome. It was his idea to bring her to Hartfield; he had thought of no other place.

This was the amount of the whole story—of his communication and of Harriet's, as soon as she had recovered her senses and speech. He dared not stay longer than to see her well; these several delays left him not another minute to lose; and Emma engaging to give assurance of her safety to Mrs Goddard, and notice of there being such a set of people in the neighbourhood to Mr Knightley, he set off, with all the grateful blessings that she could utter for her friend and herself.

Such an adventure as this—a fine young man and a lovely young woman thrown together in such a way—could hardly fail of suggesting certain ideas to the coldest heart and the steadiest brain. So Emma thought, at least. Could a linguist, could a grammarian, could even a mathematician have seen what she did, have witnessed their appearance together, and heard their history of it, without feeling that circumstances had been at work to make them peculiarly interesting to each other? How much more must an imaginist, like herself, be on fire with speculation and foresight? especially with such a groundwork of anticipation as her mind had already made.

It was a very extraordinary thing! Nothing of the sort had ever occurred before to any young ladies in the place, within her memory; no rencontre, no alarm of the kind; and now it had happened to the very person, and at the very hour, when the other very person was chancing to pass by to rescue her! It certainly was very extraordinary! And knowing, as she did, the favourable state of mind of each at this period, it struck her the more. He was wishing to get the better of his attachment to herself, she just recovering from her mania for Mr Elton. It seemed as if everything united to promise the most interesting consequences. It was not possible that the occurrence should not be strongly recommending each to the other.

In the few minutes' conversation which she had yet had with him, while Harriet had been partially insensible, he had spoken of her terror, her *näiveté*, her fervour as she seized and clung to his arm, with a sensibility amused and delighted; and just at last, after Harriet's own account had been given, he had expressed his indignation at the abominable folly of Miss Bickerton in the warmest terms. Everything was to take its natural course, however, neither impelled nor assisted. She would not stir a step nor drop a hint. No, she had had enough of interference. There could be no harm in a scheme, a mere passive scheme. It was no more than a wish. Beyond it she would on no account proceed.

Emma's first resolution was to keep her father from the knowledge of what had passed, aware of the anxiety and alarm it would occasion; but she soon felt that concealment must be impossible. Within half an hour it was known all over Highbury. It was the very event to engage those who talk most—the young and the low; and all the youth and servants in the place were soon in the happiness of frightful news. The last night's ball seemed lost in the gipsies. Poor Mr Woodhouse trembled as he sat, and, as Emma had foreseen, would scarcely be satisfied without their promising never to go beyond the shrubbery again. It was some comfort to him that many inquiries after himself and Miss Woodhouse (for his neighbours knew that he loved to be inquired after), as well as Miss Smith, were coming in during the rest of the day; and he had the pleasure of returning for answer, that they were all very indifferent; which, though not exactly true, for she was perfectly well, and Harriet not much otherwise, Emma would not interfere with. She had an unhappy state of health in general for the child of such a man, for she hardly knew what indisposition was; and if he did not invent illnesses for her, she would make no figure in a message.

The gipsies did not wait for the operations of justice; they took themselves off in a hurry. The young ladies of Highbury might have walked again in safety before their panic began, and the whole history dwindled soon into a matter of little importance but to Emma and her nephews: in her imagination it maintained its ground; and Henry and John were still asking every day for the story of Harriet and the gipsies, and still tenaciously setting her right if she varied in the slightest particular from the original recital.

40

A VERY few days had passed after this adventure; when Harriet came one morning to Emma with a small parcel in her hand, and after sitting down and hesitating, thus began:

'Miss Woodhouse—if you are at leisure, I have something that I should like to tell you: a sort of confession to make—and then, you know, it will be over.'

Emma was a good deal surprised; but begged her to speak. There was a seriousness in Harriet's manner which prepared her, quite as much as her words, for something more than ordinary.

'It is my duty, and I am sure it is my wish,' she continued, 'to have no reserves with you on this subject. As I am, happily, quite an altered creature, in *one respect*, it is very fit that you should have the satisfaction of knowing it. I do not want to say more than is necessary; I am too much ashamed of having given way as I have done, and I dare say you understand me.'

'Yes,' said Emma, 'I hope I do.'

'How I could so long a time be fancying myself,' cried Harriet warmly. 'It seems like madness! I can see nothing at all extraordinary in him now. I do not care whether I meet him or not, except that, of the two, I had rather not see him; and, indeed, I would go any distance round to avoid him; but I do not envy his wife in the least: I neither admire her nor envy her, as I have done. She is very charming, I dare say, and all that; but I think her very ill-tempered and disagreeable: I shall never forget her look the other night. However, I assure you, Miss Woodhouse, I wish her no evil. No; let them be ever so happy together, it will not give me another moment's pang; and, to convince you that I have been speaking truth, I am now going to destroy—what I ought to have destroyed long ago—what I ought never to have kept: I know that very well' (blushing as she spoke). 'However, now I will destroy it all; and it is my particular wish to do it in your presence, that you may see how rational I am grown. Cannot you guess what this parcel holds?' said she, with a conscious look.

'Not the least in the world. Did he ever give you anything?'

'No—I cannot call them gifts; but they are things that I have valued very much.'

She held the parcel towards her, and Emma read the words *Most precious treasures* on the top. Her curiosity was greatly excited. Harriet unfolded the parcel, and she looked on with impatience.

Within abundance of silver paper was a pretty little Tunbridge-ware box, which Harriet opened: it was well lined with the softest cotton; but, excepting the cotton, Emma saw only a small piece of court-plaster.

'Now,' said Harriet, 'you *must* recollect.'

'No, indeed, I do not.'

'Dear me! I should not have thought it possible you could forget what passed in this very room about court-plaster, one of the very last times we ever met in it. It was but a very few days before I had my sore throat—just before Mr and Mrs John Knightley came; I think the very evening. Do not you remember his cutting his finger with your new penknife, and your recommending court-plaster? But, as you had none about you, and knew I had, you desired me to supply him; and so I took mine out and cut him a piece: but it was a great deal too large, and he cut it smaller, and kept playing some time with what was left, before he gave it back to me. And so then, in my nonsense, I could not help making a treasure of it; so I put it by, never to be used, and looked at it now and then as a great treat.'

'My dearest Harriet!' cried Emma, putting her hand before her face, and jumping up, 'you make me more ashamed of myself than I can bear. Remember it? Aye, I remember it all now; all, except your saving this relic: I knew nothing of that till this moment—but the cutting the finger, and my recommending court-plaster, and saying I had none about me. Oh! my sins! my sins!—And I had plenty all the while in my pocket! One of my senseless tricks. I deserve to be under a continual blush all the rest of my life. Well' (sitting down again), 'go on: what else?'

'And had you really some at hand yourself? I am sure I never suspected it, you did it so naturally.'

'And so you actually put this piece of court-plaster by for his sake!' said Emma, recovering from her state of shame and feeling divided between wonder and amusement; and secretly she added to herself, 'Lord bless me! when should I ever have thought of putting by in cotton a piece of court-plaster that Frank Churchill had been pulling about! I never was equal to this.'

'Here,' resumed Harriet, turning to her box again, 'here is something still more valuable—I mean that *has been* more valuable —because this is what did really once belong to him, which the court-plaster never did.'

Emma was quite eager to see this superior treasure. It was the end of an old pencil, the part without any lead.

'This was really his,' said Harriet. 'Do not you remember one morning?—no, I dare say you do not. But one morning—I forget exactly the day—but perhaps it was the Tuesday or Wednesday before *that evening*, he wanted to make a memorandum in his pocket-book; it was about spruce-beer. Mr Knightley had been telling him something about brewing spruce-beer, and he wanted to put it down; but when he took out his pencil, there was so little lead that he soon cut it all away, and it would not do, so you lent him another, and this was left upon the table as good for nothing. But I kept my eye on it; and, as soon as I dared, caught it up, and never parted with it again from that moment.'

'I do remember it,' cried Emma; 'I perfectly remember it. Talking about spruce-beer. Oh! yes. Mr Knightley and I both saying we liked it, and Mr Elton's seeming resolved to learn to like it too. I perfectly remember it. Stop—Mr Knightley was standing just here, was not he? I have an idea he was standing just here.'

'Ah! I do not know. I cannot recollect. It is very odd, but I cannot recollect. Mr Elton was sitting here, I remember, much about where I am now.'

'Well, go on.'

'Oh! that's all. I have nothing more to show you, or to say, except that I am now going to throw them both behind the fire, and I wish you to see me do it.'

'My poor dear Harriet! and have you actually found happiness in treasuring up these things?'

'Yes, simpleton as I was! but I am quite ashamed of it now, and wish I could forget as easily as I can burn them. It was very wrong of me, you know, to keep any remembrances after he was married. I knew it was—but had not resolution enough to part with them.'

'But, Harriet, is it necessary to burn the court-plaster? I have not a word to say for the bit of old pencil, but the court-plaster might be useful.'

'I shall be happier to burn it,' replied Harriet. 'It has a disagreeable look to me. I must get rid of everything. There it goes, and there is an end, thank Heaven! of Mr Elton.'

'And when,' thought Emma, 'will there be a beginning of Mr Churchill?'

She had soon afterwards reason to believe that the beginning was already made, and could not but hope that the gipsy, though she had *told* no fortune, might be proved to have made Harriet's.

About a fortnight after the alarm they came to a sufficient explanation, and quite undesignedly. Emma was not thinking of it at the moment, which made the information she received more valuable. She merely said in the course of some trivial chat, 'Well, Harriet, whenever you marry, I would advise you to do so and so '—and thought no more of it, till after a minute's silence she heard Harriet say, in a very serious tone, 'I shall never marry.'

Emma then looked up, and immediately saw how it was; and after a moment's debate, as to whether it should pass unnoticed or not, replied:

'Never marry! This is a new resolution.'

'It is one that I shall never change, however.'

After another short hesitation, 'I hope it does not proceed from—I hope it is not in compliment to Mr Elton? '

'Mr Elton, indeed!' cried Harriet indignantly. 'Oh! no '—and Emma could just catch the words, 'so superior to Mr Elton!'

She then took a longer time for consideration. Should she proceed no further? should she let it pass, and seem to suspect nothing? Perhaps Harriet might think her cold or angry if she did; or, perhaps, if she were totally silent, it might only drive Harriet into asking her to hear too much; and against anything like such an unreserve as had been, such an open and frequent discussion of hopes and chances, she was perfectly resolved. She believed it would be wiser for her to say and know at once all that she meant to say and know. Plain dealing was always best. She had previously determined how far she would proceed, on any application of the sort; and it would be safer for both to have the judicious law of her own brain laid down with speed. She was decided, and thus spoke:

'Harriet, I will not affect to be in doubt of your meaning. Your resolution, or rather your expectation of never marrying, results from an idea that the person whom you might prefer would be too greatly your superior in situation to think of you. Is not it so? '

'Oh, Miss Woodhouse, believe me, I have not the presumption to suppose—indeed I am not so mad. But it is a pleasure to me to admire him at a distance, and to think of his infinite superiority to all the rest of the world, with the gratitude, wonder, and veneration which are so proper, in me especially.'

'I am not at all surprised at you, Harriet. The service he rendered you was enough to warm your heart.'

'Service! oh, it was such an inexpressible obligation! The

very recollection of it, and all that I felt at the time, when I saw him coming—his noble look, and my wretchedness before. Such a change! In one moment such a change! From perfect misery to perfect happiness!'

'It is very natural. It is natural, and it is honourable. Yes, honourable, I think, to choose so well and so gratefully. But that it will be a fortunate preference is more than I can promise. I do not advise you to give way to it, Harriet. I do not by any means engage for its being returned. Consider what you are about. Perhaps it will be wisest in you to check your feelings while you can: at any rate do not let them carry you far, unless you are persuaded of his liking you. Be observant of him. Let his behaviour be the guide of your sensations. I give you this caution now, because I shall never speak to you again on the subject. I am determined against all interference. Henceforward I know nothing of the matter. Let no name ever pass our lips. We were very wrong before; we will be cautious now. He is your superior, no doubt, and there do seem objections and obstacles of a very serious nature; but yet, Harriet, more wonderful things have taken place: there have been matches of greater disparity. But take care of yourself; I would not have you too sanguine; though, however it may end, be assured that your raising your thoughts to *him* is a mark of good taste which I shall always know how to value.'

Harriet kissed her hand in silent and submissive gratitude. Emma was very decided in thinking such an attachment no bad thing for her friend. Its tendency would be to raise and refine her mind—and it must be saving her from the danger of degradation.

41

IN this state of schemes and hopes, and connivance, June opened upon Hartfield. To Highbury, in general, it brought no material change. The Eltons were still talking of a visit from the Sucklings, and of the use to be made of their barouche-landau, and Jane Fairfax was still at her grandmother's; and as the return of the Campbells from Ireland was again delayed, and August, instead of Midsummer, fixed for it, she was likely to remain there full two months longer, provided at least she were able to defeat Mrs Elton's activity in her service, and save herself from being hurried into a delightful situation against her will.

Mr Knightley, who, for some reason best known to himself, had certainly taken in early dislike to Frank Churchill, was only growing to dislike him more. He began to suspect him of some double dealing in his pursuit of Emma. That Emma was his object appeared indisputable. Everything declared it; his own attentions, his father's hints, his mother-in-law's guarded silence; it was all in unison; words, conduct, discretion and indiscretion, told the same story. But while so many were devoting him to Emma, and Emma herself making him over to Harriet, Mr Knightley began to suspect him of some inclination to trifle with Jane Fairfax. He could not understand it; but there were symptoms of intelligence between them—he thought so at least —symptoms of admiration on his side, which, having once observed, he could not persuade himself to think entirely void of meaning, however he might wish to escape any of Emma's errors of imagination. *She* was not present when the suspicion first arose. He was dining with the Randalls family and Jane at the Eltons'; and he had seen a look, more than a single look, at Miss Fairfax, which, from the admirer of Miss Woodhouse, seemed somewhat out of place. When he was again in their company, he could not help remembering what he had seen; nor could he avoid observations which, unless it were like Cowper and his fire at twilight,

Myself creating what I saw,

brought him yet stronger suspicion of there being a something of private liking, of private understanding even, between Frank Churchill and Jane.

He had walked up one day after dinner, as he very often did, to spend his evening at Hartfield. Emma and Harriet were going to walk; he joined them; and, on returning, they fell in with a larger party, who, like themselves, judged it wisest to take their exercise early, as the weather threatened rain; Mr and Mrs Weston and their son, Miss Bates and her niece, who had accidentally met. They all united; and, on reaching Hartfield gates, Emma, who knew it was exactly the sort of visiting that would be welcome to her father, pressed them all to go in and drink tea with him. The Randalls party agreed to it immediately; and after a pretty long speech from Miss Bates, which few persons listened to, she also found it possible to accept dear Miss Woodhouse's most obliging invitation.

As they were turning into the grounds, Mr Perry passed by on horseback. The gentlemen spoke of his horse.

'By the bye,' said Frank Churchill to Mrs Weston presently, 'what became of Mr Perry's plan of setting up his carriage?'

Mrs Weston looked surprised, and said, 'I did not know that he ever had any such plan.'

'Nay, I had it from you. You wrote me word of it three months ago.'

'Me! impossible!'

'Indeed you did. I remember it perfectly. You mentioned it as what was certainly to be very soon. Mrs Perry had told somebody and was extremely happy about it. It was owing to *her* persuasion, as she thought his being out in bad weather did him a great deal of harm. You must remember it now?'

'Upon my word, I never heard of it till this moment.'

'Never! really never! Bless me! how could it be? Then I must have dreamt it—but I was completely persuaded—Miss Smith, you walk as if you were tired. You will not be sorry to find yourself at home.'

'What is this? What is this?' cried Mr Weston, 'about Perry and a carriage? Is Perry going to set up his carriage, Frank? I am glad he can afford it. You had it from himself, had you?'

'No, sir,' replied his son, laughing. 'I seem to have had it from nobody. Very odd! I really was persuaded of Mrs Weston's having mentioned it in one of her letters to Enscombe, many weeks ago, with all these particulars; but as she declares she never heard a syllable of it before, of course it must have been a dream. I am a great dreamer. I dream of everybody at Highbury, when I am away; and when I have gone through my particular friends, then I begin dreaming of Mr and Mrs Perry.'

'It is odd, though,' observed his father, 'that you should have had such a regular connected dream about people whom it was not very likely you should be thinking of at Enscombe. Perry's setting up his carriage! and his wife's persuading him to it, out of care for his health—just what will happen, I have no doubt, some time or other; only a little premature. What an air of probability sometimes runs through a dream! And at others, what a heap of absurdities it is! Well, Frank, your dream certainly shows that Highbury is in your thoughts when you are absent. Emma, you are a great dreamer, I think?'

Emma was out of hearing. She had hurried on before her guests to prepare her father for their appearance, and was beyond the reach of Mr Weston's hint.

'Why, to own the truth,' cried Miss Bates, who had been trying in vain to be heard the last two minutes, 'if I must speak on this subject, there is no denying that Mr Frank Churchill might have—I do not mean to say that he did not dream it—I am sure I have sometimes the oddest dreams in the world—but if I am questioned about it, I must acknowledge that there was such an idea last spring; for Mrs Perry herself mentioned it to my mother, and the Coles knew of it as well as ourselves—but it was quite a secret, known to nobody else, and only thought of about three days. Mrs Perry was very anxious that he should have a carriage, and came to my mother in great spirits one morning because she thought she had prevailed. Jane, don't you remember grandmamma's telling us of it when we got home? I forget where we had been walking to—very likely to Randalls; yes, I think it was to Randalls. Mrs Perry was always particularly fond of my mother—indeed I do not know who is not—and she had mentioned it to her in confidence; she had no objection to her telling us, of course, but it was not to go beyond; and from that day to this I never mentioned it to a soul that I know of. At the same time, I will not positively answer for my having never dropt a hint, because I know I do sometimes pop out a thing before I am aware. I am a talker, you know; I am rather a talker; and now and then I have let a thing escape me which I should not. I am not like Jane; I wish I were. I will answer for it *she* never betrayed the least thing in the world. Where is she? Oh! just behind. Perfectly remember Mrs Perry's coming. Extraordinary dreams, indeed!'

They were entering the hall. Mr Knightley's eyes had preceded Miss Bates's in a glance at Jane. From Frank Churchill's face, where he thought he saw confusion suppressed or laughed away, he had involuntarily turned to hers; but she was indeed behind, and too busy with her shawl. Mr Weston had walked in. The two other gentlemen waited at the door to let her pass. Mr Knightley suspected in Frank Churchill the determination of catching her eye—he seemed watching her intently—in vain, however, if it were so. Jane passed between them into the hall, and looked at neither.

There was no time for further remark or explanation. The dream must be borne with, and Mr Knightley must take his seat with the rest round the large modern circular table which Emma had introduced at Hartfield, and which none but Emma could have had power to place there and persuade her father to use, instead of the small-sized Pembroke, on which two of his daily meals had for forty years been crowded. Tea passed pleasantly, and nobody seemed in a hurry to move.

'Miss Woodhouse,' said Frank Churchill, after examining a table behind him, which he could reach as he sat, 'have your nephews taken away their alphabets—their box of letters? It used to stand here. Where is it? This is a sort of dull-looking evening, that ought to be treated rather as winter than summer. We had great amusement with those letters one morning. I want to puzzle you again.'

Emma was pleased with the thought; and producing the box, the table was quickly scattered over with alphabets, which no one seemed so much disposed to employ as their two selves. They were rapidly forming words for each other, or for anybody else who would be puzzled. The quietness of the game made it particularly eligible for Mr Woodhouse, who had often been distressed by the more animated sort, which Mr Weston had occasionally introduced, and who now sat happily occupied in lamenting, with tender melancholy, over the departure of the 'poor little boys,' or in fondly pointing out, as he took up any stray letter near him, how beautifully Emma had written it.

Frank Churchill placed a word before Miss Fairfax. She gave a slight glance round the table, and applied herself to it. Frank was next to Emma, Jane opposite to them; and Mr Knightley so placed as to see them all; and it was his object to see as much as he could, with as little apparent observation. The word was discovered, and with a faint smile pushed away. If meant to be immediately mixed with the others, and buried from sight, she should have looked on the table instead of looking just across, for it was not mixed; and Harriet, eager after every fresh word, and finding out none, directly took it up, and fell to work. She was sitting by Mr Knightley, and turned to him for help. The word was *blunder*; and as Harriet exultingly proclaimed it, there was a blush on Jane's cheek which gave it a meaning not otherwise ostensible. Mr Knightley connected it with the dream; but how it could all be, was beyond his comprehension. How the delicacy, the discretion of his favourite could have been so lain asleep! He feared there must be some decided involvement. Disingenuousness and double dealing seemed to meet him at every turn. These letters were but the vehicle for gallantry and trick. It was a child's play, chosen to conceal a deeper game on Frank Churchill's part.

With great indignation did he continue to observe him; with great alarm and distrust, to observe also his two blinded companions. He saw a short word prepared for Emma, and given to her with a look sly and demure. He saw that Emma had soon made it out, and found it highly entertaining, though it was something which she judged it proper to appear to censure; for she said, ' Nonsense! for shame!' He heard Frank Churchill next say, with a glance towards Jane, ' I will give it to her— shall I?' and as clearly heard Emma opposing it with eager laughing warmth, ' No, no, you must not, you shall not, indeed.'

It was done, however. This gallant young man, who seemed to love without feeling, and to recommend himself without complaisance, directly handed over the word to Miss Fairfax, and with a particular degree of sedate civility entreated her to study it. Mr Knightley's excessive curiosity to know what this word might be, made him seize every possible moment for darting his eye towards it, and it was not long before he saw it to be *Dixon*. Jane Fairfax's perception seemed to accompany his; her comprehension was certainly more equal to the covert meaning, the superior intelligence, of those five letters so arranged. She was evidently displeased; looked up, and, seeing herself watched, blushed more deeply than he had ever perceived her, and saying only, ' I did not know that proper names were allowed,' pushed away the letters with even an angry spirit, and looked resolved to be engaged by no other word that could be offered. Her face was averted from those who had made the attack, and turned towards her aunt.

' Aye, very true, my dear,' cried the latter, though Jane had not spoken a word: ' I was just going to say the same thing. It is time for us to be going, indeed. The evening is closing in, and grandmamma will be looking for us. My dear sir, you are too obliging. We really must wish you good night.'

Jane's alertness in moving proved her as ready as her aunt had preconceived. She was immediately up, and wanting to quit the table; but so many were also moving that she could not get away; and Mr Knightley thought he saw another collection of letters anxiously pushed towards her, and resolutey swept away by her unexamined. She was afterwards looking for her shawl— Frank Churchill was looking also: it was growing dusk, and the room was in confusion; and how they parted Mr Knightley could not tell.

He remained at Hartfield after all the rest, his thoughts full of what he had seen; so full, that when the candles came to assist his observations, he must—yes, he certainly must, as a friend—an anxious friend—give Emma some hint, ask her some

question. He could not see her in a situation of such danger
without trying to preserve her. It was his duty.

'Pray, Emma,' said he, 'may I ask in what lay the great
amusement, the poignant sting of the last word given to you
and Miss Fairfax? I saw the word, and am curious to know how
it could be so very entertaining to the one, and so very distressing
to the other.'

Emma was extremely confused. She could not endure to give
him the true explanation; for, though her suspicions were by
no means removed, she was really ashamed of having ever imparted them.

'Oh!' she cried, in evident embarrassment, 'it all meant
nothing, a mere joke among ourselves.'

'The joke,' he replied gravely, 'seemed confined to you and
Mr Churchill.'

He had hoped she would speak again, but she did not. She
would rather busy herself about anything than speak. He sat
a little while in doubt. A variety of evils crossed his mind. Interference—fruitless interference. Emma's confusion, and the
acknowledged intimacy, seemed to declare her affection engaged.
Yet he would speak. He owed it to her, to risk anything that
might be involved in an unwelcome interference, rather than her
welfare; to encounter anything, rather than the remembrance
of neglect in such a cause.

'My dear Emma,' said he at last, with earnest kindness, 'do
you think you perfectly understand the degree of acquaintance
between the gentleman and lady we have been speaking of?'

'Between Mr Frank Churchill and Miss Fairfax? Oh! yes,
perfectly. Why do you make a doubt of it?'

'Have you never at any time had reason to think that he admired her, or that she admired him?'

'Never, never!' she cried with a most open eagerness. 'Never,
for the twentieth part of a moment, did such an idea occur to
me. And how could it possibly come into your head?'

'I have lately imagined that I saw symptoms of attachment
between them; certain expressive looks, which I did not believe
meant to be public.'

'Oh! you amuse me excessively. I am delighted to find that
you can vouchsafe to let your imagination wander; but it will
not do—very sorry to check you in your first essay, but indeed
it will not do. There is no admiration between them, I do assure
you: and the appearances which have caught you, have arisen
from some peculiar circumstances; feelings rather of a totally

different nature; it is impossible exactly to explain—there is a good deal of nonsense in it—but the part which is capable of being communicated, which is sense, is, that they are as far from any attachment or admiration for one another as any two beings in the world can be. That is, I *presume* it to be so on her side, and I can *answer* for its being so on his. I will answer for the gentleman's indifference.'

She spoke with a confidence which staggered, with a satisfaction which silenced Mr Knightley. She was in gay spirits, and would have prolonged the conversation, wanting to hear the particulars of his suspicions, every look described, and all the wheres and hows of a circumstance which highly entertained her; but his gaiety did not meet hers. He found he could not be useful, and his feelings were too much irritated for talking. That he might not be irritated into an absolute fever by the fire which Mr Woodhouse's tender habits required almost every evening throughout the year, he soon afterwards took a hasty leave, and walked home to the coolness and solitude of Donwell Abbey.

42

AFTER being long fed with hopes of a speedy visit from Mr and Mrs Suckling, the Highbury world were obliged to endure the mortification of hearing that they could not possibly come till the autumn. No such importation of novelties could enrich their intellectual stores at present. In the daily interchange of news, they must be again restricted to the other topics, with which for a while the Sucklings' coming had been united, such as the last accounts of Mrs Churchill, whose health seemed every day to supply a different report, and the situation of Mrs Weston, whose happiness, it was to be hoped, might eventually be as much increased by the arrival of a child, as that of all her neighbours was by the approach of it.

Mrs Elton was very much disappointed. It was the delay of a great deal of pleasure and parade. Her introductions and recommendations must all wait, and every projected party be still only talked of. So she thought at first; but a little consideration convinced her that everything need not be put off. Why should not they explore to Box Hill though the Sucklings did not come? They could go there again with them in the autumn. It was settled that they should go to Box Hill. That there was to be such a party had been long generally known; it had even given the idea of another. Emma had never been to Box Hill; she wished to see what everybody found so well worth seeing, and she and Mr Weston had agreed to choose some fine morning and drive thither. Two or three more of the chosen only were to be admitted to join them, and it was to be done in a quiet, unpretending, elegant way, infinitely superior to the bustle and preparation, the regular eating and drinking, and picnic parade of the Eltons and the Sucklings.

This was so very well understood between them that Emma could not but feel some surprise, and a little displeasure, on hearing from Mr Weston that he had been proposing to Mrs Elton, as her brother and sister had failed her, that the two parties should unite, and go together; and that as Mrs Elton had very readily acceded to it, so it was to be, if she had no objection. Now, as her objection was nothing, but her very great dislike of Mrs Elton, of which Mr Weston must already be perfectly aware, it was not worth bringing forward again: it could not be done without a reproof to him, which would be giving pain to his wife; and she found herself, therefore, obliged to consent to an arrangement which she would have done a great deal to avoid; an arrangement which would, probably, expose her even to the degradation of being said to be of Mrs Elton's party! Every feeling was offended; and the forbearance of her outward submission left a heavy arrear due of secret severity in her reflections, on the unmanageable goodwill of Mr Weston's temper.

'I am glad you approve of what I have done,' said he, very comfortably. 'But I thought you would. Such schemes as these are nothing without numbers. One cannot have too large a party. A large party secures its own amusement. And she is a good-natured woman after all. One could not leave her out.'

Emma denied none of it aloud, and agreed to none of it in private.

It was now the middle of June and the weather fine; and Mrs Elton was growing impatient to name the day, and settle with Mr Weston as to pigeon-pies and cold lamb, when a lame carriage-horse threw everything into sad uncertainty. It might be weeks, it might be only a few days, before the horse were usable; but no preparations could be ventured on, and it was all melancholy stagnation. Mrs Elton's resources were inadequate to such an attack.

'Is not this most vexatious, Knightley?' she cried; 'and such weather for exploring! these delays and disappointments are quite odious. What are we to do? The year will wear away at this rate, and nothing done. Before this time last year, I assure you, we had had a delightful exploring party from Maple Grove to Kings Weston.'

'You had better explore to Donwell,' replied Mr Knightley. ' That may be done without horses. Come and eat my strawberries; they are ripening fast.'

If Mr Knightley did not begin seriously, he was obliged to proceed so; for his proposal was caught at with delight; and the ' Oh! I should like it of all things,' was not plainer in words than manner. Donwell was famous for its strawberry-beds, which seemed a plea for the invitation; but no plea was necessary; cabbage-beds would have been enough to tempt the lady, who only wanted to be going somewhere. She promised him again and again to come—much oftener than he doubted—and was extremely gratified by such a proof of intimacy, such a distinguishing compliment as she chose to consider it.

'You may depend upon me,' said she; ' I certainly will come. Name your day, and I will come. You will allow me to bring Jane Fairfax?'

'I cannot name a day,' said he, ' till I have spoken to some others, whom I would wish to meet you.'

'Oh, leave all that to me; only give me a *carte blanche*. I am Lady Patroness, you know. It is my party. I will bring friends with me.'

'I hope you will bring Elton,' said he; ' but I will not trouble you to give any other invitations.'

'Oh, now you are looking very sly; but consider—you need not be afraid of delegating power to *me*. I am no young lady on her preferment. Married women, you know, may be safely authorised. It is my party. Leave it all to me. I will invite your guests.'

'No,' he calmly replied, ' there is but one married woman in the world whom I can ever allow to invite what guests she pleases to Donwell, and that one is——'

'Mrs Weston, I suppose,' interrupted Mrs Elton, rather mortified.

'No—Mrs Knightley; and till she is in being, I will manage such matters myself.'

'Ah, you are an odd creature!' she cried, satisfied to have no one preferred to herself. ' You are a humorist, and may say what you like. Quite a humorist. Well, I shall bring Jane with me—Jane and her aunt. The rest I leave to you. I have no objections at all to meeting the Hartfield family. Don't scruple, I know you are attached to them.'

'You certainly will meet them, if I can prevail; and I shall call on Miss Bates in my way home.'

'That's quite unnecessary; I see Jane every day; but as you like. It is to be a morning scheme, you know, Knightley; quite a simple thing. I shall wear a large bonnet, and bring one of my little baskets hanging on my arm. Here—probably this basket with pink ribbon. Nothing can be more simple, you see. And Jane will have such another. There is to be no form or parade—a sort of gipsy party. We are to walk about your gardens, and gather the strawberries ourselves, and sit under trees; and whatever else you may like to provide, it is to be all out of doors; a table spread in the shade, you know. Everything as natural and simple as possible. Is not that your idea?'

'Not quite. My idea of the simple and the natural will be to have the table spread in the dining-room. The nature and the simplicity of gentlemen and ladies, with their servants and furniture, I think is best observed by meals within doors. When you are tired of eating strawberries in the garden, there shall be cold meat in the house.'

'Well, as you please; only don't have a great set-out. And, by the bye, can I or my housekeeper be of any use to you with our opinion? Pray be sincere, Knightley. If you wish me to talk to Mrs Hodges, or to inspect anything——'

'I have not the least wish for it, I thank you.'

'Well—but if any difficulties should arise, my housekeeper is extremely clever.'

'I will answer for it that mine thinks herself full as clever, and would spurn anybody's assistance.'

'I wish we had a donkey. The thing would be for us all to come on donkeys, Jane, Miss Bates, and me, and my *caro sposo* walking by. I really must talk to him about purchasing a donkey. In a country life I conceive it to be a sort of necessity; for, let a woman have ever so many resources, it is not possible for her to be always shut up at home; and very long walks, you know—in summer there is dust, and in winter there is dirt.'

'You will not find either between Donwell and Highbury. Donwell Lane is never dusty, and now it is perfectly dry. Come on a donkey, however, if you prefer it. You can borrow Mrs Cole's. I would wish everything to be as much to your taste as possible.'

'That I am sure you would. Indeed, I do you justice, my good friend. Under that peculiar sort of dry, blunt manner, I know you have the warmest heart. As I tell Mr E., you are a thorough humorist. Yes, believe me, Knightley, I am fully sensible of your attention to me in the whole of this scheme. You have hit upon the very thing to please me.'

Mr Knightley had another reason for avoiding a table in the shade. He wished to persuade Mr Woodhouse, as well as Emma, to join the party; and he knew that to have any of them sitting down out of doors to eat would inevitably make him ill. Mr Woodhouse must not, under the specious pretence of a morning drive, and an hour or two spent at Donwell, be tempted away to his misery.

He was invited on good faith. No lurking horrors were to upbraid him for his easy credulity. He did consent. He had not been at Donwell for two years. ' Some very fine morning, he, and Emma, and Harriet could go very well; and he could sit still with Mrs Weston while the dear girls walked about the gardens. He did not suppose they could be damp now, in the middle of the day. He should like to see the old house again exceedingly, and should be very happy to meet Mr and Mrs Elton, and any other of his neighbours. He could not see any objection at all to his, and Emma's, and Harriet's going there some very fine morning. He thought it very well done of Mr Knightley to invite them; very kind and sensible; much cleverer than dining out. He was not fond of dining out.'

Mr Knightley was fortunate in everybody's most ready concurrence. The invitation was everywhere so well received, that it seemed as if, like Mrs Elton, they were all taking the scheme as a particular compliment to themselves. Emma and Harriet professed very high expectations of pleasure from it; and Mr Weston, unasked, promised to get Frank over to join them, if possible; a proof of approbation and gratitude which could have been dispensed with. Mr Knightley was then obliged to say that he should be glad to see him; and Mr Weston engaged to lose no time in writing, and spare no arguments to induce him to come.

In the meanwhile the lame horse recovered so fast that the party to Box Hill was again under happy consideration; and at last Donwell was settled for one day; and Box Hill for the next, the weather appearing exactly right.

Under a bright mid-day sun, at almost Midsummer, Mr Woodhouse was safely conveyed in his carriage, with one window down, to partake of this al fresco party; and in one of the most comfortable rooms in the Abbey, especially prepared for him by a fire all the morning, he was happily placed, quite at his ease, ready to talk with pleasure of what had been achieved, and advise everybody to come and sit down, and not to heat themselves. Mrs Weston, who seemed to have walked there on purpose to be tired, and sit all the time with him, remained, when all the others were invited or persuaded out, his patient listener and sympathiser.

It was so long since Emma had been at the Abbey, that as soon as she was satisfied of her father's comfort, she was glad to leave him and look around her; eager to refresh and correct her memory with more particular observation, more exact understanding of a house and grounds which must ever be so interesting to her and all her family.

She felt all the honest pride and complacency which her alliance with the present and future proprietor could fairly warrant, as she viewed the respectable size and style of the building, its suitable, becoming, characteristic situation, low and sheltered; its ample gardens stretching down to meadows washed by a stream, of which the Abbey, with all the old neglect of prospect, had scarcely a sight—and its abundance of timber in rows and avenues, which neither fashion nor extravagance had rooted up. The house was larger than Hartfield, and totally unlike it, covering a good deal of ground, rambling and irregular, with many comfortable, and one or two handsome rooms. It was just what it ought to be, and it looked what it was; and Emma felt an increasing respect for it, as the residence of a family of such true gentility, untainted in blood and understanding. Some faults of temper John Knightley had; but Isabella had connected herself unexceptionably. She had given them neither men, nor names, nor places, that could raise a blush. These were pleasant feelings, and she walked about and indulged them till it was necessary to do as the others did, and collect round the strawberry-beds. The whole party were assembled, excepting Frank Churchill, who was expected every moment from Richmond; and Mrs Elton, in all her apparatus of happiness, her large bonnet and her basket, was very ready to lead the way in gathering, accepting, or talking. Strawberries, and only strawberries, could now be thought or spoken of. ' The best fruit in England—everybody's favourite—always wholesome. These the finest beds and finest sorts. Delightful to gather for oneself—the only way of really enjoying them. Morning decidedly the best time—never tired—every sort good—hautboy infinitely superior—no comparison—the others hardly eatable—hautboys very scarce—Chili preferred—white wood finest flavour of all— price of strawberries in London—abundance about Bristol— Maple Grove—cultivation—beds when to be renewed—garden- ers thinking éxactly different—no general rule—gardeners never to be put out of their way—delicious fruit—only too rich to be eaten much of—inferior to cherries—currants more re- freshing—only objection to gathering strawberries the stooping —glaring sun—tired to death—could bear it no longer—must go and sit in the shade.'

Such, for half an hour, was the conversation; interrupted only once by Mrs Weston, who came out, in her solicitude after her son-in-law, to inquire if he were come; and she was a little uneasy. She had some fears of his horse.

Seats tolerably in the shade were found; and now Emma was obliged to overhear what Mrs Elton and Jane Fairfax were talking of. A situation, a most desirable situation, was in ques- tion. Mrs Elton had received notice of it that morning, and was in raptures. It was not with Mrs Suckling, it was not with Mrs Bragge, but in felicity and splendour it fell short only of them: it was with a cousin of Mrs Bragge, an acquaintance of Mrs Suckling, a lady known at Maple Grove. Delightful, charming, superior, first circles, spheres, lines, ranks, everything: and Mrs Elton was wild to have the offer closed with immediately. On her side, all was warmth, energy, and triumph; and she posi- tively refused to take her friend's negative, though Miss Fairfax continued to assure her that she would not at present engage in anything—repeating the same motives which she had been heard to urge before. Still Mrs Elton insisted on being authorised to write an acquiescence by the morrow's post. How Jane could bear it at all, was astonishing to Emma. She did look vexed, she did speak pointedly—and at last, with a decision of action unusual to her, proposed a removal. ' Should not they walk? Would not Mr Knightley show them the gardens—all the gardens? She wished to see the whole extent.' The pertinacity of her friend seemed more than she could bear.

It was hot; and after walking some time over the gardens in a scattered, dispersed way, scarcely any three together, they in- sensibly followed one another to the delicious shade of a broad short avenue of limes, which, stretching beyond the garden at an equal distance from the river, seemed the finish of the pleasure grounds. It led to nothing; nothing but a view at the end over a low stone wall with high pillars, which seemed intended, in their erection, to give the appearance of an approach to the house, which never had been there. Disputable, however, as might be the taste of such a termination, it was in itself a charming walk and the view which closed it extremely pretty. The considerable slope, at nearly the foot of which the Abbey stood, gradually acquired a steeper form beyond its grounds; and at half a mile distant was a bank of considerable abruptness and grandeur, well clothed with wood; and at the bottom of this bank, favourably placed and sheltered, rose the Abbey Mill Farm, with meadows in front, and the river making a close and handsome curve around it.

It was a sweet view—sweet to the eye and the mind. English verdure, English culture, English comfort, seen under a sun bright, without being oppressive.

In this walk Emma and Mr Weston found all the others assembled; and towards this view she immediately perceived Mr Knightley and Harriet distinct from the rest, quietly leading the way. Mr Knightley and Harriet! It was an odd *tête-à-tête*; but she was glad to see it. There had been a time when he would have scorned her as a companion, and turned from her with little ceremony. Now they seemed in pleasant conversation. There had been a time also when Emma would have been sorry to see Harriet in a spot so favourable for the Abbey Mill Farm; but now she feared it not. It might be safely viewed, with all its appendages of prosperity and beauty, its rich pastures, spreading flocks, orchard in blossom, and light column of smoke ascending. She joined them at the wall, and found them more engaged in talking than in looking around. He was giving Harriet information as to modes of agriculture, etc.; and Emma received a smile which seemed to say: 'These are my own concerns. I have a right to talk on such subjects, without being suspected of introducing Robert Martin.' She did not suspect him. It was too old a story. Robert Martin had probably ceased to think of Harriet. They took a few turns together along the walk. The shade was most refreshing, and Emma found it the pleasantest part of the day.

The next remove was to the house; they must all go in and eat; and they were all seated and busy, and still Frank Churchill did not come. Mrs Weston looked, and looked in vain. His father would not own himself uneasy, and laughed at her fears; but she could not be cured of wishing that he would part with his black mare. He had expressed himself as to coming with more than common certainty. 'His aunt was so much better, that he had not a doubt of getting over to them.' Mrs Churchill's state, however, as many were ready to remind her, was liable to such sudden variation as might disappoint her nephew in the most reasonable dependence; and Mrs Weston was at last persuaded to believe, or to say, that it must be by some attack of Mrs Churchill that he was prevented coming. Emma looked at Harriet while the point was under consideration; she behaved very well, and betrayed no emotion.

The cold repast was over, and the party were to go out once more to see what had not yet been seen, the old Abbey fish-ponds; perhaps get as far as the clover, which was to be begun cutting on the morrow, or, at any rate, have the pleasure of being hot, and growing cool again. Mr Woodhouse, who had already taken his little round in the highest part of the gardens, where no damps from the river were imagined even by him, stirred no more; and his daughter resolved to remain with him, that Mrs Weston might be persuaded away by her husband to the exercise and variety which her spirits seemed to need.

Mr Knightley had done all in his power for Mr Woodhouse's entertainment. Books of engravings, drawers of medals, cameos, corals, shells, and every other family collection within his cabinets, had been prepared for his old friend, to while away the morning; and the kindness had perfectly answered. Mr Woodhouse had been exceedingly well amused. Mrs Weston had been showing them all to him, and now he would show them all to Emma; fortunate in having no other resemblance to a child, than in a total want of taste for what he saw, for he was slow, constant, and methodical. Before this second looking over was begun, however, Emma walked into the hall for the sake of a few moments' free observation of the entrance and ground-plot of the house, and was hardly there when Jane Fairfax appeared, coming quickly in from the garden, and with a look of escape. Little expecting to meet Miss Woodhouse so soon, there was a start at first; but Miss Woodhouse was the very person she was in quest of.

'Will you be so kind,' said she, 'when I am missed, as to say that I am gone home? I am going this moment. My aunt is not aware how late it is, nor how long we have been absent; but I am sure we shall be wanted, and I am determined to go directly. I have said nothing about it to anybody. It would only be giving trouble and distress. Some are gone to the ponds, and some to the lime-walk. Till they all come in I shall not be missed; and when they do, will you have the goodness to say that I am gone?'

'Certainly, if you wish it; but you are not going to walk to Highbury alone?'

'Yes; what should hurt me? I walk fast. I shall be at home in twenty minutes.'

'But it is too far, indeed it is, to be walking quite alone. Let my father's servant go with you. Let me order the carriage. It can be round in five minutes.'

'Thank you, thank you—but on no account—I would rather walk. And for *me* to be afraid of walking alone! I, who may so soon have to guard others!'

She spoke with great agitation; and Emma very feelingly replied: 'That can be no reason for your being exposed to danger now. I must order the carriage. The heat even would be danger. You are fatigued-already.'

'I am,' she answered, 'I am fatigued; but it is not the sort of fatigue—quick walking will refresh me. Miss Woodhouse, we all know at times what it is to be wearied in spirits. Mine, I confess, are exhausted. The greatest kindness you can show me will be to let me have my own way, and only say that I am gone when it is necessary.'

Emma had not another word to oppose. She saw it all; and entering into her feelings, promoted her quitting the house immediately, and watched her safely off with the zeal of a friend. Her parting look was grateful; and her parting words, 'Oh! Miss Woodhouse, the comfort of being sometimes alone!' seemed to burst from an overcharged heart, and to describe somewhat of the continual endurance to be practised by her, even towards some of those who loved her best.

'Such a home, indeed! such an aunt!' said Emma, as she turned back into the hall again. 'I do pity you. And the more sensibility you betray of their just horrors, the more I shall like you.'

Jane had not been gone a quarter of an hour, and they had only accomplished some views of St Mark's Place, Venice, when Frank Churchill entered the room. Emma had not been thinking of him; she had forgotten to think of him, but she was very glad to see him. Mrs Weston would be at ease. The black mare was blameless; *they* were right who had named Mrs Churchill as the cause. He had been detained by a temporary increase of illness in her—a nervous seizure which had lasted some hours; and he had quite given up every thought of coming till very late; and had he known how hot a ride he should have, and how late, with all his hurry, he must be, he believed he should not have come at all. The heat was excessive; he had never suffered anything like it—almost wished he had stayed at home—nothing killed him like heat—he could bear any degree of cold, etc., but heat was intolerable; and he sat down, at the greatest possible distance from the slight remains of Mr Woodhouse's fire, looking very deplorable.

'You will soon be cooler, if you sit still,' said Emma.

'As soon as I am cooler I shall go back again. I could very ill be spared; but such a point had been made of my coming! You will all be going soon, I suppose; the whole party breaking up. I met *one* as I came—madness in such weather!—absolute madness!'

Emma listened, and looked, and soon perceived that Frank Churchill's state might best be defined by the expressive phrase of being out of humour. Some people were always cross when they were hot. Such might be his constitution; and as she knew that eating and drinking were often the cure of such incidental complaints, she recommended his taking some refreshment; he would find abundance of everything in the dining-room; and she humanely pointed out the door.

'No; he should not eat. He was not hungry; it would only make him hotter.' In two minutes, however, he relented in his own favour; and muttering something about spruce-beer, walked off. Emma returned all her attention to her father, saying in secret—

'I am glad I have done being in love with him. I should not like a man who is so soon discomposed by a hot morning. Harriet's sweet easy temper will not mind it.'

He was gone long enough to have had a very comfortable meal, and came back all the better—grown quite cool, and with good manners, like himself, able to draw a chair close to them, take an interest in their employment, and regret, in a reasonable way, that he should be so late. He was not in his best spirits, but seemed trying to improve them; and, at last, made himself talk nonsense very agreeably. They were looking over views in Switzerland.

'As soon as my aunt gets well I shall go abroad,' said he. 'I shall never be easy till I have seen some of these places. You will have my sketches, some time or other, to look at—or my tour to read—or my poem. I shall do something to expose myself.'

'That may be—but not by sketches in Switzerland. You will never go to Switzerland. Your uncle and aunt will never allow you to leave England.'

'They may be induced to go too. A warm climate may be

prescribed for her. I have more than half an expectation of our all going abroad. I assure you, I have. I feel a strong persuasion, this morning, that I shall soon be abroad. I ought to travel. I am tired of doing nothing. I want a change. I am serious, Miss Woodhouse, whatever your penetrating eyes may fancy—I am sick of England, and would leave it to-morrow if I could.'

' You are sick of prosperity and indulgence! Cannot you invent a few hardships for yourself, and be contented to stay? '

' *I* sick of prosperity and indulgence! You are quite mistaken. I do not look upon myself as either prosperous or indulged. I am thwarted in everything material. I do not consider myself at all a fortunate person.'

' You are not quite so miserable, though, as when you first came. Go and eat and drink a little more, and you will do very well. Another slice of cold meat, another draught of Madeira and water, will make you nearly on a par with the rest of us.'

' No—I shall not stir. I shall sit by you. You are my best cure.'

' We are going to Box Hill to-morrow: you will join us. It is not Switzerland, but it will be something for a young man so much in want of a change. You will stay and go with us? '

' No, certainly not; I shall go home in the cool of the evening.'

' But you may come again in the cool of to-morrow morning.'

' No—it will not be worth while. If I come, I shall be cross.'

' Then pray stay at Richmond.'

' But if I do, I shall be crosser still. I can never bear to think of you all there without me.'

' These are difficulties which you must settle for yourself. Choose your own degree of crossness. I shall press you no more.'

The rest of the party were now returning, and all were soon collected. With some there was great joy at the sight of Frank Churchill; others took it very composedly; but there was a very general distress and disturbance on Miss Fairfax's disappearance being explained. That it was time for everybody to go concluded the subject; and with a short final arrangement for the next day's scheme, they parted. Frank Churchill's little inclination to exclude himself increased so much, that his last words to Emma were—

' Well; if *you* wish me to stay and join the party, I will.'

She smiled her acceptance; and nothing less than a summons from Richmond was to take him back before the following evening.

43

THEY had a very fine day for Box Hill; and all the other outward circumstances of arrangement, accommodation, and punctuality, were in favour of a pleasant party. Mr Weston directed the whole, officiating safely between Hartfield and the Vicarage, and everybody was in good time. Emma and Harriet went together; Miss Bates and her niece with the Eltons; the gentlemen on horseback. Mrs Weston remained with Mr Woodhouse. Nothing was wanting but to be happy when they got there. Seven miles were travelled in expectation of enjoyment, and everybody had a burst of admiration on first arriving; but in the general amount of the day there was deficiency. There was a languor, a want of spirits, a want of union, which could not be got over. They separated too much into parties. The Eltons walked together; Mr Knightley took charge of Miss Bates and Jane; and Emma and Harriet belonged to Frank Churchill. And Mr Weston tried, in vain, to make them harmonise better. It seemed at first an accidental division, but it never materially varied. Mr and Mrs Elton, indeed, showed no unwillingness to mix, and to be as agreeable as they could; but during the two whole hours that were spent on the hill, there seemed a principle of separation between the other parties, too strong for any fine prospects, or any cold collation, or any cheerful Mr Weston, to remove.

At first it was downright dullness to Emma. She had never seen Frank Churchill so silent and stupid. He said nothing worth hearing—looked without seeing—admired without intelligence—listened without knowing what she said. While he was so dull, it was no wonder that Harriet should be dull likewise; and they were both insufferable.

When they all sat down it was better—to her taste a great deal better—for Mr Frank Churchill grew talkative and gay, making her his first object. Every distinguishing attention that could be paid, was paid to her. To amuse her, and be agreeable in her eyes, seemed all that he cared for—and Emma, glad to be enlivened, not sorry to be flattered, was gay and easy too, and gave him all the friendly encouragement, the admission to be gallant, which she had ever given in the first and most animating period of their acquaintance: but which now, in her own estimation, meant nothing, though in the judgment of most people looking on, it must have had such an appearance as no

English word but flirtation could very well describe. ' Mr Frank Churchill and Miss Woodhouse flirted together excessively.' They were laying themselves open to that very phrase—and to having it sent off in a letter to Maple Grove by one lady, to Ireland by another. Not that Emma was gay and thoughtless from any real felicity; it was rather because she felt less happy than she had expected. She laughed because she was disappointed; and though she liked him for his attentions, and thought them all, whether in friendship, admiration, or playfulness, extremely judicious, they were not winning back her heart. She still intended him for her friend.

' How much I am obliged to you,' said he, ' for telling me to come to-day! If it had not been for you, I should certainly have lost all the happiness of this party. I had quite determined to go away again.'

' Yes, you were very cross; and I do not know what about, except that you were too late for the best strawberries. I was a kinder friend than you deserved. But you were humble. You begged hard to be commanded to come.'

' Don't say I was cross. I was fatigued. The heat overcame me.'

' It is hotter to-day.'

' Not to my feelings. I am perfectly comfortable to-day.'

' You are comfortable because you are under command.'

' Your command? Yes.'

' Perhaps I intended you to say so, but I meant self-command. You had, somehow or other, broken bounds yesterday, and run away from your own management; but to-day you are got back again—and as I cannot be always with you, it is best to believe your temper under your own command rather than mine.'

' It comes to the same thing. I can have no self-command without a motive. You order me, whether you speak or not. And you can be always with me. You are always with me.'

' Dating from three o'clock yesterday. My perpetual influence could not begin earlier, or you would not have been so much out of humour before.'

' Three o'clock yesterday! That is your date. I thought I had seen you first in February.'

' Your gallantry is really unanswerable. But ' (lowering her voice) ' nobody speaks except ourselves, and it is rather too much to be talking nonsense for the entertainment of seven silent people.'

' I say nothing of which I am ashamed,' replied he, with lively

impudence. ' I saw you first in February. Let everybody on the
Hill hear me if they can. Let my accents swell to Mickleham on
one side, and Dorking on the other. I saw you first in February.'
And then whispering: ' Our companions are excessively stupid.
What shall we do to rouse them? Any nonsense will serve.
They *shall* talk. Ladies and gentlemen, I am ordered by Miss
Woodhouse (who, wherever she is, presides) to say, that she
desires to know what you are all thinking of? '

Some laughed, and answered good-humouredly. Miss Bates
said a great deal; Mrs Elton swelled at the idea of Miss Woodhouse's presiding; Mr Knightley's answer was the most distinct.

' Is Miss Woodhouse sure that she would like to hear what
we are all thinking of? '

' Oh, no, no! ' cried Emma, laughing as carelessly as she
could—' upon no account in the world. It is the very last thing
I would stand the brunt of just now. Let me hear anything rather
than what you are all thinking of. I will not say quite all. There
are one or two perhaps ' (glancing at Mr Weston and Harriet),
' whose thoughts I might not be afraid of knowing.'

' It is a sort of thing,' cried Mrs Elton emphatically, ' which
I should not have thought myself privileged to inquire into.
Though, perhaps, as the *chaperon* of the party—*I* never was in any
circle—exploring parties—young ladies—married women—— '

Her mutterings were chiefly to her husband; and he mur-
mured, in reply—

' Very true, my love, very true. Exactly so, indeed—quite
unheard of—but some ladies say anything. Better pass it off
as a joke. Everybody knows what is due to *you*.'

' It will not do,' whispered Frank to Emma, ' they are most
of them affronted. I will attack them with more address. Ladies
and gentlemen, I am ordered by Miss Woodhouse to say,
that she waives her right of knowing exactly what you may all
be thinking of, and only requires something very entertaining
from each of you, in a general way. Here are seven of you, besides myself (who, she is pleased to say, am very entertaining
already), and she only demands from each of you, either one
thing very clever, be it prose or verse, original or repeated;
or two things moderately clever; or three things very dull indeed; and she engages to laugh heartily at them all.'

' Oh! very well,' exclaimed Miss Bates; ' then I need not
be uneasy. " Three things very dull indeed." That will just do
for me, you know. I shall be sure to say three dull things as
soon as ever I open my mouth, shan't I? ' (looking round with

the most good-humoured dependence on everybody's assent).
'Do you not all think I shall?'

Emma could not resist.

'Ah! ma'am, but there may be a difficulty. Pardon me, but you will be limited as to number—only three at once.'

Miss Bates, deceived by the mock ceremony of her manner, did not immediately catch her meaning; but when it burst on her, it could not anger, though a slight blush showed that it could pain her.

'Ah! well—to be sure. Yes, I see what she means' (turning to Mr Knightley) 'and I will try to hold my tongue. I must make myself very disagreeable, or she would not have said such a thing to an old friend.'

'I like your plan,' cried Mr Weston. 'Agreed, agreed. I will do my best. I am making a conundrum. How will a conundrum reckon?'

'Low, I am afraid, sir, very low,' answered his son; 'but we shall be indulgent, especially to any one who leads the way.'

'No, no,' said Emma, 'it will not reckon low. A conundrum of Mr Weston's shall clear him and his next neighbour. Come, sir, pray let me hear it.'

'I doubt its being very clever myself,' said Mr Weston. 'It is too much a matter of fact; but here it is: What two letters of the alphabet are there that express perfection?'

'What two letters—express perfection? I am sure I do not know.'

'Ah! you will never guess. You' (to Emma), 'I am certain, will never guess. I will tell you. M and A: Emma. Do you understand?'

Understanding and gratification came together. It might be a very indifferent piece of wit, but Emma found a great deal to laugh at and enjoy in it: and so did Frank and Harriet. It did not seem to touch the rest of the party equally; some looked very stupid about it, and Mr Knightley gravely said:

'This explains the sort of clever thing that is wanted, and Mr Weston has done very well for himself: but he must have knocked up everybody else. *Perfection* should not have come quite so soon.'

'Oh! for myself, I protest I must be excused,' said Mrs Elton. '*I* really cannot attempt—I am not at all fond of the sort of thing. I had an acrostic once sent to me upon my own name which I was not at all pleased with. I knew who it came from. An abominable puppy! You know who I mean' (nodding to her husband). 'These kind of things are very well at Christmas, when one is sitting round the fire; but quite out of place, in my opinion, when one is exploring about the country in summer. Miss Woodhouse must excuse me. I am not one of those who have witty things at everybody's service. I do not pretend to be a wit. I have a great deal of vivacity in my own way, but I really must be allowed to judge when to speak, and when to hold my tongue. Pass us, if you please, Mr Churchill. Pass Mr E., Knightley, Jane, and myself. We have nothing clever to say—not one of us.

'Yes, yes, pray pass *me*,' added her husband, with a sort of sneering consciousness; '*I* have nothing to say that can entertain Miss Woodhouse, or any other young lady. An old married man—quite good for nothing. Shall we walk, Augusta?'

'With all my heart. I am really tired of exploring so long on one spot. Come, Jane, take my other arm.'

Jane declined it, however, and the husband and wife walked off. 'Happy couple!' said Frank Churchill, as soon as they were out of hearing; 'how well they suit one another! Very lucky—marrying as they did, upon an acquaintance formed only in a public place! They only knew each other, I think, a few weeks in Bath! Peculiarly lucky! for as to any real knowledge of a person's disposition that Bath, or any public place, can give—it is all nothing; there can be no knowledge. It is only by seeing women in their own homes, among their own set, just as they always are, that you can form any just judgment. Short of that, it is all guess and luck—and will generally be ill luck. How many a man has committed himself on a short acquaintance, and rued it all the rest of his life!'

Miss Fairfax, who had seldom spoken before, except among her own confederates, spoke now.

'Such things do occur, undoubtedly.' She was stopped by a cough. Frank Churchill turned towards her to listen.

'You were speaking,' said he gravely. She recovered her voice.

'I was only going to observe, that though such unfortunate circumstances do sometimes occur both to men and women, I cannot imagine them to be very frequent. A hasty and imprudent attachment may arise—but there is generally time to recover from it afterwards. I would be understood to mean, that it can be only weak, irresolute characters (whose happiness must be always at the mercy of chance), who will suffer an unfortunate acquaintance to be an inconvenience, an oppression for ever.'

He made no answer; merely looked, and bowed in submission; and soon afterwards said, in a lively tone:

' Well, I have so little confidence in my own judgment, that whenever I marry, I hope somebody will choose my wife for me. Will you? ' (turning to Emma). ' Will you choose a wife for me? I am sure I should like anybody fixed on by you. You provide for the family, you know ' (with a smile at his father). ' Find somebody for me. I am in no hurry. Adopt her; educate her.'

' And make her like myself.'

' By all means, if you can.'

' Very well. I undertake the commission. You shall have a charming wife.'

' She must be very lively, and have hazel eyes. I care for nothing else. I shall go abroad for a couple of years—and when I return, I shall come to you for my wife. Remember.'

Emma was in no danger of forgetting. It was a commission to touch every favourite feeling. Would not Harriet be the very creature described? Hazel eyes excepted, two years more might make her all that he wished. He might even have Harriet in his thoughts at the moment; who could say? Referring the education to her seemed to imply it.

' Now, ma'am.' said Jane to her aunt, ' shall we join Mrs Elton? '

' If you please, my dear. With all my heart. I am quite ready. I was ready to have gone with her, but this will do just as well. We shall soon overtake her. There she is—no, that's somebody else. That's one of the ladies in the Irish car party, not at all like her. Well, I declare—— '

They walked off, followed in half a minute by Mr Knightley. Mr Weston, his son, Emma, and Harriet only remained; and the young man's spirits now rose to a pitch almost unpleasant. Even Emma grew tired at last of flattery and merriment, and wished herself rather walking quietly about with any of the others, or sitting almost alone, and quite unattended to, in tranquil observation of the beautiful views beneath her. The appearance of the servants looking out for them to give notice of the carriages was a joyful sight; and even the bustle of collecting and preparing to depart, and the solicitude of Mrs Elton to have *her* carriage first, were gladly endured, in the prospect of the quiet drive home which was to close the very questionable enjoyments of this day of pleasure. Such another scheme, composed of so many ill-assorted people, she hoped never to be betrayed into again.

While waiting for the carriage, she found Mr Knightley by her side. He looked around, as if to see that no one were near, and then said:

'Emma, I must once more speak to you as I have been used to do; a privilege rather endured than allowed, perhaps, but I must still use it. I cannot see you acting wrong, without a remonstrance. How could you be so unfeeling to Miss Bates? How could you be so insolent in your wit to a woman of her character, age, and situation? Emma, I had not thought it possible.'

Emma recollected, blushed, was sorry, but tried to laugh it off.

'Nay, how could I help saying what I did? Nobody could have helped it. It was not so very bad. I dare say she did not understand me.'

'I assure you she did. She felt your full meaning. She has talked of it since. I wish you could have heard how she talked of it—with what candour and generosity. I wish you could have heard her honouring your forbearance, in being able to pay her such attentions, as she was for ever receiving from yourself and your father, when her society must be so irksome.'

'Oh!' cried Emma, 'I know there is not a better creature in the world; but you must allow, that what is good and what is ridiculous are most unfortunately blended in her.'

'They are blended,' said he, 'I acknowledge; and, were she prosperous, I could allow much for the occasional prevalence of the ridiculous over the good. Were she a woman of fortune, I would leave every harmless absurdity to take its chance; I would not quarrel with you for any liberties of manner. Were she your equal in situation—but, Emma, consider how far this is from being the case. She is poor; she has sunk from the comforts she was born to; and if she live to old age must probably sink more. Her situation should secure your compassion. It was badly done, indeed! You, whom she had known from an infant, whom she had seen grow up from a period when her notice was an honour—to have you now, in thoughtless spirits, and the pride of the moment, laugh at her, humble her—and before her niece, too—and before others, many of whom (certainly *some*) would be entirely guided by *your* treatment of her. This is not pleasant to you, Emma—and it is very far from pleasant to me; but I must, I will—I tell you truths while I can; satisfied with proving myself your friend by very faithful counsel, and trusting that you will some time or other do me greater justice than you can do now.'

While they talked they were advancing towards the carriage; it was ready; and, before she could speak again, he had handed her in. He had misinterpreted the feelings which had kept her face averted, and her tongue motionless. They were combined only of anger against herself, mortification, and deep concern. She had not been able to speak; and, on entering the carriage, sunk back for a moment, overcome; then reproaching herself for having taken no leave, making no acknowledgment, parting in apparent sullenness, she looked out with voice and hand eager to show a difference; but it was just too late. He had turned away, and the horses were in motion. She continued to look back, but in vain; and soon, with what appeared unusual speed, they were half way down the hill, and everything left far behind. She was vexed beyond what could have been expressed—almost beyond what she could conceal. Never had she felt so agitated, mortified, grieved, at any circumstance in her life. She was forcibly struck. The truth of his representation there was no denying. She felt it at her heart. How could she have been so brutal, so cruel to Miss Bates! How could she have exposed herself to such ill opinion in any one she valued! And how suffer him to leave her without saying one word of gratitude, of concurrence, of common kindness!

Time did not compose her. As she reflected more, she seemed but to feel it more. She never had been so depressed. Happily it was not necessary to speak. There was only Harriet, who seemed not in spirits herself, fagged, and very willing to be silent; and Emma felt the tears running down her cheeks almost all the way home, without being at any trouble to check them, extraordinary as they were.

44

THE wretchedness of a scheme to Box Hill was in Emma's thoughts all the evening. How it might be considered by the rest of the party she could not tell. They, in their different homes, and their different ways, might be looking back on it with pleasure; but in her view it was a morning more completely misspent, more totally bare of rational satisfaction at the time, and more to be abhorred in recollection, than any she had ever passed. A whole evening of backgammon with her father was felicity to it. *There*, indeed, lay real pleasure, for there she was giving up the sweetest hours of the twenty-four to his comfort; and feeling that, unmerited as might be the degree of his fond affection and confiding esteem, she could not, in her general conduct, be open to any severe reproach. As a daughter, she hoped she was not without a heart. She hoped no one could have said to her, 'How could you be so unfeeling to your father?—I must, I will tell you truths while I can.' Miss Bates should never again—no never! If attention in future could do away the past she might hope to be forgiven. She had been often remiss, for conscience told her so; remiss, perhaps, more in thought than fact; scornful, ungracious. But it should be so no more. In the warmth of true contrition she would call upon her the very next morning, and it should be the beginning on her side, of a regular, equal, kindly intercourse.

She was just as determined when the morrow came, and went early, that nothing might prevent her. It was not unlikely, she thought, that she might see Mr Knightley in her way; or perhaps he might come in while she were paying her visit. She had no objection. She would not be ashamed of the appearance of the penitence, so justly and truly hers. Her eyes were towards Donwell as she walked, but she saw him not.

'The ladies were all at home.' She had never rejoiced at the sound before, nor ever before entered the passage, nor walked up the stairs, with any wish of giving pleasure, but in conferring obligation, or of deriving it, except in subsequent ridicule.

There was a bustle on her approach; a good deal of moving and talking. She heard Miss Bates's voice, something was to be done in a hurry, the maid looked frightened and awkward; hoped she would be pleased to wait a moment, and then ushered her in too soon. The aunt and niece seemed both escaping into the adjoining room. Jane she had a distinct glimpse of, looking extremely ill; and before the door had shut them out, she heard Miss Bates saying, 'Well, my dear, I shall *say* you are laid down upon the bed, and I am sure you are ill enough.'

Poor old Mrs Bates, civil and humble as usual, looked as if she did not quite understand what was going on.

'I am afraid Jane is not very well,' said she, 'but I do not know; they *tell* me she is well. I dare say my daughter will be here presently, Miss Woodhouse. I hope you find a chair. I wish Hetty had not gone. I am very little able—have you a chair, ma'am? Do you sit where you like? I am sure she will be here presently.'

Emma seriously hoped she would. She had a moment's fear of Miss Bates keeping away from her. But Miss Bates soon came —'Very happy and obliged'—but Emma's conscience told her that there was not the same cheerful volubility as before—less ease of look and manner. A very friendly inquiry after Miss Fairfax, she hoped, might lead the way to a return of old feelings. The touch seemed immediate.

' Ah, Miss Woodhouse, how kind you are! I suppose you have heard—and are come to give us joy. This does not seem much like joy, indeed, in me ' (twinkling away a tear or two); ' but it will be very trying for us to part with her, after having had her so long; and she has a dreadful headache just now, writing all the morning; such long letters, you know, to be written to Colonel Campbell and Mrs Dixon. " My dear," said I, " you will blind yourself," for tears were in her eyes perpetually. One cannot wonder, one cannot wonder. It is a great change; and though she is amazingly fortunate—such a situation, I suppose, as no young woman before ever met with on first going out; do not think us ungrateful, Miss Woodhouse, for such surprising good fortune ' (again dispersing her tears)—' but, poor dear soul! if you were to see what a headache she has. When one is in great pain, you know, one cannot feel any blessing quite as it may deserve. She is as low as possible. To look at her nobody would think how delighted and happy she is to have secured such a situation. You will excuse her not coming to you; she is not able, she is gone into her own room. I want her to lie down upon the bed. " My dear," said I, " I shall say you arc laid down upon the bed "; but, however, she is not; she is walking about the room. But, now that she has written her letters, she says she shall soon be well. She will be extremely sorry to miss seeing you, Miss Woodhouse, but your kindness will excuse her. You were kept waiting at the door; I was quite ashamed; but somehow there was a little bustle; for it so happened that we had not heard the knock; and, till you were on the stairs, we did not know anybody was coming. " It is only Mrs Cole," said I, " depend upon it; nobody else would come so early."—" Well," said she, " it must be borne some time or other, and it may as well be now." But then Patty came in, and said it was you. " Oh," said I, " it is Miss Woodhouse, I am sure you will like to see her "—" I can see nobody," said she, and up she got, and would go away; and that was what made us keep you waiting; and extremely sorry and ashamed we were. " If you must go, my dear," said I, " you must, and I will say you are laid down upon the bed." '

Emma was most sincerely interested. Her heart had been long growing kinder towards Jane; and this picture of her present sufferings acted as a cure of every former ungenerous suspicion, and left her nothing but pity; and the remembrance of the less just and less gentle sensations of the past obliged her to admit that Jane might very naturally resolve on seeing Mrs Cole, or any other steady friend, when she might not bear to see herself. She spoke as she felt, with earnest regret and solicitude—sincerely wishing that the circumstances which she collected from Mrs Bates to be now actually determined on, might be as much for Miss Fairfax's advantage and comfort as possible.

' It must be a severe trial to them all. She had understood it was to be delayed until Colonel Campbell's return.'

' So very kind! ' replied Miss Bates; ' but you are always kind.'

There was no bearing such an ' always; ' and to break through her dreadful gratitude Emma made to direct inquiry of:

' Where, may I ask, is Miss Fairfax going? '

' To a Mrs Smallridge—charming woman—most superior—to have the charge of her three little girls—delightful children! Impossible that any situation could be more replete with comfort; if we except, perhaps, Mrs Suckling's own family, and Mrs Bragge's, but Mrs Smallridge is intimate with both, and in the very same neighbourhood—lives only four miles from Maple Grove. Jane will be only four miles from Maple Grove.'

' Mrs Elton, I suppose, has been the person to whom Miss Fairfax owes—— '

' Yes, our good Mrs Elton. The most indefatigable, true friend. She would not take a denial. She would not let Jane say " No; " for when Jane first heard of it (it was the day before yesterday, the very morning we were at Donwell), when Jane first heard of it, she was quite decided against accepting the offer, and for the reasons you mention; exactly as you say, she had made up her mind to close with nothing till Colonel Campbell's return, and nothing should induce her to enter into any engagement at present—and so she told Mrs Elton over and over again—and I am sure I had no more idea that she would change her mind! —but that good Mrs Elton, whose judgment never fails her, saw farther than I did. It is not everybody that would have stood out in such a kind way as she did, and refuse to take Jane's answer; but she positively declared she would *not* write any such denial yesterday, as Jane wished her; she would wait—and, sure enough, yesterday evening, it was all settled that Jane should go. Quite a surprise to me! I had not the least idea. Jane took Mrs Elton aside, and told her at once, that, upon think-

ing over the advantages of Mrs Smallridge's situation, she had
come to the resolution of accepting it. I did not know a word
of it till it was all settled.'

'You spent the evening with Mrs Elton?'

'Yes, all of us; Mrs Elton would have us come. It was
settled so, upon the hill, while we were walking about with Mr
Knightley. "You *must all* spend your evening with us," said
she—" I positively must have you *all* come." '

'Mr Knightley was there too, was he?'

'No, not Mr Knightley; he declined it from the first; and
though I thought he would come, because Mrs Elton declared
she would not let him off, he did not; but my mother, and Jane,
and I, were all there, and a very agreeable evening we had.
Such kind friends, you know, Miss Woodhouse, one must always
find agreeable, though everybody seemed rather fagged after the
morning's party. Even pleasure, you know, is fatiguing—and I
cannot say that any of them seemed very much to have enjoyed
it. However, *I* shall always think it a very pleasant party, and
feel extremely obliged to the kind friends who included me in it.'

'Miss Fairfax, I suppose, though you were not aware of it,
had been making up her mind the whole day?'

'I dare say she had.'

'Whenever the time may come it must be unwelcome to her
and all her friends—but I hope her engagement will have every
alleviation that is possible—I mean, as to character and manners
of the family.'

'Thank you, dear Miss Woodhouse. Yes, indeed, there is
everything in the world that can make her happy in it. Except
the Sucklings and Bragges, there is not such another nursery
establishment, so liberal and elegant, in all Mrs Elton's acquaintance. Mrs Smallridge, a most delightful woman! A style of
living almost equal to Maple Grove—and as to the children,
except the little Sucklings and little Bragges, there are not such
elegant sweet children anywhere. Jane will be treated with such
regard and kindness! It will be nothing but pleasure—a life of
pleasure. And her salary. I really cannot venture to name her
salary to you, Miss Woodhouse. Even you, used as you are to
great sums, would hardly believe that so much could be given
to a young person like Jane.'

'Ah, madam,' cried Emma, 'if other children are at all like
what I remember to have been myself, I should think that five
times the amount of what I have ever yet heard named as a
salary on such occasions dearly earned.'

'You are so noble in your ideas.'

'And when is Miss Fairfax to leave you?'

'Very soon, very soon, indeed; that's the worst of it. Within a fortnight. Mrs Smallridge is in a great hurry. My poor mother does not know how to bear it. So, then, I try to put it out of her thoughts, and say, "Come, ma'am, do not let us think about it any more."'

'Her friends must all be sorry to lose her; and will not Colonel and Mrs Campbell be sorry to find that she has engaged herself before their return?'

'Yes; Jane says she is sure they will; but yet this is such a situation that she cannot feel herself justified in declining. I was so astonished when she first told me what she had been saying to Mrs Elton, and when Mrs Elton at the same moment came congratulating me upon it! It was before tea—stay—no, it could not be before tea, because we were just going to cards— and yet it was before tea, because I remember thinking—Oh, no, now I recollect, now I have it; something happened before tea, but not that. Mr Elton was called out of the room before tea, old John Abdy's son wanted to speak with him. Poor old John—I have a great regard for him; he was clerk to my poor father twenty-seven years; and now, poor old man, he is bedridden, and very poorly with the rheumatic gout in his joints— I must go and see him to-day; and so will Jane, I am sure, if she gets out at all. And poor John's son came to talk to Mr Elton about relief from the parish; he is very well-to-do himself, you know, being head man at the Crown—ostler, and everything of that sort—but still he cannot keep his father without some help; and so, when Mr Elton came back, he told us what John ostler had been telling him, and then it came out about the chaise having been sent to Randalls to take Mr Frank Churchill to Richmond. That was what happened before tea. It was after tea that Jane spoke to Mrs Elton.'

Miss Bates would hardly give Emma time to say how perfectly new this circumstance was to her; but as without supposing it possible that she could be ignorant of any of the particulars of Mr Frank Churchill's going, she proceeded to give them all, it was of no consequence.

What Mr Elton had learned from the ostler on the subject, being the accumulation of the ostler's own knowledge, and the knowledge of the servants at Randalls, was, that a messenger had come over from Richmond soon after the return of the party from Box Hill—which messenger, however, had been no more than was expected; and that Mr Churchill had sent his nephew a few lines containing, upon the whole, a tolerable account of Mrs Churchill, and only wishing him not to delay coming back beyond the next morning early; but that Mr Frank Churchill, having resolved to go home directly, without waiting at all, and his horse seeming to have got a cold, Tom had been sent off immediately for the Crown chaise, and the ostler had stood out and seen it pass by, the boy going a good pace, and driving very steady.

There was nothing in all this either to astonish or interest, and it caught Emma's attention only as it united with the subject which already engaged her mind. The contrast between Mrs Churchill's importance in the world and Jane Fairfax's struck her; one was everything, the other nothing—and she sat musing on the difference of woman's destiny, and quite unconscious on what her eyes were fixed, till roused by Miss Bates saying:

' Ay, I see what you are thinking of, the pianoforte. What is to become of that? Very true. Poor dear Jane was talking of it just now. " You must go," said she. " You and I must part. You will have no business here. Let it stay, however," said she; " give it house-room till Colonel Campbell comes back; I shall talk about it to him; he will settle for me; he will help me out of all my difficulties." And to this day, I do believe, she knows not whether it was his present or his daughter's.'

Now Emma was obliged to think of the pianoforte; and the remembrance of all her former fanciful and unfair conjectures was so little pleasing that she soon allowed herself to believe her visit had been long enough; and, with a repetition of everything that she could venture to say of the good wishes which she really felt, took leave.

45

EMMA's pensive meditations, as she walked home, were not interrupted; but on entering the parlour, she found those who must rouse her. Mr Knightley and Harriet had arrived during her absence, and were sitting with her father. Mr Knightley immediately got up, and, in a manner decidedly graver than usual, said:

' I would not go away without seeing you, but I have no time to spare, and therefore must now be gone directly. I am going to London, to spend a few days with John and Isabella. Have you anything to send or say, besides the "love," which nobody carries?'

'Nothing at all. But is not this a sudden scheme!'

'Yes—rather—I have been thinking of it some little time.'

Emma was sure he had not forgiven her; he looked unlike himself. Time, however, she thought, would tell him that they ought to be friends again. While he stood, as if meaning to go, but not going—her father began his inquiries.

'Well, my dear, and did you get there safely?—And how did you find my worthy old friend and her daughter?—I dare say they must have been very much obliged to you for coming. Dear Emma has been to call on Mrs and Miss Bates, Mr Knightley, as I told you before. She is always so attentive to them.'

Emma's colour was heightened by this unjust praise; and with a smile and shake of the head, which spoke much, she looked at Mr Knightley. It seemed as if there were an instantaneous impression in her favour, as if his eyes received the truth from hers, and all that had passed of good in her feelings were at once caught and honoured. He looked at her with a glow of regard. She was warmly gratified—and in another moment still more so, by a little movement of more than common friendliness on his part. He took her hand; whether she had not herself made the first motion, she could not say—she might, perhaps, have rather offered it; but he took her hand, pressed it, and certainly was on the point of carrying it to his lips, when, from some fancy or other, he suddenly let it go. Why he should feel such a scruple, why he should change his mind when it was all but done, she could not perceive. He would have judged better, she thought, if he had not stopped. The intention, however, was indubitable; and whether it was that his manners had in general so little gallantry, or however else it happened, but she thought nothing became him more. It was with him of so simple, yet so dignified a nature. She could not but recall the attempt with great satisfaction. It spoke such perfect amity. He left them immediately afterwards—gone in a moment. He always moved with the alertness of a mind which could neither be undecided nor dilatory, but now he seemed more sudden than usual in his disappearance.

Emma could not regret her having gone to Miss Bates, but she wished she had left her ten minutes earlier; it would have been a great pleasure to talk over Jane Fairfax's situation with Mr Knightley. Neither would she regret that he should be going to Brunswick Square, for she knew how much his visit would be enjoyed—but it might have happened at a better time—and to have had longer notice of it would have been pleasanter. They parted thorough friends, however; she could not be deceived as to the meaning of his countenance, and his unfinished gallantry; it was all done to assure her that she had fully recovered his good opinion. He had been sitting with them half an hour she found. It was a pity that she had not come back earlier.

In the hope of diverting her father's thoughts from the disagreeableness of Mr Knightley's going to London, and going so suddenly, and going on horseback, which she knew would be all very bad, Emma communicated her news of Jane Fairfax, and her dependence on the effect was justified; it supplied a very useful check—interested, without disturbing him. He had long made up his mind to Jane Fairfax's going out as governess, and could talk of it cheerfully, but Mr Knightley's going to London had been an unexpected blow.

'I am very glad, indeed, my dear, to hear she is to be so comfortably settled. Mrs Elton is very good-natured and agreeable, and I dare say her acquaintance are just what they ought to be. I hope it is a dry situation, and that her health will be taken good care of. It ought to be a first object, as I am sure poor Miss Taylor's always was with me. You know, my dear, she is going to be to this new lady what Miss Taylor was to us. And I hope she will be better off in one respect, and not be induced to go away after it has been her home so long.'

The following day brought news from Richmond to throw everything else into the background. An express arrived at Randalls to announce the death of Mrs Churchill. Though her nephew had had no particular reason to hasten back on her account, she had not lived above six-and-thirty hours after his return. A sudden seizure of a different nature from anything foreboded by her general state, had carried her off after a short struggle. The great Mrs Churchill was no more.

It was felt as such things must be felt. Everybody had a degree of gravity and sorrow; tenderness towards the departed, solicitude for the surviving friends, and, in a reasonable time, curiosity to know where she would be buried. Goldsmith tells us, that when lovely woman stoops to folly, she has nothing to do but to die; and when she stoops to be disagreeable, it is equally to be recommended as a clearer of ill-fame. Mrs Churchill, after being disliked at least twenty-five years, was now spoken of with compassionate allowances. In one point she was fully justified. She had never been admitted before to be seriously ill. The event acquitted her of all the fancifulness, and all the selfishness of imaginary complaints.

'Poor Mrs Churchill! no doubt she had been suffering a great deal; more than anybody had ever supposed—and continual pain would try the temper. It was a sad event—a great shock —with all her faults, what would Mr Churchill do without her? Mr Churchill's loss would be dreadful, indeed. Mr Churchill would never get over it. ' Even Mr Weston shook his head, and looked solemn, and said, 'Ah, poor woman, who would have thought it!' and resolved that his mourning should be as handsome as possible; and his wife sat sighing and moralising over her broad hems with a commiseration and good sense true and steady. How it would affect Frank, was among the earliest thoughts of both. It was also a very early speculation with Emma. The character of Mrs Churchill, the grief of her husband—her mind glanced over them both with awe and compassion—and then rested with lightened feelings on how Frank might be affected by the event, how benefited, how freed. She saw in a moment all the possible good. Now an attachment to Harriet Smith would have nothing to encounter. Mr Churchill, independent of his wife, was feared by nobody; an easy, guidable man, to be persuaded into anything by his nephew. All that remained to be wished was that the nephew should form the attachment, as, with all her goodwill in the cause, Emma could feel no certainty of its being already formed.

Harriet behaved extremely well on the occasion—with great self-command. Whatever she might feel of brighter hope, she betrayed nothing. Emma was gratified to observe such a proof in her of strengthened character, and refrained from any allusion that might endanger its maintenance. They spoke, therefore, of Mrs Churchill's death with mutual forbearance.

Short letters from Frank were received at Randalls, communicating all that was immediately important of their state and plans. Mr Churchill was better than could be expected; and their first removal, on the departure of the funeral for Yorkshire, was to be to the house of a very old friend in Windsor, to whom Mr Churchill had been promising a visit the last ten years. At present, there was nothing to be done for Harriet; good wishes for the future were all that could yet be possible on Emma's side.

It was a more pressing concern to show attention to Jane

Fairfax, whose prospects were closing while Harriet's opened, and whose engagements now allowed of no delay in any one at Highbury who wished to show her kindness; and with Emma it was grown into a first wish. She had scarcely a stronger regret than for her past coldness; and the person, whom she had been so many months neglecting, was now the very one on whom she would have lavished every distinction of regard or sympathy. She wanted to be of use to her; wanted to show a value for her society, and testify respect and consideration. She resolved to prevail on her to spend a day at Hartfield. A note was written to urge it. The invitation was refused and by a verbal message. ' Miss Fairfax was not well enough to write; ' and when Mr Perry called at Hartfield the same morning, it appeared that she was so much indisposed as to have been visited, though against her own consent, by himself, and that she was suffering under severe headaches, and a nervous fever to a degree which made him doubt the possibility of her going to Mrs Smallridge's at the time proposed. Her health seemed for the moment completely deranged—appetite quite gone; and though there were no absolutely alarming symptoms, nothing touching the pulmonary complaint which was the standing apprehension of the family, Mr Perry was uneasy about her. He thought she had undertaken more than she was equal to, and that she felt it so herself, though she would not own it. Her spirits seemed overcome. Her present home, he could not but observe, was unfavourable to a nervous disorder;—confined always to one room—he could have wished it otherwise; and her good aunt, though his very old friend, he must acknowledge to be not the best companion for an invalid of that description. Her care and attention could not be questioned; they were, in fact, only too great. He very much feared that Miss Fairfax derived more evil than good from them. Emma listened with the warmest concern; grieved for her more and more, and looked around eager to discover some way of being useful. To take her—be it only an hour or two—from her aunt, to give her change of air and scene, and quiet, rational conversation, even for an hour or two, might do her good; and the following morning she wrote again to say, in the most feeling language she could command, that she would call for her in the carriage at any hour that Jane would name—mentioning that she had Mr Perry's decided opinion in favour of such exercise for his patient. The answer was only in this short note:

' Miss Fairfax's compliments and thanks, but is quite unequal to any exercise.'

Emma felt that her own note had deserved something better; but it was impossible to quarrel with words, whose tremulous inequality showed indisposition so plainly, and she thought only of how she might best counteract this unwillingness to be seen or assisted. In spite of the answer, therefore, she ordered the carriage, and drove to Mrs Bates's, in the hope that Jane would be induced to join her—but it would not do; · Miss Bates came to the carriage door, all gratitude, and agreeing with her most earnestly in thinking an airing might be of the greatest service—and everything that message could do was tried—but all in vain. Miss Bates was obliged to return without success; Jane was quite unpersuadable; the mere proposal of going out seemed to make her worse. Emma wished she could have seen her, and tried her own powers; but, almost before she could hint the wish, Miss Bates made it appear that she had promised her niece on no account to let Miss Woodhouse in. ' Indeed, the truth was, that poor dear Jane could not bear to see anybody—anybody at all—Mrs Elton, indeed, could not be denied—and Mrs Cole had made such a point—and Mrs Perry had said so much—but, except them, Jane would really see nobody.'

Emma did not want to be classed with the Mrs Eltons, the Mrs Perrys, and the Mrs Coles, who would force themselves anywhere; neither could she feel any right of preference herself—she submitted, therefore, and only questioned Miss Bates further as to her niece's appetite and diet, which she longed to be able to assist. On that subject poor Miss Bates was very unhappy, and very communicative; Jane would hardly eat anything. Mr Perry recommended nourishing food; but everything they could command (and never had anybody such good neighbours) was distasteful.

Emma, on reaching home, called the housekeeper directly to an examination of her stores; and some arrowroot of very superior quality was speedily despatched to Miss Bates, with a most friendly note. In half an hour the arrowroot was returned, with a thousand thanks from Miss Bates, but ' dear Jane would not be satisfied without its being sent back; it was a thing she could not take—and, moreover, she insisted on her saying that she was not at all in want of anything.'

When Emma afterwards heard that Jane Fairfax had been seen wandering about the meadows at some distance from Highbury, on the afternoon of the very day on which she had, under the plea of being unequal to any exercise, so peremptorily refused to go out with her in the carriage, she could have no doubt—putting everything together—that Jane was resolved to receive no kindness from *her*. She was sorry, very sorry. Her heart was grieved for a state which seemed but the more pitiable from this sort of irritation of spirits, inconsistency of action, and inequality of powers; and it mortified her that she was given so little credit for proper feeling, or esteemed so little worthy as a friend; but she had the consolation of knowing that her intentions were good, and of being able to say to herself, that could Mr Knightley have been privy to all her attempts of assisting Jane Fairfax, could he even have seen into her heart, he would not, on this occasion, have found anything to reprove.

46

ONE morning, about ten days after Mrs Churchill's decease, Emma was called downstairs to Mr Weston, who ' could not stay five minutes, and wanted particularly to speak with her.' He met her at the parlour door, and hardly asking her how she did, in the natural key of his voice, sunk it immediately, to say, unheard by her father:

' Can you come to Randalls at any time this morning? Do, if it be possible. Mrs Weston wants to see you. She must see you.'

' Is she unwell? '

' No, no; not at all; only a little agitated. She would have ordered the carriage and come to you, but she must see you *alone*, and that you know ' (nodding towards her father). ' Humph! can you come? '

' Certainly. This moment, if you please. It is impossible to refuse what you ask in such a way, but what can be the matter? is she really not ill? '

' Depend upon me; but ask no more questions. You will know it all in time. The most unaccountable business! But, hush, hush! '

To guess what all this meant was impossible even for Emma. Something really important seemed announced by his looks; but, as her friend was well, she endeavoured not to be uneasy, and settling it with her father, that she would take her walk now, she and Mr Weston were soon out of the house together, and on their way at a quick pace for Randalls.

' Now,' said Emma, when they were fairly beyond the sweep
gates—' now, Mr Weston, do let me know what has happened.'

' No, no,' he gravely replied. ' Don't ask me. I promised my
wife to leave it all to her. She will break it to you better than I
can. Do not be impatient, Emma; it will all come out too soon.'

' Break it to me!' cried Emma, standing still with terror.
' Good God! Mr Weston, tell me at once. Something has happened in Brunswick Square. I know it has. Tell me, I charge
you, tell me this moment what it is.'

' No, indeed, you are mistaken.'

' Mr Weston, do not trifle with me. Consider how many of
my dearest friends are now in Brunswick Square. Which of
them is it? I charge you by all that is sacred not to attempt concealment.'

' Upon my word, Emma—— '

' Your word! Why not your honour! why not say upon your
honour, that it has nothing to do with any of them? Good
Heavens! What can be to be *broke* to me, that does not relate to
one of that family? '

' Upon my honour,' said he very seriously, ' it does not. It
is not in the smallest degree connected with any human being
of the name of Knightley.'

Emma's courage returned, and she walked on.

' I was wrong,' he continued, ' in talking of its being *broke* to
you. I should not have used the expression. In fact, it does not
concern you, it concerns only myself; that is, we hope. Humph!
In short, my dear Emma, there is no occasion to be so uneasy
about it. I don't say that it is not a disagreeable business, but
things might be much worse. If we walk fast, we shall soon be
at Randalls.'

Emma found that she must wait; and now it required little
effort. She asked no more questions therefore, merely employed
her own fancy, and that soon pointed out to her the probability
of its being some money concern—something just come to light,
of a disagreeable nature, in the circumstances of the family; something which the late event at Richmond had brought forward.
Her fancy was very active. Half a dozen natural children, perhaps, and poor Frank cut off! This, though very undesirable,
would be no matter of agony to her. It inspired little more than
an animating curiosity.

' Who is that gentleman on horseback? ' said she, as they proceeded; speaking more to assist Mr Weston in keeping his secret
than with any other view.

'I do not know. One of the Otways—not Frank; it is not Frank, I assure you. You will not see him. He is half-way to Windsor by this time.'

'Has your son been with you, then?'

'Oh, yes! did not you know? Well, well, never mind.'

For a moment he was silent; and then added, in a tone much more guarded and demure:

'Yes, Frank came over this morning, just to ask us how we did.'

They hurried on and were speedily at Randalls. 'Well, my dear,' said he, as they entered the room, 'I have brought her, and now I hope you will soon be better. I shall leave you together. There is no use in delay. I shall not be far off, if you want me.' And Emma distinctly heard him add, in a lower tone, before he quitted the room— 'I have been as good as my word. She has not the least idea.'

Mrs Weston was looking so ill, and had an air of so much perturbation, that Emma's uneasiness increased; and the moment they were alone, she eagerly said:

'What is it, my dear friend? Something of a very unpleasant nature, I find, has occurred; do let me know directly what it is. I have been walking all this way in complete suspense. We both abhor suspense. Do not let mine continue longer. It will do you good to speak of your distress, whatever it may be.'

'Have you indeed, no idea?' said Mrs Weston in a trembling voice. 'Cannot you, my dear Emma—cannot you form a guess as to what you are to hear?'

'So far as that it relates to Mr Frank Churchill, I do guess.'

'You are right. It does relate to him, and I will tell you directly' (resuming her work, and seeming resolved against looking up). 'He has been here, this very morning, on a most extraordinary errand. It is impossible to express our surprise. He came to speak to his father on a subject—to announce an attachment——'

She stopped to breathe. Emma thought first of herself, and then of Harriet.

'More than an attachment, indeed,' resumed Mrs Weston; 'an engagement—a positive engagement. What will you say, Emma—what will anybody say—when it is known that Frank Churchill and Miss Fairfax are engaged—nay, that they have been long engaged?'

Emma even jumped with surprise; and, horror struck, exclaimed:

'Jane Fairfax! Good God! You are not serious? You do not mean it?'

'You may well be amazed,' returned Mrs Weston, still averting her eyes, and talking on with eagerness, that Emma might have time to recover—'you may well be amazed. But it is even so. There has been a solemn engagement between them ever since October—formed at Weymouth, and kept a secret from everybody. Not a creature knowing it but themselves—neither the Campbells, nor her family, nor his. It is so wonderful, that though perfectly convinced of the fact, it is yet almost incredible to myself. I can hardly believe it. I thought I knew him.'

Emma scarcely heard what was said. Her mind was divided between two ideas. Her own former conversations with him about Miss Fairfax, and poor Harriet; and for some time she could only exclaim, and require confirmation, repeated confirmation.

'Well!' said she at last, trying to recover herself, 'this is a circumstance which I must think of at least half a day before I can at all comprehend it. What! —engaged to her all the winter—before either of them came to Highbury?'

'Engaged since October—secretly engaged. It has hurt me, Emma, very much. It has hurt his father equally. *Some part* of his conduct we cannot excuse.'

Emma pondered a moment, and then replied: 'I will not pretend *not* to understand you; and to give you all the relief in my power, be assured that no such effect has followed his attentions to me as you are apprehensive of.'

Mrs Weston looked up, afraid to believe; but Emma's countenance was as steady as her words.

'That you may have less difficulty in believing this boast of my present perfect indifference,' she continued, 'I will further tell you, that there was a period in the early part of our acquaintance when I did like him—when I was very much disposed to be attached to him; nay, was attached—and how it came to cease is perhaps the wonder. Fortunately, however, it did cease. I have really for some time past—for at least these three months—cared nothing about him. You may believe me, Mrs Weston. This is the simple truth.'

Mrs Weston kissed her with tears of joy; and when she could find utterance, assured her that this protestation had done her more good than anything else in the world could do.

'Mr Weston will be almost as much relieved as myself,' said she. 'On this point we have been wretched. It was our darling wish that you might be attached to each other, and we were persuaded that it was so. Imagine what we have been feeling on your account.'

'I have escaped; and that I should escape may be a matter of grateful wonder to you and myself. But this does not acquit *him*, Mrs Weston; and I must say that I think him greatly to blame. What right had he to come among us with affection and faith engaged, and with manner so *very* disengaged? What right had he to endeavour to please, as he certainly did—to distinguish any one young woman with persevering attention, as he certainly did, while he really belonged to another? How could he tell what mischief he might be doing? How could he tell that he might not be making me in love with him? Very wrong, very wrong, indeed.'

'From something that he said, my dear Emma, I rather imagine—— '

'And how could *she* bear such behaviour? Composure with a witness! to look on, while repeated attentions were offering to another woman before her face, and not resent it. That is a degree of placidity which I can neither comprehend nor respect. '

'There were misunderstandings between them, Emma; he said so expressly. He had not time to enter into much explanation. He was here only a quarter of an hour, and in a state of agitation which did not allow the full use even of the time he could stay—but that there had been misunderstandings, he decidedly said. The present crisis, indeed, seemed to be brought on by them; and those misunderstandings might very possibly arise from the impropriety of his conduct.'

'Impropriety! Oh! Mrs Weston, it is too calm a censure. Much, much beyond impropriety! It has sunk him—I cannot say how it has sunk him in my opinion. So unlike what a man should be. None of that upright integrity, that strict adherence to truth and principle, that disdain of trick and littleness, which a man should display in every transaction of his life.'

'Nay, dear Emma, now I must take his part; for though he has been wrong in this instance, I have known him long enough to answer for his having many, very many good qualities; and—— '

'Good God!' cried Emma, not attending to her, 'Mrs Small-ridge, too! Jane actually on the point of going as governess! What could he mean by such horrible indelicacy? To suffer her to engage herself—to suffer her even to think of such a measure!'

'He knew nothing about it, Emma. On this article I can fully acquit him. It was a private resolution of hers, not communicated to him, or at least not communicated in a way to carry conviction. Till yesterday, I know, he said he was in the dark as to her plans. They burst on him, I do not know how, but by some letter or message—and it was the discovery of what she was doing, of this very project of hers, which determined him to come forward at once, own it all to his uncle, throw himself on his kindness, and, in short, put an end to the miserable state of concealment that had been carrying on so long.'

Emma began to listen better.

'I am to hear from him soon,' continued Mrs Weston. 'He told me at parting that he should soon write; and he spoke in a manner which seemed to promise me many particulars that could not be given now. Let us wait, therefore, for this letter. It may bring many extenuations. It may make many things intelligible and excusable which now are not to be understood. Don't let us be severe; don't let us be in a hurry to condemn him. Let us have patience. I must love him; and now that I am satisfied on one point, the one material point, I am sincerely anxious for its all turning out well, and ready to hope that it may. They must both have suffered a great deal under such a system of secrecy and concealment.'

'His sufferings,' replied Emma, dryly, 'do not appear to have done him much harm. Well, and how did Mr Churchill take it?'

'Most favourably for his nephew—gave his consent with scarcely a difficulty. Conceive what the events of a week have done in that family! While poor Mrs Churchill lived, I suppose there could not have been a hope, a chance, a possibility; but scarcely are her remains at rest in the family vault, than her husband is persuaded to act exactly opposite to what she would have required. What a blessing it is, when undue influence does not survive the grave! He gave his consent with very little persuasion.'

'Ah!' thought Emma, 'he would have done as much for Harriet.'

'This was settled last night, and Frank was off with the light this morning. He stopped at Highbury, at the Bates's, I fancy, some time, and then came on hither; but was in such a hurry to get back to his uncle, to whom he is just now more necessary than ever, that, as I tell you, he could stay with us but a quarter of an hour. He was very much agitated—very much indeed —to a degree that made him appear quite a different creature from anything I had ever seen him before. In addition to all the rest, there had been the shock of finding her so very unwell, which he had had no previous suspicion of, and there was every appearance of his having been feeling a great deal.'

'And do you really believe the affair to have been carrying on with such perfect secrecy? The Campbells, the Dixons—did none of them know of the engagement?'

Emma could not speak the name of Dixon without a little blush.

'None; not one. He positively said that it had been known to no being in the world but their two selves.'

'Well,' said Emma, 'I suppose we shall gradually grow reconciled to the idea, and I wish them very happy. But I shall always think it a very abominable sort of proceeding. What has it been but a system of hypocrisy and deceit, espionage and treachery? To come among us with professions of openness and simplicity; and such a league in secret to judge us all! Here have we been the whole winter and spring, completely duped, fancying ourselves all on an equal footing of truth and honour, with two people in the midst of us who may have been carrying round, comparing and sitting in judgment on sentiments and words that were never meant for both to hear. They must take the consequence, if they have heard each other spoken of in a way not perfectly agreeable.'

'I am quite easy on that head,' replied Mrs Weston. 'I am very sure that I never said anything of either to the other which both might not have heard.'

'You are in luck. Your only blunder was confined to my ear, when you imagined a certain friend of ours in love with the lady.'

'True. But as I have always had a thoroughly good opinion of Miss Fairfax, I never could, under any blunder, have spoken ill of her; and as to speaking ill of him, there I must have been safe.'

At this moment Mr Weston appeared at a little distance from the window, evidently on the watch. His wife gave him a look which invited him in; and, while he was coming round, added:

'Now, dearest Emma, let me entreat you to say and look everything that may set his heart at ease, and incline him to be satisfied with the match. Let us make the best of it—and, indeed, almost everything may be fairly said in her favour. It is not a connection to gratify; but if Mr Churchill does not feel that, why should we? and it may be a very fortunate circumstance for him— for Frank, I mean—that he should have attached himself to a girl of such steadiness of character and good judgment as I have always given her credit for, and still am disposed to give her credit for, in spite of this one great deviation from the strict rule of right. And how much may be said, in her situation, for even that error?'

'Much, indeed!' cried Emma feelingly. 'If a woman can ever be excused for thinking only of herself, it is in a situation like Jane Fairfax's. Of such, one may almost say, that "the world is not theirs, nor the world's law."'

She met Mr Weston on his entrance with a smiling countenance, exclaiming:

'A very pretty trick you have been playing me, upon my word! This was a device, I suppose, to sport with my curiosity, and exercise my talent of guessing. But you really frightened me. I thought you had lost half your property at least. And here, instead of its being a matter of condolence, it turns out to be one of congratulation. I congratulate you, Mr Weston, with all my heart, on the prospect of having one of the most lovely and accomplished young women in England for your daughter.'

A glance or two between him and his wife convinced him that all was as right as this speech proclaimed; and its happy effect on his spirits was immediate. His air and voice recovered their usual briskness; he shook her heartily and gratefully by the hand, and entered on the subject in a manner to prove that he now only wanted time and persuasion to think the engagement no very bad thing. His companions suggested only what could palliate imprudence or smooth objections; and by the time they had talked it all over together, and he had talked it all over again with Emma, in their walk back to Hartfield, he was become perfectly reconciled, and not far from thinking it the very best thing that Frank could possibly have done.

47

'HARRIET, poor Harriet!'—Those were the words; in them lay the tormenting ideas which Emma could not get rid of, and which constituted the real misery of the business to her. Frank Churchill had behaved very ill by herself—very ill in many ways—but it was not so much *his* behaviour as her *own* which made her so angry with him. It was the scrape which he had drawn her into on Harriet's account, that gave the deepest hue to his offence. Poor Harriet! to be a second time the dupe of her misconceptions and flattery. Mr Knightley had spoken prophetically when he once said, ' Emma, you have been no friend to Harriet Smith.' She was afraid she had done her nothing but disservice. It was true that she had not to charge herself in this instance, as in the former, with being the sole and original author of the mischief; with having suggested such feelings as might otherwise never have entered Harriet's imagination; for Harriet had acknowledged her admiration and preference of Frank Churchill before she had ever given her a hint on the subject; but she felt completely guilty of having encouraged what she might have repressed. She might have prevented the indulgence and increase of such sentiments. Her influence would have been enough. And now she was very conscious that she ought to have prevented them. She felt that she had been risking her friend's happiness on most insufficient grounds. Common sense would have directed her to tell Harriet that she must not allow herself to think of him, and that there were five hundred chances to one against his ever caring for her. ' But with common sense,' she added, ' I am afraid I have had little to do.'

She was extremely angry with herself. If she could not have been angry with Frank Churchill too, it would have been dreadful. As for Jane Fairfax, she might at least relieve her feelings from any present solicitude on her account. Harriet would be anxiety enough; she need no longer be unhappy about Jane, whose troubles and whose ill health having, of course, the same origin, must be equally under cure. Her days of insignificance and evil were over. She would soon be well, and happy and prosperous. Emma could now imagine why her own attentions had been slighted. This discovery laid many smaller matters open. No doubt it had been from jealousy. In Jane's eyes she had been a rival; and well might anything she could offer of assistance or regard be repulsed. An airing in the Hartfield carriage would have been the rack, and arrowroot from the Hartfield storeroom must have been poison. She understood it all; and as far as her mind could disengage itself from the injustice and selfishness of angry feelings, she acknowledged that Jane Fairfax would have neither elevation nor happiness beyond her desert. But poor Harriet was such an engrossing charge! There was little sympathy to be spared for anybody else. Emma was sadly fearful that this second disappointment would be more severe than the first. Considering the very superior claims of the object, it ought; and judging by its apparently stronger effect on Harriet's mind, producing reserve and self-command, it would. She must communicate the painful truth, however, and as soon as possible. An injunction of secrecy had been among Mr Weston's parting words. 'For the present the whole affair was to be completely a secret. Mr Churchill had made a point of it, as a token of respect to the wife he had so very recently lost; and everybody admitted it to be no more than due decorum.' Emma had promised; but still Harriet must be excepted. It was her superior duty.

In spite of her vexation, she could not help feeling it almost ridiculous, that she should have the very same distressing and delicate office to perform by Harriet which Mrs Weston had just gone through by herself. The intelligence which had been so anxiously announced to her she was now to be anxiously announcing to another. Her heart beat quick on hearing Harriet's footstep and voice; so, she supposed, had poor Mrs Weston felt when *she* was approaching Randalls. Could the event of the disclosure bear an equal resemblance! But of that, unfortunately, there could be no chance.

'Well, Miss Woodhouse,' cried Harriet, coming eagerly into the room, 'is not this the oddest news that ever was?'

'What news do you mean?' replied Emma, unable to guess, by look or voice, whether Harriet could indeed have received any hint.

'About Jane Fairfax. Did you ever hear anything so strange? Oh!—you need not be afraid of owning it to me, for Mr Weston has told me himself. I met him just now. He told me it was to be a great secret; and, therefore, I should not think of mentioning it to anybody but you, but he said you knew it.'

'What did Mr Weston tell you?' said Emma, still perplexed.

'Oh! he told me all about it; that Jane Fairfax and Mr Frank Churchill are to be married, and that they have been privately engaged to one another this long while. How very odd!'

It was, indeed, so odd; Harriet's behaviour was so extremely odd, that Emma did not know how to understand it. Her character appeared absolutely changed. She seemed to propose showing no agitation, or disappointment, or peculiar concern in the discovery. Emma looked at her, quite unable to speak.

'Had you any idea,' cried Harriet, 'of his being in love with her? You, perhaps, might. You' (blushing as she spoke) 'who can see into everybody's heart; but nobody else——'

'Upon my word,' said Emma, 'I begin to doubt my having

any such talent. Can you seriously ask me, Harriet, whether I imagined him attached to another woman at the very time that I was—tacitly if not openly—encouraging you to give way to your own feelings? I never had the slightest suspicion, till within the last hour, of Mr Frank Churchill's having the least regard for Jane Fairfax. You may be very sure that, if I had, I should have cautioned you accordingly.'

' Me! ' cried Harriet, colouring, and astonished. ' Why should you caution me? You do not think I care about Mr Frank Churchill? '

' I am delighted to hear you speak so stoutly on the subject,' replied Emma, smiling; ' but you do not mean to deny that there was a time—and not very distant either—when you gave me reason to understand that you did care about him? '

' Him!—never, never. Dear Miss Woodhouse, how could you so mistake me? ' (turning away distressed).

' Harriet,' cried Emma, after a moment's pause, ' what do you mean?—Good Heaven! what do you mean?—Mistake you! —Am I to suppose then——? '

She could not speak another word. Her voice was lost; and she sat down, waiting in great terror till Harriet should answer.

Harriet, who was standing at some distance, and with face turned from her, did not immediately say anything; and when she did speak, it was in a voice nearly as agitated as Emma's.

' I should not have thought it possible,' she began, ' that you could have misunderstood me! I know we agreed never to name him—but considering how infinitely superior he is to everybody else, I should not have thought it possible that I could be supposed to mean any other person. Mr Frank Churchill, indeed! I do not know who would ever look at him in the company of the other. I hope I have a better taste than to think of Mr Frank Churchill, who is like nobody by his side. And that you should have been so mistaken is amazing!—I am sure, but for believing that you entirely approved and meant to encourage me in my attachment, I should have considered it at first too great a presumption almost to dare to think of him. At first, if you had not told me that more wonderful things had happened; that there had been matches of greater disparity (those were your very words)—I should not have dared to give way to— I should not have thought it possible; but if *you*, who had been always acquainted with him—— '

' Harriet,' cried Emma, collecting herself resolutely, ' let us understand each other now, without the possibility of further mistake. Are you speaking of—Mr Knightley?'

'To be sure I am. I never could have an idea of anybody else; and so I thought you knew. When we talked about him it was as clear as possible.'

'Not quite,' returned Emma, with forced calmness; 'for all that you then said appeared to me to relate to a different person. I could almost assert that you had *named* Mr Frank Churchill. I am sure the service Mr Frank Churchill had rendered you, in protecting you from the gipsies, was spoken of.'

'Oh, Miss Woodhouse, how you do forget.'

'My dear Harriet, I perfectly remember the substance of what I said on the occasion. I told you that I did not wonder at your attachment; that, considering the service he had rendered you, it was extremely natural; and you agreed to it, expressing yourself very warmly as to your sense of that service, and mentioning even what your sensations had been in seeing him come forward to your rescue. The impression of it is strong on my memory.'

'Oh, dear,' cried Harriet, 'now I recollect what you mean; but I was thinking of something very different at the time. It was not the gipsies—it was not Mr Frank Churchill that I meant. No!' (with some elevation) 'I was thinking of a much more precious circumstance—of Mr Knightley coming and asking me to dance, when Mr Elton would not stand up with me, and when there was no other partner in the room. That was the kind action; that was the noble benevolence and generosity; that was the service which made me begin to feel how superior he was to every other being upon earth.'

'Good God!' cried Emma, 'this has been a most unfortunate —most deplorable mistake! What is to be done?'

'You would not have encouraged me, then, if you had understood me? At least, however, I cannot be worse off than I should have been, if the other had been the person; and now. —it *is* possible—'

She paused a few moments. Emma could not speak.

'I do not wonder, Miss Woodhouse,' she resumed, 'that you should feel a great difference between the two, as to me or as to anybody. You must think one five hundred million times more above me than the other. But I hope, Miss Woodhouse, that supposing—that if—strange as it may appear— But you know they were your own words, that *more* wonderful things had happened; matches of *greater* disparity had taken place

than between Mr Frank Churchill and me; and, therefore, it
seems as if such a thing even as this may have occurred before—
and if I should be so fortunate, beyond expression, as to—if
Mr Knightley should really—if *he* does not mind the disparity,
I hope, dear Miss Woodhouse, you will not set yourself against
it and try to put difficulties in the way. But you are too good
for that, I am sure.'

Harriet was standing at one of the windows. Emma turned
round to look at her in consternation, and hastily said:

' Have you any idea of Mr Knightley returning your affection?'

' Yes,' replied Harriet modestly, but not fearfully; ' I must
say that I have.'

Emma's eyes were instantly withdrawn; and she sat silently
meditating in a fixed attitude, for a few minutes. A few minutes
were sufficient for making her acquainted with her own heart.
A mind like hers, once opening to suspicion, made rapid progress;
she touched, she admitted, she acknowledged the whole truth.
Why was it so much worse that Harriet should be in love with
Mr Knightley than with Frank Churchill? Why was the evil
so dreadfully increased by Harriet's having some hope of a return?
It darted through her with the speed of an arrow that Mr
Knightley must marry no one but herself!

Her own conduct, as well as her own heart, was before her
in the same few minutes. She saw it all with a clearness which
had never blessed her before. How improperly had she been
acting by Harriet! How inconsiderate, how indelicate, how
irrational, how unfeeling, had been her conduct! What blindness, what madness had led her on! It struck her with dreadful
force, and she was ready to give it every bad name in the world.
Some portion of respect for herself, however, in spite of all these
demerits, some concern for her own appearance, and a strong
sense of justice by Harriet (there would be no need of *compassion* to
the girl who believed herself loved by Mr Knightley—but justice
required that she should not be made unhappy by any coldness
now) gave Emma the resolution to sit and endure further, with
calmness, with even apparent kindness. For her own advantage,
indeed, it was fit that the utmost extent of Harriet's hopes should
be inquired into; and Harriet had done nothing to forfeit the
regard and interest which had been so voluntarily formed and
maintained, or to deserve to be slighted by the person whose
counsels had never led her right. Rousing from reflection, therefore, and subduing her emotion, she turned to Harriet again,
and in a more inviting accent renewed the conversation; for as

to the subject which had first introduced it, the wonderful story of Jane Fairfax, that was quite sunk and lost. Neither of them thought but of Mr Knightley and themselves.

Harriet, who had been standing in no unhappy reverie, was yet very glad to be called from it by the now encouraging manner of such a judge, and such a friend as Miss Woodhouse; and only wanted invitation to give the history of her hopes with great, though trembling delight. Emma's tremblings, as she asked, and as she listened, were better concealed than Harriet's, but they were not less. Her voice was not unsteady, but her mind was in all the perturbation that such a development of self, such a burst of threatening evil, such a confusion of sudden and perplexing emotions, must create. She listened with much inward suffering, but with great outward patience, to Harriet's detail. Methodical, or well arranged, or very well delivered, it could not be expected to be; but contained, when separated from all the feebleness and tautology of the narration, a substance to sink her spirit; especially with the corroborating circumstances which her own memory brought in favour of Mr Knightley's most improved opinion of Harriet.

Harriet had been conscious of a difference in his behaviour ever since those two decisive dances. Emma knew that he had, on that occasion, found her much superior to his expectation. From that evening, or at least from the time of Miss Woodhouse's encouraging her to think of him, Harriet had begun to be sensible of his talking to her much more than he had been used to do, and of his having, indeed, quite a different manner towards her; a manner of kindness and sweetness. Latterly, she had been more and more aware of it. When they had been all walking together, he had so often come and walked by her, and talked so very delightfully! He seemed to want to be acquainted with her. Emma knew it to have been very much the case; she had often observed the change, to almost the same extent. Harriet repeated expressions of approbation and praise from him—and Emma felt them to be in the closest agreement with what she had known of his opinion of Harriet. He praised her for being without art or affectation; for having simple, honest, generous feelings. She knew that he saw such recommendations in Harriet; he had dwelt on them to her more than once. Much that lived in Harriet's memory, many little particulars of the notice she had received from him, a look, a speech, a removal from one chair to another, a compliment implied, a preference inferred, had been unnoticed, because unsuspected, by Emma. Circumstances that might swell to half an hour's relation, and contained multiplied proofs to her who had seen them, had passed undiscerned by her who now heard them; but the two latest occurrences to be mentioned—the two of strongest promise to Harriet—were not without some degree of witness from Emma herself. The first was his walking with her apart from the others in the limewalk at Donwell, where they had been walking some time before Emma came, and he had taken pains (as she was convinced) to draw her from the rest to himself; and at first he had talked to her in a more particular way than he had ever done before—in a very particular way indeed! (Harriet could not recall it without a blush.) He seemed to be almost asking her whether her affections were engaged. But as soon as she (Miss Woodhouse) appeared likely to join them, he changed the subject, and began talking about farming. The second was his having sat talking with her nearly half an hour before Emma came back from her visit, the very last morning of his being at Hartfield—though, when he first came in, he had said that he could not stay five minutes—and his having told her, during their conversation, that though he must go to London, it was very much against his inclination that he left home at all, which was much more (as Emma felt) than he had acknowledged to *her*. The superior degree of confidence towards Harriet which this one article marked gave her severe pain.

On the subject of the first of the two circumstances, she did, after a little reflection, venture the following question: ' Might he not?—Is not it possible, that, when inquiring, as you thought, into the state of your affections, he might be alluding to Mr Martin—he might have Mr Martin's interest in view? ' But Harriet rejected the suspicion with spirit.

' Mr Martin! No, indeed!—There was not a hint of Mr Martin. I hope I know better now than to care for Mr Martin, or to be suspected of it.'

When Harriet had closed her evidence, she appealed to her dear Miss Woodhouse to say whether she had not good ground for hope.

' I never should have presumed to think of it at first,' said she, ' but for you. You told me to observe him carefully, and let his behaviour be the rule of mine—and so I have. But now I seem to feel that I may deserve him; and that if he does choose me, it will not be anything so very wonderful.'

The bitter feelings occasioned by this speech, the many bitter feelings, made the utmost exertion necessary on Emma's side to enable her to say on reply:

'Harriet, I will only venture to declare, that Mr Knightley is the last man in the world who would intentionally give any woman the idea of his feeling for her more than he really does.'

Harriet seemed ready to worship her friend for a sentence so satisfactory; and Emma was only saved from raptures and fondness, which at that moment would have been dreadful penance, by the sound of her father's footsteps. He was coming through the hall. Harriet was too much agitated to encounter him. 'She could not compose herself—Mr Woodhouse would be alarmed—she had better go;' with most ready encouragement from her friend, therefore, she passed off through another door—and the moment she was gone, this was the spontaneous burst of Emma's feelings: 'O God! that I had never seen her!'

The rest of the day, the following night, were hardly enough for her thoughts. She was bewildered amidst the confusion of all that had rushed on her within the last few hours. Every moment had brought a fresh surprise; and every surprise must be matter of humiliation to her. How to understand it all! How to understand the deceptions she had been thus practising on herself, and living under! The blunders, the blindness of her own head and heart! She sat still, she walked about, she tried her own room, she tried the shrubbery—in every place, every posture, she perceived that she had acted most weakly; that she had been imposed on by others in a most mortifying degree; that she had been imposing on herself in a degree yet more mortifying; that she was wretched, and should probably find this day but the beginning of wretchedness.

To understand, thoroughly understand her own heart, was the first endeavour. To that point went every leisure moment which her father's claims on her allowed, and every moment of involuntary absence of mind.

How long had Mr Knightley been so dear to her, as every feeling declared him now to be? When had his influence, such influence begun? When had he succeeded to that place in her affection which Frank Churchill had once, for a short period, occupied?—She looked back, she compared the two—compared them, as they had always stood in her estimation, from the time of the latter's becoming known to her—and as they must at any time have been compared by her, had it—oh! had it, by any blessed felicity, occurred to her to institute the comparison. She saw that there never had been a time when she did not consider Mr Knightley as infinitely the superior, or when his regard for her had not been infinitely the most dear. She saw, that in persuading herself, in fancying, in acting to the contrary, she had been entirely under a delusion, totally ignorant of her own heart—and, in short, that she had never really cared for Frank Churchill at all!

This was the conclusion of the first series of reflections. This was the knowledge of herself, on the first question of inquiry, which she reached; and without being long in reaching it. She was most sorrowfully indignant; ashamed of every sensation but the one revealed to her—her affection for Mr Knightley. Every other part of her mind was disgusting.

With insufferable vanity had she believed herself in the secret of everybody's feelings; with unpardonable arrogance proposed to arrange everybody's destiny. She was proved to have been universally mistaken; and she had not quite done nothing—for she had done mischief. She had brought evil on Harriet, on herself, and, she too much feared, on Mr Knightley. Were this most unequal of all connections to take place, on her must rest all the reproach of having given it a beginning; for his attachment she must believe to be produced only by a consciousness of Harriet's; and even were this not the case, he would never have known Harriet at all but for her folly.

Mr Knightley and Harriet Smith! It was a union to distance every wonder of the kind. The attachment of Frank Churchill and Jane Fairfax became commonplace, threadbare, stale in comparison, exciting no surprise, presenting no disparity, affording nothing to be said or thought. Mr Knightley and Harriet Smith! Such an elevation on her side! Such a debasement on his! It was horrible to Emma to think how it must sink him in the general opinion, to foresee the smiles, the sneers, the merriment it would prompt at his expense; the mortification and disdain of his brother, the thousand inconveniences to himself. Could it be? No; it was impossible. And yet it was far, very far, from impossible. Was it a new circumstance for a man of first-rate abilities to be captivated by very inferior powers? Was it new for one, perhaps too busy to seek, to be the prize of a girl who would seek him? Was it new for anything in this world to be unequal, inconsistent, incongruous—or for chance and circumstance (as second causes) to direct the human fate?

Oh! had she never brought Harriet forward! Had she left her where she ought, and where he had told her she ought! Had she not, with a folly which no tongue could express, prevented her marrying the unexceptionable young man who would have made her happy and respectable in the line of life to which she ought to belong, all would have been safe; none of this dreadful sequel would have been.

How Harriet could ever have had the presumption to raise her thoughts to Mr Knightley! How she could dare to fancy herself the chosen of such a man till actually assured of it! But Harriet was less humble, had fewer scruples than formerly. Her inferiority, whether of mind or situation, seemed little felt. She had seemed more sensible of Mr Elton's being to stoop in marrying her, than she now seemed of Mr Knightley's. Alas! was not that her own doing too? Who had been at pains to give Harriet notions of self-consequence but herself? Who but herself had taught her that she was to elevate herself, if possible, and that her claims were great to a high worldly establishment? If Harriet, from being humble, were grown vain, it was her doing too.

48

TILL now that she was threatened with its loss, Emma had never known how much of her happiness depended on being *first* with Mr Knightley, first in interest and affection. Satisfied that it was so, and feeling it her due, she had enjoyed it without reflection; and only, in the dread of being supplanted, found how inexpressibly important it had been. Long, very long, she felt she had been first; for, having no female connections of his own, there had been only Isabella whose claims could be compared with hers, and she had always known exactly how far he loved and esteemed Isabella. She had herself been first with him for many years past. She had not deserved it; she had often been negligent or perverse, slighting his advice, or even wilfully opposing him, insensible of half his merits, and quarrelling with him because he would not acknowledge her false and insolent estimate of her own—but still, from family attachment and habit, and thorough excellence of mind, he had loved her, and watched over her from a girl, with an endeavour to improve her, and an anxiety for her doing right, which no other creature had at all shared. In spite of all her faults, she knew she was dear to him; might she not say very dear? When the suggestions of hope, however, which must follow here, presented themselves, she could not presume to indulge them. Harriet Smith might think herself not unworthy of being peculiarly, exclusively, passionately loved by Mr Knightley. *She* could not. She could not flatter herself with any idea of blindness in his attachment to *her*. She had received a very recent proof of its impartiality. How shocked had he been by her behaviour to Miss Bates! How directly, how strongly, had he expressed himself to her on the subject! Not too strongly for the offence—but far, far too strongly to issue from any feeling softer than upright justice and clear-sighted goodwill. She had no hope, nothing to deserve the name of hope, that he could have that sort of affection for herself which was now in question; but there was a hope (at times a slight one, at times much stronger) that Harriet might have deceived herself, and be overrating his regard for *her*. Wish it she must, for his sake—be the consequence nothing to herself, but his remaining single all his life. Could she be secure of that, indeed, of his never marrying at all, she believed she should be perfectly satisfied. Let him but continue the same Mr Knightley to her and her father, the same Mr Knightley to all the world; let Donwell and Hartfield lose none of their precious intercourse of friendship and confidence, and her peace would be fully secured. Marriage, in fact, would not do for her. It would be incompatible with what she owed to her father, and with what she felt for him. Nothing should separate her from her father. She would not marry, even if she were asked by Mr Knightley.

It must be her ardent wish that Harriet might be disappointed; and she hoped, that when able to see them together again, she might at least be able to ascertain what the chances for it were. She should see them henceforward with the closest observance; and wretchedly as she had hitherto misunderstood even those she was watching, she did not know how to admit that she could be blinded here! He was expected back every day. The power of observation would be soon given; frightfully soon it appeared when her thoughts were in one course. In the meanwhile, she resolved against seeing Harriet. It would do neither of them good, it would do the subject no good, to be talking of it further. She was resolved not to be convinced, as long as she could doubt, and yet had no authority for opposing Harriet's confidence. To talk would be only to irritate. She wrote to her, therefore, kindly, but decisively, to beg that she would not, at present, come to Hartfield; acknowledging it to be her conviction that all further confidential discussion of *one* topic had better be avoided; and hoping, that if a few days were allowed to pass before they met again, except in the company of others—she objected only to a *tête-à-tête*—they might be able to act as if they had forgotten the conversation of yesterday. Harriet submitted, and approved, and was grateful.

This point was just arranged when a visitor arrived to tear Emma's thoughts a little from the one subject which had engrossed them, sleeping or waking, the last twenty-four hours— Mrs Weston, who had been calling on her daughter-in-law elect, and took Hartfield in her way home, almost as much in duty to Emma as in pleasure to herself, to relate all the particulars of so interesting an interview.

Mr Weston had accompanied her to Mrs Bates's, and gone through his share of this essential attention most handsomely. But she having then induced Miss Fairfax to join her in an airing, was now returned with much more to say, and much more to say with satisfaction, than a quarter of an hour spent in Mrs Bates's parlour, with all the encumbrance of awkward feelings could have afforded.

A little curiosity Emma had, and she made the most of it while her friend related. Mrs Weston had set off to pay the visit in a good deal of agitation herself; and in the first place had wished not to go at all at present, to be allowed merely to write to Miss Fairfax instead, and to defer this ceremonious call till a little time had passed, and Mr Churchill could be reconciled to the engagement's becoming known; as, considering everything, she thought such a visit could not be paid without leading to reports; but Mr Weston had thought differently; he was extremely anxious to show his approbation to Miss Fairfax and her family, and did not conceive that any suspicion could be excited by it; or, if it were, that it would be of any consequence; for ' such things,' he observed, ' always got about.' Emma smiled, and felt that Mr Weston had very good reason for saying so. They had gone, in short; and very great had been the evident distress and confusion of the lady. She had hardly been able to speak a word, and every look and action had shown how deeply she was suffering from consciousness. The quiet, heartfelt satisfaction of the old lady, and the rapturous delight of her daughter, who proved even too joyous to talk us usual, had been a gratifying; yet almost an affecting, scene. They were both so truly respectable in their happiness, so disinterested in every sensation; thought so much of Jane; so much of everybody, and so little of themselves, that every kindly feeling was at work for them. Miss Fairfax's recent illness had offered a fair plea for Mrs Weston to invite her to an airing; she had drawn back and declined at first, but, on being pressed, had yielded; and, in the course of their drive, Mrs Weston had, by gentle encouragement, overcome so much of her embarrassment, as to bring her to converse on the important subject. Apologies for her seemingly ungracious silence in their first reception, and the warmest expressions of the gratitude she was always feeling towards herself and Mr Weston, must necessarily open the cause; but when these effusions were put by, they had talked a good deal of the present and of the future state of the engagement. Mrs Weston was convinced that such conversation must be the greatest relief to her companion, pent up within her own mind as everything had so long been, and was very much pleased with all that she had said on the subject.

'On the misery of what she had suffered, during the concealment of so many months,' continued Mrs Weston, 'she was energetic. This was one of her expressions: "I will not say that since I entered into the engagement I have not had some happy moments; but I can say, that I have never known the blessing of one tranquil hour:"—and the quivering lip, Emma, which uttered it was an attestation that I felt at my heart.'

'Poor girl!' said Emma. 'She thinks herself wrong, then, for having consented to a private engagement?'

'Wrong! No one, I believe, can blame her more than she is disposed to blame herself. "The consequence," said she, "has been a state of perpetual suffering to me; and so it ought. But after all the punishment that misconduct can bring, it is still not less misconduct. Pain is no expiation. I never can be blameless. I have been acting contrary to all my sense of right; and the fortunate turn that everything has taken, and the kindness I am now receiving is what my conscience tells me ought not to be." "Do not imagine, madam," she continued, "that I was taught wrong. Do not let any reflection fall on the principles or the care of the friends who brought me up. The error has been all my own; and I do assure you that, with all the excuse that present circumstances may appear to give, I shall yet dread making the story known to Colonel Campbell."'

'Poor girl!' said Emma, again. 'She loves him, then, excessively, I suppose. It must have been from attachment only that she could be led to form the engagement. Her affection must have overpowered her judgment.'

'Yes, I have no doubt of her being extremely attached to him.'

'I am afraid,' returned Emma, sighing, 'that I must often have contributed to make her unhappy.'

'On your side, my love, it was very innocently done. But she probably had something of that in her thoughts, when alluding to the misunderstandings which he had given us hints of before. One natural consequence of the evil she had involved herself in, she said, was that of making her *unreasonable*. The consciousness of having done amiss had exposed her to a thousand inquietudes, and made her captious and irritable to a degree, that must have been—that had been—hard for him to bear. " I did not make the allowances," said she, " which I ought to have done, for his temper and spirits—his delightful spirits, and that gaiety, that playfulness of disposition, which, under any other circumstances, would, I am sure, have been as constantly bewitching to me as they were at first." She then began to speak of you, and of the great kindness you had shown her during her illness; and, with a blush, which showed me how it was all connected, desired me, whenever I had an opportunity, to thank you—I could not thank you too much—for every wish and every endeavour to do her good. She was sensible that you had never received any proper acknowledgment from herself.'

' If I did not know her to be happy now,' said Emma seriously, ' which in spite of every little drawback from her scrupulous conscience, she must be, I could not bear these thanks; for, oh! Mrs Weston, if there were an account drawn up of the evil and the good I have done Miss Fairfax—— Well ' (checking herself, and trying to be more lively), ' this is all to be forgotten. You are very kind to bring me these interesting particulars; they show her to the greatest advantage. I am sure she is very good; I hope she will be very happy. It is fit that the fortune should be on his side, for I think the merit will be all on hers.'

Such a conclusion could not pass unanswered by Mrs Weston. She thought well of Frank in almost every respect; and, what was more, she loved him very much, and her defence was, therefore, earnest. She talked with a great deal of reason, and at least equal affection; but she had too much to urge for Emma's attention; it was soon gone to Brunswick Square or to Donwell; she forgot to attempt to listen; and when Mrs Weston ended with, ' We have not yet had the letter we are so anxious for, you know, but I hope it will soon come,' she was obliged to pause before she answered, and at last obliged to answer at random, before she could at all recollect what letter it was which they were so anxious for.

' Are you well, my Emma?' was Mrs Weston's parting question.

' Oh, perfectly. I am always well, you know. Be sure to give me intelligence of the letter as soon as possible.'

Mrs Weston's communications furnished Emma with more food for unpleasant reflection, by increasing her esteem and compassion, and her sense of past injustice towards Miss Fairfax. She bitterly regretted not having sought a closer acquaintance with her, and blushed for the envious feelings which had certainly been, in some measure, the cause. Had she followed Mr Knightley's known wishes, in paying that attention to Miss Fairfax which was every way her due; had she tried to know her better; had she done her part towards intimacy; had she endeavoured to find a friend there instead of in Harriet Smith; she must, in all probability, have been spared from every pain which pressed on her now. Birth, abilities, and education had been equally marking one as an associate for her, to be received with gratitude; and the other—what was she? Supposing even that they had never become intimate friends; that she had never been admitted into Miss Fairfax's confidence on this important matter—which was most probable—still, in knowing her as she ought, and as she might, she must have been preserved from the abominable suspicions of an improper attachment to Mr Dixon, which she had not only so foolishly fashioned and harboured herself, but had so unpardonably imparted; an idea which she greatly feared had been made a subject of material distress to the delicacy of Jane's feelings, by the levity or carelessness of Frank Churchill's. Of all the sources of evil surrounding the former, since her coming to Highbury, she was persuaded that she must herself have been the worst. She must have been a perpetual enemy. They never could have been all three together, without her having stabbed Jane Fairfax's peace in a thousand instances; and on Box Hill, perhaps, it had been the agony of a mind that would bear no more.

The evening of this day was very long and melancholy at Hartfield. The weather added what it could of gloom. A cold stormy rain set in, and nothing of July appeared but in the trees and shrubs, which the wind was despoiling, and the length of the day, which only made such cruel sights the longer visible.

The weather affected Mr Woodhouse; and he could only be kept tolerably comfortable by almost ceaseless attention on his daughter's side, and by exertions which had never cost her half so much before. It reminded her of their first forlorn *tête-à-tête*, on the evening of Mrs Weston's wedding-day. But Mr Knightley had walked in then, soon after tea, and dissipated every melancholy fancy. Alas! such delightful proofs of Hartfield's attractions, as those sort of visits conveyed, might shortly be over. The picture which she had then drawn of the privations of the approaching winter had proved erroneous; no friends had deserted them, no pleasures had been lost. But her present forebodings she feared would experience no similar contradictions. The prospect before her now was threatening to a degree that could not be entirely dispelled—that might not be even partially brightened. If all took place that might take place among the circle of her friends, Hartfield must be comparatively deserted; and she left to cheer her father with the spirits only of ruined happiness.

The child to be born at Randalls must be a tie there even dearer than herself; and Mrs Weston's heart and time would be occupied by it. They should lose her; and probably, in great measure, her husband also. Frank Churchill would return among them no more; and Miss Fairfax, it was reasonable to suppose, would soon cease to belong to Highbury. They would be married, and settled either at or near Enscombe. All that were good would be withdrawn; and if to these losses the loss of Donwell were to be added, what would remain of cheerful or of rational society within their reach? Mr Knightley to be no longer coming there for his evening comfort! No longer walking in at all hours, as if ever willing to change his own home for theirs! How was it to be endured? And if he were to be lost to them for Harriet's sake; if he were to be thought of hereafter, as finding in Harriet's society all that he wanted! if Harriet were to be the chosen, the first, the dearest, the friend, the wife to whom he looked for all the best blessings of existence; what could be increasing Emma's wretchedness but the reflection, never far distant from her mind, that it had been all her own work?

When it came to such a pitch as this, she was not able to refrain from a start, or a heavy sigh, or even from walking about the room for a few seconds; and the only source whence anything like consolation or composure could be drawn, was in the resolution of her own better conduct, and the hope that, however inferior in spirit and gaiety might be the following and every future winter of her life to the past, it would yet find her more rational, more acquainted with herself, and leave her less to regret when it were gone.

49

THE weather continued much the same all the following morning; and the same loneliness, and the same melancholy, seemed to reign at Hartfield; but in the afternoon it cleared; the wind changed into a softer quarter; the clouds were carried off; the sun appeared; it was summer again. With all the eagerness which such a transition gives, Emma resolved to be out of doors as soon as possible. Never had the exquisite sight, smell, sensation of nature, tranquil, warm, and brilliant after a storm, been more attractive to her. She longed for the serenity they might gradually introduce; and, on Mr Perry's coming in soon after dinner, with a disengaged hour to give her father, she lost no time in hurrying into the shrubbery. There, with spirits freshened, and thoughts a little relieved, she had taken a few turns, when she saw Mr Knightley passing through the garden door and coming towards her. It was the first intimation of his being returned from London. She had been thinking of him the moment before, as unquestionably sixteen miles distant. There was time only for the quickest arrangement of mind. She must be collected and calm. In half a minute they were together. The 'How-d'ye-do's' were quiet and constrained on each side. She asked after their mutual friends; they were all well. When had he left them? Only that morning. He must have had a wet ride.—Yes!—He meant to walk with her, she found. 'He had just looked into the dining-room, and as he was not wanted there, preferred being out-of-doors.' She thought he neither looked nor spoke cheerfully; and the first possible cause for it, suggested by her fears, was, that he had perhaps been communicating his plans to his brother, and was pained by the manner in which they had been received.

They walked together. He was silent. She thought he was often looking at her, and trying for a fuller view of her face than it suited her to give. And this belief produced another dread. Perhaps he wanted to speak to her of his attachment to Harriet, he might be watching for encouragement to begin. She did not, could not, feel equal to lead the way to any such subject. He must do it all himself. Yet she could not bear this silence. With him it was most unnatural. She considered, resolved, and trying to smile, began:

'You have some news to hear, now you are come back, that will rather surprise you.'

'Have I?' said he quietly, and looking at her; 'of what nature?'

'Oh, the best nature in the world—a wedding.'

After waiting a moment, as if to be sure she intended to say no more, he replied:

'If you mean Miss Fairfax and Frank Churchill, I have heard that already.'

'How is it possible?' cried Emma, turning her glowing cheeks towards him; for, while she spoke, it occurred to her that he might have called at Mrs Goddard's in his way.

'I had a few lines on parish business from Mr Weston this morning, and at the end of them he gave me a brief account of what had happened.'

Emma was quite relieved, and could presently say, with a little more composure:

'*You* probably have been less surprised than any of us, for you have had your suspicions. I have not forgotten that you once tried to give me a caution. I wish I had attended to it—but ' (with a sinking voice and a heavy sigh) 'I seem to have been doomed to blindness.'

For a moment or two nothing was said, and she was unsuspicious of having excited any particular interest, till she found her arm drawn within his, and pressed against his heart, and heard him thus saying, in a tone of great sensibility, speaking low:

'Time, my dearest Emma, time will heal the wound. Your own excellent sense; your exertions for your father's sake; I know you will not allow yourself—— ' Her arm was pressed again, as he added, in a more broken and subdued accent, 'The feelings of the warmest friendship—indignation—abominable scoundrel!' And in a louder, steadier tone, he concluded with, 'He will soon be gone. They will soon be in Yorkshire. I am sorry for *her*. She deserves a better fate.'

Emma understood him; and as soon as she could recover from the flutter of pleasure, excited by such tender consideration, replied:

'You are very kind, but you are mistaken, and I must set you right. I am not in want of that sort of compassion. My blindness to what was going on led me to act by them in a way that I must always be ashamed of, and I was very foolishly tempted to say and do many things which may well lay me open to unpleasant conjectures, but I have no other reason to regret that I was not in the secret earlier.'

'Emma,' cried he, looking eagerly at her, 'are you indeed?'

—but checking himself—'No, no, I understand you—forgive me; I am pleased that you can say even so much. He is no object of regret, indeed! and it will not be very long, I hope, before that becomes the acknowledgment of more than your reason. Fortunate that your affections were not further entangled! I could never, I confess, from your manners, assure myself as to the degree of what you felt—I could only be certain that there was a preference—and a preference which I never believed him to deserve. He is a disgrace to the name of man. And is he to be rewarded with that sweet young woman? Jane! Jane! you will be a miserable creature.'

'Mr Knightley,' said Emma, trying to be lively, but really confused—'I am in a very extraordinary situation. I cannot let you continue in your error; and yet, perhaps, since my manners gave such an impression, I have as much reason to be ashamed of confessing that I never have been at all attached to the person we are speaking of, as it might be natural for a woman to feel in confessing exactly the reverse. But I never have.'

He listened in perfect silence. She wished him to speak, but he would not. She supposed she must say more before she was entitled to his clemency; but it was a hard case to be obliged still to lower herself in his opinion. She went on, however.

'I have very little to say for my own conduct. I was tempted by his attentions, and allowed myself to appear pleased. An old story, probably—a common case—and no more than has happened to hundreds of my sex before; and yet it may not be the more excusable in one who sets up as I do for Understanding. Many circumstances assisted the temptation. He was the son of Mr Weston—he was continually here—I always found him very pleasant—and in short, for ' (with a sigh) ' let me swell out the causes ever so ingeniously, they all centre in this at last— my vanity was flattered, and I allowed his attentions. Latterly, however—for some time, indeed—I have had no idea of their meaning anything. I thought them a habit, a trick, nothing that called for seriousness on my side. He has imposed on me, but he has not injured me. I have never been attached to him. And now I can tolerably comprehend his behaviour. He never wished to attach me. It was merely a blind to conceal his real situation with another. It was his object to blind all about him; and no one, I am sure, could be more effectually blinded than myself—except that I was *not* blinded—that it was my good fortune—that, in short, I was somehow or other safe from him.'

She had hoped for an answer here—for a few words to say that her conduct was at least intelligible; but he was silent; and, as far as she could judge, deep in thought. At last, and tolerably in his usual tone, he said:

'I have never had a high opinion of Frank Churchill. I can suppose, however, that I may have underrated him. My acquaintance with him has been but trifling. And even if I have not underrated him hitherto, he may yet turn out well. With such a woman he has a chance. I have no motive for wishing him ill—and for her sake, whose happiness will be involved in his good character and conduct, I shall certainly wish him well.'

'I have no doubt of their being happy together,' said Emma; 'I believe them to be very mutually and very sincerely attached.'

'He is a most fortunate man,' returned Mr Knightley, with energy. 'So early in life—at three-and-twenty—a period when, if a man chooses a wife, he generally chooses ill. At three-and-twenty to have drawn such a prize! What years of felicity that man in all human calculation has before him! Assured of the love of such a woman—the disinterested love—for Jane Fairfax's character vouches for her disinterestedness; everything in his favour—equality of situation—I mean, as far as regards society, and all the habits and manners that are important; equality in every point but one—and that one, since the purity of her heart is not to be doubted, such as must increase his felicity, for it will be his to bestow the only advantages she wants. A man would always wish to give a woman a better home than the one he takes her from; and he who can do it, where there is no doubt of her regard, must, I think, be the happiest of mortals. Frank Churchill is, indeed, the favourite of fortune. Everything turns out for his good. He meets with a young woman at a watering-place, gains her affection, cannot even weary her by negligent treatment—and had he and all his family sought round the world for a perfect wife for him, they could not have found her superior. His aunt is in the way. His aunt dies. He has only to speak. His friends are eager to promote his happiness. He has used everybody ill—and they are all delighted to forgive him. He is a fortunate man, indeed!'

'You speak as if you envied him.'

'And I do envy him, Emma. In one respect he is the object of my envy.'

Emma could say no more. They seemed to be within half a sentence of Harriet, and her immediate feeling was to avert the subject, if possible. She made her plan; she would speak of something totally different—the children in Brunswick Square; and she only waited for breath to begin, when Mr Knightley startled her by saying:

'You will not ask me what is the point of envy. You are determined, I see, to have no curiosity. You are wise—but *I* cannot be wise. Emma, I must tell what you will not ask, though I may wish it unsaid the next moment.'

'Oh, then, don't speak it, don't speak it,' she eagerly cried. 'Take a little time, consider, do not commit yourself.'

'Thank you,' said he, in an accent of deep mortification, and not another syllable followed.

Emma could not bear to give him pain. He was wishing to confide in her—perhaps to consult her; cost her what it would, she would listen. She might assist his resolution, or reconcile him to it; she might give just praise to Harriet, or, by representing to him his own independence, relieve him from that state of indecision which must be more intolerable than any alternative to such a mind as his. They had reached the house.

'You are going in, I suppose?' said he.

'No,' replied Emma, quite confirmed by the depressed manner in which he still spoke, 'I should like to take another turn. Mr Perry is not gone.' And, after proceeding a few steps, she added —'I stopped you ungraciously, just now, Mr Knightley, and, I am afraid, gave you pain. But if you have any wish to speak openly to me as a friend, or to ask my opinion of anything that you may have in contemplation—as a friend, indeed, you may command me. I will hear whatever you like. I will tell you exactly what I think.'

'As a friend!' repeated Mr Knightley. 'Emma, that, I fear, is a word—no, I have no wish. Stay, yes, why should I hesitate? I have gone too far already for concealment. Emma, I accept your offer, extraordinary as it may seem, I accept it, and refer myself to you as a friend. Tell me, then, have I no chance of ever succeeding?'

He stopped in his earnestness to look the question, and the expression of his eyes overpowered her.

'My dearest Emma,' said he, 'for dearest you will always be, whatever the event of this hour's conversation, my dearest, most beloved Emma—tell me at once. Say "No," if it is to be said.' She could really say nothing. 'You are silent,' he cried, with great animation; 'absolutely silent! at present I ask no more.'

Emma was almost ready to sink under the agitation of this

moment. The dread of being awakened from the happiest dream was perhaps the most prominent feeling.

'I cannot make speeches, Emma,' he soon resumed, and in a tone of such sincere, decided, intelligible tenderness as was tolerably convincing. 'If I loved you less, I might be able to talk about it more. But you know what I am. You hear nothing but truth from me. I have blamed you, and lectured you, and you have borne it as no other woman in England would have borne it. Bear with the truths I would tell you now, dearest Emma, as well as you have borne with them. The manner, perhaps, may have as little to recommend them. God knows, I have been a very indifferent lover. But you understand me. Yes, you see, you understand my feelings—and will return them if you can. At present, I ask only to hear—once to hear your voice.'

While he spoke, Emma's mind was most busy, and, with all the wonderful velocity of thought, had been able—and yet without losing a word—to catch and comprehend the exact truth of the whole; to see that Harriet's hopes had been entirely groundless, a mistake, a delusion, as complete a delusion as any of her own—that Harriet was nothing; that she was everything herself; that what she had been saying relative to Harriet had been all taken as the language of her own feelings; and that her agitation, her doubts, her reluctance, her discouragement, had been all received as discouragement from herself. And not only was there time for these convictions, with all their glow of attendant happiness, there was time also to rejoice that Harriet's secret had not escaped her, and to resolve that it need not, and should not. It was all the service she could now render her poor friend; for as to any of that heroism of sentiment which might have prompted her to entreat him to transfer his affection from herself to Harriet, as infinitely the most worthy of the two—or even the more simple sublimity of resolving to refuse him at once and for ever, without vouchsafing any motive because he could not marry them both—Emma had it not. She felt for Harriet, with pain and with contrition; but no flight of generosity run mad, opposing all that could be probable or reasonable, entered her brain. She had led her friend astray, and it would be a reproach to her for ever; but her judgment was as strong as her feelings, and as strong as it had ever been before, in reprobating any such alliance for him, as most unequal and degrading. Her way was clear, though not quite smooth. She spoke then, on being so entreated. What did she say?

Just what she ought, of course. A lady always does. She said enough to show there need not be despair—and to invite him to say more himself. He *had* despaired at one period; he had received such an injunction to caution and silence, as for the time crushed every hope—she had begun by refusing to hear him. The change had perhaps been somewhat sudden—her proposal of taking another turn, her renewing the conversation which she had just put an end to, might be a little extraordinary. She felt its inconsistency; but Mr Knightley was so obliging as to put up with it, and seek no further explanation.

Seldom, very seldom, does complete truth belong to any human disclosure; seldom can it happen that something is not a little disguised, or a little mistaken; but where, as in this case, though the conduct is mistaken, the feelings are not, it may not be very material. Mr Knightley could not impute to Emma a more relenting heart than she possessed, or a heart more disposed to accept of his.

He had, in fact, been wholly unsuspicious of his own influence. He had followed her into the shrubbery with no idea of trying it. He had come, in his anxiety to see how she bore Frank Churchill's engagement, with no selfish view, no view at all, but of endeavouring, if she allowed him an opening, to soothe or to counsel her. The rest had been the work of the moment, the immediate effect of what he heard, on his feelings. The delightful assurance of her total indifference towards Frank Churchill, of her having a heart completely disengaged from him, had given birth to the hope that, in time, he might gain her affection himself; but it had been no present hope; he had only, in the momentary conquest of eagerness over judgment, aspired to be told that she did not forbid his attempt to attach her. The superior hopes which gradually opened were so much the more enchanting. The affection which he had been asking to be allowed to create, if he could, was already his. Within half an hour he had passed from a thoroughly distressed state of mind, to something so like perfect happiness, that it could bear no other name.

Her change was equal. This one half-hour had given to each the same precious certainty of being beloved, had cleared from each the same degree of ignorance, jealousy, or distrust. On his side, there had been a long-standing jealousy, old as the arrival or even the expectation of Frank Churchill. He had been in love with Emma, and jealous of Frank Churchill, from about the same period, one sentiment having probably enlightened him as to the other. It was his jealousy of Frank Churchill that had taken him from the country. The Box Hill party had decided him on going away. He would save himself from witnessing again such permitted, encouraged attentions. He had gone to learn to be indifferent. But he had gone to a wrong place. There was too much domestic happiness in his brother's house; woman wore too amiable a form in it; Isabella was too much like Emma—differing only in those striking inferiorities which always brought the other in brilliancy before him, for much to have been done even had his time been longer. He had stayed on, however, vigorously, day after day—till this very morning's post had conveyed the history of Jane Fairfax. Then, with the gladness which must be felt, nay, which he did not scruple to feel, having never believed Frank Churchill to be at all deserving Emma, was there so much fond solicitude, so much keen anxiety for her, that he could stay no longer. He had ridden home through the rain; and had walked up directly after dinner, to see how this sweetest and best of all creatures, faultless in spite of all her faults, bore the discovery.

He had found her agitated and low. Frank Churchill was a villain. He heard her declare that she had never loved him. Frank Churchill's character was not desperate. She was his own Emma, by hand and word, when they returned into the house; and if he could have thought of Frank Churchill then, he might have deemed him a very good sort of fellow.

50

WHAT totally different feelings did Emma take back into the house from what she had brought out! She had then been only daring to hope for a little respite of suffering; she was now in an exquisite flutter of happiness—and such happiness, moreover, as she believed must still be greater when the flutter should have passed away.

They sat down to tea—the same party round the same table —how often it had been collected! and how often had her eyes fallen on the same shrubs in the lawn, and observed the same beautiful effect of the western sun! But never in such a state of spirits, never in anything like it; and it was with difficulty that she could summon enough of her usual self to be the attentive lady of the house, or even the attentive daughter.

Poor Mr Woodhouse little suspected what was plotting against him in the breast of that man whom he was so cordially welcoming, and so anxiously hoping might not have taken cold from his ride. Could he have seen the heart, he would have cared very little for the lungs; but without the most distant imagination of the impending evil, without the slightest perception of anything extraordinary, in the looks or ways of either, he repeated to them very comfortably all the articles of news he had received from Mr Perry, and talked on with much self-contentment, totally unsuspicious of what they could have told him in return.

As long as Mr Knightley remained with them, Emma's fever continued; but when he was gone she began to be a little tranquillised and subdued, and in the course of the sleepless night, which was the tax for such an evening, she found one or two such very serious points to consider, as made her feel, that even her happiness must have some alloy. Her father—and Harriet. She could not be alone without feeling the full weight of their separate claims; and how to guard the comfort of both to the utmost was the question. With respect to her father, it was a question soon answered. She hardly knew yet what Mr Knightley would ask; but a very short parley with her own heart produced the most solemn resolution of never quitting her father. She even wept over the idea of it, as a sin of thought. While he lived, it must be only an engagement; but she flattered herself, that if divested of the danger of drawing her away, it might become an increase of comfort to him. How to do her best by Harriet was of more difficult decision; how to spare her from any unnecessary pain; how to make her any possible atonement; how to appear least her enemy? On these subjects her perplexity and distress were very great—and her mind had to pass again and again through every bitter reproach and sorrowful regret that had ever surrounded it. She could only resolve at last that she would still avoid a meeting with her and communicate all that need be told by letter; that it would be inexpressibly desirable to have her removed just now for a time from Highbury, and—indulging in one scheme more—nearly resolve that it might be practicable to get an invitation for her to Brunswick Square. Isabella had been pleased with Harriet; and a few weeks spent in London must give her some amusement. She did not think it in Harriet's nature to escape being benefited by novelty and variety, by the streets, the shops, and the children. At any rate, it would be a proof of attention and kindness in herself, from whom everything was due; a separation for the present; an averting of the evil day, when they must all be together again.

She rose early, and wrote her letter to Harriet: an employment which left her so very serious, so nearly sad, that Mr Knightley, in walking up to Hartfield to breakfast, did not arrive at all too soon; and half an hour stolen afterwards to go over the same ground again with him, literally and figuratively, was quite necessary to reinstate her in a proper share of the happiness of the evening before.

He had not left her long—by no means long enough for her to have the slightest inclination for thinking of anybody else—when a letter was brought her from Randalls—a very thick letter; she guessed what it must contain, and deprecated the necessity of reading it. She was now in perfect charity with Frank Churchill: she wanted no explanations, she wanted only to have her thoughts to herself—and as for understanding anything he wrote, she was sure she was incapable of it. It must be waded through, however. She opened the packet; it was too surely so; a note from Mrs Weston to herself, ushered in the letter from Frank to Mrs Weston:

' I have the greatest pleasure, my dear Emma, in forwarding to you the enclosed. I know what thorough justice you will do it, and have scarcely a doubt of its happy effect. I think we shall never materially disagree about the writer again; but I will not delay you by a long preface. We are quite well. This letter has been the cure of all the little nervousness I have been feeling lately. I did not quite like your looks on Tuesday, but it was an ungenial morning; and though you will never own being affected by weather, I think everybody feels a north-east wind. I felt for your dear father very much in the storm of Tuesday afternoon and yesterday morning, but had the comfort of hearing last night, by Mr Perry, that it had not made him ill. —Yours ever,

' A. W.'

[*To Mrs Weston.*]

WINDSOR.—*July.*

' MY DEAR MADAM,—If I made myself intelligible yesterday, this letter will be expected; but expected or not, I know it will be read with candour and indulgence. You are all goodness, and I believe there will be need of even all your goodness to allow for some parts of my past conduct. But I have been forgiven by one who had still more to resent. My courage rises while I write. It is very difficult for the prosperous to be humble. I have already met with such success in two applications for pardon, that I may be in danger of thinking myself too sure of yours, and of those among your friends who have had any ground of offence. You must all endeavour to comprehend the exact nature of my situation when I first arrived at Randalls; you must consider me as having a secret which was to be kept at all hazards. This was the fact. My right to place myself in a situation requiring such concealment is another question. I shall not discuss it here. For my temptation to *think* it a right, I refer every caviller to a brick house, sashed windows below, and casements above, in Highbury. I dared not address her openly; my difficulties in the then state of Enscombe must be too well known to require definition; and I was fortunate enough to prevail, before we parted at Weymouth, and to induce the most upright female mind in the creation to stoop in charity to a secret engagement. Had she refused, I should have gone mad. But you will be ready to say, What was your hope in doing this? What did you look forward to? To anything, everything—to time, chance, circumstance, slow effects, sudden bursts, perseverance, and weariness, health, and sickness. Every possibility of good was before me, and the first of blessings secured, in obtaining her promises of faith and correspondence. If you need further explanation, I have the honour, my dear madam, of being your husband's son, and the advantage of inheriting a disposition to hope for good, which no inheritance of houses or lands can ever equal the value of. See me, then, under these circumstances, arriving on my first visit to Randalls; and here I am conscious of wrong, for that visit might have been sooner paid. You will look back, and see that I did not come till Miss Fairfax was in Highbury; and as *you* were the person slighted, you will forgive me instantly; but I must work on my father's compassion, by reminding him, that so long as I absented myself from his house, so long I lost the blessing of knowing you. My behaviour, during the very happy fortnight which I spent with you, did not, I hope, lay me open to reprehension, excepting on one point. And now I come to the principal, the only important part of my conduct, while belonging to you, which excites my own anxiety, or requires very solicitous explanation. With the greatest respect, and the warmest friendship, do I mention Miss Woodhouse; my father, perhaps, will think I ought to add, with the deepest humiliation. A few words which dropped from him yesterday spoke his opinion, and some censure I acknowledge myself liable to. My behaviour to Miss Woodhouse indicated, I believe, more than it ought. In order to assist a concealment so essential to me, I was led on to make more than an allowable use of the sort of intimacy into which we were immediately thrown. I cannot deny that Miss Woodhouse was my ostensible object; but I am sure you will believe the declaration, that had I not been convinced of her indifference, I would not have been induced by any selfish views to go on. Amiable and delightful as Miss Woodhouse is, she never gave me the idea of a young woman likely to be attached; and that she was perfectly free from any tendency to being attached to me, was as much my conviction as my wish. She received my attention with an easy, friendly, good-humoured playfulness which exactly suited me. We seemed to understand each other. From our relative situation, those attentions were her due, and were felt to be so. Whether Miss Woodhouse began really to understand me before the expiration of that fortnight I cannot say; when I called to take leave of her, I remember that I was within a moment of confessing the truth, and I then fancied she was not without suspicion; but I have no doubt of her having since detected me—at least in some degree. She may not have surmised the whole, but her quickness must have penetrated a part. I cannot doubt it. You will find, whenever the subject becomes freed from its present restraints, that it did not take her wholly by surprise. She frequently gave me hints of it. I remember her telling me at the ball that I owed Mrs Elton gratitude for her attentions to Miss Fairfax. I hope this history of my conduct towards her will be admitted by you and my father as great extenuation of what you saw amiss. While you considered me as having sinned against Emma Woodhouse, I could deserve nothing from either. Acquit me here, and procure for me, when it is allowable, the acquittal and good wishes of that said Emma Woodhouse, whom I regard with so much brotherly affection as to long to have her as deeply and as happily in love as myself. Whatever strange things I said or did during that fortnight you have now a key to. My heart was in Highbury, and my business was to get my body thither as often as might be, and with the least suspicion. If you remember any queernesses set them all to the right account. Of the pianoforte so much talked of, I feel it only necessary to say, that its being ordered was absolutely unknown to Miss F——, who would never have allowed me to send it had any choice been given her. The delicacy of her mind throughout the whole engagement, my dear madam, is much beyond my power of doing justice to. You will soon, I earnestly hope, know her thoroughly yourself. No description can describe her. She must tell you herself what she is; yet not by word, for never was there a human creature who would so designedly suppress her own merit. Since I began this letter, which will be longer than I foresaw, I have heard from her. She gives a good account of her own health; but as she never complains, I dare not depend. I want to have your opinion of her looks. I know you will soon call on her; she is living in dread of the visit. Perhaps it is paid already. Let me hear from you without delay; I am impatient for a thousand particulars. Remember how few minutes I was at Randalls, and in how bewildered, how mad a state: and I am not much better yet; still insane either from happiness or misery. When I think of the kindness and favour I have met with, of her excellence and patience, and my uncle's generosity, I am mad with joy: but when I recollect all the uneasiness I occasioned her, and how little I deserve to be forgiven, I am mad with anger. If I could but see her again! But I must not propose it yet; my uncle has been too good for me to encroach. I must still add to this long letter. You have not heard all that you ought to hear. I could not give any connected detail yesterday; but the suddenness and, in one light, the unseasonableness with which the affair burst out, needs explanation; for though the event of the 26th ult., as you will conclude, immediately opened to me the happiest prospects, I should not have presumed on such early measures, but from the very particular circumstances which left me not an hour to lose. I should myself have shrunk from anything so hasty, and she would have felt every scruple of mine with multiplied strength and refinement: but I had no choice. The hasty engagement she had entered into with that woman——here, my dear madam, I was obliged to leave off abruptly, to recollect and compose myself. I have been walking over the country, and am now, I hope, rational enough to make the rest of my letter what it ought to be. It is, in fact, a most mortifying retrospect for me. I behaved shamefully. And here I can admit that my manners to Miss W., in being unpleasant to Miss F., were highly blamable. *She* disapproved them, which ought to have been enough. My plea of concealing the truth she did not think sufficient. She was displeased: I thought unreasonably so; I thought her, on a thousand occasions, unnecessarily scrupulous and cautious; I thought her even cold.

But she was always right. If I had followed her judgment, and subdued my spirits to the level of what she deemed proper, I should have escaped the greatest unhappiness I have ever known. We quarrelled. Do you remember the morning spent at Donwell? *There* every little dissatisfaction that had occurred before came to a crisis. I was late: I met her walking home by herself, and wanted to walk with her, but she would not suffer it. She absolutely refused to allow me, which I then thought most unreasonable. Now, however, I see nothing in it but a very natural and consistent degree of discretion. While I, to blind the world to our engagement, was behaving one hour with objectionable particularity to another woman, was she to be consenting the next to a proposal which might have made every previous caution useless? Had we been met walking together between Donwell and Highbury, the truth must have been suspected. I was mad enough, however, to resent. I doubted her affection. I doubted it more the next day on Box Hill; when, provoked by such conduct on my side, such shameful, insolent, neglect of her, and such apparent devotion to Miss W., as it would have been impossible for any woman of sense to endure, she spoke her resentment in a form of words perfectly intelligible to me. In short, my dear madam, it was a quarrel blameless on her side, abominable on mine; and I returned the same evening to Richmond, though I might have stayed with you till the next morning, merely because I would be as angry with her as possible. Even then I was not such a fool as not to mean to be reconciled in time; but I was the injured person—injured by her coldness —and I went away determined that she should make the first advances. I shall always congratulate myself that you were not of the Box Hill party. Had you witnessed my behaviour there, I can hardly suppose you would ever have thought well of me again. Its effect upon her appears in the immediate resolution it produced. As soon as she found I was really gone from Randalls, she closed with the offer of that officious Mrs Elton; the whole system of whose treatment of her, by the bye, has ever filled me with indignation and hatred. I must not quarrel with a spirit of forbearance which has been so richly extended towards myself; but, otherwise, I should loudly protest against the share of it which that woman has known. "Jane," indeed! You will observe that I have not yet indulged myself in calling her by that name, even to you. Think, then, what I must have endured in hearing it bandied between the Eltons, with all the vulgarity of needless repetition, and all the insolence of imaginary superior-

ity. Have patience with me, I shall soon have done. She closed
with this offer, resolving to break with me entirely, and wrote
the next day to tell me that we never were to meet again. *She
felt the engagement to be a source of repentance and misery to each: she
dissolved it.* This letter reached me on the very morning of my
poor aunt's death. I answered it within an hour; but from
the confusion of my mind, and the multiplicity of business falling
on me at once, my answer, instead of being sent with all the many
other letters of that day, was locked up in my writing-desk, and
I, trusting that I had written enough, though but a few lines,
to satisfy her, remained without any uneasiness. I was rather
disappointed that I did not hear from her again speedily; but
I made excuses for her, and was too busy, and (may I add?)
too cheerful in my views to be captious. We removed to Windsor;
and two days afterwards I received a parcel from her—my own
letters all returned! and a few lines at the same time by the post,
stating her extreme surprise at not having had the smallest reply
to her last; and adding that as silence on such a point could
not be misconstrued, and as it must be equally desirable to both
to have every subordinate arrangement concluded as soon as
possible, she now sent me, by a safe conveyance, all my letters,
and requested, that if I could not directly command hers, so as
to send them to Highbury within a week, I would forward them
after that period to her at——: in short, the full direction to
Mr Smallridge's, near Bristol, stared me in the face. I knew
the name, the place, I knew all about it, and instantly saw
what she had been doing. It was perfectly accordant with that
resolution of character which I knew her to possess; and the
secrecy she had maintained as to any such design in her former
letter, was equally descriptive of its anxious delicacy. For the
world would not she have seemed to threaten me. Imagine
the shock; imagine how, till I had actually detected my own
blunder, I raved at the blunders of the post. What was to be
done? One thing only. I must speak to my uncle. Without
his sanction, I could not hope to be listened to again. I spoke;
circumstances were in my favour; the late event had softened
away his pride, and he was, earlier than I could have anticipated,
wholly reconciled and complying; and could say at last, poor
man! with a deep sigh, that he wished I might find as much
happiness in the marriage state as he had done. I felt that it
would be of a different sort. Are you disposed to pity me for
what I must have suffered in opening the cause to him, for my
suspense while all was at stake? No; do not pity me till I

reached Highbury, and saw how ill I had made her. Do not pity me till I saw her wan, sick looks. I reached Highbury at the time of day when, from my knowledge of their late breakfast-hour, I was certain of a good chance of finding her alone. I was not disappointed; and at last I was not disappointed either in the object of my journey. A great deal of very reasonable, very just displeasure I had to persuade away. But it is done; we are reconciled, dearer, much dearer, than ever, and no moment's uneasiness can ever occur between us again. Now, my dear madam, I will release you; but I could not conclude before. A thousand and a thousand thanks for all the kindness you have ever shown me, and ten thousand for the attentions your heart will dictate towards her. If you think me in a way to be happier than I deserve, I am quite of your opinion. Miss W. calls me the child of good fortune. I hope she is right. In one respect my good fortune is undoubted, that of being able to subscribe myself, your obliged and affectionate Son,

'F. C. Weston Churchill.'

51

This letter must make its way to Emma's feelings. She was obliged, in spite of her previous determination to the contrary, to do it all the justice that Mrs Weston foretold. As soon as she came to her own name, it was irresistible; every line relating to herself was interesting, and almost every line agreeable; and when this charm ceased, the subject could still maintain itself by the natural return of her former regard for the writer, and the very strong attraction which any picture of love must have for her at that moment. She never stopped till she had gone through the whole: and though it was impossible not to feel that he had been wrong, yet he had been less wrong than she had supposed; and he had suffered and was very sorry; and he was so grateful to Mrs Weston, and so much in love with Miss Fairfax, and she was so happy herself, that there was no being severe; and could he have entered the room, she must have shaken hands with him as heartily as ever.

She thought so well of the letter, that when Mr Knightley came again she desired him to read it. She was sure of Mrs Weston's wishing it to be communicated; especially to one who, like Mr Knightley, had seen so much to blame in his conduct.

'I shall be very glad to look it over,' said he; 'but it seems long. I will take it home with me at night.'

But that would not do. Mr Weston was to call in the evening, and she must return it by him.

'I would rather be talking to you,' he replied; 'but as it seems a matter of justice, it shall be done.'

He began—stopping, however, almost directly to say: 'Had I been offered the sight of one of this gentleman's letters to his mother-in-law a few months ago, Emma, it would not have been taken with such indifference.'

He proceeded a little farther, reading to himself; and then, with a smile, observed, 'Humph! a fine complimentary opening: but it is his way. One man's style must not be the rule of another's. We will not be severe.'

'It will be natural for me,' he added shortly afterwards, 'to speak my opinion aloud as I read. By doing it, I shall feel that I am near you. It will not be so great a loss of time; but if you dislike it—— '

'Not at all. I should wish it.'

Mr Knightley returned to his reading with greater alacrity.

'He trifles here,' said he, 'as to the temptation. He knows he is wrong, and has nothing rational to urge. Bad. He ought not to have formed the engagement. " His father's disposition " —he is unjust, however, to his father. Mr Weston's sanguine temper was a blessing on all his upright and honourable exertions; but Mr Weston earned every present comfort before he endeavoured to gain it. Very true; he did not come till Miss Fairfax was here.'

'And I have not forgotten,' said Emma, 'how sure you were that he might have come sooner if he would. You pass it over very handsomely; but you were perfectly right.'

'I was not quite impartial in my judgment, Emma; but yet, I think, had you not been in the case, I should still have distrusted him.'

When he came to Miss Woodhouse, he was obliged to read the whole of it aloud—all that related to her—with a smile, a look, a shake of the head, a word or two of assent, or disapprobation, or merely of love, as the subject required; concluding, however, seriously, and, after steady reflection, thus:

'Very bad—though it might have been worse. Playing a most dangerous game. Too much indebted to the event for his acquittal. No judge of his own manners by you. Always deceived, in fact, by his own wishes, and regardless of little besides his own convenience. Fancying you to have fathomed his secret! Natural enough! his own mind full of intrigue, that he should suspect it in others. Mystery—finesse—how they pervert the understanding! My Emma, does not everything serve to prove more and more the beauty of truth and sincerity in all our dealings with each other?'

Emma agreed to it, and with a blush of sensibility on Harriet's account, which she could not give any sincere explanation of.

'You had better go on,' said she.

He did so, but very soon stopped again to say: 'The pianoforte! Ah! that was the act of a very, very young man, one too young to consider whether the inconvenience of it might not very much exceed the pleasure. A boyish scheme, indeed! I cannot comprehend a man's wishing to give a woman any proof of affection which he knows she would rather dispense with: and he did know that she would have prevented the instrument's coming if she could.'

After this, he made some progress without any pause. Frank Churchill's confession of having behaved shamefully was the first thing to call for more than a word in passing.

'I perfectly agree with you, sir,' was then his remark. 'You did behave very shamefully. You never wrote a truer line.' And having gone through what immediately followed of the basis of their disagreement, and his persisting to act in direct opposition to Jane Fairfax's sense of right, he made a fuller pause to say: 'This is very bad. He had induced her to place herself, for his sake, in a situation of extreme difficulty and uneasiness, and it should have been his first object to prevent her from suffering unnecessarily. She must have had much more to contend with in carrying on the correspondence than he could. He should have respected even unreasonable scruples, had there been such; but hers were all reasonable. We must look to her one fault, and remember that she had done a wrong thing in consenting to the engagement, to bear that she should have been in such a state of punishment.'

Emma knew that he was now getting to the Box Hill party, and grew uncomfortable. Her own behaviour had been so very improper! She was deeply ashamed, and a little afraid of his next look. It was all read, however, steadily, attentively, and without the smallest remark; and, excepting one momentary glance at her, instantly withdrawn, in the fear of giving pain, no remembrance of Box Hill seemed to exist.

'There is no saying much for the delicacy of our good friends,

the Eltons,' was his next observation. ' His feelings are natural.
What? actually resolve to break with him entirely! She felt
the engagement to be a source of repentance and misery to
each: she dissolved it. What a view this gives of her sense of
his behaviour! Well, he must be a most extraordinary——— '

' Nay, nay, read on. You will find how very much he suffers.'

' I hope he does,' replied Mr Knightley coolly, and resuming
the letter. ' " Smallridge! " What does this mean? What is
all this? '

' She had engaged to go as governess to Mrs Smallridge's
children—a dear friend of Mrs Elton's—a neighbour of Maple
Grove; and, by the bye, I wonder how Mrs Elton bears the
disappointment? '

' Say nothing, my dear Emma, while you oblige me to read—
—not even of Mrs Elton. Only one page more. I shall soon have
done. What a letter the man writes! '

' I wish you would read it with a kinder spirit towards him.'

' Well, there is feeling here. He does seem to have suffered
in finding her ill. Certainly, I can have no doubt of his being
fond of her. " Dearer, much dearer, than ever." I hope he may
long continue to feel all the value of such a reconciliation. He is
a very liberal thanker, with his thousands and tens of thousands.
" Happier than I deserve." Come, he knows himself there. " Miss
Woodhouse calls me the child of good fortune." Those were
Miss Woodhouse's words, were they? And a fine ending—and
there is the letter. " The child of good fortune! " That was your
name for him, was it? '

' You do not appear so well satisfied with his letter as I am;
but still you must, at least I hope you must, think the better of
him for it. I hope it does him some service with you.'

' Yes, certainly it does. He has had great faults—faults of
inconsideration and thoughtlessness; and I am very much of
his opinion in thinking him likely to be happier than he deserves:
but, still, as he is, beyond a doubt, really attached to Miss Fairfax, and will soon, it may be hoped, have the advantage of being
constantly with her, I am very ready to believe his character
will improve, and acquire from hers the steadiness and delicacy
of principle that it wants. And now, let me talk to you of something else. I have another person's interest at present so much at
heart, that I cannot think any longer about Frank Churchill.
Ever since I left you this morning, Emma, my mind has been
hard at work on one subject.'

The subject followed; it was in plain, unaffected, gentlemanlike English, such as Mr Knightley used even to the woman he was in love with, how to be able to ask her to marry him without attacking the happiness of her father. Emma's answer was ready at the first word. 'While her dear father lived, any change of condition must be impossible for her. She could never quit him.' Part only of this answer, however, was admitted. The impossibility of her quitting her father Mr Knightley felt as strongly as herself; but the inadmissibility of any other change he could not agree to. He had been thinking it over most deeply, most intently; he had at first hoped to induce Mr Woodhouse to remove with her to Donwell; he had wanted to believe it feasible, but his knowledge of Mr Woodhouse would not suffer him to deceive himself long; and now he confessed his persuasion that such a transplantation would be a risk of her father's comfort, perhaps even of his life, which must not be hazarded. Mr Woodhouse taken from Hartfield! No, he felt that it ought not to be attempted. But the plan which had arisen on the sacrifice of this, he trusted his dearest Emma would not find in any respect objectionable; it was, that he should be received at Hartfield! that so long as her father's happiness—in other words, his life—required Hartfield to continue her home, it should be his likewise.

Of their all removing to Donwell, Emma had already had her own passing thoughts. Like him, she had tried the scheme and rejected it; but such an alternative as this had not occurred to her. She was sensible of all the affection it evinced. She felt that, in quitting Donwell, he must be sacrificing a great deal of independence of hours and habits; that in living constantly with her father, and in no house of his own, there would be much, very much, to be borne with. She promised to think of it, and advised him to think of it more; but he was fully convinced that no reflection could alter his wishes or his opinion on the subject. He had given it, he could assure her, very long and calm consideration; he had been walking away from William Larkins the whole morning to have his thoughts to himself.

'Ah! there is one difficulty unprovided for,' cried Emma. 'I am sure William Larkins will not like it. You must get his consent before you ask mine.'

She promised, however, to think of it; and pretty nearly promised, moreover, to think of it with the intention of finding it a very good scheme.

It is remarkable that Emma, in the many, very many, points of view in which she was now beginning to consider Donwell

Abbey, was never struck with any sense of injury to her nephew Henry, whose rights as heir expectant had formerly been so tenaciously regarded. Think she must of the possible difference to the poor little boy; and yet she only gave herself a saucy conscious smile about it, and found amusement in detecting the real cause of that violent dislike of Mr Knightley's marrying Jane Fairfax, or anybody else, which at the time she had wholly imputed to the amiable solicitude of the sister and the aunt.

This proposal of his, this plan of marrying and continuing at Hartfield—the more she contemplated it the more pleasing it became. His evils seemed to lessen, her own advantages to increase, their mutual good to outweight every drawback. Such a companion for herself in the periods of anxiety and cheerlessness before her! Such a partner in all those duties and cares to which time must be giving increase of melancholy!

She would have been too happy but for poor Harriet; but every blessing of her own seemed to involve and advance the sufferings of her friend, who must now be even excluded from Hartfield. The delightful family party which Emma was securing for herself, poor Harriet must, in mere charitable caution, be kept at a distance from. She would be a loser in every way. Emma could not deplore her future absence as any deduction from her own enjoyment. In such a party, Harriet would be rather a dead weight than otherwise; but for the poor girl herself, it seemed a peculiarly cruel necessity that was to be placing her in such a state of unmerited punishment.

In time, of course, Mr Knightley would be forgotten, that is, supplanted; but this could not be expected to happen very early. Mr Knightley himself would be doing nothing to assist the cure; not like Mr Elton. Mr Knightley, always so kind, so feeling, so truly considerate for everybody, would never deserve to be less worshipped than now; and it really was too much to hope even of Harriet, that she could be in love with more than *three* men in one year.

52

I T was a very great relief to Emma to find Harriet as desirous as herself to avoid a meeting. Their intercourse was painful enough by letter. How much worse had they been obliged to meet!

Harriet expressed herself very much, as might be supposed,

without reproaches, or apparent sense of ill usage; and yet Emma fancied there was a something of resentment, a something bordering on it in her style, which increased the desirableness of their being separate. It might be only her own consciousness; but it seemed as if an angel only could have been quite without resentment under such a stroke.

She had no difficulty in procuring Isabella's invitation; and she was fortunate in having a sufficient reason for asking it, without resorting to invention. There was a tooth amiss. Harriet really wished, and had wished some time, to consult a dentist. Mrs John Knightley was delighted to be of use; anything of ill health was a recommendation to her; and though not so fond of a dentist as of a Mr Wingfield, she was quite eager to have Harriet under her care. When it was thus settled on her sister's side, Emma proposed it to her friend, and found her very persuadable. Harriet was to go; she was invited for at least a fortnight. She was to be conveyed in Mr Woodhouse's carriage. It was all arranged, it was all completed, and Harriet was safe in Brunswick Square.

Now Emma could, indeed, enjoy Mr Knightley's visits; now she could talk, and she could listen with true happiness, unchecked by that sense of injustice, of guilt, of something most painful, which had haunted her when remembering how disappointed a heart was near her, how much might at that moment, and at a little distance, be enduring by the feelings which she had led astray herself.

The difference of Harriet at Mrs Goddard's, or in London made, perhaps, an unreasonable difference in Emma's sensations; but she could not think of her in London without objects of curiosity and employment, which must be averting the past, and carrying her out of herself.

She would not allow any other anxiety to succeed directly to the place in her mind which Harriet had occupied. There was a communication before her, one which *she* only could be competent to make—the confession of her engagement to her father; but she would have nothing to do with it at present. She had resolved to defer the disclosure till Mrs Weston were safe and well. No additional agitation should be thrown at this period among those she loved—and the evil should not act on herself by anticipation before the appointed time. A fortnight, at least, of leisure and peace of mind, to crown every warmer, but more agitating, delight, should be hers.

She soon resolved, equally as a duty and a pleasure, to employ half an hour of this holiday of spirits in calling on Miss Fairfax. She ought to go—and she was longing to see her; the resemblance of their present situations increasing every other motive of goodwill. It would be a *secret* satisfaction; but the consciousness of a similarity of prospect would certainly add to the interest with which she should attend to anything Jane might communicate.

She went—she had driven once unsuccessfully to the door, but had not been into the house since the morning after Box Hill, when poor Jane had been in such distress as had filled her with compassion, though all the worst of her sufferings had been unsuspected. The fear of being still unwelcome determined her, though assured of their being at home, to wait in the passage, and send up her name. She heard Patty announcing it; but no such bustle succeeded as poor Miss Bates had before made so happily intelligible. No; she heard nothing but the instant reply of: ' Beg her to walk up '; and a moment afterwards she was met on the stairs by Jane herself coming eagerly forward, as if no other reception of her were felt sufficient. Emma had never seen her look so well, so lovely, so engaging. There was consciousness, animation, and warmth; there was everything which her countenance or manner could ever have wanted. She came forward with an offered hand; and said, in a low, but very feeling tone:

' This is most kind, indeed! Miss Woodhouse, it is impossible for me to express—I hope you will believe—Excuse me for being so entirely without words.'

Emma was gratified, and would soon have shown no want of words, if the sound of Mrs Elton's voice from the sitting-room had not checked her, and made it expedient to compress all her friendly and all her congratulatory sensations into a very, very earnest shake of the hand.

Mrs Bates and Mrs Elton were together. Miss Bates was out, which accounted for the previous tranquillity. Emma could have wished Mrs Elton elsewhere; but she was in a humour to have patience with everybody; and as Mrs Elton met her with unusual graciousness, she hoped the rencontre would do them no harm.

She soon believed herself to penetrate Mrs Elton's thoughts, and understand why she was, like herself, in happy spirits; it was being in Miss Fairfax's confidence, and fancying herself acquainted with what was still a secret to other people. Emma saw symptoms of it immediately in the expression of her face; and while paying her own compliments to Mrs Bates, and appear-

ing to attend to the good old lady's replies, she saw her with a
sort of anxious parade of mystery fold up a letter which she had
apparently been reading aloud to Miss Fairfax, and return it
into the purple and gold ridicule by her side, saying, with
significant nods:

'We can finish this some other time, you know. You and I
shall not want opportunities; and, in fact, you have heard all
the essential already. I only wanted to prove to you that Mrs S.
admits our apology, and is not offended. You see how delightfully she writes. Oh, she is a sweet creature! You would have
doted on her, had you gone. But not a word more. Let us be
discreet—quite on our good behaviour. Hush! You remember
those lines—I forget the poem at this moment:

> For when a lady's in the case,
> You know, all other things give place.

Now I say, my dear, in *our* case, for *lady*, read—mum! a word
to the wise. I am in a fine flow of spirits, an't I? But I want to
see your heart at ease as to Mrs S. *My* representation, you see,
has quite appeased her.'

And again, on Emma's merely turning her head to look at
Mrs Bates's knitting, she added, in a half whisper:

'I mentioned no *names*, you will observe. Oh no! cautious
as a minister of state. I managed it extremely well.'

Emma could not doubt. It was a palpable display, repeated
on every possible occasion. When they had all talked a little
while in harmony of the weather and Mrs Weston, she found
herself abruptly addressed with:

'Do not you think, Miss Woodhouse, our saucy little friend
here is charmingly recovered? Do not you think her cure does
Perry the highest credit?' (here was a side glance of great
meaning at Jane). 'Upon my word, Perry has restored her in
a wonderful short time! Oh, if you had seen her, as I did, when
she was at the worst!' And when Mrs Bates was saying something to Emma, whispered further: 'We do not say a word
of any *assistance* that Perry might have; not a word of a certain
young physician from Windsor. Oh! no, Perry shall have all the
credit.'

'I have scarce had the pleasure of seeing you, Miss Woodhouse,' she shortly afterwards began, 'since the party to Box Hill.
Very pleasant party. But yet I think there was something wanting. Things did not seem—that is, there seemed a little cloud
upon the spirits of some. So it appeared to me, at least, but

I might be mistaken. However, I think it answered so far as to tempt one to go again. What say you both to our collecting the same party, and exploring to Box Hill again, while the fine weather lasts? It must be the same party, you know—quite the same party, not *one* exception.'

Soon after this Miss Bates came in, and Emma could not help being diverted by the perplexity of her first answer to herself, resulting, she supposed, from doubt of what might be said, and impatience to say everything.

' Thank you, dear Miss Woodhouse, you are all kindness. It is impossible to say—yes, indeed, I quite understand—dearest Jane's prospects—that is, I do not mean. But she is charmingly recovered. How is Mr Woodhouse? I am so glad. Quite out of my power. Such a happy little circle as you find us here. Yes, indeed. Charming young man! that is, so very friendly; I mean good Mr Perry! such attention to Jane!' And from her great, her more than commonly thankful delight towards Mrs Elton for being there, Emma guessed that there had been a little show of resentment towards Jane, from the Vicarage quarter, which was now graciously overcome. After a few whispers, indeed, which placed it beyond a guess, Mrs Elton, speaking louder, said:

' Yes, here I am, my good friend; and here I have been so long, that anywhere else I should think it necessary to apologise; but, the truth is, that I am waiting for my lord and master. He promised to join me here, and pay his respects to you.'

' What! are we to have the pleasure of a call from Mr Elton? That will be a favour indeed; for I know gentlemen do not like morning visits, and Mr Elton's time is so engaged.'

' Upon my word it is, Miss Bates. He really is engaged from morning to night. There is no end of people's coming to him, on some pretence or other. The magistrates, and overseers, and churchwardens, are always wanting his opinion. They seem not able to do anything without him. " Upon my word, Mr E.," I often say, " rather you than I. I do not know what would become of my crayons and my instrument if I had half so many applicants." Bad enough as it is, for I absolutely neglect them both to an unpardonable degree. I believe I have not played a bar this fortnight. However, he is coming, I assure you: yes, indeed, on purpose to wait on you all.' And putting up her hand to screen her words from Emma: ' A congratulatory visit, you know. Oh! yes, quite indispensable.'

Miss Bates looked about her, so happily!

' He promised to come to me as soon as he could disengage himself from Knightley; but he and Knightley are shut up together in deep consultation. Mr E. is Knightley's right hand.'

Emma would not have smiled for the world, and only said: ' Is Mr Elton gone on foot to Donwell? He will have a hot walk.'

' Oh no, it is a meeting at the Crown—a regular meeting. Weston and Cole will be there too; but one is apt to speak only of those who lead. I fancy Mr E. and Knightley have everything their own way.'

' Have you not mistaken the day? ' said Emma. ' I am almost certain that the meeting at the Crown is not till to-morrow. Mr Knightley was at Hartfield yesterday, and spoke of it as for Saturday.'

' Oh no, the meeting is certainly to-day,' was the abrupt answer, which denoted the impossibility of any blunder on Mrs Elton's side. ' I do believe,' she continued, ' this is the most troublesome parish that ever was. We never heard of such things at Maple Grove.'

' Your parish there was small,' said Jane.

' Upon my word, my dear, I do not know, for I never heard the subject talked of.'

' But it is proved by the smallness of the school, which I have heard you speak of, as under the patronage of your sister and Mrs Bragge; the only school, and not more than five-and-twenty children.'

' Ah! you clever creature, that's very true. What a thinking brain you have! I say, Jane, what a perfect character you and I should make, if we could be shaken together. My liveliness and your solidity would produce perfection. Not that I presume to insinuate, however, that *some* people may not think *you* perfection already. But hush—not a word, if you please.'

It seemed an unneccessary caution; Jane was wanting to give her words, not to Mrs Elton, but to Miss Woodhouse, as the latter plainly saw. The wish of distinguishing her, as far as civility permitted, was very evident, though it could not often proceed beyond a look.

Mr Elton made his appearance. His lady greeted him with some of her sparkling vivacity.

' Very pretty, sir, upon my word; to send me on here, to be an encumbrance to my friends, so long before you vouchsafe to come. But you knew what a dutiful creature you had to deal with. You knew I should not stir till my lord and master appeared. Here have I been sitting this hour, giving these young ladies a sample of true conjugal obedience; for who can say, you know, how soon it may be wanted?'

Mr Elton was so hot and tired, that all this wit seemed thrown away. His civilities to the other ladies must be paid; but his subsequent object was to lament over himself, for the heat he was suffering, and the walk he had had for nothing.

'When I got to Donwell,' said he, 'Knightley could not be found. Very odd! very unaccountable! after the note I sent him this morning, and the message he returned, that he should certainly be at home till one.'

'Donwell!' cried his wife. 'My dear Mr E., you have not been to Donwell! you mean the Crown; you come from the meeting at the Crown.'

'No, no, that's to-morrow; and I particularly wanted to see Knightley to-day on that very account. Such a dreadful broiling morning! I went over the fields too' (speaking in a tone of great ill usage), 'which made it so much the worse. And then not to find him at home! I assure you I am not at all pleased. And no apology left, no message for me. The housekeeper declared she knew nothing of my being expected. Very extraordinary! And nobody knew at all which way he was gone. Perhaps to Hartfield, perhaps to the Abbey Mill, perhaps into his woods. Miss Woodhouse, this is not like our friend Knightley! Can you explain it?'

Emma amused herself by protesting that it was very extraordinary indeed, and that she had not a syllable to say for him.

'I cannot imagine,' said Mrs Elton (feeling the indignity as a wife ought to do), I cannot imagine how he could do such a thing by you, of all people in the world! The very last person whom one should expect to be forgotten! My dear Mr E., he must have left a message for you, I am sure he must. Not even Knightley could be so very eccentric; and his servants forgot it. Depend upon it that was the case; and very likely to happen with the Donwell servants, who are all, I have often observed, extremely awkward and remiss. I am sure I would not have such a creature as his Harry stand at our sideboard for any consideration. And as for Mrs Hodges, Wright holds her very cheap indeed. She promised Wright a receipt, and never sent it.'

'I met William Larkins,' continued Mr Elton, 'as I got near the house, and he told me I should not find his master at home, but I did not believe him. William seemed rather out of humour.

He did not know what was come to his master lately, he said, but he could hardly ever get the speech of him. I have nothing to do with William's wants, but it really is of very great importance that *I* should see Knightley to-day; and it becomes a matter, therefore, of very serious inconvenience that I should have had this hot walk to no purpose.'

Emma felt that she could not do better than go home directly. In all probability she was at this very time waited for there; and Mr Knightley might be preserved from sinking deeper in aggression towards Mr Elton, if not towards William Larkins.

She was pleased, on taking leave, to find Miss Fairfax determined to attend her out of the room, to go with her even downstairs; it gave her an opportunity, which she immediately made use of, to say:

'It is as well, perhaps, that I have not had the possibility. Had you not been surrounded by other friends, I might have been tempted to introduce a subject, to ask questions, to speak more openly than might have been strictly correct. I feel that I should certainly have been impertinent.'

'Oh!' cried Jane, with a blush and a hesitation which Emma thought more becoming to her than all the elegance of all her usual composure—'there would have been no danger. The danger would have been of my wearying you. You could not have gratified me more than by expressing an interest—— Indeed, Miss Woodhouse' (speaking more collectedly), 'with the consciousness which I have of misconduct—very great misconduct—it is particularly consoling to me to know that those of my friends whose good opinion is most worth preserving, are not disgusted to such a degree as to—I have not time for half that I could wish to say. I long to make apologies, excuses, to urge something for myself. I feel it so very due. But, unfortunately—in short, if your compassion does not stand my friend—— '

'Oh! you are too scrupulous, indeed you are,' cried Emma warmly, and taking her hand. 'You owe me no apologies; and everybody to whom you might be supposed to owe them is so perfectly satisfied, so delighted even—— '

'You are very kind, but I know what my manners were to you. So cold and artificial! I had always a part to act. It was a life of deceit! I know that I must have disgusted you.'

'Pray say no more. I feel that all the apologies should be on my side. Let us forgive each other at once. We must do whatever is to be done quickest, and I think our feelings will lose no time there. I hope you have pleasant accounts from Windsor?'

'Very.'

'And the next news, I suppose, will be, that we are to lose you—just as I begin to know you.'

'Oh! as to all that, of course nothing can be thought of yet. I am here till claimed by Colonel and Mrs Campbell.'

'Nothing can be actually settled yet, perhaps,' replied Emma, smiling—'but, excuse me, it must be thought of.'

The smile was returned as Jane answered:

'You are very right; it has been thought of. And I will own to you (I am sure it will be safe), that so far as our living with Mr Churchill at Enscombe, it is settled. There must be three months, at least, of deep mourning; but when they are over, I imagine there will be nothing more to wait for.'

'Thank you, thank you. This is just what I wanted to be assured of. Oh! if you knew how much I love everything that is decided and open! Good-bye, good-bye.'

53

Mrs Weston's friends were all made happy by her safety; and if the satisfaction of her well-doing could be increased to Emma, it was by knowing her to be the mother of a little girl. She had been decided in wishing for a Miss Weston. She would not acknowledge that it was with any view of making a match for her, hereafter, with either of Isabella's sons; but she was convinced that a daughter would suit both father and mother best. It would be a great comfort to Mr Weston, as he grew older—and even Mr Weston might be growing older ten years hence—to have his fireside enlivened by the sports and the nonsense, the freaks and the fancies of a child never banished from home; and Mrs Weston—no one could doubt that a daughter would be most to her; and it would be quite a pity that any one who so well knew how to teach, should not have their powers in exercise again.

'She has had the advantage, you know, of practising on me,' she continued—'like La Baronne d'Almane on La Comtesse d'Ostalis, in Madame de Genlis's *Adelaide and Theodore*, and we shall now see her own little Adelaide educated on a more perfect plan.'

' That is,' replied Mr Knightley, ' she will indulge her even more than she did you, and believe that she does not indulge her at all. It will be the only difference.'

' Poor child! ' cried Emma; ' at that rate, what will become of her? '

' Nothing very bad. The fate of thousands. She will be disagreeable in infancy, and correct herself as she grows older. I am losing all my bitterness against spoilt children, my dearest Emma. I, who am owing all my happiness to *you*, would not it be horrible ingratitude in me to be severe on them? '

Emma laughed, and replied: ' But I had the assistance of all your endeavours to counteract the indulgence of other people. I doubt whether my own sense would have corrected me without it.'

' Do you? I have no doubt. Nature gave you understanding: Miss Taylor gave you principles. You must have done well. My interference was quite as likely to do harm as good. It was very natural for you to say: " What right has he to lecture me? " and I am afraid very natural for you to feel that it was done in a disagreeable manner. I do not believe I did you any good. The good was all to myself, by making you an object of the tenderest affection to me. I could not think about you so much without doting on you, faults and all; and by dint of fancying so many errors, have been in love with you ever since you were thirteen at least.'

' I am sure you were of use to me,' cried Emma. ' I was very often influenced rightly by you—oftener than I would own at the time. I am very sure you did me good. And if poor little Anna Weston is to be spoiled, it will be the greatest humanity in you to do as much for her as you have done for me, except falling in love with her when she is thirteen.'

' How often, when you were a girl, have you said to me, with one of your saucy looks: " Mr Knightley, I am going to do so-and-so; papa says I may," or " I have Miss Taylor's leave " —something which, you knew, I did not approve. In such cases my interference was giving you two bad feelings instead of one.'

' What an amiable creature I was! No wonder you should hold my speeches in such affectionate remembrance.'

' " Mr Knightley," you always called me. " Mr Knightley "; and, from habit, it has not so very formal a sound. And yet it is formal. I want you to call me something else, but I do not know what.'

' I remember once calling you " George," in one of my amiable fits, about ten years ago. I did it because I thought it would offend you; but, as you made no objection, I never did it again.'

'And cannot you call me " George " now? '

'Impossible! I never can call you anything but " Mr Knightley." I will not promise even to equal the elegant terseness of Mrs Elton, by calling you Mr K. But I will promise,' she added presently, laughing and blushing, ' I will promise to call you once by your Christian name. I do not say when, but perhaps you may guess where—in the building in which N. takes M. for better, for worse.'

Emma grieved that she could not be more openly just to one important service which his better sense would have rendered her, to the advice which would have saved her from the worst of all her womanly follies—her wilful intimacy with Harriet Smith; but it was too tender a subject. She could not enter on it. Harriet was very seldom mentioned between them. This, on his side, might merely proceed from her not being thought of; but Emma was rather inclined to attribute it to delicacy, and a suspicion, from some appearances, that their friendship were declining. She was aware herself that, parting under any other circumstances, they certainly should have corresponded more, and that her intelligence would not have rested, as it now almost wholly did, on Isabella's letters. He might observe that it was so. The pain of being obliged to practise concealment towards him was very little inferior to the pain of having made Harriet unhappy.

Isabella sent quite as good an account of her visitor as could be expected; on her first arrival she had thought her out of spirits, which appeared perfectly natural, as there was a dentist to be consulted; but since that business had been over, she did not appear to find Harriet different from what she had known her before. Isabella, to be sure, was no very quick observer; yet if Harriet had not been equal to playing with the children, it would not have escaped her. Emma's comforts and hopes were most agreeably carried on, by Harriet's being to stay longer; her fortnight was likely to be a month at least. Mr and Mrs John Knightley were to come down in August, and she was invited to remain till they could bring her back.

' John does not even mention your friend,' said Mr Knightley. ' Here is his answer, if you like to see it.' It was the answer to the communication of his intended marriage. Emma accepted it with a very eager hand, with an impatience all alive to know what he would say about it, and not at all checked by hearing that her friend was unmentioned.

'John enters like a brother into my happiness,' continued Mr Knightley, 'but he is no complimenter; and though I well know him to have, likewise, a most brotherly affection for you, he is so far from making flourishes, that any other young woman might think him rather cool in her praise. But I am not afraid of your seeing what he writes.'

'He writes like a sensible man,' replied Emma, when she had read the letter. 'I honour his sincerity. It is very plain that he considers the good fortune of the engagement as all on my side, but that he is not without hope of my growing, in time, as worthy of your affection as you think me already. Had he said anything to bear a different construction, I should not have believed him.'

'My Emma, he means no such thing. He only means—— '

'He and I should differ very little in our estimation of the two '—interrupted she, with a sort of serious smile—' much less, perhaps, than he is aware of, if we could enter without ceremony or reserve on the subject.'

'Emma, my dear Emma—— '

'Oh!' she cried, with more thorough gaiety, 'if you fancy your brother does not do me justice, only wait till my dear father is in the secret, and hear his opinion. Depend upon it, he will be much further from doing *you* justice. He will think all the happiness, all the advantage, on your side of the question; all the merit on mine. I wish I may not sink into " poor Emma " with him at once. His tender compassion towards oppressed worth can go no further.'

'Ah!' he cried, 'I wish your father might be half as easily convinced as John will be, of our having every right that equal worth can give, to be happy together. I am amused by one part of John's letter—did you notice it?—where he says that my information did not take him wholly by surprise, that he was rather in expectation of hearing something of the kind.'

'If I understand your brother, he only means so far as your having some thoughts of marrying. He had no idea of me. He seems perfectly unprepared for that.'

'Yes, yes—but I am amused that he should have seen so far into my feelings. What has he been judging by? I am not conscious of any difference in my spirits or conversation that could prepare him at this time for my marrying any more than at another. But it was so, I suppose. I dare say there was a difference when I was staying with them the other day. I believe I did not play with the children quite so much as usual. I remember one evening the poor boys saying, " Uncle seems always tired now." '

The time was coming when the news must be spread further, and other persons' reception of it tried. As soon as Mrs Weston was sufficiently recovered to admit Mr Woodhouse's visits, Emma having it in view that her gentle reasonings should be employed in the cause, resolved first to announce it at home, and then at Randalls. But how to break it to her father at last! She had bound herself to do it, in such an hour of Mr Knightley's absence, or when it came to the point her heart would have failed her, and she must have put it off; but Mr Knightley was to come at such a time, and follow up the beginning she was to make. She was forced to speak, and to speak cheerfully too. She must not make it a more decided subject of misery to him, by a melancholy tone herself. She must not appear to think it a misfortune. With all the spirits she could command, she prepared him first for something strange, and then, in a few words, said, that if his consent and approbation could be obtained—which, she trusted, would be attended with no difficulty, since it was a plan to promote the happiness of all—she and Mr Knightley meant to marry; by which means Hartfield would receive the constant addition of that person's company, whom she knew he loved, next to his daughters and Mrs Weston, best in the world.

Poor man! it was at first a considerable shock to him, and he tried earnestly to dissuade her from it. She was reminded, more than once, of having always said she would never marry, and assured that it would be a great deal better for her to remain single; and told of poor Isabella, and poor Miss Taylor. But it would not do. Emma hung about him affectionately, and smiled, and said it must be so; and that he must not class her with Isabella and Mrs Weston, whose marriages taking them from Hartfield had, indeed, made a melancholy change: but she was not going from Hartfield; she should be always there; she was introducing no change in their numbers or their comforts but for the better; and she was very sure that he would be a great deal the happier for having Mr Knightley always at hand, when he were once got used to the idea. Did he not love Mr Knightley very much? He would not deny that he did, she was sure. Whom did he ever want to consult on business but Mr Knightley? Who was so useful to him, who so ready to write his letters, who so glad to assist him? Who so cheerful, so attentive, so attached to him? Would not he like to have him always on the spot? Yes. That was all very true. Mr Knightley could not be there too often; he should be glad to see him every day; but they did see him every day as it was. Why could not they go on as they had done?

Mr Woodhouse could not be soon reconciled; but the worst was overcome, the idea was given; time and continual repetition must do the rest. To Emma's entreaties and assurances succeeded Mr Knightley's, whose fond praise of her gave the subject even a kind of welcome; and he was soon used to be talked to by each on every fair occasion. They had all the assistance which Isabella could give, by letters of the strongest approbation; and Mrs Weston was ready, on the first meeting, to consider the subject in the most serviceable light; first as a settled, and, secondly, as a good one—well aware of the nearly equal importance of the two recommendations to Mr Woodhouse's mind. It was agreed upon, as what was to be; and everybody by whom he was used to be guided assuring him that it would be for his happiness, and having some feelings himself which almost admitted it, he began to think that some time or other, in another year or two, perhaps, it might not be so very bad if the marriage did take place.

Mrs Weston was acting no part, feigning no feelings in all that she said to him in favour of the event. She had been extremely surprised, never more so than when Emma first opened the affair to her; but she saw in it only increase of happiness to all, and had no scruple in urging him to the utmost. She had such a regard for Mr Knightley, as to think he deserved even her dearest Emma; and it was in every respect so proper, suitable, and unexceptionable a connection, and in one respect, one point of the highest importance, so peculiarly eligible, so singularly fortunate, that now it seemed as if Emma could not safely have attached herself to any other creature, and that she had herself been the stupidest of beings in not having thought of it, and wished it long ago. How very few of those men in a rank of life to address Emma would have renounced their own home for Hartfield! And who but Mr Knightley could know and bear with Mr Woodhouse, so as to make such an arrangement desirable! The difficulty of disposing of poor Mr Woodhouse had been always felt in her husband's plans and her own, for a marriage between Frank and Emma. How to settle the claims of Enscombe and Hartfield had been a continual impediment— less acknowledged by Mr Weston than by herself—but even he

had never been able to finish the subject better than by saying:
'Those matters will take care of themselves; the young people
will find a way.' But here there was nothing to be shifted off
in a wild speculation of the future. It was all right, all open,
all equal. No sacrifice on any side worth the name. It was
a union of the highest promise of felicity in itself, and without
one real, rational difficulty to oppose or delay it.

Mrs Weston, with her baby on her knee, indulging in such
reflections as these, was one of the happiest women in the world.
If anything could ·increase her delight, it was perceiving that
the baby would soon have outgrown its first set of caps.

The news was universally a surprise wherever it spread; and
Mr Weston had his five minutes' share of it; but five minutes
were enough to familiarise the idea to his quickness of mind. He
saw the advantages of the match, and rejoiced in them with all
the constancy of his wife; but the wonder of it was very soon
nothing; and by the end of an hour he was not far from believing that he had always foreseen it.

'It is to be a secret, I conclude,' said he. 'These matters are
always a secret till it is found out that everybody knows them.
Only let me be told when I may speak out. I wonder whether
Jane has any suspicion?'

He went to Highbury the next morning, and satisfied himself on that point. He told her the news. Was not she like a
daughter, his eldest daughter? he must tell her; and Miss
Bates being present, it passed, of course, to Mrs Cole, Mrs
Perry, and Mrs Elton, immediately afterwards. It was no more
than the principals were prepared for; they had calculated from
the time of its being known at Randalls how soon it would be
over Highbury; and were thinking of themselves, as the evening
wonder in many a family circle, with great sagacity.

In general, it was a very well approved match. Some might
think him, and others might think her, the most in luck. One
set might recommend their all removing to Donwell, and leaving Hartfield for the John Knightleys; and another might
predict disagreements among their servants; but yet, upon the
whole, there was no serious objection raised, except in one habi-
tation—the Vicarage. There, the surprise was not softened by
any satisfaction. Mr Elton cared little about it, compared with
his wife; he only hoped 'the young lady's pride would now be
contented'; and supposed 'she had always meant to catch
Knightley if she could'; and, on the point of living at Hartfield,
could daringly exclaim, 'Rather he than I!' But Mrs Elton

was very much discomposed indeed. 'Poor Knightley! poor fellow! sad business for him. She was extremely concerned; for though very eccentric, he had a thousand good qualities. How could he be so taken in? Did not think him at all in love—not in the least. Poor Knightley! There would be an end of all pleasant intercourse with him. How happy he had been to come and dine with them whenever they asked him! But that would be all over now. Poor fellow! No more exploring parties to Donwell made for *her*. Oh no; there would be a Mrs Knightley to throw cold water on everything. Extremely disagreeable; but she was not at all sorry that she had abused the housekeeper the other day. Shocking plan, living together. It would never do. She knew a family near Maple Grove who had tried it, and been obliged to separate before the end of the first quarter.'

54

TIME passed on. A few more to-morrows, and the party from London would be arriving. It was an alarming change; and Emma was thinking of it one morning, as what must bring a great deal to agitate and grieve her, when Mr Knightley came in, and distressing thoughts were put by. After the first chat of pleasure, he was silent; and then, in a graver tone, began with:

'I have something to tell you, Emma; some news.'

'Good or bad?' said she, quickly, looking up in his face.

'I do not know which it ought to be called.'

'Oh, good, I am sure. I see it in your countenance. You are trying not to smile.'

'I am afraid,' said he, composing his features, 'I am very much afraid, my dear. Emma, that you will not smile when you hear it.'

'Indeed! but why so? I can hardly imagine that anything which pleases or amuses you should not please and amuse me too.'

'There is one subject,' he replied, 'I hope but one, on which we do not think alike.' He paused a moment, again smiling, with his eyes fixed on her face. 'Does nothing occur to you? Do not you recollect? Harriet Smith.'

Her cheeks flushed at the name, and she felt afraid of something, though she knew not what.

'Have you heard from her yourself this morning?' cried he.
'You have, I believe, and know the whole.'

'No, I have not; I know nothing; pray tell me.'

'You are prepared for the worst, I see; and very bad it is.
Harriet Smith marries Robert Martin.'

Emma gave a start, which did not seem like being prepared;
and her eyes, in eager gaze, said, 'No, this is impossible!' but
her lips were closed.

'It is so, indeed!' continued Mr Knightley; 'I have it from
Robert Martin himself. He left me not half an hour ago.'

She was still looking at him with the most speaking amazement.

'You like it, my Emma, as little as I feared—I wish our opinions were the same. But in time they will. Time, you may be
sure, will make one or the other of us think differently; and in
the meanwhile, we need not talk much on the subject.'

'You mistake me, you quite mistake me,' she replied, exerting herself. 'It is not that such a circumstance would now make
me unhappy, but I cannot believe it. It seems an impossibility!
You cannot mean to say that Harriet Smith has accepted Robert
Martin! You cannot mean that he has even proposed to her
again—yet! You only mean that he intends it.'

'I mean that he has done it,' answered Mr Knightley, with
smiling but determined decision, 'and been accepted.'

'Good God!' she cried. 'Well!' Then having recourse to
her work-basket, in excuse for leaning down her face, and concealing all the exquisite feelings of delight and entertainment
which she knew she must be expressing, she added, 'Well, now
tell me everything; make this intelligibile to me. How, where,
when? Let me know it all. I never was more surprised—but it
does not make me unhappy, I assure you. How—how has it
been possible?'

'It is a very simple story. He went to town on business three
days ago, and I got him to take charge of some papers which I
was wanting to send to John. He delivered these papers to John,
at his chambers, and was asked by him to join their party the
same evening to Astley's. They were going to take the two eldest
boys to Astley's. The party was to be our brother and sister,
Henry, John—and Miss Smith. My friend Robert could not
resist. They called for him in their way; were all extremely
amused: and my brother asked him to dine with them the next
day, which he did, and in the course of that visit (as I understand) he found an opportunity of speaking to Harriet; and
certainly did not speak in vain. She made him, by her accept-

ance, as happy even as he is deserving. He came down by yesterday's coach, and was with me this morning, immediately after breakfast, to report his proceedings, first on my affairs, and then on his own. This is all that I can relate of the how, where, and when. Your friend Harriet will make a much longer history when you see her. She will give you all the minute particulars, which only woman's language can make interesting. In our communications we deal only in the great.. However, I must say, that Robert Martin's heart seemed for *him*, and to *me*, very overflowing; and that he did mention, without its being much to the purpose, that on quitting their box at Astley's, my brother took charge of Mrs John Knightley and Little John, and he followed, with Miss Smith and Henry; and that at one time they were in such a crowd as to make Miss Smith rather uneasy.'

He stopped. Emma dared not attempt any immediate reply. To speak, she was sure, would be to betray a most unreasonable degree of happiness. She must wait a moment, or he would think her mad. Her silence disturbed him; and after observing her a little while, he added:

' Emma, my love, you said that this circumstance would not now make you unhappy; but I am afraid it gives you more pain than you expected. His situation is an evil; but you must consider it as what satisfies your friend; and I will answer for your thinking better and better of him as you know him more; his good sense and good principles would delight you. As far as the man is concerned, you could not wish your friend in better hands. His rank in society I would alter if I could, which is saying a great deal, I assure you, Emma. You laugh at me about William Larkins; but I could quite as ill spare Robert Martin.'

He wanted her to look up and smile; and having now brought herself not to smile too broadly, she did, cheerfully answering:

' You need not be at any pains to reconcile me to the match. I think Harriet is doing extremely well. *Her* connections may be worse than *his*: in respectability of character, there can be no doubt that they are. I have been silent from surprise, merely— excessive surprise. You cannot imagine how suddenly it has come on me, how peculiarly unprepared I was! for I had reason to believe her very lately more determined against him, much more than she was before.'

' You ought to know your friend best,' replied Mr Knightley; ' but I should say she was a good-tempered, soft-hearted girl, not likely to be very, very determined against any young man who told her he loved her.'

Emma could not help laughing as she answered, 'Upon my word, I believe you know her quite as well as I do. But, Mr Knightley, are you perfectly sure that she has absolutely and downright *accepted* him? I could suppose she might in time, but can she already? Did not you misunderstand him? You were both talking of other things; of business, shows of cattle, or new drills; and might not you, in the confusion of so many subjects, mistake him? It was not Harriet's hand that he was certain of—it was the dimensions of some famous ox.'

The contrast between the countenance and air of Mr Knightley and Robert Martin was, at this moment, so strong to Emma's feelings, and so strong was the recollection of all that had so recently passed on Harriet's side, so fresh the sound of those words spoken with such emphasis, 'No, I hope I know better than to think of Robert Martin,' that she was really expecting the intelligence to prove, in some measure, premature. It could not be otherwise.

'Do you dare say this?' cried Mr Knightley. 'Do you dare to suppose me so great a blockhead as not to know what a man is talking of? What do you deserve?'

'Oh! I always deserve the best treatment, because I never put up with any other; and, therefore, you must give me a plain, direct answer. Are you quite sure that you understand the terms on which Mr Martin and Harriet now are?'

'I am quite sure,' he replied, speaking very distinctly, 'that he told me she had accepted him; and that there was no obscurity, nothing doubtful, in the words he used; and I think I can give you a proof that it must be so. He asked my opinion as to what he was now to do. He knew of no one but Mrs Goddard to whom he could apply for information of her relations or friends. Could I mention anything more fit to be done than to go to Mrs Goddard? I assured him that I could not. Then, he said, he would endeavour to see her in the course of this day.'

'I am perfectly satisfied,' replied Emma, with the brightest smiles, 'and most sincerely wish them happy.'

'You are materially changed since we talked on this subject before.'

'I hope so—for at that time I was a fool.'

'And I am changed also; for I am now very willing to grant you all Harriet's good qualities. I have taken some pains for your sake, and for Robert Martin's sake (whom I have always had reason to believe as much in love with her as ever), to get acquainted with her. I have often talked to her a good deal. You must have seen that I did. Sometimes, indeed, I have thought you were half suspecting me of pleading poor Martin's cause, which was never the case; but, from all my observations, I am convinced of her being an artless, amiable girl, with very good notions, very seriously good principles, and placing her happiness in the affections and utility of domestic life. Much of this, I have no doubt, she may thank you for.'

' Me! ' cried Emma, shaking her head. ' Ah, poor Harriet! '

She checked herself, however, and submitted quietly to a little more praise than she deserved.

Their conversation was soon afterwards closed by the entrance of her father. She was not sorry. She wanted to be alone. Her mind was in a state of flutter and wonder, which made it impossible for her to be collected. She was in dancing, singing, exclaiming spirits; and till she had moved about, and talked to herself, and laughed and reflected, she could be fit for nothing rational.

Her father's business was to announce James's being gone out to put the horses to, preparatory to their now daily drive to Randalls; and she had, therefore, an `immediate excuse for disappearing.

The joy, the gratitude, the exquisite delight of her sensations may be imagined. The sole grievance and alloy thus removed in the prospect of Harriet's welfare, she was really in danger of becoming too happy for security. What had she to wish for? Nothing, but to grow more worthy of him, whose intentions and judgment had been ever so superior to her own. Nothing but that the lessons of her past folly might teach her humility and circumspection in future.

Serious she was, very serious, in her thankfulness and in her resolutions; and yet there was no preventing a laugh, sometimes in the very midst of them. She must laugh at such a close—such an end of the doleful disappointment of five weeks back—such a heart—such a Harriet!

Now there would be pleasure in her returning; everything would be a pleasure; it would be a great pleasure to know Robert Martin.

High in the rank of her most serious and heartfelt felicities was the reflection that all necessity of concealment from Mr Knightley would soon be over. The disguise, equivocation, mystery, so hateful to her to practise, might soon be over. She could now look forward to giving him that full and perfect confidence which her disposition was most ready to welcome as a duty.

In the gayest and happiest spirits, she set forward with her father, not always listening, but always agreeing, to what he said; and, whether in speech or silence, conniving at the comfortable persuasion of his being obliged to go to Randalls every day, or poor Mrs Weston would be disappointed.

They arrived. Mrs Weston was alone in the drawing-room. But hardly had they been told of the baby, and Mr Woodhouse received the thanks for coming, which he asked for, when a glimpse was caught through the blind of two figures passing near the window.

'It is Frank and Miss Fairfax,' said Mrs Weston. 'I was just going to tell you of our agreeable surprise in seeing him arrive this morning. He stays till to-morrow, and Miss Fairfax has been persuaded to spend the day with us. They are coming in, I hope.'

In half a minute they were in the room. Emma was extremely glad to see him; but there was a degree of confusion, a number of embarrassing recollections, on each side. They met readily and smiling, but with a consciousness which at first allowed little to be said; and having all sat down again, there was for some time such a blank in the circle that Emma began to doubt whether the wish now indulged, which she had long felt, of seeing Frank Churchill once more, and of seeing him with Jane, would yield its proportion of pleasure. When Mr Weston joined the party, however, and when the baby was fetched, there was no longer a want of subject or animation, or of courage and opportunity for Frank Churchill to draw near her and say:

'I have to thank you, Miss Woodhouse, for a very kind, forgiving message, in one of Mrs Weston's letters. I hope time has not made you less willing to pardon; I hope you do not retract what you then said.'

'No, indeed,' cried Emma, most happy to begin; 'not in the least. I am particularly glad to see and shake hands with you, and to give you joy in person.'

He thanked her with all his heart, and continued some time to speak with serious feeling of his gratitude and happiness.

'Is not she looking well?' said he, turning his eyes towards Jane—'better than she ever used to do? You see how my father and Mrs Weston dote upon her.'

But his spirits were soon rising again; and, with laughing eyes, after mentioning the expected return of the Campbells, he named the name of Dixon. Emma blushed, and forbade its being pronounced in her hearing.

'I can never think of it,' she cried, 'without extreme shame.'

'The shame,' he answered, 'is all mine, or ought to be. But is it possible that you had no suspicion? I mean of late: early, I know, you had none.'

'I never had the smallest, I assure you.'

'That appears quite wonderful. I was once very near—and I wish I had; it would have been better. But though I was always doing wrong things, they were very *bad* wrong things, and such as did me no service. It would have been a much better transgression had I broken the bond of secrecy and told you everything.'

'It is not now worth a regret,' said Emma.

'I have some hope,' resumed he, 'of my uncle's being persuaded to pay a visit at Randalls; he wants to be introduced to her. When the Campbells are returned, we shall meet them in London, and continue there, I trust, till we may carry her northward; but now, I am at such a distance from her—is not it hard, Miss Woodhouse? Till this morning, we have not once met since the day of reconciliation. Do not you pity me?'

Emma spoke her pity so very kindly, that with a sudden accession of gay thought, he cried:

'Ah! by the bye,' then sinking his voice, and looking demure for the moment, 'I hope Mr Knightley is well?' He paused. She coloured and laughed. 'I know you saw my letter, and think you may remember my wish in your favour. Let me return your congratulations. I assure you that I have heard the news with the warmest interest and satisfaction. He is a man whom I cannot presume to praise.'

Emma was delighted, and only wanted him to go on in the same style; but his mind was the next moment in his own concerns and with his own Jane, and his next words were:

'Did you ever see such a skin? such smoothness! such delicacy! and yet without being actually fair. One cannot call her fair. It is a most uncommon complexion, with her dark eyelashes and hair—a most distinguishing complexion! So peculiarly the lady in it. Just colour enough for beauty.'

'I have always admired her complexion,' replied Emma archly; 'but do not I remember the time when you found fault with her for being so pale? When we first began to talk of her. Have you quite forgotten?'

'Oh, no! what an impudent dog I was! how could I dare—— ''

But he laughed so heartily at the recollection that Emma could not help saying:

' I do suspect that in the midst of your perplexities at that time, you had very great amusement in tricking us all. I am sure you had. I am sure it was a consolation to you.'

' Oh, no, no, no! how can you suspect me of such a thing? I was the most miserable wretch.'

' Not quite so miserable as to be insensible to mirth. I am sure it was a source of high entertainment to you, to feel that you were taking us all in. Perhaps I am the readier to suspect, because, to tell you the truth, I think it might have been some amusement to myself in the same situation. I think there is a little likeness between us.'

He bowed.

' If not in our dispositions,' she presently added, with a look of true sensibility, ' there is a likeness in our destiny; the destiny which bids fair to connect us with two characters so much superior to our own.'

' True, true,' he answered warmly. ' No, not true on your side. You can have no superior, but most true on mine. She is a complete angel. Look at her. Is not she an angel in every gesture? Observe the turn of her throat. Observe her eyes, as she is looking up at my father. You will be glad to hear ' (inclining his head, and whispering seriously) ' that my uncle means to give her all my aunt's jewels. They are to be new set. I am resolved to have some in an ornament for the head. Will not it be beautiful in her dark hair?'

' Very beautiful, indeed,' replied Emma; and she spoke so kindly that he gratefully burst out:

' How delighted I am to see you again! and to see you in such excellent looks! I would not have missed this meeting for the world. I should certainly have called at Hartfield had you failed to come.'

The others had been talking of the child, Mrs Weston giving an account of a little alarm she had been under the evening before, from the infant's appearing not quite well. She believed she had been foolish, but it had alarmed her, and she had been within half a minute of sending for Mr Perry. Perhaps she ought to be ashamed, but Mr Weston had been almost as uneasy as herself. In ten minutes, however, the child had been perfectly well again. This was her history; and particularly interesting it was to Mr Woodhouse, who commended her very much for thinking of sending for Perry, and only regretted that she had not done it. ' She should always send for Perry, if the child appeared in the slightest degree disordered, were it only for a moment. She could not be too soon alarmed, nor send for Perry too often. It was a pity, perhaps, that he had not come last night; for, though the child seemed well now—very well considering—it would probably have been better if Perry had seen it.'

Frank Churchill caught the name.

'Perry!' said he to Emma, and trying, as he spoke, to catch Miss Fairfax's eye. 'My friend Mr Perry! What are they saying about Mr Perry? Has he been here this morning? And how does he travel now? Has he set up his carriage?'

Emma soon recollected, and understood him; and while she joined in the laugh, it was evident from Jane's countenance, that she too was really hearing him, though trying to seem deaf.

'Such an extraordinary dream of mine!' he cried. 'I can never think of it without laughing. She hears us, she hears us, Miss Woodhouse. I see it in her cheek, her smile, her vain attempt to frown. Look at her. Do not you see that, at this instant, the very passage of her own letter, which sent me the report, is passing under her eye; that the whole blunder is spread before her; that she can attend to nothing else, though pretending to listen to the others?'

Jane was forced to smile completely for a moment; and the smile partly remained as she turned towards him, and said in a conscious, low, yet steady voice:

'How you can bear such recollections is astonishing to me. They *will* sometimes obtrude; but how you can *court* them!'

He had a great deal to say in return, and very entertainingly; but Emma's feelings were chiefly with Jane in the argument; and on leaving Randalls, and falling naturally into a comparison of the two men, she felt, that pleased as she had been to see Frank Churchill, and really regarding him as she did with friendship, she had never been more sensible of Mr Knightley's high superiority of character. The happiness of this most happy day received its completion in the animated contemplation of his worth which this comparison produced.

55

IF EMMA had still, at intervals, an anxious feeling for Harriet, a momentary doubt of its being possible for her to be really cured of her attachment to Mr Knightley, and really able to accept another man from unbiassed inclination, it was not long that she had to suffer from the recurrence of any such uncertainty. A very few days brought the party from London; and she had no sooner an opportunity of being one hour alone with Harriet, than she became perfectly satisfied, unaccountable as it was, that Robert Martin had thoroughly supplanted Mr Knightley; and was now forming all her views of happiness.

Harriet was a little distressed—did look a little foolish at first: but having once owned that she had been presumptuous and silly, and self-deceived before, her pain and confusion seemed to die away with the words, and leave her without a care for the past, and with the fullest exultation in the present and future: for as to her friend's approbation, Emma had instantly removed every fear of that nature, by meeting her with the most unqualified congratulations. Harriet was most happy to give every particular of the evening at Astley's, and the dinner the next day; she could dwell on it all with the utmost delight. But what did such particulars explain? The fact was, as Emma could now acknowledge, that Harriet had always liked Robert Martin; and that his continuing to love her had been irresistible. Beyond this, it must ever be unintelligible to Emma.

The event, however, was most joyful; and every day was giving her fresh reason for thinking so. Harriet's parentage became known. She proved to be the daughter of a tradesman, rich enough to afford her the comfortable maintenance which had ever been hers, and decent enough to have always wished for concealment. Such was the blood of gentility which Emma had formerly been so ready to vouch for! It was likely to be as untainted, perhaps, as the blood of many a gentleman: but what a connection had she been preparing for Mr Knightley, or for the Churchills, or even for Mr Elton! The stain of illegitimacy, unbleached by nobility or wealth, would have been a stain indeed.

No objection was raised on the father's side; the young man was treated liberally; it was all as it should be; and as Emma became acquainted with Robert Martin, who was now introduced at Hartfield, she fully acknowledged in him all the appearance of sense and worth which could bid fairest for her little friend. She had no doubt of Harriet's happiness with any good-tempered man; but with him, and in the home he offered, there would be the hope of more, of security, stability, and improvement. She would be placed in the midst of those who loved her, and who had better sense than herself; retired enough for safety, and occupied enough for cheerfulness. She would be never led into temptation, nor left for it to find her out. She would be respectable and happy; and Emma admitted her to be the luckiest creature in the world, to have created so steady and persevering an affection in such a man; or, if not quite the luckiest, to yield only to herself.

Harriet, necessarily drawn away by her engagements with the Martins, was less and less at Hartfield, which was not to be regretted. The intimacy between her and Emma must sink; their friendship must change into a calmer sort of goodwill; and, fortunately, what ought to be, and must be, seemed already beginning, and in the most gradual, natural manner.

Before the end of September, Emma attended Harriet to church, and saw her hand bestowed on Robert Martin with so complete a satisfaction, as no remembrances, even connected with Mr Elton as he stood before them, could impair. Perhaps indeed, at that time, she scarcely saw Mr Elton, but as the clergyman whose blessing at the altar might next fall on herself. Robert Martin and Harriet Smith, the latest couple engaged of the three, were the first to be married.

Jane Fairfax had already quitted Highbury, and was restored to the comforts of her beloved home with the Campbells. The Mr Churchills were also in town; and they were only waiting for November.

The intermediate month was the one fixed on, as far as they dared, by Emma and Mr Knightley. They had determined that their marriage ought to be concluded, while John and Isabella were still at Hartfield; to allow them the fortnight's absence in a tour to the sea-side, which was the plan. John and Isabella, and every other friend, were agreed in approving it. But Mr Woodhouse—how was Mr Woodhouse to be induced to consent? he, who had never yet alluded to their marriage but as a distant event.

When first sounded on the subject, he was so miserable that they were almost hopeless. A second allusion, indeed, gave less pain. He began to think it was to be, and that he could not prevent it—a very promising step of the mind on its way to resignation. Still, however, he was not happy. Nay, he appeared so much otherwise that his daughter's courage failed. She could not bear to see him suffering; to know him fancying himself neglected; and though her understanding almost acquiesced in the assurance of both the Mr Knightleys, that when once the event were over, his distress would be soon over too, she hesitated—she could not proceed.

In this state of suspense, they were befriended, not by any

sudden illumination of Mr Woodhouse's mind, or any wonderful change of his nervous system, but by the operation of the same system in another way. Mrs Weston's poultry-house was robbed one night of all her turkeys—evidently by the ingenuity of man. Other poultry-yards in the neighbourhood also suffered. Pilfering was *house-breaking* to Mr Woodhouse's fears. He was very uneasy; and but for the sense of his son-in-law's protection, would have been under wretched alarm every night of his life. The strength, resolution, and presence of mind of the Mr Knightleys commanded his fullest dependence. While either of them protected him and his, Hartfield was safe. But Mr John Knightley must be in London again by the end of the first week in November.

The result of this distress was, that, with a much more voluntary, cheerful consent than his daughter had ever presumed to hope for at the moment, she was able to fix her wedding-day; and Mr Elton was called on, within a month from the marriage of Mr and Mrs Robert Martin, to join the hands of Mr Knightley and Miss Woodhouse.

The wedding was very much like other weddings, where the parties have no taste for finery or parade; and Mrs Elton, from the particulars detailed by her husband, thought it all extremely shabby, and very inferior to her own. 'Very little white satin, very few lace veils; a most pitiful business! Selina would stare when she heard of it.' But, in spite of these deficiencies, the wishes, the hopes, the confidence, the predictions of the small band of true friends who witnessed the ceremony, were fully answered in the perfect happiness of the union.